U0732471

万里皆鹏程

那些年，勇闯世界的深圳前辈们

深圳市人民政府侨务办公室
深圳市归国华侨联合会　编
深 圳 市 海 外 交 流 协 会

Flying Far and High

Pioneers from Shenzhen Who Explored the World

暨南大学出版社
JINAN UNIVERSITY PRESS

中国·广州

图书在版编目（CIP）数据

万里皆鹏程：那些年，勇闯世界的深圳前辈们 =
Flying Far and High:Pioneers from Shenzhen Who
Explored the World：汉英对照 / 深圳市人民政府侨务
办公室，深圳市归国华侨联合会，深圳市海外交流协会编.
广州：暨南大学出版社，2025. 4.
ISBN 978-7-5668-4106-3

Ⅰ. Ⅰ25

中国国家版本馆 CIP 数据核字第 2024VH1873 号

万里皆鹏程：那些年，勇闯世界的深圳前辈们（Flying Far and High: Pioneers
from Shenzhen Who Explored the World）
WANLI JIE PENGCHENG：NAXIE NIAN, YONGCHUANG SHIJIE DE SHENZHEN
QIANBEI MEN

编　者：深圳市人民政府侨务办公室　深圳市归国华侨联合会　深圳市海外交流协会

出 版 人：阳　翼
责任编辑：冯　琳　雷晓琪　杨柳牧菁
责任校对：王燕丽　梁安儿　黄亦秋
责任印制：周一丹　郑玉婷

出版发行：暨南大学出版社（511434）
电　　话：总编室（8620）31105261
　　　　　营销部（8620）37331682　37331689
传　　真：（8620）31105289（办公室）　37331684（营销部）
网　　址：http://www.jnupress.com
排　　版：广州尚文数码科技有限公司
印　　刷：深圳市新联美术印刷有限公司
开　　本：787mm×1092mm　1/16
印　　张：29.75
字　　数：600 千
版　　次：2025 年 4 月第 1 版
印　　次：2025 年 4 月第 1 次
定　　价：180.00 元

（暨大版图书如有印装质量问题，请与出版社总编室联系调换）

序　言

近年我们面临世界百年未有之大变局，国际形势日趋严峻，各种风险挑战加剧，又叠加了三年新冠疫情、国内机构调整、人员新老交替等因素。但深圳侨务部门迎难而上，紧紧围绕市委、市政府中心工作，充分发挥侨乡优势，提早布局，率先发力，在为侨服务、引进高端人才、探索创新发展、招商引资和涵养侨力资源等方面取得显著成效，为全力推进粤港澳大湾区建设、打造更具全球影响力的经济中心城市和现代化国际大都市做好服务。

说实话，在答应为本书写序之初，我有些诚惶诚恐，但当我拜读完26篇文章后，心灵受到极大震撼。美国华人刘惠强坚定爱国，克服重重阻力带领爱国侨团在纽约华埠中心升起第一面五星红旗；97岁高龄的巴拿马华人章辞修，十几年前四处奔波，打破外交先例，力促中国华为公司在拉美地区设立第一家公司总部；清代名将后人、英国华人赖荣茂，一贯爱心报国，带领侨社与英国政府进行艰苦不懈的努力协调，助力流失海外的国宝文物回归中国；澳大利亚华人何沈慧霞，积极融入主流社会，成为澳大利亚首位华裔立法议员，致力于为华人社区争取权益；还有王兆凯、李大西、马介璋、马伟武、杨华根、已故老友毕传有的胞弟毕传铭和毕传发等，都是我们侨务系统的老朋友。他们白手起家，艰苦创业，爱国爱乡，热心公益，乐善好施，热心为侨服务，为深圳发展和祖（籍）国民族复兴伟业作出了重大贡献。

本书介绍的28位侨胞来自亚洲、欧洲、北美洲、南美洲、非洲和大洋洲全球6大洲的12个国家和地区，身世不同，经历各异，最长者97岁高龄，最小者66岁，平均年龄78.6岁。全书以写实、接地气、朴实无华的文风揭示侨胞们平凡的人生轨迹和不平凡的业绩，展现他们艰苦创业的奋斗经历、勤奋拼搏的高尚品行、扶危济困的大爱之德和爱国爱乡的坚定情怀。这本书不仅记录了深圳的发展历史，也是中华人民共和国成立75年来逐步走向振兴的生动写照，讴歌了海外6000万侨胞的历史功绩，更是中国现当代历史发展的精彩缩影。

作为一名老侨务工作者，我深感责任重大，责无旁贷。2023年考察深圳侨务工作时，我就深感深圳侨务部门用心用情用力。他们是统战侨务工作的有心人，在繁忙之余编写了这部《万里皆鹏程：那些年，勇闯世界的深圳前辈们》，希望此书能够成为鲜活生动的爱国主义教材，成为海内外侨界的一部现实版教科书。感谢深圳侨务部门为侨界做了一件大好事，这是不忘初心、牢记使命的真实体现。

2017年我在全国政协十二届五次会议第四次全体会议上作了"'一带一路'建设要充分发挥海外侨胞的独特作用"的发言，在专题调研的基础上总结提出海外侨胞的八大优势，即：牵线搭桥，提供商机；融通资金；利用人脉，提供法律保护；提供中高端人才；做好华文媒体宣传，讲好中国故事；熟悉国情，防范风险；协调沟通，合作共赢；充当中外友好的桥梁和使者。发言在海内外引起强烈共鸣。本书中28位侨胞的感人事迹，再次佐证了这些独特优势。可以自豪地说，没有海外侨胞的一贯大力支持，中国的改革开放事业就不可能取得今天这样巨大的成就。

在我们迈向新长征的关键时刻，本书的出版旨在提示统战侨务工作者和年青一代牢记这段难忘的历史，继承与发扬中华民族爱国爱乡的光荣传统，我们的民族解放事业需要"打侨牌"，新中国建设和改革开放事业需要"打侨牌"，实现第二个百年奋斗目标、以中国式现代化全面推进强国建设和民族复兴伟业仍然需要"打好侨牌"。侨务工作永远不会过时，统战侨务是我们党进行革命和建设的重要法宝，需要后来者永远铭记和传承。

2020年10月，习近平总书记在广东考察时强调，我们的改革开放和发展建设事业同大批心系桑梓、心系祖国的华侨是分不开的。他还曾指出："中国梦是国家梦、民族梦，也是每个中华儿女的梦。广大海外侨胞有着赤忱的爱国情怀、雄厚的经济实力、丰富的智力资源、广泛的商业人脉，是实现中国梦的重要力量。"我也相信，只要我们海内外的中华儿女紧密团结起来，一心奋斗，就一定能够汇聚起实现梦想的强大力量。

赵　阳

国务院侨务办公室原副主任

全国政协参政议政人才库特聘专家

2024年12月

Preface

In recent years, we have faced a world with great changes that have not been seen in a century. The international situation has become increasingly severe, and various risks and challenges have intensified. In addition, there are some other factors such as the three-year COVID-19 pandemic, the adjustment of domestic institutions, and the replacement of old staff with the new. Overseas Chinese Affairs office of the People's Govemment of Shenzhe Municipality has risen to the challenge, closely centered on the core work of the municipal Party committee and the municipal government, given full play to the city's advantages as the hometown of overseas Chinese, made early layout and efforts, and achieved remarkable results in serving overseas Chinese, introducing high-end talents, exploring innovative development, attracting investment, and conserving overseas Chinese resources, thus providing excellent service to fully promote the construction of the Guangdong-Hong Kong-Macao Greater Bay Area and build a more influential economic hub and a modern international metropolis.

To be honest, I was a bit apprehensive when I agreed to write the preface to *Flying Far and High: Pioneers from Shenzhen Who Explored the World*. However, after reading the 26 articles, I was absolutely astounded. Whether it is in regard to Lou Wai Keing, a Chinese American with steadfast love to China, who overcame the opposition of others and numerous obstacles to lead patriotic overseas Chinese groups to raise the first five-star red flag in the center of Chinatown in New York; Guillermo John Chava, a 97-year-old Chinese Panamanian, who ran around to break diplomatic precedents and pushed for the establishment of Huawei's first corporate headquarters in Latin America more than a decade ago; Lai Kayming, a descendant of a famous Qing Dynasty general, and a Chinese British devoted to serving China with love, who led the overseas Chinese community to make arduous and unremitting efforts to coordinate with the British government when they helped a Chinese cultural treasure lost overseas return home; Helen Wai-Har Sham-Ho, a Chinese Australian, who has actively integrated into mainstream society and served as the first elected Chinese-born member of an Australian parliament for a long time, committed to fighting for the rights of the Chinese community; or Jaw-Kai Wang, Daxi Li, Ma Kai Cheung, Ma Wai Mo, Wah Kun Yeung, and Pat Chuen Ming and Pat Chuen Fa, the younger brothers of my late friend Chuen You But, they are all old friends of our overseas Chinese affairs system. They have started from scratch, worked hard to start their businesses, and loved China and their hometown. Enthusiastic about public welfare, benevolent and kind-hearted, and keen to serve overseas Chinese, they have made significant contributions to the development of Shenzhen and the great cause of national rejuvenation.

The 28 overseas Chinese introduced in this book are from six continents including Asia, Europe, North America, South America, Africa, and Oceania. They are from 12 countries and regions, with different backgrounds and experiences. The oldest is 97 years old, the youngest is 66 years old, and their average age is 78.6. The authors use a realistic, down-to-earth, and simple writing style to reveal the ordinary life trajectories and extraordinary achievements of those overseas Chinese, showcasing their arduous entrepreneurial struggles, noble character of hard work, humanity of helping the needy, and steadfast patriotism and love for their hometown. The book not only records the development history of Shenzhen, but also vividly depicts the gradual revitalization of the People's Republic of China over the past 75 years, praises the historical achievements of 60 million overseas Chinese, presenting itself as a wonderful epitome of China's modern historical development.

As an experienced overseas Chinese affairs worker, I deeply feel a great sense of responsibility and duty. When inspecting the overseas Chinese affairs work in Shenzhen in 2023, I deeply felt that the Overseas Chinese Affairs office of the People's Government of Shenzhe Municipality is dedicated, passionate, and hardworking. They are persons who set their mind on doing united front and overseas Chinese affairs work. Despite their busy schedule, they have compiled this book, *Flying Far and High: Pioneers from Shenzhen Who Explored the World*, which I hope that it can become a vivid patriotic textbook as well as a realistic textbook for the overseas Chinese community at home and abroad. Thanks to the Overseas Chinese Affairs office of the People's Government of Shenzhe Municipality for doing a great job for the overseas Chinese community, which is a true reflection of "remaining true to our original aspiration and keeping our mission firmly in mind."

In 2017, I made a speech at a meeting of the 12th National Committee of the CPPCC, saying "the Belt and Road construction should give full play to the unique role of overseas Chinese." On the basis of special research, I summarized and proposed eight advantages of overseas Chinese, namely, matching buyers and sellers to provide business opportunities; financing; utilizing personal connections to provide legal protection; providing mid-end and high-end talents; publicizing through Chinese language media to tell the story of China well; being familiar with the condition of relevant countries and preventing risks;

coordinating, communicating, and achieving win-win cooperation; and acting as bridges and messengers of friendship between China and foreign countries. The speech resonated strongly at home and abroad. The touching stories of the 28 overseas Chinese in this book once again prove these unique advantages. It can be proudly said that without the consistently strong support of overseas Chinese, China's reform and opening-up cause would not gain such great achievements as it does today.

Today, at a critical moment when we are heading for the New Long March, the publication of this book is intended to remind the united front and overseas Chinese affairs workers and the young generation to remember this unforgettable history and inherit and carry forward the glorious tradition of the Chinese nation's patriotism and love for their hometown. Our national liberation cause needed to "play the overseas Chinese card," the national construction and the reform and opening-up cause needed to "play the overseas Chinese card," and to achieve the second centennial goal and comprehensively advance Chinese modernization construction still needs to "play the overseas Chinese card well." Overseas Chinese affairs work will never be outdated. The united front and overseas Chinese affairs work is an important magic weapon for our party to carry out revolution and construction, which needs to be remembered and inherited by later generations.

In October 2020, during his inspection in Guangdong, General Secretary Xi Jinping emphasized that our reform and opening-up, development and construction undertakings are inseparable from a large number of overseas Chinese who care about their hometown and motherland. He once pointed out, "The Chinese Dream is the dream of the country, the dream of the nation, and the dream of every Chinese. With a sincere patriotic sentiment, strong economic strength, abundant intellectual resources, and extensive business networks, the numerous overseas Chinese are an important force for realizing the Chinese Dream." I also believe that as long as we Chinese people at home and abroad unite closely and work hard with one heart, we will be able to gather a powerful force for realizing our dreams.

Zhao Yang

Former deputy director of

the Overseas Chinese Affairs Office of the State Council,

Specially appointed expert of the CPPCC National Committee's

talent pool for political participation and deliberation

December 2024

第
一
章

赤子之心

目 录

Chapter Two: Building a strong country through industry

第二章

实业强国

行路难，行路难，多歧路，今安在？
长风破浪会有时，直挂云帆济沧海。
——〔唐〕李白《行路难·其一》

Hard is the way, hard is the way. Don't go astray!
Whither today? A time will come to ride the wind and
cleave the waves; I'll set my cloudlike sail to cross the
sea which raves.
—*Hard Is the Way I*, by Li Bai (Tang Dynasty)

Chapter Three: Caring about the hometown

第
三
章

桑梓情深

露从今夜白，月是故乡明。

——〔唐〕杜甫《月夜忆舍弟》

Dew turns into frost since tonight; The moon viewed at home is more bright.

—*Thinking of My Brothers on a Moonlit Night*, by Du Fu (Tang Dynasty)

Chapter Four: Passing on the torch

第
四
章

江山代有才人出，各领风骚数百年。
——〔清〕赵翼《论诗五首·其二》

Talented poets are brought forth in their times; Each will lead the literary excellence for hundreds of years.
—*On Poetry Ⅱ*, by Zhao Yi (Qing Dynasty)

薪
火
相
传

Chapter Five: Building bridges

相知无远近，万里尚为邻。

——〔唐〕张九龄《送韦城李少府》

Distance cannot separate true friends afar; They are like neighbors although thousands of miles apart.

—*Farewell to County Captain Li of Weicheng*, by Zhang Jiuling (Tang Dynasty)

第五章

以侨为桥

第一章
Chapter One

赤子之心
Loving the motherland

力微任重久神疲，再竭衰庸定不支。

苟利国家生死以，岂因祸福避趋之。

——〔清〕林则徐《赴戍登程口占示家人》

I have felt exhausted from shouldering heavy responsibilities for my country with my meager strength. If I continue to exhaust myself, neither my weakened physique nor mediocre abilities will be able to sustain me. Were it to benefit my country, I would lay down my life. What then is risk to me?

—*Casually Composing a Poem for My Family When Embarking on a Journey to Defend the Border*, by Lin Zexu (Qing Dynasty)

詹伟光

国家强大了，我们华侨走路腰都直了

詹伟光　Jim Wai Kwong

　　詹伟光，又名詹宝泉，1940年1月出生于深圳大鹏龙岐村。旅荷林堡华侨总会永远名誉会长、荷兰中国和平统一促进会荣誉会长、香港大鹏同乡会永远名誉顾问，曾任中华全国归国华侨联合会海外顾问、深圳市海外交流协会海外名誉理事、深圳大鹏归国华侨联合会名誉主席、旅荷深圳大鹏同乡会会长、旅荷林堡华侨总会会长、林堡荷兰中文学校校董会校监等。

　　曾获荷兰王室骑士勋章，受邀参加中华人民共和国成立50周年、成立60周年国庆观礼。

采访时间：2022年。

据《深圳侨务史志》记载，深圳人移居荷兰始于 20 世纪初。1911 年，荷兰爆发海员罢工，为了平息工潮，荷兰船务公司从中国聘请了一批广东籍海员前往荷兰工作，随后有些人留下来取代荷兰船员的司炉工作（在船上铲煤烧锅炉）。这批人中，深圳大鹏人占了很大比例，这就是早期移居荷兰的深圳人。

詹伟光，又名詹宝泉，1940 年 1 月出生于深圳大鹏龙岐村。如今定居在荷兰林堡省的他有多个身份：旅荷林堡华侨总会永远名誉会长、荷兰中国和平统一促进会荣誉会长、香港大鹏同乡会永远名誉顾问……

"我捐了 50 港元，当时我的工资是 60 港元"

17 岁时，詹伟光就离开家乡大鹏出外谋生。不过，当时的他并没有走多远，只是去了离大鹏只有 3 公里的香港。"大鹏人历来都有去香港谋生的传统，我们家族里也有很多人在海外谋生，当时我的兄长就在新加坡谋生，堂姐在香港居住。"詹伟光说道。

在詹伟光的印象中，1957 年的香港其实没什么工业，也没多少高楼大厦。初到香港的他，生活很不容易，酒楼餐馆、制衣厂等许多地方都曾留下他的足迹。

詹伟光到香港后不久，家乡在筹建大鹏华侨中学。当时有乡亲代表大鹏华侨中学在香港募捐。"见到一群同乡在给华侨中学捐款，我也捐了 50 港元，当时我的月工资是 60 港元。"詹伟光透露，钱捐出去之后，那个月他连吃饭都成了问题，后来不得不到大排档赊账才能吃上饭。

"这件事如果告诉别人，别人或许会说我是个傻瓜，但我不是这么想的。"詹伟光知道大鹏子弟求学心切，更是亲身体会过大鹏小孩读完小学就没有地方可去的那种痛苦滋味。

在大鹏华侨中学创办之前，大鹏半岛原来唯一设有初中的德光中学在 1953 年下半年被取消，当地的小孩读完小学如果还想继续升学的话，就得去坪山、龙岗、淡水甚至南头等地。

但对大部分学生来说，外出求学谈何容易，一是家里没钱，二是交通不便、路途遥远。过去，能在大鹏读中学的人，实在是凤毛麟角。也难怪有人戏言："那个年代，在大鹏考中学真的就像古时候考状元一样。"

合流聚海，集腋成裘。在 470 多名旅居香港及海外的大鹏乡亲合力捐献了 20 万港元之后，大鹏华侨中学建设工程终于在 1958 年顺利完工。

在 470 多名的捐赠者中，有像王少清女士这样的慷慨捐献者——她个人捐出 10 万港元，占了总捐款额的一半（1960 年大鹏华侨中学扩建校舍，王少清又捐出 15 万港元，使校舍面积增加了一倍），但更多的还是像詹伟光这种经济状况一般的华侨华人和居港乡亲，即使只捐出 50 港元，也是平时省吃俭用一点一滴攒下来的。

"在荷兰升起了五星红旗，我们全体理事都非常紧张、激动"

史料记载，"二战"以后，一些靠航海为生的大鹏人受雇于香港的外轮公司，当轮船抵达荷兰后，船员看到当地的华人餐馆能挣到更多的钱，于是部分人就留在荷兰当厨师或侍应，他们站稳脚跟之后，又把在国内或其他地方的亲戚朋友接到当地；另外，有部分原居住在香港地区或英国的深圳人看到了荷兰中餐业的发展良机，也纷纷前往荷兰闯天下。

在香港工作生活了近 10 年之后，詹伟光去了荷兰。"因为我有亲友在荷兰那边工作生活，他们经营饮食业，需要人手帮忙，于是我在 1966 年就过去了。"詹伟光解释道。

在异乡工作的詹伟光不但非常勤奋，而且很节俭，这是绝大部分海外华侨华人的基本品格。经过几年打拼，1971 年，詹伟光开始创业，经营自己的餐馆一直到退休。在荷兰的餐馆经营上了正轨之后，詹伟光终于有了空闲的时间。从 20 世纪 80 年代起，他开始参加荷兰的侨团工作。"过去 40 多年，除了我自己的餐馆和私人工作，我大部分的时间几乎都在为侨团服务。"詹伟光自豪地说。

詹伟光最初参加的侨团名叫"旅荷华侨总会"，他曾经担任理事，后来又被选为副秘书长、副会长。这是一个在荷兰有着悠久历史传统的华人侨团，其前身是在

2018 年，詹伟光（前排左四）参加"全荷华侨华人庆祝中华人民共和国成立 69 周年"活动。（来源：北欧绿色邮报网）

Jim Wai Kwong (fourth from the left in the front row) takes part in an event named "Overseas Chinese Across the Netherlands Celebrate the 69th Anniversary of the Founding of the People's Republic of China" in 2018. (Photo: greenpost.se)

1947 年主要由温州籍华侨华人成立的瓯海同乡会（后来曾更名为"瓯海华侨会"）。
1951 年 10 月 1 日，在庆祝中华人民共和国成立两周年的活动中，当时中荷尚未建立外交关系，旅荷华侨总会在阿姆斯特丹升起了第一面五星红旗，大大震惊了整个欧洲社会。自此以后，每年 10 月 1 日，旅荷华侨总会都会组织庆祝中国国庆活动。加入旅荷华侨总会之后，每一年侨团的国庆活动，詹伟光都踊跃参加。

"在庆祝中华人民共和国成立两周年的活动上，华侨总会在荷兰升起了五星红旗，我也有幸参加，其间我们全体理事都非常紧张、激动，同时非常担心。"詹伟光解释，主要是担心升旗仪式不能顺利完成，会有外来的骚扰，毕竟是在别人的国家里升起五星红旗。

"幸好，最后一切顺利完成，大家都兴奋莫名，因为我们做了一件应该做的事情。旅荷华侨总会是整个欧洲大陆第一个升起五星红旗的侨团，这是一件值得我们永远纪念的事情。"

"有同乡会这个组织，就可以为我们同乡争取到正当的权益"

位于深圳东南部的大鹏半岛，三面环海，东临大亚湾，与惠州接壤，西抱大鹏湾，遥望香港新界。千百年来，大鹏人深受海洋文化洗礼，与海外联系密切，这里是知名的侨乡。

数据统计，如今的深圳大鹏新区有海外侨胞、港澳同胞约 5.2 万人，分布在世界 20 多个国家和地区。以"大鹏"命名的侨团也不少：香港大鹏同乡会、美国纽约大鹏同乡会、美国纽约大鹏育英总社、旅荷深圳大鹏同乡会、德国大鹏同乡会……

1987 年初，旅居荷兰的大鹏乡亲本着"同心同德，加强乡亲团结，维护乡亲利益"的宗旨，成立了"荷兰大鹏平洲同乡会"筹备组，并向旅居在荷兰的 1000 多位乡亲发出倡议书，号召他们加入荷兰大鹏平洲同乡会。

1988 年 12 月 28 日，荷兰大鹏平洲同乡会在海牙皇上皇大酒楼举行成立大会，当时有 400 多名会员参加了大会，成员均为祖籍深圳大鹏、香港平洲（香港方面更习惯称为"东平洲"）的海外乡亲。2007 年，荷兰大鹏平洲同乡会召开第十一届理事会，并正式更名为"旅荷大鹏同乡会"。2020 年 3 月，为了让更多人知道和认识大鹏就在深圳，同乡会重新命名为"旅荷深圳大鹏同乡会"，会员 1100 多人。

詹伟光表示："有了同乡会，就可以给我们大鹏乡亲一个聚会的地方，有困难大家互相帮助，互相传递家乡的信息，以及进行工作上的交流。比如我们都是经营餐馆的，就可以利用同乡会这个平台在各个餐馆间进行人力调配。"

一直在荷兰热心侨团工作的詹伟光，就是在 2007 年接棒成为第十一届旅荷大鹏同乡会会长的。上任之后，他首先着手抓的工作就是同乡会的正规化，比如组织常规的春节、中秋联欢会活动，将同乡会登记为荷兰的合法社团。

2014 年，詹伟光参加旅荷大鹏同乡联欢晚会。
Jim Wai Kwong takes part in an evening party held by the Tai Peng Association in The Netherlands in 2014.

詹伟光透露，华侨华人在外国经营餐馆，时不时会有多种骚扰。"有了同乡会这个组织，就可以为我们同乡争取到正当的权益，以及促进大鹏同乡的团结，互相支持同乡融入荷兰当地社会，提高我们侨胞的社会地位和经济实力。"

"最主要的是，可以架起我们跟当地政府沟通的桥梁。平时乡亲们有什么事要跟政府沟通，就是通过同乡会这个平台来进行的，有这么一个组织，跟政府沟通起来会比较容易一些。"

不过，詹伟光觉得，现在同乡会有一项更迫切的工作要去做，就是发动更多的青年参加同乡会，否则就可能会面临后继无人的窘境。

"在荷兰土生土长的后一辈华人，家乡观念比较薄弱，即使你告诉他，他是大鹏人，他也不知道大鹏在哪里。所以我经常发动年轻人来参与同乡会，如果不这样做，就很难有人传承。老一辈人虽然爱国爱乡，但是毕竟已经老了，对于同乡会工作有心无力了。"

"国家强大了，我们华侨在外面走路腰都直了"

詹伟光是 1957 年离开大鹏的，但是他告诉记者："无论人走多远，我的心永远都记挂着家乡。"中国改革开放之后，詹伟光在 1979 年第一次回到了大鹏老家，"那个时候的深圳（市区）还没有像现在这样繁华"。

詹伟光透露，旅荷大鹏同乡会成立之后，历任会长都非常注重跟家乡大鹏、南澳的侨务部门紧密联系，经常沟通、交流。"我们每次回家乡，都会专门去拜访大鹏、南澳的侨办、侨联等机构。"

在回忆往事的时候，詹伟光特别提到了 2011 年旅荷大鹏同乡会组织的那次回乡寻根之旅。当时詹伟光还是同乡会的会长，观光团成员大概有 50 人，而且有很多乡亲都是离开大鹏之后第一次"返乡下"。

"这一次的返乡寻根之旅，收获很丰富。每一位同乡回荷兰的时候，都是欢天喜地、喜气洋洋的。"詹伟光表示，"这一次的返乡经历，真是回味无穷。"

在家乡大鹏和南澳，旅荷的侨胞们受到地方侨务部门的热情接待，在大鹏多个地方参观之后，同乡会成员强烈地感受到几十年来家乡翻天覆地的变化。

"以前我们住的平房，现在都变成高楼大厦了。交通方面，以前砂石泥泞的小路现在也不见了，出入有公路了。"说起家乡的变化，詹伟光顿时热情高涨。"以前我们出门都是'行路'（靠双脚走路），现在有了公共交通，出去外面方便多了。我们最感动的是，大鹏现在也有了医院，人们看病、接受诊治服务方便多了。"

在大鹏期间，詹伟光和乡亲们还专门到学校去参观。他们看到学生在教室里上课时每一张桌子上都配有教学电脑，回想起过去没有机会上学的艰苦日子，詹伟光惊讶地说："这是进步，是我们国家走上现代化的一个标志。"

"每一个爱国的华侨华人都希望我们的国家能够强大起来。国家强大了，我们华侨在外面走路腰都直了，不会被别人看不起。如果国家不够强大，没有人会看得起你，你走在外面，人家都会耻笑你的。是真的，我这种感受就特别深，所以说我们有一颗中国心。"詹伟光补充道。

2011 年，旅荷大鹏同乡会组织的回乡观光团在深圳大鹏合影留念。

A homecoming tour group organized by the Tai Peng Association in the Netherlands has a group photo taken in Dapeng, Shenzhen in 2011.

"虽然我们都在国外生活，但我们的心始终是向着祖国的"

老一辈的大鹏人原来在荷兰从事餐饮业的比较多，而年青一代基本已经融入荷兰当地的生活了。

"因为有了新的知识，子承父业的就比较少。"詹伟光表示，在荷兰的大鹏子弟都非常争气，第二、第三代读书的成绩也不错，出来工作之后从事律师、医生、工程师等各种职业的都不少。"我们大鹏人历来还是比较注重教育的，子弟也能读书。每一个家庭都希望子女能够学有所成，都'几标青'（粤语"出类拔萃"的意思）。"

移居荷兰的大鹏人多数生活在阿姆斯特丹、海牙以及鹿特丹等几个主要大城市，但詹伟光早年是在荷兰南部的林堡省经营餐馆。在詹伟光看来，林堡是个好地方，与德国、比利时、卢森堡三个国家接壤，很方便。林堡的省会和最大城市马斯特里赫特（Maastricht），其实也是非常有名的一个地方，欧洲共同体（欧盟的前身）的第一次会议就在这里召开。

詹伟光年过80，早已退休，因为5个子女都不想继续从事餐饮行业，所以他早就把餐馆卖掉了，不过他平时还是会参与旅荷深圳大鹏同乡会和旅荷林堡华侨总会的会议和工作。

旅荷林堡华侨总会是詹伟光在1985年11月5日跟一帮志同道合的朋友组织创办的，成员来自香港、广东、浙江等中国各地区以及马来西亚、印度尼西亚、新加坡、苏里南等国家。总会成立后，经过40多年的发展，下面又成立了妇女会、青年会、松柏会（老人会），还创办了三所（现在剩下两所）中文学校。

2010 年，詹伟光出席旅荷林堡华侨总会下属中文学校结业典礼，与师生合影留念。

Jim Wai Kwong attends the graduation ceremony of a Chinese school under the Chinese Association Limburg in the Netherlands, and has a group photo taken with the teachers and students in 2010.

　　"旅荷林堡华侨总会在荷兰的声誉很高，和大使馆的联系也非常密切。1990年北京亚运会、2008年北京奥运会，国内曾邀请我们荷兰华侨团体去参观。我也曾受邀参加中华人民共和国（成立）50周年、60周年国庆观礼活动。"詹伟光自豪地介绍，旅荷林堡华侨总会的宗旨是爱国爱乡，为侨胞谋福利，为当地经济和社会发展、为祖国建设和家乡公益事业作贡献。

　　"每当国家出现一些大灾害，比如之前发生的华东水灾、华南冰雪灾、四川汶川地震等，只要大鹏同乡会和旅荷林堡华侨总会向大家号召，我们华侨同胞都会非常积极地支持，并尽力去筹款捐钱。"

　　"虽然我们都在国外生活，但我们的心始终是向着祖国的。大家都是中国人，血浓于水嘛。生活在国外，这种感觉会更深一些。"身处荷兰林堡省的詹伟光在微信里深情地说道。

　　（除署名外，本文图片均由受访者詹伟光提供。参考资料：《深圳侨务史志》《桑梓情深　赤子丹心——大鹏侨情口述史》。）

Jim Wai Kwong

As China becomes strong, overseas Chinese walk tall

Jim Wai Kwong, also known as Jim Po Chuen, was born in January 1940 in Longqi Village, Dapeng, Shenzhen. He is permanent honorary president of the Chinese Association Limburg in the Netherlands, honorary president of the Netherlands Association of the Unification of China, and permanent honorary adviser to the Tai Pang Residents Association (Hong Kong). He was overseas consultant to the All-China Federation of Returned Overseas Chinese, overseas honorary director of the Shenzhen Overseas Exchange Association, honorary president of the Shenzhen Dapeng Federation of Returned Overseas Chinese, president of the Shenzhen Tai Peng Association in the Netherlands, president of the Chinese Association Limburg in the Netherlands, and supervisor of the school board of Chinese schools in Limburg.

He was awarded Knight in the Order of Orange-Nassau (Ridder in de Orde van Oranje-Nassau) of the Netherlands, and was invited to attend the 50th and 60th National Day celebrations of the founding of the People's Republic of China.

According to the *Historical Records of Shenzhen Overseas Chinese Affairs*, the migration of Shenzhen people to the Netherlands could date back to the early 20th century. In 1911, a seamen's strike broke out in the Netherlands. In order to cope with the labor unrest, Dutch shipping companies hired a group of Cantonese seamen from China. Later, some of them stayed to replace Dutch seamen as stokers, shoveling coal and burning boilers on the ship. Among these Chinese people, those from Dapeng, Shenzhen accounted for a large proportion. They were the Shenzhen people who immigrated to the Netherlands in the early days.

Jim Wai Kwong, also known as Jim Po Chuen, was born in Longqi Village, Dapeng, Shenzhen in January 1940. Now living in Limburg, the Netherlands, he has a lot of identities: permanent honorary president of the Chinese Association Limburg in

The interview took place in 2022.

the Netherlands, honorary president of the Netherlands Association of the Unification of China, and permanent honorary adviser of the Tai Pang Residents Association (Hong Kong)…

"I donated HK$50 when my monthly wage was HK$60."

At the age of 17, Jim left his hometown Dapeng to make a living. However, at that time, he did not go far, but went to Hong Kong, only three kilometers away from Dapeng. "People in Dapeng had the tradition of making a living in Hong Kong. Many people in my family also made a living overseas. At that time, my elder brother made a living in Singapore, and my cousin lived in Hong Kong," Jim said.

In his impression, there were not many industries or high-rise buildings in Hong Kong in 1957. Life was not easy when he first arrived. He left his footprints in many places, such as restaurants and garment factories.

Shortly after he arrived in Hong Kong, Jim's hometown was preparing to build the Dapeng Overseas Chinese Middle School. Some natives of Dapeng raised funds in Hong Kong on behalf of the school. "When I saw a group of fellow Dapeng immigrants donating money to the Overseas Chinese Middle School, I also donated 50 Hong Kong dollars. At that time, my monthly wage was 60 Hong Kong dollars," Jim said. After the donation, he was left without enough money for meals in that month. Then he had to eat on credit at food stalls.

"If I had told others about this, they would have said that I was a fool, but I didn't think so," Jim said. He knew that children in Dapeng were eager to study, and he had experienced the painful feeling as a child in Dapeng when he could go nowhere after finishing primary school.

Before the Dapeng Overseas Chinese Middle School was established, the Deguang Middle School, the only junior high school in Dapeng Peninsula, was cancelled in the second half of 1953. Local children who wanted to continue their studies after finishing primary school had to go to Pingshan, Longgang, Danshui and even Nantou.

But for most of the students, it was not easy because their families were poor while those places were far way with transportation difficulties. In the past, few people in Dapeng could go to middle school. No wonder people joked, "In those days, getting oneself into a high school was really like winning the first place in the imperial examination in the ancient times."

Many rivers make the sea, and many a little makes a mickle. More than 470 natives of

Dapeng living in Hong Kong and overseas donated a total of 200,000 Hong Kong dollars, and the construction of the Dapeng Overseas Chinese Middle School was successfully completed in 1958.

Among those donors, there were generous ones like Ms. Wong Siu Ching, who donated 100,000 Hong Kong dollars, accounting for half of the total donation (in 1960, when the Dapeng Overseas Chinese Middle School needed to expand the school building, she donated another 150,000 Hong Kong dollars, helping to increase the school building's area by half). Most of the donors were overseas Chinese and Hong Kong residents from modest economic backgrounds like Jim, who lived frugally to save 50 Hong Kong dollars bit by bit.

"When the five-star red flag was raised in the Netherlands, all the directors were very nervous and excited."

According to historical records, after World War II, some sea-going Dapeng people were employed by foreign shipping companies in Hong Kong. When the ships arrived in the Netherlands, some crew members found that Chinese restaurants there offered better wages. Thus, some of the people stayed in the Netherlands as chefs or waiters. After they gained a firm foothold, they received their relatives and friends from home or other places. In addition, some people from Shenzhen who had lived in Hong Kong or the United Kingdom moved to the Netherlands because they saw a good opportunity for Chinese restaurants to develop.

After working and living in Hong Kong for nearly 10 years, Jim went to the Netherlands. "It was because I had relatives and friends working and living in the Netherlands. They were running catering business and needed more workers, so I went there in 1966," Jim explained.

Working in a strange land, Jim was very diligent and frugal, which is a basic character of most overseas Chinese. After several years of hard work, Jim started his own business in 1971, running his own restaurant until retirement. When his restaurant business in the Netherlands got on track, Jim began to have free time. In the 1980s, he began to participate in the work of overseas Chinese associations in the Netherlands. "In the past 40 years, except for my own restaurant and personal work, I have spent most of my time serving overseas Chinese associations," Jim said proudly.

Jim initially joined an overseas Chinese group called Algemene Chinese Vereniging in Nederland (the General Chinese Association in the Netherlands). He once served as a director, and later was elected deputy secretary general and the vice president. This is an overseas Chinese association in the Netherlands with a long history. Its predecessor was the Ouhai Natives Association, founded in 1947 mainly by overseas Chinese from Wenzhou, which was once renamed "Ouhai Overseas Chinese Association." On October 1, 1951, in the celebration of the second anniversary of the founding of the People's Republic of China, when China and the Netherlands had yet to establish diplomatic relations, the General Chinese Association in the Netherlands raised the first five-star red flag in Amsterdam, which greatly shocked the entire European society. Since then, the General Chinese Association in the Netherlands has organized activities to celebrate China's National Day on October 1 each year. After joining the association, Jim actively participated in the National Day activities of overseas Chinese groups every year.

"In the celebration of the second anniversary of the founding of the People's Republic of China, the General Chinese Association in the Netherlands raised the five-star red flag in the Netherlands, and I was lucky to witness the scene. During the process, we, all the directors, were very nervous, excited and worried."

Jim explained that they were mainly worried about whether the flag raising ceremony could be successfully completed and whether there would be external harassment. After all, it was raising the five-star red flag in a country of others.

"Fortunately, in the end, everything was smoothly done. Everyone was excited because we did something we should do. The General Chinese Association in the Netherlands was the first overseas Chinese group to raise the five-star red flag in the whole European continent, which is something we should always remember."

"With the association, we can win legitimate rights and interests for our fellow townsmen."

Dapeng Peninsula, located in the southeast of Shenzhen, is surrounded by the sea on three sides. It adjoins Daya Bay and Huizhou in the east and Dapeng Bay in the west, and looks towards New Territories, Hong Kong. For thousands of years, people in Dapeng have been baptized by marine culture, and have kept close overseas ties. It is a well-known hometown of overseas Chinese.

According to statistics, there are about 52,000 overseas Chinese and Hong Kong and Macao compatriots from Dapeng New District of Shenzhen, spreading in more than 20 countries and regions in the world. There are also many overseas Chinese groups named after Dapeng: the "Tai Pang Residents Association (Hong Kong)," the "Tai Pun Residents

Association in New York, USA," the "Yook Ying Association, New York," the "Shenzhen Tai Peng Association in The Netherlands," and the "Tai Peng Association in Germany"…

In early 1987, some natives of Dapeng living in the Netherlands set up a preparatory group for the "Tai Peng and Ping Chau Residents Association in the Netherlands" in line with the purpose of "being of one heart and one mind, strengthening the solidarity, and safeguarding the interests of fellow townsmen." They issued a proposal to more than 1,000 fellow Dapeng immigrants living in the Netherlands, calling on them to join the "Tai Peng and Ping Chau Residents Association in the Netherlands."

On December 28, 1988, the Tai Peng and Ping Chau Residents Association in the Netherlands held its inaugural meeting at the Wong Sheung Wong Restaurant in the Hague, and more than 400 members attended the meeting. All of the association's members were natives of Dapeng, Shenzhen and Ping Chau, Hong Kong (the Hong Kong side is more accustomed to calling the place Tung Ping Chau). In 2007, the Tai Peng and Ping Chau Residents Association in the Netherlands held its 11th council, when it was officially renamed "Tai Peng Association in the Netherlands." In March 2020, in order to let more people know that Dapeng is in Shenzhen, the association was renamed "Shenzhen Tai Peng Association in the Netherlands." It had more than 1,100 members at that time.

Jim said, "With the association, we can have a gathering place for natives of Dapeng. In case of difficulties, we can help each other. We also pass on information about our hometown, and communicate about our work. We all run restaurants. For example, we are able to use the association as a platform to deploy manpower for different restaurants."

Jim has always been enthusiastic about working with overseas Chinese groups in the Netherlands. He took over as president of the 11th Tai Peng Association in the Netherlands in 2007. The first thing he did after taking office was to regularize the association, such as organizing regular Spring Festival and Mid-Autumn Festival get-together activities, and registering the association as a legal association in the Netherlands.

Jim revealed that overseas Chinese running restaurants in foreign countries had encountered all kinds of harassment from time to time. "With the association as our own organization, we can win legitimate rights and interests for our fellow townsmen, promote the unity of fellow immigrants from Dapeng, support each other to integrate into the local Dutch society, and improve the social status and economic strength of our overseas Chinese."

"The most important thing is that we can build a bridge to communicate with the local government. Usually, when the fellow Dapeng immigrants need to communicate with the government, they do it through the platform of the association. It's easier to communicate with the government through an organization of ours," he said.

However, Jim thinks that the association has a more urgent task now: to mobilize more young people to join the association. Otherwise, the association may face the dilemma of lacking successors.

"The younger generation of overseas Chinese born and raised in the Netherlands has a relatively weak sense of hometown. Even if you tell him that he is from Dapeng, he does not know where Dapeng is. So I often mobilize young people to join the association. If you do not do this, it will be difficult to inherit. Although the older generation loves their motherland and hometown, they are old after all, and the association's work is beyond their ability."

"As China becomes strong, overseas Chinese walk tall outside."

Jim left Dapeng in 1957, but he told us, "No matter how far I go, my heart will always remember my hometown." After China began its reform and opening-up, Jim returned to hometown for the first time in 1979. "At that time, (the downtown of) Shenzhen was not as prosperous as it is now."

Jim said that after the establishment of the Tai Peng Association in the Netherlands, each president had attached importance to keeping close contact with the overseas Chinese affairs offices in their hometown, including Dapeng and Nan'ao. Both sides have frequently communicated with each other and exchanged opinions. "Every time we returned to our hometown, we would pay a special visit to the overseas Chinese offices and federations of returned overseas Chinese in Dapeng and Nan'ao."

Recalling the past, Jim specifically mentioned a trip to find roots organized by the Tai Peng Association in the Netherlands in 2011, when he was president. There were about 50 people in that sightseeing group, and it was the first time for many of them to "return to the countryside" after leaving Dapeng.

"This trip back home to find roots yielded a lot. All the fellow Dapeng immigrants returned to the Netherlands with great joy," Jim said. "This experience of returning to the hometown is really memorable."

In their hometown, including Dapeng and Nan'ao, the overseas Chinese from the Netherlands were warmly received by the local overseas Chinese affairs offices. After visiting several places in Dapeng, the members of the association were impressed with the dramatic changes in their hometown over the past decades.

"The single-storey houses we lived in have turned into tall buildings. In terms of transportation, sandy and muddy pathways are gone. There are roads to get in and out," Jim immediately became excited when speaking of the changes in his hometown. "In the past, we had to go out on foot. Now we have public transportation, making it easier to go outside. What touches us most is that we have hospitals in Dapeng now, making it easier for people to see doctors and receive treatment."

During their stay in Dapeng, Jim and the fellow Dapeng immigrants also visited schools. They saw students in classrooms where each desk was equipped with a computer for teaching, while Jim remembered the hard old days when children had no chance to go to school. Jim said in surprise, "This is very progressive, and it is a symbol of our country's modernization."

"Every patriotic overseas Chinese hopes that our motherland will become stronger. As China becomes strong, we overseas Chinese walk tall outside, and we are not looked down upon by others. If the country is not strong enough, no one will respect you, and people will laugh at you when you walk outside. It's true. I have had especially deep feeling about this. So I would like to say that we have a Chinese heart," Jim added.

"Although we all live abroad, our hearts always sides with our motherland."

The older generation from Dapeng used to work in the catering industry in the Netherlands, while the younger generation has basically integrated into the local life there.

"Few children inherit their father's work, because they have learned new knowledge," Jim said. The children of Dapeng natives in the Netherlands are very successful. The second and third generations are doing well in school. After graduation, many of them are engaged in various professions such as lawyers, doctors and engineers. "We Dapeng people have always laid stress on education, and our children are good at study. Every family hopes that their children can learn something and be outstanding."

Most Dapeng immigrants to the Netherlands live in several major cities, including Amsterdam, the Hague, and Rotterdam. However, Jim settled down and operated his restaurant in Limburg Province in the south of the Netherlands. In his view, Limburg is a good and convenient place, bordering Germany, Belgium and Luxembourg. Maastricht, the capital and the largest city of Limburg, is very famous. The first meeting of the European Community (the predecessor of the European Union) was held here.

Jim, who is 82 years old, has already retired. As his five children did not want to continue working in the catering industry, he sold the restaurant a long time ago. However, he still participates in the meetings and work of the Shenzhen Tai Peng Association in the Netherlands and the Chinese Association Limburg in the Netherlands.

The Chinese Association Limburg in the Netherlands was founded by Jim and a group of like-minded friend on November 5, 1985. Its member included overseas Chinese from Hong Kong, Guangdong, Zhejiang and other parts of China, as well as those from Malaysia, Indonesia, Singapore, Suriname and other countries. After more than 40 years of development, the federation has established the Women's Association, the Youth Association, the Pine and Cypress Association (the elderly association) and three Chinese schools (there are two left now).

"The Chinese Association Limburg in the Netherlands enjoys a very high reputation in the Netherlands, and has a very close relationship with the Chinese embassy. During the 1990 Beijing Asian Games and the 2008 Beijing Olympic Games, China invited overseas Chinese groups in the Netherlands to visit. I was also invited to attend the celebrations of the 50th and 60th anniversaries of the People's Republic of China," Jim said. He proudly said that the purpose of the Chinese Association Limburg in the Netherlands is to love the motherland, seek welfare for overseas Chinese, contribute to the local economic and social development, and contribute to the construction of the motherland and the public welfare of the hometown.

"Whenever major disasters took place in China, such as the flood in East China, the ice and snow disaster in South China, and the Wenchuan earthquake in Sichuan, as long as the Shenzhen Tai Peng Association in the Netherlands and the Chinese Association Limburg in the Netherlands issued a call, the overseas Chinese compatriots were very active in supporting us and did their best to raise money and donate."

"Although we all live abroad, our hearts always sides with our motherland. We are all Chinese, and blood is thicker than water. When living abroad, this feeling will be deeper," Jim said affectionately in Limburg Province, the Netherlands, through WeChat.

(Photos courtesy of Jim Wai Kwong, except for the one with credit. References: *Historical Records of Shenzhen Overseas Chinese Affairs* and *Deep Love for the Hometown and Sincere Loyalty to the Motherland: Oral History of Overseas Chinese from Dapeng.*)

毕传铭、毕传发兄弟

走出大鹏，在荷兰打造中国名片

毕传铭（右）、毕传发兄弟在深圳大鹏家中。（来源：《晶报》）
Pat Chuen Ming (right) and his younger brother Pat Chuen Fa at home in Dapeng, Shenzhen.
(Photo: *Daily Sunshine*)

毕传铭，荷兰著名侨领毕传有（已故）的弟弟，1949年出生于深圳大鹏乌冲村。深圳海外交流协会第三届理事会海外理事、第四届理事会名誉理事，曾任旅荷深圳大鹏同乡会会长、深圳市大鹏归国华侨联合会名誉主席、荷兰广东总会名誉会长。

毕传发，又名毕瑜，毕传有和毕传铭的弟弟，1951年出生于深圳大鹏乌冲村。1967年前往香港谋生，1971年去荷兰；1975年与哥哥、姐姐合作，在荷兰经营餐馆；1992年，响应国家号召，与兄弟一起回国投资，建设家乡。

采访时间：2022年。

位于深圳市东部海边的大鹏所城，原是明代为了抗击倭寇而设立的"大鹏守御千户所城"，有"沿海所城，大鹏为最"之美誉。这里是明清两代中国南部的海防军事要塞，还曾是鸦片战争的肇始地。深圳今又名"鹏城"，正是源于此。今天，大鹏所城及其旁边的较场尾（中国古时的练兵场称为"校场"，这里的"较场"其实是"校场"的讹传），已经成为深圳著名的旅游景点和民宿客栈聚集地。

从大鹏所城往西大约 1 公里，有一个乌冲村（又叫"乌涌村"）。1949 年，毕传铭就出生在这里。两年以后，毕传铭的弟弟毕传发也来到这个世上。

从大鹏到香港，再到海牙

毕传铭表示，自己小时候是在家乡大鹏所城里的鹏城小学接受教育的，但是因为家里生活困难，读书并不多。15 岁时，他便离开家乡，去了香港。自清末起，大鹏一带的村民就有去香港或海外谋生的习惯。起初是务工，挣钱回来养家，后来逐渐在外定居，落地生根。

"原本我是想到香港继续读书的，但到了香港之后才发现，那里的生活也很困难，根本就不可能读书。"毕传铭说道。于是，他开始在香港做童工。一开始，毕传铭学习修理汽车，希望日后有一技之长可以在香港立足，然而这谈何容易，他不得不转行进入酒楼工作。

毕传发的回忆跟哥哥的差不多。"我们小时候家里很穷，没有饭吃，只能吃那些喂鸡、喂猪的东西——用糠混合番薯做成的食物——来充饥。"毕传发是 1967 年去香港的，那个时候，他的哥哥、姐姐们已经在香港基本站稳了脚跟。

毕传铭在香港酒楼工作几年之后，已经在荷兰海牙从事餐饮业的哥哥姐姐问他，想不想也到荷兰发展。"由于文化程度低，当时在香港觉得前途很渺茫，所以我还是决定去那边闯一闯。"只是，在哪里生活都不容易。初到荷兰时，毕传铭发现，当地的工作比在香港更加辛苦，每天工作十二三个小时是常有的事儿，有时候晚上还要继续加班加点。但开弓没有回头箭，"我不想被人看不起，唯有咬牙硬撑下去，"毕传铭说。

在荷兰，毕传铭认识了妻子刘艳萍。刘艳萍祖籍也是大鹏的，不过她在香港出生。"当时在荷兰的华侨都想拼命多赚一些钱，老公出去工作，老婆也去工作，子女没有人带。"毕传铭无奈地说，"后来我们请了一个外国妇女帮忙带子女，但她教我们的小孩叫她妈妈，和她一起睡觉，孩子不认我们夫妇，我们很心痛。"迫不得已，毕传铭夫妇将子女送回了香港，请孩子的外婆来帮忙照顾。

毕传发回忆，自己是在 1971 年到荷兰的，比两个哥哥要晚一些。"当时，我姐和姐夫告诉我，荷兰大赦，我如果过去可能拿到合法居留身份。"在海牙，毕传发工作了半年，居留申请没有成功，于是就去了德国发展。在德国工作了一年多之

毕传铭（右）与毕传发（左）兄弟年轻时的照片。

A photo of Pat Chuen Ming (right), and Pat Chuen Fa (left) when they were young.

后，毕传发又回到了香港办理赴荷劳工证。

1972年9月，毕传发拿到了劳工居留权，重新返回荷兰工作。当时，他们兄弟几个正考虑在荷兰创业开餐馆。这也是那个时候在荷兰的大鹏人从事的主要职业。据《深圳侨务史志》记载："到20世纪70年代，荷兰华人的职业仍以餐馆业为主，华人餐馆的数量每年以18%的速度增长。"两个哥哥在荷兰做餐馆，后来毕传发也自立门户，出来做外卖餐馆。

荷兰运河上，建起了一座"海上皇宫"

2022年6月20日晚间，一则新闻在网上流传：香港仔饮食集团旗下的水上餐厅珍宝海鲜舫，在驶离香港的过程中，于中国西沙群岛附近海域遇上风浪入水翻转……承载几代港人近半个世纪集体记忆的珍宝海鲜舫，慢慢沉入南海之中。

而在阿姆斯特丹莱茵河入海口，碧波荡漾的运河上，矗立着一座具有浓郁中国特色、可同时容纳700人就座的豪华餐厅——海上皇宫。这是一艘四层雕栏玉砌的仿宫廷画舫，它将中国的古典建筑和经典烹饪淋漓尽致地展现给来自全球各地的游客。

毕传铭毫不讳言地表示，他们兄弟和几个华侨在阿姆斯特丹一起筹建经营海上皇宫，最初的灵感就是来自香港的珍宝海鲜舫。在阿姆斯特丹，来自大鹏半岛的深圳毕家兄弟经营海上皇宫，一开始是向当地政府租赁停泊的码头船位，后来他们为了餐厅的可持续发展，与政府沟通，买下了码头泊位的永久使用权。

如今，香港的珍宝海鲜舫已经沉入海中，但是在欧亚大陆另一端的阿姆斯特丹，海上皇宫与风车、木鞋、郁金香并列成为荷兰的代名词。在荷兰，流传着这样两句话——"未到阿姆斯特丹等于没有来过荷兰""到了阿姆斯特丹，必到海上皇宫"，由此足见，漂浮于阿姆斯特丹运河上的这座中国海上皇宫在旅行者心中的分量之重。

自1984年落成以来，海上皇宫不但慢慢成了游客在阿姆斯特丹的网红打卡点，而且逐渐成为一张在荷兰的中国名片，这里是荷兰王室和许多明星非常喜欢光顾的一个地方。荷兰对华的重要活动，以及当地的中国侨团、中资企业举办的一些盛大

位于阿姆斯特丹运河上的海上皇宫。
The Sea Palace on a canal in Amsterdam.

招待会都会特意选在海上皇宫举行，例如中国海洋石油集团有限公司与荷兰皇家壳牌石油公司在广东大亚湾的合作项目，北京与阿姆斯特丹结为友好城市，厦门航空与荷兰皇家航空的携手合作，这些签约仪式都是在海上皇宫举行的。

海上皇宫给毕家兄弟及其下一代留下了太多美好回忆。毕传铭人生的第一次"触电"，就是在海上皇宫完成的。这就要提到

毕传铭在电影《古惑仔3：只手遮天》中的"跑龙套"经历。（来源：《古惑仔3：只手遮天》电影截图）
C. M. Pat plays a small role in the movie *Young and Dangerous 3: Covering the Sky with One Hand.* (Photo: video screenshot)

由漫画改编而成的港产系列动作电影《古惑仔》了。20 世纪 90 年代中期，《古惑仔3：只手遮天》到荷兰取景拍摄，其中一个拍摄地点就是海上皇宫。而作为海上皇宫老板之一的毕传铭，则在片中客串了一个在荷兰养老的"老叔父"（黑帮教父）角色。虽然是人生的第一次也是唯一一次拍电影，但是坐镇主场的毕传铭，在与张耀扬饰演的"乌鸦"演对手戏时，一点儿也不怵。

回忆起 20 多年前的那一次"触电"经历，毕传铭笑言，自己只是个"茄哩啡"（临时演员）而已。在最后上映的电影中，他露脸了 6 秒钟，说了 4 句台词。

"你支持国家建设，国家也支持你赚钱"

通过海上皇宫，毕家兄弟在之后几十年的时间里，缔造出了一个享誉欧洲华人社会的企业王国。除了广大华人赖以谋生的传统餐饮业之外，他们的产业还涉及酒店、房地产、旅行社等多个行业。

毕传铭透露，大约在1989年，他们兄弟就已经计划回国进行投资了。"中国的地方政府非常支持海外华侨回国投资建设，比如投资房地产、建工厂、开酒店等，给了一系列的优惠政策。当时，政府给我们的土地价格非常优惠。"毕传铭说，"这是国家的支持，也是我们的荣幸，你支持国家建设，国家也支持你赚钱。"

只是那个时候，毕家兄弟刚刚在荷兰开始自己经营酒店，资金比较紧张，只能用从海上皇宫赚来的利润来填补酒店的亏损，以及偿还建酒店时的银行贷款。抽调不出更多的资金，他们兄弟也不敢在国内进行大型的投资建设。"其实，家乡这边的政府是非常支持我们回国投资的，那时候我们想要多少地、想要什么地方，基本不成问题。当然，政府也是有条件的，如果买下土地，两年之内就要发展建设。"毕传铭遗憾表示，"然而，我们没有眼光，因为在荷兰那边也要发展投资，实在是抽不出更多的资金。如果买下了家乡这边的土地，又无法发展，届时真的不知道怎么跟政府解释。"

不过，毕家兄弟确实非常想为家乡的建设出一份力量。后来，深圳市龙岗区政府（当时大鹏归龙岗区管辖）到海外招商引资，他们在大鹏镇上与人合作投资建设了千禧大厦和新世纪大厦。2022年10月12日，在位于大鹏新区勤政路附近的新世纪大厦内，记者见到从荷兰回国的毕传铭、毕传发兄弟及他们俩的夫人。站在大厦三楼的阳台往东望去，秋日下的大鹏，蓝天白云，晴空万里，绿荫掩映，阵阵清风徐徐吹来，让人心旷神怡。"那座山的脚下，就是我们小时候出生的地方——乌冲村。"毕传铭指着不远处的群山说道。

"我们当初投资建设新世纪大厦，还有一个想法，就是想让一些在海外奔波劳碌的华侨同胞回到大鹏之后，有一个可以长期定居的地方。"毕传铭坦言。以前，毕传铭经常在荷兰和中国两头跑。因为新冠疫情，最近几年两地来回跑不太方便。2021年3月，毕传铭、毕传发两兄弟偕妻子从阿姆斯特丹直飞广州，几经辗转，终于回到了小时候出生的地方——大鹏。

后来，毕传铭又回了荷兰一趟，并于2022年3月经香港中转，再在5月回到大鹏的家中。"我们在外面的华侨都有一种'思乡病'，这里是我们的根，这里也有我们的产业。"毕传铭说。

弟弟毕传发表示，1992年邓小平视察南方，他看到新闻说中国要搞市场经济，感觉机会来了。"市场经济就意味着我们可以回来投资，国家将会转换另外一条道路，会跟以前完全不一样。"

关于回国投资，毕传发还讲了一个故事。1998 年，长江发生特大洪水灾害，他们在荷兰街头为祖国同胞募捐，后来就想把筹得的资金加上自己的捐款汇回国内灾区。本来在荷兰捐款是不需要缴税的，但当时荷兰的税务人员认为这笔钱是捐回中国内地的，中国是他们的祖籍国和出生地，所以不能免税，即便是捐给中国的红十字会也不行，然而捐给越南、非洲或荷兰的红十字会又可以免税。"当时我们咨询的时候，相关的工作人员说得很清楚，我的会计也在旁边。我非常生气，一怒之下就回到国内了。"

"一开始，我们在国内的投资都是以买地的方式进行的。例如，在龙岗和顺德都买了地。"为什么会投资房地产？毕传发解释："如果做其他行业，比如开工厂或做餐馆，需要有人天天盯着才行。可我们在荷兰那边还有生意，又长期不在国内，所以只能采取这种'隔山买牛'的投资方法。"对于这种投资方式，毕传发也承认，如果他们当初投资其他生意，可能对促进国内的就业会有更多的贡献。

毕传有，荷兰华人的传奇

在荷兰华人世界里，毕传有（有时写作"毕传友"，又名毕通）就是一个传奇。而他，就是毕传铭、毕传发的兄长，一个出生在大鹏乌冲村的深圳人。1963 年，16 岁的毕传有前往香港艰难谋生。1969 年，他抵达荷兰海牙，在姐夫家的餐馆打工。5 年之后，他开设了第一家属于自己的餐馆。1984 年，他成为全荷兰乃至西欧最大的中餐馆海上皇宫的创办者之一。1989 年，他打破荷兰华人原来只从事餐饮行业的传统，将业务拓展到了酒店、房地产、旅行社等多个领域。1999 年，他又担任阿姆斯特丹新中国城基金会主席。在短短二三十年时间里，毕传有一跃成了欧洲华人企业家中的一个重量级人物。

在荷兰，他是欧洲著名侨领，是旅荷华人联谊会会长，是全荷华人社团联合会主席，是荷兰中国和平统一促进会会长，是荷比卢崇正总会名誉会长，是旅荷大鹏同乡会会长；在中国，他是知名爱国华侨，是暨南大学校董，是深圳市荣誉市民、市政协委

在荷兰华人世界里，毕传有是一个传奇。
Chuen You But, a legend in the Dutch Chinese community.

员，是浙江省政协委员，还曾应邀列席过十届全国人大和政协会议，被誉为"传播友谊与文化的使者"。

事业有成的毕传有，时刻不忘支援建设祖国与家乡。他出钱出力，在深圳捐建了大鹏华侨中学、大鹏华侨医院、鹏城老人中心，在黑龙江、贵州、广西、浙江、江苏等地捐建了多间"传有"希望小学。

毕传有是毕家兄弟的主心骨。说起哥哥毕传有，毕传发依然记得，当初刚到香港时，哥哥不但要带他们去吃饭，还要给他们洗衣服、洗裤子，细心照顾他们。在他心目中，哥哥毕传有拥有超乎常人的毅力和智慧。"他的超常能力，就是他可以做出让人刮目相看的成绩，比如将海上皇宫搞得非常成功，这是令我非常佩服的地方。"毕传发说。

"哥哥毕传有是我们几兄弟中最早到荷兰的，一直以来，除了工作，他还非常热心侨团的各种事务。兄弟之中，我主内（搞好海上皇宫等生意），他则是主外（做侨团的工作）。"毕传铭表示，自己后来会从事侨团的工作，完全是受到哥哥毕传有的影响。"我是在 2007 年哥哥逝世之后，才开始逐渐接触侨团工作的。"

2013 年至 2015 年，毕传铭担任旅荷大鹏同乡会会长。2016 年 1 月，他又成为大鹏新区归国华侨联合会名誉主席。虽然毕传铭非常谦虚地表示，自己没有什么经验，时间也不够，做不好侨团的工作，但不可否认的是，他还是做了一件影响深远的事情。

在毕传铭的推动之下，2020 年 3 月，旅荷大鹏同乡会正式更名为"旅荷深圳大鹏同乡会"。对此，他的解释是，"为了让更多的人知道和认识大鹏就在深圳"。现在毕传铭的一个身份，就是旅荷深圳大鹏同乡会永远名誉会长。

目前，旅荷深圳大鹏同乡会有 1100 多名会员，但是毕传铭忧心忡忡。他说："现在荷兰的华侨二代好像不是那么热心参与侨团，对祖国的了解也不多，我呼吁政府应该多邀请华侨子女回国参观访问。"

在毕传铭、毕传发兄弟看来，其实 99% 的华侨都是爱国的。"当国家有困难的时候，最能显示出华侨的热心和力量，他们总是竭尽所能地帮助祖国。"毕传铭说道。

（除署名外，本文图片均由受访者毕传铭、毕传发提供。参考资料：《深圳侨务史志》《桑梓情深 赤子丹心——大鹏侨情口述史》。）

Pat Chuen Ming and Pat Chuen Fa

Going out of Dapeng and creating a business card for China in the Netherlands

Pat Chuen Ming (C. M. Pat), is one of the younger brothers of the famous Dutch overseas Chinese leader Chuen You But (C.Y. But, deceased). He was born in Wuchong Village, Dapeng, Shenzhen in 1949. He is the overseas director of the third council of the Shenzhen Overseas Exchange Association, and honorary director of the fourth council of the Shenzhen Overseas Exchange Association, and used to be president of the Shenzhen Tai Peng Association in the Netherlands, honorary chairman of the Shenzhen Dapeng Federation of Returned Overseas Chinese, honorary president of the Guangdong Federation Netherlands overseas director of the third council of the Shenzhen Overseas Exchange Association, and honorary director of the fourth council of the Shenzhen Overseas Exchange Association.

Pat Chuen Fa, also known as Pat Yu, is the younger brother of C.Y. But and C.M. Pat. He was born in Wuchong Village, Dapeng, Shenzhen in 1951. He went to Hong Kong to make a living in 1967, and went to the Netherlands in 1971. In 1975, he cooperated with his elder brothers and sister to run a restaurant in the Netherlands. In 1992, in response to the call of the motherland, he returned to China with his brothers to invest in and build their hometown.

Located on the east coast of Shenzhen, Dapeng Fortress was originally established in the Ming Dynasty to fight against Japanese pirates, with the full name of Dapeng Defense Fortress of a Thousand Households. Enjoying the reputation of "the best fortress along the coast," it was a coastal defense fortress in southern China during the Ming and Qing Dynasties, and was also one of the places where the Opium War started. Pengcheng (meaning "Peng City"), another name for Shenzhen, stems from Dapeng Fortress. Today, Dapeng Fortress and the adjacent Jiaochangwei (the training ground in ancient China was called "Jiaochang") have become Shenzhen's famous tourist attractions, which also gather a lot of homestay inns.

The interview took place in 2022.

About one kilometer west from Dapeng Fortress, it is Wuchong Village, near Pengcheng Garden. C. M. Pat was born in the village in 1949. Two years later, his younger brother Pat Chuen Fa came into this world.

From Dapeng to Hong Kong, then to the Hague

C.M. Pat said that when he was a child, he was educated at the Pengcheng Primary School in Dapeng Fortress in his hometown. However, because his family was poor, he didn't get much education. At the age of 15, he left his hometown and went to Hong Kong. Since the late Qing Dynasty, villagers in the Dapeng area used to travel to Hong Kong or overseas to make a living. At first, they were migrant workers who earned money to support their family back home. Later, they gradually settled outside and took root there.

"Originally, I intended to continue studying in Hong Kong. But after arriving in Hong Kong, I found that life there was also very difficult, and it was impossible for me to go to school at all," C. M. Pat said. So he started working as a child laborer in Hong Kong. At the beginning, C. M. Pat learned to repair cars, hoping to gain a foothold in Hong Kong in the future with his skills. But it turned out to be not easy, and he had to switch to restaurants.

Pat Chuen Fa's memories are similar to those of his brother. "When we were young, our family was very poor, and we had no food to eat. We had to eat what was fed to chickens and pigs—food made of bran mixed with sweet potatoes—to satisfy our hunger." Pat Chuen Fa went to Hong Kong in 1967, when his elder brothers and sister had basically gained a firm foothold there.

After C. M. Pat worked in Hong Kong restaurants for a few years, his elder brother and sister, who had gone to the Hague, the Netherlands to work in the catering industry, asked him if he wanted to develop in the Netherlands as well. "Because of my low level of education, the future looked bleak for me in Hong Kong, so I decided to go there." But life was not easy anywhere. C. M. Pat arrived in the Netherlands only to find that he had to work even harder than he had done in Hong Kong. He often worked 12 or 13 hours a day, and sometimes had to work overtime at night. But there was no turning back. "I didn't want to be looked down upon, so I just gritted my teeth and got on with it," C. M. Pat said.

In the Netherlands, C. M. Pat met his wife, Lau Yim Ping. Her ancestral home is also in Dapeng, but she was born in Hong Kong. "Back then, the overseas Chinese in the Netherlands were desperately trying to earn more money. The husbands went out to work, and so did the wives, but no one took care of their children," C. M. Pat said helplessly. "Later we hired a foreign woman to help take care of the children, but she taught our children to call her mother and had them sleep with her. Our children did not recognize me and my wife, and we were heartbroken." As a last resort, C. M. Pat and his wife sent their children back to Hong Kong and asked his wife's mother to take care of them.

Pat Chuen Fa recalled that he came to the Netherlands in 1971, later than his two elder brothers. "At that time, my elder sister and her husband told me that I might obtain legal residence status in the Netherlands because of an amnesty there." Pat Chuen Fa worked in the Hague for half a year, but his application for residence failed, so he moved to Germany. After working in Germany for more than a year, he returned to Hong Kong to apply for a labor permit in the Netherlands.

In September 1972, Pat Chuen Fa obtained the labor residence permit and returned to work in the Netherlands. At the time, the brothers were considering starting their own business by opening a restaurant in the Netherlands. This was also the main occupation of the Dapeng people in the Netherlands at that time. *Historical Records of Shenzhen Overseas Chinese Affairs* said, "In the 1970s, the occupation of the Chinese in the Netherlands was still dominated by the restaurant industry, and Chinese restaurants were increasing at a rate of 18% every year." Pat Chuen Fa's two elder brothers ran a restaurant in the Netherlands, and later he came out to open his own takeaway restaurant.

A "Sea Palace" built on a Dutch canal

On the evening of June 20, 2022, a piece of news was widely shared on the Internet: the Jumbo Floating Restaurant under Aberdeen Restaurant Enterprises encountered wind and waves in the waters near China's Xisha Islands while leaving Hong Kong. The seafood restaurant on a boat, which has been collectively remembered by Hong Kong people for nearly half a century, slowly sank into the South China Sea.

At the mouth of the Rhine River in Amsterdam, on the rippling water of the canal, stands the Sea Palace, a luxurious restaurant with strong Chinese characteristics, which can accommodate 700 people at the same time. This is a four-storey gaily painted boat with carved railings and marble inlays, which vividly displays Chinese classical architecture and classic cooking to tourists from all over the world.

C. M. Pat made no secret that it was the Jumbo Floating Restaurant in Hong Kong that had inspired him, his brothers, and several overseas Chinese to build and operate the Sea Palace in Amsterdam. The brothers from Dapeng Peninsula, Shenzhen ran the Sea Palace after renting a berth from the local government at the beginning. Later, for the sustainable development of the restaurant, they discussed with the government and bought the permanent right to use the berth.

Today, Hong Kong's Jumbo Floating Restaurant has sunk into the sea, but on the other side of the Eurasian continent, in Amsterdam, the Sea Palace has become synonymous with the Netherlands alongside windmills, wooden shoes, and tulips. In the Netherlands, there are two sayings, "If you haven't been to Amsterdam, you haven't been to the Netherlands." "When you arrive in Amsterdam, you must go to the Sea Palace." This shows the importance of this Chinese-style Sea Palace floating on an Amsterdam canal in the hearts of travelers.

Since its completion in 1984, the Sea Palace has not only gradually become a very popular tourist attraction in Amsterdam, but also presented as a business card for China in the Netherlands. It is a place that the Dutch royal family and many celebrities like to visit. The important events of the Netherlands towards China and some grand receptions held by local overseas Chinese groups and Chinese-funded enterprises are specially held in the Sea Palace. Many signing ceremonies were held there, such as those of the cooperation project between CNOOC and Royal Dutch Shell Group in Daya Bay, Guangdong, the sister cities partnership between Beijing and Amsterdam, and the cooperation between Xiamen Airlines and KLM Royal Dutch Airlines.

The Sea Palace has left too many good memories for the Pat brothers and their next generation. C. M. Pat's first performance in a movie was done there. This brings us to the Hong Kong action movie series of *Young and Dangerous*, which were adapted from comics. In the mid-1990s, *Young and Dangerous 3: Covering the Sky with One Hand* was filmed in the Netherlands, and one of the filming locations was the Sea Palace. As one of the bosses of the Sea Palace, C. M. Pat played the role of an "old uncle" (godfather of gangsters) living in the Netherlands after retirement. Although it was the first and only time in his life to perform in a movie, C. M. Pat, who was on his home ground, was not afraid at all when he played opposite "the Crow" played by Roy Cheung Yiu Yeung.

Recalling his performance in the movie more than 20 years ago, C. M. Pat said with a smile that he was just a "carefree" extra. When the movie was released, he appeared for six seconds and spoke four lines.

"You supported the country's construction, and the country supported you to make money."

Through the Sea Palace, the Pat brothers have created a business empire in the following decades that is well-known in the European Chinese community. In addition to the traditional industry of catering, which many overseas Chinese rely on for a living, they have also been involved in hotels, real estate, travel agencies and many other industries.

C. M. Pat revealed that around 1989, the brothers already planned to return to China for investment. "Local governments in China were very supportive of overseas Chinese returning home to invest in construction, such as investing in real estate, building factories, opening hotels, and so on, offering a series of preferential policies. At that time, the governments offered very favorable land prices to us," C. M. Pat said. "This showed the support from the country, and was also our honor. You supported the country's construction, and the country supported you to make money."

But by then, the Pat brothers had just started to run their own hotels in the Netherlands, and they suffered from financial strain. They had to use the profits they earned from the Sea Palace to make up for the loss of the hotels and repay the bank loan for building the hotels. Unable to mobilize more funds, the brothers didn't dare to carry out large-scale investment and construction in China. "Actually, the government of my hometown was very supportive of us returning to China to invest. At that time, the amount and location of land, if we asked for, was basically not a problem. Of course, the government set prerequisites. If we bought the land, we should develop it within two years," C. M. Pat said regretfully. "However, we had no vision. Because we also needed to develop and invest in the Netherlands, we really couldn't spare more funds. If we bought land in our hometown and failed to develop it, we really didn't know how to explain it to the government."

However, the Pat brothers really wanted to contribute to the construction of their hometown. Later, the Longgang District Government of Shenzhen (Dapeng was under the jurisdiction of Longgang District then) went overseas to attract investment, and then the brothers cooperated with others to invest in the construction of the Millennium Building and the New Century Building in Dapeng Township. On October 12, 2022, in the New Century Building near Qinzheng Road, Dapeng New District, we saw C. M. Pat, Pat Chuen Fa and their wives, who had returned from the Netherlands. Standing on the balcony on the third floor of the building and looking eastward, Dapeng was in the autumn sun, with blue and clear sky, white clouds, and green shades. The slow breeze was quite refreshing. "At the foot of that mountain is where we were born, Wuchong Village," C. M. Pat said, pointing to the mountains not far away.

"At first, when we invested in the construction of the New Century Building, we had an idea, which was to provide some overseas Chinese compatriots who had worked hard abroad with a place where they could settle for a long time after returning to Dapeng," C. M. Pat said frankly. In the past, C. M. Pat often traveled between the Netherlands and China. The COVID-19 pandemic made it inconvenient to travel back and forth between the two countries in recent years. In March 2021, the two brothers, C. M. Pat and Pat Chuen Fa, together with their wives, flew directly from Amsterdam to Guangzhou. After several transfers, they finally returned to Dapeng, the place where they were born.

Later, C. M. Pat went back to the Netherlands, and returned to his home in Dapeng in May 2022 after transiting through Hong Kong in March 2022. "We overseas Chinese all have a kind of 'homesickness.' We have our roots and business here," C. M. Pat said.

His younger brother Pat Chuen Fa said that after Deng Xiaoping's South Tour in 1992, he saw the news that China was going to develop a market economy, and he felt that the opportunity was coming. "A market economy meant that we could come back to invest, and the country would switch to another path, which would be completely different from the one before."

Pat Chuen Fa also told a story about how they returned to China to invest. In 1998, when the Yangtze River was flooded, they raised donations on the streets of the Netherlands for the compatriots back in the motherland. Later, they wanted to remit the funds they had raised together with their own donations to the disaster-stricken areas in China. Donations in the Netherlands were not supposed to be taxable, but the Dutch tax officials said that the money, even if it was donated to the Red Cross Society of China, couldn't be exempted from tax, because it was donated back to Chinese mainland, the brothers' home country and birthplace. But donations to the Red Cross in Vietnam, Africa or the Netherlands were tax-free. "When we consulted, the relevant staff made it very clear. My accountant was also there. I was very angry and went back to China in a fit of anger."

"In the beginning, our domestic investment was all carried out in the form of buying land. For example, we bought land in Longgang and Shunde." Why did they invest in real estate? Pat Chuen Fa explained, "If you were in other industries, such as opening a factory or running a restaurant, you needed someone to monitor the business every day. But we also had business in the Netherlands, and we were out of China for most of the time, so we could only adopt the investment method of 'buying cattle across the mountain.'" Regarding this investment method, Pat Chuen Fa also admitted that if they had invested in other businesses, they might have made more contributions to promoting China's employment.

C. Y. But, a legend of the Dutch Chinese

In the Dutch Chinese community, Chuen You But (C. Y. But) was a legend. A native of Shenzhen, born in Wuchong, Dapeng, he was C. M. Pat and Pat Chuen Fa's elder brother. In 1963, the 16-year-old C. Y. But went to Hong Kong and struggled to make a living there. In 1969, he arrived in the Hague, the Netherlands, and worked in the restaurant of his brother-in-law's family. Five years later, he opened the first restaurant of his own. In 1984, he became one of the founders of the Sea Palace, the largest Chinese restaurant in the Netherlands and even in Western Europe. In 1989, he broke the tradition that the Chinese in Dutch were engaged only in the catering industry, and expanded his business to hotels, real estate, travel agencies and other fields. In 1999, he became chairman of Amsterdam's New Chinatown Foundation. In just 20 to 30 years, he became a heavyweight among Chinese entrepreneurs in Europe.

In the Netherlands, he was a famous leader of overseas Chinese in Europe, president of the Chinese Association in the Netherlands 'Fa Yin' (Chinese Vereniging in Nederland 'Fa Yin'), chairman of the Foundation National Federation of Chinese Organizations in the Netherlands (Stichting Landelijke Federatie van Chinese Organisaties in Nederland), president of the Netherlands Association of the Unification of China, honorary president of the Benelux Tsung Tsin Hakka Association, and president of the Tai Peng Association in the Netherlands. In China, he was a well-known patriotic overseas Chinese, a member of the school board of Jinan University, an honorary citizen of Shenzhen, a member of the CPPCC (Chinese People's Political Consultative Conference) Shenzhen Municipal Committee, and a member of the CPPCC Zhejiang Provincial Committee. He was invited to attend the annual sessions of the 10th National People's Congress and the CPPCC National Committee as a nonvoting delegate. He was known as "a messenger of friendship and culture."

C. Y. But had a successful career and never forgot to support the construction of his motherland and hometown. He donated money and made efforts to build the Dapeng Overseas Chinese Middle School, the Dapeng Overseas Chinese Hospital, and the Pengcheng Elderly Center in Shenzhen, and donated to build many "Chuen You" Hope Primary Schools in Heilongjiang, Guizhou, Guangxi, Zhejiang, Jiangsu and other places.

C. Y. But was the backbone of the brothers. Pat Chuen Fa still remembers that when they first arrived in Hong Kong, his elder brother C. Y. But not only took them to dinner, but also washed their clothes and trousers and took good care of them. In his mind, his elder brother C. Y. But possessed extraordinary perseverance and wisdom. "His extraordinary ability was that he could make impressive achievements, such as making the Sea Palace very successful. This is why I admire him very much," Pat Chuen Fa said.

"My elder brother C. Y. But was the first among the brothers to go to the Netherlands. In addition to his work, he was always enthusiastic about various affairs of overseas Chinese groups. Among the brothers, I was in charge of internal affairs (managing our businesses such as the Sea Palace), he was in charge of external affairs (working for overseas Chinese groups)." C. M. Pat said that he later started working for overseas Chinese groups just because he was influenced by his brother C. Y. But. "I gradually began to work for overseas Chinese groups after my brother passed away in 2007."

From 2013 to 2015, C. M. Pat served as president of the Tai Peng Association in the Netherlands. In January 2016, he became honorary chairman of the Federation of Returned Overseas Chinese of Dapeng New District. Although C. M. Pat said modestly that he could not do the work of overseas Chinese groups well because he did not have much experience and time, it is undeniable that he did something far-reaching.

Under the promotion of C. M. Pat, in March 2020, the Tai Peng Association in the Netherlands was officially renamed the Shenzhen Tai Peng Association in the Netherlands. "It was in order to let more people know that Dapeng is in Shenzhen," he explained. One of his current identities is permanent honorary president of the Shenzhen Tai Peng Association in the Netherlands.

At present, there are more than 1,100 members in the Shenzhen Tai Peng Association in the Netherlands, but C. M. Pat is a little worried. He said, "Now the second generation of overseas Chinese in the Netherlands doesn't seem to be so enthusiastic about joining overseas Chinese groups, and they don't know much about their motherland. I call on the government to invite more children of overseas Chinese to return to China for visits."

According to C. M. Pat and Pat Chuen Fa, in fact, 99% of overseas Chinese are patriotic. "When the country is in trouble, the enthusiasm and strength of overseas Chinese can be best shown. They always try their best to help the motherland," C. M. Pat said.

(Photos courtesy of C. M. Pat and Pat Chuen Fa, except for the ones with credit. References: *Historical Records of Shenzhen Overseas Chinese Affairs* and *Deep Love for the Hometown and Sincere Loyalty to the Motherland: Oral History of Overseas Chinese from Dapeng*.)

陈玉昌

为国为乡常怀赤子之心，引资助推深圳发展

2015 年 4 月 25 日，陈玉昌（右一）带领在港乡亲到广东开平参加香港观澜同乡总会组织的"情系港亲千人行"活动。

Chan Yuk Cheong (first from right) leads fellow immigrants in Hong Kong to Kaiping, Guangdong during the "Trip for a Thousand Hometown Fellows in Hong Kong" organized by the Federation of Hong Kong Guanlan Association on April 25, 2015.

　　陈玉昌，1951 年出生于深圳观澜松元厦（今属龙华区观湖街道），1969 年赴香港谋生，先后在餐饮、贸易、电子配件加工等行业工作，1987 年回家乡投资兴业。深圳市荣誉市民，现任香港观澜同乡总会主席、香港观湖同乡会会长。曾任香港观澜同乡总会会长，中国海外交流协会理事，深圳市宝安区政协第一、二、三、四届常委，观澜商会第二、三、四届会长。

　　陈玉昌帮助深圳引进投资项目 100 多个，资金总额近 10 亿元人民币，为全国各项公益慈善事业累计捐款 1600 万元。参与创办观澜商会，积极参与旅港同乡会事务，团结爱国爱港爱家乡的乡亲，为家乡的招商引资工作牵线搭桥。曾获"全国归侨侨眷先进个人""全国先进爱国企业家"等荣誉称号。

采访时间：2023 年。

陈玉昌在办公室接受采访。（来源：《晶报》）
Chan Yuk Cheong is interviewed in his office.
(Photo: *Daily Sunshine*)

陈玉昌的故事里，浓缩了厚重的家族故事、历史的风云际会。

在深圳市龙华区观湖街道松元厦社区的昌玮工业区里，陈玉昌有一间宽敞的办公室。他办公桌旁边的墙上高挂着一块红底金字的牌匾，"义门世家"几个大字十分醒目。

这块牌匾是广东省梅州市五华县陈氏开基祖陈景旺的后裔宗亲在 2013 年送来的，为的是感谢陈玉昌等 5 人捐资建设景旺公纪念堂门楼。陈氏又称为"义门陈氏"，发祥于江西省德安县车桥镇。

谈起这块牌匾，陈玉昌谦虚地说，自己就是为景旺公纪念堂门楼的建设组织了一下捐款活动，为铭记本族历史出了点力。

松元厦陈氏的始祖陈振能，就是陈景旺的十世孙。深圳教育史上记载的华侨学校——振能学校，就是陈振能的后人创办的，陈玉昌也为这所学校的发展壮大作过贡献。

他为家族出力的事还有很多。比如，他和陈锦明、陈煌胜等人为恢复江西省德安县陈氏故居捐款十余万元，为资助出版《义门陈文史考》一书捐款 4.5 万元。

树高千尺不忘根，陈玉昌念兹在兹的不仅仅是家族的荣辱兴衰，他身上还有着深厚的家国情怀。在改革开放大潮中，他不但自己回乡投资，还为大批台商、港商牵线搭桥，汇聚成了深圳早期发展的一股重要力量。他积极投身商会、同乡会事务，还为公益事业慷慨解囊。

"我就是帮着做桥梁。我感觉，我做了好事，自己开心，心里安泰。"陈玉昌对自己的总结，是那样朴实无华。

客家后代，闯荡香港当厨师

1951 年，陈玉昌出生在深圳松元厦大布头村，是客家人陈振能的九世孙。松元厦这个地名，就是陈振能起的。1751 年，年近六旬的陈振能响应当时清朝政府的"复界招垦"政策，毅然率家眷和堂弟等十几人从广东省长乐县（今五华县）的大山里向外迁徙，寻求更大的发展空间。

他们辗转经过紫金、惠州、东莞等地，甚至到过香港的九龙半岛，最后在当时的新安县观澜镇七都洞落脚。这里背山面水，青松遍地，人烟稀少，陈振能觉得这是一处宝地。他带领众人在背夫山边的松林下搭起茅寮，将此地称为"松园厦"。"松园厦"后来演变为"松元厦"，并且逐渐取代了"七都洞"这个地名。

据客家文化研究者杨宏海考证，深圳的客家人多数来自梅州市的梅县、兴宁、五华等地。而陈玉昌在日常生活中说的客家话，正是梅州一带的口音。

陈玉昌年少时种过田、放过牛。18岁的时候，他只身去香港谋生，还学会了粤语（俗称"白话"）。因为文化水平不高，他选择了学厨，边学边做，先后在多家餐馆当厨师。"我没什么拿手菜，最拿手的是客家焖猪肉。"

话虽这么说，但时至今日，陈玉昌的厨艺依然出众。2023年8月的一天，他在办公室接受《晶报》采访时，热情地招呼大家吃月饼，还强调说："我自己做的馅！"

月饼的包装盒上印着"亚昌配方"。在粤语里，"亚昌"和"阿昌"发音相似，指的就是陈玉昌。"你慢慢嚼，里面有火腿的味道。"陈玉昌介绍说。这是他买来金华火腿之后，自己用刀慢慢地切细，加到馅料里，另外还加入了五仁、陈皮等原料。然后他安排人照这个配方去做。这几年，他的公司都是这样制作月饼，自用或者馈赠，包括送给附近的几所老人院。

层层开嶂，变身商人、企业家

陈玉昌的办公室里高挂着一幅题为《层层开嶂》的油画，标注着"阿昌构思"。这是他请朋友创作的，描绘了他在福建见过的类似景色：层层叠叠的山峰，由近到远延伸开去，山一座比一座高。在自己的人生之路上，"阿昌"也是一步一个台阶往上走的，难怪他对这样的景色很有感触。

在香港做厨师时，陈玉昌增长了见识，结交了很多朋友，其中一些人后来去了国外。这样的经历和人脉，为陈玉昌转换赛道埋下了伏笔。

陈玉昌回忆说，有些朋友后来去日本工作，他去探访他们时，在交流中发现，海外侨胞对中国土特产有比较强烈的需求，但是不容易买到。那是1978年，中国还没有改革开放，直接出口的商品很有限。陈玉昌觉得这是个商机，于是做起了这方面的生意。

"在国外的侨胞想要国内的什么，我就在香港寄给他们。"那几年，陈玉昌常常前往日本，每次带些特产过去。这有点像今天的"代购""海淘"，只不过反了过来，把中国货送到海外侨胞手上。

当然，这样"小打小闹"是不够的。后来，陈玉昌开拓了贸易渠道，"搞点小出口"，帮中国的国货公司把产品推销到日本。他经销的特产包括药材、茶叶、人参、燕窝、虫草等，生意越做越大，一方面满足了侨胞的物质需求，让侨胞一解乡

2020 年 8 月 1 日，时任苏里南驻华大使陈家慧（左三）和丈夫（左二）前来探望家乡父老，到访陈玉昌公司，合影的背景里就有陈玉昌构思的油画《层层开嶂》。

Patty Chen (third from left), then ambassador of Suriname to China, and her husband (second from left) visit Chan Yuk Cheong's company on August 1, 2020 during a trip to her hometown. In the background of this group photo, there is the oil painting *Beyond the Peaks* conceived by Chan.

愁，另一方面让他积累了第一桶金。

在香港，陈玉昌还跟人合伙经营电子配件加工生意。"买塑胶和铜，把它们做成配件卖给贸易商。"

回乡兴业，助力深圳跨越式发展

20 世纪 80 年代，随着国家一系列鼓励政策的出台和深圳投资环境的不断完善，越来越多的华侨和港澳同胞来到深圳投资。从厨师转型为商人、企业家的陈玉昌，一直牵挂着家乡的发展。家乡的亲友陆续捎来"春天的信息"，家乡的干部还带来观澜的荔枝，邀请在港乡亲们回去投资做生意、建设家乡。陈玉昌心潮澎湃，决定回家乡投资。"我想把故乡建设得和香港一样好！"

经过一番紧锣密鼓的准备，陈玉昌在 1987 年回到深圳观澜投资兴业。他在松元厦创办了昌兴五金塑料厂，后来又投资兴建了昌玮工业区及商业城。

陈玉昌说，最初，他的工厂是做"三来一补"业务的，就像深圳发展的一个缩影：深圳靠这个起步，吸引了人才，把整个城市带旺了，而陈玉昌则完成了他在深圳投资发展的起步。

"三来一补"是改革开放初期的一种企业贸易形式，即"来料加工""来样加工""来件装配"与"补偿贸易"，由外商提供设备、原材料、来样等，由中方提供工地、厂房、劳动力，按照外商要求组织生产、加工装配，全部产品外销，中方收取加工费。积极发展"三来一补"贸易，对深圳经济的起步和跨越式发展起到了巨大的推动作用。1993 至 1994 年，"三来一补"贸易在深圳的发展到达顶峰阶段。

现在回望这段历史，陈玉昌返乡投资可谓恰逢其时。他总结自己的创业经验时也说："胆子可以大一点，碰到机会就要抓住。跟着国家政策走，跟上产业的风口，就容易发现机会。"

招商引资，为家乡聚合大量资源

陈玉昌在深圳的投资是当时的一个重大招商引资项目，生产的产品远销日本、欧美等地。项目的成功起到了很好的带动作用，令不少港商注意到改革开放的成效和商机。

除了自己投资办厂、形成榜样的力量，陈玉昌还通过商会和同乡会为家乡发展聚合资源、链接人脉，引领、协助港商、台商投资深圳。

1994 年 9 月，陈玉昌参与创办的观澜商会应运而生，陈玉昌担任副会长。从 1998 年开始，他连续担任第二、三、四届会长，长达 16 年。观澜商会成立时，正值 1992 年邓小平南方谈话后，广东掀起新一轮深化改革、扩大开放、加快发展的热潮。天时地利人和再次共振，有力地推动了观澜经济的发展。

1985 年，陈玉昌的叔叔陈官新参与创立了观澜旅港同乡会。这个组织后来改名为"香港观澜同乡总会"。从 20 世纪 80 年代末开始，陈玉昌连续担任了 30 多年会长。总会坚持"爱国爱港爱乡"的办会宗旨，发挥桥梁纽带作用，广泛联系和团结居港乡亲，带领乡贤回乡投资置业，为家乡发展献策出力，为落实"一国两制"、维护香港长期繁荣稳定和推动深港交流合作做了大量的工作。

陈玉昌用浅显的语言解释："我们同乡会主要是聚集一批爱国爱港爱家乡的老乡，为家乡说好话、做桥梁。通过大家互相介绍，宣传观澜、宣传龙华、宣传深圳。有好的项目，就介绍乡亲们参与投资。如果想回来投资的乡亲有顾虑，我们同乡会就去牵线，深入介绍家乡的情况，把事情促成。"

2015 年，原观澜街道拆分为观湖、福城、观澜街道。2018 年，香港观湖同乡会、香港福城同乡会、香港观澜同乡会成立，迈出了龙华区居港乡亲社团组织精细化建设的重要一步，陈玉昌出任香港观湖同乡会会长。

据陈玉昌介绍，这些新成立的同乡会做的事情也差不多。"全世界的同乡会都是一样的，都是聚集老乡，大家讲得开（谈得来）。"他说，认同中华儿女身份、认同中国发展道路的侨胞，最在意的就是同乡会，因此谈得来。加上同乡会与深圳各级侨务部门有密切联系，所以是很好的沟通桥梁。

经过多年的努力，陈玉昌成功介绍 60 多位台商、50 多位港商到观澜投资办厂，引进资金近 10 亿元。

热心公益，延续崇文重教光荣传统

组织居港乡亲到深圳参观考察、促进深港交流合作是陈玉昌的重要工作。他还依托商会、同乡会，携手香港同胞、观澜企业家投身公益事业，回馈社会，展现人间大爱。陈玉昌为社会公益事业累计捐资 1600 万元，发动商会会员捐资近 1 亿元。他带领商会、同乡会成员多次在广东河源等地出资建桥修路。商会成员多次赴广东省龙川县、五华县等地开展扶贫助发展活动。

教育事业是陈玉昌支持的重点之一。在这方面，他可谓是延续了"崇文重教，耕读传家"的家族传统。其中，他为家乡的振能小学捐资 30 多万元，用于改善办学条件；在五华县赤径村，他捐资 30 多万元，支持兴建五华赤径振能学校。"振能"两字，镌刻着深圳教育史上延续数百年的一段佳话。

观澜是著名的侨乡，也是远近闻名的教育之乡。松元厦陈氏一族从第三代起就开办了家族私塾。1914 年，在族中先贤和侨领推动下，陈氏家族的 9 所私塾合并，开办了永修小学，这是深圳最早的现代学堂之一。1929 年，海内外族人共 499 人筹资在新址建设的学校落成，命名为"振能学校"以纪念先祖陈振能。这是当时宝安县最负盛名的学校，吸引了邻近大批青少年前来就读。1946 年，海内外族人共 154 人捐款创办了振能中学。

中华人民共和国成立后，振能中学并入了今天的深圳市观澜中学；小学部一度改名为"松元小学"，1982 年复名"振能小学"，后来又多次扩建，政府为此投入巨资，陈氏海内外族人也踊跃捐款。2019 年，振能小学升级为九年一贯制学校，更名为"深圳市龙华区振能学校"，成为全市同级同类学校中办学规模最大的学校之一。看到自己家族创办的百年名校焕发新光彩，陈玉昌颇感欣慰。

2007 年，国务院侨办启动"侨爱工程"，这是专为海外侨胞、港澳同胞、归侨侨眷关注和支持国内各项公益事业、扶贫济困、回馈社会、奉

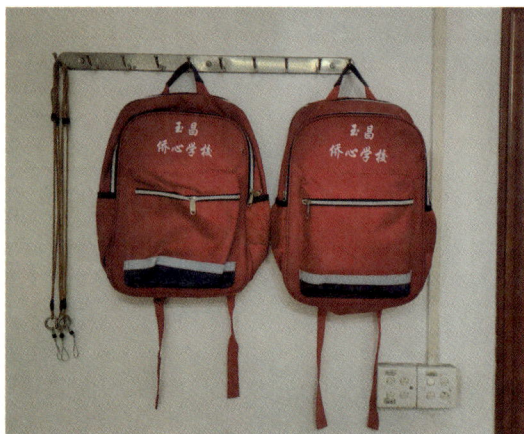

陈玉昌办公室的墙上挂着玉昌侨心学校的书包。
（来源：《晶报》）
Schoolbags of Yuchang Qiaoxin School hung on a wall of Chan Yuk Cheong's office. (Photo: *Daily Sunshine*)

献爱心提供服务而搭建的平台，陈玉昌积极参与其中。2007 年，随同国务院侨务办公室前往河北省贫困山区考察扶贫工作时，陈玉昌看到承德市兴隆县上石洞乡中心小学低矮破旧、岌岌可危的教室，当即捐款 20 万元重建学校。同时，陈玉昌联系观澜的工商企业家，共同捐资 60 万元，支持江西省新建县建起一所"观澜希望小学"，解决了当地小学生缺少校舍的困难。

2009 年，陈玉昌捐建的上石洞乡新学校落成投入使用，命名为"玉昌侨心小学"。陈玉昌又与两位澳门同胞追加捐款，改善办学条件。

陈玉昌扶贫济困的善举还有很多。2008 年，四川省汶川县发生 8.0 级特大地震，陈玉昌先后捐出 150 多万元；2011 年，陈玉昌等几位香港同胞一起为"侨爱工程——点亮藏区牧民新生活计划"捐款 100 万元……

女儿接棒，侨团事业薪火相传

由于在经济和社会领域的突出贡献，陈玉昌获得了"全国归侨侨眷先进个人""全国先进爱国企业家""深圳市首届慈善个人大奖"等荣誉。2011 年，他被授予"深圳市荣誉市民"称号。他应邀赴北京人民大会堂出席国庆招待会 10 余次，3 次登上天安门城楼阅兵观礼台，其中包括 2015 年的纪念中国人民抗日战争暨世界反法西斯战争胜利 70 周年活动。

"我的经济条件还不错，所以，在社会有需要的时候，我就帮一点点。"陈玉昌这样总结自己做公益的初心。

如今，73 岁的陈玉昌处于退而不休的状态，依然在帮助家乡招商引资。"有好的项目，就介绍过来，因为我是做商会出身嘛。我现在非常忙，好多事情要用心去过问。"

他的侨团事业已经后继有人。为了适应观澜片区行政区划的变化，2019 年，香港观澜同乡总会改名为"香港大观澜同乡总会"，陈玉昌出任主席，他的小女儿陈秋娴出任会长，接过了这个老牌侨团的重担。陈秋娴还是深圳市政协委员、中国侨联青年委员、香港深圳社团总会常务副会长兼常务副秘书长。在父亲言传身教下，她积极参与社会和侨团事务。

陈玉昌有一个儿子、两个女儿，他们都很好地传承了陈玉昌的爱国爱乡精神。陈玉昌希望，年青一代都不要忘记自己的根在哪里。

（除署名外，本文图片均由受访者陈玉昌提供。参考资料：新华社、中新网、《南方》杂志、深圳政府在线、《深圳特区报》、《宝安日报》、《梅州日报》、《龙华侨史》、《深圳风物志·第二辑·家族记忆卷》、《特区丰碑——特区历史文献丛书·卷二》、《义门陈文史续考》。）

Chan Yuk Cheong

Devoted to his motherland and hometown, attracting investment to promote Shenzhen's development

Chan Yuk Cheong was born in Songyuanxia, Guanlan, Shenzhen in 1951. (Songyuanxia now belongs to Guanhu Subdistrict, Longhua District.) In 1969, he went to Hong Kong to make a living and worked successively in catering, trading, electronic accessories processing and other industries. In 1987, he returned to his hometown to invest in business. He is an Honorary Citizen of Shenzhen Municipality, and currently serves as chairman of the Federation of Hong Kong Guanlan Association and president of the Hong Kong Guanhu Natives Association. He used to be president of the Federation of Hong Kong Guanlan Association, a director of the China Overseas Exchange Association, a member of the standing committee of the first, second, third and fourth sessions of the Bao'an District Committee of the Chinese People's Political Consultative Conference, and the second, third and fourth president of the Guanlan Chamber of Commerce.

Chan has helped Shenzhen introduce more than 100 investment projects with a total capital of nearly 1 billion yuan, and has donated a total of 16 million yuan to various public welfare and charity causes across China. He was one of the founders of the Guanlan Chamber of Commerce. He has actively participated in the affairs of hometown associations in Hong Kong, united the fellow immigrants who love the motherland, Hong Kong and their hometown, and helped to attract investment to his hometown. He has won honorary titles such as the "National Advanced Individual of Returned Overseas Chinese and Relatives of Overseas Chinese Nationals Residing in China" and the "National Advanced Patriotic Entrepreneur."

Chan Yuk Cheong's story condenses weighty family tales and historical events.

Chan has a spacious office in the Changwei Industrial Zone in Songyuanxia Community, Guanhu Subdistrict, Longhua District, Shenzhen Municipality. On the wall

---

The interview took place in 2023.

next to his desk, a plaque with gold characters on a red background is hanging high. The characters "Yimen Clan" are very eye-catching.

This plaque was sent in 2013 by the descendants of Chen Jingwang, the founder of the Chen clan in Wuhua County, Meizhou City, Guangdong Province, in order to thank Chan and four other people for donating to build the gate tower of the Jingwang Gong Memorial Hall. The Chen clan, also known as the "Yimen Chen clan," originated in Cheqiao Town, De'an County, Jiangxi Province.

Talking about this plaque, Chan said modestly that he had organized the donation for the construction of the gate tower of the Jingwang Gong Memorial Hall in a bid to contribute to remembering the history of his clan.

Chen Zhenneng, the ancestor of the Chen clan in Songyuanxia, is the 10th-generation descendant of Chen Jingwang. Zhenneng School, an overseas Chinese school recorded in the history of education in Shenzhen, was founded by Chen Zhenneng's descendants. Chan Yuk Cheong also contributed to the development and growth of this school.

He has done many other things for his clan. For example, Chan Yuk Cheong, Chen Jinming, Chen Huangsheng and others donated more than 100,000 yuan to restore the Chen clan's former residence in De'an County, Jiangxi Province, and donated 45,000 yuan to fund the publication of the book *Cultural and Historical Research on the Yimen Chen Clan*.

A thousand-feet-tall tree never forgets its roots. Chan has been concerned about the honor of his clan, and has deep feelings for his motherland. In the tide of reform and opening-up, he not only returned to his hometown to invest, but also helped attract a large number of businessmen from Taiwan and Hong Kong, China, forming an important force in the early development of Shenzhen. He has actively participated in the affairs of the chamber of commerce and hometown associations, and has donated generously to public welfare undertakings.

"I have just offered help and acted as a bridge. I feel happy and at ease when I have done good things," Chan's summary of himself is so simple and unpretentious.

A Hakka descendant who worked as a cook in Hong Kong

In 1951, Chan was born in Dabutou Village, Songyuanxia. He is a ninth-generation descendant of Chen Zhenneng, a Hakka man, who created the place name, Songyuanxia. In 1751, Chen, who was nearly 60 years old, responded to the Qing Dynasty government's policy of "restoring borders and recruiting people for reclamation" and resolutely led his family and cousins, amounting to more than a dozen people, to migrate out of the mountains in Changle County (now Wuhua County), Guangdong Province, seeking greater space for development.

They traveled through Zijin, Huizhou, Dongguan and other places, and even went to the Kowloon Peninsula of Hong Kong. They finally settled in Qidudong, Guanlan Township, Xin'an County. With mountains in the back, water in the front, and green pines around, this sparsely populated area was a treasured place in Chen's eyes. He led his family members to build thatched cottages under the pine forest on the edge of Beifu Mountain, and named the place "Songyuanxia," meaning "Pine Garden Mansions." The Chinese name of "Songyuanxia" later evolved a little and gradually replaced the name of "Qidudong."

According to the research by Yang Honghai, a researcher on Hakka culture, most of the Hakkas in Shenzhen were from Meixian, Xingning, Wuhua and other places in Meizhou City. The Hakka dialect that Chan speaks in his daily life belongs to the accent around Meizhou.

When Chan was young, he farmed and herded cattle. When he was 18 years old, he went to Hong Kong alone to make a living, where he learned Cantonese (commonly known as "the vernacular"). Not well-educated, he chose to learn cooking and learned it from work. Then he worked as a cook in many restaurants. "I didn't have many specialties, but I was good at Hakka braised pork."

However, to this day, Chan's cooking skills are still outstanding. One day in August 2023, when the *Daily Sunshine* interviewed him in his office, he warmly invited everyone there to eat mooncakes. He emphasized, "I made the fillings myself!"

The packaging box of the mooncakes was printed with "Recipe by Nga Cheong." In Cantonese, "Nga Cheong" and "Ah Cheong" have similar pronunciations, and both are the nicknames of Chan Yuk Cheong. "Chew it slowly, and you will find the taste of ham inside." Chan said that after purchasing Jinhua ham, he slowly chopped it into fine pieces with a knife and added it to the filling. He also added ingredients such as "five kernels" and tangerine peel. Then, he asked his subordinates to follow this recipe. In the past few years, his company has been making mooncakes like this for personal use or as gifts given to several nearby nursing homes and others.

Beyond the peaks: becoming a businessman and entrepreneur

An oil painting hung in Chan's office, was titled "Beyond the Peaks" and marked "Ah Cheong's Conception." It was drawn by a friend at Chan's request, depicting a similar scene Chan had seen in Fujian: Layers of mountain peaks extended from near to far, with each higher than the one before it. On the road of his own life, "Ah Cheong" also walked up step by step. No wonder he is very touched by such scenery.

While working as a cook in Hong Kong, Chan gained a lot of knowledge and made many friends, some of whom later went abroad. Such experience and connections paved the way for Chan to change his career track.

Chan recalled that some friends later went to work in Japan. When he visited them, he discovered through their chats that overseas Chinese had a strong demand for Chinese local specialties, which were not easy to buy abroad. That was in 1978, the eve of China's reform and opening-up, when the country directly exported few goods. Chan saw this as a business opportunity, so he started a business in this area.

"When the overseas Chinese wanted something made in China, I would send it to them by post from Hong Kong." In those years, Chan often traveled to Japan, bringing some specialties with him each time. That was a bit like today's "purchasing agents" and "overseas shopping," but, in reverse, he was delivering Chinese goods to overseas Chinese.

Certainly, such a "small-scale business" was not enough. Later, Chan was "engaged in small exports." He opened up trade channels to help Chinese domestic product companies sell their products to Japan. The specialties he distributed include medicinal materials, tea, ginseng, bird's nest, and cordyceps fungus, among others. The business grew fast. On the one hand, it met the material needs of overseas Chinese and relieved their homesickness. On the other hand, Chan earned his first pot of gold by doing this.

In Hong Kong, Chan partnered with others to run an electronic accessories processing business. "We bought plastic and copper, made them into accessories, and sold them to traders."

Returning to hometown to start business, helping Shenzhen develop by leaps and bounds

In the 1980s, when China introduced a series of incentive policies and Shenzhen's investment environment kept improving, more and more overseas Chinese and compatriots from Hong Kong and Macao came to Shenzhen to invest. Chan, who had transformed from a cook to a businessman and entrepreneur, had always been concerned about the development of his hometown. Relatives and friends from his hometown brought "messages of spring" one after another. Officials from Guanlan brought lychees to Hong Kong, and invited Guanlan immigrants to go back to invest in business and build their hometown. Chan was very excited and decided to return to his hometown to invest. "I wanted to build my hometown into a place as good as Hong Kong!"

After intensive preparations, Chan returned to Guanlan, Shenzhen in 1987 to invest and start a business. He founded Changxing Hardware and Plastic Factory in Songyuanxia, and later invested in the construction of the Changwei Industrial Zone and Commercial City.

At the beginning, Chan's factory was engaged in the "three supplies and one compensation" trade, which, he said, was like a microcosm of Shenzhen's development: Shenzhen started with this trade, attracted talents and made the entire city prosperous, while Chan started his investment and development in Shenzhen.

"Three supplies and one compensation" was a form of trade among enterprises at the beginning of reform and opening-up, namely "processing with supplied materials, processing according to supplied samples, assembling with supplied parts, and compensation trade." Foreign clients provided equipment, raw materials, and samples while Chinese enterprises provided land, workshops and labor and organized production, processing and assembly in accordance with the requirements of foreign clients. All the products were exported, and the Chinese enterprises charged processing fees only. The active development of the "three supplies and one compensation" trade greatly promoted the subsequent leap-forward growth of Shenzhen's economy. 1993 and 1994 witnessed the peak of this trading mode.

Looking back at this history, Chan found that he had returned to his hometown to invest at the right time. "You can be bolder and seize opportunities when you encounter them. If you follow the country's policies and keep up with industry trends, it will be easier to find opportunities," he said when summarizing his entrepreneurial experience.

Attracting investment and gathering a lot of resources for hometown

Chan's investment in Shenzhen was a major investment promotion project at that time, and his products were exported to Japan, European countries and the United States. The success of the project played a very good promotive role, leading many Hong Kong businessmen to notice the effects and business opportunities of Chinese mainland's reform and opening-up.

Chan not only set an example by investing to start his factory, but also gathered resources and contacts for the development of his hometown through the chamber of commerce and hometown associations, leading and assisting businessmen from Hong Kong and Taiwan, China, to invest in Shenzhen.

In September 1994, the Guanlan Chamber of Commerce, which Chan co-founded, came into being at the right time, with Chan serving as vice president. Starting in 1998, he served as the chamber's second, third and fourth president for 16 years. This chamber of commerce was established when Guangdong set off a new boom in deepening reform, expanding opening-up, and accelerating development after Deng Xiaoping's Southern Talks in 1992. The right time, right place and right people once again resonated to effectively promote the economic development of Guanlan.

In 1985, Chan Yuk Cheong's uncle Chan Koon San co-founded the Hong Kong Guanlan Hometown Association. This organization later changed its name to the Federation of Hong Kong Guanlan Association. Starting in the late 1980s, Chan Yuk Cheong served as the federation's president for more than 30 years. The federation has adhered to its purpose of "loving the country, loving Hong Kong, and loving the hometown," played the role of a bridge and link, extensively contacted and united hometown fellows living in Hong Kong, and led the elites of them to return to their hometown to invest and buy property. The federation has made suggestions and contribution to the development of the hometown, and done a lot of work to implement "one country, two systems," maintain Hong Kong's long-term prosperity and stability, and promote exchanges and cooperation between Shenzhen and Hong Kong.

Chan Yuk Cheong explained in plain language, "Our federation has focused on gathering a group of hometown fellows who love the country, love Hong Kong and love our hometown, and putting in a good word and serving as a bridge for our hometown. Through mutual introductions, we have promoted Guanlan, Longhua and Shenzhen. When there are good projects, we will invite the hometown fellows to participate in the investment. If the hometown fellows who want to return to invest have concerns, we will act as a bridge, introduce the hometown in depth, and facilitate the investment."

In 2015, the original Guanlan Subdistrict was split into Guanhu, Fucheng and Guanlan subdistricts. In 2018, the Hong Kong Guanhu Natives Association, the Hong Kong Fucheng Natives Association, and the Hong Kong Guanlan Natives Association were established, taking an important step in the refined construction of community organizations for Hong Kong residents from Longhua District. Chan became president of the Hong Kong Guanhu Natives Association.

According to Chan, these newly established hometown associations do similar things. "Hometown associations all over the world are the same. They gather fellow immigrants, who can get along well." Overseas Chinese who identify themselves as Chinese descendants and agree on China's development path care most about hometown associations, so they get along well with the associations, he said. In addition, the hometown associations have close contact with the overseas Chinese affairs offices at all levels in Shenzhen, so they are good bridges of communication.

After years of hard work, Chan has successfully introduced more than 60 Taiwan merchants and more than 50 Hong Kong merchants to Guanlan for investing and setting up factories, bringing in nearly 1 billion yuan in capital.

Enthusiastic about public welfare, continuing glorious tradition of advocating culture and education

Organizing hometown fellows living in Hong Kong to visit Shenzhen and promoting exchanges and cooperation between Shenzhen and Hong Kong have been important tasks for Chan. Through the chamber of commerce and hometown associations, he has joined hands with Hong Kong compatriots and Guanlan entrepreneurs to devote themselves to public welfare undertakings and give back to society, showing love for humanity. Chan has donated a total of 16 million yuan to social welfare undertakings and mobilized members of the chamber of commerce to donate nearly 100 million yuan. He led members of the chamber of commerce and hometown associations to finance the construction of bridges and roads in Heyuan City, Guangdong Province and other places. Members of the chamber of commerce have visited Longchuan County, Wuhua County and other places in Guangdong Province many times for poverty alleviation and development promotion.

Education has been one of the key fields supported by Chan. In this regard, he has continued his clan's tradition of "advocating culture and education, sticking to farming and study." He donated more than 300,000 yuan to Zhenneng Primary School in his hometown to improve school conditions. In Chijing Village, Wuhua County, he donated more than 300,000 yuan for the construction of Wuhua Chijing Zhenneng School. The characters of "Zhenneng" are engraved with a story that has lasted for hundreds of years in the history of Shenzhen's educational undertakings.

Guanlan is a famous hometown of overseas Chinese and a town famous for education. The Chen clan in Songyuanxia began to run private schools since the third generation. In 1914, driven by sages and overseas leaders in the Chen clan, nine private schools of the clan merged to establish Yongxiu Primary School, which was one of the earliest modern schools in Shenzhen. In 1929, a total of 499 members of the clan at home and abroad raised funds to build a school at a new site and named it "Zhenneng School" in memory of their ancestor Chen Zhenneng. It was the most prestigious school in Bao'an County at the time, attracting a lot of young students from nearby areas. In 1946, a total of 154 members of the Chen clan at home and abroad donated money to establish Zhenneng Middle School.

After the founding of the People's Republic of China in 1949, Zhenneng Middle School was merged into today's Shenzhen Guanlan Middle School. The primary school was once renamed Songyuan Primary School, and was renamed Zhenneng Primary School in 1982. Later, it was expanded several times as the government invested huge sums of money and the Chen clan members at home and abroad enthusiastically donated. In 2019, Zhenneng Primary School was upgraded to a nine-year school and renamed "Shenzhen Longhua Zhenneng School," becoming one of the largest schools of its kind in the city. Chan is quite pleased to see the new glory of the century-old prestigious school founded by his clan.

In 2007, the Overseas Chinese Affairs Office of the State Council launched the "Overseas Chinese Love Project," a platform specially built to provide services for overseas Chinese, Hong Kong and Macao compatriots, returned overseas Chinese and relatives of overseas Chinese nationals residing in China to follow and support various domestic public welfare undertakings, help the poor, give back to society, and send their care and love. Chan has actively participated in the project. In 2007, when he accompanied the Overseas Chinese Affairs Office of the State Council to inspect poverty alleviation work in impoverished mountainous areas of Hebei Province, Chan saw the low, dilapidated and precarious classrooms of Shangshidong Township Central Primary School in Xinglong County, Chengde City, and immediately donated 200,000 yuan to rebuild the school. At the same time, he contacted industrial and commercial entrepreneurs in Guanlan, and they jointly donated 600,000 yuan to support the construction of a "Guanlan Hope Primary School" in Xinjian County, Jiangxi Province, solving the lack of school buildings for local primary school students.

In 2009, the new school in Shangshidong Township that Chan donated to build was completed and put into use, named "Yuchang Qiaoxin Primary School." Chan and two Macao compatriots made additional donations to improve school conditions.

Chan has done many other charitable deeds to help the poor. In 2008, when an 8.0-magnitude earthquake occurred in Wenchuan County, Sichuan Province, Chan donated more than 1.5 million yuan. In 2011, Chan and several Hong Kong compatriots donated 1 million yuan in total for the "Overseas Chinese Love Project—Plan of Lighting up New Life for Herdsmen in Tibetan Areas."

Daughter carries on his cause of overseas Chinese community

Due to his outstanding contributions in the economic and social fields, Chan has won honors such as the "National Advanced Individual of Returned Overseas Chinese and Relatives of Overseas Chinese Nationals Residing in China," the "National Advanced Patriotic Entrepreneur," and the "First Individual Charity Award of Shenzhen." In 2011, he was awarded the title of "Honorary Citizen of Shenzhen Municipality." He was invited to the National Day reception at the Great Hall of the People in Beijing for more than 10 times. He mounted Tiananmen Square's military parade viewing platform three times, including for the event to commemorate the 70th anniversary of the victory of the Chinese People's War of Resistance against Japanese Aggression and the World Anti-Fascist War in 2015.

"My financial situation is not bad, so when the society is in need, I will help a little," Chan summed up his original intention of doing charity.

Today, the 73-year-old Chan has retired but is still busy helping his hometown attract investment. "When there are good projects, I'll introduce them here, because I used to be engaged in the chamber of commerce. I am very busy now, and there are many things that I need to keep an eye on."

His cause of overseas Chinese community has already had a successor. To adapt to the changes in the administrative division of the Guanlan area, in 2019, the Federation of Hong Kong Guanlan Association added "Greater" before "Guanlan" in its Chinese name. Chan became chairman of the federation while his youngest daughter Alison Chen became president, taking over the responsibilities of this established overseas Chinese organization. Alison Chen is also a member of the Shenzhen Municipal Committee of the Chinese People's Political Consultative Conference, a youth member of the All-China Federation of Returned Overseas Chinese, and executive deputy president and executive deputy secretary-general of the Federation of Hong Kong Shenzhen Associations. Under the guidance of her father's words and deeds, she has actively participated in social and overseas Chinese affairs.

Chan has a son and two daughters, all of whom have well inherited the spirit of loving their motherland and hometown. Chan hopes that the younger generation will never forget where their roots are.

(Photos courtesy of Chan Yuk Cheng, except for the ones with credit. References: Xinhua News Agency; China News Service; *Southern*; Shenzhen Government Online; *Shenzhen Special Zone Daily*; *Bao'an Daily*; *Meizhou Daily*; *History of Longhua Overseas Chinese*; *Shenzhen Scenery and Culture, Volume 2: Family Memories*; *Monument to the Special Economic Zone: Historical Document Series of the Special Economic Zone, Volume 2*; and *Continued Cultural and Historical Research on the Yimen Chen Clan*.)

刘惠强

情系故土，率先在纽约华埠中心
升起五星红旗

刘惠强　Lou Wai Keing

　　刘惠强，1954年出生，深圳大鹏王母石禾塘人。曾在深圳的无线电厂工作，其父母于1964年至美国定居，从事餐饮行业。1982年，刘惠强前往美国谋生，早年从事汽车运输和维修工作，后于1988年开办贸易公司。曾任美国纽约大鹏同乡会主席，组织同乡会在纽约华埠中心升起第一面五星红旗，创办奖学金，提供敬老餐，修缮已逝老华侨墓碑。

采访时间：2022年。

去美国那年，刘惠强 28 岁。一晃，40 年过去了。在深圳的时候，刘惠强是个"多面手"。其中一些本领，他在美国也用上了，比如开车、修车，那是他的谋生手段；又比如舞麒麟，那是他传承给后辈的传统文化技艺。

他办的几件大事被广为称道：在纽约华埠中心升起第一面五星红旗，修缮已逝老华侨墓碑，办奖学金，提供敬老餐；他做的点滴小事也挺实在：去外地送货时，顺便采购物美价廉的物品，帮同乡会节省开支……

这些大大小小的事情、各种各样的细节，他有的历历在目、如数家珍，有的却记不清了，那是因为他在 2008 年做过脑部手术。在康复期间，他甚至有三年不能正常走路。除了那段时间之外，他长期坚持给多家侨团帮忙。驱使他这样做的，是挥之不去的故土情和守望相助的热心肠。

大鹏"林冲"，多才多艺

刘惠强回忆说，自己年轻的时候学技术挺快的，干过很多不同的活儿。1972 年到 1973 年，生产大队安排他参与"打山洞"的工作，就是从山里水库引水出来灌溉农田。后来，他又被派去学开汽车、开拖拉机、修汽车。1977 年，他被调往宝安县城深圳镇的无线电厂工作。

1980 年，大鹏把他调了回去，让他带徒弟修车。当时，刚参加工作的年轻人每月工资有十几二十元，但刘惠强的徒弟们能拿到二三十元，因为他把徒弟修车赚来的钱都分给他们了，自己没有留。因为这点，他的徒弟颇令旁人羡慕。

刘惠强会吹军号，又学过射击和修枪，所以在公社当过司号员，又帮着训练过民兵，人送绰号"林冲"。林冲是《水浒传》里的禁军枪棒教头，刘惠强的这个绰号当然只是戏说。刘惠强还会舞麒麟，十来岁时就偷学过。他小时候有时在姑妈家住，那个村里有舞麒麟、打武术的，他就借机偷师了一番。

20 岁的时候，刘惠强在大队拉手风琴，大队书记看见了，问他会不会舞麒麟，然后让老师傅教他，帮他提高。这下，刘惠强才算是科班出身的了。学成之后，他又教起了年轻人。那时，他可能没想到，自己日后还会把这门技艺带到美国，传给在那里生长的后生们。

美国谋生，干的主要是老本行

1964 年，刘惠强的父母就去了美国。他大姨一家去得更早。在那边，他们都以开餐馆为生。1982 年，刘惠强和妻子也移居美国，先到了威斯康星州，那里华人不多。刘惠强大舅子一家人都在纽约，第二年，刘惠强开车带妻子去纽约探亲，发现那里有很多华人。妻子喜欢上了纽约，就先住下了。刘惠强回到威斯康星州待了一段时间之后，当年年底也搬到了纽约。

刘惠强找了一份开货车的工作，周薪大约 250 美元。那家公司有十几辆奔驰货车，还有一辆装卸货物用的铲车，刘惠强后来承担了这些车的修理工作，周薪加到 350 美元。老本行得心应手，干得还不错。

但是，刘惠强被公司老板娘无端指责了两次之后，很不愉快，就跳槽去了另一家公司，负责开车给餐馆配送物资。当时，对方告诉他，工资可以随便开。但他是个老实人，也不敢多要，就要了大约 390 美元的周薪。

1986 年，刘惠强开起了餐馆。他不会下厨，有时在厨房打打下手，有时帮帮外面。因为弟弟、妹妹在美国出生，会英语，刘惠强也跟着学了点，可以简单招呼客人。

1988 年，刘惠强开了一家"深圳贸易公司"，自己开车送货。公司的名字，是老朋友李广镇的主意，李广镇当时是深圳市副市长。1969 年到 1975 年，李广镇在大鹏公社当过党委书记。听说刘惠强要开贸易公司，李广镇就建议把"深圳"放进公司名字里，别人一看就明白老板来自深圳，身居美国的同乡们也会更乐意帮衬公司的生意。这招确实起了作用。当然，刘惠强的生意伙伴也不限于华侨华人。

勤勤恳恳几十年，刘惠强在美国养大了一个女儿、两个儿子。女儿排行老大，生下的一双儿女也都长大了：儿子已经大学毕业，女儿在读法律专业。刘惠强的大儿子开了家运输公司，自己驾着货柜车跑外州，一去就是一个星期以上。小儿子在犹太人的疗养院负责维护电脑。

点点滴滴，为侨团出一份力

在平淡无奇的工作中，刘惠强也善于发掘机会，为侨团作贡献。比如，他开车送货去纽约隔壁的新泽西州，就顺便帮同乡会采购物资，那里的物价比纽约低很多，这样能帮同乡会节省一些开支。虽然已经退休多年，但刘惠强至今还记得当年的价格：同乡会搞活动要用的汽水，纽约每箱卖 8 美元多，新泽西州只卖 3～5 美元；纽约的打印纸每包卖 20 多美元，新泽西州只要十几美元……

因为经常送货，刘惠强跟一家水果批发公司比较熟。他有时就自掏腰包，买些水果送给同乡会。

有一次，刘惠强在同乡会会所附近的街边看到有老人站在寒风里等救济餐，但救济餐的分量很少。于是，他决定由同乡会出面，每月派送两次敬老餐，启动资金是他自己出的。他开的深圳贸易公司在给一家餐馆送货，他就从餐馆采购炒米粉作为敬老餐，餐费从货款里扣除。炒好的米粉，也是他自己开车从餐馆拉到同乡会楼下的。

那是 1998 年。那年，刘惠强当选纽约大鹏同乡会主席，办了几件大事，提供敬老餐就是其中之一。为了办敬老餐，刘惠强动员了同乡会的一些元老捐款。同乡

2019 年，刘惠强（左一）出席纽约大鹏同乡会 100 周年庆典暨春节联欢晚会。
Lou Wai Keing (first from left) attends the 100th anniversary celebration of the Tai Pun Residents Association in New York and its Chinese New Year gala in 2019.

会搞春宴的时候，有舞麒麟、舞狮拜年的环节，他就跟会员们说，大家包给麒麟队的红包可以留名，善款会一分不少地用于敬老餐。经过他们发动，很多人积极包红包。此后每年都有会员、职员和爱心人士捐款。

敬老餐主要派送给同乡会里的退休人士，每月两次，每次大约有 200 人领取。最开始派的是米粉或者饭，后来改成一次餐包、一次饭。一直坚持到 2020 年新冠疫情暴发后，敬老餐才暂停了。

飘扬的五星红旗，隔不断的血脉联系

1998 年 7 月 9 日，刘惠强组织纽约大鹏同乡会在会所升起五星红旗。这是纽约华埠中心升起的第一面五星红旗，轰动全城。当时的中国国务院侨务办公室主任郭东坡、中国驻纽约总领事邱胜云主持了升旗仪式，到场的还有纽约地区 70 多个侨团的领导。

华埠，就是唐人街。纽约的华埠中心，是指唐人街的中心地带，有几条街的范围。这里是华侨华人的聚集地，也是各国、各族裔人士领略中国风情的热门去处。历史原因，华埠中心迟迟没有升起五星红旗。

纽约大鹏同乡会升旗仪式大会留影。

A group photo of some of the attendees at the flag-raising ceremony of the Tai Pun Residents Association in New York.

　　原来，中华人民共和国成立初期，遭到西方封锁，国内外环境复杂，对外宣传没能很好地传播到华侨华人群体。不少海外华侨华人对新中国不太了解，没有迅速建立起认同感。1979 年中美建交后，纽约的部分侨团挂起了五星红旗，但华埠中心仍然没有悬挂五星红旗。刘惠强说，很多华侨华人都是早年移居美国的，纽约大鹏同乡会的很多元老、顾问也对新中国不了解。20 世纪 80 年代中期，曾有一位顾问建议挂五星红旗，但有些老华侨不同意，最后开会决定：挂同乡会会旗，不挂五星红旗。

　　但刘惠强一直觉得，应该在华埠中心升起五星红旗。直到 1998 年，天时地利人和促成了这件事。那年是改革开放 20 周年，中国综合国力和国际影响力日益强大，海外的华侨华人有了越发坚实的后盾。就在前一年，香港回归祖国，极大地激发了海外侨胞的民族自豪感，纽约大鹏同乡会也组织了庆祝活动，充满深圳文化特色的舞麒麟表演让人眼前一亮。

　　刘惠强当上纽约大鹏同乡会主席后，为了升五星红旗的事情积极奔走，做了很多说服、协调的工作。刘惠强对同乡会的元老和顾问们说："我们的家乡就在中华人民共和国的土地上，所以应该挂中华人民共和国的国旗。"经过刘惠强的一番思想工作之后，元老和顾问们都同意了他的意见。1998 年 2 月 2 日，同乡会会员大会一致通过：在会所悬挂中华人民共和国国旗。

刘惠强又跟中华公所以及熟悉台湾地区的侨团打好招呼："纽约大鹏同乡会要升五星红旗了，希望大家相安无事。"

台湾地区闻讯后，写信给纽约大鹏同乡会，想阻止此事。刘惠强坚决回绝："我如果挂了你们的旗子，以后还怎么回大陆？我就是要升中华人民共和国的国旗。"为了避免升起五星红旗后遇到麻烦，刘惠强还找人跟唐人街的社团人员沟通，让他们不要惹事，对方也同意了。

美东华人社团联合总会的主席帮忙致信中国国务院侨务办公室，请郭东坡主任为纽约大鹏同乡会的升国旗仪式授旗。

1998 年 7 月 9 日，郭东坡利用访美的机会，出席了升旗仪式，并向刘惠强授旗。众多侨团代表和华侨华人共襄盛举，会所门前的马路被围得水泄不通，醒狮欢舞，锣鼓喧天。在同乡会的二楼阳台上，刘惠强小心翼翼地把五星红旗挂出，郭东坡在他身旁托旗、展旗。鲜艳的五星红旗在纽约华埠中心迎风飘扬，现场掌声响成一片。

刘惠强回忆说："大家都非常激动，他们都认同我说的——祖国是我们海外华侨华人的坚强后盾，只有祖国强大，我们海外华人的腰杆才挺得直，不会被人欺负。"仪式进行得很顺利，刘惠强悬着的心也放了下来。

太平洋隔不断华侨华人与祖（籍）国、与家乡的血脉联系。每当中国遭遇重大灾害，比如汶川大地震、雅安芦山地震，同乡会成员慷慨解囊捐助，爱心如潮。每逢中国传统节日和大事喜事，同乡会的庆祝活动也少不了。在活动中助兴的舞狮、舞麒麟表演，都得到过刘惠强的指导。他回家乡大鹏探访的时候，也会帮助当地的龙狮协会传授技艺。

大鹏同乡会升旗现场。（来源：视频截图）
The flag-raising ceremony. (Photo: video screenshot)

刘惠强赴美后第一次返乡是在 1999 年，他应邀出席了首届中国国际高新技术成果交易会（简称"高交会"）。正是在那届高交会上，腾讯公司的马化腾拿着 20 多页的商业计划书到处推销，最终拿到了公司发展史上最为关键的第一笔风险投资——IDG（美国国际数据集团）与盈科数码共同投资 220 万美元。

现在，腾讯已是全球顶级

互联网公司，深圳成为闪耀世界的科技创新之城。记者对刘惠强的采访，也是通过腾讯开发的微信软件完成的。时代的巧合，总是这么别有意味。

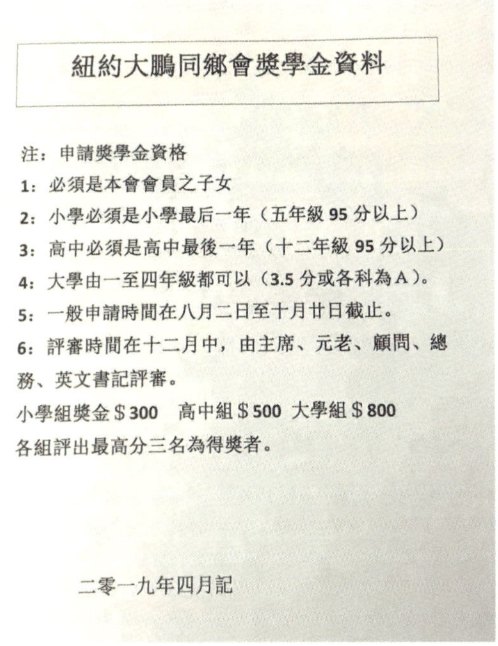

奖学金让后辈记住来处

刘惠强在同乡会设立奖学金，出发点也是对传统的继承、对血脉的延续。

有一回，刘惠强的小儿子带着一个六七岁的小女孩到家里，刘惠强就问她是哪里人。她回答："我不知道我是哪里人，但是我知道我妈妈是大鹏人。"

这让刘惠强很有感触。他也知

紐約大鵬同鄉會獎學金資料

注：申請獎學金資格
1：必須是本會會員之子女
2：小學必須是小學最後一年（五年級 95 分以上）
3：高中必須是高中最後一年（十二年級 95 分以上）
4：大學由一至四年都可以（3.5 分或各科為 A）。
5：一般申請時間在八月二日至十月廿日截止。
6：評審時間在十二月中，由主席、元老、顧問、總務、英文書記評審。
小學組獎金 $300　高中組 $500　大學組 $800
各組評出最高分三名為得獎者。

二零一九年四月記

2019 年记录存档的奖学金规则。
The scholarship rules recorded and archived in 2019.

道，在美国长大的很多华裔孩子不清楚这些。"所以，我打算办一个奖学金，让大鹏人的后代知道自己是'大鹏人'。等他们工作了，也可以来同乡会帮忙，甚至捐助同乡会，或者孝敬同乡会的老人家。"奖学金就这么在 1998 年创立并延续至今。

2019 年记录存档的奖学金规则显示，每年评奖一次，同乡会会员的子女都有资格参评。奖励对象是小学毕业生、高中毕业生、大学一年级到四年级学生，各组的奖金分别是每人 300 美元、500 美元、800 美元，每组评出学习成绩的前三名获奖。

客家人的侨团纽约崇正会也设立了类似的奖学金。有一年，有四个华裔孩子考大学都是满分，但按规定只能有两位获奖者，要抽签决定。刘惠强当时身兼崇正会会董，他说："难得有四个都满分的，全都给他们吧！"大家一听，觉得很有道理，就都同意了。

慎终追远，功德无量

除了帮助年青一代传承中华优秀传统文化、记住故乡深圳，刘惠强还很重视慎终追远。

他在中华公所的墓园里发现，很多碑石都被泥土掩埋了。1998 年，他自己开车买来材料，然后运到墓园，修缮墓碑。同乡会有十几位成员也报名参加。他们清理了掩埋墓碑的泥土，发现大鹏籍人士的墓碑就扶起来，用木棍、水泥加固，弄得整整齐齐。冒着小雨干了两个星期，他们最终修缮了 90 多块墓碑。

此事还有个插曲，快完工的时候，沙子不够用了，他们想向墓园借用一点，途中遇到了墓园的老板。对方一度误以为他们是来"抢生意"的，所以很不乐意，甚至想破坏他们的成果。

不过，这老板也确实观察到刘惠强他们冒雨干了两个星期，又了解到刘惠强是同乡会主席，干这事并不是为了赚钱，而是为了故乡的先人们，所以很感动，认可了他们的行为。

刘惠强他们就是抱着义务劳动的念头去做的，但同乡会的元老、顾问们觉得，事情办得很好，还是应该拿点报酬。同乡会最后研究决定了报酬的标准：每人每天30美元。

这些墓碑修缮完成后，中国、澳大利亚、加拿大都有人闻讯前来祭拜先人，刘惠强开车带他们去现场。他们要给刘惠强酬劳，他都一一谢绝，而是请他们把钱捐给同乡会。

热心公益，大爱无疆

刘惠强不但在华侨华人中很有人缘，他的名声还早就"出圈"了。他家不在华埠，邻居里除了华侨华人，更多的是其他族裔，但整条街的人都认识他，见到他都会打招呼。这是因为，他是个"资深"热心人，从1999年就开始做义工：早上帮着搬运垃圾到垃圾车上。

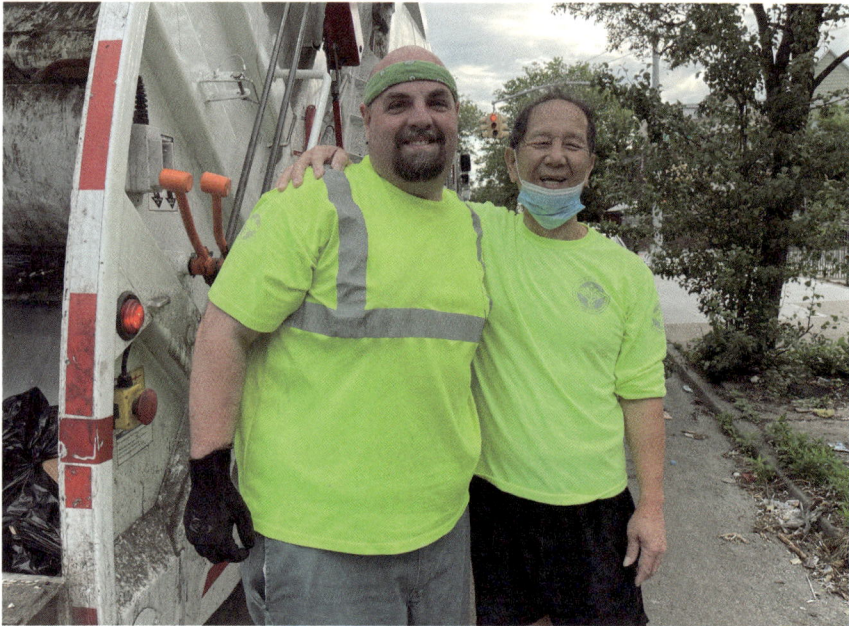

刘惠强帮忙搬运垃圾。
Lou Wai Keing helps to carry garbage.

2022 年，刘惠强做义工时偶遇一位已退休的车长，对方感叹："你还在帮忙啊！"刘惠强说："是呀！就当是做运动啦！"他还告诉对方，自己退休后，服务范围从一条街扩展到了四条街，一个星期做两天，每次从半小时增加到两小时。从一场大病复原后，他的负重能力从 20 磅（约 9 公斤）提高到了现在的几十甚至上百磅（45 公斤以上），可以一下子把一袋垃圾抛上车。

不过，人们已经不肯让他搬太重的垃圾了。他的那场大病发生在 2008 年：他正开着车，脑血管瘤破裂，失去意识，头都砸到方向盘上了。幸好那次妻子坐在旁边，她刹停了车，向路过的司机求助。

在医院里，刘惠强进行了脑部手术，有三年时间不能正常行走，义工工作也就暂停了。但他下定决心，坚持运动，然后逐渐康复了。

刘惠强的微信名字叫"青松"，有种"名如其人"的感觉。在他微信头像的照

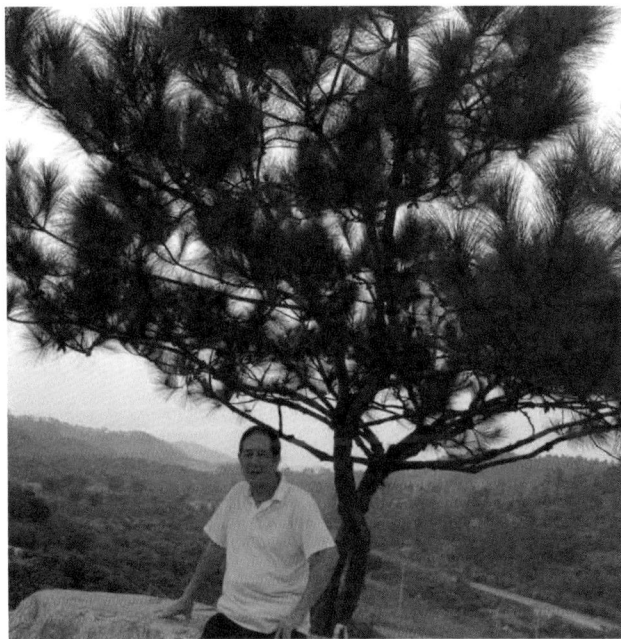

刘惠强微信头像照片。
Lou Wai Keing's WeChat profile picture.

片里，他的身后也是一棵松树，那是在广东省惠东县跟同学聚会时拍的。

他还说，在纽约，他家附近的路旁有很多松树，也有很多樱花，但樱花没开多久就会凋谢，唯有松树四季常青、不惧风雪，很有生命力。他希望自己像青松一样，无论何时都是那么坚强。

吃苦耐劳，坚韧不拔，守望相助，大爱无疆，正是海外众多中华儿女共同的闪光点。

（本文图片均由受访者刘惠强提供。参考资料：《桑梓情深　赤子丹心——大鹏侨情口述史》《大鹏侨情：文史研究报告》《深圳侨报》以及深圳市档案馆门户网站。）

Lou Wai Keing

Loving the homeland, raising the first five-star red flag in the center of New York's Chinatown

Lou Wai Keing, born in 1954, is a native of Shihetang, Wangmu, Dapeng, Shenzhen. He used to work in a radio factory in Shenzhen. His parents settled in the United States in 1964 and worked in the catering industry. In 1982, he went to the United States to make a living. He was engaged in trucking and automobile maintenance in early years before he opened a trading company in 1988. When serving as president of the Tai Pun Residents Association in New York, he led the association to raise the first five-star red flag in the center of New York's Chinatown, launched a scholarship for students and a free meal project for the elderly, and repaired the tombstones of deceased overseas Chinese.

Lou Wai Keing was 28 years old when he went to the United States. In a flash, 40 years have passed. He was a generalist in Shenzhen. He has made use of some of these skills in the United States, such as driving and repairing cars and trucks, as means of earning a living, and the kylin dance, as a traditional cultural skill he passes on to younger generations.

Several big things he has done are widely praised, such as raising the first five-star red flag in the center of Chinatown in New York, repairing the tombstones of old overseas Chinese, and launching a scholarship for students and a free meal project for the elderly. Some little things he has done are practical, such as purchasing high-quality and inexpensive items while he was delivering goods out of town, in a bid to help the Tai Pun Residents Association save money...

Some of these things and details are still vivid in his memory, but some can't be remembered clearly because he had a brain surgery in 2008. On his way to recovery, he couldn't even walk normally for three years. Except for that period, he has been helping many overseas Chinese groups for a long time. What drives him is the lingering love for his homeland and his enthusiasm for helping others.

The interview took place in 2022.

A versatile man nicknamed "Lin Chong in Dapeng"

Lou recalled that when he was young, he learned skills quickly and did many different jobs. From 1972 to 1973, the production brigade sent him to "dig caves," diverting water from a mountain reservoir to irrigate farmland. Later, he was sent to learn car driving, tractor driving and car repairing. In 1977, he was transferred to work in a radio factory in Shenzhen Township, Bao'an County.

In 1980, Dapeng transferred him back and asked him to train apprentices in repairing automobiles. At that time, young people who just started working had a monthly salary of 10 to 20 yuan, but Lou's apprentices could get 20 to 30 yuan because he did not get a percentage for the automobiles his apprentices repaired but distributed all the money to them. So his apprentices were envied by others.

Lou could also blow the bugle, and knew how to shoot and repair guns, so he worked as a trumpeter in the commune and helped train the militia. He was nicknamed "Lin Chong." Lin is the spear and stick instructor of the Forbidden Army in the Chinese novel *Water Margin*, and Lou's nickname was of course just a joke. Lou could also play the kylin dance, or the Chinese unicorn dance, which he learned secretly when he was a teenager sometimes living at his aunt's house. There were kylin dancers and martial arts practitioners in that village, so he took the opportunity to learn.

When Lou was 20 years old, the brigade secretary saw him playing the accordion in the brigade and asked him whether he could play the kylin dance. Then the secretary had some masters teach Lou and help him improve. Thus, he became a kylin dancer by training. After finishing his professional learning, he went on to teach young people. He might not have imagined that he would bring this craft to the United States in the future and pass it on to the younger generations who grew up there.

Taking up his old jobs in U.S.

In 1964, Lou's parents went to the United States. The family of his mother's elder sister went there earlier. They all made a living running restaurants. In 1982, Lou and his wife also migrated to the United States. They first went to Wisconsin, where there were not many Chinese. As his brother-in-law's family was in New York, Lou drove his wife to New York the next year to visit relatives, finding many Chinese there. His wife fell in love with New York and stayed there. Lou returned to Wisconsin, before moving to New York at the end of that year.

Lou got a job as a truck driver for about $250 a week. That company had more than a dozen Mercedes-Benz trucks and a forklift for loading and unloading goods. Later, Lou also took over the repair work of these vehicles, and his weekly salary was increased to $350. He did well in this old job.

However, he was very unhappy after his boss's wife criticized him twice for no reason. So he switched to another company to deliver supplies to restaurants. That company told him to ask for a salary at will. But he was honest and didn't dare to ask for too much, so he got a weekly salary of about $390.

In 1986, Lou opened a restaurant. Not knowing how to cook, he just helped in the kitchen, and sometimes helped outside. One of his younger brothers and two of his younger sisters were born in the United States and could speak English, so he learned a little bit from them, enabling him to greet guests.

In 1988, Lou opened a "Shenzhen Trading Company" and drove a truck to deliver goods. The company's name was the idea of an old friend, Li Guangzhen, who was then vice mayor of Shenzhen. From 1969 to 1975, Li served as Party secretary of Dapeng Commune. Hearing that Lou was going to open a trading company, Li suggested putting "Shenzhen" in its name, so that others would know that the boss was from Shenzhen, and fellow Shenzhen immigrants living in the United States would be more willing to help the company's business. The idea worked. Of course, Lou's business partners were not limited to overseas Chinese.

After decades of hard work, Lou raised a daughter and two sons in the United States. The daughter is the eldest, and her son and daughter have grown up: The son has graduated from college, while the daughter is studying law. Lou's elder son runs a transportation company and drives a container truck to other states, with each trip lasting for more than a week. The younger son maintains computers in a Jewish nursing home.

Little by little, contributing to overseas Chinese groups

During his ordinary work, Lou was good at discovering opportunities to contribute to overseas Chinese groups. For example, when driving to deliver goods to New Jersey, which is next to New York, he helped the Tai Pun Residents Association purchase supplies at prices much lower than those in New York. In this way, he helped the association cut down expenses. Although he has been retired for many years, Lou still remembers the prices back then: the soda water used for the association's activities cost more than $8 per box in New York, but only $3 to $5 in New Jersey. Printing paper in New York sold for more than $20 a pack, but only a dozen dollars in New Jersey...

As a result of frequent deliveries, Lou became familiar with a fruit wholesale company. Sometimes he paid out of his own pocket to buy some fruit for the Tai Pun Residents Association in New York.

One day, Lou saw elderly people stand in the cold wind waiting for a relief meal on the street near the association's building, and the relief meal turned out to be in small portions. Therefore, he decided that the association would provide free meals for the elderly twice a month, and he paid for the start-up funds himself. The Shenzhen Trading Company he opened was delivering goods to a restaurant, and he purchased fried rice noodles from the restaurant as meals for the elderly, with the cost deducted from the payment that the restaurant owed him. He drove to carry the fried rice noodles to the downstairs of the association's building.

That was in 1998. That year, Lou was elected president of the Tai Pun Residents Association in New York, and did several big things, one of which was the free meal project for the elderly. Lou asked some veterans of the association to donate for the meals for the elderly. During the association's spring banquet, where the kylin dance and lion dance were staged to pay Chinese New Year's greetings, he told the members that they could have their name recorded for the red envelopes they gave to the kylin dance team, and that all the money would be used for the elderly's meals. After his mobilization, many people actively offered red envelopes. Moreover, members, staff and caring people have been donating money every year since then.

The free meals for the elderly have been mainly distributed to retirees who are members of the Tai Pun Residents Association in New York, twice a month. About 200 people came to receive it each time. The meals used to be rice noodles or rice, and later changed to buns and rice in turn. It was not until the outbreak of the COVID-19 pandemic in 2020 that the free meals were suspended.

The flying five-star red flag and continuous blood connection

On July 9, 1998, Lou led the Tai Pun Residents Association in New York to raise the five-star red flag in its building. This was the first five-star red flag raised in the center of New York's Chinatown, causing a sensation throughout the city. Guo Dongpo, then director of the Overseas Chinese Affairs Office of the State Council of China, and Qiu Shengyun, then Chinese consul general in New York, presided over the flag-raising ceremony. Leaders of more than 70 overseas Chinese groups in the New York area were also present.

The center of Chinatown in New York covers several streets. It is a magnet for overseas Chinese and a popular destination for people from all countries and ethnicities to appreciate Chinese culture. Due to historical reasons, the five-star red flag was absent in the center of Chinatown for a long time.

The People's Republic of China (PRC) was blocked by Western countries after it was founded. The environment was complicated at home and abroad, so the PRC's external publicity did not work well among overseas Chinese, many of whom knew little about the new country and failed to quickly establish a sense of acceptance. After the PRC established diplomatic relations with the United States in 1979, some overseas Chinese groups in New York raised the five-star red flag, but the center of Chinatown still did not see the flag. Lou said that many overseas Chinese migrated to the United States in the early years. Many veterans and consultants of the Tai Pun Residents Association in New York did not know much about the PRC either. In the mid-1980s, a consultant suggested hanging the five-star red flag, but some old overseas Chinese disagreed, and the association finally decided at a meeting to hang the association's flag instead of the five-star red flag.

However, Lou stuck to his idea that the five-star red flag should be raised in the center of Chinatown. In 1998, the right time and place as well as the unity of thought contributed to this matter. That year marked the 20th anniversary of China's reforms and opening-up. Its comprehensive national strength and international influence became stronger and stronger, giving overseas Chinese a more solid backing. The year before, Hong Kong returned to the motherland, which greatly inspired the national pride. The Tai Pun Residents Association in New York also organized celebrations of Hong Kong's return, while the kylin dance performance full of Shenzhen cultural characteristics was quite eye-catching.

After he became president of the association, Lou worked hard to prepare for raising the five-star red flag. He visited many people and did a lot of persuasion and coordination. Lou told the veterans and consultants of the association, "Our hometown is on the soil of the PRC, so the national flag of the PRC should be hung." After his persuasion, the veterans and consultants agreed with him. On February 2, 1998, the members' meeting of the association unanimously agreed to hang the national flag of the PRC in the association's building.

Lou then told the Chinese Consolidated Benevolent Association and overseas Chinese groups with close ties to the Taiwan region, "The Tai Pun Residents Association in New York is about to raise the five-star red flag, and let's keep the peace between us."

After hearing the news, the Taiwan region wrote to the Tai Pun Residents Association in New York in the hope of stopping it. Lou resolutely refused. "If I hang your flag, how can I return to Chinese mainland in the future? I just want to raise the national flag of the PRC," he said. To avoid trouble after raising the five-star red flag, Lou also asked someone to communicate with community members in Chinatown, telling them not to make trouble. The community members agreed.

The president of the U.S. East Coast Federation of Chinese Associations helped by writing a letter to the Overseas Chinese Affairs Office of the State Council of China, asking Director Guo Dongpo to present the flag for the flag-raising ceremony of the Tai Pun Residents Association in New York.

On July 9, 1998, Guo took advantage of his visit to the United States to attend the flag-raising ceremony and presented the flag to Lou. Many representatives of overseas Chinese groups and a lot of overseas Chinese participated in the grand event. The road in front of the association's building was crowded, featuring the joyful lion dance and the sound of gongs and drums. On the balcony on the second floor of the association's building, Lou carefully hung up the five-star red flag, and Guo held and displayed the flag beside him. The bright five-star red flag fluttered in the breeze in the center of New York's Chinatown, and the crowd burst into applause.

"Everyone was very excited. They all agreed with what I said—the motherland is the strong backing of our overseas Chinese. Only when the motherland is strong can our overseas Chinese stand tall and be rid of bully," Lou recalled. The ceremony went smoothly, and Lou felt relieved.

The Pacific Ocean has not cut off the blood connection between overseas Chinese and their ancestral country and hometown. When China suffers major disasters, such as the Wenchuan Earthquake and the Lushan Earthquake in Ya'an, members of the Tai Pun Residents Association in New York will generously donate, forming tides of love. Whenever there are traditional Chinese festivals and important events, the Tai Pun Residents Association in New York will hold celebrations. The lion dance and kylin dance that add to the fun in the events have been guided by Lou. When he visited Dapeng, his hometown, he helped the local dragon and lion dance association teach skills.

In 1999, Lou returned to his hometown for the first time after going to the United States. He was invited to attend the first China Hi-Tech Fair (CHTF). At that year's high-tech fair, Tencent's Ma Huateng, also known as Pony Ma, tried to sell his business plan of more than 20 pages to many investors he met, and finally got the first and most critical venture capital investment in the company's history: $2.2 million co-invested by IDG (International Data Group) and PCCW (Pacific Century Cyber Works).

Now, Tencent is one of the top Internet companies globally, and Shenzhen has become a city of technological innovation that shines in the world. Our interview with Lou was done through the WeChat software developed by Tencent. The coincidence of the times is always so interesting.

Scholarship allows younger generations to remember their roots

Lou set up a scholarship in the association. It was also to inherit the tradition and continue the blood lineage.

His younger son once brought home a girl who was about 6 or 7 years old, and Lou asked her where she was from. She replied, "I don't know where I am from, but I know my mother is from Dapeng."

Lou was touched by what she said. He knew that many children of Chinese origin growing up in the United States did not know such things. "So, I planned a scholarship to let the descendants of Dapeng residents know that they are 'Dapeng people.' When they have a job later, they can come to our association to help and even donate, or look after the elderly in the association." The scholarship was thus established in 1998 and continues to this day.

According to the scholarship rules recorded and archived in 2019, the scholarship is awarded once a year, and the children of the association's members are eligible to apply. The recipients should be elementary school graduates, high school graduates or first-year to fourth-year college students. The prizes for the three groups are $300, $500 and $800 per person, awarded to the top three students in each group.

The Tsung Tsin Association, New York, an overseas Chinese group of the Hakka people, had a similar scholarship. One year, there were four Chinese children who got full marks in the college entrance examination, but according to the scholarship regulations, there could be only two winners, who should be selected by drawing lots. "It's rare to see four students get full marks, so let's give scholarship to them all!" said Lou, who was also a director of the Tsung Tsin Association at the time. The others thought it made sense, and all agreed.

A great service remembering the ancestors

In addition to helping the younger generations inherit the excellent traditional Chinese culture and remember their hometown Shenzhen, Lou has placed a high value on remembering the ancestors.

In the cemetery of the Chinese Consolidated Benevolent Association, he found that many tombstones were buried with soil. In 1998, he drove to buy materials and then transported them to the cemetery to repair the tombstones. More than a dozen members of the Tai Pun Residents Association in New York volunteered to join him. They cleaned up the soil that buried the tombstones. When they saw the tombstones of natives of Dapeng, they lifted them up, reinforced them with wooden sticks and cement, and made them neat. After two weeks of work in light rain, a total of more than 90 tombstones were repaired.

Here was an episode. When the work was almost finished, they ran out of sand and wanted to borrow some from the cemetery. They met the boss of the cemetery on the way, who mistakenly thought that they were there to "compete for business." He was very unhappy and even wanted to destroy their achievements.

However, the boss did see them work in the rain for two weeks, and learned that Lou was president of the Tai Pun Residents Association in New York, who did this not for money but to remember the ancestors from his hometown. The boss was touched and recognized their work.

Lou and the others did it as volunteer work, but the veterans and consultants of the association thought that they had done a good job and should get paid. After discussion, the association finally offered a remuneration of $30 per person per day.

After the restoration of these tombstones, people from China, Australia and Canada heard the news and came to worship their ancestors. Lou drove them to the scene. They wanted to pay him, but he declined all of them. Instead, he asked them to donate to the Tai Pun Residents Association in New York.

Enthusiasm about public welfare, fame for boundless love

Lou is popular not only among overseas Chinese. His reputation has long been "out of the circle." He does not live in Chinatown. His neighbors are more of other ethnicities than overseas Chinese. But everyone along the street knows him and greets him when seeing him. This is because he is a "senior" enthusiastic person who has been doing volunteer work since 1999, helping to carry garbage to the garbage truck in the morning.

When Lou was doing the volunteer work in 2022, he ran into a retired garbage truck driver, who exclaimed, "You are still helping with this!" Lou said, "Yes! I just take it as exercise!" Lou told him that after he retired, his scope of service expanded from one street to four. He did it two days a week, two hours each time, an increase from half an hour each time in the past. After recovering from a serious illness, his loading ability has increased from 20 pounds (about nine kilograms) to dozens of pounds or more than 100 pounds (more than 45 kilograms), and he can throw a bag of garbage into the truck in one go.

However, people now stop him from carrying heavy garbage. His serious illness occurred in 2008: When he was driving a car, a brain hemangioma ruptured, he lost consciousness, and his head hit the steering wheel. Fortunately, his wife was sitting next to him. She stopped the car and asked passing drivers for help.

In the hospital, Lou underwent brain surgery and was unable to walk normally for three years, so his volunteer work was suspended. But he made up his mind, kept exercising, and gradually recovered.

Lou's WeChat nickname is "Qingsong," meaning "green pine." The name feels like the person. In his WeChat profile picture, there is also a pine tree behind him. That photo was taken during a reunion with his classmates in Huidong County, Guangdong Province.

There are many pine trees and cherry blossoms on the roadside near his home in New York, but the cherry blossoms will wither after a short period of time. Only the pine trees are evergreen all year round, not afraid of wind and snow, showing great vitality. He hopes that he will be always as strong as a pine tree.

Many overseas Chinese share the same shining points. They can bear hardships and stand hard work, they show great perseverance, they are ready to help each other, and they have boundless love.

(Photos courtesy of Lou Wai Keing. References: *Deep Love for the Hometown and Sincere Loyalty to the Motherland: Oral History of Overseas Chinese from Dapeng*, *Facts About Overseas Chinese from Dapeng: A Cultural and Historical Research Report*, *Shenzhen Overseas Chinese News*, and the official website of the Shenzhen Municipal Archives.)

第二章
Chapter Two

实业强国
Building a strong country through industry

行路难，行路难，多歧路，今安在？

长风破浪会有时，直挂云帆济沧海。

——〔唐〕李白《行路难·其一》

Hard is the way, hard is the way. Don't go astray!
Whither today? A time will come to ride the wind and
cleave the waves; I'll set my cloudlike sail to cross
the sea which raves.

—*Hard Is the Way I*, by Li Bai (Tang Dynasty)

王兆凯：

退休后坚持创业，
一心"为中国做一点事"

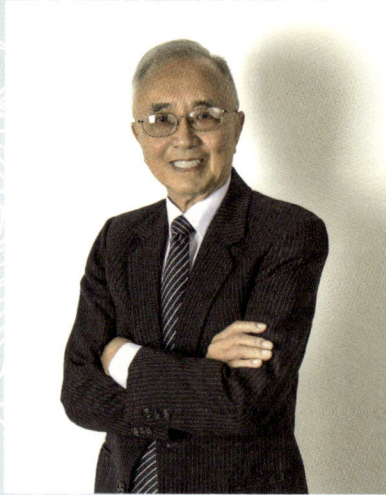

王兆凯　Jaw-Kai Wang

　　王兆凯，1932年3月出生于江苏南京，祖籍浙江省温州市瓯海区郭溪镇任桥村，1955年赴美国。世界著名水产工程学家、深圳市第四批荣誉市民、美国国家工程院院士、美国水产业工程学会创立人之一和首任主席、中国国务院侨务办公室"海外专家咨询委员会"首批委员、中国水产科学研究院渔业机械仪器研究所首席专家、南方科技大学－泰利硅藻材料联合实验室名誉主任、深圳市兆凯生物工程研发中心有限公司总裁。曾任联合国粮农组织、世界银行、美国农业部、洛克菲勒基金会等机构顾问。曾在夏威夷大学任教。

　　王兆凯院士长期从事水产养殖工程的研究工作，在开放式微藻规模养殖这一世界性技术难题上取得了突破。

采访时间：2022年。

"老骥伏枥，志在千里。烈士暮年，壮心不已。"曹操的这几句诗，是王兆凯的真实写照。

76 岁的时候，王兆凯开始在深圳创业，研究户外硅藻养殖。

80 多岁的时候，他穿梭于大江南北，做水产科技调研，为产业发展支招，给普罗大众讲学。

90 岁的时候，他发现自己离创业目标越来越近了。"能做到在户外低价连续高产养殖硅藻，并且已找到大量用硅藻壳的路子，为世界创立在农业中生产工业原料的途径，虽然若要在三五年内达到商业化的水平尚待努力，但是我觉得可以庆幸了。"

少小离家老大回，从 1979 年起，王兆凯就多次回到中国，受到过邓小平、陈云、王震、方毅等老一辈国家领导人的接见。2005 年，国务院侨务办公室"海外专家咨询委员会"成立，王兆凯受聘成为首批委员。那批委员由 30 位海外华侨华人知名专家学者组成，包括了杨振宁、丘成桐等大名鼎鼎的人物。

被改革开放的春风"吹"回中国的王兆凯，当初可能并没有预料到，自己终极梦想的落脚地会是改革开放的发源地之一——深圳。王兆凯在深圳创办了公司，后来又牵手深圳另一家公司继续推进自己的梦想，这家公司还跟南方科技大学（简称"南科大"）成立了联合实验室，共同探索硅藻生态产业链，王兆凯担任联合实验室的名誉主任，在大方向上做指导。

他乐意提携后辈。南科大有位毕业多年的学生创业研发免洗洗手液，在他指点下，用到了硅藻提取物。

为中国做一点事，是王兆凯在学生时代就埋下的心愿。

一次偶遇改变志向，功成名就不忘师恩

王兆凯的祖籍地温州市瓯海区是著名侨乡，现有超过 12 万名华侨华人旅居意大利、法国、西班牙等上百个国家和地区。王兆凯的父亲被清政府派去美国留学，在哥伦比亚大学读心理学，获得硕士学位后回国任教，在中央大学当教授期间，王兆凯出生了。

王兆凯先是在南京生活，上了幼儿园就跟随父母到了重庆，一待就是 8 年，后来又回南京待了几年。1948 年底，他们到了广州，王兆凯在中山大学附属中学读高三。1949 年，他考入了台湾大学（简称"台大"）。考台大时，王兆凯报的是机械专业。他的总分绰绰有余，但数学只考了 29 分，比工学院的录取标准少 1 分。学校给了他"额外录取，强迫转系"的待遇，他就先读了地质专业，一年后转系。

王兆凯想转到机械系，但一次偶遇改变了他的人生轨迹。当时，他已经填好了表格，但在送表格的路上遇见了农田水利专家金城教授。金城教授把他领到办公室喝茶，并告诉他，为了帮助中国，应该学农业工程。一席话让这个少年动了心，改了主意，付出了一生。

1953年，王兆凯从台大农工系毕业。1955年，他远赴美国密歇根州立大学深造，先后拿到了硕士和博士学位。

学成之后，王兆凯来到夏威夷大学任教，一干就是40多年，并且从农业工程改行到养殖工程，一路做到了教授。这中间，他有很多机会可以离开夏威夷，但有三大原因让他决定留下来：一来，夏威夷大学对他不薄，给过他很大的帮助；二来，夏威夷远离美国本土，种族歧视方面的问题要好很多，他希望他的三个孩子可以在夏威夷长大；三来，虽然夏威夷大学不是一流学府，但也无妨。"一个人做事，你靠学校固然是很好。你不靠学校，你自己做出来，也有一定的好处。"

事实证明，王兆凯确实"做出来"了。

他在海藻抗菌物质提取、微藻生物反应器、循环水养殖技术等方面进行了系统研究，在国际性刊物上发表学术论文170篇，出版专著3部，申请专利7项。

他获得的各种荣誉、头衔也不计其数。夏威夷州政府、州议会多次表彰他对水产工程推广事业的贡献。1993年，他参与创立了美国水产业工程学会并担任首任主席。1995年，他当选为美国国家工程院院士，这个身份是美国工程界的最高荣誉。

"我今天的成就，一来，是在大学的时候受到老师们的熏陶；二来，与我在美国受到我的教授们的教导密切相关。"功成名就的王兆凯对师恩念念不忘。

古稀之年养硅藻，破解世界级难题

王兆凯去美国之前，台大的老师也再三跟他讲，将来有机会就应该回中国。"我退休以后就决定，我要回国去做一点事。"王兆凯回忆说，"我在中国这些年来是一分钱的薪水都没有拿过，完全是以服务的态度（做事）。"（他只是获得了生活补贴和住处。）或许，这就是王兆凯"回国去做一点事"的原则吧。

在王兆凯的字典里，似乎没有"颐养天年"的概念。76岁的时候，他跑到深圳，守着海边的池子，养起了硅藻。

那是2008年，王兆凯由深圳市政府作为人才引进。他创办了深圳市兆凯生物工程研发中心有限公司，带领几十个年轻人在大鹏半岛的海边研发开放式硅藻养殖。

这个项目的投入很大，有一个时期，由于资金紧张，项目推进异常艰难。王兆凯毅然卖了台湾的房子，将资金投入项目。

2017年，深圳泰利能源有限公司向王兆凯发出邀请，共同推进硅藻养殖项目。硅藻属于微藻，开放式微藻规模养殖是世界性的技术难题。功夫不负有心人，王兆凯在深圳耕耘了十几年，取得了决定性的突破，首次成功实现了户外大规模养殖。

王兆凯在深圳大鹏研发硅藻养殖技术。（来源：泰利集团）
Jaw-Kai Wang develops diatom cultivation technology in Dapeng, Shenzhen. (Photo: Taili Group)

"我大概是世界上唯一的一个人，知道怎么不用任何化学药品去养硅藻的，就是说，不用防虫，也不用防其他微藻侵入。"王兆凯透露。

但他也坦承："我的办法只能用在少数几种硅藻上。其他的藻类，我的办法也没有用。"

这样养殖硅藻是要做什么用呢？

王兆凯瞄准的是工业原料。因为，硅藻壳是目前所知的唯一天然生产的纳米材料，如果用低成本的方式生产出来，前途将不可限量。"硅藻是种很奇怪的藻类。单细胞植物外面的一层壳，也就是细胞壁，一般都是有机的东西，是软的。唯有硅藻的细胞壁是无机的，是硬的，是二氧化硅。"

通常，纳米材料的制造成本很高，限制了纳米材料的应用范围。"我们是用农业的方法去大量生产，假设我们需要的话，一年几百万吨没问题。这可以说是唯一能通过农业生产直接供给工业做原料的。"王兆凯说。

硅藻壳要怎么大批量运用，属于材料学范畴，王兆凯为此又"改行"了。他在做了很多研究后发现，把硅藻壳用作工业原料，有很好的热稳定性和水热稳定性、高生物适应性、低毒性等，在大分子催化、生物过程、选择吸附、功能材料等方面有广泛的应用前景。

"我不是学材料学的人，所以这次改行非常辛苦。"他说，"总而言之吧，我现在走到了路子上，大概再有两三年的功夫，可以有小小的成功。"他举了个例子：硅藻壳和铝做复合物就非常好，但是铝跟硅藻壳的接触不是很好，强度不够。"我们现在已经找到办法，可以做出来了，同时尽量发挥硅藻的强度、高温、防腐、硬度等好处。大概再有个5年，我们可以开始商业化。"

结缘深圳"黑马"高校，助推硅藻材料应用

在深圳，王兆凯还跟南科大结了缘。南科大是深圳在中国高等教育改革发展的时代背景下创建的一所高起点、高定位的公办新型研究型大学，成立于2012年。短短的10年里，这所大学发展迅猛，成为中国高校里的一匹"黑马"。在2022年10月公布的2023年泰晤士世界大学排名中，南科大跻身前200强，排在全球第166名、中国内地第8名，超越了武汉大学、华中科技大学、中山大学等老牌名校。

2019年8月，南科大与深圳泰利能源有限公司签署合作协议，共建"南方科技大学－泰利硅藻材料联合实验室"，主要就硅藻材料的综合应用展开研究与开发。身为泰利能源首席科学家的王兆凯，出任这个联合实验室的名誉主任。2020年8月，在联合实验室一周年工作总结会议上，王兆凯参与学术交流，提出了自己的独到见解。

另外，南科大和浙江省台州市政府合作孵化的一家科技公司研制了一款免洗洗手液，已经投入市场，这里面也有王兆凯的功劳。这家公司的董事长兼总经理郭恬子是南科大的校友。2019年，她从香港科技大学硕士毕业后，她在南科大的本科导师孙大陟邀请她加入这个孵化科创公司的项目。这款洗手液前期研发时，孙大陟为她引荐了王兆凯。能跟这样的顶尖专家合作开发产品，对年轻的创业者来说是一件幸事。郭恬子和王兆凯合作的成果是在这款洗手液里添加了能有效灭菌的硅藻提取物，既提升了科技含量，又形成了产品的特色。

鼓励后辈创新，赞赏中国速度

耄耋之年的王兆凯，在中国东奔西走，开展推广、交流、合作。他为一些地方的水产科技企业支招，向一些地方的市民、师生普及科学知识和科学精神。除了广东，他还去过北京、福建、山东、四川……在广东外语外贸大学办讲座时，王兆凯鼓励青年学生们多动脑思考，敢于提出疑问。"一个社会的进步，不仅依靠前人的智慧，还需要我们开拓进取。一件事情的成功，都是一代人发现它的可行之处后，全力以赴所造就的。"

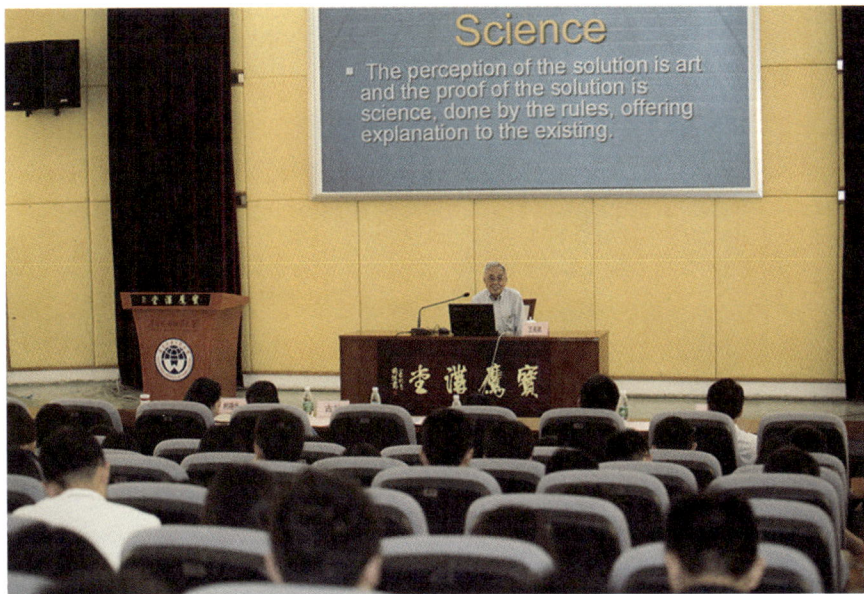

2016 年 5 月 12 日，王兆凯在广东外语外贸大学举办讲座。（来源：宝鹰集团）
Jaw-Kai Wang gives a lecture at the Guangdong University of Foreign Studies on May 12, 2016.
(Photo: Bauing Group)

在佛山市里水镇的"上善"教育科技节活动讲座上，王兆凯语出惊人，叮嘱孩子们不要做"好学生"。"创新就是做跟以前不一样的事。要是老听前人的话，怎么去创新？要懂得什么时候听话、什么时候不听话。"他还指出，培养孩子的创新思维，与教育环境有很大关系。"老师要有热情和动力，这样才能点燃学生的激情。而且，老师要能接受学生的质疑。"

王兆凯是个雷厉风行的人。在北京的一个论坛上，他得知硅藻可以在某项材料领域做得很好，顿时来了兴致，向发言的专家提出，希望在会后深入交流。"在这方面我不太懂，想向你们请教学习。如果允许，我还希望能去你们实验室参观。"第二天一大早，他就去了对方的实验室。

王兆凯还体验过"中国速度"。在山东自贸试验区青岛片区，他与人合办了一家致力于海洋科技成果转化的企业。当时，他在青岛只停留 1 天，他们来到政务服务大厅已是上午 10 点，手上只有身份证和原来公司的营业执照。由于时间紧张，他们连新公司的名字都没准备好。大厅工作人员手把手地帮着准备，包括公司起名、手续办理以及需要准备好的材料。11 点开始办，下午 1 点半就办出了营业执照。对此，王兆凯非常赞赏。他感慨，中国自贸区的效率非常高，这在国外是很少见的。

想当"领头羊"，就不要急于求成

山重水复疑无路，柳暗花明又一村。困难能在关键时刻化解，总是令人欣慰的。

2020 年 10 月 16 日，王兆凯在深圳出席中国海洋经济博览会的海洋科技产业创新发展论坛。
（来源：凤凰网）

Jaw-Kai Wang attends the Marine Science and Technology Industry Innovation and Development Forum of the China Marine Economy Expo in Shenzhen on October 16, 2020. (Photo: ifeng.com)

对于回中国工作的这十几年，王兆凯感到非常满意。对于中国海洋经济的发展，对于深圳建设全球海洋中心城市，他也有一些观察和思考。从海洋产业的发展情况和创新潜力来看，他认为，海洋经济将成为深圳乃至整个中国经济增长的又一支柱。

不过，中国海洋经济行业跟国外仍然有一定差距。中国是海洋养殖大国，但缺乏对水产工程的专业性研究，所以他建议：加强海洋基础研究和相关人才的培养，提高水产养殖的科技含量和可持续发展能力。深圳有漫长的海岸线，在粤港澳大湾区发展的过程中，深圳可以利用好的资源、好的条件来发展海洋产业，把水产创新和工业革命结合起来，这将有助于深圳制造业和新材料技术的创新。

王兆凯通过自己创业的亲身经历发现，在先进技术领域做出点成绩大概要 15 年。"15 年其实是个很短的时间，你能做出一个有用的东西，那是非常难得的。"

他不讳言，在中国搞科研，时间压力比较大，很多人希望能在三五年内出成果。但他相信，这种心态是会改变的。"基础科技的发展，十几年算什么？你要是做老二，把人家做好的东西拿出来自己做，三年也许可以。但是，你要想做'领头羊'，那么，三五年是不够的。"

"能够有个机会，满足我的初心，不取薪水，在有生之年为中国做一点事，吾愿足矣。"他为记者的采访写下这样的小结。

（除署名外，本文图片均由受访者王兆凯提供。参考资料：今日瓯海、读特、泰利能源网站、广东外语外贸大学新闻网、里水教育、信网。）

Jaw-Kai Wang

Starting a business after retirement, dedicated to "doing something for China"

Jaw-Kai Wang, native of Renqiao Village, Guoxi Township, Ouhai District, Wenzhou City, Zhejiang Province, was born in Nanjing, Jiangsu Province in March 1932. He went to the United States in 1955. One of the fourth batch of honorary citizens of Shenzhen Municipality, he is a world-renowned aquaculture engineer, and a member of the National Academy of Engineering of the United States. He was one of the founders and the first president of the Aquaculture Engineering Society of the United States. He was among the first batch of members of the "Overseas Expert Advisory Committee" of the Overseas Chinese Affairs Office of the State Council of China. He is the chief science advisor to the Fishery Machinery and Instrument Research Institute of the Chinese Academy of Fishery Sciences, honorary director of the SUSTech-Taili Joint Laboratory of Diatom Materials, and president of Shenzhen Jawkai Bioengineering R&D Center Co., Ltd. He was consultant to the Food and Agriculture Organization of the United Nations, the World Bank, the United States Department of Agriculture, and the Rockefeller Foundation. He used to teach at the University of Hawaii.

Engaged in the research of aquacultural engineering for a long time, Professor Wang has made a breakthrough in large-scale open-pond cultivation of microalgae, which is a world-class technical problem.

"Although the stabled steed is old, he dreams to run for mile and mile. In life's December heroes bold won't change indomitable style." These lines from a poem by Cao Cao are a true portrayal of Jaw-Kai Wang.

At the age of 76, Wang started his own business in Shenzhen, researching outdoor diatom cultivation.

When he was more than 80 years old, he shuttled across the country, researching aquaculture science and technology, offering advice for industrial development, and giving

---

The interview took place in 2022.

lectures to the general public.

At the age of 90, he found that he was getting closer to his entrepreneurial goal. "We can realize continuous and high-yield cultivation of diatoms outdoors at a low price, and have found a way to use diatom frustules in large numbers, creating a way for the world to produce industrial raw materials in agriculture. Although hard work is still needed to see whether it can reach the level of commercialization within three to five years, I think I can be thankful now."

He left home young and came back old. Since 1979, Wang has returned to China many times, received by leaders of the older generation such as Deng Xiaoping, Chen Yun, Wang Zhen, and Fang Yi. In 2005, the "Overseas Expert Advisory Committee" of the Overseas Chinese Affairs Office of the State Council was established, and Wang was appointed as one of the first batch of members, which consisted of 30 well-known overseas Chinese experts and scholars, including famous figures such as Chen Ning Yang and Shing-Tung Yau.

Wang, who was attracted back to China by its reform and opening-up, may not have expected that his ultimate dream would be settled in Shenzhen, one of the birthplaces of the reform and opening-up. Wang founded a company in Shenzhen, and later joined hands with another company in Shenzhen to pursue his dream. In addition, that company established a joint laboratory with the Southern University of Science and Technology (SUSTech) to explore the diatom ecological industry chain, with Wang as the laboratory's honorary director to guide the general direction.

He is happy to support the younger generation. A former SUSTech student graduating many years ago started a business to develop hand sanitizer, using diatom extract under his guidance.

To do something for China has always been his wish since he was a student.

A chance encounter changed his ambition, and he never forgets his teachers after achieving success and fame

Wang's ancestral home is in Ouhai District, Wenzhou City, which is a famous hometown of overseas Chinese. More than 120,000 overseas Chinese originating from Ouhai are living in more than 100 countries and regions including Italy, France, and Spain. Wang's father was sent by the Qing government to study psychology at Columbia University, the United States. With a master's degree, he returned to China to teach. Wang was born while his father was a professor at Central University.

Wang first lived in Nanjing, and went to Chongqing with his parents after entering kindergarten. He stayed there for eight years and returned to live in Nanjing for a few more years. At the end of 1948, they went to Guangzhou, and Wang was in the third year of high school in the Middle School Attached to Sun Yat-sen University. In 1949, he was admitted to Taiwan University. He applied for the Mechanical Engineering Department, but, while his total score was more than enough, he scored only 29 points in mathematics, one point less than what was required for the College of Engineering. The college treated him with "exceptional admission and forced transfer to another department," so he first studied geology and then transferred to another department a year later.

At that time, Wang wanted to transfer to the Mechanical Engineering Department, but a chance encounter changed his life trajectory. He had already filled out the form, but on his way to hand in the form, he met Professor Chin Cheng, an expert in farmland water conservancy. Professor Chin took him to the office for tea and told him to study agricultural engineering to help China. Those words moved the young man, who then changed his mind and devoted his whole life to agriculture.

In 1953, Wang graduated from the Department of Agricultural Engineering. In 1955, he went to study at Michigan State University in the United States, where he obtained a master's degree and a Ph.D.

After completing his studies, Wang went to teach at the University of Hawaii. Working there for more than 40 years, he switched from agricultural engineering to aquacultural engineering, and became a professor. During this period, he had many opportunities to leave Hawaii, but decided to stay mainly for three reasons:

Firstly, the university treated him well and gave him a job when he desperately needed one. Secondly, far away from the continental United States, Hawaii is much better in terms of racial discrimination. He has three children and he wants them to grow up in Hawaii. Thirdly, although the university is not a first-class one, it doesn't matter for him. "Of course, when you are starting, it's advantageous for you have a well-known university to back you up. But if you make it by yourself, there are also some benefits."

It turned out that Wang "made it" indeed.

He has conducted systematic research on the extraction of antibacterial substances from seaweed, microalgae bioreactors, and recirculating aquaculture technology. He has published more than 170 papers in international journals, published three monographs, and received seven patents.

He has received countless honors and titles. The Hawaii state government and state legislatures have commended his contribution to the field. In 1993, he co-founded the Aquaculture Engineering Society in the United States and served as its first president. In 1995, he was elected as member of the National Academy of Engineering, the highest honor in the U.S. engineering community.

"My achievements today are due to the influence of my teachers when I was in college, and are closely related to the teachings I received from my professors in the United States," said Wang, who has achieved success and fame, and never forgets his teachers.

Starting to raise diatom in his 70s, and solving world-class problem

Before Wang went to the United States, his teachers at Taiwan University repeatedly told him that he should return to China in the future once he had the opportunity. "After I retired, I decided to go back to China to do something," Wang recalled. "I have not got a single penny of salary during these years in China, because I have done these just to provide my service." (But he did receive living expenses and housing.) Perhaps this is Wang's idea of "going back to China to do something."

It seems that his dictionary doesn't have the concept of "enjoy retirement." When he was 76, he went to Shenzhen to raise diatom in pools by the sea.

That was in 2008. Wang was introduced by the Shenzhen Municipal Government as a talent. He founded Shenzhen Jawkai Bioengineering R&D Center Co., Ltd. and led dozens of young people to develop diatom cultivation in outdoor ponds on the seaside of Dapeng Peninsula.

This project needs substantial investment. There was a period when the project progress was extremely difficult because of the shortage of funds. Wang resolutely sold his house in Taiwan to invest in the project.

In 2017, Shenzhen Taili Energy Co., Ltd. invited Wang to jointly promote the diatom cultivation project. Diatoms are microalgae. Large-scale open cultivation of microalgae is a worldwide technical problem. Hard work pays off. Wang has worked in Shenzhen for more than 10 years and has made a decisive breakthrough, successfully realizing outdoor large-scale cultivation for the first time.

"I'm probably the only person in the world who knows how to raise diatoms without using any chemicals to control insects or the invasion of other microalgae," Wang revealed.

But he also admitted, "My method can be used on only a few types of diatoms. It doesn't work on other algae."

Why cultivate diatoms in this way?

Wang is targeting industrial raw materials. Because diatom frustule is the only naturally produced nanomaterial known so far, if it is produced in a low-cost way, the future will almost be limitless. "Diatoms are very strange algae. The outer shell of single-celled plants, which is the cell wall, is generally organic and soft. Only the cell wall of diatoms is inorganic and hard, which is silicon dioxide."

Usually, the manufacturing cost of nanomaterials is high, which limits the application range of nanomaterials. "We use an agricultural method to produce large quantities. It is no problem to reach an annual yield of millions of tons, if necessary. I can say this is the only raw material that can be supplied to industry directly through agricultural production," Wang said.

How to use diatom frustule in large quantities is within the domain of materials science. So Wang switched his field of specialization once again and did a lot of research. He found that frustules, when used as industrial raw materials, have good thermal stability, high biological adaptability, and low toxicity, showing broad application prospects in macromolecular catalysis, biological processes, selective adsorption, and medically functional materials.

"I did not major in material science, so the switch this time has been very difficult," he said. "All in all, I believe I'm on the right track. I will probably achieve a moderate success in two or three years." For example, the composite of diatom frustule and aluminum is very good, but the aluminum and diatom frustule are not well connected, so the strength of the composite is not enough. "We have found a way to make it while taking advantage of the strength, high temperature, anti-corrosion, hardness and other advantages of diatoms as much as possible. In about five years, we can start commercialization."

Working with a "dark horse" university in Shenzhen to boost the application of diatom materials

In Shenzhen, Wang also cooperates with the Southern University of Science and Technology (SUSTech). Founded by the Shenzhen Municipal Government in 2012, SUSTech is a new type of research-oriented public university with a high starting point and high positioning in the background of China's higher education reform. In just 10 years, this university has developed rapidly and has become a "dark horse" among Chinese universities. In the Times Higher Education World University Rankings 2023, released in October 2022, SUSTech was among the top 200, ranking 166th in the world and 8th in Chinese mainland, surpassing some established prestigious ones such as Wuhan University, the Huazhong University of Science and Technology, and Sun Yat-sen University.

In August 2019, SUSTech and Shenzhen Taili Energy Co., Ltd. signed a cooperation agreement to jointly build the SUSTech-Taili Joint Laboratory of Diatom Materials, which mainly conducts research and development on the comprehensive application of diatom materials. Wang, as chief scientist of Taili Energy, serves as honorary director of this joint laboratory. In August 2020, at a work summary meeting to mark the lab's first anniversary, Wang participated in academic exchanges and put forward his unique insights.

A technology company co-incubated by SUSTech and the Taizhou City Government of Zhejiang Province developed a hand sanitizer, which has been put into the market, and Wang also contributed to this product. Guo Tianzi, chairwoman and general manager of this company, is an alumnus of SUSTech. In 2019, after she graduated from The Hong Kong University of Science and Technology with a master's degree, her undergraduate tutor at SUSTech, Sun Dazhi, invited her to join this project for incubating technology innovation companies. During the early development of this hand sanitizer, Sun introduced Wang to her. It is a blessing for a young entrepreneur to cooperate with such a top expert to develop products. The cooperation between Guo and Wang resulted in a kind of diatom extract, which can effectively sterilize. The extract was added to the hand sanitizer, making it more advanced and unique.

Encouraging younger generations to innovate, appreciating "China Speed"

In his 80s, Wang travelled all over China for technology promotion, exchange and cooperation. He has provided advice to some aquaculture technology enterprises, and popularized scientific knowledge and spirit to citizens, teachers and students. In addition to Guangdong, he has been to Beijing, Fujian, Shandong, Sichuan... When giving a lecture at the Guangdong University of Foreign Studies, Wang encouraged young students to think more and dare to ask questions. "The progress of a society not only depends on the wisdom of the predecessors, but also requires our pioneering and enterprising. The success of something is achieved by a generation of people who discover its feasibility and go all out to make it happen."

At a lecture during the "Shangshan" Education and Technology Festival in Lishui Township, Foshan City, Wang surprisingly told the children not to be "good students".

"Innovation is doing something different from before. If you always listen to the predecessors, how can you innovate? You need to know when to be obedient and when to be disobedient." He also pointed out that cultivating children's innovative thinking had a lot to do with the educational environment. "Teachers must offer enthusiasm and motivation to ignite the passion of students. Moreover, teachers must be able to accept students' doubts."

Wang is vigorous and resolute. At a forum in Beijing, when learning that diatoms could work well with a certain material, he immediately became interested, and proposed in-depth exchanges with the expert who spoke. "I don't know much about this, and I want to learn from you. If allowed, I hope to visit your laboratory." Early the next morning, he visited that expert's laboratory.

Wang has experienced "China Speed." In the Qingdao Area of China (Shandong) Pilot Free Trade Zone, he co-founded an enterprise dedicated to the transformation of marine scientific achievements. At that time, he stayed in Qingdao for only one day, and it was already 10 a.m. when they arrived at the government service hall, with only their ID cards and the business license of the original company in hand. They even had no time to name the new company. The staff in the service hall helped with the preparation, including the company's name, the formalities and materials needed. It started at 11 a.m., and the new business license was issued at 1:30 pm. Wang appreciated it very much. He praised the high efficiency of China's free trade zones, which is rare in foreign countries.

"Don't rush for success if you want to be a leader."

"After endless mountains and rivers that leave doubt whether there is a path out, suddenly one encounters the shade of a willow, bright flowers and a lovely village." As an ancient Chinese poem indicates, it is always gratifying that difficulties can be resolved at critical moments.

Wang is very satisfied with the past decade after returning to work in China. He also has some observations and thoughts on the development of China's marine economy (or ocean economy) and Shenzhen's construction of a global ocean center. From the perspective of the development and innovation potential of the marine industry, he believes that the marine economy will become another pillar of economic growth in Shenzhen and even in China as a whole.

However, China's marine industries still lag behind their foreign counterparts. Although a big country in marine aquaculture, China lacks professional research on aquaculture engineering. Therefore, he suggests strengthening marine basic research and the cultivation of talents, and improving the scientific and technological level and sustainable development capabilities of aquaculture. With a long coastline, Shenzhen, and the Guangdong-Hong Kong-Macao Greater Bay Area, can make use of good resources and good conditions to develop the marine industry and combine aquaculture innovation with industrial revolution, during the development of the Guangdong-Hong Kong-Macao Greater Bay Area. This will boost the innovation in Shenzhen's manufacturing industry and new material technology.

Through his own entrepreneurial experience, Wang has found that it takes about 15 years to make some achievements in a field of advanced technology. "It is very rare that you can make something useful within 15 years, which is actually a very short time."

He admits that conducting scientific research in China faces a lot of time pressure, and that many people expect results within three to five years. But he believes that mentality will change. "A dozen years are no big deal for the development of basic technology. If you are in second place, you can take something that others have made and make it yourself, maybe within three years. But if you want to be a 'leader,' three to five years are not enough."

"I'm satisfied to have a chance to fulfill my original wish, doing something for China in my lifetime without taking a salary," he wrote such a summary for our interview.

(Photo courtesy of Jaw-Kai Wang, except for the ones with credit. References: Ouhai Today, Dute News, the website of Taili Energy, the news website of the Guangdong University of Foreign Studies, Lishui Education, and qdxin.cn.)

马介璋

善于跨界的潮商，有颗不变的初心

马介璋（图片来源：《晶报》） Ma Kai Cheung (Photo: *Daily Sunshine*)

马介璋，1942年出生于广东汕头潮阳。第九、十、十一届全国政协委员，中国侨商联合会荣誉会长，粤港澳大湾区企业家联盟常务副主席，深圳市首届荣誉市民，深圳市侨联荣誉主席，深圳市侨商国际联合会创始人之一、永远名誉会长，深圳外商投资企业协会永远名誉会长，深圳市社会治安基金会（今为深圳市见义勇为基金会）创办人，香港潮属社团总会永远名誉主席，香港潮州商会永远名誉会长，佳宁娜集团控股有限公司名誉主席，华南城控股有限公司荣誉顾问，分别于2003年、2009年获香港特区政府颁发"铜紫荆星章""银紫荆星章"。

采访时间：2022年。

"1983 年，祖国改革开放的消息传来，犹如一阵春风，振奋人心。当时我马上就想到，我在国外有这么多的投资，现在是不是也可以回到祖国去投资？我是个商人，做生意肯定要考虑有没有商机，我们国家人口那么多，又地大物博，改革开放了，这个发展潜力肯定巨大。回来投资，一方面支持祖国的改革开放，另一方面也是发展壮大我的事业。"

2022 年 11 月的一个下午，在位于深圳罗湖区佳宁娜友谊广场 5 楼的办公室内，马介璋对来访的记者道出了上述肺腑之言。从 1985 年正式来深投资兴业，至今已有 37 个年头，马介璋仍然没有忘记自己的初心。

马介璋现在的身份是佳宁娜集团控股有限公司名誉主席，除此之外，他还有中国侨商联合会荣誉会长、深圳市侨联荣誉主席、深圳市侨商国际联合会永远名誉会长、深圳外商投资企业协会永远名誉会长、香港潮州商会永远名誉会长等多个头衔。

第一天上班，被炒了鱿鱼

1942 年，马介璋出生在广东潮阳成田镇（现属汕头市潮南区）一个名为家美村的地方。成田镇是当地著名的侨乡，最新统计数据显示，该镇旅外侨胞和港澳台同胞超过 20 万人，是汕头市的重点侨乡。

马介璋 7 岁那一年，其父马明耀带着一家人从潮阳成田老家到香港谋生。初到香港，马明耀做的是小贩生意，即使每天早出晚归，也常常是入不敷出，全家蜗居在一个徙置区的小木屋阁楼上。徙置区对内地人来说是一个陌生的概念，却是 20 世纪许多港人熟悉的记忆。比如"歌神"许冠杰就曾在名曲《有酒今朝醉》中唱道："行年十八岁，懒风趣，有名高级徙置区。"所谓的徙置区，其实并不高级，就是香港早期的出租公共房屋，原是为了安置无家可归的灾民而建。

潮汕人相信"工字不出头"，意思是"打工永无出头之日"，所以一有积蓄便想着做生意。后来，攒了点本钱的马明耀在香港与人合伙开了间米铺，勉勉强强可以糊口，毕竟家中有 5 个子女要养。

马介璋是家中长子，15 岁时，为了帮父母分忧，他不得不中途辍学，出来闯荡天下。初入社会，马介璋到母亲打工的毛衣厂做抓毛学徒。只是没想到，第一天上班他就被老板炒了鱿鱼。当时由于没有工作经验，他跑去向母亲请教，结果老板误以为他贪玩偷懒，就让他回家了。走出厂门，马介璋气愤难平，但仍安慰母亲说："不要紧的，他的厂这么小，我将来开一间工厂，要比他的大 10 倍以上。"见儿子有如此雄心壮志，母亲顿时就笑了。

后来，马介璋进入一家生产牛仔裤的工厂，很快就从学徒工变成熟练工。那时候马介璋很辛苦，白天在工厂上班，晚上又做裁缝补贴家用。当时由于香港地区享受英联邦特惠税制，英国进口商在港大量进货，各类服装加工订单络绎不绝。马介璋看到这个商机，在黄大仙区租下一个地铺，买了两台二手缝纫机，从大厂接单拿材料来做代加工。有时候活儿太多做不过来，就分发给周围一些家庭主妇来做。靠这个家庭式的作坊，经过3年奋斗拼搏，马介璋赚到了人生第一桶金。

到了20世纪80年代初，除了港澳地区外，马介璋名下的公司还在南非、泰国等海外7个国家设立了生产基地，组建起了以生产牛仔裤为主，兼营布匹、拉链、纽扣等辅料的香港达成集团，产品畅销欧美市场。

当然，马介璋也早早就洗掉了过去"第一天上班就被炒鱿鱼"的"屈辱"。2021年8月，马介璋在接受凤凰卫视采访时还回应了当年的雄心壮志："我在世界各地的工厂，光是厂房面积就超过30万（平方英）尺。回顾以前我第一天（上班）就被炒鱿鱼，那个老板的那间厂最多也就是3000（平方英）尺，现在我的厂比他的大了几十倍。说起来真是一个巧合。"

马介璋的生意做得越来越大，在香港也小有名气，人称"牛仔裤大王"。不过，对于这个称号，马介璋在接受采访时却感觉有点不好意思，连忙解释"都是外人封的"。在那个年代，香港除了"牛仔裤大王"马介璋，还有"塑料花大王"首富李

1988年，马介璋与同事在香港达成旧厂房（永祥工业大厦）庆祝生日。
Ma Kai Cheung and his colleagues celebrate his birthday in Tak Sing's old factory building (Wing Cheung Industrial Building) in Hong Kong in 1988.

嘉诚、"制衣大王"林百欣和"钟表大王"庄静庵，他们四人都有一个共同特点，就是"潮商"。

跨过罗湖桥，投资深圳

20世纪80年代，马介璋是最早一批跨过罗湖桥回到深圳投资兴业的港商之一。至今，他依然清晰记得当时的情景："1984年，我和几个香港的朋友一起来内地考察。当时的过关口岸是罗湖口岸，只提供'朝九晚五'的通关服务。那时过关不仅要排很长的队，而且还要经过边防人员的层层询问，一边询问一边手写登记。过完关，还得去中国银行将港币换成人民币，办完整个入境手续就得两三个小时。"

"那时候出关口到了罗湖，抬眼望去，到处都是黄土路，交通也不方便。路上汽车不多，单车多，风一吹，骑单车的人就像在灰尘里飞起来似的。但出乎我意料的是，沿路都是一派热火朝天的大开发景象。"马介璋回忆道。

1985年，马介璋在深圳南头与内地的一家企业合作，斥资兴建了一家纺织、印染、服装"一条龙"大型服装加工厂。不过，在南头的服装加工厂建设期间，闲不住的马介璋在罗湖黄贝岭投资的一个小纺织服装厂先开张了。"正好黄贝岭有一个闲置的老毛纺厂，我们就把厂房租下来了，还是生产牛仔裤。"马介璋解释，"在深圳请工人容易，人工成本也比香港低很多。"

来深圳后，马介璋发现很难找到一个吃饭的好地方。"不管是出品味道还是卫生环境，都不是很好，很难找到高档一点的饭店。"他当时已经在香港开了一家佳宁娜潮州菜酒楼，何不照样在深圳也开一家？一方面自己有吃饭的地方，另一方面很多港商来到深圳也有地方吃饭。

在潮州话里，"佳宁娜"就是"自己人"的意思。在装饰、卫生、管理与服务方面，香港佳宁娜酒楼都跟世界接轨，而且高薪聘请名厨主理，在色、香、味、形、器等方面做到精益求精，只为追求原汁原味的潮州特色家乡菜。马介璋如此费尽苦心，酒楼开业后顾客自然是络绎不绝。

于是，1988年，马介璋在刚落成的深圳晶都酒店开办了内地第一家大型港资潮州菜酒楼——深圳佳宁娜大酒楼，按照香港佳宁娜酒楼高标准打造，连厨师和楼面管理人员也大部分是从香港派过来的，同时对内地员工进行了一系列的"港式服务"培训。开业后，深圳佳宁娜大酒楼生意异常火爆。

"那时候我们的菜品价格并不低，印象中有人吃完了说贵，但是过了几天，我又在酒楼碰到他。"马介璋笑着说。顾客嘴里喊贵身体却很诚实，其实原因很简单："我们的东西都是真材实料，所以成本就高，但是好吃，而且服务好。"

佳宁娜大酒楼在深圳的成功，坚定了马介璋走高端潮菜的品牌连锁道路。随后，佳宁娜又相继在广州、北京、海口、昆明、武汉、佛山、益阳等地，以及加拿大、泰国等国家开设多家分店，分店遍布全球，佳宁娜成为一家跨国的中餐饮食集团。

慢慢地，深圳成为马介璋事业布局的重要版图或者说他投资内地城市的桥头堡。1991 年，他相中了毗邻深圳火车站的一块土地，在此建成佳宁娜友谊广场。这里原来只有连片低矮的平房以及闹哄哄的夜市大排档，一下雨就会被淹得一塌糊涂，如今已经成了繁荣的罗湖商圈的重要组成部分。2002 年，马介璋又与孙启烈、马伟武、郑松兴、梁满林 4 位侨商共同投资 26 亿元在深圳平湖兴建了华南国际工业原料城。随后，马介璋将华南国际工业原料城的模式在全国进行复制，在南昌投资"华中城"，在连云港建设"华东城"……

携手侨商，逐梦大湾区

前人披荆斩棘，闯出一条大道，定会引来他人跟上，络绎不绝。20 世纪 80 年代后期，不少港商、侨商看到"牛仔裤大王"马介璋在深圳投资兴业取得成功，也纷纷来深圳寻找商机。为加强与港商、侨商的联系，马介璋牵头创办了深圳外商投资企业协会。"我在全球各地做生意，多少会接触到一些华侨朋友，考虑到他们对内地不熟悉，为了向这些前来投资的华侨、外商提供一些力所能及的帮助和便利，同时服务国家对外开放的大局，所以创办了这个协会。"

马介璋当时是深圳外商投资企业协会的常务副会长。他透露，协会把如何吸引侨商外资、他们进来之后应该如何投资、有哪些流程都一一总结归纳到章程里。"之后我们常常会带动外商来深圳投资，有好的项目我们也会推荐给深圳市政府；其他地方需要招商引资，也会找我们协会给他们提供人选。在这个过程中，深圳外商投资企业协会为很多侨商外商排忧解难，获得了大家的认可，很多侨商外资就是通过这个协会进入内地投资的。直到今天，外商投资企业协会仍然是深圳市培育民间组织最成功的范例之一。"

深圳市侨商国际联合会成立于 2000 年，是全国第一批成立的侨商组织之一，马介璋也是这个联合会的创始人之一。从 2002 年起，马介璋连续三届担任会长。利用自身在海内外商界的影响力以及人脉广的优势，马介璋邀请大批实力雄厚的侨商入会，在骨干会员中，全国、省、市三级人大代表、政协委员达 50 多人。

"我经常带领侨商在内地考察调研、寻找发展机会，也带领企业出国学习走访，深圳市侨商国际联合会成为提供良好投资环境的考察平台。现在回过头看，虽然当时回来投资的侨胞有的做得很成功，也有做得一般甚至失败的，这是市场经济发展的规律，但是，我觉得无论发展得成功与否，当时能回来投资的侨胞都是爱国、爱党的。"马介璋感慨道，过去这么多年，特别是过去 10 年国家发展向前迈进了一大步，企业发展非常迅速，大家感觉在内地办事更加顺畅、做事更加踏实和放

2003 年，马介璋获颁"铜紫荆星章"。
Ma is awarded the "Bronze Bauhinia Star" in 2003.

心。"这主要得益于国家和平稳定的政治经济环境，还有政府更加廉洁、法治条件更为成熟、交通和信息流通更加便捷等等，为企业发展创造了得天独厚的条件，我们觉得在国内经营企业比在海外更加方便快捷。"

2021 年 10 月 6 日，时任香港特首林郑月娥在任期最后一份《施政报告》中透露了一则重磅消息：建设北部都会区。同一天，香港特区政府发布《北部都会区发展策略》。对此，外界的解读是：这是在粤港澳大湾区的框架下，香港特区政府第一次以港深融合的规划理念做出的一份重要规划，将有助于加速深港一体化进程。

作为一名常年在深港两地来回奔波的商人，马介璋对深港双城一体化的思考比绝大多数人都要超前得多。2008 年，全国两会期间，身为全国政协委员的马介璋就在全国政协第十一届一次会议提出：深港合作应纳入国家战略层面，并建议建立深港共建国际大都会的联合机构。他甚至还大胆提出，为了在未来发展中更好地发挥深港两地作用，可以考虑尝试"深港（市场）一体化"。马介璋认为，这个设想对祖国的统一大业大有好处，他说："这一举措如果实施，可以让全世界各国看到，国家对香港的大力支持和鼓励。"

2017 年政府工作报告指出，"要推动内地与港澳深化合作，研究制定粤港澳大湾区城市群发展规划，发挥港澳独特优势，提升在国家经济发展和对外开放中的地位与功能"。至此，粤港澳大湾区已经上升为国家战略。2019 年 2 月 18 日，中共中央、国务院印发《粤港澳大湾区发展规划纲要》，标志着粤港澳大湾区建设进入全面实施阶段。

尽管马介璋已经 80 岁了，但依然密切关注着国家的发展，他表示："港澳同胞、海外侨胞应把握粤港澳大湾区建设和国家'十四五'规划等重大机遇，更好融入国家发展大局，为中华民族伟大复兴作出应有贡献。"

知恩图报，支援家乡建设

如今，马介璋在内地的产业早已经从当初的服装厂转变成汇集餐饮食品、房地产、商贸物流等多个板块的大型国际企业集团。无论在哪个行业打拼，他都懂得知恩图报，时刻不忘支援祖国和家乡的建设。"我的父母经常教育我们兄弟姐妹几个，做人一定要爱国、爱家乡，我们身上流的是中国血，我们的根在中国，无论走到哪里都要记得自己是中国人。"马介璋说。

尽管时隔40多年，但第一次随父母回家乡探亲时的情景，马介璋至今仍记忆犹新。20世纪80年代初，家乡父老乡亲生活贫苦拮据，村民用水仅靠一条水沟，大家既在水沟里洗菜、洗衣服，又用水沟里的水煮饭；小孩上学的教室破旧不堪，而且没有课桌和椅子，只能坐在泥地上上课……看到这一幕，马介璋的眼睛湿润了，当即捐出了120万元，其中60万元用作修建小学，60万元用作修建自来水厂。

此后，马介璋密切关注家乡的发展情况，不遗余力地支持家乡教育卫生、道路修缮等各项建设事业。2000年，他再次捐资1000多万元在家乡建起了马介璋中学（图南学校），包括教学楼、图书馆、大礼堂、教师宿舍以及操场等配套设施。从2002年起，他又在1984年出资为家乡设立奖教奖学金的基础上，追加到每年30万元，为马介璋中学、家美学校设立奖教奖学金。

2006年，马介璋捐出赈灾款100万元。
Ma Kai Cheung donates 1 million yuan for disaster relief in 2006.

马介璋说："我捐的钱不算多，但希望能起到榜样的作用，激励年轻一代奋发图强，为家乡作出更大的贡献。"在他的带动下，一代又一代在外的潮汕乡贤反哺家乡蔚然成风，成为支持祖国和家乡发展的重要力量。

2008 年 1 月 29 日，马介璋（前排左四）赞助香港科技大学研究生奖学金。
Ma Kai Cheung (fourth from the left in the front row) sponsors to set up postgraduate scholarships at The Hong Kong University of Science and Technology on January 29, 2008.

2008 年 5 月 12 日，四川汶川地震灾情传出，当时马介璋身在海外，获悉灾情后，他立即打电话给香港潮州商会和深圳市侨商国际联合会会员，动员全体同仁捐款赈灾，并以最快的速度筹集资金。3 天之后，首笔救灾款就送到香港中联办，并转交内地灾区，香港潮州商会也由此成为最早捐出善款的机构之一。

香港潮州商会是香港历史最悠久、最具代表性的工商团体之一，至今已有过百年的历史，在东南亚以至全球华人世界都有重要的影响力。在担任香港潮州商会会长时，马介璋曾表示，潮州人在发展自己事业的同时，也要热心公益。"希望大家更加努力参与社会事务，关心公益事业，继续发扬潮人热心公益的传统，服务社会。"

马介璋还是深圳市见义勇为基金会（原深圳市社会治安基金会）创办人之一。20 世纪 90 年代初，在深圳市经济突飞猛进的同时，大量外来人口涌入，一时间产生了严峻的治安问题。1992 年，马介璋、李贤义（信义集团董事局主席）等港商及深圳市 30 多家企事业单位共同发起成立深圳市社会治安基金会，后来该基金会更名为"深圳市见义勇为基金会"。2022 年是基金会成立 30 周年，截至 2022 年，共表彰见义勇为先进群体 77 个、先进个人 3562 名，对深圳见义勇为的人士给予经济和精神的双重奖励，让他们摆脱了"光荣一阵子，痛苦一辈子""流血又流泪"的尴尬局面。2022 年 11 月 11 日，深圳市见义勇为基金会成立 30 周年致敬典礼在深圳会堂举行，佳宁娜、信义玻璃等 20 家企业荣获"深圳市见义勇为突出贡献奖"。

鉴于马介璋对深圳经济建设与社会发展所作出的贡献，早在 1994 年，他就与李嘉诚、胡应湘、余彭年等知名港商一起获颁首届"深圳市荣誉市民"称号。在深圳投资兴业 37 年，马介璋早已把这里当成了自己的第二故乡，并积极地以主人翁的姿态为这座城市的发展贡献自己的智慧和力量。

"我做过三届全国政协委员，一直积极参与政治协商工作，我的一些想法和建议被国家各级政府采纳，对地方发展起到一定作用，令我感到十分高兴。但更多的是，我从中学到了为人民服务的理念，我们经营企业就要有这样的初心和理念，一切从消费者出发，为消费者提供健康安全、匠心品质的产品和优质服务，才能在激烈的市场竞争中脱颖而出，获得消费者的认可和喜爱。"马介璋说。

（除署名外，本文图片均由受访者马介璋提供。参考资料：《侨心向党 追梦百年》、《深圳特区报》、罗湖发布。）

Ma Kai Cheung

A Chaoshan businessman good at crossing borders maintains his original aspiration

Ma Kai Cheung was born in Chaoyang, Shantou, Guangdong in 1942. He was member of the 9th, 10th and 11th National Committee of the Chinese People's Political Consultative Conference. He is honorary chairman of the China Federation of Overseas Chinese Entrepreneurs, and executive vice chairman of the Guangdong-Hong Kong-Macao Greater Bay Area Entrepreneurs Alliance. He was one of the first honorary citizens of Shenzhen. He is honorary chairman of the Shenzhen Federation of Returned Overseas Chinese, co-founder and permanent honorary chairman of the Shenzhen Overseas Chinese International Association, permanent honorary chairman of the Shenzhen Association of Enterprises with Foreign Investment, founder of the Shenzhen Social Security Foundation (now the Shenzhen Foundation for Justice and Courage), permanent honorary president of the Federation of Hong Kong Chiu Chaw Community Organizations, permanent honorary president of the Hong Kong Chiu Chow Chamber of Commerce, honorary chairman of Carrianna Group Holdings Company Limited, and honorary consultant to China South City Holdings Limited. He was awarded the "Bronze Bauhinia Star" and "Silver Bauhinia Star" by the Government of the Hong Kong Special Administrative Region in 2003 and 2009 respectively.

"In 1983, the news of the reform and opening-up of the motherland came like a spring breeze. It was exciting. I immediately thought: Since I have so much investment abroad, can I return to the motherland to invest now? I am a businessman. When doing business, I must consider whether there are business opportunities. Our country has such a large population, as well as vast land and resources, plus the reform and opening-up, so there must be huge potential in development. Returning to invest, on the one hand, can support the reform and opening up of the motherland, and, on the other hand, can develop and strengthen my business."

The interview took place in 2022.

One afternoon in November 2022, sitting in his office on the fifth floor of the Carrianna Friendship Plaza in Luohu District, Shenzhen, Ma Kai Cheung said the above heartfelt words to us. It has been 37 years since he formally came to Shenzhen to invest and start a business in 1985, and he still has not forgotten his original aspiration.

Ma is currently honorary chairman of Carrianna Group Holdings Company Limited. In addition, he has many other titles, such as honorary chairman of the China Federation of Overseas Chinese Entrepreneurs, honorary chairman of the Shenzhen Federation of Returned Overseas Chinese, permanent honorary chairman of the Shenzhen Overseas Chinese International Association, permanent honorary chairman of the Shenzhen Association of Enterprises with Foreign Investment, and permanent honorary president of the Hong Kong Chiu Chow Chamber of Commerce.

Fired on his first day at work

In 1942, Ma was born in a place called Jiamei Village in Chengtian Township, Chaoyang, Guangdong Province (now in Chaonan District, Shantou City). Chengtian Township is a famous hometown of overseas Chinese. The latest statistics show that more than 200,000 overseas Chinese and compatriots in Hong Kong, Macao and Taiwan are from that town. It is a key hometown of overseas Chinese in Shantou City.

When Ma Kai Cheung was 7 years old, his father, Ma Ming Yiu, took the family to travel from their hometown in Chengtian, Chaoyang to Hong Kong to make a living. When they first arrived in Hong Kong, Ma Ming Yiu was a hawker. Even if he went out early and returned late every day, he often couldn't make ends meet. The whole family lived in the attic of a small wooden house in a resettlement area. The resettlement area is an unfamiliar concept to mainlanders, but it is a familiar memory for many Hong Kong people in the 20th century. For example, the pop legend Sam Hui once sang in his famous song *Enjoy While You Can*, "When I was 18 years old, I pretended to be humorous. I was nicknamed High-end Resettlement Area." Actually, the so-called resettlement areas were not high-end at all. They were rental public housing in Hong Kong in the early years to accommodate homeless disaster victims.

The Chaoshan people believe that "working for others will never make it to the top." They want to start a business as soon as they have some savings. Later, Ma Ming Yiu, who saved some capital, opened a rice shop in Hong Kong in partnership with others, barely making ends meet for his family with five children.

Ma Kai Cheung is the eldest son in the family. When he was 15 years old, to share his parents' burdens, he had to drop out of school and go out to work and explore. First, he worked as an apprentice to grab wool at the sweater factory where his mother worked. Unexpectedly, he was fired by his boss on the first day of work. It was because he, with no work experience, went to ask his mother for advice. But the boss mistakenly thought that he was playful and lazy, so he let him go home. Walking out of the factory, Ma was very angry, but he comforted his mother and said, "It doesn't matter. His factory is so small. I will open a factory in the future, more than 10 times bigger than his." His mother immediately laughed after seeing his ambition.

Later, Ma entered a factory that produced jeans, and soon grew from an apprentice to a skilled worker. He worked very hard, working in the factory during the day, and working as a tailor at night to subsidize his family. As Hong Kong enjoyed the preferential tax system of the Commonwealth, British importers purchased many goods from Hong Kong, and various orders for garment processing came in an endless stream. Seeing this business opportunity, Ma rented a ground-floor shop in Wong Tai Sin District, bought two second-hand sewing machines, and got orders and materials from large factories for contract manufacturing. When there were too many orders, he distributed some of them to housewives around. Through this family-style workshop, after three years of hard work, Ma made the first pot of gold in his life.

In the early 1980s, in addition to Hong Kong and Macao, Ma's companies also established production bases in seven foreign countries such as South Africa and Thailand. He founded Tak Sing Alliance Holdings Limited in Hong Kong, mainly producing jeans and also selling accessories such as cloth, zippers, and buttons. The products sold well in the European and American markets.

Of course, Ma also washed away the "humiliation" of "being fired on the first day of work" in the past. In August 2021, in an interview with Phoenix TV, Ma responded to his ambition in the early years, "My factories all over the world have an area of more than 300,000 square feet. Looking back on my being fired on my first day at work, that boss had a factory of at most 3,000 square feet. Now my factories are dozens of times larger than his. It's really a coincidence."

Ma's business was getting bigger and bigger, and he made a name for himself in Hong Kong, known as the "King of Jeans." However, Ma felt a little embarrassed when talking about this title, and quickly explained, "It was just given by outsiders." In those days in Hong Kong, in addition to this "King of Jeans," there were also the "King of Plastic Flowers" and the richest man (Li Ka-shing), the "King of Clothing" (Lim Por

Yen), and the "King of Watches" (Chong Ching Um). All four of them share a common characteristic, that is, they are all "Chaoshan businessmen."

Crossing the Luohu Bridge to invest in Shenzhen

In the 1980s, Ma was one of the first Hong Kong businessmen to cross the Luohu Bridge and return to Shenzhen to invest and start a business. To this day, he still clearly remembers the scenes: "In 1984, I visited the mainland with a few friends from Hong Kong. I still remember that the customs clearance port at that time was Luohu Port, which provided 'nine-to-five' customs clearance services only. Back then, when passing the customs, people not only stood a long queue, but also went through layers of questioning by the border guards, who even wrote down the questions and answers. After passing the customs, we had to go to Bank of China to exchange Hong Kong dollars into renminbi. It took two or three hours to complete the entry formalities."

"At that time, when I got out of the customs and arrived at Luohu, I looked up to find dirt roads everywhere, and the traffic was not convenient. There were not many cars on the road, but many bicycles. When the wind blew, the cyclists seemed to fly in the dust. But to my surprise, there was scenes of large-scale development in full swing along the road," Ma recalled.

In 1985, Ma cooperated with a mainland enterprise to invest to build a large "one-stop" garment processing factory in Nantou, Shenzhen, involved in textile, printing, dyeing, and clothing. However, while the garment processing factory in Nantou was still under construction, the diligent Ma opened a small textile and garment factory in Huangbeiling, Luohu. "It happened that there was an old idle wool spinning factory in Huangbeiling, so we rented the factory and continued to produce jeans," Ma explained. "It was easier to hire workers in Shenzhen, and the labor cost was much lower than that in Hong Kong."

After coming to Shenzhen, Ma found it difficult to find a good place to have meals. "Neither the taste of the food nor the environment was very good. It was difficult to find a high-end restaurant." He had already opened a Carrianna Chiu Chow Restaurant in Hong Kong, so why not open another in Shenzhen? On the one hand, he would have a place to have meals. On the other hand, it would also be a place for many Hong Kong businessmen to dine in Shenzhen.

In Chaozhou dialect, "Carrianna" means "one of our own." In terms of decoration, sanitation, management and service, the Carrianna Restaurant in Hong Kong was in line with the world. It employed famous chefs with high salaries, and kept on improving the color, aroma, taste, shape, and utensils just to pursue original and authentic cuisine with characteristics of the hometown, Chaozhou. With Ma's painstaking efforts, the restaurant naturally had a continuous stream of customers after its opening.

Therefore, in 1988, Ma opened the first large-scale Hong Kong-funded Chaozhou restaurant in the mainland, the Shenzhen Carrianna Restaurant, in the newly completed Oriental Regent Hotel in Shenzhen. The restaurant copied the high standards of its counterpart in Hong Kong. Even the chefs and floor managers were mostly sent from Hong Kong, and a series of "Hong Kong-style service" trainings were conducted for the mainland employees. Business was booming after the Shenzhen restaurant opened.

"The price of our dishes was not low. I remember that someone said it was expensive after eating, but a few days later, I ran into him again in the restaurant," Ma said with a smile. Although that customer complained about the price, His body was honest. The reason was very simple. "Our dishes are all made of quality materials, so the cost is high. But they are delicious, and our service is good."

The success of the restaurant in Shenzhen strengthened Ma's determination to run high-end Chaozhou cuisine chain restaurants. Subsequently, the Carrianna Restaurant opened branches in places such as Guangzhou, Beijing, Haikou, Kunming, Wuhan, Foshan, and Yiyang, as well as Canada, Thailand and other countries, spreading all over the world and becoming a multinational Chinese food group.

Gradually, Shenzhen has also become an important territory for Ma's business layout, or a bridgehead for him to invest in mainland cities. In 1991, he chose a piece of land adjacent to the Shenzhen Railway Station to build the Carrianna Friendship Square. There used to be stretches of low-rise bungalows and noisy night market stalls in that area, which would be flooded when it rained. Now it has become an important part of the prosperous Luohu commercial area. In 2002, Ma and four overseas Chinese businessmen, Cliff Sun Kai-lit, Ma Wai Mo, Cheng Chung Hing, and Leung Moon Lam, jointly invested 2.6 billion yuan to build the China South International Industrial Materials City in Pinghu, Shenzhen. Later, Ma copied the model of the China South City (China South City) across the country, investing in the "China Central City" in Nanchang, and the "China East City" in Lianyungang...

Joining hands with overseas Chinese entrepreneurs to pursue dreams in Greater Bay Area

When the predecessors blaze a broad road through brambles, it will definitely attract others to follow in an endless stream. In the late 1980s, many Hong Kong businessmen and overseas Chinese businessmen came to Shenzhen for business opportunities after seeing the success of Ma, the "King of Jeans," in investing in Shenzhen. To strengthen the connection with Hong Kong businessmen and overseas Chinese businessmen, Ma took the lead in founding the Shenzhen Association of Enterprises with Foreign Investment. "I did business all over the world, and I got in contact with some overseas Chinese friends, more or less. Considering that they were not familiar with the mainland, we founded this association in a bid to provide some help and convenience to these overseas Chinese and foreign businessmen who came to invest, and, at the same time, to serve the overall situation of the country's opening up to the outside world."

Ma was then executive vice chairman of the Shenzhen Association of Enterprises with Foreign Investment. He revealed that the association summarized in its charter how to attract overseas Chinese businessmen and foreign capital, how they would invest after they come in, and what processes would be involved. "Afterwards, we often led foreign businessmen to invest in Shenzhen, and we recommended good projects to the Shenzhen Municipal Government. When some other places needed to attract investment, they would also ask our association to recommend candidates. In this process, the Shenzhen Association of Enterprises with Foreign Investment has helped solve problems for many overseas Chinese and foreign businessmen, and has gained widespread recognition. Many overseas Chinese and foreign investors have invested in the mainland through this association. To this day, the association is still one of the most successful examples of cultivating non-governmental organizations in Shenzhen."

The Shenzhen Overseas Chinese International Association was established in 2000, as one of the first overseas Chinese business organizations in the country. Ma is one of the founders of this association. Starting in 2002, he served as chairman for three consecutive terms. Taking advantage of his influence in the business circles at home and abroad and his extensive contacts, Ma invited many powerful overseas Chinese businessmen to join the association. Among its key members, more than 50 are deputies to the People's Congress or members of the Chinese People's Political Consultative Conference at the national, provincial, or municipal level.

"I often led overseas Chinese businessmen to investigate and find development opportunities in the mainland, and I also led companies to study abroad. The Shenzhen Overseas Chinese International Association has acted as an investigation platform to provide a good investment environment. Looking back now, although some overseas

Chinese who returned to invest at that time turned out to be very successful, and some were mediocre or even failed, which is the law of the development of a market economy, but I think that no matter whether they were successful or not in their development, the overseas Chinese who came back to invest at that time all loved the country and the Party," Ma said. So many years have passed. Especially in the past decade, China's development has taken a big step forward, and enterprises have developed very rapidly. People find it smoother to handle affairs in the mainland, and feel more reassured and relaxed when doing things. "This is mainly because of the country's peaceful and stable political and economic environment, as well as the cleaner government, more mature conditions for the rule of law, more convenient transportation and information circulation, and so on, which have created unique conditions for the development of enterprises. We feel that operating enterprises in China is more convenient and efficient than doing it overseas."

On October 6, 2021, the then chief executive of Hong Kong, Carrie Lam Cheng Yuet-ngor, revealed a piece of big news in her last Policy Address: the construction of the Northern Metropolis. On the same day, the Government of the Hong Kong Special Administrative Region released the Northern Metropolis Development Strategy. The interpretation by the outside was: Under the framework of the Guangdong-Hong Kong-Macao Greater Bay Area, this was the first time that the Government of the Hong Kong Special Administrative Region had made an important plan based on the planning concept of Hong Kong-Shenzhen integration, which would help accelerate the integration process of Shenzhen and Hong Kong.

As a businessman who travels back and forth between Shenzhen and Hong Kong all the year round, Ma's thinking on the integration of Shenzhen and Hong Kong has been much ahead of most people. In 2008, during the national Two Sessions, Ma, as a member of the National Committee of the Chinese People's Political Consultative Conference (CPPCC), proposed to the First Session of the 11th National Committee of the CPPCC that Shenzhen-Hong Kong cooperation should be incorporated into the national strategy, and suggested the establishment of a joint institution for Shenzhen and Hong Kong to jointly build an international metropolis. He even boldly proposed trying "Shenzhen-Hong Kong (market) integration" to better play the role of Shenzhen and Hong Kong in future development. Ma believes that this idea is of great benefit to the great cause of the motherland's reunification. He said, "If this measure is implemented, all countries in the world can see our country's strong support and encouragement for Hong Kong."

The Government Work Report in 2017 said, "We will promote closer cooperation between the mainland and Hong Kong and Macao. We will draw up a plan for the development of a city cluster in the Guangdong-Hong Kong-Macao Greater Bay Area, give full play to the distinctive strengths of Hong Kong and Macao, and elevate their positions and roles in China's economic development and opening up." By then, the Guangdong-Hong Kong-Macao Greater Bay Area (GBA) became a national strategy. On February 18, 2019, the Central Committee of the Communist Party of China and the State Council issued the Outline Development Plan for the Guangdong-Hong Kong-Macao Greater Bay Area, marking the start of the full implementation of the construction of the GBA.

Although he is 80 years old, Ma still pays close attention to the development of the country. He said, "Compatriots in Hong Kong and Macao and overseas Chinese should seize major opportunities such as the construction of the GBA and the national '14th Five-Year Plan' to better integrate into the country's overall development and make due contributions to the great rejuvenation of the Chinese nation."

Supporting the construction of his hometown with gratitude

Today, Ma's businesses in the mainland have already transformed from garment factories into a large international enterprise group that integrates multiple sectors such as catering and food, real estate, and trade and logistics. No matter which industry he works in, he knows how to repay the kindness he has received, and never forgets to support the construction of his motherland and hometown. "My parents often taught me and my siblings that we must be patriotic and love our hometown, we have Chinese blood in our body, our roots are in China, and we must remember that we are Chinese wherever we go," Ma said.

Ma still remembers the scenes when he returned to his hometown with his parents to visit relatives for the first time, although it was more than 40 years ago. In the early 1980s, the villagers in his hometown were living in poverty. They relied on a ditch for water, washing vegetables and clothes there, and cooking with water from the ditch. The classrooms where children studied were dilapidated. Without desks and chairs, the students had to sit on the muddy floor for class... Seeing this, Ma's eyes brimmed with tears, and he immediately donated 1.2 million yuan, of which 600,000 yuan was used to build a primary school and 600,000 yuan was used to build a tap water factory.

Since then, Ma has paid close attention to the development of his hometown and spared no effort to support various construction undertakings in his hometown such as education, health, and road repairs. In 2000, he donated more than 10 million yuan to build the Ma

Kai Chung Middle School (namely the Tunan School) in his hometown, including the teaching building, library, auditorium, teachers' dormitory, playground, and other supporting facilities. He founded teaching awards and scholarships in his hometown in 1984. From 2002 onwards, he has increased the amount to 300,000 yuan each year, setting up teaching awards and scholarships for the Ma Kai Chung Middle School and the Jiamei School.

Ma said, "The money I have donated is not too much, but I hope to serve as an example and inspire the younger generation to work hard and make greater contributions to their hometown." Inspired by him, it has become a common practice for generations of overseas Chaoshan people to repay their hometown, forming an important force to support the development of their motherland and hometown.

On May 12, 2008, Ma was overseas when news came that an earthquake hit Wenchuan in Sichuan Province. After learning about the disaster, he immediately called the members of the Hong Kong Chiu Chow Chamber of Commerce and the Shenzhen Overseas Chinese International Association to mobilize all colleagues to donate for disaster relief. He also raised funds as quickly as possible. Three days later, their first disaster relief funds were sent to the Liaison Office of the Central People's Government in Hong Kong and transferred to the disaster-stricken areas in the mainland. The Hong Kong Chiu Chow Chamber of Commerce became one of the organizations that donated early for the earthquake.

The Hong Kong Chiu Chow Chamber of Commerce is one of the oldest and most representative industrial and commercial organizations in Hong Kong. It has a history of more than 100 years and an important influence in Southeast Asia and Chinese communities worldwide. When he was president of the chamber of commerce, Ma once said that Chaozhou people should also be enthusiastic about public welfare while developing their own business. "I hope that everyone will make more efforts to participate in social affairs and care about public welfare, continue to carry forward Chaozhou people's tradition of being enthusiastic about public welfare, and serve the society."

Ma is also one of the founders of the Shenzhen Foundation for Justice and Courage (formerly the Shenzhen Social Security Foundation). In the early 1990s, while Shenzhen's economy was developing by leaps and bounds, a lot of people flocked to the city, which also brought serious public security problems. In 1992, some Hong Kong businessmen, including Ma and Lee Yin Yee (chairman of Xinyi Group), and more than 30 enterprises and institutions in Shenzhen jointly initiated the Shenzhen Social Security Foundation, which was later renamed the Shenzhen Foundation for Justice and Courage. The year

2022 marked the 30th anniversary of the foundation, which has commended 77 advanced groups and 3,562 advanced individuals for performing outstanding acts of bravery. Giving financial and spiritual rewards to those who have acted bravely in Shenzhen has freed them from the embarrassing situation of "glory for a while, pain for a lifetime" and "shedding both blood and tears." On November 11, 2022, the tribute ceremony for the 30th anniversary of the Shenzhen Foundation for Justice and Courage was held in the Shenzhen Hall. A total of 20 companies including Carriana and Xinyi Glass won the award for "Outstanding Contribution to Justice and Courage in Shenzhen."

In view of Ma's contribution to Shenzhen's economic construction and social development, as early as 1994, he became a "Shenzhen Honorary Citizen" together with Li Ka-shing, Gordon Wu, Yu Pang-lin and other well-known Hong Kong businessmen when the title was awarded for the first time. Having invested in Shenzhen for 37 years, Ma has long regarded it as his second hometown, and has actively contributed his wisdom and strength to the development of this city with a sense of being the master.

"I acted as member of the National Committee of the CPPCC for three terms and have been actively participating in political consultations. I am very happy that some of my ideas and suggestions have been adopted by governments at all levels of the country and have played a certain role in local development. But more importantly, I have learned from it the concept of serving the people. We must have such an original aspiration and concept when running businesses. Everything we do should be done for consumers. We should provide consumers with healthy and safe products with ingenious quality as well as high-quality services. Only in this way can we stand out from the fierce market competition and gain the recognition and love of consumers," Ma said.

(Photos courtesy of Ma Kai Cheung, except for the one with credit. References: *Hearts of Overseas Chinese Turn to the Party, Pursuing Dreams for a Hundred Years*; *Shenzhen Special Zone Daily*; and Luohu News Release.)

吴荣基

投资大鹏的先锋，敬老慈幼的好人

吴荣基（来源：《晶报》） Ng Wing Kee (Photo: *Daily Sunshine*)

吴荣基，祖籍广东潮阳（现汕头市潮阳区），1944 年出生于香港，深圳市大鹏新区大鹏商会永远名誉会长。自 1987 年来到深圳大鹏投资后，他积极参与慈善公益事业，曾为大鹏第二小学等学校和有关单位捐款超过 1000 万元，捐建的河源市连平县三角镇吴荣基卫生院是当地首个侨捐项目。2011 年他被授予"深圳市荣誉市民"称号，2013 年再获大鹏新区"鹏城好人"嘉奖。

采访时间：2024 年。

《孟子·告子下》有云："敬老慈幼，无忘宾旅。"

在吴荣基看来，这是中华民族自古以来流传的一种美德，也是他一直以来为人处世信奉的一条重要准则。

2024 年 6 月底，一个炎热的下午，在深圳大鹏新区较场尾附近的一处住宅中，记者如约见到了刚刚从香港赶过来的吴荣基。

"先要做人，再谈做事。"已进入耄耋之年的吴荣基感慨道，"每个人有不同的处事方式，有的人一生以赚钱为主，有的人则以服务群众为主，但是无论什么时候，都要学会尊重他人，最主要的就是'敬老慈幼'。"

祖籍潮阳，小作坊孕育出大生意

吴荣基祖籍广东潮阳，父母一辈是从内地到香港谋生的"潮州人"（旧时，整个潮汕地区外出谋生的人都自称潮州人）。吴父一开始是在当时潮州人聚集的尖沙咀附近码头做苦力，后来积攒了一些本钱，就自己经营了一间米铺。再后来，吴父跟人合作，又开办了一间小规模的塑胶加工厂。

1944 年，吴荣基在香港九龙出生。潮汕人向来崇尚"多子多福"，在吴荣基之后，吴家又陆续增添了 7 个子女。一个并不算太富裕的小商人家庭，有 8 个嗷嗷待哺的孩子，吴父当年肩负的压力可不一般。在吴荣基的记忆中，父亲是一个对家庭非常有责任感且信守承诺的男人。

作为长子的吴荣基自小就非常懂事，放学后常常穿梭于繁忙的米铺与塑胶加工厂之间，协助父亲经营生意。这一时期积累的经验伴随着他步入商界，成为他事业道路上的坚实基石。不久后，他便继承了父亲的塑胶加工厂。1972 年，28 岁的吴荣基另外注册了一家有限公司，开始从事出口贸易生意。

20 世纪 60 至 70 年代是香港工业发展的鼎盛时期，塑胶产业在当时更是香港的几大支柱产业之一。据学者沈元章在研究文章《战后香港制造业的发展》中介绍，1972 年，以塑胶为主要原材料的港产玩具出口数量超过了日本，跃居世界第一位；到 1979 年，港产玩具出口总值则达到了 51.56 亿港元，占本埠塑胶产品出口总值的85%（详见《亚太经济》1985 年第 6 期）。

多年来，许多媒体津津乐道的一件事就是，20 世纪 60 至 70 年代，香港地区的塑胶花出口量居全球首位，市场占有率一度高达八成，当年的"塑胶花大王"潮商李嘉诚，后来更是成了香港首富。

踩中风口的吴荣基，同样在塑胶行业赚到了人生的第一桶金。经过十多年的艰苦奋斗，他将原来只有两三个员工的小作坊发展成为一家有一定规模和影响力的企业。

大鹏建厂，做个开心快乐鹏城人

20世纪70年代末，在香港事业蒸蒸日上的吴荣基，愈发强烈地感觉到工厂发展的瓶颈。"主要是那个时候的香港工厂很难请到人。"吴荣基告诉记者。

与此同时，中国开始实行改革开放，这股春风也吹进了吴荣基的心中。他毅然决定北上发展，将目光投向了充满机遇和挑战的内地，开始在珠三角寻找合适的新厂址。"我曾经去东莞、六约（现属深圳市龙岗区）等地考察过，但那时候这些地方太热门了，有很多港商涌过去，不是很适合我。"吴荣基表示。

机缘巧合下，吴荣基来到当时属于宝安县的大鹏镇鹏城村（现鹏城社区），一眼便爱上了这里。"虽然当时的鹏城村周围看起来比较荒芜，但这个地方的空气非常好，人又朴实，我立即就下定了决心在这里投资。"吴荣基还透露了自己当时的小算盘，"在这个地方建厂，工人在本地住宿舍、吃饭堂，我估计没有什么问题。只是我每周从香港过来大鹏一次，个人辛苦一点点而已。更重要的是，这个地方可发展的空间非常大，生意比较容易做到一定规模"。

潮汕人会做生意，被认为是基因里自带的，他们独具慧眼，善于把握商机。虽然是在香港出生和长大的，但是吴荣基血液里流淌着的还是潮汕人天生的商业基因。果然，吴荣基的工厂在鹏城的蓬勃发展跟他当初所预料的差不多。当然，这都是后话。

"那时鹏城村这边刚好有已经建好的厂房，于是我就立即将工厂从香港搬了过来。"1987年，吴荣基在内地投资的华凯塑胶制品（深圳）有限公司在鹏城村创立，这就是当地居民口中常说的"鹏城华凯厂"。工厂生产的主要是塑胶、五金、石膏、布饰等产品，一开始做的都是来料加工业务。"我们通过在香港的公司拿订单，在鹏城村的工厂加工生产，再转运回香港，出口到美国、加拿大。"吴荣基介绍。

当时，深圳大鹏半岛周边的环境条件还是比较艰苦的，光是交通这一点就让吴荣基吃了不少苦头。尽管只是每周从香港来大鹏的工厂一次，但是每一次从罗湖或者文锦渡口岸过关后，他常常需要再花四五个小时才能到达鹏城村的工厂。

"过去从深圳（市区）来大鹏，还要绕山路、走小道的。那时候，来大鹏可不像现在有高速这么方便，走的差不多都是烂泥路。"吴荣基说，"我上午从香港家中出发，一般都是傍晚才能来到工厂。如果遇上下雨天，那更不知道要多长时间才能来到鹏城这边的工厂了。"再回想起当年的这些经历，恍若隔世。现在深港交通发达，来来往往非常便利，再无当年的路途艰辛。

如今，虽已80岁高龄，但吴荣基仍旧每周往返香港大鹏两地。"我这个人自小就非常喜欢大海，鹏城这里靠海环境好、空气清新，而且很安静，我住在这边很开心。"吴荣基笑着说。

吴荣基曾任大鹏新区大鹏商会第三届会长，目前处于半退休的状态，平日就在香港陪陪太太，周末则会返回大鹏。"一般是逗留一个晚上，第二天又回去香港。过来这边一是为了处理原来工厂遗留的一些事务，二是跟一些老朋友、旧同事见见面、聊聊天。"吴荣基说。

吴荣基口中的"老朋友"就包括现任的大鹏商会会长李建齐。"老会长每次回来大鹏都会主动联系我。他是我们商会的永远名誉会长，至今依然非常关心商会和大鹏经济的发展。"在李建齐看来，在改革开放初期，由于交通不便，大鹏当地的招商工作其实特别困难，但是吴荣基选择投资大鹏、落户鹏城社区，为本地的经济发展作出了重要贡献。

吴荣基曾任大鹏商会第三届会长。

Ng Wing Kee was the third president of the Dapeng Chamber of Commerce.

宴请长者，三十多年依然坚持着

几百年来，大鹏所城附近的鹏城社区都有宴请长者吃饭的敬老优良传统，当地著名的"千人将军宴"是每五年举办一次的盛大活动。每当将军宴举办时，鹏城社区内的天后宫、老人中心和西北大楼将摆设几百张圆桌，几千名宾客共进将军宴的场景蔚为壮观。

据曾任鹏城社区党总支书记的余少林介绍，将军宴源于清道光年间镇守大鹏所城的赖恩爵将军，过去逢年过节或打仗凯旋时，他就会设家宴，宴请将士和四方乡邻。将军宴上的都是当地的家常菜：长命菜（酸菜）、将军黄金块（烧猪肉）、豆腐丸子、肉丸、炒面、云菜、炸鸡翼、炸猪肉、白切鸡、猪皮、大杂烩……

今天，在鹏城社区，能够与将军宴齐名的恐怕就是一年一度的"吴老板请老人吃饭"活动了。当地居民口中的"吴老板"，正是吴荣基。自20世纪90年代初起，吴荣基便坚持每年在农历年末或春节期间，邀请鹏城当地的长者们共聚一堂，享用丰盛的团圆饭。"同一时间，几百名长者坐在一起吃饭，这是非常难得的机会。"吴荣基说："我希望可以提供一个平台，让长者们一起吃吃饭、聊聊天，开心开心。"聊起请鹏城当地长者吃饭的起因，吴荣基表示"纯属巧合"。"鹏城社区老年人协

2024年1月19日，吴荣基携手嘉霖集团林氏兄弟宴请长者活动准备的大鹏本地家常菜。（来源：刘玉芬）

A banquet for the elderly co-organized by Ng Wing Kee and the Lin brothers of Jialin Group provides home-cooked dishes in Dapeng on January 19, 2024. (Photo: Liu Yufen)

会曾经请我去吃过当地的'老人宴'，我觉得这是一种好风气。之后，我就请老年人协会一定要给我一个机会，让我每年都宴请本地的长者吃一顿饭。"

近些年，鹏城社区老年人协会会长刘玉芬一直是"吴老板请老人吃饭"活动的协助执行人。她告诉记者，过去30多年，除了新冠疫情期间不能组织群体性聚会之外，"吴老板请老人吃饭"从未间断，规模大的时候有五六十桌、近600人进餐。

"即使是新冠疫情期间，不能请本地的老人吃饭，但是每年吃完饭的例行活动——吴老板给长者派发利是，依然坚持着。"刘玉芬透露。

"请长者吃饭，这真的是一件非常有意义的事情。"吴荣基希望有人能够把这件好事传承下去："这几年，我一直在物色合适人选，希望能将这个传统坚持下去。老实说，做这件事的经济压力不算太大，就是看你有没有这个心，毕竟不是天天请长者吃饭，只是一年一次而已。"

"每一次，在请长者吃饭的现场，看到大家载歌载舞，欢声笑语，吃完之后再领一份礼物带回家去，那一刻，我觉得非常开心。"吴荣基说。

慷慨解囊，积极捐资助学做慈善

距离吴荣基在深圳的家约一公里处，就是大鹏第二小学。该校的官方介绍里有这么一段文字："2001年9月由苏晃南先生、黄真秀女士、吴荣基先生、黄启泰先生捐资，各级政府和鹏城社区居委会大力支持，于现址建成新校。"

据吴荣基透露，建学校的规划和图纸都由当时镇政府定，他们几个厂商只负责出资建造。为了建造一间质量过硬的学校，他和苏晃南（原籍鹏城村，与黄真秀为夫妻）、黄启泰等几个在鹏城开厂的港商还特别找来了相熟的建筑商承建学校。"建筑商是我们认识的，这样就可以监控学校的建筑质量。我们希望捐出的每一分钱都能发挥最大效用，将一所质量有保障的学校交给政府，我们也就安心了。"

除了捐资建校，当时吴荣基还特别捐出了150万元在鹏城村设立奖教奖学金，对教学成果优异的教师和学习成绩优秀，考取中、大专学校的学生分别给予奖励。

2001 年 9 月，吴荣基（左二）与其他捐建学校的港商一起出席大鹏第二小学启用仪式。
Ng Wing Kee (second from left) attends the opening ceremony of Dapeng No. 2 Primary School in September 2001 with other Hong Kong businessmen who donated funds to build the school.

大鹏第二小学。（来源：深圳政府在线）
Dapeng No. 2 Primary School. (Photo: Shenzhen Government Online)

据媒体报道，这可是"全龙岗区（未设新区前，大鹏原属龙岗区管辖）第一个村级奖学基金"。

吴荣基的善举并未止步于此。据《深圳侨报》2009年1月12日报道，吴荣基敬老爱老、热心公益的爱心故事在大鹏一直都被传为佳话。比如，他曾捐资70万元帮助鹏城社区修建了安老院，添置健身器材，让老人的活动更加丰富多彩；捐资5万港元，助力大鹏华侨医院改建；捐资150万元，修建鹏城文化广场；捐资60万元，完善鹏城公园的配套设施建设。

吴荣基捐建的河源市连平县三角镇卫生院被确定为当地首个侨捐项目。

The Sanjiao Township Health Center in Lianping County, Heyuan City, which Ng Wing Kee donated funds to build, is identified as the first overseas Chinese donation project in that area.

一份大鹏商会成立15周年的内部特刊记载：1999年，吴荣基曾为兴建大鹏商会大厦捐资25万元；2012年6月，他更是以629万元的捐款总额，名列"大鹏商会慈善公益群芳谱"榜眼。他也因此被公认"为促进大鹏慈善公益事业发挥了极其重大的作用"。

而且，吴荣基播撒的爱心并没有局限于深圳本地。2004年，在当时的深圳市外事（侨务）办公室的牵线搭桥下，他出资60万元，在河源市连平县三角镇捐建了一所卫生院，改善了当地的医疗卫生条件，为当地群众就医提供了方便。2008年7月，吴荣基捐建的这所卫生院被广东省人民政府侨务办公室确定为当地首个侨捐项目。

几十年间，吴荣基为公益慈善事业做出的个人捐款已超过1000万元。2011年，鉴于为深圳市建设做出了突出贡献，吴荣基等48人被授予"深圳市荣誉市民"称号；2013年，他再获大鹏新区"鹏城好人"嘉奖。

对于吴荣基的善行义举，大鹏新区文艺界人士罗育灿曾特别为其作诗一首，并手书"鹏飞万里春光好，诚育千家厚德人"对联相赠。对此，吴荣基再三强调只是"在做自己能力范围之内的一点小事"，就是"取之于社会，用之于社会"。

2011年，吴荣基被授予"深圳市荣誉市民"称号。

Ng Wing Kee is awarded the title of "Honorary Citizen of Shenzhen Municipality" in 2011.

　　有着630年历史的大鹏所城被誉为"鹏城之根"，深圳又名"鹏城"即源于此。这里是"深圳之源"，也是吴荣基在深圳的根。如今吴荣基在深圳的家，就安在大鹏新区的鹏城社区，距离大鹏所城一公里多。

　　诚如庄子所云，"水击三千里，抟扶摇而上者九万里"。今日的新鹏城社区发展得越来越好，乘着改革开放的春风，已从昔日的沿海旧所城、小渔村，摇身变成"全国重点文物保护单位"、"中国历史文化名村"、"深圳八景"之首、"深圳十大文化名片"之一……看到这些巨大的变化，吴荣基感到非常欣慰。

　　"在鹏城工作生活了30多年，我的心早已跟大鹏系在了一起，也将这里当成了我的第二故乡、第二个家。"吴荣基动情地说道。

　　（深圳市大鹏新区大鹏侨联副主席李添奎先生对本文亦有贡献，特此鸣谢。除署名外，本文图片均由受访者吴荣基提供。参考资料：《深圳特区报》、《深圳侨报》、"深圳政府在线"网站。）

Ng Wing Kee

A pioneer in investing in Dapeng, a good man who respects the elderly and loves the young

Ng Wing Kee, or Sunny Ng, whose ancestral home is Chaoyang, Guangdong (now Chaoyang District, Shantou City), was born in Hong Kong in 1944. He is the permanent honorary president of the Dapeng Chamber of Commerce in Dapeng New District, Shenzhen. Since he came to Dapeng, Shenzhen to invest in 1987, he has actively participated in charity and public welfare undertakings. He has donated more than 10 million yuan to Dapeng No. 2 Primary School and other schools and units. The Ng Wing Kee Health Center in Sanjiao Township, Lianping County, Heyuan City, which he donated funds to build, is the first overseas Chinese donation project there. In 2011, he was awarded the title of "Honorary Citizen of Shenzhen Municipality." In 2013, he was awarded "Good Man of Pengcheng" by Dapeng New District.

Gaozi II, Mencius says, "Respect the elderly and love the young, and never forget the homeless."

In Ng Wing Kee's view, this is a virtue that has been passed down by the Chinese nation since ancient times, and it is also an important principle that he has always believed in when dealing with people.

On a hot afternoon at the end of June 2024, in a house near Jiaochangwei in Dapeng New District, Shenzhen, we met Ng, who had just rushed over from Hong Kong, as scheduled.

"Be a good person first, before talking about doing things," Ng, who is already in his 80s, said with emotion. "Everyone has a different way of doing things. Some people spend their whole life making money, while others focus on serving the masses. But no matter when, we must learn to respect others, and the most important thing is to 'respect the elderly and love the young.'"

The interview took place in 2024.

Originally from Chaoyang, he turned a small workshop into a big business

Ng's ancestral home is Chaoyang, Guangdong. His parents were "Chaozhou people" who came to Hong Kong from the mainland to make a living. (In the old days, people from the Chaoshan area called themselves Chaozhou people when they went out to make a living.) Ng's father started out as a coolie at a dock near Tsim Sha Tsui, where Chaozhou people gathered at the time. Later, he saved some capital and ran a rice shop by himself. Later, he cooperated with others to open a small-scale plastic processing factory.

In 1944, Ng was born in Kowloon, Hong Kong. Chaoshan people have always advocated the concept of "more children, more blessings." After Ng, the family added seven children. The small merchant family was not too wealthy but had eight children to feed, and Ng's father was under extraordinary pressure. In Ng's memory, his father was a very responsible man for his family and kept his promises.

As the eldest son, Ng has been very sensible since he was a child. After school, he often shuttled between the busy rice shop and plastic processing factory to help his father run the businesses. These experiences accompanied him as he entered the business world and became a solid foundation for his career path. Soon after, he inherited his father's plastic processing factory. In 1972, the 28-year-old Ng registered another limited company to engage in export trade.

The 1960s and 1970s were the heyday of Hong Kong's industrial development, when plastic industry became one of Hong Kong's pillar industries. According to the essay "The Development of Hong Kong's Manufacturing Industry after the War" by scholar Shen Yuanzhang, the export volume of Hong Kong-made toys with plastic as the main raw material exceeded that of Japan in 1972, ranking first in the world, and by 1979, the total export value of Hong Kong-made toys reached HK$5.156 billion, accounting for 85% of the total export value of local plastic products (See *Asia-Pacific Economy*, No. 6, 1985).

Over the years, many media outlets have liked to report that from the 1960s to the 1970s, the export volume of plastic flowers in Hong Kong ranked first in the world, and its market share was as high as 80%. Li Ka-shing, a Chaozhou businessman dubbed "Plastic Flower King," later became the richest man in Hong Kong.

Ng, who hit the right spot, also made his first pot of gold in the plastic industry. After more than 10 years of hard work, he developed a small workshop with only two or three employees into an enterprise with a certain scale and influence.

Building a factory in Dapeng and becoming a happy person in Pengcheng

In the late 1970s, Ng's career was booming in Hong Kong, but he strongly felt the bottleneck of his factory's development. "The main problem was the difficulty in finding employees for factories in Hong Kong," Ng said.

Meanwhile, China's mainland began to implement reform and opening-up, and this "spring breeze" also blew into Ng's heart. He resolutely decided to develop northward, set his sights on the mainland, where was full of opportunities and challenges. He began to look for a suitable new factory site in the Pearl River Delta. "I visited Dongguan, Liuyue (which now belongs to Longgang District, Shenzhen) and other places, but these places were too popular, with many Hong Kong businessmen flocking there. So they were not very suitable for me," Ng said.

By chance, Ng came to Pengcheng Village (now Pengcheng Community), Dapeng Township, which belonged to Bao'an County at that time, and fell in love with the place at first sight. "Although the area around Pengcheng Village looked rather desolate at the time, the air here was very good and the people were simple, so I immediately made up my mind to invest here," Ng also revealed his calculations back then. "I didn't think there would be any problem in building a factory here, with workers living in dormitories and dining in the canteen here. It was a little bit hard for me to come to Dapeng from Hong Kong once a week. But more importantly, there would be a lot of room for development in this place, and it was easier for my business to reach a certain scale here."

The Chaoshan people are good at doing business, which is a skill thought to be in their genes. They have a unique vision and a genius for seizing business opportunities. Although born and raised in Hong Kong, Ng still has the Chaoshan people's natural business genes flowing in his blood. Sure enough, his factory in Pengcheng flourished as he expected. But that's another story.

"At that time, there happened to be a factory building that had been completed in Pengcheng Village, so I immediately moved my factory here from Hong Kong." In 1987, Huakai Plastic Products (Shenzhen) Co., Ltd., Ng's investment project in the mainland, was established in Pengcheng Village. Local residents often called it "Pengcheng Huakai Factory." It mainly produced plastics, hardware, plaster, and fabrics, among others. At the beginning, it was all processing business. "We got orders through my company in Hong Kong, processed and produced in the factory in Pengcheng Village, and then transported the products back to Hong Kong for export to the United States and Canada," Ng said.

Back then, the conditions around Dapeng Peninsula in Shenzhen were still relatively tough, and Ng suffered a lot from transportation alone. Although he came to the factory in Dapeng from Hong Kong only once a week, he often needed to spend another four or five hours to get to the factory in Pengcheng Village every time after he passed through Luohu Port or Wenjindu Port.

"In the past, to come to Dapeng from (the downtown of) Shenzhen, you had to go around mountain roads and take small paths. At that time, it was not as convenient to come to Dapeng as it is now with the highways there. Almost all the roads I took were muddy roads," Ng said. "I set off from my home in Hong Kong in the morning and usually arrived at the factory in the evening. If it rained, I would never know how long it would take to get to the factory in Pengcheng." Looking back on these experiences of the past, it seems like a lifetime ago. Now the traffic between Shenzhen and Hong Kong is well developed, and it is very convenient to travel back and forth. There is no longer the hard journey as people saw in the past.

Today, although at 80 years old, Ng still travels back and forth between Hong Kong and Dapeng every week. "I have loved the sea since I was a child. Pengcheng locates by the sea. The environment here in is good, the air is fresh, and it is very quiet. I am very happy living here," Ng said with a smile.

Ng was the third president of the Dapeng Chamber of Commerce in Dapeng New District, and is semi-retired now. He usually stays with his wife in Hong Kong and returns to Dapeng on weekends. "I usually stay overnight and return to Hong Kong the next day. I come here to deal with some affairs left over from the old factory, and to meet and chat with some old friends and former colleagues," Ng said.

The "old friends" mentioned by Ng include Li Jianqi, the current president of the Dapeng Chamber of Commerce. "The old president will contact me every time he comes back to Dapeng. He is the permanent honorary president of our chamber of commerce and still cares about the development of the chamber and Dapeng's economy." In Li's view, in the early days of reform and opening up, Dapeng's investment promotion was "particularly difficult" as a result of inconvenient transportation, but Ng chose to invest in Dapeng and settle in Pengcheng Community, making important contributions to the local economic development.

Persisting in treating the elderly for more than 30 years

For hundreds of years, Pengcheng Community, which is near Dapeng Fortress, has a fine tradition of treating the elderly to dinner. The famous "General's Banquet for

Thousands" is a grand event held there every five years. Whenever the General's Banquet is held in Pengcheng, there are hundreds of round tables set at the Tianhou Palace, the Elderly Center and the Northwest Building in the community, forming a spectacular scene of thousands of guests attending the General's Banquet.

Yu Shaolin, who was secretary of the Pengcheng Community General Branch Committee of the Communist Party of China, said that the General's Banquet originated from General Lai Enjue, who guarded Dapeng Fortress during the Daoguang period of the Qing Dynasty. In the past, in the occasion of a festival or a victorious return from the war, the General would hold a family banquet to entertain soldiers and neighbors from all directions. The General's Banquet serves local home-cooked dishes: longevity vegetables (pickled vegetables), General's golden nuggets (roasted pork), tofu balls, meatballs, fried noodles, braised pork, fried chicken wings, fried pork, white-cut chicken, pig skin, and hodgepodge, among others.

Today, in Pengcheng Community, the only event as famous as the General's Banquet is probably the annual "Boss Ng's Dinner for the Elderly." The "Boss Ng" in the mouths of local residents is Ng Wing Kee. Since the early 1990s, Ng has persisted in inviting the elders in Pengcheng to gather at the end of the lunar year or during the Spring Festival every year for a sumptuous reunion feast. "It is a very rare opportunity for hundreds of elders to sit together for dinner at the same time," Ng said. "I want to provide a platform for the elders to eat and chat together and have fun."

Talking about the reason for inviting the elders in Pengcheng to dinner, Ng said it was "purely coincidental." "The Pengcheng Community Elderly Association once invited me to a local 'banquet for the elderly,' and I thought this was a good trend. After that, I asked the Elderly Association to give me a chance to treat local elders to a meal every year."

In recent years, Liu Yufen, president of the Pengcheng Community Elderly Association, has assisted in holding the "Boss Ng's Dinner for the Elderly." Except for the COVID-19 pandemic when group gatherings could not be organized, the "Boss Ng's Dinner for the Elderly" has never been interrupted in the past 30 years, she said. There were up to 50 to 60 tables for nearly 600 people dining at the same time.

"Even during the COVID-19 pandemic, when he couldn't treat local elders to dinner, the annual after-dinner routine—Boss Ng distributing red envelopes to the elders was held as usual," Liu said.

"Inviting the elderly to dinner is really a very meaningful thing," Ng hopes that someone can pass on this good deed. "In the past few years, I have been looking for suitable successors, hoping to keep this tradition going. To be honest, there's not too much financial pressure in doing this is. It just depends on whether you have the intention. After all, you don't invite the elderly to dinner every day, but only once a year."

"Every time when I invite the elderly to dinner, I see them singing, dancing, laughing and talking. After eating, they get a gift to take home. At that moment, I feel very happy," Ng said.

Generous donation to education and charity

About one kilometer away from Ng's home in Shenzhen is Dapeng No. 2 Primary School. A paragraph in the school's official introduction says: "In September 2001, with the funds donated by Mr. So Fong Nam, Ms. Wong Chun Sau, Mr. Ng Wing Kee and Mr. Wong Kai Tai, as well as the strong support from governments at all levels and the Pengcheng Community Residents' Committee, a new school was built at the current site."

According to Ng, the planning and drawings of the school were determined by the then township government, and several Hong Kong businessmen were only responsible for funding the construction. In order to build a high-quality school, those Hong Kong businessmen, who opened factories in Pengcheng, including Ng, So Fong Nam (originally from Pengcheng Village, husband of Wong Chun Sau) and Wong Kai Tai, deliberately found a familiar construction company to build the school. "We knew the builder, so we could monitor the quality of the school's construction. We hoped that every penny of the donation could be used to the maximum effect. We felt at ease when a school with guaranteed quality was handed over to the government."

In addition to donating money to build the school, Ng also donated 1.5 million yuan to set up scholarships and teaching awards in Pengcheng Village for teachers with excellent teaching results and students with excellent academic performance or admitted to technical secondary schools, colleges and universities. According to media reports, this was "the first village-level scholarship fund in Longgang District." (Dapeng was under the jurisdiction of Longgang District before the establishment of Dapeng New District.)

Ng's good deeds do not stop there. According to the *Shenzhen Overseas Chinese News* on January 12, 2009, Ng's caring story of respecting and loving the elderly and being enthusiastic about public welfare had always been praised far and wide in Dapeng. For example, he donated 700,000 yuan to help Pengcheng Community build a nursing home and purchase fitness equipment to make the activities of the elderly more colorful; he donated 50,000 Hong Kong dollars to help rebuild the Dapeng Overseas Chinese Hospital; he donated 1.5 million yuan to build the Pengcheng Cultural Square; and he donated 600,000 yuan to improve the supporting facilities of Pengcheng Park.

In an internal special publication for the 15th anniversary of the Dapeng Chamber of Commerce, we found that in 1999, Ng donated 250,000 yuan to build the Dapeng Chamber of Commerce Building; and in June 2012, with a total donation of 6.29 million yuan, he ranked second in the "Dapeng Chamber of Commerce Charity and Public Welfare Honor Roll." He is therefore generally accepted to have "played an extremely important role in promoting Dapeng's charity and public welfare."

Moreover, Ng's love is not limited to Shenzhen. In 2004, with the help of the then Foreign Affairs (Overseas Chinese Affairs) Office of Shenzhen Municipality, he donated 600,000 yuan to build a health center in Sanjiao Township, Lianping County, Heyuan City, improving local medical and health conditions and providing convenience for local people to seek medical treatment. In July 2008, the health center was identified as the first overseas Chinese donation project in that area by the Overseas Chinese Affairs Office of the Guangdong Provincial People's Government.

Over the past decades, Ng's personal donations to public welfare and charity have exceeded 10 million yuan. In 2011, in view of his outstanding contributions to the construction of Shenzhen, Ng, together with 47 others, was awarded the title of "Honorary Citizen of Shenzhen Municipality." In 2013, he was awarded "Good Man of Pengcheng" by Dapeng New District.

Regarding Ng's good deeds, Luo Yucan, a literary and artistic figure in Dapeng New District, once wrote a poem for him and gave him a handwritten couplet, which read, "The roc flies for thousands of miles in bright spring, while sincerity cultivates people with great virtue in thousands of households." Talking about this, Ng repeatedly emphasized that he had just "done some small things within my ability," which was "taking from society and giving back to society."

With a history of 630 years, Dapeng Fortress is known as the "root of Pengcheng," and it is why Shenzhen is also known as "Pengcheng."(Pengcheng literally means Peng Fortress or Peng City.) It is the "source of Shenzhen" and also the root of Ng in Shenzhen. His home in Shenzhen is in Pengcheng Community, Dapeng New District, just more than one kilometer away from Dapeng Fortress.

As Zhuangzi said, "(The roc) flaps its wings on the surface of the water to stir up waves of 3,000 miles, and it flies up to a height of 90,000 miles around the whirlwind."

Today, the new Pengcheng Community is developing better and better. Riding on the spring breeze of reform and opening-up, it has transformed from an old coastal fortress and a small fishing village into a "national key cultural relic protection unit," a "famous historical and cultural village of China," the first among the "Eight Scenes of Shenzhen," and one of the "Top 10 Cultural Name Cards of Shenzhen," among others. Ng is gratified to see these huge changes.

"I have worked and lived in Pengcheng for more than 30 years. My heart has long been tied to Dapeng, and I have regarded this place as my second hometown and second home," Ng said emotionally.

(Special thanks to Mr. Li Tiankui, vice chairman of the Dapeng Returned Overseas Chinese Federation of Dapeng New District, Shenzhen, who has contributed to this article. Photos courtesy of Ng Wing Kee, except for those with credit. References: *Shenzhen Special Zone Daily*, *Shenzhen Overseas Chinese News*, and Shenzhen Government Online.)

马伟武：

从包装印刷到创意文化，
这位潮商一直很"潮"

马伟武　Ma Wai Mo

马伟武，1946 年出生，祖籍广东省汕头市潮阳区。深圳市荣誉市民、力嘉国际集团董事长、中国包装联合会参事会副主席、深圳市侨商国际联合会名誉会长。曾任深圳市政协委员、深圳市侨商国际联合会常务副会长等职务。

马伟武 1970 年在香港成立力嘉纸品公司，1986 年到深圳横岗投资，1994 年成立力嘉国际集团。2011 年创建力嘉创意文化产业园，该园区连续 8 年成为深圳文博会分会场。2013 年，在东莞市桥头镇创建力嘉环保包装印刷产业园，致力于促进包装印刷业发展和实现企业转型升级。

多年来，他热心公益事业，累计捐赠额超 1 亿元。先后荣获深圳市光彩事业贡献奖、"南方·华人慈善盛典"慈善人物奖、全国优秀包装工作者、毕昇印刷杰出成就奖、世界杰出华人奖、中国纸包装行业终身荣誉成就奖等称号及奖项。

采访时间：2023 年。

清晨 5 点，起床。这是马伟武几十年来养成的习惯。然后，他会在园区做运动，在泳池里游上大约半个小时。马伟武身材魁梧，今年 77 岁了，但是依然神采奕奕，外貌看上去也比实际年龄要小很多，或许这就是他多年来一直坚持体育锻炼的结果。

吃完早餐，马伟武就去工厂巡视。有时候看到一些不规范的地方，他会立即提出整改的要求。工厂位于他在园区居所的同一栋楼楼下。"我们以厂为家。"马伟武告诉《晶报》记者，"我认为这是人生的一种享受，当然，在厂区巡查也是我做运动的一种方式。我就是抱着这样一种心态，希望力嘉可以一直延续下去"。

马伟武接受《晶报》采访。（来源：《晶报》）
Ma Wai Mo was interviewed by the *Daily Sunshine*.
(Photo: *Daily Sunshine*)

香港打拼：9000 港元起家

1946 年，马伟武出生在广东汕头市潮阳区和平镇里美村的一个普通家庭。1959 年，马伟武和母亲、弟弟马馀雄以及一个堂妹一起申请单程证去了香港，投靠在那边的父亲。

马伟武的父亲最初在香港是做小生意的潮州商人，只是后来生意失败了，不得不到外面去打零工。"主要是在码头做'咕喱'，给人搬东西。"马伟武这样介绍他父亲的工作。在广东话中，"咕喱"是英语 coolie 的音译词，就是"苦力"的意思。

"我爸爸当时主要是在香港广东道九龙仓码头（如今的海港城位置），这个很多潮籍人聚集的地方做'咕喱'。有活干人家就叫他一起去干，没有的话他就只能坐在那里'食白果'（广东话，指白忙活）。"马伟武说，"那时候我们在香港有上顿没下顿，生活其实还是很辛苦的。"

迫于无奈，初到香港不久的马伟武只能出来打工，尽管当时他只有 13 岁。一开始，他只能去熟人的大排档洗碗。马伟武解释，因为进工厂打工是需要身份证的，起码要 16 岁才行，而他当时年纪太小了，只能干洗碗这种不需要身份证的活。

一年之后，在申报身份证的时候，马伟武就把年龄虚报大了 2 岁。后来他又在一个也到了香港的小学同学的介绍下，进了一家纸品厂工作。时至今日，马伟武仍然清楚记得，他进纸品厂的时间是 1960 年的下半年，月薪 30 港元。

"进去之后，因为有熟人照顾，很快就熟悉了这一行，慢慢地也算是入行了。不像你们年轻人现在喜欢做哪一行才入哪一行，我入行算是被迫的。我也就是从那个时候开始做一些纸箱包装之类的工作。"马伟武说。

由于有熟人领入行，再加上年轻学东西快，人又努力肯干，很快马伟武就成了纸品厂的技术工。有了技术之后，马伟武就一边做工一边跳槽，工作之余，还到夜校进修，到20岁的时候已经当上了厂长。

"但是，你知道我们潮州人的啦，不会甘心打一辈子工的，个个都想做老板。"马伟武告诉《晶报》记者，1970年，他用大约9000港元积蓄在香港观塘康宁道租了一个阁楼，创办了力嘉纸品公司，正式走上创业之路。

"我自己买了几台原始的手工设备，主要是一些订盒机、缝线机、压纹机。"马伟武表示，最初他既是公司的老板，也是唯一的员工，"白天出去接单、送货，晚上回来生产加工……"实在是忙不过来就叫家人来帮工，或者找以前的老工友下班后来帮忙。

关于"力嘉"两个字，马伟武有一个解释，就是"力不到不为财，还要精神可嘉"。这句话最终也内化成了力嘉公司的企业精神。通过奋斗，工厂一步步地发展壮大。1973年，他在观塘瑞宁街50号地下（底楼）连阁楼租下200多平方米的地方，扩大了生产经营规模。

1970年，力嘉纸品公司在香港观塘康宁道创立。
Luk Ka Paper was founded on Hong Ning Road, Kwun Tong, Hong Kong in 1970.

1978 年，力嘉在香港观塘鸿图道自购厂房。

In 1978, Luk Ka purchased a factory building on Hung To Road, Kwun Tong, Hong Kong.

20 世纪 70 年代中，香港电子工业高速发展，计算机、收音机和电子表非常流行，也带动了彩色印刷业的发展。马伟武敏锐地抓住了这个机遇，拿到了不少订单，企业得到升级拓展，业务开始涉及印刷。

1978 年，马伟武的弟弟马馀雄正式加盟力嘉，并且他们在香港观塘鸿图道购置了新厂房，扩大发展。1980 年，马伟武的长兄马余略又从广州来港加入力嘉，马氏"兄弟班"情同手足，同甘共苦，不断把企业做强做大。

投资深圳：爬上工厂天台找手机信号

到 20 世纪 80 年代中期，力嘉在香港鸿图道已发展成为拥有 200 多名工人和 2 万多平方呎（约 1900 平方米）厂房的大型企业。但与此同时，力嘉在香港也面临着土地成本高、招工难和劳动力成本不断攀升等发展瓶颈。

让人振奋的是，时值改革开放，乘此东风，马伟武兄弟跨过罗湖桥，到深圳实地考察。"之前我曾经在眼镜行业做过，认识了一些朋友，他们当时在横岗投资建厂。我们聊天的时候，有人就说：国家搞改革开放，内地现在也开始发展了，而且内地有很多年轻人，工人也便宜、容易请。"

因此，马伟武兄弟最后选择了具有优越地理位置，但当时还是一片荒芜的横岗（那时候还叫横岗村），作为力嘉在内地投资的第一站。

1986年，马伟武在横岗村。
Ma Wai Mo in Henggang Village in 1986.

1986年，力嘉在深圳横岗的观音山脚，租用了一处600平方米的厂房，他从香港带来10多位技术人员，通过以师带徒的方式，带领数十名内地年轻工人，开始投入生产。

中国的改革开放最初是"摸着石头过河"，在深圳的力嘉同样也是"摸着石头过河"。刚到横岗，马伟武看到人们衣着多是灰色调的、简单朴素，房屋低矮陈旧，街道狭窄，车辆不多，晚间灯火昏暗、一片寂静。

"那时候我们横岗的厂房外都是菜地，那里真是穷乡僻壤。过去横岗是很缺电的，还有水、物流、通信等，都不像现在这么方便。"马伟武给《晶报》记者讲了一件趣事："当时我们在深圳的工厂要跟香港公司联络，要拿个'大哥大'电话，爬上高高的天台，到处去找手机信号，才联系得上。"

"所有这些，都是我们需要克服的困难。没有水，我们就自己打井。没有电，我们就自己买发电机。但最初从香港过去，交通确实很不方便，我们从罗湖到横岗的工厂就差不多要两个小时。"

马伟武说，当时最怕的就是雨天，每逢下雨，深惠路（如今的龙岗大道）就会出现内涝，货车在路上一堵就是大半天，回不了香港，损失比较大。

后来，深圳各地建设热火朝天，经济高速增长，内地纸品市场需求旺盛。在这种经济形势下，力嘉接到的订单如雪片飞来，年产值屡创新高。

马氏兄弟乘胜追击，1989年投资兴建横岗力嘉纸品大厦（即现在的力嘉创意文化产业园一期），并斥资购买了横岗观音山下十万多平方米的荒地；1990年引进美国制造的瓦楞纸板生产线；1992年自资购地建立力嘉工业城；1993年引进德国生产的高宝、海德堡等先进印刷设备，扩展了印刷业务；1994年，力嘉工业城一期落成，同年力嘉国际集团成立，彼时集团已拥有4000多名员工与13家附属和联营企业，业务遍及瓦楞纸板纸箱、彩盒和纸制精品三大领域，实现了从中型企业到大型企业的成功跨越；1996年力嘉进入高速发展期，到20世纪90年代末，力嘉客户遍及欧美、日韩和东南亚，下游厂商涵盖众多国际知名品牌，每年营业额约6亿港元。

到21世纪初，力嘉公司显露出强劲的发展态势，自2004年至今，每年都跻身"中国印刷百强企业"行列。在这种利好形势下，力嘉尝试开创多元化的发展格局，将市场的"触角"陆续延伸到全国各地。

2002年，力嘉携手佳宁娜、民生、香港建业和京晖，五大集团共同投资26亿元（总投资超60亿元）兴建深圳平湖华南城，创建了国内首个华南城印刷纸品包装交易中心。

"我和佳宁娜集团董事长马介璋当时都是深圳市政协委员，在他跟我提到在深圳建设一座原料城的想法后，我兴趣很大。他们几个手里有皮草、服装、电子这些资源，但没有印刷包装，我正好能补上这块，于是就成了华南城早期的股东之一。"马伟武说。

2009年9月，华南城控股有限公司在香港上市。（右一为马伟武）
Ma Wai Mo (first from right) attends a press conference after China South City Holdings Limited was listed in Hong Kong in September 2009.

深耕粤港澳大湾区：创意纸凳被嘉宾抢着带走

2008 年，受国际金融危机的冲击，力嘉同广东其他外向型企业一样，面临着订单减少、利润率下降、人民币升值、原材料上涨等严峻考验。

也是在这一年，深圳成为国内第一个被联合国教科文组织授予"设计之都"称号的城市。当时联合国教科文组织评审团给深圳的评语是："深圳在设计产业方面拥有巩固的地位。它鲜活的平面设计和工业设计部门，快速发展的数字内容和在线互动设计，以及采用先进技术和环保方案的包装设计，均享有特别的声誉。"

马伟武认为，力嘉的品牌价值要得到提升，必须通过文化产业。

Ma Wai Mo believes that only through the cultural industry should Luk Ka improve its brand value.

马伟武敏锐地察觉到，这是一个契机，"三来一补"型企业的时代已经过去，与文化产业相结合将是包装印刷业未来发展的出路，力嘉的品牌价值要得到提升，必须通过文化产业。

2011 年 5 月，马伟武带领团队改造旧厂房，将印刷包装与文化创意相结合，在深圳横岗创办了力嘉创意文化产业园。该园区连续 8 届成为深圳文博会分会场，先后荣获"国家级 AAA 旅游景区""国家科普教育基地""国家高新技术企业"等多项荣誉。

2015 年 12 月 4 日，第十一届"创意十二月"暨 2015"创客 +"狂欢节开幕式在深圳欢乐海岸举行。开幕式结束后，参加活动的众多嘉宾纷纷把自己在现场坐的凳子或座椅带回家。而这些使用瓦楞纸板做成的凳子和座椅，都是力嘉创意文化产业园的杰作，是根据人体力学设计的，不但结实耐用，而且可回收再利用，体现出环保与创新的理念。在当日的开幕式上，上百位嘉宾全都坐在力嘉做的"纸"上，让无人机、机器人这类高科技产品都略显失色。

在致力于印刷包装与文化创意互融的同时，近年来，力嘉国际集团继续深耕大湾区，在香港、深圳、东莞等地积极布局。

2013年，力嘉集团在东莞市桥头镇建立了力嘉环保包装印刷产业园，又在该产业园内先后打造了一个粤港澳大湾区3D科创实验基地，首个包装印刷行业产业学院——东职力嘉包装产业学院，以及一个户外社会实践基地——力嘉生态农场。2023年，更是在该产业园二期园区建设"力嘉数字城"，推动产业数字化转型，打造数字经济时代产业创新集群。

"当然，我们在深圳那边的力嘉创意文化产业园也不会放弃，目前深圳的二期项目也正在加紧建设中。"马伟武补充道。

"力嘉决定在东莞桥头镇发展，是因为这边是国家指定的环保包装名镇。我们这边的产业园功能分区非常清晰，厂归厂，园区归园区，有企业馆、博物馆、展示厅、多功能厅，还有创客空间、3D打印区、数字印刷区、产业孵化基地等。"说到此，马伟武非常自豪地指出，"我们的园区现在可是'广东省工业旅游精品线路'上的一站啊，而且还在2024年4月获得了2023年度'广东省省级文化产业示范园区'称号。"

力嘉创意产品"纸上咖啡馆"。
The "paper cafe," a creative product of Luk Ka.

2023 年 6 月 28 日，《晶报》记者在东莞桥头镇的力嘉环保包装印刷产业园内采访马伟武时，见到了面积更大、更结实耐用、完全由瓦楞纸制作而成的力嘉创意产品"纸上咖啡馆"——人坐上去休息，跟在普通咖啡馆的体验并无二致。

热心公益：捐 8000 万元建设家乡中学

跟很多潮商一样，马伟武继承了爱国爱乡、热心公益的传统，在事业上取得成功后不忘回报家乡、回报社会。

力嘉中学位于汕头市潮阳区和平镇里美村，是潮阳南侨中学的高中校区。这是马伟武和弟弟马馀雄合力捐建的一所中学。2010 年，马伟武和马馀雄兄弟筹集 4000 万元，捐建了学校的教学楼、科学楼、行政楼、教师宿舍和体育馆等一期工程。接着，马伟武又分别在 2013 年和 2014 年捐款续建了两栋学生宿舍楼，在 2020 年续建了学校综合楼和 400 米标准运动场，进而令他们在这所学校的总捐款额达到了 8000 万元。

马伟武告诉《晶报》记者，自己在年纪很小的时候就已经出来闯世界，"最遗憾的事，就是读书读得少了"。

"大概是 2010 年 6 月的时候，当时潮阳区和平镇的领导带我们去南侨中学参观。"在学校教学楼的天台上，在一间用铁皮加建起来的临时教室里，马伟武看到 108 名学生正挤在里面上课。"教室里只有几把牛角扇在那里不停地吹着，虽然风是吹过来了，但依然是热辣辣的，我站在那里一会儿都受不了，更何况是他们学生一直坐在那里上课？我真的被震撼到了。"

"老实说，我们'做厂的'挣钱不算多，都是一边做，一边买设备、扩建厂房的，平时口袋里没有多少余钱，我们很多钱都是靠融资向银行借的。"马伟武表示，"但是，那一刻我就和弟弟马馀雄商量，无论如何，我们都要想办法帮忙把学校建好。"

为了确保学校建设工程顺利进行，他们把一处位于黄金地段的工厂卖了，同时用自家的产业作抵押向银行贷了款，合在一起才凑足了 4000 万元捐款。

在力嘉中学规划建设的过程中，马伟武、马馀雄兄弟每个周末都要轮流从香港或深圳回到潮阳，在学校的建设工地上亲自检查施工进展，严格把好工程质量关。

"捐建学校这件事，一定不能失败，因为我们兄弟都是在那里出生的，所以我们都要亲力亲为。"马伟武解释。

学校建成以后，马伟武兄弟还时刻关心学校发展，出资 130 多万元设立了汕头市潮阳区南侨中学力嘉集团教学金与奖学金，用于奖励那些教学和学业成绩优异的师生。

马伟武（右）与胞弟马馀雄。
Ma Wai Mo (right) and his younger brother Ma Yu Hung.

除了捐建力嘉中学，马伟武也曾为汶川、玉树地震捐款赈灾，为广东省的扶贫事业和深圳市的公益事业捐款捐物。迄今为止，他已累计向社会捐款超过 1 亿元。

鉴于其在包装印刷领域及社会慈善方面作出的贡献，多年来他先后荣获深圳市光彩事业贡献奖、"南方·华人慈善盛典"慈善人物奖、深圳市荣誉市民、汕头市荣誉市民、全国优秀包装工作者、毕昇印刷杰出成就奖、世界杰出华人奖、中国纸包装行业终身荣誉成就奖等多个荣誉称号及奖项。

"力嘉是我创立的，到今年已经 53 年了。我最大的感想就是，如果你选择了某个目标，就一定要坚持下去，并做好它，做到有成绩出来为止，对家庭、对社会、对国家有贡献。就像我们兄弟捐建力嘉中学那样，尽你所能，做能做的事，是非常有意义的。"马伟武感慨道。

（除署名外，本文图片均由受访者马伟武提供。参考资料：广东侨商网、龙岗政协、精彩横岗、《汕头日报》。）

Ma Wai Mo

From packaging and printing to creative culture, this Chaoshan businessman has always been trendy

Ma Wai Mo, born in 1946, originally from Chaoyang District, Shantou City, Guangdong Province, is an honorary citizen of Shenzhen Municipality, chairman of Luk Ka International Limited, vice chairman of the Council of Counselors of the China Packaging Federation, and honorary president of the Shenzhen Overseas Chinese International Association. He once served as a member of the Shenzhen Municipal Committee of the Chinese People's Political Consultative Conference and executive vice president of the Shenzhen Overseas Chinese International Association.

He founded "Luk Ka Paper" in Hong Kong in 1970, went to Henggang, Shenzhen to invest in 1986, and founded Luk Ka International Limited in 1994. In 2011, he founded the Luk Ka Creative & Cultural Centre, which has been a parallel venue of the China (Shenzhen) International Cultural Industries Fair for eight consecutive years. In 2013, he founded the Luk Ka Green Packaging and Printing Industrial Park in Qiaotou Township, Dongguan City, committed to promoting the development of the packaging and printing industry and realizing the transformation and upgrading of his company.

Over the years, he has been enthusiastic about public welfare and has donated more than 100 million yuan in total. He has won honors such as the Shenzhen Guangcai Program Contribution Award, the Charity Figure Award of "The Grand Charity Ceremony," the National Outstanding Packaging Worker, the Bi Sheng Printing Outstanding Achievement Award, the World Outstanding Chinese Award, and the China Paper Packaging Industry Lifetime Honorary Achievement Award.

Getting up at 5 o'clock in the morning is a habit that Ma Wai Mo has developed over decades. Then, he starts exercising in the industrial park and swims in the swimming pool

---

The interview took place in 2023.

for about half an hour. As a 77-year-old large man, Ma is still energetic and looks much younger than his actual age. Perhaps this is the result of his persistence in physical exercise for many years.

After breakfast, Ma goes to the factory to carry out inspections. When seeing irregularities, he will immediately request rectification. The factory is located downstairs in the same building where he lives in the industrial park. "We regard the factory as our home," Ma told the *Daily Sunshine*. "I think this is a kind of enjoyment in life. Naturally, inspecting the factory is also a way for me to exercise. With this mentality, I hope that Luk Ka can last forever."

Working hard in Hong Kong: Starting a business with 9,000 Hong Kong dollars

In 1946, Ma was born into an ordinary family in Limei Village, Heping Township, Chaoyang District, Shantou City, Guangdong. In 1959, Ma, his mother, his younger brother—Ma Yu Hung, or Samuel Ma—and a cousin got a one-way permit to Hong Kong to seek refuge with his father there.

Ma Wai Mo's father used to be a Chaozhou businessman doing small business in Hong Kong, but later his business failed and he had to go out to do odd jobs. "He mainly worked as a 'gu lei' at the dock, moving things for people," Ma described his father's job. In Cantonese, "gu lei" is the transliteration of "coolie," an offensive English word for a worker in Eastern countries with no special skills or training.

"My father worked as a 'gu lei' mainly at the Kowloon Wharves (in the location of today's Harbor City) on Canton Road in Hong Kong, where many Chaozhou people gathered. If there was work to do, others would ask him to do it together. If not, he would have to sit there 'eating ginkgo' (Cantonese, meaning ending up in vain)," Ma said. "Back then in Hong Kong, we didn't know where the next meal was coming from. The life was actually very hard."

Ma, who had just arrived in Hong Kong, had no choice but to work out, even though he was only 13 years old. At first, he went to an acquaintance's food stall to wash dishes. Ma explained that to work in a factory required an ID card, which was issued for people at least 16 years old. He was so young that he could only do work such as washing dishes that didn't require an ID card.

A year later, when applying for his ID card, Ma presented himself as two years older than he actually was. Later, he worked in a paper product factory after a primary school classmate, who also came to Hong Kong, recommended him. To this day, Ma still clearly remembers that he entered the paper product factory in the second half of 1960, with a monthly salary of 30 Hong Kong dollars.

"After I entered the factory, I quickly became familiar with this industry because I had the acquaintance to take care of me, and I gradually entered the profession. Unlike you young people who choose to enter an industry you prefer, I was forced to enter the industry. At that time, I started doing something like carton packaging," Ma said.

Because he was introduced to the industry by an acquaintance, coupled with the fact that he was young and hard-working, and learned things quickly, Ma soon became a technician in the paper product factory. After acquiring the skills, Ma changed jobs while working. After work, he went to night school for further studies. By the time he was 20, he had become a factory director.

"But, as you know, we Chaozhou people are not willing to work for others all the lifetime. We all want to be bosses," Ma told the *Daily Sunshine* that in 1970, he spent about 9,000 Hong Kong dollars out of savings to rent "a mezzanine" on Hong Ning Road in Kwun Tong, Hong Kong to found Luk Ka Paper and formally embarked on the road of entrepreneurship.

"I bought several pieces of primitive manual equipment, mainly box-binding machines, sewing machines, and embossing machines." Ma said that at first he was both the boss and the only employee in the company. "I went out to take orders and deliver products during the day, and came back for production and processing in the evening... " When he was too busy, he would ask his family to help, or ask his former coworkers to help after work.

Regarding the name of "Luk Ka," Ma has an explanation, "If you don't work hard enough, you can't make money. You should also have admirable intentions." This has eventually become the corporate spirit. Through hard work, the factory has developed and grown step by step. In 1973, he rented more than 200 square meters of space at No. 50 Shui Ning Street, Kwun Tong, including the ground floor and the mezzanine, where he expanded the scale of production and operations.

In the mid-1970s, Hong Kong's electronics industry developed rapidly, and computers, radios, and electronic watches were very popular, which also boosted the development of the color printing industry. Ma keenly seized this opportunity to get a lot of orders, and the company was upgraded and expanded, beginning to involve printing.

Ma Yu Hung, Ma Wai Mo's younger brother, officially joined Luk Ka in 1978, and they bought a new factory building on Hung To Road, Kwun Tong, Hong Kong to expand their business. In 1980, Ma Wai Mo's eldest brother, Ma Yu Leuk, came to Hong Kong from Guangzhou to join Luk Ka. The brothers shared joys and sorrows together and continued to make the company stronger and bigger.

Investing in Shenzhen: Climbing onto the factory rooftop to find mobile phone signal

By the mid-1980s, Luk Ka had developed into a large-scale enterprise with more than 200 workers and more than 20,000 square feet (approximately 1,900 square meters) of factory space on Hung To Road, Hong Kong. But at the same time, Luk Ka was also facing development bottlenecks in Hong Kong, such as high land costs, difficulty in recruiting workers and rising labor costs.

It was exciting that the mainland began its reform and opening-up. Taking advantage of that, the Ma brothers crossed the Luohu Bridge and went to Shenzhen for field investigation. "I used to work in the spectacles industry and knew some friends who invested to build factories in Henggang. When we were chatting, some of them said, 'The country is engaged in reform and opening-up, and the mainland is now starting to develop. And there are many young people in the mainland, so workers are cheap and easy to hire.'"

Therefore, the Ma brothers finally chose Henggang (still called Henggang Village at that time), which had a superior geographical location but was still deserted, as the first stop for Luk Ka's investment in the mainland.

In 1986, Luk Ka rented a 600-square-meter factory building at the foot of Guanyin Mountain in Henggang, Shenzhen. More than 10 technicians from Hong Kong led dozens of young mainland workers in a master-apprentice manner to start production.

In the beginning, China's reform and opening-up was like "crossing the river by feeling the stones," and so did Luk Ka. When he first arrived in Henggang, Ma Wai Mo saw that most people were wearing gray, simple and plain clothing. The houses were low and old, the streets were narrow with few vehicles, and it was dim and quiet at night.

"At that time, there were vegetable fields outside our factory in Henggang, which was really a remote place. In the past, Henggang was very short of electricity, while water, logistics, communications and so on were not as convenient as they are now." Ma told the *Daily Sunshine* an interesting story, "At that time, our factory in Shenzhen needed to contact the Hong Kong company. We had to bring a 'Big Brother' mobile phone, climb onto the high rooftop, and look for mobile phone signals here and there before we could contact them in Hong Kong."

"We had to overcome all these difficulties. With no water, we dug our own wells. With no electricity, we bought our own generators. But at first, when we went there from Hong Kong, the transportation was really inconvenient. It took us almost two hours to travel from Luohu to the factory in Henggang."

Ma said that he feared rainy days most. Whenever it rained, there would be waterlogging in Shenhui Road (now Longgang Avenue). The trucks would be stuck for more than half a day and were unable to return to Hong Kong in time, causing big losses.

Later, the construction of various parts of Shenzhen was in full swing, the economy grew rapidly, and the demand for paper products in the mainland market was strong. In this economic situation, orders came in to Luk Ka like snowflakes, and its annual output value repeatedly hit new highs.

The Ma brothers continued the triumphant pursuit and invested in the construction of the Henggang Luk Ka Paper Products Building (now the first phase of the Luk Ka Creative & Cultural Centre) in 1989, and purchased more than 100,000 square meters of wasteland at the foot of Guanyin Mountain in Henggang. In 1990, they introduced corrugated cardboard production lines made in the United States. In 1992, they purchased land with their own capital to establish the Luk Ka Industrial City. In 1993, advanced German printing equipment, such as the products of KBA and Heidelberg, was introduced to expand the printing business. In 1994, the first phase of the Luk Ka Industrial City was completed, and Luk Ka International Limited was established, which had more than 4,000 employees and 13 subsidiaries and associated companies, with its business covering the three major fields of corrugated cardboard boxes, color boxes and fine paper products, achieving a successful leap from a medium-sized enterprise to a large enterprise. In 1996, Luk Ka entered a period of rapid development. By the end of the 1990s, Luk Ka had customers in countries and regions such as the United States, Europe, Japan, South Korea, and Southeast Asia. Its customers covered many world-renowned brands, with an annual turnover of approximately 600 million Hong Kong dollars.

At the beginning of the 21st century, Luk Ka showed strong momentum. Since 2004, it has been ranked among the "Top 100 Printing Enterprises in China" every year. In this favorable situation, Luk Ka tried diversified development, extending its "tentacles" to many parts of the country.

In 2002, Luk Ka joined hands with Carrianna, Man Sang, Kinox and Kings Faith. The five groups jointly invested 2.6 billion yuan (the total investment exceeded 6 billion yuan) to build the China South City in Pinghu, Shenzhen, establishing the country's first China

South City exchange center for printed paper products and packaging.

"Ma Kai Cheung, chairman of Carrianna Group, and I were both members of the Shenzhen Municipal Committee of the Chinese People's Political Consultative Conference at the time. After he told me the idea of building a raw material city in Shenzhen, I was very interested. They had resources such as fur, clothing, and electronics, but no resources in printing and packaging, and I happened to be able to make up for this. So I became one of the early shareholders of China South City," Ma Wai Mo said.

Deep cultivation in the Guangdong-Hong Kong-Macao Greater Bay Area: Creative paper stools were well popular in guests

In 2008, affected by the global financial crisis, Luk Ka, like other export-oriented enterprises in Guangdong, endured severe tests such as reduced orders, declining profit margins, renminbi appreciation, and rising raw material prices.

In the same year, Shenzhen was designated by UNESCO as China's first City of Design. The UNESCO jury commented, "Shenzhen has established a strong footing in the design industry. Shenzhen enjoys a high reputation for its vibrant graphic design and industrial design sectors, fast-developing digital content and online interactive design, and package design featuring advanced technology and environmental-friendly portfolio."

Ma was keenly aware of this opportunity: The era had passed for enterprises processing imported raw materials, and "three supplies and one compensation" as a whole. ("Three supplies" means processing imported raw materials, manufacturing products according to imported samples, and assembling imported parts, while "one compensation" refers to "compensation trade," which means repaying loans for imported equipment and technologies with products.) Combining with the cultural industry would be the way out for the future development of the packaging and printing industry. Only through the cultural industry should Luk Ka improve its brand value.

In May 2011, Ma led his team to establish the Luk Ka Creative & Cultural Centre in Henggang, Shenzhen by renovating the old factory building, combing printing and packaging with cultural creativity. It has been a parallel venue of the China (Shenzhen) International Cultural Industries Fair for eight consecutive years, and has won many honors such as the national "AAA Tourist Attraction," "National Science Education Base" and "National High-tech Enterprise."

On December 4, 2015, the opening ceremony of the 11th "Shenzhen Creative December" and 2015 "Maker+" Carnival was held at the OCT Harbour in Shenzhen. After the opening ceremony, many guests at the event took home the stools or chairs they had just sat on. These stools and chairs made of corrugated cardboard were masterpieces of the Luk Ka Creative & Cultural Centre. Designed in accordance with human body mechanics, they were not only strong and durable, but also recyclable, reflecting the concepts of environmental protection and innovation. At the opening ceremony that day, more than 100 guests all sat on the "paper" made by Luk Ka, which slightly "overshadowed" high-tech products such as drones and robots.

While committed to the combination of printing and packaging with cultural creativity, in recent years, Luk Ka International Limited has continued to deeply explore the Guangdong-Hong Kong-Macao Greater Bay Area and actively deployed in Hong Kong, Shenzhen, Dongguan and other cities in the Greater Bay Area.

In 2013, the Luk Ka Green Packaging and Printing Industrial Park was established in Qiaotou Township, Dongguan City. In addition, the industrial park was home to a 3D science and technology innovation experimental base for the Guangdong-Hong Kong-Macao Greater Bay Area, the first industrial college for the packaging and printing industry—the Dongguan Polytechnic Luk Ka Packaging Institute, and an outdoor social practice base—the Luk Ka Ecological Farm. In 2023, the Digital City is being built in the second phase of Luk Ka's Dongguan industrial park to promote the digital transformation of the industry and create an industrial innovation cluster in the era of digital economy.

"Certainly, we will not give up the Luk Ka Creative & Cultural Centre in Shenzhen, and the second phase of the project in Shenzhen is under construction," Ma added.

"Luk Ka decided to develop in Qiaotou Town, Dongguan, because it is a famous town for environmentally friendly packaging designated by the country. The functional division of our industrial park is very clear. The factories are the factories, and the industrial park is the industrial park. There are enterprise halls, a museum, exhibition halls, multi-functional halls, as well as maker space, 3D printing zone, digital printing zone, industrial incubation bases, and so on," Ma said proudly. "Our industrial park is now a 'fine route of industrial tourism in Guangdong Province,' and, in April, it won the title of 'Guangdong Provincial Cultural Industry Demonstration Park' for 2023."

On June 28, 2023, in the Luk Ka Green Packaging and Printing Industrial Park in Qiaotou Town, Dongguan, the *Daily Sunshine* saw a larger, stronger and more durable creative product of Luk Ka: a "paper cafe" made entirely of corrugated paper, where people sit and have a rest. The experience is no different from that in an ordinary cafe.

Enthusiastic about public welfare: Donating 80 million yuan to build a middle school in his hometown

Like many Chaoshan businessmen, Ma has inherited the tradition of loving his country and hometown and being enthusiastic for public welfare. After achieving success in his career, he has never forgotten to give back to his hometown and society.

He and his younger brother, Ma Yu Hung, donated to build Luk Ka Middle School in Limei Village, Heping Town, Chaoyang District, Shantou City. It is the senior high school campus of Chaoyang Nanqiao Middle School. In 2010, the two brothers raised 40 million yuan to build the first phase of the school, including the teaching building, science building, administrative building, teachers' dormitory and gymnasium. Then, Ma Wai Mo donated to build two student dormitory buildings in 2013 and 2014 respectively, and a school complex and a 400-meter standard sports field in 2020, bringing their total donation to this school to 80 million yuan.

Ma told the *Daily Sunshine* that he had entered the workforce at a very young age. "The most regrettable thing is that I'm not well-educated."

"In June 2010 or so, the leaders of Heping Town, Chaoyang District took us to visit Nanqiao Middle School." On the rooftop of the school's teaching building, Ma saw that 108 students huddled in a temporary classroom built with iron sheets. "There were only several industrial fans blowing constantly in the classroom. Although the wind was blowing, it was still very hot. I couldn't bear to stand there for a while, let alone the students sitting there all the time in class. I was really blown away by them."

"Honestly, as 'factory runners,' we don't make much money. We buy equipment and expand factories while doing business. We usually don't have much money in our pockets. We borrow a lot from banks through financing," Ma said. "But at that moment, I discussed with my brother Ma Yu Hung and decided that we must find ways to help build the school, no matter how."

To ensure the smooth progress of the school's construction project, they sold a factory in a prime location and used their property as collateral to borrow money from a bank, thus collecting a donation of 40 million yuan.

During the planning and construction process of Luk Ka Middle School, the Ma brothers took turns returning to Chaoyang from Hong Kong or Shenzhen every weekend to check the progress in person at the school's construction site and strictly control the project quality.

"The donation to build the school must not fail, because we brothers were born there.

So we should do it ourselves," Ma explained.

Since the school was built, the Ma brothers have been caring about the development of the school. They spent more than 1.3 million yuan to establish the Luk Ka Group Teaching Award and Scholarship at Nanqiao Middle School, Chaoyang District, Shantou City to reward teachers and students for their outstanding teaching or academic achievements.

In addition to donating to build Luk Ka Middle School, Ma Wai Mo donated money for the Wenchuan and Yushu earthquake relief, and donated money and materials for poverty alleviation in Guangdong Province and public welfare undertakings in Shenzhen. So far, he has donated more than 100 million yuan to society.

In view of his contribution to the field of packaging and printing and social charity, he has won many honorary titles over the years, such as the Shenzhen Guangcai Program Contribution Award, the Charity Figure Award of "The Grand Charity Ceremony," the Honorary Citizen of Shenzhen Municipality, the Honorary Citizen of Shantou City, the National Outstanding Packaging Worker, the Bi Sheng Printing Outstanding Achievement Award, the World Outstanding Chinese Award, and the China Paper Packaging Industry Lifetime Honorary Achievement Award.

"Luk Ka was founded by me, and it has been 53 years since then. My biggest reflection is that if you choose a certain goal, you must stick to it and do it well until you achieve results, which will contribute to your family, society and the country. Just as we brothers donated to build Luk Ka Middle School, it is very meaningful to try your best and do what you can do," Ma said with emotion.

(Photos courtesy of Ma Wai Mo, except for the one with credit. References: www. gocea.net, the CPPCC Longgang District Committee, Wonderful Henggang, and *Shantou Daily*.)

李大西

穿越历史风云，
助力深圳打造"创新之城"

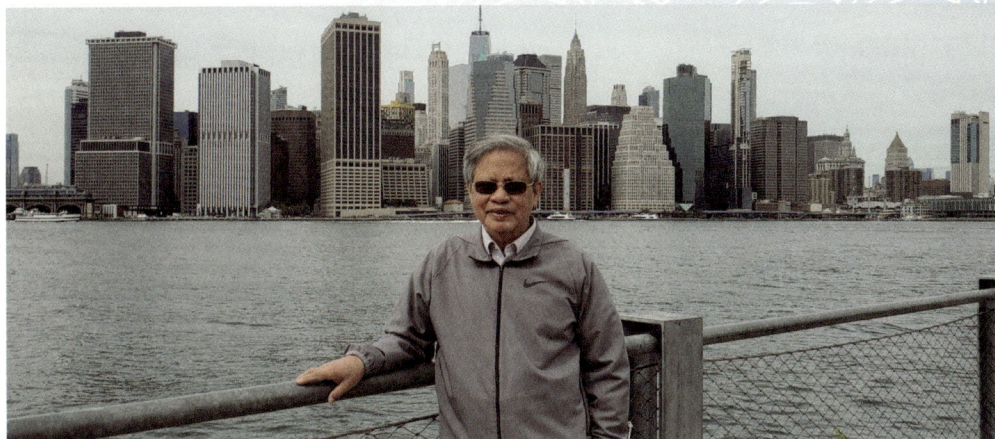

李大西　Daxi Li

　　李大西，1948 年出生于广东普宁。1975 年毕业于广东师范学院（华南师范大学前身），1980 年中山大学硕士毕业后赴美留学。国际华人科技工商协会主席，多家上市公司董事，中国全国政协十届三次会议特邀海外列席人员，中国侨联海外委员，深圳海外潮人经济促进会名誉主席，深圳市普宁商会荣誉会长。

　　李大西博士曾从事高能物理和超弦理论研究，1991 年后转向金融领域，曾任职于美国著名投资银行所罗门兄弟公司、雷曼兄弟公司，参与多项重要 IPO（首次公开募股）和风险投资项目。1997 年发起组织国际华人科技工商协会，为科技与工商搭桥，为中国和世界搭桥；1999 年，李大西与该协会的核心成员成立创业投资公司，主要为留学生和科技工作者回国创业提供帮助。该公司参与创立的深圳市留学生创业园是国内首家以中外合作形式组建的股份制留学生创业园，并首创"政府引导，留学生管理"的运作模式，已孵化朗科、迅雷、光峰科技等 1000 多家企业，为深圳成长为"创新之城"作出了积极贡献。

采访时间：2022 年。

在中美科技界、投资圈，李大西是大名鼎鼎的人物。他回到祖国"干大事业"产生的影响，其实早已出圈。很多人用过的U盘和下载的软件，很多电影院采用的激光放映技术，乃至深圳这座"创新之城"的崛起，都有这位幕后英雄的一份功劳。

李大西的人生充满传奇色彩。他多次见证历史，并努力实践自己的理想，最终让梦想的光亮照进了现实。

在那个出国不易的年代，李大西和其他900多位留学生一样，遇到了伯乐——诺贝尔物理学奖得主李政道。李政道推动设立的"中美联合招考物理研究生项目"（China-U.S. Physics Examination and Application，CUSPEA，俗称"李政道奖学金"），让他们得以赴美深造，进而深刻地改变了世界科技人才格局。

李大西亲历了"9·11"事件。与死神擦肩而过的他决定：回国，投身风险投资领域，推动中国高新科技的发展。

就这样，他变身为"伯乐""筑巢者""引路人"，搭建中外交流的平台和渠道，吸引海外人才回国投资、创业，引入国外创新技术和项目。他参与创办的深圳市留学生创业园就是"海归"创业热潮最早的沃土之一，孵化了朗科、迅雷、光峰科技等明星企业。

钻研物理，幸得大师引路

李大西1948年出生于广东普宁，在那里度过了童年。他的父亲和母亲都在年轻时参加了革命。父亲被国民党政府追捕，逃到越南，定期寄钱回来养家。中华人民共和国成立后，父亲变卖财产，坐飞机回到故乡，担任普宁师范学校校长多年。母亲则在小学老师的岗位上耕耘了一辈子。

1964年，李大西到广州读高中。上山下乡时，他又回到普宁插队落户。在农村劳动4年后，他进入广东师范学院物理系学习，1975年毕业后留校工作3年，然后考上了中山大学高能物理专业研究生，

李大西一家三口和李大西父母早年的合影。

Daxi Li's family of three and his parents.

1980 年获得硕士学位。

他在中学时学的外语是俄语，想象中的出国目的地是苏联。改革开放、科教兴国，给他的人生带来了重大转折。

教育部开始派人出国留学，中山大学派李大西参加出国留学英语考试，他突击学了一二十个句型，居然通过了。

考试通过者要自己联系学校。1979 年，李大西给美国几所大学写了信，但都石沉大海。很多人都有类似的遭遇。

也是在 1979 年，诺贝尔物理学奖得主、美籍华裔科学家、哥伦比亚大学教授李政道应邀在北京友谊宾馆进行为期 7 周的讲学，开设两门课程，轰动一时，并对中国物理学的发展起到了积极作用。李大西就是听讲者之一。这次授课，把他带进了粒子物理研究的大门。

1979 年，李政道在北京授课。
（来源：李政道图书馆馆藏）
Tsung-Dao Lee gives a lecture in Beijing in 1979.
(Photo: Tsung-Dao Lee Library archive)

抓住历史机遇赴美，薪火相传埋伏笔

李政道此行，不仅传播了知识，还选拔了人才。他在讲学中发现中国有不少很有才华的年轻学子，想帮助他们赴美留学，成为国际一流人才。当时，中国学生赴美非常困难，没有 TOEFL（托福）和 GRE（留学研究生入学考试）等考试可以参加，而美国方面也对中国学生的水平不了解。

于是，李政道发起了选拔中国优秀学子赴美留学的"中美联合招考物理研究生项目"。李大西把 CUSPEA 的性质概括为"自费公派"："美国的大学出奖学金让我们过去，但是，我们在身份上还算是国家派出去的。"

1979 年，李政道为这个项目组织了两次试点考试。那年 12 月，李大西赴京通过了笔试。1980 年 1 月，李政道来到广州从化，亲自面试李大西，用日常英语跟他交谈，最后宣布，他被哥伦比亚大学录取了。

后来，美国另外两所名校也录取了李大西，他最终选择了纽约市立大学。李大西选择纽约市立大学，有一个重要原因是那里的导师研究的范围是大统一理论，而李大西对大统一理论比较有兴趣，而且总结出大统一理论也是爱因斯坦没有完成

的梦想。那所大学的基本粒子组实力强大，其中的罗伯特·E. 马夏克（Robert E. Marshak）教授是美国物理学会的会长。另外，该校也把吸引李大西去他们那里学习视为重要的事情，学校承诺"他去了以后可以马上参与科研项目"。

就这样，李大西去了纽约市立大学。他们那批赴美学生表现很优秀，也为后续更多中国学生去美国打开了大门。

李政道对李大西最终没选择哥伦比亚大学并不介意，后来还当了李大西的博士论文指导小组成员。

恩师长期尽心尽力为祖国发展作贡献的精神，也感召了李大西，为他后来投身中外交流事业埋下了伏笔。

CUSPEA 先后培养了 915 位学者，他们在科学、金融、互联网、芯片等领域取得了令人瞩目的成就，深刻地改变了世界科技人才格局。比如，中国互联网的先锋人物张朝阳 1986 年从清华大学物理系毕业后，获得了 CUSPEA 奖学金，赴美国麻省理工学院（MIT）深造，1993 年获得博士学位，后来拿到 MIT 两位教授的风险投资，创立了搜狐公司。

随着出国留学渠道的日益畅通，这个项目完成了历史使命，在 1989 年终止。受 CUSPEA 的成功影响，美国高校的其他一些学科也设立过类似的选拔考试。

据粗略估计，CUSPEA 的相关事务曾经用去了李政道每年三分之一的时间，与中国方面沟通所产生的邮费、电话费也是他自付的，但他无怨无悔。

李大西（左）和李政道讨论问题。（来源：广东文史网）
Daxi Li (left) and Tsung-Dao Lee discuss questions. (Photo: www.gdwsw.gov.cn)

科学壮志未酬，转战华尔街

初到美国时，李大西很受震撼，"汽车在高速公路上飞驰，给人的感觉很神奇"，"超市里的商品琳琅满目，想要什么就可以往购物车里搬，无需凭票供应"。

这些中国留学生也引起了美国媒体的关注。李大西说："我们 1980 年到纽约的时候，虽然此前已经来过几批，但人都不多。所以，对我们的到来，（媒体）还是觉得非常新鲜。"

他在超市里抱着一个大西瓜的画面被记者拍了下来，登在了《新闻日报》上。他身旁站着的同学王波明，回国后推动创立了上海证券交易所。

纽约市立大学兑现了承诺，李大西到那里的第一年就参与了一个研究项目，成果发表在世界上最重要的物理刊物《物理评论》上。参与合作研究的包括访问学者冼鼎昌，他后来成了中科院院士。

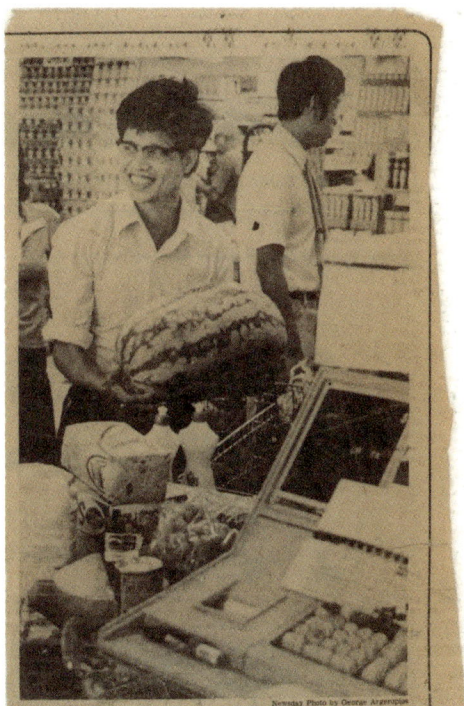

《新闻日报》刊登的李大西抱西瓜照片。
A clipping from the *Newsday* carries a photo of Daxi Li holding a watermelon.

李大西（左）在宿舍里与冼鼎昌（中）讨论问题。
Daxi Li (left) discusses questions with Xian Dingchang (middle) in the dormitory.

在美国的头十年，李大西潜心研究高能物理，包括基本粒子、超弦理论，想着拿个诺贝尔奖给中国人争光。1985 年获得博士学位后，他再接再厉，进站博士后研究。但他和一些知名数学家交流之后，明白了自己的处境：超弦理论要有重大突破，至少还需要 50 年的时间。

李大西开始思考怎样扬长避短。巧的是，他在一次学术报告中提出的宇宙模型吸引了华尔街金融人士的注意。他们觉得，李大西改行做金融模型绝对没问题，而且可以很快看到成效。

物理博士闯荡华尔街的传奇，就此拉开了序幕。从 1991 年到 2002 年，李大西先后任职于美国著名投资银行所罗门兄弟公司和雷曼兄弟公司，参与了多项重要的 IPO 和风险投资项目，一路做到了雷曼兄弟的副总裁。

亲历 "9·11"，再次转身

但是，李大西又急流勇退，结束投行生涯，出来创业。促成这个重大转折决定的，是他在 "9·11" 事件中的死里逃生。

当时，李大西的办公室在纽约世贸中心 1 号楼（北塔）的 40 层。2001 年 9 月 11 日，他上班迟到了十几分钟。从地铁站出来，就看到大楼已经有一个大洞了，那是一架客机撞击造成的。

李大西对事情的严重性估计不足，还想去办公室。但现场有很多 FBI（美国联邦调查局）的人把道路封锁了，他走来走去都进不了大楼。很快，另一架客机撞向 2 号楼（南塔）。李大西确信：这是恐怖袭击！

那个时候，手机信号已经不通了。李大西就到世贸中心旁边一座大楼的地下室找到固定电话打给妻子报平安，突然听到外面传来 "轰隆" 一声巨响，他以为是旁边一座老旧的教堂倒了。他冲出地面，跟很多逃命的人一起朝着与大楼倒塌相反的方向跑。跑了两个街口，到了纽约市政厅前面，站定往后一看，发现世贸中心的双子塔只剩下一座了，也就是北塔。没过多久，北塔也倒塌了。

面对废墟，想起不幸罹难的同事们，李大西陷入了深深的思考：这辈子究竟应该干些什么？他最终的决定是："出来做自己想做的事，为祖国、为家乡做更多该做的事情。"

1997 年，李大西发起成立了国际华人科技工商协会，参与创会的有多位著名华人科学家，很多骨干是 CUSPEA 学生，李政道欣然同意担任协会顾问。1999 年，李大西与协会的 80 名核心成员成立了一家海外创业投资公司，协助科技界人士创业，推动中国高新科技的发展。

"我们做的科研只是自己的小事业。真正要干大事业，还是要回到祖国，把科研成果更好地转化为生产力，让更多的人受益。我们要做科技与资本互动的事情。"李大西说。

他还感慨：人在比较安逸的环境里下这样的决心不容易，而"9·11"事件给了他非常大的触动，使他能够痛下决心，专注于中美科技投资领域的交流合作。

这次转身，也让他避开了几年后次贷危机的风暴。2007年至2008年，美国次级抵押贷款引发的金融危机席卷全球，雷曼兄弟公司因为巨额亏损而宣布破产就是标志性事件之一。

那次危机中，李大西也没有袖手旁观。为了给中国的决策者提供参考，2008年，他和诺贝尔经济学奖得主、"欧元之父"罗伯特·蒙代尔（Robert A. Mundell）教授一起给中国领导人写信，建议出台经济刺激措施，发放万亿元级别的人民币消费券。那年11月，中国推出了4万亿元的投资计划。

其实，早在1997年，亚洲金融危机的乌云刚出现，李大西请教蒙代尔教授之后，就给中国领导人写过一封信，建议中国早做准备，支持香港，并且保持人民币汇率不变。1998年，香港特区政府在中央政府支持下，拼尽全力赢得了金融保卫战。中国顶着巨大的压力，坚持人民币不贬值，为缓解亚洲经济紧张形势发挥了重要作用。

如今，李大西的独子在顶级投行摩根大通工作，也有点子承父业的味道。

结缘深圳，孵化众多明星企业

国际华人科技工商协会按照"立足科技与工商，面向中国与世界，倡导归国创业"的宗旨，经过25年发展，已经成为比较有影响力的华侨华人科技社团，会员有3000多人。主要成员是在美获得高学历的中国留学生，活跃于科技、教育、金融、商业管理等领域。

"协会的主要工作是，在中美两国之间介绍具有良好发展前景和合作基础的科研项目，让中国了解我们的科研项目取得的研究成果，让我们了解中国正在开展和需要开展的科研项目，在中美之间架设合作的桥梁。"李大西说。

他们到中国各地考察、洽谈、参展，落地的项目不计其数。李大西的足迹当然也少不了故乡广东。

1998年12月底，第一届中国（广州）留学人员科技交流会召开，组委会的主任是时任广州市市长林树森，副主任是李大西，他带了100多位留学生来参加。会后，深圳市方派了几辆大巴，把他们接到深圳参观，时任深圳市市长李子彬在五洲宾馆接待了他们。李大西答应了李子彬的邀请：带留学生参加第一届中国国际高新技术成果交易会（简称"高交会"）。

1999年，李大西带着100多位留学生到深圳参加第一届高交会，从此揭开了留学人员通过高交会了解深圳、寻找机会的序幕。汪建就在李大西带来的这支队伍里。

那年 9 月，为了承接人类基因组计划的中国部分，汪建在北京主导创建了华大基因。到了 2007 年，他率团队南下深圳，创办深圳华大基因研究院（后来更名为"深圳华大生命科学研究院"）。现在，华大集团已成为全球领先的生命科学前沿机构。

1999 年，第一届高交会期间，李大西（左二）主持留学生展团新闻发布会，汪建（右一）等人发言。

Daxi Li (second from left) presides over the overseas students press conference during the first China High-Tech Fair in 1999. Wang Jian (first from right) and others made speeches at the press conference.

首届高交会期间，当时的深圳市委主要领导接见了留学生展团。李大西向领导提出，中国好几个城市有留学生创业园了，深圳也应该搞一个。"留学生回来创业，有他们特别的困难。如果有一个留学生创业园，特别是由我们协会和深圳市政府来合办，有民间的力量，又有政府的力量，这样就更好。"李大西说。

一番交流之后，李大西的建议获得了深圳支持。留学生创业园的筹建工作就紧锣密鼓地开始了。到了 2000 年，第二届高交会的时候，深圳市留学生创业园就正式成立了。这是国内首家以中外合作形式组建的股份制留学生创业园，美国国际华人科技工商协会海外创业投资有限公司是创业园的三家股东之一。李大西回忆说，这个创业园是从一个很小的地方办起来的，深圳市政府大力支持，给了留学生创业园一块更大更好的地方。

这个创业园首创了"政府引导，留学生管理"的运作模式。李大西担任副董事长，负责挑选留学生当总经理。李大西说，很多地方的留学生创业园由政府主导，而深圳走市场化路线，主要由海外留学生组织负责操作，注重引进企业的质量。他们在海外建立了专业化引才网络，成立了专家委员会，选拔企业的标准比较严，加上深圳良好的创新生态和创业园提供的"一揽子"服务，所以成功率高。

李大西说的"一揽子"服务，包括了基础设施、创业辅导、融资、人才引进、交流培训、市场推广、管理咨询、项目推介、联谊沟通等。如今，深圳市留学生创业园已经成为深圳市政府吸引海外留学人员回国创业、扶持留学生企业发展的重要平台，还被人社部批准为与深圳市政府共建的"中国深圳留学人员创业园"。20多年来，这里孵化了1000多家企业，包括朗科、迅雷、光峰科技、奥比中光、华傲数据等明星企业。

朗科在1999年研发出全球第一款USB闪存盘（U盘），后来在中国和美国都获得了闪存盘的基础发明专利。在创业初期入驻深圳市留学生创业园时，创始人邓国顺带来了一个打火机大小的U盘，说抵得上10张软盘，大家觉得不可思议。如今，U盘已成为众多电脑用户的标配。

迅雷2003年入驻创业园，短短几年时间，他们开发的下载软件就成了市场上的王者。

光峰科技发明的激光显示技术已成为国际主流，全国影院8万多块银幕中将近三分之一装备了这一技术。

…………

深圳成长为"创新之城"的过程中，高交会这个"窗口"、留学生创业园这个"家"以及幕后的"家长"李大西都功不可没。

不畏艰难，初心不改

除了多次带队到深圳参加高交会，李大西还在美国多次协办了深圳的招商引资活动。他推动了一些重要项目落户深圳，比如广大·康奈尔中美科技转移中心、微纳米芯片研究院、精准医疗研究院等。

李大西透露，广大·康奈尔中美科技转移中心是常春藤名校康奈尔大学在中国参股的唯一公司，而他自己也参了股。他也坦承，2018年发生中美经贸摩擦以后，这个中心运行不容易。

和耶鲁大学合作的芯片研究院落户在留学生创业园二期，牵头参与这个项目的耶鲁大学教授、美国工程院院士马佐平是世界半导体界的权威专家。

李大西不讳言，2020年暴发的新冠疫情给跨国交流造成了困难。"因为没有回深圳，所以很多事情要推动也就不太容易。"但他依然和各方面保持着联系，也希望芯片研究院等项目能取得新进展。

李大西也积极参与、支持深圳一些民间组织的工作，比如深圳海外潮人经济促进会、深圳市普宁商会等，通常的方式是在他们的研讨会上发表演讲，促进各种交流与合作。

任凭国际风云变幻，李大西为中国、为家乡做事情的初心未改。

（除署名外，本文图片均由受访者李大西提供。参考资料来源：中新社、第一财经、广东文史网、《南方日报》、《广州日报》、《华南师大校友》、《现代物理知识》。）

Daxi Li

Witnessing historical moments, helping Shenzhen build "innovative city"

Daxi Li, born in Puning, Guangdong in 1948, graduated from the Guangdong Normal University in 1975, and went to study in the United States in 1980 after graduated with a master's degree from Sun Yat-sen University. He is chairman of the Chinese Association for Science and Business, and director of several listed companies. He was one of the specially invited overseas representatives to the Third Session of the 10th National Committee of the Chinese People's Political Consultative Conference. He is overseas member of the All-China Federation of Returned Overseas Chinese, honorary chairman of the Shenzhen Chaoren Overseas Economic Promotion Association, and honorary chairman of the Shenzhen Puning Chamber of Commerce.

Dr. Li was engaged in the research of high-energy physics and superstring theory. After 1991, he turned to the financial sector. He worked for the famous U.S. investment banks Salomon Brothers and Lehman Brothers, and participated in many important IPO (initial public offering) and venture capital projects. In 1997, he initiated the Chinese Association for Science and Business, building a bridge between technology and business, as well as between China and the world. In 1999, he and other core members of the association established a venture capital company, mainly to assist overseas students and scientific and technological workers to return to China to start businesses. The company participated in the founding of the Shenzhen Overseas Chinese High-Tech Venture Park, China's first joint-stock overseas students venture park in the form of Sino-foreign cooperation, which initiated the modus operandi of "guided by the government, operated by the returned overseas students". It has incubated more than 1,000 enterprises including Netac, Xunlei, and Appotronics, making positive contributions to Shenzhen's growth into an "innovative city."

Daxi Li is a well-known figure in Chinese and U.S. science, technology, and

---

The interview took place in 2022.

investment circles. The impact of his return to the motherland to "do a big business" has extended out of these circles. This behind-the-scenes hero can claim credit for the USB flash drives and download software used by many people, the laser projection technology used in many movie theaters, and even the rise of Shenzhen as an "innovative city."

Li's life is full of legends. He has witnessed some turning points in history, worked hard to implement his ambitious plans, and finally achieved some remarkable accomplishments.

In an era when it was not easy to go abroad, Li, like more than 900 other Chinese students, met his talent scout, Tsung-Dao Lee, the Nobel Prize laureate in physics. Lee pushed for the establishment of the "China-U.S. Physics Examination and Application" (CUSPEA for short, commonly known as the "Tsung-Dao Lee Scholarship"), creating opportunities for talented Chinese students to study physics at universities in the United States. The project profoundly changed the global scientific and technological talent structure.

Li personally experienced the "9/11" attacks. After brushing shoulders with death, he decided to do something meaningful. He began to dedicate himself to introducing venture capital into China and promoting the development of China's high technology.

Over time, he has transformed himself into a talent scout, a nest builder, and a guide, building platforms and channels for Sino-foreign exchanges, attracting overseas talents to return to China to invest and start businesses, and introducing new technologies and projects. The Shenzhen Overseas Chinese High-Tech Venture Park, which he co-founded, is one of the earliest fertile grounds for the "overseas returnees" entrepreneurial boom, incubating star companies such as Netac, Xunlei, and Appotronics.

A physics student fortunately guided by a master

Li was born in Puning, Guangdong in 1948 and spent his childhood there. His father and mother joined the revolution when they were young. His father was hunted by the Kuomintang government and fled to Vietnam, regularly sending money back to support the family. After the founding of the People's Republic of China, Li's father sold his property and flew back to his hometown. He then served as principal of the Puning Normal School for many years. Li's mother worked as an elementary school teacher before retirement.

In 1964, Li went to Guangzhou to attend high school. During the national campaign to send urban youth to the countryside, he returned to settle in Puning. After working in the countryside for four years, he enrolled in the Physics Department of the Guangdong

Normal University. He graduated in 1975 and stayed to work at the university for three years. Then he was admitted to Sun Yat-Sen University as a graduate student in high-energy physics, and obtained a master's degree in 1980.

The foreign language he learned in middle school was Russian, and his dream destination abroad was the Soviet Union. China's reform and opening-up, as well as the national strategy to develop the country through science and education, brought a major turning point in his life.

The Ministry of Education began to send people to study abroad, and Sun Yat-sen University sent Li to take the English test for studying abroad. He learned a dozen or so sentence patterns in a short time and, surprisingly, passed the test.

It was up to those who passed the test to find a university. In 1979, Li wrote letters to several universities in the United States but received no response. Many people had similar experiences.

Also in 1979, Tsung-Dao Lee, the Nobel Prize laureate in physics, a Chinese American scientist, and professor at Columbia University, was invited to teach two courses at the Beijing Friendship Hotel for seven weeks. It was a sensation and played a positive role in the development of Chinese physics. Li was one of the attendees. This lecture brought him to the door of particle physics research.

Seizing historical opportunity to go to U.S., and then passing on the torch

During his trip to China, Lee not only spread knowledge, but also identified talent. He found many talented young Chinese students during his lectures, so he wanted to help them to study in the United States and become world-class talents. At that time, it was very difficult for Chinese students to go to the United States. There were no exams such as TOEFL (the Test of English as a Foreign Language) and the GRE (the Graduate Admissions Examination), and the U.S. side did not know the academic level of Chinese students.

Therefore, Lee initiated the CUSPEA to select outstanding Chinese students to study in the United States. Li states that the CUSPEA students can be seen as "state-sent but self-financed." "Universities in the United States provided scholarships for us to go there, but in terms of our identity, we were still sent by the state."

In 1979, Lee organized two pilot exams for this project. In December of that year, Li went to Beijing and passed the physics examination. In January 1980, Lee came to Conghua, Guangzhou to interview Li in person. He talked with Li in everyday English, and finally announced that he was admitted to Columbia University.

Later, two other famous universities in the United States also admitted Li, and he ultimately chose The City University of New York (CUNY). An important reason why Li chose CUNY was that the research domain of his supervisor there was the grand unified theory, which was also Li's field of interest and Albert Einstein's unfulfilled dream. The elementary particle group of that university was strong, and Professor Robert E. Marshak was the president of the American Physical Society. In addition, to attract Li, CUNY made a generous promise to him that he could immediately participate in research projects once enrolled.

As a result, Li went to CUNY. He and his peers performed very well in the United States, opening the door for more Chinese students to go there.

Lee didn't mind that Li didn't choose Columbia University in the end, and later became a member of Li's doctoral dissertation committee.

Lee's long-term dedication to the development of the motherland also inspired Li, laying the groundwork for him to devote himself to the cause of Sino-foreign exchanges.

CUSPEA helped 915 scholars in total, many of whom have made remarkable achievements in science, finance, Internet, chips and other fields, and have profoundly changed the global scientific and technological talent structure. For example, after graduating from the Physics Department of Tsinghua University in 1986, Zhang Chaoyang (Charles Zhang), a pioneer of the Internet in China, received a CUSPEA scholarship and went to study at the Massachusetts Institute of Technology (MIT). Later, he got the venture capital from two MIT professors and founded Sohu.

When studying abroad became more and more convenient, this project completed its historical mission and was terminated in 1989. Inspired by the success of CUSPEA, other disciplines in U.S. universities set up similar selection examinations.

According to a rough estimate, Dr. Lee spent a third of his time on CUSPEA-related affairs every year before the project ended in 1989, and he paid out of his own pocket the cost of the postage and long-distance telephone communication. His dedication and contribution have been widely admired and appreciated.

Leaving academy for Wall Street

When he first arrived in the United States, Li was very shocked. "The cars were running fast on the expressway. It was amazing." "The supermarket was full of goods. You could move anything you want into the shopping cart without showing tickets."

These Chinese students also attracted the attention of the American media. Li said, "Before we arrived in New York City in 1980, several batches of students had come, but there were very few of them. Therefore, (the media) were still very interested in our arrival."

The moment of him holding a large watermelon in a supermarket was photographed and published in the *Newsday*. Wang Boming, a fellow student standing next to him, promoted the establishment of the Shanghai Stock Exchange after returning to China.

The CUNY kept its promise, and Li participated in a research project in his first year there, with the results published in the world's most important physics journal, the *Physical Review*. Xian Dingchang, a visiting scholar, also participated in the collaborative research, who later became an academician of the Chinese Academy of Sciences.

In his first decade in the United States, Li devoted himself to the study of high-energy physics, including elementary particles and superstring theory, dreaming of winning a Nobel Prize to honor the Chinese. After receiving his Ph.D. in 1985, he continued his efforts and started postdoctoral research. But after communicating with some well-known mathematicians, he understood his situation: It would take at least 50 years to achieve a major breakthrough in superstring theory.

Li began to think about how to maximize his strengths and avoid his weaknesses. It so happened that the universe model he proposed in an academic report attracted the attention of Wall Street. They thought that Li could seamlessly switch to financial modeling and make immediate progress.

This was the prelude to the legend of a doctor of physics breaking into Wall Street. From 1991 to 2002, Li successively worked at famous American investment banks Salomon Brothers and Lehman Brothers, participated in a number of important IPO and venture capital projects, and became a vice president at Lehman Brothers.

Taking a new path after experiencing "9/11"

However, Li resigned from his Wall Street job at the height of his successful career in investment banking, and took a new path in life. What contributed to this major turning point was his narrow escape in the 9/11 attacks.

Back then, his office was on the 40th floor of 1 World Trade Center (the North Tower) in New York. On September 11, 2001, he was a dozen minutes late for work. When he got out of the subway station, he saw a big hole and fire in the building, which was caused by the impact of a passenger plane.

Underestimating the seriousness of the matter, Li still wanted to go to his office. But there were many FBI (Federal Bureau of Investigation) personnel blocking the road, and he found no way to enter the building. Soon, another plane crashed into 2 World Trade Center (the South Tower). Li now realized that this was a terrorist attack!

Mobile phone signal was not available then. Li went to the basement of a building next to the World Trade Center to find a telephone to tell his wife that he was safe. Suddenly he heard a loud "bang" from outside, and he thought that an old church nearby was collapsing. He rushed to the ground and ran in the opposite direction from the building with many fleeing people until he was two blocks away. He stood in front of the New York City Hall and looked back to find that only one of the Twin Towers of the World Trade Center was left, which was the North Tower. Moments later, the North Tower also collapsed.

Facing the ruins and lamenting his colleagues who died tragically, Li began to ponder: What should I do in the rest of my life? Eventually he decided that he would do something he want, and he'd do more things for his motherland and hometown.

Back in 1997, Li initiated and founded the Chinese Association for Science and Business. Many famous Chinese scientists joined this organization, including some CUSPEA students. Tsung-Dao Lee readily agreed to serve as adviser for the association. In 1999, Li and 80 core members of the association founded an overseas venture capital company to assist people in the scientific and technological circles to start businesses and to promote the development of high technology in China.

"The scientific research we did was just our own small business. If we really wanted to do something bigger, we should return to the motherland to help applying scientific research results to economic growth and benefit more people. We would do something about the interaction between technology and capital," Li said.

He said that it was not easy for people to make such a decision in a relatively comfortable environment, but the "9/11" attack prompted him to make the decision and devote himself to the exchanges and cooperation in the field of Sino-U.S. technology investment.

This turnaround also kept him away from the storm of the subprime mortgage crisis a few years later. From 2007 to 2008, the financial crisis triggered by U.S. subprime mortgages swept the world, with the bankruptcy of Lehman Brothers due to huge losses as one of the landmark events.

During that crisis, Li did not stand by. Together with Professor Robert A. Mundell, a

Nobel laureate in economics and the "father of the euro," he wrote to the Chinese leaders in 2008, suggesting economic stimulus measures such as issuing trillion yuan scale of consumer vouchers. In November of that year, China launched an investment plan of 4 trillion yuan.

In 1997, when the dark clouds of the Asian financial crisis just appeared, Li consulted with Professor Mundell and wrote a letter to the Chinese leaders, suggesting that China should prepare early, support Hong Kong, and keep the renminbi exchange rate unchanged. In 1998, with the support of the Central Government, the Government of the Hong Kong Special Administrative Region made every effort to win the financial defense war. Under tremendous pressure, China insisted on not depreciating the renminbi, playing an important role in alleviating the economic tensions in Asia.

Li's only son now works for the top investment bank J. P. Morgan Chase, very much "following in his father's footsteps."

Working with Shenzhen to incubate many star enterprises

With the purpose of "based on science, technology and business, facing China and the world, and advocating returning to start a business in China," after 25 years of development, the Chinese Association for Science and Business has become an influential overseas Chinese science and technology association with more than 3,000 members, most of whom are Chinese graduates who have obtained higher degrees in the United States and are active in such fields as science and technology, education, finance, and business management.

"The main work of the association is to introduce, between China and the United States, scientific research projects with good prospects and cooperation foundations, to inform China of the research results of our scientific research projects, to learn the Chinese scientific research projects that are being carried out and need to be carried out, and to build a bridge of cooperation between China and the United States," Li said.

They have visited various parts of China to inspect, negotiate and participate in exhibitions, and countless projects have been implemented. Of course, Li has left footprints in his hometown Guangdong.

In late December 1998, the first China (Guangzhou) Convention of Overseas Chinese Scholars in Science and Technology was held. The director of the organizing committee was Lin Shusen, the mayor of Guangzhou at that time, while Li was deputy director, who led more than 100 overseas students to participate. After the event, Shenzhen sent several buses to take them to Shenzhen for a visit. Li Zibin, then mayor of Shenzhen, received them at Wuzhou Guesthouse. Daxi Li agreed to the mayor's invitation to bring overseas students to the first China High-Tech Fair (CHTF for short).

In 1999, Daxi Li led more than 100 overseas students to Shenzhen to participate in the first CHTF, which was the beginning for overseas students to understand Shenzhen and look for opportunities through the CHTF. Wang Jian was in the team brought by Li. In September of that year, to undertake the Chinese part of the Human Genome Project, Wang founded BGI in Beijing. In 2007, he led his team to go south to found the Shenzhen BGI Research Institute (currently BGI-Research). Now, BGI Group has become one of the world's leading life science research institutes.

During the first CHTF, the top leaders of the Shenzhen Municipal Committee of the Communist Party of China received the returned overseas student group. Li told them that several cities in China had venture parks for returned overseas students, and suggested that Shenzhen should also set up one. "Returned overseas students have special difficulties when they come back to start a business. It would be better if there is a returned overseas student venture park, especially jointly run by our association and the Shenzhen Municipal Government, supported by both the government and the private sector," Li explained.

After the dialog, Li's suggestion gained support from Shenzhen. The preparatory work for the returned overseas students venture park was actively carried out. The Shenzhen Overseas Chinese High-Tech Venture Park was formally established during the second CHTF in 2000. This was China's first joint-stock returned overseas students venture park established in the form of Sino-foreign cooperation. CASB Ventures LLC is one of the three shareholders of the park. Li recalled that the park started in a very small place, and the Shenzhen Municipal Government strongly supported it and later gave it a bigger and better place.

This venture park pioneered the modus operandi of "guided by the government, operated by the returned overseas students." Li serves as vice chairman and is responsible for selecting the general manager from overseas scholars. The overseas student venture parks in many places are led by the government, while Shenzhen takes a market-oriented route to have the park mainly operated by overseas student organizations, attaching importance on the quality of the enterprises introduced, Li said. They have established a professional network overseas for talent introduction, set up an expert committee, and have relatively strict standards for selecting companies. These, coupled with Shenzhen's good innovation ecology and the "package" services provided by the venture park, have resulted in a high success rate.

The "package" services mentioned by Li includes infrastructure, guidance on venture setup, financing, talent introduction, exchange and training, marketing, management consulting, project promotion, networking and so on. Today, the venture park has become an important platform for the Shenzhen Municipal Government to attract overseas students to return to China to start businesses and support the development of overseas students' enterprises. It has been granted by the Ministry of Human Resources and Social Security as a state-level overseas Chinese students venture park jointly constructed with the Shenzhen Municipal Government. In more than 20 years, it has incubated more than 1,000 enterprises, including star enterprises such as Netac, Xunlei, Appotronics, Orbbec, and Audaque.

Netac developed the world's first USB flash drive (U disk) in 1999, and later obtained the basic invention patents of the flash drive in both China and the United States. When the company entered the Shenzhen Overseas Chinese High-Tech Venture Park in the early days, its founder, Deng Guoshun, brought a USB flash drive just the size of a lighter, saying that it was equivalent to 10 floppy disks. But everyone felt incredible. Nowadays, the U disk has become a must-have for many computer users.

Xunlei settled in the venture park in 2003. In just a few years, the download software they developed became the king in the market.

The laser display technology invented by Appotronics has become a mainstream globally, equipping nearly one-third of the more than 80,000 cinema screens across China.

......

In the process of Shenzhen growing into an "innovative city," the CHTF as a "window," the venture park as a "home", and Li as a "parent" behind the scenes all contributed a lot.

Original aspiration never changed despite difficulties

In addition to leading teams to Shenzhen to attend the CHTF many times, Li has co-organized Shenzhen's investment promotion activities in the United States. He also pushed some important projects to settle in Shenzhen, such as the Guangda Cornell International Technology Center (GCITC), the Micro-Nano Chip Research Institute, and the Precision Medicine Research Institute.

Li revealed that the GCITC is the only Chinese company in which Cornell University, an Ivy League member, has a shareholding. Li has a shareholding in the GCITC too.

He admitted that the operation of the center had not been easy since the Sino-U.S. trade friction in 2018.

The Chip Research Institute, which is joint operated with Yale University, is in the second phase of the Shenzhen Overseas Chinese High-Tech Venture Park. Tso-Ping Ma, who led this project, was a professor at Yale University, a member of the National Academy of Engineering, the United States, and a top expert in the world's semiconductor sector.

Li acknowledged that the outbreak of the COVID-19 pandemic in 2020 made it difficult for cross-border exchanges. "Since I haven't visited Shenzhen for a couple of years, it's not easy to promote a lot of things." But he keeps in touch with relative parties, and hopes that projects such as the Chip Research Institute can make new progress.

Li also actively participates in and supports the work of some non-governmental organizations in Shenzhen, such as the Shenzhen Chaoren Overseas Economic Promotion Association, and the Shenzhen Puning Chamber of Commerce, usually by giving speeches at their seminars and promoting various exchanges and cooperation.

Despite the changing international developments, his original aspiration to do things for China and his hometown has never changed.

(Photos courtesy of Daxi Li, except for those with credit. References: China News Service, Yicai, www.gdwsw.gov.cn, *Nanfang Daily*, *Guangzhou Daily*, *South China Normal University Alumni*, and *Modern Physics*.)

孙启烈

功勋模范侨商，
与深圳改革开放同频共振

孙启烈　Sun Kai-lit

　　孙启烈，1953 年出生于香港。太平绅士，中国侨商联合会常务副会长、广东省侨商会监事长、深圳市侨商国际联合会永远荣誉主席、深圳市侨联荣誉主席、香港工业总会名誉会长，香港建乐士企业有限公司、建业五金塑胶厂有限公司董事长。

　　作为最早参与改革开放和深圳经济特区建设的企业家之一，孙启烈团结广大侨商，为深圳发展作出了积极的贡献。他曾连任两届（第五届、第六届）深圳市侨商国际联合会会长，带领该商会充分发挥政企桥梁作用，在凝聚侨心侨力、积极建言献策、助力公益事业以及深圳国际化城市建设等方面发挥了积极作用。他曾获得香港铜紫荆星章、深圳市荣誉市民、影响深圳经济特区 30 年"十大港商领袖"、深圳市侨商国际联合会"功勋模范侨商"等荣誉。

采访时间：2024 年。

教授、铜紫荆星章、太平绅士，这是孙启烈递给记者名片正面上写着的头衔。除此之外，他还拥有中国侨商联合会常务副会长等众多称谓。

2024年3月中旬，一个阳光灿烂的下午，在位于深圳市罗湖区人民南路的香港工业总会深圳代表处，记者见到了从香港匆匆赶过来的孙启烈。

在记者面前的孙启烈精神矍铄，说起自己的过往经历和家族故事，思维清晰、逻辑缜密而且语速极快，一点都看不出他已经迈入了古稀之年。

"我祖籍是深zhèn的！"初听到孙启烈说出的这句话，记者非常吃惊，还以为自己听错了。

"但是，这个'zhèn'是'田'字边的'甽'。"孙启烈解释道。在《现代汉语词典》中，"甽"是一个异体字，同"圳"，都是指"田边的水沟"。孙启烈口中的这个"深甽"，是地处浙江省宁波市宁海县西北部的一个小镇。

原来，冥冥之中，孙启烈与"深圳（甽）"早有某种特别的渊源。

香港出生，子承父业

历史学家许纪霖认为，上海与宁波有太多的基因同源，无论是商业精神还是文化精神，宁波都是上海近代城市文化最重要的血脉之一。而宁波商帮（上海商帮）与香港商帮，又有着千丝万缕的关系。

20世纪30年代，一个名叫孙建超的少年离开家乡宁波的宁海县，到上海拜师当学徒。出师之后，少年就跟着师傅在工厂里打工。不久，抗日战争全面爆发，他所在的工厂被政府征用，变成了兵工厂，生产军需物资。上海沦陷后，孙建超随工厂迁往浙江丽水，直到抗日战争胜利之后，才重返上海。

1948年，孙建超从上海辗转漂泊到了香港。经一位之前在上海认识的朋友介绍，他进入了一家维修纺织机的机械厂打工。一年后，自己积攒了一点本钱，孙建超开了一间小作坊，主要是承接机械厂的维修工作。

20世纪50年代，塑胶制品在香港热销。看到商机，孙建超在1953年开始制造塑胶家庭用品，生产的第一个产品就是红色的塑料小酒杯，一经面世，就大受市场欢迎，比传统的白色陶瓷小酒杯吃香多了。

同一年，孙建超的儿子孙启烈出生。身为家中长子，孙启烈自幼常到父亲的工厂帮忙。在加拿大修读完物理和机械工程大学课程后，20世纪70年代末，他回到香港，帮助父亲打理家族生意。

孙启烈父亲孙建超如今已经105岁高龄，身体依然健朗。"家父在香港创立建业公司，当时只是一间小型制模工厂，制造塑胶家庭用品。随后家父开始研发及制造不锈钢保温杯和保温瓶，奠定公司的产品基础。到了20世纪60年代，建业通过洋行将产品出口到海外市场。"孙启烈说。

1980 年，孙启烈创立名为"建乐士"的品牌，商标同时在香港和北京注册，并在同年成立了建乐士企业有限公司，主要生产咖啡壶、咖啡炉、保温壶、不锈钢厨具等产品。

他向记者透露了自己创立这个品牌的详细过程。"我将建业公司的英文名上半部分'Kin'与不锈钢的法文'inoxydable'的前几个字母合并成'Kinox'，中文翻译为'建乐士'。英文名读起来铿锵响亮，中文名则营造出了一种高端的企业品牌形象。"

正是源于多年在厨具、其他金属及塑料产品批发分销与制造业方面的管理经验，孙启烈在 2009—2011 年期间成为香港工业总会的主席，还曾经担任香港优质标志局主席超过 6 年时间。

要知道，"Q 唛（Q Mark）"就是由香港优质标志局颁发的一个认证。在香港，"Q 唛"就是优质产品的代名词，就是产品质量过硬的信心保证。

进军内地，投资深圳

风起南海，潮涌珠江。在中国改革开放伟大历史进程中涌现出一批代表区县，创造了很多改革开放的宝贵经验，其中就包括地处珠江三角洲腹地的广东南海县（今佛山市南海区）。

在《迈向城乡融合文明新形态：南海案例》一书中，学者刘守英等人披露，1978 年，南海县委、县政府提出了"以县办为龙头、镇办为主体、村办为支柱、个体联合体为补充"的工业发展思路；还利用港澳同胞众多的优势，积极引进港资、外资，发展"三来一补"企业和"三资"企业。

孙启烈无比自豪地介绍，他们就是第一批参与内地开发建设的港商企业。当时他从媒体和华润公司的朋友那里听说国家正在广东和福建试办"出口特区"的消息，便萌生了去内地创业的念头。

他们落脚内地的第一站就是广东的南海县。1979 年，孙启烈引进新式的注塑、冲压和电镀设备，带着几个员工到当时的南海县以"补偿贸易"的方式，开办了一家小型五金加工厂，产品加工完成之后，再运回香港包装和出口。

孙启烈解释，那时候香港工业发展进入全盛期，建业公司在香港厂房的空间远远不够用，另寻新址的土地成本又太高；而且，香港制造业工人不足，人工成本大增。

他讲了一个细节：20 世纪 70 年代末，香港很多行业尤其是玩具厂、电子厂都在千方百计抢工人，不少厂房为此还特别安装了空调，但建业的五金厂没有空调，以致经常有订单却无法请到足够的人手，非常头痛。

适逢改革开放，他们当机立断，将生产线迁移到内地。有了在南海县的经验之后，他们随后又在东莞、广州和深圳等地开设加工厂。"从 1988 年起，我们将投入重点放在深圳，做来料加工。"孙启烈透露，"20 世纪 80 年代末，当时有港商暂时撤离内地，令不少土地闲置，但我们与深圳当地的村委会商议扩大厂房面积，最后建业公司以每平方米 100 港元的价格在平湖拿到地皮，并获银行贷款，兴建大规模的现代化厂房"。

1992 年，建业公司在深圳成立了独资企业，深圳从此成了孙启烈事业发展的大本营。"不像在其他地方设厂，在深圳我们可以自己拿主意，最重要的是拥有自主权，可以自己请工人，自己发工资。"孙启烈说，那时他们在深圳投资可以获得相当大的优惠和自主度，有关报批手续和环节也大大缩减，就算是现在看，这些措施都是十分超前的。

以侨为桥，聚商力量

"真的很幸运，我们赶上改革开放这个热潮，我们有参与也有付出，同时有更多的收获和回报，我自己对深圳的感情就很深厚。"2010 年 8 月，孙启烈在接受新华社采访时曾说过这样一番话："深圳是我另外一个家，也是我另外一个发源地。"

跟大多香港企业家一样，孙启烈起步在香港，但是借着改革开放的东风，在内地尤其是深圳获得稳定的财富增长，事业蒸蒸日上。因此，他非常感恩深圳，感恩国家。只要有机会，他就联系更多的侨商侨胞朋友，凝聚更多的侨商力量，尽可能地为深圳、为国家做更多的事情。

2000 年 3 月，孙启烈与林立方、马介璋等联袂发起成立了深圳市侨商国际联合会（以下简称"侨商会"）。这是一个由在深圳投资的华侨华人和港澳同胞、归侨侨眷、港澳属企业或个人组成的社会组织。

一开始，孙启烈他们几个创始元老借鉴香港商会的管理模式，经费由会员自筹，办公用房由会员集资购买，实行"民间非官方"运作，团队没有任何编制，侨商会也无官员担任领导，这在当时都是属于了不起的创新。深圳市侨商会率先采用的这种"侨商自主领导管理"的模式，后来被国务院侨办、中国侨联称为"深圳模式"，认为值得全国侨商组织借鉴和复制。

2012 年 6 月 29 日，孙启烈当选第五届深圳市侨商会会长。2015 年 7 月，他继续连任。他提出，要进一步改变侨商会的办会理念、办会形式和活动内容，要有大胸怀，加强合作意识，向优秀联合类、行业类社会团体学习，打"侨牌"、打"国际牌"，把国家发展战略与侨商事业、社会责任结合起来。

孙启烈知道，侨商会本身就是一个难得的天然"商业智库"。于是，他和团队利用侨商会这个平台，经常组织会员召开或参加集思会、研讨会和论坛，了解侨商侨胞们的想法、困难以及在投资经营中遇到的问题。

2012 年 6 月 29 日，孙启烈（右）成为第五届深圳市侨商会会长，图左为前一任会长马介璋。
（来源：深圳市侨商会）

Sun Kai-lit (right) becomes the fifth president of the Shenzhen Overseas Chinese International Association on June 29, 2012. On the left is his predecessor, Ma Kai Cheung. (Photo: Shenzhen Overseas Chinese International Association)

　　对一些共性的问题，孙启烈还利用深圳市政协委员的身份，从参政议政的渠道反馈给政府相关部门去解决。像他提出的一个关于深港便捷通关的提案，就惠及不少在内地投资的侨商侨胞。

　　对侨商侨胞在深圳招商引资中所起的重要作用，孙启烈曾有一个非常形象的说法——"以侨为桥"，就是充分发挥侨商侨胞"民间大使"的作用，在"走出去、请进来"上双向发力。

　　他先后组织会员和会员企业到前海蛇口、南沙、横琴三大自贸片区考察，寻找粤港澳大湾区建设与共建"一带一路"的对接点；还组团赴美国、墨西哥开展侨务考察，参加"东盟华商论坛""世界华商大会"，与澳大利亚、泰国、马来西亚、意大利等国的华人商会和社团进行定向交流；与希腊雅典市政议会、西班牙经济部投资局、德国政府顾问、澳大利亚墨尔本政府顾问建立了合作关系，为深圳企业到当地投资建厂架桥铺路。

　　多年来，孙启烈先后获颁"深圳市荣誉市民"和"影响深圳经济特区 30 年'十大港商领袖'"等称号，也被香港特区政府授予"太平绅士""铜紫荆星章"。

孙启烈等 6 人荣获"功勋模范侨商"称号。（来源：深圳市侨商会）
Sun Kai-lit and five others are awarded the title of "Meritorious Model Overseas Chinese Entrepreneur."
(Photo: Shenzhen Overseas Chinese International Association)

2024 年 4 月 24 日晚，在深圳市侨商会第八届理监事会就职典礼暨优秀侨商颁奖盛典上，孙启烈与马介璋、马伟武等 6 人一起荣获"功勋模范侨商"称号。

扶贫助学，亲力亲为

"太平绅士巡视，有投诉要求就举手。"你如果看过周润发和梁家辉主演的电影《监狱风云》，或许对这经典一幕多少会有些印象。

孙启烈曾经做过香港廉政公署香港商业道德发展咨询委员会主席（2014—2020 年），现在也是香港的太平绅士，他每隔几个月就要去监狱里巡视一次。在巡视期间，他见过人生百态，也在里面遇到过几个曾在外面非常风光的旧相识。

"人真的不能走错路，只要走错了一步，就可能会终生遗憾。"孙启烈感慨道。

作为一位在商界摸爬滚打数十载的前辈，孙启烈非常关心年轻一辈的创业成长道路。他说，年轻人创业，如果之前是一张白纸，就很容易"撞板"（广东话，"碰壁、遇到挫折"之意）。

孙启烈自己有一个信念，无论哪个儿子，毕业后出来工作，先得在外面打工几年，积累一定的人生经验，才能回来接班。"英文有句俗语，'Ruin someone else's company before you ruin mine'（先毁了别人的公司，再来毁我的公司）。"说完此话，他立即哈哈大笑，并补充道："年轻人在外边'撞了一次板'，也算是拿到了一点人生经验，再失败的概率就小得多了。"

他的儿子孙荣良，在澳大利亚一所大学就读电子机械工程专业，毕业后先是在澳大利亚一个矿场工作了两年，之后才回到家族企业上班。

孙启烈告诉记者，他现在的"主业"就是从事一些社会服务工作。此前，他曾带领侨商企业家积极支持深圳市侨商关爱公益基金会开展扶贫助学活动，连续多年对深圳各区困难归侨侨眷子女开展助学活动，有超过百名学子受益。

"我是一个不会算计别人的人。现在儿子孝顺，孙辈健康成长，我感到非常欣慰，所以我非常感恩。"孙启烈说。

2016 年，在宁波大学建校 30 周年之际，孙启烈的儿子孙荣良捐资人民币 1000 万元，兴建宁波大学孙荣良科技楼。在捐资仪式上，孙荣良表示，祖父辈们情系桑梓，捐资助学，他希望能够沿着父辈们走过的道路，为家乡高等教育发展尽一份绵薄之力。

为了帮助香港中小学生了解国家的历史和社会发展，从 2013 年起，孙启烈就与中华精忠慈善基金会合作，定期组织香港青少年游学团赴内地参观学习交流。除了捐赠 200 多万元经费支持活动外，他还亲自带队考察、亲自讲授，用亲身经历激发学生们的爱国情怀。

"下个月，我将带领香港宁波公学、香港宁波第二中学、北角苏浙公学等学校的 180 余名师生到我的家乡宁波去交流访问，让香港的青少年以此为契机，感受国家日新月异的变化。"孙启烈说。

（除署名外，本文图片均由受访者孙启烈提供。参考资料：《深圳特区报》、《深圳商报》、《深圳侨报》、"深圳市侨商会"微信公众号等。）

Cliff Sun Kai-lit

A "meritorious model overseas Chinese entrepreneur" keeping pace with Shenzhen's reform and opening-up

Cliff Sun Kai-lit, who born in Hong Kong in 1953, is a Justice of the Peace, executive vice president of the China Federation of Overseas Chinese Entrepreneurs, supervising president of the Guangdong Overseas Chinese Enterprises Association, permanent honorary chairman of the Shenzhen Overseas Chinese International Association, honorary chairman of the Shenzhen Municipal Federation of Returned Overseas Chinese, honorary president of the Federation of Hong Kong Industries, and chairman of Kinox Enterprises Limited and Kin Hip Metal & Plastic Factory Ltd., Hong Kong.

As one of the first entrepreneurs to participate in the reform and opening-up and the construction of the Shenzhen Special Economic Zone, Sun united a lot of overseas Chinese entrepreneurs and made positive contributions to the development of Shenzhen. He was president of the Shenzhen Overseas Chinese International Association for two consecutive terms (the fifth and sixth terms), leading the association to fully play the role of a bridge between government and business, and to play an active role in gathering the hearts and strength of overseas Chinese, actively making suggestions, facilitating public welfare undertakings and building Shenzhen into an international city. He has won honors such as the Bronze Bauhinia Star of Hong Kong, Honorary Citizen of Shenzhen Municipality, Top 10 Hong Kong Business Leaders Who Have Influenced the Shenzhen Special Economic Zone in 30 Years, and "Meritorious Model Overseas Chinese Entrepreneur" granted by the Shenzhen Overseas Chinese International Association.

Professor, Bronze Bauhinia Star, and Justice of the Peace are the titles on the front side of the business card that Cliff Sun Kai-lit handed to us. In addition, he has many titles such as executive vice president of the China Federation of Overseas Chinese Entrepreneurs.

The interview took place in 2024.

On a sunny afternoon in mid-March 2024, at the Shenzhen Representative Office of the Federation of Hong Kong Industries on Renmin South Road, Luohu District, Shenzhen, we met Sun, who hurried over from Hong Kong.

He was in high spirits in front of us. When talking about his past experiences and family stories, he had clear thinking and careful logic, and spoke extremely fast. It was hard to tell that he was in his seventies.

"My ancestral home is in Shenzhen!" It was so surprising to hear Sun say this that we thought we had heard wrong.

"But the 'zhen' here is 甽, with the component of 田 (meaning the field)," Sun explained. In the *Modern Chinese Dictionary*, 甽 is a variant character for 圳, both referring to "a ditch beside the field." The "Shenzhen" that Sun mentioned is a small town located in the northwest of Ninghai County, Ningbo Municipality, Zhejiang Province.

So it turns out that Sun was somehow destined to have a special connection with "Shenzhen" a long time ago.

Born in Hong Kong, he inherited his father's business

Historian Xu Jilin believes that Shanghai and Ningbo share too many genetic origins. Whether it comes to business spirit or cultural spirit, Ningbo is one of the most important bloodlines of Shanghai's modern urban culture. The Ningbo business group (Shanghai business group) has countless ties with the Hong Kong business group.

In the 1930s, a teenager named Sun Kin Chao left his hometown of Ninghai County, Ningbo, and went to the big city of Shanghai to become an apprentice. After his apprenticeship was completed, the teenager worked in a factory with his master. Soon, the War of Resistance Against Japanese Aggression broke out, and the factory was requisitioned by the government and turned into an arsenal to produce military supplies. After the fall of Shanghai, Sun Kin Chao moved to Lishui, Zhejiang Province with the factory, and did not return to Shanghai until the victory of the war.

In 1948, Sun Kin Chao left Shanghai and finally reached Hong Kong. Recommend by a friend he had met in Shanghai, he entered a machinery factory that repaired textile machines. A year later, he saved up a little capital and opened a small workshop, mainly undertaking maintenance work for machinery factories.

In the 1950s, plastic products sold well in Hong Kong. Seeing the business opportunity, Sun Kin Chao began to manufacture plastic household products in 1953. His first product was a small red plastic liquor glass. Once launched, it was favored by the market, much more popular than the traditional small white ceramic liquor glass.

In the same year, Sun Kin Chao's son Sun Kai-lit was born. As the eldest son in the family, Sun Kai-lit often helped with the matters at his father's factory even when he was a child. After completing university courses in physics and mechanical engineering in Canada, he returned to Hong Kong in the late 1970s to help his father run the family business.

Sun's father, Sun Kin Chao, is 105 years old now and still in good health. "My father founded Kin Hip in Hong Kong. Back then, it was just a small mold-making factory that manufactured plastic household products. Later, my father began to develop and manufacture stainless steel thermos cups and thermos bottles, laying the foundation for the company's products. In the 1960s, Kin Hip exported its products to overseas markets through trading companies," said Sun Kai-lit.

In 1980, Sun founded the Kinox brand, and the trademark was registered in Hong Kong and Beijing at the same time. In the same year, Kinox Enterprises Limited was established, mainly producing coffee pots, coffee stoves, thermos pots and stainless steel kitchenware.

He revealed to us in detail how he created the brand. "I combined the first half of the Kin Hip company's English name with the first few letters of 'inoxydable,' the French word for stainless steel, to form Kinox, which is translated into Chinese as 建乐士 . The English name sounds sonorous, and the Chinese name creates a high-end corporate brand image."

It was precisely because of his many years of management experience in the wholesale distribution and manufacturing of kitchenware as well as other metal and plastic products that Sun Kai-lit became chairman of the Federation of Hong Kong Industries from 2009 to 2011, and served as chairman of the Hong Kong Q Mark Council for more than six years.

You may know that the "Q Mark" is a certification issued by the Hong Kong Q Mark Council. In Hong Kong, the "Q Mark" is synonymous with high-quality products and a confidence guarantee of high product quality.

Entering the mainland and investing in Shenzhen

The wind rises in the South China Sea, and the tide surges in the Pearl River. In the great historical process of China's reform and opening-up, a number of representative districts and counties have emerged, creating many valuable experiences for reform and opening-up. Among them is Nanhai County (now Nanhai District, Foshan City), Guangdong Province, which is located in the hinterland of the Pearl River Delta.

In the book *Towards a New Form of Urban-Rural Integrated Civilization: The Case of Nanhai*, Liu Shouying and other scholars revealed that in 1978, the Nanhai County Committee of the Communist Party of China and the Nanhai County Government proposed the industrial development idea of "taking county-run industry as the leader, township-run industry as the main force, village-run industry as the pillar, and individual associations as the supplement." They also took advantage of the large number of Hong Kong and Macao compatriots to actively introduce Hong Kong and foreign capital to develop "three supplies and one compensation" enterprises and "three types of foreign funded enterprises."

Sun Kai-lit said proudly that he was among the first batch of Hong Kong businessmen to participate in the development and construction of the mainland. At that time, after he heard from the media and friends in China Resources that the country was trying "export special zones" in Guangdong and Fujian, he came up with the idea of starting a business in the mainland.

Their first stop in the mainland was Nanhai County, Guangdong. In 1979, Sun introduced new-type injection molding, stamping and electroplating equipment, and led several employees to Nanhai County to open a small hardware processing factory in the form of "compensatory trade." The products processed there were shipped back to Hong Kong for packaging and export.

Sun explained that Hong Kong's industrial development was in its heyday at that time, and Kin Hip's factory space in Hong Kong was far from enough. However, the land cost of finding a new site was too high; and there was a shortage of workers in Hong Kong's manufacturing industry, resulting in significantly increased labor costs.

He told us a detail: In the late 1970s, many industries in Hong Kong, especially toy factories and electronics factories, were trying every means to "grab" workers, and many factories even installed air conditioners for this purpose, but Kin Hip's hardware factory did not have air conditioners, causing frequent headaches when the company received orders but failed to hire enough people.

Coinciding with the reform and opening-up of the mainland, they made a quick decision to move the production lines to the mainland. After gaining experience in Nanhai County, they opened processing plants in Dongguan, Guangzhou and Shenzhen. "Beginning in 1988, we focused our investment on Shenzhen, processing material provided by clients," Sun revealed. "In the late 1980s, some Hong Kong entrepreneurs temporarily withdrew from the mainland, leaving a lot of land idle, but we discussed with the local villagers' committee in Shenzhen to expand our factory area. Finally, Kin Hip obtained land in Pinghu at a price of HK$100 per square meter and got bank loans to build a large-scale modern factory."

In 1992, Kin Hip established a wholly-owned enterprise in Shenzhen, and Shenzhen has since become the base camp for Sun's career. "Unlike setting up factories in other places, we could make our own decisions in Shenzhen, and the most important thing was that we had autonomy, hiring workers and paying wages on our own will." Sun said that when investing in Shenzhen at that time, they could get considerable preferential treatment and autonomy, and the relevant approval procedures and processes were greatly reduced. In retrospect, these measures are still very advanced.

Connecting overseas Chinese to gather business forces

"We have been really lucky to catch the wave of reform and opening-up. We have participated and contributed, and at the same time we have gained more and received higher returns. So I have a deep affection for Shenzhen," Sun said in an interview with Xinhua News Agency in August 2010. "Shenzhen is another home of mine, and another birthplace of mine."

Like most Hong Kong entrepreneurs, Sun started in Hong Kong, but, with the help of the reform and opening-up, has achieved stable wealth growth and a booming career in the mainland, especially in Shenzhen. Therefore, he is very grateful to Shenzhen and the country. Whenever having the opportunity, he has contacted more overseas Chinese entrepreneurs and friends, gathered more strength of overseas Chinese entrepreneurs, and done as much as possible for Shenzhen and the country.

In March 2000, Sun Kai-lit, Lam Lap Fong, Ma Kai Cheung and others jointly initiated the establishment of the Shenzhen Overseas Chinese International Association (SOCIA). It is a social organization composed of overseas Chinese, Hong Kong and Macao compatriots, returned overseas Chinese, family members of overseas Chinese, and Hong Kong and Macao enterprises or individuals who have invested in Shenzhen.

At the beginning, Sun and other founding members borrowed the management model of chambers of commerce in Hong Kong. The members of SOCIA raised funds by themselves, and collected capital to purchase the office space. The operation of the association was "civilian and non-official," with the team members having no governmental status, and the association having no government officials as its leaders. All these were great innovations at the time.

The model of "independent leadership and management by overseas Chinese entrepreneurs" first adopted by SOCIA was later named the "Shenzhen Model" by the

Overseas Chinese Affairs Office of the State Council and the All-China Federation of Returned Overseas Chinese, who thought that it was worthy of reference and replication by overseas Chinese business organizations across the country.

Sun was elected as the fifth president of SOCIA on June 29, 2012. He was re-elected in July 2015. He proposed that the concept, form and activity content of the SOCIA should be further changed, and that it should have a broad mind, strengthen the sense of cooperation, learn from excellent joint and industry social groups, play the "overseas Chinese card" and the "international card," and combine the national development strategy with the cause of overseas Chinese business and social responsibility.

Sun knew that the association was a rare natural-born "business think tank." Therefore, he and his team used the platform of the association to frequently organize its members to participate in brainstorming sessions, seminars and forums to understand the thoughts and difficulties of overseas Chinese entrepreneurs and compatriots as well as the problems they encountered in investment and management.

As a member of the Shenzhen Municipal Committee of the Chinese People's Political Consultative Conference, Sun reported some common problems to relevant government departments through the channel of participating in politics and policy-making in a bid to solve them. For example, a proposal he put forward on convenient customs clearance between Shenzhen and Hong Kong has benefited many overseas Chinese entrepreneurs and compatriots investing in the mainland.

Regarding the important role of overseas Chinese entrepreneurs and compatriots in attracting investment to Shenzhen, Sun had a very vivid description: "using overseas Chinese as a bridge." It means to give full play to the role of overseas Chinese entrepreneurs and compatriots as "civilian ambassadors" and make two-way efforts in "going out and inviting in."

He organized SOCIA's members and member companies to visit the three major free trade zones of Qianhai Shekou, Nansha and Hengqin to find the connection points between the construction of the Guangdong-Hong Kong-Macao Greater Bay Area and the joint construction of the "Belt and Road." He organized delegations to conduct overseas Chinese affairs investigations in the United States and Mexico, participate in the "ASEAN Overseas Chinese Entrepreneurs Forum" and "World Chinese Entrepreneurs Convention," and have targeted exchanges with Chinese chambers of commerce and associations in Australia, Thailand, Malaysia, Italy and other countries. He established cooperative relations with the Athens Municipal Council of Greece, the Investment Bureau of the

Spanish Ministry of Economy, the German government consultants, and the Melbourne government consultants of Australia, paving the way for Shenzhen companies to invest and build factories in those places.

Over the years, Sun has been awarded titles such as "Honorary Citizen of Shenzhen Municipality" and "Top 10 Hong Kong Business Leaders Who Have Influenced the Shenzhen Special Economic Zone in 30 Years," and has been awarded the honors of "Justice of the Peace" and "Bronze Bauhinia Star" by the Government of the Hong Kong Special Administrative Region.

On the evening of April 24, 2024, at the inauguration ceremony of the eighth board of directors and board of supervisors of SOCIA and the award ceremony for outstanding overseas Chinese entrepreneurs, Sun Kai-lit, Ma Kai Cheung, Ma Wai Mo and three others were awarded the title of "Meritorious Model Overseas Chinese Entrepreneur."

Hands-on approach to poverty alleviation and education development

"Justices of the Peace are on patrol. Raise your hand if you have a complaint." If you have seen *Prison on Fire*, a movie starring Chow Yun-fat and Tony Leung Ka-fai, you may have some impression of this classic scene.

Sun was chairman of the Hong Kong Business Ethics Development Advisory Committee under the Independent Commission Against Corruption (2014—2020), and is a Justice of the Peace in Hong Kong. He visits prisons every few months. During the visits, he has seen the spectrum of life and met several old acquaintances who were very successful outside.

"People really can't take the wrong path. If you take a wrong step, you may regret it for the rest of your life," Sun sighed.

As a senior who has been working hard in the business world for decades, Sun is very concerned about the entrepreneurial growth path of the younger generation. If young people start a business with a blank sheet of paper and have not "hit the board" before, they will easily "hit the board," he said. In Cantonese, "hit the board" means "to be rebuffed and encounter setbacks."

Sun has a belief that no matter which of his sons comes out to work after graduation, he must work outside for a few years and accumulate certain life experience before returning to take over the family business. "There is an English saying, 'Ruin someone else's company before you ruin mine.'" After saying this, he immediately laughed and added, "Once young people 'hit the board' outside, they are supposed to gain some life experience, and the chance of more failures is much smaller."

His son Warren Sun Yung Liang studied electronic mechanical engineering at a university in Australia. After graduation, he worked in a mine in Australia for two years before returning to work for the family business.

Sun Kai-lit said that his current "main business" is to engage in social service work. He has led overseas Chinese entrepreneurs to actively support the Shenzhen Overseas Chinese Entrepreneur Charity Foundation to carry out activities alleviating poverty and helping education development. For many years, they have given financial aid for the impoverished children of returned overseas Chinese and family members of overseas Chinese in various districts of Shenzhen, benefiting more than 100 students.

"I am someone who does not scheme against others. Now my sons show filial obedience and my grandchildren are growing up healthily. I feel very gratified, so I am very grateful," Sun said.

In 2016, on the occasion of the 30th anniversary of Ningbo University, Sun Kai-lit's son Warren Sun Yung Liang donated 10 million yuan to build the Warren Sun Yung Liang Science and Technology Building of Ningbo University. At the donation ceremony, Warren Sun Yung Liang said that the generations of his grandfather and father had been concerned about their hometown and donated money to support education. He hoped to follow the path of the elder generation and do his part for the development of higher education in his hometown.

In order to help primary and secondary school students in Hong Kong understand the country's history and social development, Sun Kai-lit has cooperated with the Chinese Patriot Elites Charity Foundation since 2013 to regularly organize Hong Kong youth study tours in the mainland for study and exchange. In addition to donating more than 2 million yuan to support the activities, he also led the tours and gave lessons in person, inspiring the students' patriotic feelings with his own experience.

"Next month, I will lead more than 180 teachers and students from Ning Po College, Hong Kong, Ning Po No. 2 College, Hong Kong, and Kiangsu-Chekiang College, North Point, among others, to visit my hometown Ningbo for exchange, so that young people in Hong Kong can take this opportunity to feel the rapid changes in the country," Sun said.

(Photos courtesy of Sun Kai-lit, except for those with credit. References: *Shenzhen Special Zone Daily*, *Shenzhen Economic Daily*, *Shenzhen Overseas Chinese News*, the WeChat public account of "Shenzhen Overseas Chinese International Association," etc.)

第三章
Chapter Three

桑梓情深
Caring about the hometown

露从今夜白，月是故乡明。

——〔唐〕杜甫《月夜忆舍弟》

Dew turns into frost since tonight; The moon viewed at home is more bright.
—*Thinking of My Brothers on a Moonlit Night*, by Du Fu (Tang Dynasty)

赖荣茂

清代名将后人，大鹏所城的"活字典"

赖荣茂（来源:《晶报》） Lai Kayming (Photo: *Daily Sunshine*)

　　赖荣茂，1931 年 9 月出生于深圳大鹏所城，系清代名将赖恩爵后人。现为英国朴次茅斯华人协会荣誉会长，曾任英国朴次茅斯华人协会会长、全英华人社团联合总会名誉会长。

　　1966 年，赖荣茂以劳工身份抵达英国，侨居朴次茅斯市，曾在餐饮行业打工，后开快餐店。赖荣茂在经营"中央酒楼"时期，于 1980 年 6 月团结当地的爱国侨胞，一起创立了英国朴次茅斯华人协会。他热心公益事业、乐于助人，2019 年 5 月获英国朴次茅斯市政府颁发"荣誉市民"称号。

采访时间：2023 年。

深圳博物馆内再现九龙海战一幕。（来源：《晶报》）
A scene of the Battle of Kowloon is recreated in the Shenzhen Museum.
(Photo: *Daily Sunshine*)

"沿海所城，大鹏为最。"这是清嘉庆《新安县志》关于大鹏所城的一句描述。今天，在深圳大鹏所城南门右侧的赖府巷内，有一座辉煌气派的古建筑"振威将军第"——清代广东水师提督、振威将军赖恩爵的府邸，格外引人瞩目。

1839年（清道光十九年）9月4日，英国驻华商务监督义律率领军舰炮轰清军水师船和九龙炮台，时任大鹏营参将的赖恩爵率领官兵还击，取得了九龙海战的胜利。

2023年9月中旬，在大鹏所城里，《晶报》记者见到了回乡探亲访友的赖恩爵第六代孙赖荣茂。92岁的赖荣茂如今侨居英国朴次茅斯，现在是英国朴次茅斯华人协会荣誉会长。

所城旧事：穿越时空与先祖偶遇

1931年9月，赖荣茂出生在大鹏所城西南角将军第巷（现址为大鹏所城将军第巷1号101）的一户人家里，当时这个家庭里已经有了一个3岁大的儿子赖荣启。

大鹏所城的赖氏家族是深圳历史上的名门望族，家族中曾经"三代出了五位将军"，在中国历史上都属罕见，故有"宋朝杨家将、清代赖家帮"之美誉。"我们这一支是赖恩爵大儿子的后人。"不过，赖荣茂告诉《晶报》记者，家族里到他们父

173

辈这一代就已经不再习武、入伍了，像其父亲赖六宜就是"行船嘅（海员）"。

只是天有不测风云，赖六宜出远洋时在船上患病，30多岁就在美国纽约不幸去世，现还葬在纽约华人墓园里。父亲去世之后，赖荣茂的母亲很快就改嫁了，从此再也没有音信。

"我们两兄弟很小就没有了父母，全靠老祖母抚养长大，跟老祖母的感情也非常好。"说起自己的祖母赖潘氏（潘瑞英），赖荣茂声音有点哽咽，眼眶也湿润了起来。

"我和哥哥赖荣启都是在大鹏所城里读完高小（高级小学）的，当时学校叫'鹏一中心小学'，学校地址就在古城北门的太公庙（关帝庙）那边。"赖荣茂口中的"鹏一中心小学"，拥有"宝安县鹏一乡中心学校""大鹏乡中心国民学校""鹏城学校""鹏城小学"等多个称谓。后来被誉为"中国改革开放的最初实践者"的袁庚，在20世纪30年代末就曾在大鹏所城里教书育人，并曾担任过小学校长。

由祖母抚养的赖荣启、赖荣茂兄弟二人从小就很懂事，在校读书非常勤奋，学习成绩也一直名列前茅。

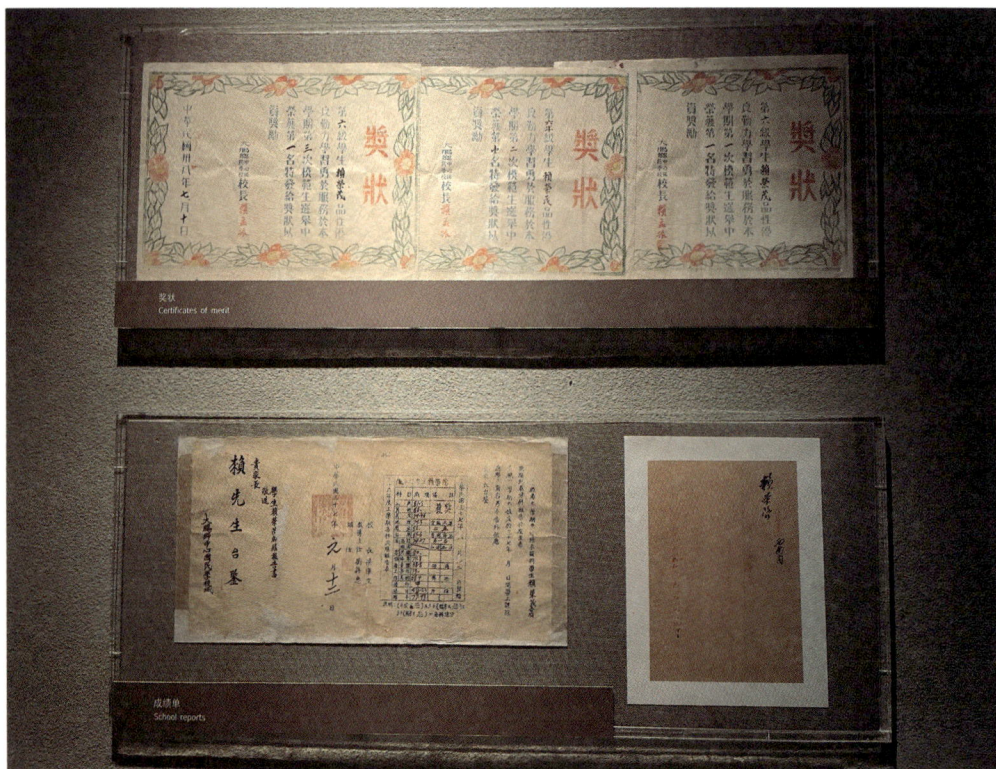

深圳博物馆内收藏的赖荣茂的奖状和成绩单。（来源：《晶报》）
Lai Kayming's certificates of commendation and transcript collected by the Shenzhen Museum.
(Photo: *Daily Sunshine*)

如今，在深圳博物馆二楼"近代深圳展厅"临近出口处附近，有一个新中国成立前宝安县葵涌、大鹏地区学校概况的展柜，里面展示了一批 20 世纪 40 年代的历史档案，其中就有一张赖荣茂在五年级上学期时考了全级第一名的成绩单，以及在六年级第二学期的三次模范生选举中全都荣获第一名的三张奖状。按照现在的理解，70 多年前在大鹏所城里读书的赖荣茂，那可是妥妥的学霸，以及让人羡慕的"别人家的孩子"。

有趣的是，在深圳博物馆同一展厅里，一进去便可见到由仿真人、背景油画、影像、声效、光构成等合成现代艺术手段再现的九龙海战一幕，以及一个关于大鹏赖氏"三代五将"史料与文物的专门展柜。赖荣茂居然在这样一个特殊场合中，穿越时空与 184 年前的自家先祖赖恩爵偶然相遇。

香港打工：艰难维持生计

1949 年 7 月，赖荣茂和几个同学离开家乡大鹏，去了香港打工。"我们是在叠福那边搭火船（蒸汽轮船）离开的，坐了大概两个小时的船，就到香港新界的大埔，然后再坐火车到九龙油麻地。我们有一些亲戚在香港那边，多是一些我们叫'阿叔'的长辈。"当年的赴港经历，赖荣茂仍记忆犹新。

在香港，赖荣茂投靠的是堂叔赖六凯。赖六凯自小就在香港接受西式的教育，精通英文，当时在九龙一家由英国人经营的酒店里工作。"那家酒店就在尖沙咀，叫海景酒店，我堂叔在里面做部长。"赖荣茂透露，在堂叔的介绍下，他也顺利进入海景酒店的茶水部打工。

"因为之前一直都在大鹏乡下，初到香港的我其实什么都不懂，但我那个堂叔很能干，也挺关照我的。他跟我说，你先做着，然后学一点英文，再慢慢升职。"赖荣茂说。

在海景酒店工作了几年之后，经朋友介绍，赖荣茂去了香港洋务工会的服务部工作。在当时，洋务工会与海员工会、摩托工会等都是香港比较大的工会。最初他是在工会的服务部做售卖员，再后来就转做了书记员，负责收会费等事务工作。

1954 年，赖荣茂申请从香港回到家乡大鹏结婚。"我老婆冼桂玲跟我同读一所小学，只是我年级比她高一点。"那个年代，女孩要耕田、做家务，读书其实是很少的，因此，能娶到这样的女子，赖荣茂感到非常幸运。

随后几年，赖荣茂两个女儿也在大鹏所城将军第巷的老屋里陆续出生。到了 1962 年，赖荣茂申请妻子和二女儿一起去香港，但把大女儿赖坚贞留在了大鹏老家。

被问到为什么要将大女儿留在老家，赖荣茂无奈地回答："因为乡下还有老祖母需要照顾。"当然，到了 1976 年，赖荣茂又帮助大女儿申请签证到了英国，一家终于团圆，不过，这都是后话了。

赖荣茂与妻子冼桂玲的结婚照。
（摄于 1954 年 2 月）
The marriage registration photo
of Lai Kayming and his wife Sin
Kwailing, taken in February 1954.

妻子到了香港之后，又相继生下一子一女。"当时要养家，还要交房租，生活真的很困难。"赖荣茂坦言，在香港工作的那十几年其实很辛苦，但是，也就是在这一时期，他组建了自己的家庭，后又有几个子女陆续出生，令他感到非常欣慰。

朴次茅斯落脚：成为华人协会创始人之一

1966 年 8 月，因生活所迫，赖荣茂带着一种相当复杂的心情，去了英国的朴次茅斯，在一家中餐馆里打工。

一开始，是在餐馆里的水吧做冲茶等服务工作，但赖荣茂并不甘于此，坚持进厨房学习，"因为掌握了一些厨房工作的技能，就可以自己开快餐店了。当时很多大鹏人在英国都是做厨房工作的"。

一年之后，在同乡黄音（后来成为著名的荷兰侨领）的帮助下，赖荣茂在朴次茅斯开了一家外卖餐厅。"黄音是大鹏所城东南角人，我是西南角的，我们曾在同一所小学读书。他爸爸是做厨房工作的，他也比我早到英国。我当时其实没有多少钱，但他说：'开餐馆你有多少钱就出多少钱，不够我给你垫。'真的非常关心我。"赖荣茂至今都非常感谢黄音当初的仗义相助。

在朴次茅斯逐渐站稳脚跟之后，赖荣茂也在用实际行动回馈社会，尤其是当地的华人社区。为了给华侨华人争取利益，也为了提升华人在朴次茅斯的社会地位，赖荣茂和一批志同道合的朋友在 1980 年 6 月正式成立了英国朴次茅斯华人协

赖荣茂年轻时的照片。（1983 年摄于朴次茅斯）
A photo of Lai Kayming taken in
Portsmouth in 1983.

会，并于同年 9 月创办了朴次茅斯华人协会中文学校。

由于之前曾经在香港的工会工作过，对社团的事务比较熟悉，赖荣茂曾在华人协会里担任多届秘书长以及第八届的会长。协会章程的起草、修改以及会长演讲稿的撰写等很多工作，都是由他负责完成的。"当然，修改会章不是我一个人决定的，一切都以协会的整体利益为重，不能夹杂个人私利。"赖荣茂补充道。

赖荣茂自豪地表示，现在朴次茅斯华人协会在英国的华侨组织里，算是影响力比较大的。

"我们的会务搞得不错，经济也搞得很好，得到了很多人的赞赏。"他透露，最初协会是没有固定会所的，都是租别人的地方来运作，直到 1992 年大家才下决心筹钱购买了现在的协会会所。

"当时有些华侨有钱，就捐得比较多，有的捐了 5000 英镑，我那时比较穷，但也捐了 3000 英镑，因为我是会里的骨干，在这件事上可不能落后于别人。"

赖荣茂的女儿赖坚贞现在是朴次茅斯华人协会名誉会长兼妇女部主任。她介绍说："43 年来，华人协会积极服务当地华人社区，已经成为沟通政府和华人之间的

2023 年 7 月 16 日，赖荣茂以朴次茅斯华人协会中文学校创始人之一的嘉宾身份为学校优秀教师颁奖。
Lai Kayming, as a founder of the Portsmouth Chinese Association Sunday School, presents an award to the school's outstanding teacher on July 16, 2023.

桥梁。协会目前有 400 多位会员、20 位执行委员，协会中文学校最高峰的时候学生有 200 多人，目前学生也有 180 名左右。"

爱国行动：助力流落海外国宝文物回家

几个世纪以来，朴次茅斯一直都是英国皇家海军的主要基地之一。

1900 年 6 月 17 日，由英、法等国组成的八国联军攻陷天津的大沽炮台，悬挂于炮台上的大沽铁钟被英国士兵作为战利品掠夺走，并运回到英国，存放在朴次茅斯市的维多利亚公园内。从此，大沽铁钟开始了在朴次茅斯的 100 多年海外流浪生涯。

2003 年，英国维多利亚艺术中心主任马可·刘易斯和中国留学生范辉偶然发现了铁钟，后来在中英两国政府和朴次茅斯华人协会的多方努力下，2005 年 5 月 25 日，英国政府通过了将大沽铁钟无偿返还中国的提案。

同年 7 月 20 日，大沽铁钟重新回到了故土。2006 年，天津市政府等比例复制了一口铁钟回赠给了朴次茅斯市，并悬挂在该市维多利亚公园内。

2007 年 7 月 1 日，赖荣茂（右四）到伦敦参加全英华人侨团联合举办的庆祝香港回归祖国 10 周年活动。

Lai Kayming (fourth from right) participates in an event in London jointly organized by overseas Chinese groups across Britain to celebrate the 10th anniversary of Hong Kong's return to the motherland on July 1, 2007.

2014 年，大沽铁钟因其特殊意义入选成为国家一级文物。如今，铁钟真品收藏在天津大沽口炮台遗址博物馆内，并成为该博物馆的镇馆之宝。而朴次茅斯华人协会特别是协会会长叶锦洪先生的努力奔走，促成了大沽铁钟回归中国，此事也成为中英两国间通过政府协商并由英国政府主动无偿归还文物的一个典范。回忆此事，赖荣茂自豪地说："这是我们协会这些年以来做的众多爱国行动之一。"

为表示对华人协会多年来所作贡献的感谢及尊重，朴次茅斯市政府特别给予了协会一项极高的礼遇：在每年的中国春节、中国国庆节以及香港回归祖国纪念日等重要时刻，都可以在当地的市政厅广场进行升五星红旗的仪式。

而且，在现任会长蔡润泉先生的努力下，朴次茅斯华人协会还促成了朴次茅斯市与珠海市、湛江市结为友好城市，以及中英两地多所院校结为友好学校。赖荣茂也因为热心公益事业和服务社区，在 2019 年 5 月获得朴次茅斯市政府颁发的"荣誉市民"称号。

"在华人协会服务了四十几年，我从来没有从协会支取过一分钱，只是出钱出力，为华侨华人服务好，并尽量宣传好我们的国家政策。"赖荣茂说。

重返大鹏：犹如所城的"活字典"

2023 年是新安县（今深圳、香港所在地的旧称）建县 450 周年。2023 年 9 月 4 日是九龙海战取得胜利 184 周年，当日，清代鸦片战争将领赖恩爵将军铜像在大鹏所城振威将军第落成揭幕。铜像落成揭幕后一周，《晶报》记者在大鹏所城里见到了赖恩爵的六世孙赖荣茂、赖荣平，以及七世孙女赖坚贞及其丈夫余锦培。

当日下午，在振威将军第参观时，屋外突然下起了倾盆大雨。因为新冠疫情，有 3 年没有回家乡大鹏的赖荣茂突然感慨道："真是'下雨天，留客天'啊！"

赖荣茂很早就离开了家乡，但跟所城众多的赖氏后人一样，不管走了多远，他始终心系大鹏，会经常回来看看这座建于明洪武廿七年（1394）的古城。

为了查清楚鹏城赖氏的世系家谱，他从 1993 年开始研究，到处去搜集资料，并访问了还在世的一些老前辈。最后，他用 6 年时间，编纂出了一本原广东省宝安县《大鹏城赖氏世系简谱》。2014 年，他又编出了一本《大鹏城赖氏敦厚堂简谱》。

对此，曾经担任深圳鹏城赖氏宗亲理事会会长的赖荣茂说："我是赖府的后代，我如果不去做，就很可能没有其他人会去编这个家谱了。"今天大鹏新区博物馆内有不少介绍资料，引用的都是《大鹏城赖氏世系简谱》里的内容。

《晶报》记者留意到，虽然已经是 90 多岁高龄，腿脚有些不大灵便，但赖荣茂对过去的一些人和事记得很清楚，就像是一本大鹏所城的"活字典"。大鹏新区博物馆副馆长黄文德每当有新发现，遇到拿不准的地方，都要向赖荣茂这位前辈请教。

2023 年 9 月 12 日，赖荣平、赖荣茂、赖坚贞、余锦培（从左至右）在大鹏所城赖恩爵铜像前合影。（来源：《晶报》）

Lai Wingping, Lai Kayming, Chien Chen Yu and her husband Yu Kampui (from left to right) in front of a bronze statue of Lai Enjue in Dapeng Fortress on September 12, 2023. (Photo: *Daily Sunshine*)

　　"我是在这里长大的，对这里的很多地方都记忆犹新。"赖荣茂动情地说，"而且我之前访问过很多所城里的老人和一些曾经在大鹏工作过的东江纵队老游击队队员，掌握了不少的一手资料。"

　　《晶报》记者还注意到一个细节，这次从海外回来，赖荣茂在大鹏所城选择下榻的民宿酒店，居然就是他 20 世纪 80 年代在所城兴建的一座房屋（现产权已经出售给了别人）。"我爸爸是一个非常念旧的人，在自己旧屋住着，见到熟悉的场景，他会睡得更安稳一些。"女儿赖坚贞说道。

　　（除署名外，本文图片均由赖坚贞提供。参考资料：深圳政府在线、廉洁深圳网、大沽口炮台遗址博物馆微信公众号。）

Lai Kayming

Descendant of a famous Qing Dynasty general, "living dictionary" of Dapeng Fortress

Lai Kayming (also known as Lai Wingmau or Lai Rongmao), born in Dapeng Fortress, Shenzhen in September 1931, is a descendant of Lai Enjue, a famous general in the Qing Dynasty. He is honorary president of the Portsmouth Chinese Association (PCA) in Britain. He used to be president of the PCA and honorary president of the Confederation of Chinese Associations UK.

In 1966, Lai arrived in Britain as a laborer and lived in Portsmouth. He worked in the catering industry and later opened a fast food restaurant. When he ran the Centre Chinese Restaurant, he united local patriotic overseas Chinese to found the PCA in June 1980. He is enthusiastic about public welfare and helpful to others. In May 2019, he was awarded the title of Honorary Citizen by the Portsmouth City Council.

"Of all the fortresses along the coast, Dapeng is the best." This is a description of Dapeng Fortress in *Xin'an County Chronicles* written during the Jiaqing period of the Qing Dynasty. Today, in Laifu Lane on the right side of the south gate of Dapeng Fortress in Shenzhen, there is a splendid and eye-catching ancient building, the "Mansion of General Zhenwei," the residence of Lai Enjue, commander of the Guangdong navy in the Qing Dynasty, who was given the title of General Zhenwei.

On September 4, 1839 (the 19th year of the Daoguang Emperor's reign in the Qing Dynasty), Charles Elliot, the British commercial supervisor in China, led warships to bombard the Qing navy ships and the Kowloon Fort. Lai Enjue, then general of the Dapeng Battalion, led the officers and soldiers to fight back and won the skirmish, known as the Battle of Kowloon, or the Kowloon Sea Battle.

In mid-September 2023, in Dapeng Fortress, a reporter from the *Daily Sunshine* met Lai Kayming, a sixth-generation descendant of Lai Enjue, who returned to his hometown to visit relatives and friends. The 92-year-old Lai Kayming is based in in Portsmouth,

---

The interview took place in 2023.

181

Britain, and is honorary president of the Portsmouth Chinese Association.

Past events in the fortress: traveling through time and space to encounter his ancestor

In September 1931, Lai Kayming was born in a family in Jiangjundi Lane at the southwest corner of Dapeng Fortress (the current address is No. 101, Jiangjundi Lane, Dapeng Fortress). The family already had a 3-year-old son, Lai Wingkay.

The Lai clan in Dapeng Fortress is a renowned one in the history of Shenzhen. With five Qing Dynasty generals in three generations, which was rare in Chinese history, the clan's fame paralleled the Yang clan in the Northern Song Dynasty. "Our family belongs to the offspring of Lai Enjue's eldest son," Lai Kayming said. However, he told the *Daily Sunshine* that by his father's generation, the family had stopped practicing martial arts and joining the army. His father, Lai Lokye, was a sailor.

However, something unexpected happened. Lai Lokye fell ill on the ship when he was on an ocean voyage, and died in New York City in his 30s. He is still buried in a Chinese cemetery in New York. After his death, her wife remarried soon and was never heard from again.

"We two brothers lost our parents when we were very young. We were raised by our grandmother, and have a very good relationship with her," speaking of his grandmother, Mrs. Lai Pan (Pan Ruiying), Lai Kayming suddenly choked up and his eyes became moist.

"My brother Lai Wingkay and I both finished senior primary school in Dapeng Fortress. Back then, the school was called 'Pengyi Central Primary School' and it was right next to the Taigong Temple (Guandi Temple) at the north gate of the ancient city." The "Pengyi Central Primary School" he mentioned has had many titles, such as "Bao'an County Pengyi Township Central School," "Dapeng Township Central National School," "Pengcheng School" and "Pengcheng Primary School." Yuan Geng, later known as "the original practitioner of China's reform and opening-up," taught in Dapeng Fortress in the late 1930s and served as principal of the primary school.

The two brothers, Lai Wingkay and Lai Kayming, who were raised by their grandmother, have been very sensible since childhood. They studied diligently in school and their academic performance was always among the best.

Today, near the exit of the "Exhibition Hall of Modern Shenzhen" on the second floor of the Shenzhen Museum, there is a showcase showing the overview of schools in Kuichong and Dapeng areas of Bao'an County before the founding of the People's Republic of China. It shows a collection of historical archives from the 1940s, including a transcript of Lai Kayming who finished first in the first semester of the fifth grade, as well as three certificates of commendation for his winning first place in all the three model student elections in the second semester of the sixth grade. According to today's understanding, Lai Kayming, who studied in Dapeng Fortress more than 70 years ago, was a perfect student and an enviable "child of others."

Interestingly, as soon as you enter the same exhibition hall of the Shenzhen Museum, you can see a scene of the Battle of Kowloon recreated using synthetic modern art methods such as polymer dummies, background oil paintings, images, sound effects, and light composition, as well as a cabinet for historical materials and cultural relics about the "Five Generals in Three Generations" from the Lai clan in Dapeng. On such a special occasion, Lai Kayming traveled through time and space to meet Lai Enjue, his ancestor from 184 years ago.

Working in Hong Kong: trying to make ends meet

In July 1949, Lai Kayming and several classmates left his hometown of Dapeng and went to Hong Kong to work. "We took a fire-ship (steamship) from Diefu and it took about two hours to get to Tai Po in the New Territories of Hong Kong. Then we took a train to Yau Ma Tei, Kowloon. We had some relatives over there in Hong Kong, and most of them are elders we call uncle," Lai Kayming still remembers his experience of going to Hong Kong that year.

In Hong Kong, Lai Kayming turned to his father's cousin, Lai Lokkwu, who had received a Western education in Hong Kong since he was a child and was proficient in English. He was working in a hotel in Kowloon run by Britons. "That hotel, in Tsim Sha Tsui, was called the Seaview Hotel, and my uncle was a captain there," Lai Kayming said. He was recommended by his uncle to the Seaview Hotel, working in the tea department.

"Because I had been living in the countryside of Dapeng, I actually knew nothing when I first arrived in Hong Kong. But that uncle in Hong Kong was very capable and took good care of me. He told me to do that job for the time being, learn a little bit English, and then seek gradual promotion," Lai Kayming said.

After working in the Seaview Hotel for several years, he went to work in the service department of the Hong Kong Union of Chinese Workers in Western Style Employment (HKUCWWSE), recommended by a friend. The HKUCWWSE, the Hong Kong Seamen's Union, and the Motor Transport Workers General Union were relatively large trade unions in Hong Kong. At first, Lai worked as a shop assistant in the service department of the HKUCWWSE. Later he became a clerk, responsible for collecting membership dues and other matters.

In 1954, Lai applied to return to his hometown Dapeng from Hong Kong to get married. "My wife Sin Kwailing went to the same primary school as me, but I was in a higher grade." In that era, girls had to farm fields and do housework, and rarely went to school. Therefore, Lai felt very lucky to marry such a woman.

In the following years, Lai's two daughters were born in his old house in Jiangjundi Lane, Dapeng Fortress. In 1962, he applied for his wife and younger daughter's move to Hong Kong, but left his elder daughter Chien Chen Yu in his hometown of Dapeng.

When asked why he left his elder daughter in his hometown, Lai replied helplessly, "Because there was still an old grandmother in the countryside who needed to be taken care of." Suitably, in 1976, Lai applied for his elder daughter's move to Britain from Dapeng, and the family was finally reunited. But that is another story.

After Lai's wife arrived in Hong Kong, she gave birth to a son and a daughter. "At that time, I had to support my family and pay the rent. Life was really difficult." Lai said frankly that the more than 10 years he worked in Hong Kong was actually very hard, but it was during this period that he started his own family and later several children were born one after another, which made him very happy.

Settling in Portsmouth: becoming one of the founders of the Chinese Association

In August 1966, due to the pressure of life, Lai went to Portsmouth in Britain with a rather complicated mood and began to work in a Chinese restaurant.

At first, Lai worked in a restaurant's beverage bar, making tea and providing other services, but he was not content with this and insisted on learning in the kitchen. "Because when you have mastered some kitchen work skills, you can open your own fast food restaurant. A lot of people from Dapeng worked in kitchens in Britain at that time."

A year later, with the help of fellow Dapeng immigrant Wong Yan, who later became a famous overseas Chinese leader in the Netherlands, Lai opened a takeaway restaurant in Portsmouth. "Huang Yin is from the southeast corner of Dapeng Fortress, and I am from the southwest corner. We went to the same primary school. His father worked in the kitchen, and he came to the UK earlier than me. I actually didn't have much money at the time, but he said, 'You can invest as much as you have to open the restaurant. If it's not enough, I'll give you some money.' He really cared about me." Lai is still very grateful to Huang for his help.

After gradually establishing a foothold in Portsmouth, Lai began to give back to the society, especially the local Chinese community, through practical action. In order to strive for the interests of the overseas Chinese and improve the social status of the Chinese in Portsmouth, Lai and a group of like-minded friends formally established the

Portsmouth Chinese Association (PCA) in June 1980, and founded the Portsmouth Chinese Association Sunday School in September of the same year.

Since he had worked in a trade union in Hong Kong and was familiar with community affairs, Lai served as secretary-general of the PCA for several terms and its eighth president. He was responsible for many tasks, including drafting and revising the association's charter and writing the president's speech. "Certainly, how to amend the association's charter was not up to me. Everything was based on the overall interests of the association and could not be mixed with a little bit of personal gain," Lai added.

The Portsmouth Chinese Association is now relatively influential among overseas Chinese organizations in Britain, Lai said proudly.

"We do well in the affairs of the association, and our finances are good. So we are praised by many people." He revealed that at first, the association did not have a fixed location, and it rented other's property for its operation. It was not until 1992 that they made a decision and raised money to purchase the present house of the association.

"At the time, some overseas Chinese donated more money because they were rich, some of which donated 5,000 pounds. I was relatively poor back then, but I donated 3,000 pounds because I was a backbone member of the association and I couldn't lag behind others in this matter."

Lai's daughter Chien Chen Yu is honorary president of the Portsmouth Chinese Association and director of its women's department. She said, "For 43 years, the Chinese Association has actively served the local Chinese community and has become a bridge between the government and the Chinese. The association has more than 400 members and 20 executive members. The association's Chinese school had more than 200 students at its peak, and now has about 180 students."

Patriotic action: helping China's national treasure abroad return home

For centuries, Portsmouth has been one of the main bases of the Royal Navy.

On June 17, 1900, the Eight-Nation Alliance composed of Britain, France and other countries captured the Dagu Fort in Tianjin. The Dagu Iron Bell hanging on the fort was plundered by British soldiers as a trophy, transported to Britain, and stored in Victoria Park in Portsmouth. From then on, the Dagu Iron Bell began its wandering in Portsmouth for more than 100 years.

In 2003, Mark E.W. Lewis, director of the Lodge Arts Centre in Victoria Park, and Fan Hui, a Chinese student studying abroad, accidentally discovered the iron bell. On May 25, 2005, with the efforts of the Chinese and British governments and the Portsmouth

Chinese Association, the British government passed a proposal to return the Dagu Iron Bell to China free of charge.

On July 20, 2005, the Dagu Iron Bell returned to its homeland. In 2006, Tianjin Municipality made a proportional replica the iron bell and gave it to the City of Portsmouth. Then the bell was hung in Victoria Park.

In 2014, the Dagu Iron Bell was selected as a national first-class cultural relic due to its special significance. Today, the authentic iron bell is collected in the Dagukou Fort Ruins Museum in Tianjin and has become the museum's top treasure. The hard work of the Portsmouth Chinese Association, especially Mr. Ip Kum Hung, president of the association, contributed to the return of the Dagu Iron Bell to China. It has also become an example of the return of cultural relics free of charge by the British government through government consultation between China and Britain. Recalling this, Lai said proudly, "This is one of the many patriotic actions our association has done over the years."

In order to express its gratitude and respect for the contributions made by the Portsmouth Chinese Association over the years, the Portsmouth City Council has given the association special treatment: At important moments such as the Spring Festival, the Chinese National Day and the anniversary of Hong Kong's return to China every year, a ceremony of raising the five-star red flag can be held at the city hall square.

Moreover, with the efforts of the current president, Mr. Albert Choi, the Portsmouth Chinese Association has promoted the City of Portsmouth to form sister cities with Zhuhai City and Zhanjiang City, and many universities in China and Britain to form sister schools. Lai was awarded the title of "Honorary Citizen" by the Portsmouth City Council in May 2019 because of his enthusiasm for public welfare and serving the community.

"Having served in the Chinese Association for more than 40 years, I have never earned a penny from the association. I have just contributed money and efforts to serve the overseas Chinese and tried my best to promote China's national policies," Lai said.

Returning to Dapeng: a "living dictionary" of the fortress

The year of 2023 marks the 450th anniversary of the founding of Xin'an County, which today's Shenzhen and Hong Kong used to belong to. On September 4, 2023, the 184th anniversary of the victory in the Battle of Kowloon, a bronze statue of General Lai Enjue, a general in the Opium War of the Qing Dynasty, was inaugurated in the Mansion of General Zhenwei in Dapeng Fortress. One week after the inauguration and unveiling of the bronze statue, a reporter from the *Daily Sunshine* met Lai Enjue's sixth-generation descendants Lai Kayming and Lai Wingping, as well as his seventh-generation descendant

Chien Chen Yu and her husband Yu Kampui in Dapeng Fortress.

On the afternoon of that day, while we visited the Mansion of General Zhenwei, there was a heavy downpour outside. Lai Kayming, who had not been back to his hometown of Dapeng in the past three years due to the COVID-19 pandemic, suddenly said with emotion, "It's really 'a rainy day to ask the guest to stay'!"

Lai Kayming left his hometown very early, but like many descendants of the Lai clan from the fortress, no matter how far he has gone, he has always cared about Dapeng and has often come back to visit this fortress, which was built in the 27th year of the Hongwu period in the Ming Dynasty (A.D. 1394).

In a bid to clean up the family tree of the Lai clan in Dapeng Fortress, Lai Kayming began research in 1993, collecting information wherever he could and interviewing some seniors still alive. It took him six years to compile the *Simplified Genealogy of the Lai Family in Dapeng Fortress*. In 2014, he compiled another book, *Simplified Genealogy of Dunhoutang of the Lai Family in Dapeng Fortress*.

In this regard, Lai Kayming, who once served as chairman of the Shenzhen Pengcheng Lai Clan Council, said, "I am a descendant of the Lai family. If I hadn't done it, it would have been likely that no one else would compile this family tree." Now, a lot of introductory materials in the Dapeng New District Museum have cited the *Simplified Genealogy of the Lai Family in Dapeng Fortress*.

Although he is over 90 years old and is not so surefooted, Lai remembers some people and events in the past very clearly, like a "living dictionary" of Dapeng. Even Huang Wende, deputy director of the Dapeng New District Museum, will consult Lai when he is unsure for something about his new discoveries.

"I grew up here, and I still remember many places here," Lai said emotionally. "And I have interviewed many elderly people in the fortress and some old guerrillas of the Dongjiang Column who worked in Dapeng, so I have a lot of first-hand information."

The *Daily Sunshine* also noticed a detail. During his stay in Dapeng Fortress this time, Lai chose to stay at a homestay inn. That was actually the house he built in the 1980s, and its property rights have been sold to others. "My father is a very nostalgic person. Living in his old house and seeing familiar scenes, he will sleep more soundly," said his daughter, Chien Chen Yu.

(Photos courtesy of Chien Chen Yu, except for those with credit. References: Shenzhen Government Online, Clean Shenzhen, and the official WeChat account of the Dagukou Fort Ruins Museum.)

江运灵

一呼百应赤子心，涌泉相报故园情

江运灵把金婚时拍摄的全家福挂在客厅墙上。（来源：《晶报》）
Kong Wan Ling hangs a family photo taken during his golden anniversary on the wall of his living room.
(Photo: *Daily Sunshine*)

江运灵，1935年12月出生于深圳布吉李朗（今属龙岗区南湾街道下李朗社区）。深圳市荣誉市民，深圳市龙岗区布吉街道侨联（以下简称"布吉侨联"）主席，龙岗区侨联荣誉主席，香港深圳布吉同乡总会理事长，香港深圳坂田同乡总会永远荣誉会长。1956年前往香港求学，后留港发展，经营进出口贸易等。曾为众多乡亲纾困救急，向家乡捐赠生产物资。改革开放以来，他积极宣传家乡投资环境，影响和带动了一批港澳同胞和海外华侨回乡投资办厂，为布吉片区的经济建设和各项事业发展作出了较大贡献。

江运灵热心社会公益，从事侨联工作40年，长期担任布吉侨联主席，2000年带领旅港乡亲成立香港深圳布吉同乡总会。布吉侨联发动海内外乡亲和热心人士捐资建设的布吉侨联大厦于2007年落成，进一步增强了为侨服务能力。江运灵于2004年获广东省侨联系统"侨联事业贡献奖"、深圳市"从事侨务工作二十年贡献奖"，2006年获中国侨联颁发的从事侨联工作二十年以上证书，还曾获"深圳市侨务工作贡献奖""深圳市侨联系统先进个人"等荣誉。

采访时间：2023年。

2023 年 10 月的一天中午，在香港九龙一家酒店 3 楼的餐厅里，江运灵环顾四周，发现了好几张熟面孔，都是他在香港的老朋友。

江运灵常来这家酒店。13 年前，他和妻子庆祝金婚（结婚 50 周年），就在这里的 6 楼设宴 30 多桌。2020 年，他俩迎来钻石婚（结婚 60 周年），也在这里订了 30 桌，但因为新冠疫情而取消，这成了他最遗憾的事。"假如庆祝钻石婚，有一张相片，岂不是就完美了？"

"可是，她在 2023 年 1 月离我而去了。"将近 88 岁的江运灵精神矍铄、思路清晰、谈吐风趣，但说到妻子，他几度哽咽落泪。携手相伴 60 多年，不管是经营事业，还是帮扶乡亲、支援家乡、投身侨务，都得到妻子无条件的支持，让他能心无旁骛，一步步追寻、实现心中梦想。

在江运灵的故事里，有一见钟情、相濡以沫的幸福，也有心系桑梓、知恩图报的功绩。他重情重义、讲信誉，言语深入浅出、接地气，这些或许都是他打动人心、打开局面的法宝。

童年坎坷，自知奋发上进

据江运灵介绍，他出生、长大的地方原先叫李朗村，是一个客家村落，后来分为上李朗、下李朗。他家就属于下李朗，江姓是本地的第一大姓。

江运灵的人生开局很坎坷。在他只有 8 个月大的时候，父亲就远去马来亚谋生（1963 年，马来亚与其他几个地方合并组成马来西亚）；4 岁时，母亲就去世了。他和姐姐相依为命，由姑妈、叔婆带大。李朗村的小学是江姓族人开办的，江姓子弟可免费就读，但在日本侵华期间，办学资金短缺，不再免费，江运灵虽然学业优异，但因家境贫寒交不起学费而一度辍学。校长得知后甚感可惜，特别为他申请免除了费用，他才得以继续学业。

1945 年抗战结束后，江运灵父亲有了音信，开始寄钱回来，支撑他读完初中。江运灵奋发上进，成绩一直不错。老师们用粤语教学，也为他后来闯荡香港奠定了语言基础。

1951 年，李朗村的学校缺人手，江运灵成为一名小学老师。因为教得不错，逐渐在当地小有名气，3 年后调任布吉中心小学。随着时局的变化，身有海外关系带来了一些不确定的影响，他被调到了偏远的乌石岩（今宝安区石岩街道），对前途感到迷茫。适逢归侨、侨眷可以申请出境，江运灵决定到香港读书，高中毕业再回来考大学。

由于形势的变化和个人的际遇，江运灵的计划终究没能实现。"我这一辈子没读成大学，到现在都耿耿于怀。"

好在，这扇门关上了，另一扇窗却打开了。

赴港求学，邂逅万里姻缘

1956 年 9 月 16 日，江运灵抵达香港。他白天去学习英语，晚上读会计学校。1957 年，他去马来亚见了父亲。父亲经营收音机、自行车等生意，想让江运灵留下来接手。但江运灵住了 3 个月，还是决定回香港。

当时，江运灵体弱多病，父亲不放心让他自己住，就安排他寄宿在香港一家公司。1960 年，一个叫郑素萍的年轻女子到这家公司玩，邂逅了江运灵，对他一见钟情。

这家公司是李朗籍的凌姓乡亲开的，郑素萍是公司一位股东的亲戚。她来自特立尼达和多巴哥（老一辈华侨华人口中的"千里达"），郑家是千里达当地最富有的侨商，母亲是深圳观澜人。郑素萍在千里达出生、长大，从小接受英式教育，不会说中文，中学毕业后就在家帮父母打理生意。这次，她是在母亲建议下到香港小住，为的是接触一下中国人的社会。谁知有缘千里来相会，这一来就从此留在了香港。

刚开始，郑素萍的父母很不放心，但见女儿心意已定，就只好写信邀请他俩一起到千里达生活，郑素萍让江运灵做主。因为不想远离家乡，也考虑到未来的发展，江运灵决定，要凭借自己的双手在香港开创一番事业。1960 年 10 月 1 日，江运灵特意挑在中华人民共和国国庆节这一天，在香港九龙最"气派"的酒楼设下婚宴，与郑素萍喜结连理。

江运灵夫妇年轻时的合影。（《晶报》翻拍照片）
Kong Wan Ling and his wife when they were young. (Reproduced by *Daily Sunshine*)

帮困救急，情系故土与乡亲

1961 年，江运灵在香港中环开了间贸易公司，起名为"百顺行"，从此走上经商之路。由于好学上进、精通英语，他很快在行业内崭露头角，站稳脚跟。除此之外，他还相继开办过制线厂、旅游公司，在英国投资开办外卖店。

对家乡人，江运灵总是充满信任，制线厂是跟李朗籍的一位同乡合伙开办，外卖店则是出资给李朗籍的几个同乡经营。江运灵的一个表妹对此有不同看法，她对江运灵说："你出本钱给人家经营工厂，结果人家住别墅、坐大车，你呢？"江运灵倒是不太计较这些，他回答道："住别墅、坐大车那个人也是姓江的啊！难道姓江的去做乞丐，你才会高兴吗？"

江运灵还得到了妻子的大力支持。"太太对我的所作所为从来没有抱怨过，从来不会责怪说：'你那么相信别人？那些都是钱啊！'"

香港是江运灵开拓事业的地方，家乡则是他长久的牵挂。他深知，正是依靠亲人和乡亲们的支持，自己才能在艰难的岁月里完成学业、积累阅历。饮水思源、知恩图报，事业成功的他为乡亲们和家乡的各项事业提供各种资助，改革开放后更是带头回乡投资，把满腔热情投入侨联、同乡会事务中，妻子一直默默相伴，全力支持，无怨无悔。

1961 年，深圳遭遇大旱，农田灌溉需要从河里、池塘里引水。得知灾情，江运灵购买了 3 台抽水机和几吨肥料，找运输公司送到下李朗。后来，他还向下李朗的学校捐赠了书籍、乐器、体育用品等。1979 年，为了支持家乡发展，江运灵响应号召，动员在港乡亲捐资，买了两辆货车，送给下李朗。

那些年，江运灵经常收到亲友、故交的求助信，热心肠的他总是提供力所能及的资助。家中不时收留初到香港的乡亲，"不但请吃饭，还给家乡人出钱买衣服"。

响应召唤，带头回乡投资

改革开放之初，家乡传讯，希望江运灵回去看看，但他和很多在港乡亲一样，仍心存顾虑，不敢轻易回去。1982 年 7 月，布吉公社派出 3 位干部到香港，召集在港乡亲见面。江运灵全力相助，在大埔一家酒楼订好酒席。七八十位乡亲纷纷从香港各个地方赶到，都想获得更多关于家乡的消息。就在江运灵准备独自买单承担聚会酒席的费用时，坂田籍乡亲刘泉坚持跟他平摊花销。两人因此互相留下深刻印象，并在后来回乡创办侨联时成为携手合作的好伙伴。

那晚的聚会很成功。布吉来的干部向在港乡亲们宣讲了最新的改革开放政策和华侨政策，介绍了家乡的情况，号召大家回乡投资、捐建学校。乡亲们和家乡干部相谈甚欢，种种顾虑也逐渐消除。

1983 年，布吉由公社改为区。这年 9 月，借着区政府新办公大楼落成之机，布吉邀请海外侨胞和港澳同胞回乡观礼。江运灵带着妻子，第一次踏上返乡之旅。家乡的道路坑坑洼洼，坐在车里很是颠簸，人不时会被弹起来，头"咚"的一声就撞到顶棚。路途虽然辛苦，他们内心却充满了久别重逢的喜悦。

那次回乡，江运灵做了两个决定。一是，他向布吉捐赠了 3000 港元，用于购置办公桌椅。二是，布吉的领导正式邀请他担任布吉侨联主席，他认真考虑后，决定接受邀请，勇挑重担。

不久，江运灵投资 300 多万港元，在下李朗建设了厂房。他还发挥自己朋友多、人脉广的优势，积极宣传家乡的投资环境。在他的带动和动员下，布吉籍的港澳同胞和加拿大、美国、英国、荷兰等国的布吉籍侨胞纷纷回乡投资建厂，大大促进了布吉的经济发展。

江运灵很注意招商引资的后续工作，会常常跟返乡投资者谈心，及时了解他们的需求，稳定他们的信心。"有什么风吹草动，你传我，我传你，事情就夸大了，投资信心就会动摇。"他说："所以需要一个有说服力的人跟大家聊一聊。"

投身侨务，尽心尽力数十载

布吉侨联在筹办期间，就承担了为布吉中学建设筹款的工作，共筹集捐款几十万元。1983 年 12 月 11 日，布吉侨联正式成立，江运灵出任主席。从此，他长期往返奔波于深圳和香港之间，为侨务工作尽心尽力，义务奉献。

2015 年 4 月 11 日，江运灵率队前往河源市和平县礼士镇深圳侨联中心小学，带去了布吉侨联捐赠的新书桌和课外读物。

On April 11, 2015, Kong Wan Ling led a team to Shenzhen Federation of Returned Overseas Chinese Central Primary School in Lishi Township, Heping County, Heyuan City, bringing new desks and extracurricular books donated by the Buji Federation of Returned Overseas Chinese.

宣传家乡、凝聚侨心、招商引资、落实侨房政策、关爱困难归侨侨眷、支持社会公益慈善事业……江运灵带领布吉侨联在很多方面都取得了显著的成绩。在他和布吉侨联的带动下，华侨、归侨和港澳同胞也积极为扶贫救灾、助教助学等慷慨解囊。

逢年过节走访布吉敬老院是布吉侨联常年坚持的工作之一，每次江运灵都会用心地为老人们准备礼物和生活用品。几十年如一日的繁忙工作不仅没有让他退却，反而让他保持了良好的工作状态，使他常常忘记自己比敬老院的一些老人还年长。

在龙岗区的支持下，2000年12月，江运灵带领旅港乡亲成立了香港深圳布吉同乡总会并担任理事长。在他的带领下，同乡总会由理事们共同捐资兴办，很快就红红火火地运转起来。这是1993年龙岗建区后最早成立的香港同乡会。

江运灵清楚地记得，2001年3月3日，星期六，香港深圳布吉同乡总会在港举行成立庆典，这个日子寓意着"三三不尽，六六无穷"。这句话原意是指用3或6去除10，永远除不尽。选这一天，就是希望同乡总会永永远远、长长久久地办下去。

多年来，香港深圳布吉同乡总会坚持"爱国、爱港、爱乡"的宗旨，广泛联系和团结旅港同乡，在推动深港合作、促进家乡发展等方面发挥了桥梁和纽带作用。

通过侨联和同乡总会的平台，以及自己的广阔人脉，江运灵推动了很多事项的落地，比如兴建布吉侨联大厦。江运灵竭尽全力，带领、发动海内外乡亲、好友和热心人士为这座大厦的建设捐资。2007年，总投资1200万元、总建筑面积7000平方米、楼高9层的布吉侨联大厦建成，进一步增强了为侨服务的能力，也让广大归侨、侨眷以及海外侨胞有了一个布吉的"侨之家"。

近些年，布吉的行政区划经历了多次调整，从布吉区改为布吉镇，又改为布吉街道，后来又分设为布吉、南湾、坂田、吉华共4个街道。与此相对

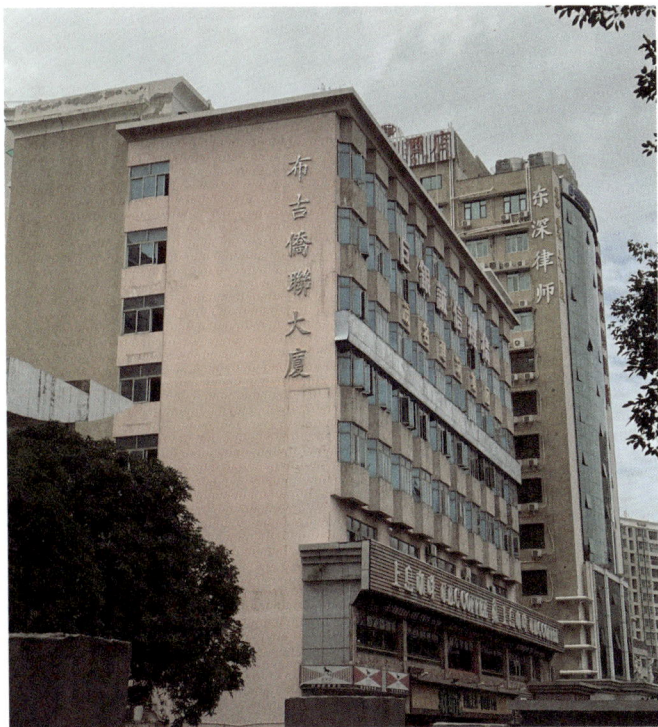

布吉侨联大厦。

The Building of the Buji Federation of Returned Overseas Chinese.

应，南湾、坂田、吉华的在港同乡会也建立了起来，对每一个组织的成长，江运灵都投入了长久的关心。4 个同乡会在港购置办公场所，他总是率先捐资相助。前不久，他还出资在香港组织了一场布吉、坂田、南湾、吉华乡亲联谊会，邀请 4 个同乡会的现任和前任理事近 100 人，共话乡情，共谋和谐发展。

2023 年 10 月 20 日，江运灵（中）在布吉、坂田、南湾、吉华乡亲联谊会上祝酒。
Kong Wan Ling (middle) toasts at a gathering for hometown fellows from Buji, Bantian, Nanwan and Jihua on October 20, 2023.

牵线搭桥，参访行程有讲究

侨联是党和政府联系广大归侨侨眷和海外侨胞的纽带和桥梁。每次到国外出差、旅行，江运灵总是把握一切机会向当地华侨华人宣传中国的政策、家乡的情况，随后也会把在海外的所见所闻汇报给政府，不断促进双方彼此深入了解，起到了很好的沟通桥梁作用。

他还引导和组织美国、加拿大、英国、马来西亚、特立尼达和多巴哥等国的侨胞和国际友人相继来深圳参观访问，亲身了解今时今日的中国。

2018 年，美国新奥尔良的 11 位友好人士应布吉侨联之邀访问深圳，他们中有医生、教师、律师、工程师、建筑师等，此前都没有到访过深圳。江运灵悉心安排了行程：从罗湖乘车，沿滨河大道、滨海大道到南头，在五星级酒店吃午餐，再经深南大道来到位于市民中心的深圳博物馆参观，一日尽览深圳今昔；然后在京基100大厦里的酒店下榻，次日参观温馨的布吉敬老院、江运灵在下李朗的祖屋、充满客家风情的甘坑小镇、现代化的盐田港码头，从多个角度感受这座都市的发展步伐。

江运灵在策划同乡总会到内地的参访活动时，也特别花心思，把爱国主义教育悄无声息地体现在行程中。他们去过香港供水的重要水源地——河源万绿湖，去过长沙、韶山、井冈山等革命圣地，还参访过叶剑英元帅的故乡梅县以及台山等侨乡。所到之处有故事更有历史，深深震撼了每一位前往的香港同胞。

2018年11月，广深港高铁香港段开通不久，香港深圳东部各同乡会湖南参访团一行约600人坐高铁专列由香港西九龙直达长沙。江运灵以香港深圳布吉同乡总会理事长的身份带队，对湖南进行了4天的参观考察。江运灵在港湘联谊晚会上表示："短短三个半小时，我们就来到了长沙，亲身体验了一日千里的高铁线路和'一地两检'的便利，共享国家发展红利，让我等深感自豪。"

重视教育，喜看后辈成栋梁

江运灵深信知识可以改变命运，对子女的教育更是分外重视。他有两儿两女，小女儿早年因风湿性心脏病不幸去世，其他三个都学业有成，现在从事建筑师、律师等专业工作。江运灵供孩子们上学很舍得投入。比如，大儿子在美国留学时，一年学费4万多美元。那时候，4万多美元在香港买套房都绰绰有余，但江运灵和妻子宁愿拿这些钱供孩子完成学业。

江运灵特别强调，在孩子的教育上，妻子功劳很大。孩子在家里全靠她辅导功课，特别是英语。"我英文当然没有她那么好啦！"每天，孩子们做完作业，她会检查一遍，收拾好书包，还会检查校服熨烫得"靓不靓、直不直"。这种细心和爱温暖了整个家庭。

看到家乡一些后辈成才，江运灵也感到由衷的欣慰。有一次，几位老同学说起他们的孙子已经大学毕业了，江运灵说："我最喜欢听的就是这些！"

江运灵还注意到，下李朗现在的领导班子都很年轻，大概40岁出头。看到后辈们这么年轻有为，他由衷地高兴。

2023年10月，12位在港发展的青年同乡找到江运灵，登门请教，"运灵叔"满心欢喜地招待了他们，面授机宜，毫无保留地分享人生所得。

为什么乡亲们爱找"运灵叔"？为什么他能做成那么多事情？江运灵解释，自己有信誉，所以"江运灵"3个字"值钱"。"因为信誉在，一心为大家办事，我一出声，个个都支持、赞助，所以事情就办成了。"

江运灵总结说："家乡时时刻刻都在我脑海里。我的付出并不为求多大回报，只要家乡好就行。"

在下李朗的一次千人大盆菜活动中，江运灵上台演讲，让众人乐开了花。他记得当时自己这么说："我今天回来，好开心啊！因为车一进来，就看到那么多高楼大厦。你们不要误会啊，没有一栋是我的。虽然没有我的，但我也一样开心，因为假如我们村人人都拥有大厦，我回到家乡，肯定个个要争着请吃饭，这个不请，那个也会请，因为大家都是有钱人了嘛！"

"布政从仁，唯愿人民衣食足；吉临桑梓，遵行法令国家强。"这是 30 多年前江运灵送给家乡的一副藏头对联，里面就藏着"布吉"两字。如今，家乡的发展变化，已经远远超出了他当初的期待。

［除署名外，本文图片均由受访者江运灵提供。参考资料：《绿叶对根的深情》、深圳市委统战部网站、红网。布吉街道党政综合办（统侨办）汪娟而对本文亦有贡献。］

Kong Wan Ling

A key motivator with a pure heart goes all out to repay his hometown

Kong Wan Ling was born in Lilang, Buji, Shenzhen in December 1935. (His birthplace now belongs to Xialilang Community, Nanwan Subdistrict, Longgang District.) Kong is an honorary citizen of Shenzhen Municipality, chairman of the Shenzhen Buji Federation of Returned Overseas Chinese, honorary chairman of the Longgang District Federation of Returned Overseas Chinese, board chairman of the Shenzhen Buji Society Hong Kong, and permanent honorary president of the Shenzhen Bantian Association of Hong Kong. He went to Hong Kong in 1956 to study, and later stayed in Hong Kong to develop his career in import and export trade, among others. He used to provide emergency relief for many fellow villagers and donated production materials to his hometown. Since the reform and opening-up, he has actively promoted the investment environment in his hometown, inspiring a group of Hong Kong and Macao compatriots and overseas Chinese to return to their hometown to invest and set up factories, and making great contributions to the economic growth and the development of various undertakings in the Buji area.

Kong is enthusiastic about social welfare and has been engaged in the work of the federations of returned overseas Chinese for 40 years. He has been chairman of the Buji Federation of Returned Overseas Chinese for a long time. In 2000, he led fellow immigrants in Hong Kong to establish the Shenzhen Buji Society Hong Kong. The Buji Federation of Returned Overseas Chinese mobilized fellow residents and enthusiasts at home and abroad to donate money to build the Building of the Buji Federation of Returned Overseas Chinese, which was completed in 2007, further enhancing the federation's ability to serve overseas Chinese. In 2004, Kong won the "Award for Contribution to the Undertaking of the Federations of Returned Overseas Chinese" of the system of the federations of returned overseas Chinese in Guangdong Province and the "Contribution Award for 20 Years' Work in Overseas Chinese Affairs" of Shenzhen Municipality. In

---

The interview took place in 2023.

2006, he was awarded the certificate of working for more than 20 years for the federations of returned overseas Chinese by the All-China Federation of Returned Overseas Chinese. He has also won the "Contribution Award for Working for Overseas Chinese Affairs of Shenzhen Municipality," "Advanced Individual of the System of the Federations of Returned Overseas Chinese in Shenzhen Municipality" and other honors.

One noon in October 2023, Kong Wan Ling looked around in a restaurant on the third floor of a hotel in Kowloon, Hong Kong. He found several familiar faces, all of whom were his old friends in Hong Kong.

Kong often comes to this hotel. Thirteen years ago, he and his wife hosted a banquet of more than 30 tables on the sixth floor here to celebrate their golden wedding (the 50th wedding anniversary). In 2020, they celebrated their diamond wedding (the 60th wedding anniversary) and booked 30 tables here. However, the banquet was canceled because of the COVID-19 pandemic, which became his biggest regret. "Wouldn't it be perfect to celebrate the diamond wedding and have a photo taken?"

"But she left me in January 2023." Kong, who is nearly 88 years old, is energetic, clear in thinking, and funny in conversation. However, when talking about his wife, he choked up and shed tears several times. They were together for more than 60 years. When he ran businesses, helped his fellow villagers, supported his hometown, and dealt with overseas Chinese affairs, he always received unconditional support from his wife, allowing him to focus on pursuing and realizing what he wanted step by step.

In Kong's story, there are the happiness of love at first sight and lifelong mutual support, as well as the achievements of caring for his hometown and repaying all the kindness. He values emotional ties and friendship, has good credit, and explains the profound in simple and down-to-earth terms. These may be his magic weapons to impress people and get the ball rolling.

Having a rocky childhood, knowing how to work hard and make progress

According to Kong, the place where he was born and grew up was a Hakka village originally called Lilang Village, which was later divided into Shanglilang (meaning "Upper Lilang") and Xialilang (meaning "Lower Lilang"). His family belongs to Xialilang, and Kong (Jiang) is the most common surname there.

But his life had a rough start. When he was 8 months old, his father went to Malaya to make a living. (Malaya merged with several other places to form Malaysia in 1963.)

When he was 4 years old, his mother died. He and his sister depended on each other and were raised by his aunt and grandaunt. Lilang's primary school was run by members of the Jiang clan, and enrolled children in the clan free of charge. However, during the Japanese invasion of China, the school was not free as a result of underfunding. Although Kong had excellent academic performance, he dropped out of school because his poor family could not afford the tuition. The principal felt very sorry when learning about it, and specially applied for a fee exemption for him, so that he could continue his studies.

After the Anti-Japanese War ended in 1945, Kong's father was heard from and began to send money back to support him through junior high school. Kong worked hard and achieved good results all the way. The teachers taught in Cantonese, which also laid the language foundation for him to venture into Hong Kong later.

In 1951, when Lilang's school was short of hands, Kong became a primary school teacher. With his good teaching skills, he gradually became famous in that area. Three years later, he was transferred to Buji Central Primary School. Later, as the political situation changed, his overseas relations brought uncertainty for him. He was transferred to the remote Wushiyan (today's Shiyan Subdistrict, Bao'an District), feeling confused about his future. It was a time when returned overseas Chinese and relatives of overseas Chinese could apply to leave, so Kong decided to study in Hong Kong, finish high school there and come back to take the college entrance.

Because of changes in the situation and his personal circumstances, Kong's plan failed to come true. "I never went to college in my life, and now I still feel regretful about it."

Fortunately, although a door closed, a window opened.

Studying in Hong Kong, meeting a happy fate from thousands of miles away

On September 16, 1956, Kong arrived in Hong Kong. He went to study English during the day and went to accounting school at night. In 1957, he went to Malaya to meet his father, who sold goods such as radios and bicycles and wanted him to stay and take over the businesses. But Kong decided to return to Hong Kong after staying there for three months.

At that time, Kong was frail and sickly, and his father wouldn't be at ease to let him live alone, so he arranged for him to stay in a company in Hong Kong. In 1960, a young woman named Shirley Chang went to play in the company, where she met Kong and fell in love with him at first sight.

This company was opened by a fellow villager surnamed Ling from Lilang, and Chang was a relative of one of the company's shareholders. She came from Trinidad and Tobago (called "Qianlida" by the older generation of overseas Chinese). Her family was the richest overseas Chinese merchant in Trinidad and Tobago, and her mother was from Guanlan, Shenzhen. Born and raised in Trinidad and Tobago, Chang had received a British-style education since childhood and could not speak Chinese. After graduating from high school, she helped her parents run the family business. This time, she came to Hong Kong for a short stay at the suggestion of her mother in order to get in touch with Chinese society. Unexpectedly, it turned out to be a happy fate coming from thousands of miles away, and she stayed in Hong Kong after that.

At first, Chang's parents were very worried about this. However, seeing that she had made up her mind, they had no choice but to write a letter inviting the young couple to move to Trinidad and Tobago and live together with them. Chang then let Kong make the decision. As he didn't want to be far away from his hometown and took his future development into account, Kong decided to stay in Hong Kong and start a career with his own hands. On October 1, 1960, Kong married Chang. He specially chose the National Day of the People's Republic of China to held a wedding banquet in the most "magnificent" restaurant in Kowloon.

Helping the poor and those in emergencies, showing affection for his homeland and fellow villagers

In 1961, Kong opened a trading company named "Bak Seon Hong" in Central, Hong Kong, embarking on the road of doing business. Due to his eagerness to learn and his proficiency in English, he quickly rose to prominence in the industry and gained a foothold. In addition, he successively opened a sewing thread factory and a tourism company, and invested in a takeaway restaurant in Britain.

Kong has always been full of trust in his fellow villagers. The sewing thread factory was a partnership with a fellow villager from Lilang, and the takeaway restaurant was funded by Kong and operated by several fellow villagers from Lilang. A cousin of Kong had a different view on this. She said to Kong, "You have provided money for the other people to run the factory. Now he lives in a villa and rides in a big car, but what about you?" Kong didn't care much about this. He replied, "The one living in a villa and riding in a big car is also surnamed Kong! Would you be happy only when someone surnamed Kong becomes a beggar?"

Kong also received strong support from his wife. "My wife never complained about what I did. She never blamed me by saying, 'You trust others so much? That's all money!'"

Hong Kong is where Kong has developed his career, while his hometown is his long-term concern. He knows very well that it was the support of his relatives and fellow villagers that enabled him to complete his studies and accumulate experience in these difficult years. When drinking water, one should remember where it comes from. After receiving kindness from others, one should seek ways to repay it. With a successful career, Kong has provided various financial aids to his fellow villagers and various undertakings in his hometown. After the reform and opening-up, he took the lead in returning to his hometown to invest, and has devoted his enthusiasm to the affairs of the federations of returned overseas Chinese and hometown associations. His wife always silently accompanied him and gave him full support, harboring no regrets.

In 1961, Shenzhen suffered a severe drought, when farmland irrigation needed water pumped from rivers and ponds. After learning about the disaster, Kong bought three water pumps and several tons of fertilizer, and asked a transportation company to deliver them to Xialilang. Later, he donated books, musical instruments and sports equipment, among others, to Xialilang's school. In 1979, in a bid to support the development of his hometown, Kong responded to the call of the hometown and mobilized fellow villagers in Hong Kong to donate money to buy two trucks, which was given to Xialilang.

In those years, Kong often received letters asking for help from his relatives, friends and old acquaintances, and he was so warm-hearted that he always provided assistance within his ability. From time to time, he took in fellow villagers who had just arrived in Hong Kong. "I not only treated them to meals, but also gave money to the fellow villagers for buying clothes."

Responding to the call, taking the lead in investing in his hometown

At the beginning of the reform and opening-up, Kong's hometown sent messages to him, hoping that he could go back for a visit. However, like many fellow immigrants in Hong Kong, he still had concerns and did not dare to go back rashly. In July 1982, Buji Commune sent three officials to Hong Kong to convene a meeting with Buji natives in Hong Kong. Kong gave his full help and booked a banquet at a restaurant in Tai Po. About 70 to 80 people came from all over Hong Kong, wanting to get more news about their hometown. When Kong was about to pay for the banquet alone, Lau Cyun, a native of Bantian, insisted on sharing the expenses equally with him. They were both impressed by each other, and became good partners when they went back to their hometown to found the federation of returned overseas Chinese.

The party that night was a success. The officials from Buji explained the latest reform and opening-up policies and overseas Chinese policies to the Buji natives in Hong Kong, introduced the situation in their hometown, and called on them to return to invest and donate to build schools. The immigrants had a great time chatting with the officials from their hometown, and their worries were gradually eliminated.

In 1983, Buji changed from a commune to a district. In September of that year, taking advantage of the completion of the district government's new office building, Buji invited overseas Chinese and compatriots in Hong Kong and Macao to return to their hometown for the opening ceremony. Kong took his wife on their first trip back to his hometown. The roads in his hometown were potholed, and their ride in a car was very bumpy. They were bounced up from time to time, with their heads thumping against the roof. Although the journey was hard, his heart was filled with the joy of reunion after a long absence.

On that trip back to his hometown, Kong made two decisions. First, he donated 3,000 Hong Kong dollars to Buji for purchasing office desks and chairs. Second, the leaders of Buji formally invited him to serve as chairman of the Buji Federation of Returned Overseas Chinese, and, after careful consideration, he decided to accept the invitation and shoulder the heavy responsibility.

Soon, Kong invested more than 3 million Hong Kong dollars on factory buildings in Xialilang. He also took advantage of having many friends and extensive contacts to actively promote the investment environment in his hometown. With his leadership and mobilization, compatriots in Hong Kong and Macao and overseas Chinese in Canada, the United States, Britain, the Netherlands and other countries, who were natives of Buji, returned to their hometown to invest and build factories, which greatly promoted Buji's economic development.

Kong paid close attention to the follow-up work of attracting investment. He often talked with returning investors to understand their needs and stabilize their confidence in a timely manner. "When there was a sign of trouble, you would tell me, or I would tell you. Then the matter would be exaggerated, and investor confidence would be shaken," he said. "So a persuasive person was needed to talk to others."

Dedicated to overseas Chinese affairs for decades

When the Buji Federation of Returned Overseas Chinese was being prepared, it took on the task of raising funds for the construction of Buji Middle School, and ended up with hundreds of thousands of yuan in donations. On December 11, 1983, the Buji Federation of Returned Overseas Chinese was formally established, with Kong as chairman. Since then, he has been traveling back and forth between Shenzhen and Hong Kong, working hard and dedicated to overseas Chinese affairs without pay.

Kong has led the federation to achieve remarkable results in many aspects, such as promoting the hometown, uniting overseas Chinese, attracting investment, implementing the policy for the houses of overseas Chinese, caring for the needy among returned overseas Chinese and relatives of overseas Chinese nationals residing in Buji, and supporting social welfare and charity. Inspired by him and the federation, overseas Chinese, returned overseas Chinese, and compatriots in Hong Kong and Macao have also actively contributed generously to poverty alleviation, disaster relief, and financial aid to teachers and students.

Visiting the Buji Nursing Home during festivals has been one of the tasks of the Buji Federation of Returned Overseas Chinese in all the years. Kong has carefully prepared gifts and daily necessities for the elderly every time. Decades of busy work has not deterred him, but has pushed him to maintain such a good mood that he often forgets that he is older than some of the elderly in the nursing home.

With the support of Longgang District, in December 2000, Kong led fellow immigrants in Hong Kong to establish the Shenzhen Buji Society Hong Kong and served as board chairman. Under his leadership, the society was founded with donations from the board members, and it soon began to prosper. This was Longgang's earliest hometown association in Hong Kong after the establishment of Longgang District in 1993.

Kong clearly remembers that on Saturday, March 3, 2001, the Shenzhen Buji Society Hong Kong held its founding celebration in Hong Kong. That day refers to "three and six are endless," which originally means that 3 or 6 will never divide into 10. That day was chosen in the hope that this hometown society would last forever.

Over the years, the Shenzhen Buji Society Hong Kong has adhered to its purpose of loving the country, loving Hong Kong and loving the hometown, and has extensively contacted and united hometown fellows in Hong Kong. It has acted as a bridge and a link in promoting cooperation between Shenzhen and Hong Kong and promoting the development of the hometown.

Through the platforms of the Buji Federation of Returned Overseas Chinese and the Shenzhen Buji Society Hong Kong, as well as his extensive network of contacts, Kong has promoted the implementation of many projects, such as the construction of the Building of the Buji Federation of Returned Overseas Chinese. Kong tried his best to lead and mobilize fellow residents, immigrants, friends and enthusiasts at home and abroad to donate funds for the construction of the building. In 2007, with a total investment of 12 million yuan and a total construction area of 7,000 square meters, the nine-story Building of the Buji Federation of Returned Overseas Chinese was completed, further enhancing the federation's ability to serve overseas Chinese and providing a "home" to returned overseas Chinese, relatives of overseas Chinese nationals residing in Buji, and overseas Chinese.

In recent years, the administrative division of Buji has undergone several adjustments. Buji District changed to Buji Township, and then to Buji Subdistrict, which was later divided into four subdistricts: Buji, Nanwan, Bantian, and Jihua. Correspondingly, Nanwan, Bantian and Jihua's hometown associations in Hong Kong were also established. Kong has devoted long-term care to the growth of each organization. When the four hometown associations purchased office space in Hong Kong, he was always the first to donate money to help. Not long ago, he funded and organized a gathering in Hong Kong for immigrants from Buji, Bantian, Nanwan and Jihua, inviting nearly 100 current and former board members of the four hometown associations to talk about their hometown and seek harmonious development.

Acting as a bridge, carefully planning tour itineraries

The federations of returned overseas Chinese are a kind of link and bridge for the Communist Party of China and the government to contact the vast number of returned overseas Chinese, relatives of overseas Chinese nationals residing in China, and overseas Chinese. Every time he goes on a business trip or travels abroad, Kong always seizes every opportunity to publicize China's policies and the situation in his hometown to overseas Chinese. When he comes back, he reports to the government what he has seen and heard overseas. Thus he constantly promotes mutual understanding, and plays a good role in communication.

He has also guided and organized overseas Chinese and foreign friends from the United States, Canada, Britain, Malaysia, Trinidad and Tobago and other countries to visit Shenzhen to learn firsthand about today's China.

In 2018, 11 friendly people from New Orleans in the United States visited Shenzhen at the invitation of the Buji Federation of Returned Overseas Chinese. Among them were doctors, teachers, lawyers, engineers, and architects, and they had never been to Shenzhen before. Kong carefully arranged the itinerary: taking a bus from Luohu to Nantou along Binhe Avenue and Binhai Avenue, having lunch at a five-star hotel, and then going to the Shenzhen Museum in the Civic Center via Shennan Avenue, so as to see the past and present of Shenzhen in one day; staying at a hotel in the Kingkey 100 building, and, the next day, visiting the cozy Buji Nursing Home, Kong's ancestral house in Xialilang, the Hakka-style town of Gankeng and the modern Yantian Port Terminal, in a bid to experience the pace of development of the city from multiple angles.

When planning the visits of members of the Shenzhen Buji Society Hong Kong to the mainland, Kong has also put special thought into quietly embodying patriotic education in the itineraries. They have been to the Wanlv Lake, the source of Hong Kong's water supply, and to revolutionary sites such as Changsha, Shaoshan and the Jinggang Mountains. They have also visited Meixian, the hometown of Marshal Ye Jianying, and hometowns of overseas Chinese such as Taishan. Wherever they went, all the Hong Kong compatriots were deeply moved by the stories and history there.

In November 2018, shortly after the Hong Kong section of the Guangzhou-Shenzhen-Hong Kong high-speed railway was opened, a team of about 600 people from eastern Shenzhen's hometown associations in Hong Kong visited Hunan Province. They took a high-speed train from West Kowloon, Hong Kong to Changsha. Kong, as board chairman of the Shenzhen Buji Society Hong Kong, led the team on a four-day visit to Hunan. He said at a Hong Kong-Hunan friendship evening party, "In just three and a half hours, we came to Changsha, experiencing firsthand the rapid development of the high-speed rail network and the convenience of 'co-location, two inspections,' and sharing the dividends of the country's development, which has made us very proud."

Valuing education, delighted to see younger generation become pillars of society

Kong firmly believes that knowledge can change destiny, and has attached great importance to the education of his children. He has had two sons and two daughters. His younger daughter died of rheumatic heart disease in her early years. The other three were all successful in their studies and are engaged in professional jobs such as architect and lawyer. Kong invested heavily on his children's education. For example, when his elder son studied in the United States, the tuition was more than US$40,000 a year, which was more than enough to buy an apartment in Hong Kong, but Kong and his wife would rather use the money to support their son in completing his studies.

Kong emphasized that his wife made a great contribution to their children's education. It was she who helped them with their homework, especially English. "Certainly, my English is not as good as hers!" Every day, after the children finished their homework, she would check it, pack their schoolbags, and make sure whether their school uniforms were "pretty and crisp" after ironing. This kind of care and love warmed the whole family.

Kong has also felt sincerely gratified to see some young people in his hometown become useful talents. One day, several former classmates of Kong said that their grandson had graduated from college. Kong said, "These are the things I most like to hear!"

Kong has also noticed that Xialilang's current leadership team is young, approximately in their early 40s. He is truly happy to see these promising young people.

In October 2023, 12 young hometown fellows developing in Hong Kong visited Kong for advice. "Uncle Wan Ling" entertained them with joy and taught them face to face, sharing his gains of life without reservation.

Why do Kong's hometown fellows like to seek help from "Uncle Wan Ling"? Why can he accomplish so many things? He has credibility, so the three characters of "Kong Wan Ling" are valuable, Kong explained. "Because I have credibility and am committed to doing things for all, everyone supports and sponsors me as soon as I ask for something. That's how the things have been done."

"My hometown is in my mind all the time. I don't seek much reward for what I have given, because I just want to benefit my hometown," Kong concluded.

At a treasure pot banquet for more than 1,000 people in Xialilang, Kong mounted the platform and gave a speech, which made the audience burst into laughter. He still remembers what he said at that time: "I'm so happy to come back today, because I saw so many high-rise buildings as soon as the car came in! Don't get me wrong. None of them are mine. Even though they are not mine, I am equally happy, because if everyone in our village owns a building, when I return to my hometown, everyone will definitely be vying to treat me to dinner. If this guy doesn't treat me, that guy will, because everyone gets rich!"

"May the government be benevolent, and I only hope that the people will have enough food and clothing. May good luck come to my hometown, and may the country be strong by obeying the laws and orders." This is an acrostic couplet Kong gave to his hometown more than 30 years ago, with the word "Buji" hidden in it. Today, the development and changes in his hometown have far exceeded his expectations.

[Photos courtesy of Kong Wan Ling, except for those with credit. References: *Green Leaves' Deep Affection for Roots*, the website of the United Front Work Department of the CPC Shenzhen Municipal Committee, and rednet.cn. Wang Juaner from the Party and Government Comprehensive Office (United Front Work and Overseas Chinese Affairs Office) of Buji Subdistrict has also contributed to this article.]

萧树强

"钢铁大王"对故乡的似水柔情，绵延到了东江源头

萧树强　Siu Shu Keung

　　萧树强，1942年出生，深圳宝安松岗江边人，1960年赴香港谋生，1969年开始创业，从事钢铁安装工程。香港深圳社团总会创会会长兼主席、世界深东社团联会创会会长兼主席、深圳市首届荣誉市民、深圳市政协第四届常委、深圳市归国华侨联合会荣誉主席、深圳侨商国际联合会创会名誉会长。

　　萧树强积极在深圳投资兴业，协助深圳招商引资，推动深港交流合作，热心社会公益，资助建设松岗人民医院和多所学校，牵头创立世界深东社团联会和香港深圳社团总会，团结居港深圳籍和海外深圳籍乡亲，为香港繁荣稳定和深圳改革创新发展发挥了积极作用。在萧树强领导下，世界深东社团联会积极支持举办世界东安恳亲大会；香港深圳社团总会在河源市出资建设一所小学，为洪灾受灾群众重建住房，为贫困学生提供奖学金；与深圳市侨办共同发起"思源之旅"青少年夏令营活动，常年组织深港青年学生及海外华裔青少年赴东江源头——江西安远县考察，萧树强在当地捐建两所小学，并为中小学生提供资助。

采访时间：2022年。

"萧树强"在深港侨界是个响当当的名字。改革开放初期，他就回到家乡深圳办实业，投身社会公益事业。他用乡情"搭桥"，促进深港民间交流，拉近海外乡亲与家乡、与祖（籍）国的距离。他带头捐款救灾、兴学、扶贫，还参与发起"思源之旅"青少年夏令营活动，带领青少年认识深圳、探访东江源头、铭记血浓于水的同胞情谊。

他说："做人不能忘本，永远不要忘记自己的根在哪里。在力所能及的范围内，要多做有益于社会的事情，不要求回报。每一代人都有时代赋予的不同机遇和挑战，成功的道路从来不会是一条坦途，无论何时何地，青年人必须有一颗爱国的心和艰苦奋斗的精神。"

他经历过香港的大旱灾和非典疫情，也抓住了很多历史机遇。走过几十年风风雨雨，他感念祖国对香港一贯的关怀和支持。

"'爱国爱港爱深圳'的情怀以及对家乡的思念，一直深深烙印在我的心里。"他说。

公司取名，记挂家乡

萧树强出生长大的地方，是今天的深圳市宝安区松岗街道江边社区。顾名思义，这是一个依江靠水的地方。

据史料记载，萧氏先祖在南宋时从河南开封珠玑巷南迁到广东东莞麻涌，后又迁到东莞霄边，在明朝年间逐步迁到宝安松岗江边定居。他们的足迹，是古代中原汉族为躲避战乱和灾害而大量南迁的一个缩影。广东省南雄市也有一条著名的珠玑巷，因宋时从开封移居此地的官吏士民眷恋故土而得名。

萧树强 1942 年出生，18 岁离开家乡去香港谋生，从建筑钢铁安装工程学徒做起。1969 年，他开始创业，承接香港各类楼宇和基础设施建设的钢铁安装工程。

萧树强把这门生意做得风生水起，所以在香港有了"钢铁大王"的称号。经过多年艰苦拼搏，他的公司完成了超过 500 个钢铁安装工程项目。其中比较有代表性的，包括香港国际机场客运大楼、铜锣湾时代广场及中环交易广场等富有挑战性、对技术要求很高的工程项目。公司多次获得香港特区政府房屋署颁授的最佳钢铁安装奖项。除了老本行，公司还参与了房地产开发和项目投资等业务，迈向多元化发展。萧树强在业界享有很高的声望，被推选为香港建筑扎铁商会创会会长。

在萧树强名下的公司里，有两家的名字很有特色。

一是他早年创办的"萧强记钢铁工程有限公司"，选取了他自己名字的两个字，这也是香港很多大小老板的习惯。

二是"宝安工程有限公司"，但它并不在深圳宝安，而是地地道道的香港公司。这个名字，寄托了萧树强对家乡的强烈思念。再细细品味，它还镂刻着深圳和香港的历史渊源。宝安在东晋时的公元 331 年建县，当时的管辖范围大致相当于今天的深圳、东莞、香港、澳门、中山、珠海。

投资兴业，助力公益

深圳取得的发展成就，离不开萧树强这样的香港同胞的大力支持。他们投资家乡、发展经济，还热心参与公益事业。20 世纪 80 年代初，萧树强初次回到老家，乡亲们敲锣打鼓欢迎他，老婆婆、老叔公拄着拐杖走过来，孩子们打着赤脚跑过来。萧树强被乡情温暖着，但也发现，家乡还比较穷，基础设施也很落后。

据当年的村干部回忆，20 世纪 80 年代的江边村是一个以农业为主的贫困村，主要种植水稻、甘蔗、荔枝等。村民们除了做农活，还要出海打鱼。村里人出行去福永、沙井、东莞等地主要靠乘船，陆路只有几条泥巴土路，没有公交车，全靠步行，个别村民家里有自行车。

百业待兴的深圳，推行了一系列优惠政策，激发了广大侨胞、港澳同胞投资的热情。萧树强的回乡之旅也让他下定决心，要助力家乡的经济社会发展和慈善公益事业。

萧树强和家乡有关方面讨论得出了一揽子计划，建设幼儿园、小学、中学、敬老院、医院、桥梁、道路，都在这个规划之中。萧树强深知工程启动难，自己就率先投资甚至无偿捐助。

萧树强从 1985 年开始回乡办实业，在宝安松岗投资 1 亿多港元发展水产养殖、房地产等。他还大力宣传改革开放，协助深圳方在香港开展招商引资工作，联系深圳籍侨胞和港商，鼓励和协助他们回深圳投资兴业。

1986 年，萧树强捐资 13 万港元兴建松岗江边小学，捐资 23 万港元兴建松岗中学教学大楼，捐资 30 万港元兴建沙井中学教学大楼，并为一些困难学生提供每人 3000 元的奖学金。1987 年，他倡导并捐资 130 万港元兴建松岗萧树强医院，这就是后来的松岗人民医院。他还把医院大楼前的一块地买下来，捐赠给医院作未来扩建之用，后来的事实证明了他的远见。他还多次向宝安区和龙岗区的

深圳市宝安区松岗人民医院。
The Songgang People's Hospital, Bao'an District, Shenzhen.

残联、儿童福利基金会等社会福利机构捐款。多年来，他对家乡的捐助总计将近1000 万元。

在萧树强的带动下，很多香港同胞和海外侨胞纷纷在深圳投资兴业或捐资兴办公益事业，蔚然成风。

1994 年，深圳首次颁授"荣誉市民"称号，以此表彰对深圳有突出贡献的人士，萧树强就在其中。

创办社团，凝聚乡情

萧树强用乡情"搭桥"，还做了很多事情，促进了深港民间交流，拉近了海外的深圳籍乡亲与家乡、与祖国的距离。2001 年 11 月，萧树强在香港牵头成立世界深东社团联会并出任会长。

这里的"深东"，是深圳和东莞的合称，跟有些侨团用的"东安"（东莞和宝安）是同样的含义。历史上，宝安县曾改名为东莞县，后来又从东莞县分出了新安县。尽管行政区划时合时分，但两地乡亲渊源深厚，去海外发展也不忘抱团。世界深东社团联会把深圳、东莞乡亲组成的 100 多个各类社团、商号组织到一起，弘扬中华文化，加强经贸交流，助力祖国和平统一和家乡经济社会繁荣进步。联会创立时，恰逢中国加入世界贸易组织，这也为海外华商回乡投资带来了新的历史机遇。

联会成立不久，就参与主办了 2002 年的第五届世界东安恳亲大会。这个恳亲大会始于 1992 年，是马来西亚、新加坡和中国香港等地的东莞、深圳籍乡亲发起的活动，后来发展为每三年举办一次。世界深东社团联会创立后，每逢恳亲大会召开，都积极支持和参与。

联会的成立，还为后来打造香港深圳社团总会这艘深港乡亲社团"航母"奠定了基础。萧树强回忆说，创立联会那年，他就有了成立香港深圳社团总会的念头。当时深圳已是一个新兴大都会，旅港深圳乡亲多达几十万人，但散落在港的深圳乡亲组织只有原来的同乡会，例如宝安同乡会等，甚至深圳有些新设立的区在港没有对应的、组织完善的同乡会，要组织深圳各区的旅港乡亲一起活动很不容易。

随着中国加入世界贸易组织以及香港与内地的联系日益紧密，把旅港乡亲更好地组织起来，可以更好地发挥优势，为香港的繁荣稳定和家乡发展作出更大的贡献。萧树强觉得，这事刻不容缓，而且自己责无旁贷。深圳市人大外事侨务工委、市侨办、市政协港澳台侨和外事委、市侨联也很支持他筹建香港深圳社团总会。

大疫之年，风雨兼程

筹建香港深圳社团总会的日子里，萧树强披星戴月，东奔西走，联络在港的深圳籍知名人士。他每天至少 15 个小时在外奔波，其中 8 小时是做社团工作，对个人事业都没有这么用心用情用力，但他觉得自己的付出是值得的。他说："创办社团，需要很多愿意出钱，或愿意出力，或既愿出钱又愿出力的有心人，我有幸遇到了很多这样的乡亲。"

经过大约两年的准备，2003年初，香港深圳社团总会到了酝酿成立筹备委员会的阶段。这一年，对于香港，对于总会，都可谓峰回路转、柳暗花明。

那是一个艰难的年份，非典型肺炎（英文缩写SARS，香港音译为"沙士"）肆虐香港，社会上弥漫着一股悲观的情绪。这个时候，总会在提振社会信心、团结乡亲联络乡情、凝聚爱国爱港力量方面的责任显得更重了。

但也有现实的困难：市民们害怕感染病毒，无事不出门，所以约人谈事很不容易。凭着满腔诚意和念兹在兹的乡情，萧树强引导大家做好个人防护，克服对病毒的恐惧，保持了有效的沟通。总会的筹备委员会终于在当年6月成立，萧树强被推举为筹委会主任。

同样是在6月，发生了一件意义非凡的大事：《内地与香港关于建立更紧密经贸关系的安排》（CEPA）由商务部和香港特别行政区财政司签署并实施。这是内地第一个全面实施的自由贸易协议，帮助众多香港制造企业站稳脚跟、快速发展，为香

2003年12月28日，香港深圳社团总会在深圳五洲宾馆举行成立大会，萧树强（右）和时任深圳市委副书记庄礼祥在大会上。

Siu Shu Keung (right) and Zhuang Lixiang, then deputy secretary of the Shenzhen Municipal Committee of the Communist Party of China, attend the inaugural meeting of the Federation of Hong Kong Shenzhen Associations on December 28, 2003.

港企业和专业服务者打开了内地的广阔市场，巩固和提升了香港的国际金融中心地位与竞争力，也拉开了内地居民个人赴港旅游的序幕。CEPA在非典之年横空出世，后续又签署了一些补充协议。CEPA的成功实践证明，内地始终是香港抵御风浪、战胜挑战的坚强后盾。

2003年12月，香港深圳社团总会成立，萧树强出任会长兼主席。在他的带领下，深圳籍的香港乡亲们更加团结了。他们抓住CEPA带来的大好机遇，发挥优势，为香港的繁荣稳定和深圳的改革创新发展作出了积极贡献。

萧树强说，香港的繁荣稳定，也是融入国家发展大局的结果。香港同胞大力支持改革开放，而改革开放也对香港的发展起到了推动作用。

精打细算，购置会址

香港深圳社团总会的创办过程，除了家国情怀的宏大叙事，还有一段体现眼光和魄力的"小插曲"。

人不论贫富，总希望有个属于自己的家。有见识的总会筹委们，也意识到要为这个新组织找个"家"。香港先后遭受了亚洲金融危机和非典疫情的冲击，房价在几年里跌了一半才企稳，置业的好时机有可能稍纵即逝。如果等香港深圳社团总会完成注册之后再出手抄底，还来得及吗？

难题很快被萧树强破解了。在咨询律师意见后，他联合另外两位深圳籍在港贤达，跟筹委会签订了一份合约，承诺先由他们购买物业，日后以原价卖给香港深圳社团总会。就这样，他们用200多万港元买下了九龙的一处房产作为会址，筹委会的6名正副主任都出钱垫资。后来总会发展壮大了，搬到了别的地点办公，但这个旧会址依然是社团的重要资产。

萧树强在香港深圳社团总会连续担任了三届会长，为总会的蓬勃发展打下了良好的基础。总会一直热心社会公益，弘扬传统美德，心系青年成长，促进深港交流。

感恩回报，饮水思源

发动居港的深圳乡亲捐款救灾、兴学、扶贫，是香港深圳社团总会一直在做的事情，也是萧树强身体力行的事情。

2004年，总会斥资400万元，在广东省河源市和平县兴建了下车镇香港深圳社团总会中心小学。2006年、2007年，和平县接连遭遇洪灾，总会先后捐出50万元，帮助受灾村民重建家园。

2005年，总会与深圳市侨办共同发起"思源之旅"青少年夏令营活动，每年暑假组织香港、深圳的青年学生及海外华裔青少年认识深圳，感受深圳的蓬勃发展，再赴江西安远县考察。萧树强坚持多年亲身参加，还在那里捐建学校、资助学生。

2008 年，四川汶川地震，他捐款 500 万元；湖南雪灾，他捐款 60 万元。

萧树强与参加"思源之旅"的青少年交流。
Siu Shu Keung communicates with young people participating in the "Journey to the Source" youth summer camp.

总会在河源和安远的善举生动诠释了什么叫"饮水思源"。香港的淡水主要来自东江 – 深圳供水工程（简称"东深供水工程"），河源的万绿湖是主要蓄水源，东江的源头则在安远县。

"清清的东江水，日夜向南流。流进深圳，流进，流进了港九。"张也在《多情东江水》这首歌里唱的，就是东深供水工程。

香港三面环海，曾饱受淡水资源短缺的困扰。1963 年，香港遭受百年一遇的干旱，最严重时每 4 天才能供水 1 次，每次 4 个小时。广东施以援手，欢迎香港派船到珠江免费抽取淡水。1963 年 12 月，经周恩来总理特批，中央财政拨款 3800 万元，用于建设东深供水工程，引东江之水济香港同胞。

在艰苦的条件下，广东省动用上万人力，全国各地大力支援，只用了 1 年时间就完工。1965 年 3 月，东深供水工程正式向香港供水，终结了香港缺水的历史。经过 4 次扩建、改造，东深供水工程惠及沿线各地，满足了香港约 80% 的淡水需求，成为香港的一条生命线，支撑了香港的繁荣稳定。

萧树强在香港亲历过水荒。他深知，没有东江水，就不会有香港经济的腾飞，他的事业也不会有那么大的发展。

他在香港深圳社团总会会长任上参与发起"思源之旅"，就是希望青年一代能深入了解内地对香港一以贯之的关怀和深港两地"共饮一江水，情同手足"的故事，传承中国人饮水思源的良好品德。

2006年7月，萧树强带领深港学子考察东江源头时，发现三百山脚下的天心镇五龙小学只有几间低矮破旧的瓦房，他立即决定捐款重建。第二年5月，五龙小学就有了新的教学楼，圆了孩子们多年来的梦。后来，他又在天心镇捐建了心怀小学。

萧树强捐款重建的五龙小学。
The Wulong Primary School, which Siu Shu Keung donated to rebuild.

2007年，天心镇五龙村的钟富平、钟荣福兄弟俩同时考上了大学，但家里为学费犯了愁。在五龙小学开展"思源之旅"夏令营活动的萧树强了解到情况，当场决定帮助兄弟俩，资助他们大学四年的学费和一部分生活费。活动结束后，萧树强就把首期1万元爱心捐款送到他们手中，嘱咐他俩努力学习。一年后，萧树强又带领"思源之旅"夏令营的队伍来了，钟富平、钟荣福早早地到了五龙小学等候，再次当面感谢恩人。

同样在2007年，萧树强牵头捐资，以香港深圳社团总会的名义，在三百山建设了一座"思源亭"，多年后又斥资数十万元修葺翻新。

在"思源之旅"中，萧树强还为安远一中的学生以及五龙小学、心怀小学的师

萧树强夫妇（左四、左二）等人在思源亭前留影。

Siu Shu Keung (fourth from left), his wife (second from left) and others in front of the Pavilion for Thinking of the Source.

生分别提供助学金和奖教金。他跟安远一中对接，搭建了深港及安远三地学生互动交流的平台。一位受助学生的家长亲手纳了一双鞋垫送给萧树强，上面工工整整绣着四个字"好人平安"。

爱国爱港，家风传承

萧树强乐善好施，也惠及了香港社会大众。他曾担任香港著名慈善机构"保良局"总理，连续 29 年参与大型筹款活动，多次担任筹款活动联席主席。在他带动下，家人也积极参与慈善活动，有 5 名家庭成员曾担任"保良局"总理。人们经常看到萧树强夫妇带着儿女共同出席公益和社会活动。

萧树强在港创办社团，回乡投资、做公益，组织"思源之旅"并捐资助学，都有妻子萧莫静璇的助力和参与。她还是香港深圳社团总会的常务副会长和妇女委员会主任，她组织举办的"优秀父母"颁奖典礼已成为总会的品牌活动。

萧莫静璇活跃在多个社团，通过自己的方式支持深圳经济社会建设。1989 年，她携手香港同胞和海外侨胞成立了宝安县妇女儿童福利会。作为香港侨媛会创会会

萧树强夫妇　Siu Shu Keung and his wife

长，她多次组织香港及海外侨界女性回深圳参观交流。她目前担任香港特区选举委员会委员、深圳市侨联副主席等职务，还曾担任深圳市政协常委。

作为港澳侨界人士中的年青一代，萧树强的女儿萧燕珍一边打理家里公司的业务，一边积极投身社会活动，担任香港深圳社团总会副会长、深圳市政协委员、深圳市侨联常委、广东省青联委员等职务。2020年3月在新冠疫情初期，留守深圳的她受父母所托，向宝安区妇女儿童福利会捐赠了一批防疫物资。

她还记得，从小到大，"爱国爱港爱深圳"就是家庭教育和精神传承的重要部分。

在她身上，这种传承已经开花结果。

（本文图片均由受访者萧树强提供。参考资料：《深圳侨务史志》、《深圳古代史》、《宝安日报》、《深圳侨报》，新华社、河南省人民政府网站、中国侨网、中国水利网、中国文明网、金羊网。）

Siu Shu Keung

The Steel King's tenderness for his hometown extends to the source of Dongjiang River

Siu Shu Keung, born in 1942, is a native of Jiangbian, Songgang, Bao'an, Shenzhen. He went to Hong Kong to make a living in 1960, and started his business in 1969, engaged in steel installation projects. He is founding president and founding chairman of the Federation of Hong Kong Shenzhen Associations, and founding president and founding chairman of the World Organisation of Shenzhen and Dongguan Associations. He was one of the first honorary citizens of Shenzhen Municipality, and member of the Standing Committee of the Fourth Shenzhen Municipal Committee of the Chinese People's Political Consultative Conference. He is honorary chairman of the Shenzhen Federation of Returned Overseas Chinese, and founding honorary president of the Shenzhen Overseas Chinese International Association.

Siu has actively invested in Shenzhen, assisted Shenzhen in attracting investment, promoted exchanges and cooperation between Shenzhen and Hong Kong. He has also been enthusiastic about social welfare. He funded the construction of the Songgang People's Hospital and several schools. He led the founding of the World Organisation of Shenzhen and Dongguan Associations and the Federation of Hong Kong Shenzhen Associations, which has united immigrants from Shenzhen living in Hong Kong and overseas to play a positive role in the prosperity and stability of Hong Kong and the reform, innovation and development of Shenzhen. Under his leadership, the World Organisation of Shenzhen and Dongguan Associations actively supported the holding of the Dong-An World Conference, the Federation of Hong Kong Shenzhen Associations funded the construction of a primary school, rebuilt houses for flood victims, and provided scholarships for poor students in Heyuan City, and jointly launched the "Journey to the Source" youth summer camp with the Overseas Chinese Affairs Office of the Shenzhen Municipal People's Government, organizing young students from Shenzhen and Hong Kong as well as overseas Chinese youths to visit the source of the Dongjiang River in Anyuan County, Jiangxi Province.

The interview took place in 2022.

Siu donated to build two primary schools in Anyuan and provided financial support for primary and secondary students there.

Siu Shu Keung is a well-known name in the overseas Chinese communities in Shenzhen and Hong Kong. In the early days of China's reform and opening-up, he returned to his hometown of Shenzhen to start businesses and devote himself to social welfare undertakings. He has "built bridges" based on homesickness, promoting non-governmental exchanges between Shenzhen and Hong Kong, and bringing overseas Chinese closer to their hometown and home country. He took the lead in donating money for disaster relief, building schools, and helping the poor. He participated in the launch of the "Journey to the Source" youth summer camp, leading young people to know Shenzhen, visit the source of the Dongjiang River, and remember the compatriot relationship showing that blood is thicker than water.

He said, "One should never forget his origin or forget where his roots are. One should do as many things as possible that are beneficial to the society without asking for rewards. Every generation has different opportunities and challenges given by the times. The road to success is never a smooth one. No matter when and where, young people must have a patriotic heart and the spirit of hard work."

He experienced a severe drought in Hong Kong and the SARS epidemic, and seized many historical opportunities. After decades of ups and downs, he is grateful for the motherland's consistent care and support for Hong Kong.

"The feeling of 'love the country, love Hong Kong, and love Shenzhen' and the nostalgia for my hometown have always been deeply imprinted in my heart," he said.

Naming his companies after his hometown

The place where Siu was born and raised is today's Jiangbian Community, Songgang Subdistrict, Bao'an District, Shenzhen. As its name suggests, that community is by the river.

According to historical records, Siu's ancestors moved from Zhuji Lane, Kaifeng, Henan Province to Machong, Dongguan, Guangdong Province in the Southern Song Dynasty, and then moved to Xiaobian, Dongguan, before gradually moving to Jiangbian, Songgang, Bao'an to settle during the Ming Dynasty. Their journey was a microcosm of the ancient Han people in the Central Plains who migrated southward in large numbers to escape wars and disasters. There is also a famous Zhuji Lane in Nanxiong City,

Guangdong Province, which was named because the officials and people who moved there from Kaifeng in the Song Dynasty were nostalgic for their homeland.

Siu was born in 1942. At the age of 18, he left his hometown and went to Hong Kong to make a living. He started as an apprentice in steel installation for construction projects. In 1969, he started his business, undertaking steel installation projects for various buildings and infrastructure construction in Hong Kong.

He got the title of "Steel King" in Hong Kong as a result of his flourishing business. After years of hard work, his companies have completed more than 500 steel installation projects. The representative ones include the terminal buildings of the Hong Kong International Airport, Times Square in Causeway Bay, and Exchange Square in Central, which are challenging and have high technical requirements. The companies have won the best steel installation award for many times from the Housing Department of the Hong Kong government. In addition to their traditional business, the companies are also involved in real estate development and project investment, moving towards diversified development. Siu enjoys a high reputation in the industry and was elected as founding president of the Hong Kong Bar-Bending Contractors Association.

Among his companies, there are two with distinctive names.

One is Siu Keung Kee Constructions & Iron Works Limited, which he founded in the early years. He put two of the three characters of his name to the company's name, as many bosses in Hong Kong have done.

The other is Po On Engineering Ltd. As an out-and-out Hong Kong company, it's not in Bao'an (Po On), Shenzhen. The name shows Siu's strong longing for his hometown. It you savor it carefully, you can find the historical ties between Shenzhen and Hong Kong. Bao'an was established as a county in AD 331 during the Eastern Jin Dynasty, and its jurisdiction at that time was roughly equivalent to today's Shenzhen, Dongguan, Hong Kong, Macao, Zhongshan, and Zhuhai.

Investing in business and helping with public welfare

Shenzhen's development achievements are inseparable from the strong support of Hong Kong compatriots like Siu. They have invested in their hometown to develop the economy, and enthusiastically participated in public welfare undertakings. In the early 1980s, when Siu returned to his hometown for the first time, the villagers welcomed him with drums and gongs. The elderly walked over with crutches, and children ran over barefoot. Siu was touched by their warmth, but also found that his hometown was still relatively poor, with backward infrastructure.

Some village officials at that time recalled to the media that Jiangbian Village in the 1980s was a poor village dominated by agriculture, mainly growing rice, sugarcane, and litchi. In addition to doing farm work, some villagers also went fishing at sea. When people in the village went to Fuyong, Shajing, Dongguan and other places, they traveled mainly by boat. There were only a few dirt roads, and, with no buses, the villagers heavily relied on walking. Only a few villagers had bicycles at home.

With all kinds of industries waiting to be developed, Shenzhen implemented a series of preferential policies, stimulating the enthusiasm for investment from overseas Chinese and compatriots in Hong Kong and Macao. Siu's trip back to his hometown also made him determined to help with the hometown's economic and social development as well as charity and public welfare undertakings.

Siu discussed with relevant parties in his hometown and came up with a package plan. Kindergartens, primary schools, middle schools, nursing homes, hospitals, bridges, and roads were all included in the plan. Siu knew that it was difficult to start the projects, so he took the lead in investing and even donating.

In 1985, Siu began to start businesses in his hometown, investing more than 100 million Hong Kong dollars to develop aquaculture and real estate in Songgang, Bao'an. He also vigorously publicized reform and opening-up, and assisted Shenzhen in attracting investment from Hong Kong. He contacted overseas Chinese and Hong Kong businessmen from Shenzhen, and encouraged and assisted them to invest and start businesses in Shenzhen.

In 1986, Siu donated 130,000 Hong Kong dollars to build the Songgang Jiangbian Primary School, 230,000 Hong Kong dollars to build the teaching building of the Songgang Middle School, and 300,000 Hong Kong dollars to build the teaching building of the Shajing Middle School, and provided scholarships of 3,000 yuan to some needy students. In 1987, he advocated and donated 1.3 million Hong Kong dollars to build the Songgang Siu Shu Keung Hospital, which later became the Songgang People's Hospital. He also bought a piece of land in front of the hospital building and donated it to the hospital for future expansion, and his foresight was proved later. He also donated money many times to social welfare organizations such as the disabled persons' federations and the children's welfare foundations in Bao'an District and Longgang District. Over the years, his donations to his hometown have totaled nearly 10 million yuan.

Driven by Siu, many Hong Kong compatriots and overseas Chinese invested in

Shenzhen or donated money to start public welfare undertakings, which became a common practice.

In 1994, Shenzhen awarded the title of Honorary Citizen for the first time in recognition of people who had made outstanding contributions to the city, and Siu was among the recipients.

Founding mass organizations to unite fellow immigrants

Siu has "built bridges" based on homesickness and done a lot of things to promote non-governmental exchanges between Shenzhen and Hong Kong, and to bring overseas Shenzhen folks closer to their hometown and motherland. In November 2001, Siu led the establishment of the World Organisation of Shenzhen and Dongguan Associations, in Hong Kong, and served as president.

The "Shen-Dong" in its Chinese name is the collective name of Shenzhen and Dongguan, with the same meaning as the "Dong-An" (Dongguan and Bao'an) used by some overseas Chinese groups. In history, Bao'an County was renamed Dongguan County, and Xin'an County was later separated from Dongguan County. Although the administrative divisions changed from time to time, the folks in the two places have a deep connection, and do not forget to stick together for development when they go overseas. The World Organisation of Shenzhen and Dongguan Associations unites more than 100 various associations and firms composed of people from Shenzhen and Dongguan to promote Chinese culture, strengthen economic and trade exchanges, and help the peaceful reunification of the motherland and the economic and social prosperity and progress of their hometown. Its establishment of the federation coincided with China's entry into the World Trade Organization, which also brought new historical opportunities for overseas Chinese businessmen to invest in their hometown.

Soon after the World Organisation of Shenzhen and Dongguan Associations was established, it co-hosted the fifth Dong-An World Conference in 2002. This conference was initiated in 1992 by folks from Dongguan and Shenzhen living in Malaysia, Singapore, and Hong Kong, China, and later developed to an event held every three years. Since the World Organisation of Shenzhen and Dongguan Associations was established, it has actively supported and participated in the conference.

The establishment of the World Organisation of Shenzhen and Dongguan Associations also laid the foundation for the birth of the Federation of Hong Kong Shenzhen Associations, an "aircraft carrier" of Shenzhen and Hong Kong folk associations.

Siu recalled that in the year he founded the World Organisation of Shenzhen and

Dongguan Associations, he had the idea of establishing the Federation of Hong Kong Shenzhen Associations. Back then, Shenzhen was already an emerging metropolis, and there were hundreds of thousands of folks from Shenzhen living in Hong Kong. However, the Shenzhen folks organizations scattered in Hong Kong were only some hometown associations, such as the Bao'an association, and there were no well-organized associations for some newly established districts of Shenzhen. It was not easy to organize activities for folks from different districts of Shenzhen.

With China's accession to the World Trade Organization and Hong Kong's increasingly close ties with the mainland, if the Shenzhen folks in Hong Kong were better organized, they world better leverage their advantages and make greater contributions to the prosperity and stability of Hong Kong and the development of their hometown. Siu thought that there was no time to lose, and felt duty-bound. The Foreign Affairs and Overseas Chinese Affairs Committee of the Shenzhen Municipal People's Congress, the Overseas Chinese Affairs Office of the Shenzhen Municipal People's Government, the Hong Kong, Macao, Taiwan, Overseas Chinese and Foreign Affairs Committee of the Shenzhen Municipal Committee of the Chinese People's Political Consultative Conference, and the Shenzhen Municipal Federation of Returned Overseas Chinese also supported him in preparing for the establishment of the Federation of Hong Kong Shenzhen Associations.

Going through hardships in a year of the SARS epidemic

During the preparations for the federation, Siu went out early and came home late, rushing around to contact well-known figures from Shenzhen living in Hong Kong. He worked outside for at least 15 hours a day, of which eight hours were spent on community work. He didn't put so much effort into his personal career, but he felt that it was worthwhile. He said, "The establishment of an organization needs a lot of people who are willing to contribute money or labor, or both. I was fortunate to meet many such folks."

After about two years of preparations, at the beginning of 2003, it was time to consider the establishment of a preparatory committee for the Federation of Hong Kong Shenzhen Associations. This year, the road turned back and forth before a way out was found, both for Hong Kong and the federation.

It was a difficult year. Severe acute respiratory syndrome (SARS) ravaged Hong Kong, which was immersed in a sense of pessimism. In such a period, the federation was expected to bear heavier responsibility in boosting social confidence, uniting the Shenzhen folks, and gathering patriots and those loving Hong Kong.

But there were also practical difficulties. Afraid of contracting the virus, people seldom went out, so it was not easy to meet people and discuss things. With all his sincerity and a sense of homesickness, Siu guided those involved to take good personal protection, overcome the fear of the virus, and maintain effective communication. The preparatory committee was finally established in June of that year, and Siu was elected director.

Also in June of that year, a significant event took place: The Mainland and Hong Kong Closer Economic Partnership Arrangement (CEPA for short) was implemented after it was signed by the Ministry of Commerce and the financial secretary of the Hong Kong Special Administrative Region. As the first free trade agreement fully implemented in the mainland, it helped many Hong Kong manufacturing companies gain a firm foothold and develop rapidly, opened a vast market in the mainland for Hong Kong companies and professional service providers, consolidated and enhanced Hong Kong's status and competitiveness as an international financial center, and raised the curtain on mainland residents' individual travel to Hong Kong. CEPA came in the year of SARS, and some supplementary agreements were signed later. The successful practice of CEPA proves that the mainland has always been the strong backing for Hong Kong to weather storms and overcome challenges.

In December 2003, the Federation of Hong Kong Shenzhen Associations was established, and Siu served as president and chairman. Under his leadership, the Shenzhen folks in Hong Kong were more united. They seized the great opportunity brought by CEPA, gave full play to their advantages, and made positive contributions to the prosperity and stability of Hong Kong and the reform, innovation, and development of Shenzhen.

The prosperity and stability of Hong Kong is also the result of integrating into the overall development of the country, Siu said. The compatriots in Hong Kong strongly support reform and opening-up, and reform and opening-up also promotes the development of Hong Kong, he said.

Careful calculation in real estate purchase

In the process of founding the Federation of Hong Kong Shenzhen Associations, in addition to the grand narrative of national feelings, there was also an "episode" featuring vision and courage.

No matter rich or poor, people always want a home of their own. The knowledgeable members of the preparatory committee were aware that they needed to find a "home" for the federation. When Hong Kong was hit by the Asian financial turmoil and the SARS epidemic successively, housing prices fell by half in a few years before stabilizing. It might be a good but fleeting opportunity to buy a property. Would it be too late to wait until the federation completed the registration process to buy the bottom?

The problem was quickly solved by Siu. After consulting lawyers, he and two other prominent persons from Shenzhen signed a contract with the preparatory committee, promising that they would buy a property first and then sell it to the federation at the original price. In this way, they bought a real estate in Kowloon for more than 2 million Hong Kong dollars, which became the federation's office, and all the six directors and deputy directors of the preparatory committee advanced money together. Later, the federation grew and moved to another office, but the old venue is still an important asset of the federation.

Siu served as president of the Federation of Hong Kong Shenzhen Associations for three consecutive terms, laying a good foundation for its vigorous development. The federation has always been enthusiastic about social welfare, promoting traditional virtues, caring about the growth of youth, and promoting exchanges between Shenzhen and Hong Kong.

Thinking of the source when drinking water

The Federation of Hong Kong Shenzhen Associations has mobilized Shenzhen folks living in Hong Kong to donate for disaster relief, education and poverty alleviation, and Siu has personally taken part.

In 2004, the federation invested 4 million yuan to build the Federation of Hong Kong Shenzhen of Associations Central Primary School of Xiache Township in Heping County, Heyuan City, Guangdong Province. In 2006 and 2007, Heping County was hit by floods, and the federation donated 500,000 yuan in total to help the affected villagers rebuild their homes.

In 2005, the federation and the Overseas Chinese Affairs Office of the Shenzhen Municipal People's Government jointly launched the "Journey to the Source" youth summer camp. Every summer, young students from Hong Kong and Shenzhen and overseas Chinese youths are organized to know Shenzhen, feel its vigorous development, and then go to Anyuan County, Jiangxi Province for investigation. Siu has taken part in it for many years, and donated to build schools and support students there.

In 2008, he donated 5 million yuan for the Wenchuan earthquake in Sichuan Province and 600,000 yuan for the snow disaster in Hunan Province.

The federation's good deeds in Heyuan and Anyuan have vividly explained what it means to "think of the source when drinking water." Hong Kong's fresh water mainly comes from the Dongjiang-Shenzhen Water Supply Project (often referred to as "Dongshen Water Supply Project"). The Wanlv Lake in Heyuan is the project's main source of water storage, and the source of the Dongjiang River is in Anyuan County.

"The clear Dongjiang water flows southward all day long. It flows into Shenzhen, and flows into Hong Kong and Kowloon." What Zhang Ye sings about in the song *Passionate Dongjiang Water* is the Dongshen Water Supply Project.

Surrounded by sea on three sides, Hong Kong was once plagued by a shortage of fresh water resources. In 1963, Hong Kong suffered from a once-in-a-century drought. At its worst, water was supplied only once every four days, for four hours at a time. Guangdong offered a helping hand and welcomed Hong Kong to send boats to the Pearl River to pump fresh water for free. In December 1963, with Premier Zhou Enlai's special approval, the Central Government allocated 38 million yuan for the construction of the Dongshen Water Supply Project to divert water from the Dongjiang River for the compatriots in Hong Kong.

Under difficult conditions, Guangdong Province mobilized more than 10,000 people, and, with strong support from all over the country, it took only one year to complete the project. In March 1965, the Dongshen Water Supply Project officially began to supply water to Hong Kong, ending the history of water shortage in Hong Kong. After four expansions and renovations, the project has benefited all places along the route and met about 80% of Hong Kong's fresh water needs. It has become a lifeline for Hong Kong, supporting Hong Kong's prosperity and stability.

Siu experienced water shortage in Hong Kong. He knows very well that without the water from the Dongjiang River, Hong Kong's economy would not have taken off, and he would not have had such great development in his career.

He participated in launching the "Journey to the Source" when he was president of the Federation of Hong Kong Shenzhen Associations in the hope that the younger generation can deeply understand the mainland's consistent care for Hong Kong and the story of "drinking water from the same river and feeling like brothers," which happens to Shenzhen and Hong Kong, and inherit the good moral character of Chinese people to think of the source while drinking water.

In July 2006, when Siu led students from Shenzhen and Hong Kong to investigate the source of the Dongjiang River, he found that there were only a few low and dilapidated tile-roofed houses in the Wulong Primary School in Tianxin Township at the foot of Sanbai Mountain. He immediately decided to donate money to rebuild the school. In May of the following year, the Wulong Primary School had a new teaching building, fulfilling the children's dream for many years. Later, he donated to build the Xinhuai Primary School in Tianxin Township.

In 2007, two brothers, Zhong Fuping and Zhong Rongfu, from Wulong Village in Tianxin Township were admitted to college at the same time, but their family was worried about their tuition fees. Siu learned about this when he attended the "Journey to the Source" youth summer camp at the Wulong Primary School, and decided to help the brothers by subsidizing their four-year college tuition and part of their living expenses. After the event, Siu gave his first donation of 10,000 yuan to them and encouraged them to study hard. A year later, when Siu led the team of the "Journey to the Source" youth summer camp to the village again, the two brothers went to the Wulong Primary School early to wait for him, and thanked their benefactor face to face again.

Also in 2007, Siu took the lead in donating money to build the "Pavilion for Thinking of the Source" in Sanbai Mountain in the name of the Federation of Hong Kong Shenzhen Associations. Years later, he spent hundreds of thousands of yuan on repairs and renovations.

During the "Journey to the Source," Siu also provided grants to the students of the Anyuan No. 1 Middle School, as well as grants and teaching awards to the students and teachers of the Wulong Primary School and the Xinhuai Primary School. He worked with the Anyuan No. 1 Middle School to build an interaction and exchange platform for students from Shenzhen, Hong Kong and Anyuan. A parent of a student who was subsidized made a pair of insoles for Siu, which were neatly embroidered with "May the nice man be safe and sound."

Passing on the family tradition of loving the country and Hong Kong

Siu's generosity has also benefited the public in Hong Kong. He used to be member of the board of directors of the well-known Hong Kong charity "Po Leung Kuk," taking part in large-scale fundraising activities for 29 consecutive years and serving as co-chairman of fundraising activities many times. Led by him, his family has also actively participated in charity. Five of his family members have served as member of the board of directors of Po Leung Kuk. People often see Siu and his wife taking their children to attend charity and social events.

Siu founded mass organizations in Hong Kong, returned to his hometown to invest and conduct charity work, organized the "Journey to the Source" and donated to help the development of education, all with the help and participation of his wife, Siu Mok Ching Suen. She is executive vice president of the Federation of Hong Kong Shenzhen Associations and director of the Women's Committee of the federation. The Excellent Parents Award Ceremony organized by her has become a brand event of the federation.

Active in a lot of associations, Siu Mok Ching Suen supports Shenzhen's economic and social development in her own way. In 1989, she joined hands with Hong Kong compatriots and overseas Chinese to establish the Bao'an County Women and Children's Welfare Association. As founding president of the Hong Kong Chinese Women Association, she has organized Hong Kong and overseas women to return to Shenzhen for visits and exchanges. She currently serves as member of the Election Committee of the Hong Kong Special Administrative Region, and vice chairwoman of the Shenzhen Municipal Federation of Returned Overseas Chinese, among others. She used to be member of the Standing Committee of the Shenzhen Municipal Committee of the Chinese People's Political Consultative Conference (CPPCC).

As the younger generation of overseas Chinese in Hong Kong and Macao, Siu Shu Keung's daughter Catherine Y.C. Siu actively participates in social activities while taking care of the business of the family's companies. She serves as vice president of the Federation of Hong Kong Shenzhen Associations, member of the Shenzhen Municipal Committee of the CPPCC, member of the Standing Committee of the Shenzhen Federation of Returned Overseas Chinese, and member of the Guangdong Youth Federation, among others. In March 2020, at the early stage of the COVID-19 outbreak, she stayed in Shenzhen and was entrusted by her parents to donate a batch of anti-epidemic materials to the Bao'an District Women and Children's Welfare Association.

She remembers that "love the country, love Hong Kong and love Shenzhen" has been an important part of her family's education and spiritual inheritance since she was a child.

Such inheritance is already bearing fruit, as we can see from her.

(Photos courtesy of Siu Shu Keung. References: *Historical Records of Shenzhen Overseas Chinese Affairs*, *Ancient History of Shenzhen*, *Bao'an Daily*, *Shenzhen Overseas Chinese News*, Xinhua News Agency, the website of the Henan Provincial People's Government, www.chinaqw.com, www.chinawater.com.cn, www.wenming.cn, and www. ycwb.com.)

赖钦

奋斗成就幸福生活，
祖国与故乡挂心头

赖钦　Lai Yen

　　赖钦，1945年出生，深圳大鹏王母中山村人。1971年因家贫与弟弟前往香港谋生。1973年移居美国，当过海员、制衣厂工人，后从事餐饮行业，担任多家餐馆东主，3次在美国电视节目中展示中国厨艺。

　　曾任美国纽约大鹏育英总社主席和顾问、纽约大鹏同乡会主席、纽约中国和平统一促进会顾问团副主席和常务顾问、纽约中华公所常务议员、纽约华侨学校校董等。曾受邀参加中国人民抗日战争暨世界反法西斯战争胜利70周年纪念活动。

采访时间：2022年。

身在纽约的赖钦，名片上印的头衔是"大鹏侨鹰"。他的微信昵称则是"鹏鹰"。他说，自己就像一只流浪的怀念故乡的鹰。

赖钦发来一段社交媒体上流传的视频，那是大鹏南澳月亮湾的美景，然后感叹："横跨此海湾，流浪了人一生。"早年，他就是从大鹏湾畔出发，来到一个叫东平洲的小岛，踏入了香港地界。他还说，大鹏半岛是世外桃源，是最适宜生活的好地方。可以想象，他对多少人分享过家乡的好。

"人凭一张嘴，摆袖走四海。命生一股劲，勤劳不后悔。敢走天涯路，坎坷一样走。幸福自己闯，安逸度日子。"这是他对自己的总结。

他觉得，人生在世，就应该顺水行舟，随环境而改变自己，寻找

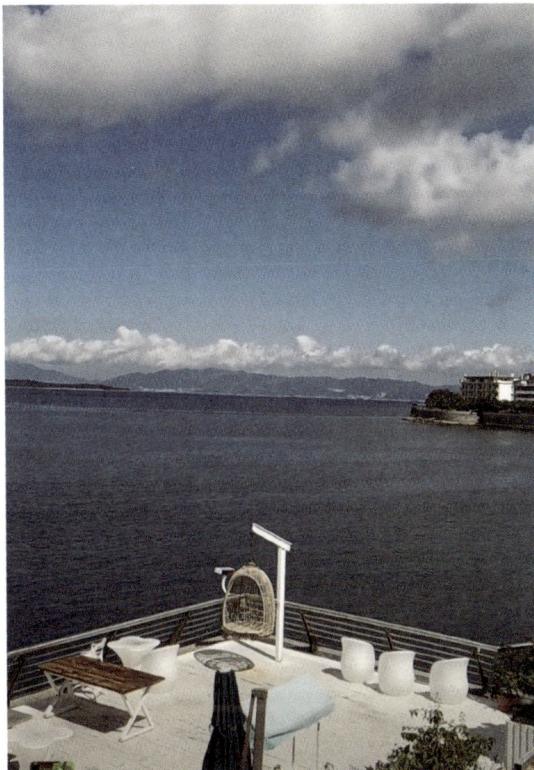

大鹏南澳月亮湾美景。
The screenshot of a video about the beautiful scenery of Moon Bay in Nan'ao, Dapeng.

出路。当年，他在大鹏也算个人物，能文能武，见证过历史风云，还推动过教育改革。后来远走他乡，白手起家，如今一大家子在美国枝繁叶茂，令他深感欣慰。祖国和故乡却依然是他心底的牵挂。

能文能武，走遍大鹏

在美国，赖钦的一大爱好是射击。他的微信头像就是他在射击场手握步枪的英姿。几乎每年秋天，他都会去打打猎。有时回故乡探访，他也会练练打靶。这个爱好，其实也是"深圳"刻在赖钦骨子里的印记。他回忆说，初中没有毕业的时候，就在大鹏武装部的安排下学了射击。那是大办民兵师的年代，他当过大鹏民兵的教练，还去广州参加过民兵师表演，"可精彩了"。

1967年，香港爆发对抗港英政府的"六七暴动"，持续了大约半年之久，其间还波及深港交界地带的沙头角。7月初，沙头角民兵连与港英军警有过一场激战。赖钦说，他也参加过战斗，直奔沙头角支援。对方的队伍里有英国人，也有雇佣兵。

赖钦在练习射击。
Lai Yen practices shooting.

"当时我们 11 挺重机枪和他们打得砰砰响。"对于这段风云历史，赖钦记忆犹新。

这场战斗，史称"岗下之战"，让沙头角"英雄民兵连"的威名传遍全国。沙头角民兵张天生牺牲了，记个人一等功。港英方面则有 14 人阵亡，49 人受伤，1 辆装甲指挥车被炸毁。

除了会练兵、打仗，赖钦还有个角色是"秀才"。

他初中毕业后，又到东莞师范学校学习。那所中专始建于 1932 年，见证过抗日战争的烽火。到了 21 世纪，几经整合，变身为东莞理工学院教育学院（师范学院）。

赖钦课余喜欢读小说、传记，还经常给报刊投稿。时至今日，他还经常把人生感悟写成诗句。

在 20 世纪 60 年代那个特殊的时期，赖钦没有完成师范学校的学业，就回到家乡工作了。当时大力发展林业，他的第一份工作就在林场，边学边干。嫁接竹子、饲养蜜蜂等，他都接触过。他还当过会计和副场长。

后来大搞民兵建设，赖钦如鱼得水，也很辛苦。他经常带着民兵连长、排长们训练，去山里，去海边。他们守望过的海岸线上，多年后崛起了大亚湾核电站、岭澳核电站。

1965 年，赖钦来到社区工作团帮忙，做文书等方面的工作。之后，他又去了大队工作。70 年代初，基层大办文化教育。在一些地方，生产队办小学，大队办初中，公社办高中。赖钦大显身手，组织了初中、高中的教学，还发动大鹏的所有学校开展教学改革——教师读课文时用普通话，解释的时候可以用大鹏话。

在当时的大鹏，日常语言是大鹏话和客家话，但有些孩子没学过大鹏话，在学校只听过普通话和客家话，结果回到家都很难跟长辈交流。另外，很多人不愿意去大鹏工作，一是因为位置偏远，二是因为语言不通。

这样的背景下，赖钦的改革就显得很有意义了。

在那些年的工作中，他走遍了大鹏半岛的村庄。他自豪地说，没几个人做到这点。

远赴美国，练就好厨艺

赖钦教书的工资是每月 30 元，比当大队干部时的十一二元高多了。但家里人口多，日子还是紧巴巴的。他后来曾跟孙女说起，自己年轻时没饭吃，结果孙女的回答让他哭笑不得："爷爷，因为你懒啊！你不去做工，当然没饭吃了。"

1971 年，赖钦和弟弟跑到香港去谋生。1973 年，他坐上了去美国的船。回首在祖（籍）国度过的岁月，赖钦说，一个时代有一个时代的任务。"现在，国家安定，能够去搞经济，就很好啊！"的确，他已经竭尽所能，为祖（籍）国、为家乡奉献了自己的青春、汗水和聪明才智。远走他乡，则是为了个人和家庭的未来去闯荡。

赖钦初到美国的时候，身边很少见到中国人（他称为"唐人"）。华人就业的选择也不多，大多是武馆、医馆、餐馆之类。他当过海员、制衣厂工人，后来进入餐饮业，从洗碗工干起，还端盘子、送外卖。

他说，当时华人还经常被其他族裔欺负，比如，有些"西班牙仔"见到华人就抢，不管华人身上带的是什么东西。"我们那时候啊，成天都带着一把枪去上班，下班也背着把枪，好像那些便衣警察一样。在餐馆工作，有时也是带着枪。"

赖钦这么不认命的人，当然不肯一辈子打下手，于是学起了厨艺，只用了 9 个月左右就当了大厨。他总结说，学厨艺，靠的是用心。看着别人做，自己肯学，再看看烹饪书，自己动脑筋发挥一下，做到色香味俱全，就可以了。

当时，赖钦打工的那家餐馆的老板来自中国台湾，很有人脉，也热衷宣传，就叫电视台来拍摄，让赖钦给外国观众表演做中国新年菜，还安排台湾地区来的一位老师傅同台竞技。

这是赖钦第一次在美国上电视展示厨艺。他做的是广东菜，结果最受欢迎，被一扫而光，每个人给的评价都很好。赖钦先后在电视上表演过 3 次。做过面，还做过锅贴、葱油饼、广东海鲜炒面等。

他记得，当年外国食客来厨房给小费，出手阔绰，一给就是十几二十美元。他还记得，到了 1977 年前后，唐人街变得很旺了。那时候，他还没有美国绿卡。他本来想着赚几年钱就走人了。"洋人的地方怎么会适合我呢？没想到，混着混着，混到自己都变成'洋人'了。"

生动诠释中国人的家庭观念和奋斗精神

赖钦有时会这样思考人生：美国，特别是纽约，到底是天堂还是地狱呢？他的回答是："要看你自己怎么去做了。有些人去做坏事，但我们是从中国出来的，始终是雄心一个，去坚持，去挣钱，去为家庭。"赖钦把中国人的家庭观念和奋斗精神体现得淋漓尽致。刚到美国时，他过得很辛苦。但他告诉自己：一定要改变自己的家庭，宁可累死，也不可以放弃。

他的愿望，最终实现了。

赖钦能取得这样的成就，有个原因是，他不满足于当大厨，而是自己开起了餐馆。究竟开过多少家，他也不记得了。"从1980年就开始带着我弟弟他们，开了大鹏酒家。"

赖钦经营餐馆，有一种独到的模式。"最没有生意的那家，我就买下来。把生意做好了，我就卖给别人。"家里现有十几家餐馆，已经上了轨道，交给子女们去经营了。赖钦自己彻底退休，颐养天年。

赖钦有两个儿子、一个女儿。大儿子是美国电话电报公司的经理人，小儿子是摩根大通的精算师。女儿排行老大，以前当过教师，家里的餐馆现在主要由她管理。

赖钦感到最高兴的是，他的9个孙辈都学业有成。其中，最大的孙女在哈佛大学读了硕士，毕业后在纽约当律师。其他孙子、孙女中，有学医的，也有学财务、会计、计算机和法律的。

赖钦与家人的合照。
Lai Yen and his family.

赖钦和两个弟弟三家人时常小聚。
The families of Lai Yen and his two younger brothers often get together.

记得自己的根在哪里

供孩子们读完大学，对祖（籍）国、对家乡念念不忘的赖钦找到了发挥余热的地方。他空出手来，帮华人社群做了不少事。他服务过的机构包括纽约大鹏育英总社、纽约大鹏同乡会、纽约中国和平统一促进会，甚至客家人团体纽约崇正会。

"也没什么。从基本的会员到职员，从职员到主席，我都做过。"说起这些，赖钦有点轻描淡写。但明眼人知道，他对祖（籍）国、对同胞的感情是根植于心的。作为侨领，他曾参与接待中国来的访问团，也为中国组织过赈灾筹款、义卖等活动。"家乡一声号召，我当然就会在这里发动老乡们不断地支持。"他出席过中国多位国家领导人访美时会见华侨华人代表的活动，感到十分荣耀。

祖（籍）国和家乡方面也欢迎赖钦常回去看看。"新冠疫情之前，我差不多每年都回祖国大陆各个地方参观考察，并且回到家乡，地方上的领导都很热情地接待我。"他说。

2002年，他应邀回中国参观，国宾式的待遇、领导的接见都让他倍感温暖。2015年，他应邀参加了中国人民抗日战争暨世界反法西斯战争胜利70周年纪念活动。

北京、上海、广东、海南、重庆、新疆、黑龙江……在多年来的近距离接触中，赖钦为中国的大好河山而惊叹，为中国的飞速发展而自豪，也在为中国略尽绵薄之力。在河南、山东等地，他给那里的贫困地区捐过款。

2002年赖钦回中国留念照片。
Lai Yen returns to China for a visit in 2002.

"北京水立方那个砖墙里也有我赖钦的名字在啊！"他这是指水立方里的"港澳台侨同胞捐资共建北京奥运场馆留名纪念廊"，又叫"留名廊""留名墙"。这背后还有一段动人的故事。

北京申办2008年奥运会时，郑重向国际奥委会承诺，中国政府的财力没有任何问题。但北京申奥成功后，港澳台同胞和海外华侨华人强烈要求捐款作贡献。北京市政府只好破例接受他们的捐赠，用于建设国家游泳中心"水立方"。最终，来自100多个国家和地区的超过35万名华侨华人、港澳台同胞捐了款，共折合9.4亿元人民币。

水立方赛后改造时，建立了纪念馆，设立了留名墙。水立方是全世界华侨华人对祖（籍）国的赤子情怀的最好见证之一，赖钦在这段辉煌的历史里面留下了自己

2010 年 7 月 27 日，参加"中国寻根之旅"夏令营的华裔青少年在水立方内的"留名廊"上寻找父母或亲朋好友的名字。（来源：中新网）

Teenagers Chinese origin participating in a "Root-seeking Trip to China" summer camp search for the names of their parents or relatives and friends on the "Name Gallery" in the "Water Cube" on July 27, 2010. (Photo: chinanews.com)

的名字。在纽约家中，他挂着很多面五星红旗。更不要说，他常常跟人讲起深圳有多好、大鹏有多好。

他做的这一切，也是在提醒子孙们：要记得自己的根在哪里。

［除署名外，本文图片均由受访者赖钦提供。参考资料：《桑梓情深　赤子丹心——大鹏侨情口述史》、《人民日报（海外版）》、中新网、水立方报道。］

Lai Yen

Striving to achieve a happy life, caring about the motherland and hometown

Lai Yen, born in 1945, is a native of Zhongshan Village, Wangmu, Dapeng, Shenzhen. In 1971, because of family poverty, Lai and one of his two younger brothers went to Hong Kong to make a living. In 1973, Lai migrated to the United States, where he worked as a sailor and a garment factory worker. Later, he worked in the catering industry, and owned some restaurants. He performed Chinese cooking skills on American TV programs three times.

Lai used to be president and advisor of the Yook Ying Association, New York, president of the Tai Pun Residents Association in New York, vice chairman and executive advisor of the Advisory Group of the New York Association for China's Peaceful Reunification, executive member of the Chinese Consolidated Benevolent Association, and director of the New York Chinese School. He was invited to the commemoration of the 70th anniversary of the victory of the Chinese People's War of Resistance against Japanese Aggression and the Anti-Fascist War.

Lai Yen, who lives in New York, has the title of "Overseas Eagle from Dapeng" printed on his business card. His WeChat nickname is "Pengying," meaning "Eagle from Dapeng." He is like a wandering eagle missing its hometown.

He sent us a video from social media, showing the beautiful scenery of Moon Bay in Nan'ao, Dapeng. "Across this bay, I have been wandering all my life," he sighed. In his early years, he set off from the shore of Dapeng Bay, went to a small island called Tung Ping Chau, and thus stepped into the boundary of Hong Kong. He also said that Dapeng Peninsula is a paradise and the most suitable place for people to live in. It is conceivable that he has shared the merits of his hometown with many people.

"A person can travel all over the world with one mouth while swinging his sleeves. Life is full of vigor, and hard work results in no regrets. You should dare to walk on the road to the end of the world, even if it is bumpy. Strive for your own happiness, and life

---

The interview took place in 2022.

will be comfortable." This is his summary of himself.

He thought that anyone living in the world should sail with the current, change himself in accordance with the environment, and find a way out. He was quite a figure in Dapeng, adept with both the pen and the gun. He witnessed historical events, and promoted educational reform. Later, he left his hometown and started from scratch. Now he is gratified to see his big family thriving in the United States. He still has the motherland and hometown in his heart.

Versed in both literature and military affairs, traveling all over Dapeng

In the United States, one of Lai's hobbies is shooting. His WeChat profile picture is his heroic posture holding a rifle on the shooting range. He goes hunting almost every autumn. When visiting his hometown, he sometimes practices shooting. This hobby is an imprint of Shenzhen engraved on him. He recalled that before graduating from junior high school, he learned shooting under the arrangement by the Dapeng Armed Forces Department. It was a time when militia divisions were widely established. He became a coach of the Dapeng militia, and he also participated in a militia division performance in Guangzhou, which "was very wonderful."

In 1967, the "1967 riots" against the British Hong Kong government broke out in Hong Kong, which lasted for about half a year. It also affected Shatoujiao, or Sha Tau Kok, on the border between Shenzhen and Hong Kong. In early July, there was a fierce battle between the Shatoujiao militia company and the British Hong Kong military and police. Lai said that he also joined the battle and went straight to Shatoujiao to support. The opponent's team included Britons and mercenaries.

"At that time, we had 11 heavy machine guns to fight with them, and the guns went 'bang, bang'," Lai still remembers this history.

This battle, known in history as the "Battle in Gangxia," spread the prestige of Shatoujiao's "Heroic Militia Company" throughout the country. Zhang Tiansheng, a militiaman in Shatoujiao, died in the battle and was awarded individual first-class merit. On the British Hong Kong side, 14 people were killed, 49 were injured, and an armored command vehicle was blown up.

In addition to training soldiers and fighting wars, Lai also had a role as a "scholar."

After graduating from junior high school, he went to the Dongguan Normal School to study. That technical secondary school was founded in 1932 and witnessed the War of Resistance against Japanese Aggression. In the 21st century, after several integrations, it was transformed into the School of Education (Normal School) of Dongguan University of Technology.

Lai liked reading novels and biographies after school, and often contributed to newspapers and periodicals. Now he still often writes his life insights into poems.

In the special period of the 1960s, Lai returned to his hometown to work without completing his normal school studies. At a time when forestry was vigorously developed, he got his first job in a forest farm, where he learned by doing. He was involved in grafting bamboo, raising bees and so on. He also worked as accountant and deputy director of the forest farm.

Later, when militias were widely developed, Lai was comfortably back on familiar ground, although it was also very hard. He often took militia company commanders and platoon leaders to train in the mountains and by the seaside. Many years later, the Daya Bay Nuclear Power Plant and the Ling'ao Nuclear Power Station appeared on the coastline they had watched.

In 1965, Lai went to the community work group to help with paperwork and something else. After that, he worked in the production brigade. In the early 1970s, cultural education was massively organized at the grassroots level. In some places, production teams ran primary schools, production brigades ran junior high schools, and communes ran senior high schools. Lai showed his talents. He organized the teaching in junior high schools and senior high schools, and mobilized all schools in Dapeng to carry out teaching reforms for teachers to speak Mandarin when reading texts and the Dapeng dialect when explaining.

At that time, the daily languages in Dapeng were the Dapeng dialect and Hakka, but some children had never learned the Dapeng dialect, and heard only Mandarin and Hakka at school. As a result, it was difficult for them to communicate with their elders at home. In addition, many people were reluctant to work in Dapeng because of the remote location and the language barrier.

Against this background, Lai's reforms were very meaningful.

During his work over those years, he traveled to all the villages on Dapeng Peninsula. He proudly said that few people made it.

Going to the U.S. and developing cooking skills

Lai's salary as a teacher was 30 yuan per month, much more than the 11 or 12 yuan he had earned as a brigade cadre. But there were so many people in his family that they lived from hand to mouth. Many years later, he told his granddaughter that he had no food when he was young, but her answer made him feel ridiculous. "Grandpa, it was because you were lazy! If you didn't work, of course you had no food," she said.

In 1971, Lai and one of his two younger brothers went to Hong Kong to make a living. In 1973, he boarded a ship to the United States. Looking back on the years he spent in his homeland, Lai said that each era had its own tasks. "Now, it is good for the country to keep stable and to engage in economic development!" Indeed, he did his best to dedicate his youth, sweat and ingenuity to his home country and hometown. He then went away from home for his and his family's future.

When Lai arrived in the United States, he rarely saw Chinese people around him, whom he called "Tang people." There were not many employment options for Chinese people, and most of them worked for martial arts schools, clinics, restaurants and the like. He worked as a sailor and a garment factory worker, and later entered the catering industry, starting as a dishwasher. He also served dishes and delivered takeaway food.

Lai said that Chinese were often bullied by other ethnic groups at that time. For example, some "Spanish boys" would rob Chinese people whenever they saw them, no matter what the Chinese were carrying with them. "At that time, we carried a gun to work all day long, and carried a gun after work, just like those plainclothes policemen. When working in restaurants, we sometimes carried a gun too."

As a person declining to accept his fate, Lai was, of course, unwilling to work as an assistant for the rest of his life. So he learned to cook, and became a chef in about only nine months. He concluded that diligence was the key when learning to cook. "I watched others cooking, and I was willing to learn," he said. "I also read some cookbooks, and thought a bit to show some creativity. The food ended up with excellence in color, aroma and taste. That's it."

The owner of the restaurant where Lai worked then was from Taiwan, China. The boss was very well-connected and keen on publicity, so he asked a TV station to film how Lai cooked Chinese New Year dishes for foreign audiences. He also had a senior chef from Taiwan compete with Lai in the program.

This was Lai's first television cooking show in the United States. He made Cantonese food, which turned out to be the most popular. It was eaten up, and everyone spoke highly of it. Lai performed on TV three times in total. He made noodles, pan-fried meat dumplings, scallion pancakes, Cantonese seafood fried noodles, and so on.

He remembers that some foreign diners were generous when coming to the kitchen to give tips between 10 and 20 dollars. He also remembers that Chinatown was booming around 1977. He did not have a U.S. green card then. He originally wanted to stay there for a few years to make some money before leaving. "How could a foreign place suit me? Unexpectedly, I have been living here so long that I have become a 'foreigner.'"

Vividly interpreting Chinese family values and fighting spirit

Lai sometimes thinks about life in this way: Is the United States, especially New York, heaven or hell? His own answer: "It depends on what you do. Some people do bad things, but, as we are from the Chinese mainland, we are always ambitious, and we persevere in our attempts to earn money and to serve our family." Lai has given full play to the family values and fighting spirit of Chinese people. He had a hard time when he first arrived in the United States. But he told himself that he must change his family, and that he would rather work himself to death than give up.

His wish finally came true.

One reason why Lai can achieve such success is that he was not satisfied with being a chef but opened his own restaurants. He can't remember how many houses he has run. "In 1980, I began to run the Dapeng Restaurant with my two younger brothers."

Lai had a unique way of running restaurants. "I would buy the one with the worst business. When the business turned good, I would sell it to others." Now his family has more than a dozen restaurants, which are already on track. After handing them over to his children, Lai has retired completely to live an easy life.

Lai has two sons and a daughter. His elder son is a manager at AT&T, and the younger son is an actuary at J.P. Morgan. The family's restaurants are mainly run by Lai's daughter, the eldest among his children, who used to be a teacher.

For Lai, the happiest thing is that all his nine grandchildren have achieved academic success. His eldest granddaughter, who got a master's degree at Harvard University, works as a lawyer in New York after graduation. The other grandsons and granddaughters have studied medicine, finance, accounting, computer or law.

Remember where your roots are

Lai has never forgotten his home country and hometown. After supporting his children in finishing college, he found a way to make contributions to the society. He spent his time doing a lot of things for the overseas Chinese community. Organizations he served include: the Yook Ying Association, New York; the Tai Pun Residents Association in New York; the New York Association for China's Peaceful Reunification; and the Tsung Tsin Association, New York, a Hakka group.

"It's nothing. I first acted as an ordinary member, then a staff member, and then president," Lai was quite low-key while speaking of these. But people of good sense know that his fond feelings for his homeland and compatriots are rooted in his heart. As an overseas Chinese leader, he received visiting delegations from China, and organized disaster relief fundraising, charity sales and other activities for China. "Whenever my hometown called, I would of course mobilize the fellow villagers here to give their constant support." He was much honored to attend several activities where Chinese leaders met with representatives of overseas Chinese when they visited the United States.

His home country and hometown also welcome him back. "Before the COVID-19 pandemic, I visited various places in the mainland and returned to my hometown almost every year, and the local leaders in my hometown received me warmly," he said.

In 2002, he was invited to visit China. He was treated like a state guest and received by leaders, which made him feel very warm. In 2015, he was invited to the commemoration of the 70th anniversary of the victory of the Chinese People's War of Resistance against Japanese Aggression and the Anti-Fascist War.

Beijing, Shanghai, Guangdong, Hainan, Chongqing, Xinjiang, Heilongjiang... During the close contact over the years, Lai marveled at the beautiful rivers and mountains of China, and was proud of its rapid development. He has also made his contribution to China. He has donated to impoverished areas in Henan, Shandong and some other places.

"My name, Lai Yen, is also on that brick wall of the Water Cube in Beijing!" He was referring to the "Memorial Gallery for Compatriots from Hong Kong, Macao, Taiwan and Overseas Chinese Who Donated to Jointly Build a Venue of Beijing Olympics," also known as the "Name Gallery" or "Name Wall." Behind this wall is a touching story.

When Beijing bid to host the 2008 Olympic Games, it made a solemn promise to the International Olympic Committee that the Chinese government had no problem with its financial resources. However, after Beijing's successful bid for the Olympic Games, compatriots from Hong Kong, Macao and Taiwan and overseas Chinese insisted on donating to make their contributions. The Beijing Municipal Government had to make an exception to accept their donations for the construction of the National Aquatics Center, also known as the "Water Cube." In the end, more than 350,000 overseas Chinese, from more than 100 countries and regions, and compatriots from Hong Kong, Macao and Taiwan donated a total of 940 million yuan.

When the Water Cube was remodeled after the Olympic Games, a memorial hall was built, together with a "Name Wall." The Water Cube is one of the best witnesses of the unconditional love that overseas Chinese worldwide have for their ancestral or home country. Lai has left his name in this glorious history. He hangs many five-star red flags at his home in New York. Not to mention that he often tells people how good Shenzhen and Dapeng are.

He has done all this to remind his descendants: remember where your roots are.

(Photos courtesy of Lai Yen, except for the one with credit. References: *Deep Love for the Hometown and Sincere Loyalty to the Motherland: Oral History of Overseas Chinese from Dapeng, People's Daily Overseas Edition*, chinanews.com, and Water Cube Report.)

黄水娣

华裔"巾帼之光"，
纽约大鹏同乡会首位女主席

黄水娣　Shui Tai Wong Chung

　　黄水娣，深圳大鹏南澳东涌人，1951 年出生，美国金海餐馆副董事长，曾任美国纽约大鹏同乡会主席。1975 年移民美国，1980 年与家人一起在宾夕法尼亚州费城开办金星餐馆，1992 年创办金海餐馆。

　　她积极参与社团公益活动，是美国纽约大鹏同乡会百年历史上首位和迄今唯一的女主席，为乡亲、社区和中美两国友谊尽心尽力，并发挥女性"半边天"的积极作用，曾获纽约华人模范母亲、全美华裔妇女会"妇女精英　再创辉煌""巾帼之光"等多项荣誉。

采访时间：2022 年。

"我非常感恩有个幸福的家，有个勤劳的好丈夫，有个孝顺上进的儿子，有间我们夫妇经营了三十多年的餐馆。可以为两国搭桥，为家乡大鹏尽一份力所能及的心意，为美国纽约大鹏同乡会的会员乡亲，也做了一些造福乡梓、敬老扶幼的工作。我真的感觉不枉此生。"接受记者正式访问之后，黄水娣又通过微信发来了上述一段感言。

从离开家乡，去了香港，再到美国，然后成家立业，服务海外乡亲，支持家乡和国家建设，黄水娣这个大鹏湾走出来的女儿，已经在外闯荡了近半个世纪。

美国艰苦创业

《中国国家地理》杂志曾经评选出"中国最美的八大海岸"，深圳大鹏半岛海岸就名列其中。1951 年，黄水娣出生在大鹏半岛的东涌大围村。回忆起小时候在大鹏上学的时光，黄水娣脑海里几乎全都是一些艰苦的画面，"说起来就像讲故事一样"。

从东涌小学毕业之后，黄水娣考上了大鹏华侨中学。那个时候，能读中学的人很少，黄水娣那一届只有两个人考上了中学。在过去那个没有车的年代，从南澳东涌走路去大鹏王母的中学，单程都要四个小时，黄水娣周日去学校，到了周六再回家。中学难考，路途又遥远，黄水娣的同龄人中很少有能读完初中的，她就是东涌的第二个初中毕业生。

黄水娣和弟弟黄伟星都是奶奶抚养大的，大约在黄水娣七岁的时候，他们的父母就离开了家乡，经香港去到了美国。23 岁时，黄水娣重走了一次父母当年漂洋过海时走过的路，姐弟两人一起坐船，一路颠簸去了香港，一年之后再到美国和父母团聚。至今她仍然清楚地记得，赴美的时间是 1975 年 4 月 20 日，落脚的第一个城市就是纽约。

过去的老华侨在美国大多从事餐饮、制衣（裁缝）、洗衣三个行业，大鹏出来的华侨以从事餐饮行业的居多，黄水娣的父亲在美国也是做餐馆的。不过，跟那时候大多数到美国的华人女子一样，黄水娣一开始在制衣厂里当工人，并且一干就是七年。

1980 年 3 月 12 日，黄水娣的丈夫钟仕庭与她父亲黄金联、弟弟黄伟星一起合伙开办的金星餐馆，在宾夕法尼亚州费城郊区霍舍姆正式营业。未来充满了不确定性，但是一家人都满怀希望。两年多以后的某一天，黄金联跟黄水娣说："你出来帮家里一起打理餐馆生意，我给两条路你选择，一是洗碗盘、倒垃圾，二是慢慢学会收银和接听电话。"那时黄水娣在制衣厂里打工，连 ABC 都不认识几个，要出来进入社会跟人打交道，其实她的内心充满了忐忑。

1983 年 8 月，黄水娣从纽约搬到了费城郊区和家人一起生活、工作。在金星餐

黄水娣与丈夫钟仕庭。
Shui Tai Wong Chung and her husband Sze Ting Chung (Jack Chung).

馆工作时，黄水娣学习英文，学习开车。"我原来一点儿英文都不懂，到后来可以用英语读出两百多个菜名，和客人沟通。"黄水娣透露，自己的秘诀就是死记硬背。当然，在餐厅做"企台"（前台服务员），面对客人最重要的还是要学会微笑。

黄家人与女婿合力经营的餐厅蒸蒸日上。1992 年 12 月 5 日，钟仕庭与黄水娣夫妇又在费城中央广场开了另外一家餐厅"金海餐馆"。虽然金星餐馆早已经没有了，但是金海餐馆经营至今已近三十年了。钟仕庭现已七十五岁，可是他一点儿都没有退休的想法。"我对餐馆有一种感恩的心态，不想不做。"钟仕庭说。

无论身处何地，望子成龙几乎都是中国家长的普遍心愿。那段创业的日子过得很辛苦，但是，黄水娣对儿子钟子威的教育一点儿也不马虎。1983 年，黄水娣拿到了汽车驾照，她常常一边在餐馆工作，一边开车送儿子去学钢琴、小提琴，上各种培训班，就像一些在美的中国"虎妈"一样。黄水娣还记得这样一件糗事：刚刚学会开车的时候，她其实是一个路盲，有一次从学习班接儿子回家的时候，居然走反了方向……

纽约大鹏同乡会首位女主席

美国纽约大鹏同乡会的前身是美国纽约大鹏慈善会，由原籍大鹏半岛的华侨华人组建，是纽约华埠传统侨团、中华公所六十侨团之一，美东联成公所十八侨团所属，也是美东华人社团联合总会创办侨团之一。

20 世纪初期，移居美国的大鹏侨胞语言不通，人生地不熟，找工作非常困难。为求生存和互相帮助，1919 年，当时在美国谋生的大鹏乡亲周水田、周石生、周水容、张南友、戴葵等人发起成立了美国纽约大鹏慈善会，并在纽约中央街租赁一所公寓作为办公场地。

20 世纪上半叶，纽约大鹏慈善会会址迁至现址纽约市摆也街 51 号。1981 年到 1983 年，慈善会募捐改造旧楼。在王少清、梁锦浩等著名老侨的努力和赞助下，五层高的新会所大楼于 1983 年落成，与此同时，慈善会更名为"美国纽约大鹏同乡会"。

迄今，纽约大鹏同乡会已经有百余年的历史，而黄水娣一家人跟同乡会的渊源还颇深。和大多数侨胞一样，黄水娣的父亲黄金联初到美国也是做餐馆的，工作之余就为乡亲服务。1974 年，黄金联开始在纽约大鹏同乡会做总务，在纽约侨社帮忙。在 1990 年到 1991 年期间，黄金联还被乡亲们推举为纽约大鹏同乡会主席，卸任之后也一直给同乡会当顾问。

黄水娣的丈夫钟仕庭是大鹏南澳西涌西贡人，两人 1976 年在美国经亲友介绍认识，之后便结婚组建家庭。2008 年至 2009 年，钟仕庭也成为纽约大鹏同乡会的主席。隔了一届之后，也就是在 2012 年，黄水娣成为纽约大鹏同乡会百年历史上首位女主席（任期 2012 年至 2013 年），一时成为佳话。

钟仕庭与黄水娣家庭荣获深圳大鹏新区南澳新时代先进人物最美家风奖。

The family of Sze Ting Chung and Shui Tai Wong Chung wins the Most Beautiful Family Values Award for Advanced Figures in the New Era of Nan'ao, Dapeng New District, Shenzhen.

黄水娣的父亲黄金联。
Shui Tai Wong Chung's father, Kam Lin Wong.

纽约大鹏同乡会现任主席黄伟星，是黄水娣的弟弟。黄伟星和姐姐一样，现在也是家住费城，但在纽约活动，常常在两地来回走动。黄伟星社会职务比较多，曾是费城东安公所的主席。东安公所就是由原来东莞县、宝安县（包括现在的深圳市）的华侨华人组成的一个团体。2021年，他又当选为客属侨团——费城崇正会的会长。纽约大鹏同乡会的主席是由3000多名会员民主推选出来的，黄伟星是该会2020年至2021年的主席，但由于新冠疫情会员不方便出来投票，所以大家一致同意，他们这一届委员留任两年，黄伟星仍继续担任主席。

（从左到右）钟仕庭、黄水娣与弟弟黄伟星。
(From left to right) Sze Ting Chung, Shui Tai Wong Chung and her younger brother, Wai San Wong.

黄水娣表示，她和丈夫钟仕庭、弟弟黄伟星做服务乡亲的社区工作，都是因为多年来受到父亲黄金联的言传身教。"从我做主席开始，每年的同乡会春节联欢晚餐都是免费的，就是想让乡亲们一起聚会，一起庆祝。在晚会上，同乡会都会颁发奖学金给成绩好的大鹏子弟，有小学的、中学的、大学的，也是想帮助和鼓励他们继续读好书。""虽然我是女主席，但我做了两年主席后，很多会员都希望我连任。"黄水娣透露，一直以来自己服务乡亲的理念没有改变，只是儿子希望她保重身体、多休息，所以她就没有继续参选。

全美华裔妇女"巾帼之光"

2012年1月2日，全美华裔妇女会给黄水娣颁发了"妇女精英 再创辉煌"牌匾。2013年3月5日，全美华裔妇女会又给黄水娣颁发了"巾帼之光"的荣誉称号。

"那时我是纽约大鹏同乡会的主席，是同乡会 90 多年来的第一位女主席。女人都可以做主席，这不但在大鹏同乡会里算是破天荒的，而且在美国的侨团里也不多见。"曾被纽约市华人家长学生联合会评为"模范母亲"的黄水娣解释，"另外一个原因，可能就是我们儿子教得还算成功吧。"

黄水娣的儿子钟子威 1977 年出生，曾在初中、高中两次获得宾夕法尼亚州数学比赛冠军；高中毕业时还被美国媒体（*USA Today*）评选为"全美最优秀的 60 名高中毕业生"，并顺利进入哈佛大学应用数学系就读。从哈佛毕业后，他又到宾夕法尼亚大学沃顿商学院继续深造，并拿到了工商管理硕士（MBA）学位。

钟子威现在是创投公司科威资本的创始人兼总裁，投资先进技术以应对全球面临的可持续发展和卫生保健等方面的挑战，过去 20 年，他经常因公务前往中国。在接受采访时，说起儿子，钟仕庭和黄水娣两人的脸上都洋溢着幸福的喜悦，他们特别提起，钟子威向哈佛大学捐赠了大笔资金，为新的科学与工程大楼的两个教室冠名，其中一个以钟子威夫妇的名字命名，另一个以钟仕庭、黄水娣的名字命名。他目前还在哈佛工程与应用科学学院的院长内阁任职。

2022 年 10 月 3 日，黄水娣从微信给记者传来了一张合照，并备注了一段话："1999 年我在哈佛大学参加了儿子钟子威的毕业典礼。2001 年我们又在哈佛大学参加我妹黄沛云的工商管理硕士毕业典礼。能在世界顶级的哈佛大学参加两次毕业典礼，我觉得自己很幸运。钟子威、黄沛云是大鹏人的骄傲，我为他们感到非常开心。"

2001 年，黄水娣和弟弟黄伟星在哈佛大学参加妹妹黄沛云的工商管理硕士毕业典礼。（从左至右分别是：黄伟星、黄沛云、黄水娣、钟子威）

Shui Tai Wong Chung and her younger brother Wai San Wong attend her younger sister Pui Wan Wong's MBA graduation ceremony at Harvard University in 2001. (From left to right: Wai San Wong, Pui Wan Wong, Shui Tai Wong Chung, and Andrew Gee Wai Chung)

黄水娣和丈夫钟仕庭经常教育儿子钟子威不要忘了中国的传统：做人一定要有人品，这是最重要的；要以德服人，不欺骗他人；无论多么富裕，都不要盛气凌人；要学会勤劳，因为天道酬勤；要学会孝顺父母，珍惜和父母在一起的时间。他们相信，这些中国古人的训诫，就是海外侨胞的生存智慧。

"虽然我儿子在纽约出生，在美国长大，但是他就像土生土长的中国人，会说中国话，会唱中国国歌。"钟仕庭自豪地说。在他们夫妇担任纽约大鹏同乡会主席期间，钟子威经常会在春茗宴会上为几千名乡亲会员用中英双语演唱中美国歌。钟子威曾经是全美中文歌曲大赛的冠军，并获得过在香港地区举办的知名歌唱大赛"香港偶像"决赛资格（有数千选手参赛），演唱水平完全可以跟专业歌手相媲美。

热心家乡公益事业

2008 年 5 月 12 日，四川汶川发生大地震，当时黄水娣的丈夫钟仕庭担任纽约大鹏同乡会主席，立即带头捐出了 3500 美元，同乡会捐了 5000 美元，并积极发动会员捐款，最后将募集到的全部款项交给了中国驻纽约总领事馆，再代为转交四川有关部门，为灾区重建尽一份力。

2013 年 4 月 20 日，四川雅安发生地震，身为纽约大鹏同乡会主席的黄水娣率先捐出 1000 美元，同乡会又捐了 1000 美元，并迅速发动乡亲继续踊跃捐款，然后联合同乡会和崇正会等几个美国客属侨团，一起将 3 万多美元的捐款交给了总领事馆，再代转给受灾的芦山地区。

2009 年 9 月 30 日，联合国教科文组织保护非物质文化遗产政府间委员会决定，将"妈祖信俗"（又称"神女信俗""天妃信俗""天后信俗"等）列入世界非物质文化遗产，这是中国首个信俗类世界遗产。

妈祖文化是中华传统文化的一个组成部分，在全球华人当中具有很强的凝聚力。目前世界上 20 多个国家和地区有 5000 多座颇具规模的天后宫（妈祖庙），而在黄水娣的家乡南澳东涌码头附近就有一座始建于明末清初的天后宫。以海为生的南澳人，对妈祖有着一种与生俱来的虔诚信仰。每年的农历三月廿三日天后诞，附近的村民及海外乡亲都会赶来庙里拜祭妈祖，祈求风调雨顺，出海平安。

2010 年 9 月，在当地居民和香港、纽约大鹏同乡会等各方的支持下，东涌社区开始对破旧的天后宫进行重建整修。黄水娣透露，为了发动乡亲们捐建家乡的天后宫，她在美国想方设法联系了住在不同州的乡亲。当然，黄水娣自己和家人先起了个带头作用。

"我们夫妻捐了 8000 美元，我儿子钟子威捐了 2000 美元，我弟弟黄伟星捐了 2000 美元，妹妹黄沛云捐了 300 美元。为了纪念我父母黄金联夫妇，我们夫妻代表他们也捐了 1000 美元。"在黄水娣的多方游说和努力下，在美国的大鹏乡亲为重建

黄水娣一家人在钟子威以父母名义捐赠命名的哈佛大学教室前留影。图片从左至右分别是：钟心懿（黄水娣孙女）、陈中珊（黄水娣儿媳）、钟子威、黄水娣和钟仕庭。

Shui Tai Wong Chung and her family in front of the Sze Ting & Shui Tai Wong Chung Room, a classroom donated by Andrew Gee Wai Chung and named after his parents, at Harvard University. From left to right: Aria Chung (granddaughter of Shui Tai Wong Chung), Coral Chen Cheung (daughter-in-law of Shui Tai Wong Chung), Andrew Gee Wai Chung, Shui Tai Wong Chung, and Sze Ting Chung.

东涌天后宫共募集了 44100 美元（当时兑换成人民币是 26 万多元）的捐款。

2011 年 12 月 2 日，位于深圳大鹏东涌社区的天后宫重建落成。为参加天后宫重建落成庆典仪式，有移居美国的老华侨甚至坐了 16 个小时的飞机赶回家乡，就是为了亲眼见证这一重要时刻。重建后的东涌天后宫，不但可以让本地居民了解到更多优秀的中华文化，而且在无形之中也成为海外乡亲联系家乡大鹏的精神纽带。

一直以来，黄水娣及丈夫钟仕庭都非常关心家乡大鹏的建设，除了带头捐钱重建东涌天后宫外，他们一家对家乡的公益事业也几乎是"有求必应"：资助大鹏南澳龙舟队去马来西亚参加国际比赛，捐建西涌小学、大鹏王母老人活动中心……

2022 年 4 月，香港新冠疫情肆虐，远在美国的钟仕庭、黄水娣夫妇和弟弟黄伟星依然时刻惦记着在港的大鹏乡亲，慷慨解囊，共捐出 3000 美元，由香港大鹏同乡会给乡亲采购抗疫物资，渡过难关。

说起这些往事，黄水娣和丈夫钟仕庭三番四次地强调："其实钱不多，成绩也很小，我们只是想力所能及地为家乡、为中国的建设尽自己的一点心意。"

（本文图片均由受访者钟仕庭、黄水娣提供。参考资料：《桑梓情深 赤子丹心——大鹏侨情口述史》《大鹏港澳台及海外乡亲社团和人物简介》。）

Shui Tai Wong Chung

A "Heroic Female Role Model" among Chinese American, first female president of Tai Pun Residents Association in New York

Shui Tai Wong Chung (Amy Chung), a native of Dongchong, Nan'ao, Dapeng (also known as "Tai Pun"), Shenzhen, was born in 1951. She is vice chairwoman of the Golden Sea Chinese Restaurant in Pennsylvania and former president of the Tai Pun Residents Association in New York. She immigrated to the United States in 1975, opened the Golden Lights Chinese Restaurant with her family in 1980 and founded the Golden Sea Chinese Restaurant in 1992 — both in suburban Philadelphia.

Shui Tai has actively participated in community service activities throughout her life in the United States. She was the first and only female president in the 100-year history of the Tai Pun Residents Association in New York. She has done her best to better the lives of fellow immigrants, improve her community, represent her two countries well, and serve as a positive role model for other women. Shui Tai has won many honors, such as the "Outstanding Chinese Mother of New York," as well as the "Elite Woman Making an Impact" and the "Heroic Female Role Model," both awarded by the National Chinese Women Association U.S.A.

"I am very grateful for having a happy family, a good hardworking husband, a filial and highly motivated son, and a restaurant that my husband and I have run for more than 30 years. I have done my best to serve as a bridge between my motherland and adoptive homeland, committed my time to better my hometown of Dapeng, respect the elderly and support the next generation of youth from the families of the members and fellow immigrants in the Tai Pun Residents Association in New York. I strive to live my life without regret, and believe my work is worthwhile," Shui Tai sent the words through WeChat after our interview.

The interview took place in 2022.

Shui Tai grew up in Dapeng Bay and departed for a new life nearly half a century ago. She first left her hometown for Hong Kong, and then immigrated to the United States, where she started a family. She has devoted herself to supporting fellow Dapeng immigrants overseas and supporting extensive renovations in her hometown and other regions of China.

Overcoming challenges in the U.S.

The *Chinese National Geography* magazine once named "China's Eight Most Beautiful Coasts" and included the coast of Dapeng Peninsula, Shenzhen. In 1951, Shui Tai was born on that very coast in Dawei Village, Dongchong. Recalling the time when she went to school in Dapeng as a child, all she can see are images of hard times. "It's like telling a story."

After graduating from the Dongchong Primary School, Shui Tai was admitted to the Dapeng Overseas Chinese Middle School. Very few people were chosen to attend middle school during that time, and only two students in her primary school were chosen that year. At a time with no cars or buses, it took four hours to walk from Dongchong, Nan'ao to the middle school in Wangmu, Dapeng. Shui Tai made the long journey to school on Sundays and returned home on Saturdays. It was so rare to be admitted into the middle school and required such lengthy travel that few of her peers could successfully complete junior high school. She was only the second junior high school graduate ever in the history of Dongchong.

Shui Tai and her younger brother Wai San were both raised by their grandmother. When she was 7 years old, her parents left her hometown and went to the United States via Hong Kong. At the age of 23, she took the same path her parents took when they crossed the sea. She and her brother made the torturous journey to Hong Kong together by boat, and reunited with their parents in the United States a year later. She still vividly remembers that she went to the United States on April 20, 1975, arriving first in New York City.

In the past, many overseas Chinese in the United States worked in industries like food service, tailoring, and laundry. Men from Dapeng often worked in the food business, and indeed, Shui Tai's father operated a restaurant. However, like most Chinese women newly arriving in the United States, she worked as a seamstress in a garment factory for seven years.

On March 12, 1980, the Golden Lights Chinese Restaurant was founded by Shui Tai's husband Sze Ting Chung (Jack Chung), her father Kam Lin Wong and her younger brother

Wai San Wong in Horsham, a suburb of Philadelphia, Pennsylvania. The future was full of uncertainty, but the family was full of hope. Two years after the restaurant opened, her father encouraged her to join the business: "You should help the family manage the restaurant. I will give you two choices. One is to wash dishes and take out the garbage, and the other is to gradually learn how to be a cashier and answer the phone." Working in a garment factory at that time, Shui Tai spoke very little English, so she was not sure she could comfortably deal with people in society.

In August 1983, Shui Tai moved from New York to the suburbs of Philadelphia to be with her family. Not too long after she started to work at Golden Lights, she learned English and learned to drive. "I barely knew any English at first, but later I could read the names of more than 200 dishes in English and communicate with customers," she said. She revealed that her secret was having a good memory and ability to learn by rote. Of course, the most important thing for her was to smile when facing customers.

Over time, the restaurant jointly run by the Wong family and Sze Ting, the son-in-law, was thriving. On December 5, 1992, Shui Tai and her husband opened another restaurant, the Golden Sea Chinese Restaurant, in Center Square, Philadelphia, Pennsylvania. Golden Lights closed several years later, but Golden Sea has continued to operate for over 30 years. Sze Ting is now 75 years old, but he has no intention of retiring at all. "I'm so grateful for what the restaurant has given to me and my family, and I can't imagine not working," he said.

Chinese parents everywhere share a common mentality of having ambitious plans for their children. Those days of starting a business were very hard, but Shui Tai was very careful to prioritize education for her son, Andrew Gee Wai Chung. She got her driver's license in 1983. While she worked in the restaurant, she also drove Andrew to learn piano and violin, and to attend classes outside of school. She still remembers an embarrassing incident: When she just learned to drive, she got lost and went to the wrong address to pick up her son from a class!

First female president of Tai Pun Residents Association in New York

The predecessor of the Tai Pun Residents Association in New York was the Tai Pun Benevolent Association, which was established by overseas Chinese originally from Dapeng Peninsula. Based in New York's Chinatown, it was one of the 60 overseas Chinese groups under the Chinese Consolidated Benevolent Association, one of the 18 overseas Chinese groups under the Lin Sing Association, and one of the overseas Chinese groups that founded the U.S. East Coast Federation of Chinese Associations.

In the early 20th century, overseas Chinese immigrating from Dapeng found it difficult to find jobs in the United States, because they were strangers to a new shore who could not speak English. To survive and help each other, some of the Dapeng immigrants who established themselves in the United States, such as Chow Shui Tin, Chow Sek Sang, Chow Shui Yung, Cheung Nam Yau and Dai Kwai, established the Tai Pun Benevolent Association in New York in 1919. They rented an apartment on Center Street in New York as an office space.

In the first half of the 20th century, the Tai Pun Benevolent Association moved to its current location at 51 Bayard Street, New York City. From 1981 to 1983, the association raised funds to renovate the old building. With the efforts and sponsorship of well-known overseas Chinese such as Wong Siu Ching and Leung Gam Hou, the five-floor new building was completed in 1983. At the same time, the association was renamed the Tai Pun Residents Association.

The association has a history of more than a century and deep ties to Shui Tai's family. Like most overseas Chinese, her father, Kam Lin Wong, worked in a restaurant when he first came to the United States and did community service to help his fellow immigrants from Dapeng in his spare time. In 1974, he began to manage the general affairs at the Tai Pun Residents Association and helped out at other overseas Chinese groups in New York. From 1990 to 1991, he was elected president of the association. After his term ended, he served as an advisor to the association.

Shui Tai's husband, Sze Ting, is from Xigong, Xichong, Nan'ao, Dapeng. They met in the United States through relatives and friends in 1976, and then married and started a family. From 2008 to 2009, Sze Ting became president of the Tai Pun Residents Association. In 2012, Shui Tai was elected the first female president in the century-long history of the association, serving from 2012 to 2013, which was a storied achievement.

Her brother, Wai San, was later elected and serves as the current president of the association. Like his sister, he lives in Philadelphia but works in New York, often traveling back and forth between the two cities. He has many social positions. He used to be president of the Tung On Association in Philadelphia, an organization of overseas Chinese from Dongguan County and Bao'an County (including the current Shenzhen Municipality). In 2021, Wai San was elected president of the Tsung Tsin Association in Philadelphia, an overseas Chinese group with Hakka origins. The president of the Tai Pun Residents Association in New York is democratically elected by more than 3,000 members. Originally, Wai San was elected president from 2020 to 2021. However, because it was not safe to vote in person during the COVID-19 pandemic, it was unanimously agreed that the officers would continue to serve for two more years.

Shui Tai said that she, her husband and younger brother performed such community service to better the lives of fellow Dapeng immigrants because her father had served as a role model over the years. "Since my term as president, the Spring Festival gala dinner of the association has been free of charge every year to allow all fellow Dapeng immigrant families to get together and celebrate. At the gala, the association awards scholarships to distinguished children of Dapeng immigrants with good grades, including primary school, high school and college students, in a bid to help and encourage them to continue to do well." "Although I was the first female president, after I served for two years, many members hoped that I would be re-elected." Shui Tai revealed that she strongly considered serving her fellow Dapeng immigrants in that capacity again. However, her son Andrew wanted her to take care of herself and get more rest, so she did not run for reelection.

"Heroic Female Role Model" among Chinese Americans

On January 2, 2012, the National Chinese Women Association U.S.A. awarded Shui Tai a plaque of "Elite Woman Making an Impact." On March 5, 2013, the association awarded her the honorary title of "Heroic Female Role Model."

"At that time, I was president of the Tai Pun Residents Association. I was the association's first female head in more than 90 years, which was not only unprecedented for the Tai Pun Residents Association, but also rare in overseas Chinese groups in the United States. Another reason for receiving the distinguished honor might be our success in raising our son," explained Shui Tai, who was once named "Outstanding Chinese Mother of New York" by the Chinese American Parent-Student Council.

Her son Andrew Gee Wai Chung, born in 1977, won Pennsylvania state mathematics contests twice, in junior and senior high school. He was among the 60 top high school graduates in the United States selected by *USA Today*, and studied Applied Mathematics at Harvard University. After graduating from Harvard, he attended the Wharton School of the University of Pennsylvania and received a Master of Business Administration (MBA) degree.

He is the founder and managing partner of 1955 Capital, a Wyoming-based venture capital firm, investing in advanced technologies to solve global challenges in sustainability and healthcare. Over the past two decades, he has traveled to China on numerous occasions on behalf of his companies. Sze Ting and Shui Tai beam when talking about their son, especially when sharing that Andrew made a significant donation to Harvard to name two classrooms in the new Science & Engineering building—one named for him and his wife, and a second room named after his parents. He currently serves on the Dean's Cabinet for the Harvard School of Engineering and Applied Sciences.

On October 3, 2022, Shui Tai sent a group photo to us via WeChat and wrote, "In 1999, I attended my son Andrew Chung's graduation ceremony at Harvard University. In 2001, we attended my younger sister Pui Wan Wong's MBA graduation ceremony at Harvard University. I feel very lucky to be able to attend two graduation ceremonies at the world-class Harvard University. Andrew Chung and Pui Wan Wong are the pride of the Dapeng people. I am very happy for them."

Shui Tai and her husband Sze Ting often taught their son Andrew not to forget Chinese traditions: One should have excellent character, which is most important; convince others by virtue and do not deceive others; no matter how rich you are, don't be arrogant; learn to work hard, because God rewards the diligent; and learn to be filial to your parents and cherish the time you spend with them. They believe that such ancient Chinese maxims are how the overseas Chinese survive.

"Although my son was born in New York and grew up in the United States, he is like a native Chinese. He can speak Chinese and sing national anthems of China," Sze Ting said proudly. When the couple chaired the Tai Pun Residents Association, their son often sang the Chinese and American national anthems in both Chinese and English for thousands of fellow members at spring banquets. He won a national Chinese singing contest in the United States, and was a finalist in "Hong Kong Idol," a celebrated singing competition held in Hong Kong with thousands of contestants. There is no doubt that he can rival professional singers.

Enthusiastic about revitalizing her hometown

On May 12, 2008, a major earthquake hit Wenchuan, Sichuan Province. At that time, Shui Tai's husband, Sze Ting, was president of the Tai Pun Residents Association. He immediately took the lead by donating $3,500. The association donated $5,000 and called on its members to donate. Finally, all the money collected was contributed through the Chinese consulate general in New York, and then passed on to the authorities in Sichuan, helping with the reconstruction of the stricken areas.

On April 20, 2013, an earthquake occurred in Ya'an, Sichuan. As chairwoman of the

Tai Pun Residents Association, Shui Tai took the lead by donating $1,000. The association donated another $1,000, and quickly mobilized fellow villagers to donate. It joined hands with several American Hakka groups, including the Tsung Tsin Association, to raise more than $30,000 in donations and presented to the consulate general, which was then transferred to the disaster-stricken Lushan area.

On September 30, 2009, the UNESCO Intergovernmental Committee for the Safeguarding of Intangible Cultural Heritage decided to inscribe the "Mazu belief and customs" (also known as the "Goddess belief and customs," the "Tianfei belief and customs," the "Tianhou belief and customs," etc.) on the Representative List of the Intangible Cultural Heritage of Humanity. It became China's first world heritage of beliefs and customs.

The Mazu culture is part of traditional Chinese culture and has a strong cohesion among Chinese people around the world. At present, there are more than 5,000 large-scale Tianhou temples (Mazu temples) in more than 20 countries and regions in the world, including a Tianhou temple built in the late Ming and early Qing dynasties near the Dongchong Wharf in Nan'ao, Shui Tai's hometown. People in Nao'ao, whose livelihood relies on the sea, have an innate devout belief in Mazu. Every year, on the 23rd day of the third month of the lunar calendar, which is called "Tianhou's Birthday," nearby villagers and fellow villagers overseas will come to the temple to worship Mazu, praying for good weather and safe sailing.

In September 2010, with the support of local people, relevant persons in Hong Kong, the Tai Pun Residents Association in New York, and other parties, Dongchong Community began to rebuild and renovate the dilapidated Tianhou temple. Shui Tai revealed that she tried every means to contact fellow Dapeng immigrants living in different U.S. states to donate for the rebuilding of the Tianhou temple in her hometown. Of course, she and her family took the lead in donating.

"My husband and I donated $8,000, my son Andrew Chung donated $2,000, my younger brother Wai San donated $2,000, and my younger sister Pui Wan donated $300. To commemorate my parents, Kam Lin and his wife, my husband and I donated $1,000 on their behalf," Shui Tai said. Thanks to her lobbying and efforts, the Dapeng community in the United States raised a total of $44,100 (converted into more than 260,000 yuan at that time) in donations for the reconstruction of the Tianhou temple in Dongchong.

On December 2, 2011, the reconstruction of the Tianhou temple in Dongchong was completed. Some overseas Chinese in the United States took the 16-hour flight back to their hometown, just to attend the completion ceremony and witness this important moment with their own eyes. The rebuilt Tianhou temple in Dongchong not only will allow local residents to learn more about their local history and Chinese culture, but also becomes a spiritual link between overseas Chinese and their hometown of Dapeng.

Shui Tai and her husband have always been very concerned about the longer-term sustainability of Dapeng. In addition to taking the lead in donating money for the rebuilding of the Tianhou temple in Dongchong, their family has supported numerous public welfare undertakings in their hometown: They funded the Nan'ao Dragon Boat Team to participate in an international competition in Malaysia, and donated to build the Xichong Primary School and the Wangmu Elderly Activity Center.

In April 2022, when the COVID-19 pandemic raged in Hong Kong, the couple and Shui Tai's younger brother, who were far away in the United States, were so concerned about Dapeng families in Hong Kong that they donated $3,000 for Tai Pun Residents Association (Hong Kong) to purchase anti-viral medications and equipment for fellow villagers during the toughest of times.

Speaking of these contributions, Shui Tai and her husband repeatedly emphasized, "Actually it was not much money. We have contributed very little, but we just want to do something within our means for Dapeng and beyond."

(Photos courtesy of Sze Ting Chung and Shui Tai Wong Chung. References: *Deep Love for the Hometown and Sincere Loyalty to the Motherland: Oral History of Overseas Chinese from Dapeng* and *Brief Introduction to Dapeng Associations and Characters in Hong Kong, Macao, Taiwan and Overseas.*)

第四章
Chapter Four

薪火相传
Passing on the torch

江山代有才人出，各领风骚数百年。

——〔清〕赵翼《论诗五首·其二》

Talented poets are brought forth in their times; Each
will lead the literary excellence for hundreds of years.
—*On Poetry II* , by Zhao Yi (Qing Dynasty)

陈观玉

言传身教，中英街上的"活雷锋"

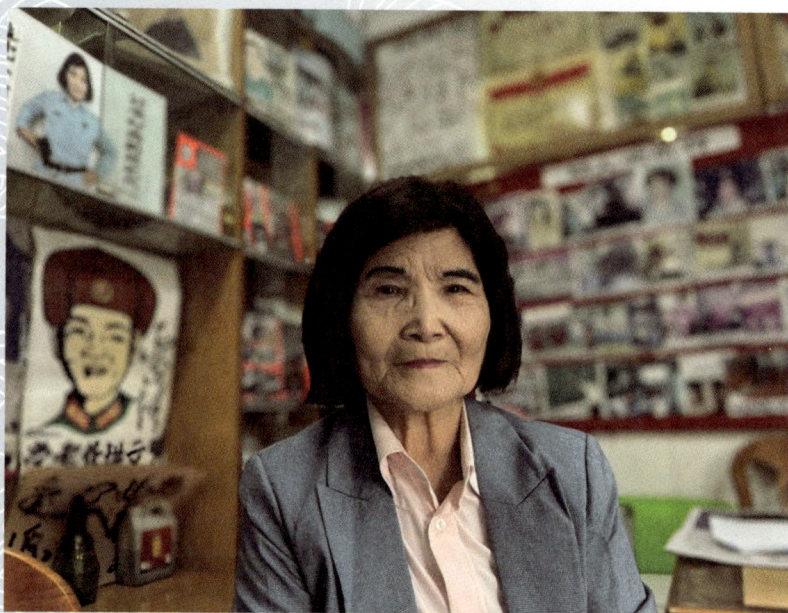

陈观玉（来源：《晶报》） Chen Guanyu (Photo: *Daily Sunshine*)

陈观玉，新加坡归侨，深圳市沙头角水产公司退休职工。1939 年 11 月出生于新加坡一个华侨家庭，10 岁时回沙头角定居。1966 年加入中国共产党，1997 年作为党代表出席在北京召开的中国共产党第十五次全国代表大会。

她数十年如一日照顾孤寡，救助穷困，拥军优属，关心青少年健康成长，热心公益事业，被誉为"中英街上的活雷锋"。曾获全国归侨侨眷先进个人、全国三八红旗手（两次）、全国老有所为奉献奖、全国学雷锋标兵、广东省学雷锋标兵、广东省优秀共产党员、广东省劳动模范、深圳市"文明市民"等众多殊荣。

采访时间：2022 年。

2022 年 10 月的一个下午，深圳市盐田区沙头角中英街关口，往日排长龙进关的热闹场面早已不见，只有三三两两的人员从居民通道进进出出。受新冠疫情影响，游客已经不能再进入中英街，但是，在关闭的游客通道入口，仍然站着两位穿着红马甲的义工。他们是中英街雷锋爱心义工队的成员，是负责劝返那些慕名远道来中英街游玩的客人的。

2017 年 10 月，"中英街活雷锋"陈观玉牵头在深圳市义工联注册了"深圳市中英街雷锋爱心义工队"。沙头角中英街关口外边的"观玉之家"就是义工队服务的一个爱心驿站。

坐在记者面前的陈观玉很健谈。她做的好事背后，藏了很多鲜活的故事。

宁可自己吃苦，也不要欺负人

1939 年 11 月，陈观玉出生在新加坡（当时为英国殖民地）一个贫苦的华侨家庭。陈观玉自小体弱多病，3 岁就患了哮喘，但是穷人的孩子早当家，五六岁时，她就要帮家里照顾弟弟妹妹。8 岁时，就要早早起床，到橡胶园去割橡胶。陈观玉回忆："割橡胶的日子很苦的。凌晨 3 点钟，就要戴着头灯出门。400 棵橡胶树，一棵一棵地割。到了 6 点钟，太阳出来，橡胶就不流出来了。有时候还会被蜈蚣咬到，痛得要命。"

不过，那时在新加坡割橡胶的小陈观玉最怕的还是老虎。她说："好怕被老虎吃掉。"原本以为这只是小孩子脑海中的臆想，然而，在翻查相关的历史文献资料之后，记者发现陈观玉所言不虚。在学者郭舜平撰写的与海外华侨研究相关的学术论文《华工与战前马来亚的开发》中，就有这么一段记述："新加坡，原柔佛邦领土，曾是中世纪淡马锡岛国的旧址，只有少数马来人和中国人在那里居住。红树林漫山遍野，沼泽处处，老虎出没无常。"（见《福建师范大学学报》哲学社会科学版，1986 年第 2 期）

10 岁时，陈观玉随父母和家人从新加坡回到深圳沙头角定居。回忆起小时候的艰苦生活，陈观玉说着说着突然就哽咽了起来。陈观玉家居住的沙头角沙栏吓村，距离香港只有一街之隔。在 13 岁之前，陈观玉都在香港大埔几个大户人家里打工，受尽了冷眼和欺凌。

"后来，我们回沙头角种田，我虽然很小，但是我干的活比一些大人还要多。我很勤快，人家吃饱饭，要休息 5 分钟，我从来不休息的，还曾经被评为先进小社员。"陈观玉说，"我很小就学会了犁田，经常挑一百多斤。什么都干，但是家里年年都超支。"

在 20 世纪的集体化时期，生产队在年终结算时，会将农户一年获得的工分收入用来抵扣从生产队得到的粮食、实物和借款等，当农户支大于收，就是超支。由于家里人口数量多而劳动力少，陈观玉家是沙头角有名的超支大户。生产队长知道陈观玉家里非常困难，平时会接济一些地瓜（番薯）给他们。

或许是打小就形成的饥饿记忆，陈观玉告诉我们，一直以来她都非常喜欢吃咸菜焖猪肉（以咸菜、五花肉为主要材料制作而成的一道客家菜），而且特别喜欢挑里面的肥肉来吃，如今依然如故，尽管她现在因为肠胃消化功能不好，不敢吃太多。

可就是在家里连野菜粥都吃不上的艰难困境下，陈观玉的母亲还是经常会在路边救济一些无家可归的老人。"在我五六岁的时候，我妈妈就教我读《三字经》《增广贤文》，教我做人的道理，告诉我'救人一命，胜造七级浮屠'。宁可自己吃苦，也不要欺负别人。"

"春种一粒粟，秋收万颗子。"在母亲的言传身教下，一颗乐于助人的爱心种子在陈观玉的心中慢慢生根发芽。

学雷锋做好事，就是为了感恩

陈观玉是深圳侨界的杰出代表，同时也是这座充满爱心的城市的模范代表。全国归侨侨眷先进个人、全国三八红旗手（1983 年、1996 年两次）、全国老有所为奉献奖、全国学雷锋标兵、广东省学雷锋标兵、广东省优秀共产党员、广东省劳动模范、改革开放 30 周年感动广东人物、深圳市"文明市民"、鹏城慈善 40 年致敬人物……迄今，陈观玉获得的各种大小荣誉已经超过百项。

陈观玉与丈夫李桂胜以及一对儿女的家庭合照。
Chen Guanyu with her husband, Li Guisheng, and their son and daughter.

2010 年 9 月 2 日，"深圳经济特区 30 年 30 位杰出人物"评选结果揭晓，陈观玉被评为其中的 10 位"杰出模范人物"之一。关于陈观玉，当时的介绍材料中有这么一段话："她 1966 年加入中国共产党，数十年如一日照顾孤寡，救助穷困，拥军优属，关心青少年健康成长，热心公益事业，做了大量好事，被誉为'中英街上的活雷锋'。"

为什么要学雷锋，为什么要做好事？这或许是许多采访陈观玉的媒体向她问得最多的一个问题。对此，陈观玉的回答就是两个字——"感恩"。

原来陈观玉婚后不久，因为小产得了癫痫病，常在发作时神志不清，曾掉到河沟里、水井边，是沙头角附近的驻军战士一次次将她从死亡的边缘拉了回来。"为了感谢解放军的救命之恩，我与爱人商量，将两个孩子分别改名为'拥军''爱民'。"陈观玉透露，以前每年的八一建军节，她都会带着两个小孩挑着柴火去慰问家附近的边防官兵，"莲塘、石坳（今罗芳村附近）、长岭、梧桐山哨所，凡是有部队的地方，我们都会去"。当然，后来致富了的陈观玉还是一如既往地热心支援当地驻军的建设，不是给部队送去慰问金，就是捐款购买图书和康乐设施等。

从 20 世纪 60 年代起，陈观玉就在沙头角坚持义务为周围的居民理发，几十年来从未间断。不仅如此，她还曾先后义务帮忙照顾 13 名"五保户"，给他们缝洗晾晒衣物，帮助他们看病取药。尽管那个时候，陈观玉家里的情况也不算好，但是，平时有好吃的，她还是会先送到这些孤寡老人家里，剩下的才是孩子和丈夫的，以致有人说她家的孩子像是"后娘养的"。过年过节，陈观玉都是和这些老人们一起度过，有几位老人是握着她的手离开人世的。

陈观玉目前居住在沙头角中英街里。她家一楼客厅的玻璃橱窗里，展示着她获得的各种奖牌、奖杯、奖状，墙上则挂满了她亲手绘制的雷锋、焦裕禄、麦贤得、钟南山等英雄人物画像，以及她抄写的拥军歌曲。其中一张已经有点泛黄的奖状上面写着"赠给：陈观玉奶奶／让同一兰（蓝）天下的孩子有一个美好的明天／献爱心送温暖"。看落款，应该是河北一个名叫"张素珍"的学生，在 1995 年 3 月 12 日，

河北张家口张北县学生张素珍赠陈观玉的奖状。
A certificate presented to Chen Guanyu by Zhang Suzhen, a student in Zhangbei County, Zhangjiakou, Hebei Province.

以这种特别的方式给她写的"感谢信"。

原来，1995 年，陈观玉在电视上看到河北张家口张北县馒头营乡的女孩张素珍因家境贫困而辍学的新闻后，彻夜难眠。第二天一大早，她就赶到邮局给小素珍寄了一封信和 1000 元钱。后来陈观玉又提出，由她一家捐助张北县 22 名儿童复学。陈观玉的义举带动了当时的沙头角镇和张北县之间的"1+1"助学活动。很快沙头角各界人士捐赠了 140 多万元，兴建了 4 所"沙头角希望小学"，并与张北县 519 名失学和面临失学的学生结成了对子。

意外发了财，就要捐出去

陈观玉告诉我们，关于她发财的故事很多人都很喜欢听，但其实一开始她就不是冲着发财去的。

深圳发展银行（现在的平安银行前身之一）是中国第一家面向社会公众公开发行股票并上市的商业银行，其前身又可以追溯到1987年由深圳本地21家农信社合并成立的深圳市联合信用银行。1987年5月9日，尽管还没有拿到正式的"准生证"，但深圳市政府决定，由中国人民银行深圳分行批准深圳发展银行首次以公募方式，采取自由认购办法，向社会公开发行39.65万股，每股面额20元，筹集资金793万元作为股本金。

然而，由于公众对股票的认识不够，在那个年代，要想向储户配售深发展的认股证非常困难，毕竟股票这东西可不像存款那样，是能够保本的。当时一则报纸新闻也记录了这样一件事：有单位为了完成发行任务，规定凡认购者每股个人出一半的钱，单位再补贴一半，非党员每人1000股，党员须认购2000股。

在1987年，像陈观玉这样主动购买深发展股票的储户并不多。当时银行业务员上门来动员陈观玉买股票，她立即说："我不赌钱的，不好的事我从来都不干的。但是，如果是能够帮人的话，要我把命搭上我都愿意。"对方告诉她，这不是赌博，是支援国家建设，因为国家还不富裕，需要大家去支援，但是本钱有可能会没了的。

其实，当时的陈观玉身体并不好，长期生病，饱受胃出血、胃下垂、十二指肠溃疡等各种疾病的困扰，医生曾经一度跟她讲"你吃不了过年饭了"。但是，一听到是支援国家建设，陈观玉立即就把自己的存款和在香港的弟弟、妹妹资助她治病的钱，全部转入信用社，兑换了6万深发展股票。"我想我就算是死了，这也是我为深圳特区人民做的最后一件善事。"

当陈观玉在给人理发时，说起自己买了股票的事，很多人都说她是"神经病"，说你平时都需要人家支援，出什么风头支援国家建设啊。3年之后，陈观玉的身体有了好转，与此同时，她当初购买的深发展股票也翻了好几倍。原沙头角公社书记张润添等人劝陈观玉把股票卖了，起初她说："我是支援国家建设的，我不要钱。"

不过，陈观玉最后还是把股票兑现，领回了45万元巨款。当晚她便和家人开家庭会议，拿出了30万元来资助那些有需要的单位和贫困、残疾个人，其中，陈观玉给妇幼中心捐了5万元，给沙头角镇小学捐了1万元，给沙头角幼儿园捐了3000元，其余的她就按1000元、2000元、3000元不等的份额，塞进几十个信封里，给她所知道的困难家庭、残疾人、山区失学儿童等汇了出去。

剩下的十多万元，陈观玉就给她弟弟妹妹在中英街外建了一间三层楼的房子，只是由于他们人都在香港，不回来住，陈观玉就把建好的房屋租了出去。但是，陈观玉记得《增广贤文》里的"钱财如粪土，仁义值千金"。过去 30 多年，她把房屋出租得来的 200 多万元，又陆续捐了出去。"我们的江山都是先烈们用鲜血换来的。我们现在发财了，去帮助他人，有什么好心疼的。"陈观玉说道。

陈观玉家在 2011 年召开的一次家庭会议。
Chen Guanyu holds a family meeting in 2011.

夫妻争相做好事，大数目互相"包庇"

学雷锋，做好事，数十年如一日，当记者问陈观玉：你有没有因为自己的善良而被人骗过呢？"有啊。"她爽朗地回答，"知道被骗了之后，一开始我会有点伤心，但后来想通了，我大人不记小人过。社会上有好多种人，如果没有那么多坏人，政府就不用去干预，就不用派那么多人去做保卫工作了。这样去想，我就想开了，不会很烦恼。"

"他骗我的钱十万八万，他不会发财，我亏了十万八万，我也不会穷。我始终觉得，人在做，天在看。做人一定要有信念，一定要行正道。我们没有做坏事，问心无愧，就能半夜敲门心不惊。"

在学雷锋的路上，陈观玉也曾受过委屈。1969 年，她上医院去照顾一个穷苦的癌症病人，因为对方是男性，结果回来之后，闹得满城风雨。"我本来是全心全意为人民服务的，却因为做好事差点连老公都没有了。那时候我很委屈，觉得好冤枉，差点想放弃。但是我想到了之前学习过的'老三篇'（即由毛泽东写的《纪念白求恩》《为人民服务》《愚公移山》三篇短文），还有毛主席说的'一个人做点好事并不难，难的是一辈子做好事，不做坏事'。我想，这也许是考验我一个共产党员的时候。正是因为难，我们共产党员就要向前，向困难挑战，不要低头。"

陈观玉的丈夫名叫李桂胜，退休前是沙头角一所学校的老师，已在2013年因中风去世。在丈夫中风住院期间，曾经有一个年轻女孩拿着2000元找上门，陈观玉很惊讶。对方说，她现在已经读大学，请李老师不要再给她寄钱了。

陈观玉表示，丈夫李桂胜始终是她做好事的最大支持者，离开丈夫和家人的支持，她什么也做不成，更不可能几十年都还在坚持学雷锋，做好事。"在捐款的问题上，我们夫妻小的数目互相沟通，大的数目互相'包庇'。他怕我不够大方，我又怕他不够大方，怕产生矛盾。"陈观玉口中的捐款"小数目"是指5000元、1万元，而"大数目"就是十万八万元。"其实我们夫妻两个都很大方的。我在偷偷摸摸做好事，他也在偷偷摸摸做好事。"

陈观玉还有个爱好，喜欢随身携带相机，将一切有意义的事情透过镜头记录下来。现在她用的一台数码相机就是妹妹从香港买回来给她的。她还习惯将拍下来的照片冲洗出来，一式两份，一份自己保存，一份写下自己的感受送给对方，并附送5元钱作为感谢。她现在每个月光是洗照片，都要花一千几百元。

陈观玉解释，5元钱代表着五谷丰登，代表着中国越来越好。更主要的还是，小时候家里困难，当时有个解放军战士在学校作报告时给了她5元钱，让她拿回家去买米。"我现在快84岁了，就是这5块钱给了我一辈子的力量，特别是当我碰到困难的时候。"

至于给人写感谢的话，陈观玉始终相信，良言一句三冬暖，恶语伤人六月寒。"每天讲好话，可以带动很多人做好事。有时候虽然只有一封信，但是可以救到很多人。"曾经有一个未婚少女给陈观玉写信，说自己怀孕了，男朋友不要她了，想去死。陈观玉立即给对方回信，劝说女孩不要寻死，要坚强，没有什么大不了的。后来，想通了的女孩再一次给陈观玉写信，道："阿姨，你救了我的命。我以后要好好地活着，好好地工作。"

爱心队伍壮大，共添世间美好

"送人玫瑰，手有余香。"这原本是一句源于古印度的谚语，现在已经成为"深圳十大观念"之一，深圳人对此可谓是耳熟能详。其实，这句话一直以来也是深圳义工坚持的一个理念。

在深圳义工联里，陈观玉的义工号为"530"号，也就是说，她是深圳义工联的第530位义工。"我是1995年在丛飞（深圳爱心大使，原深圳义工联艺术团团长）的推荐下，申请成为义工的。"陈观玉透露，"成为义工后，我觉得自己的生活内容更丰富了，圈子更广了，朋友更多了。"2005年，陈观玉获得"深圳市五星级

"观玉之家"爱心驿站橱窗。（来源：《晶报》）
The show window at the "Guanyu House" kindness station. (Photo: *Daily Sunshine*)

义工"的光荣称号。

　　至今，陈观玉仍然是深圳义工联爱心组的一员。因为得了白内障，陈观玉看书、写东西时，视力都很模糊，一见到强光眼睛就很痛，所以现在她都习惯戴着一副墨镜。再加上年纪大了，腿脚不灵便了，陈观玉出门开始越来越少。但是，只要身体许可，她都会坚持去家附近的中英街历史博物馆或中英街关口的义工站做义工。早在 2017 年 10 月 9 日，在陈观玉的牵头下，"深圳市中英街雷锋爱心义工队"在深圳市义工联注册成立。2018 年 4 月 23 日，"深圳市观玉学雷锋志愿服务学会"在深圳市民政局注册成功。

　　中英街雷锋爱心义工队的注册地址就在陈观玉的家，联系人就是陈观玉的儿子李大成（即她口中的"爱民"）。在母亲长期的言传身教之下，李大成现在也经常利用周末去做义工，为中英街雷锋爱心义工队出力。他还是深圳市观玉学雷锋志愿服务学会的副会长。

　　中英街雷锋爱心义工队平时主要负责维护中英街进出通关秩序、为观光购物的游客提供便民服务、提升市容环境等工作。在中英街因为疫情进行封闭管理时，义工们主要是负责给远道而来的游客做耐心的解释、疏导工作。在义工队里，大家都叫陈观玉为"陈妈妈"。为了激励更多的人来参加雷锋爱心义工队，"陈妈妈"坚持与每一位义工合影，并制作专属的工作牌送给他们。

在中英街关口外边的"观玉之家"爱心驿站橱窗里，记者见到很多义工队队员写下的一则则感言。其中一位署名为"肖柳"的义工的留言令人印象特别深刻，她这么写道：

2017年的某天，通过朋友介绍，第一次报名参加中英街雷锋爱心义工队的无偿义工服务活动。

弹指一挥间，已经六年了，在这六年中虽没时时参与，但稍有空闲时间就会想起义友们！对于参与而言，说不上全力以赴，但我想至少需要一份坚持与热爱。

当坚持与热爱成为一种习惯，当人们愿意为自己无法享用的树荫栽树，当不平凡的美德成为平凡！

想想……这人世间又何等的美好。

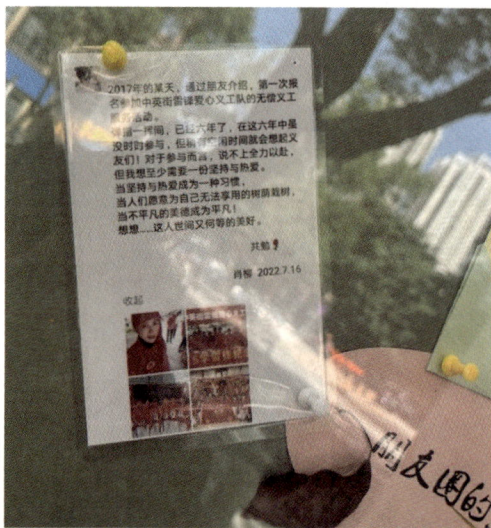

义工肖柳的留言。（来源：《晶报》）
A message from Xiao Liu, a volunteer. (Photo: *Daily Sunshine*)

在"陈妈妈"的感召之下，中英街雷锋爱心义工队迅速壮大。除了沙头角、盐田区本地的义工外，义工队还吸引了一批来自罗湖、福田、南山等区的义工。尽管现在年事已高，但是陈观玉"学雷锋，做好事"的初心依然未改。她说："只要身体允许，我会一直做下去。"

（除署名外，本文图片均由受访者陈观玉提供。参考资料：《华工与战前马来亚的开发》《侨心向党 追梦百年》。）

Chen Guanyu

"The living Lei Feng" on Zhongying Street influences others by her word and deed

Chen Guanyu is a returned overseas Chinese from Singapore, and a retired employee of Shenzhen Shatoujiao Aquatic Products Company. Born in an overseas Chinese family in Singapore in November 1939, she returned to Shatoujiao to settle down when she was 10 years old. She joined the Communist Party of China (CPC) in 1966 and attended the 15th National Congress of the CPC held in Beijing as a representative in 1997.

For decades, she has taken care of orphans and widows, helped the poor, supported the army, helped the families of army men and martyrs, cared about the healthy growth of young people, and has been enthusiastic about public welfare. Known as "the living Lei Feng on Zhongying Street," She has been awarded many honors, including the National Advanced Individual of Returned Overseas Chinese and Relatives of Overseas Chinese Nationals Residing in China, the National March 8th Red Banner Pacesetter (twice), the National Contribution Award for the Elderly, the National Model in Learning from Lei Feng, the Guangdong Provincial Model in Learning from Lei Feng, the Excellent Communist Party Member of Guangdong Province, the Guangdong Provincial Model Worker, and the Good Citizen of Shenzhen Municipality.

It was an afternoon in October 2022. At the gate of Zhongying Street, Shatoujiao, Yantian District, Shenzhen, the lively scene of long queues at the checkpoint had long disappeared. There were only people in twos and threes coming in and out through the resident passage. Because of the COVID-19 pandemic, tourists could not enter Zhongying Street, but at the entrance of the closed tourist passage, there still stood two volunteers in red vest. As members of the Lei Feng Kindness Volunteer Team on Zhongying Street, they explained the matter to guests attracted by the street's reputation.

The Lei Feng Kindness Volunteer Team on Zhongying Street of Shenzhen was registered at the Shenzhen Volunteer Association in October 2017 under the leadership of Chen Guanyu,

The interview took place in 2022.

"the living Lei Feng on Zhongying Street." The "Guanyu House" outside the checkpoint of Zhongying Street in Shatoujiao is a kindness station served by the volunteer team.

Sitting in front of us, Chen turned out to be very talkative. There are many vivid stories behind the good deeds she did.

"Better to bear hardships than to bully others"

In November 1939, Chen was born in a poor overseas Chinese family in Singapore (then a British colony). Chen has been weak and sick since she was a child, and she suffered from asthma at the age of 3. But, as a Chinese proverb says, poor children are early masters. When she was five or six years old, she had to help the family take care of her younger siblings. When she was 8 years old, she had to get up early and go to the rubber plantation to cut rubber. Chen recalled, "The days of rubber cutting were bitter. At 3 o'clock in the morning, I had to go out with a headlight. I cut 400 rubber trees one by one. At 6 o'clock, when the sun came out, the rubber would not flow out. Sometimes I was bitten by centipedes, and it hurt badly."

However, as a child cutting rubber in Singapore, Chen was most afraid of tigers. She said, "I'm afraid of being eaten by a tiger." It seemed a fantasy in the mind of a child, but, after searching relevant historical documents, we found that she told the truth. In an academic paper about overseas Chinese, *Chinese Laborers and the Development of Malaya Before the War*, written by a scholar named Guo Shunping, there is a description: "Singapore used to be a territory of Johor State, and was once the site of Temasek, an island country, in the Middle Ages. Only a few Malays and Chinese lived there, where mangrove forests and swamps were everywhere, while tigers came and went without regularity." (From the *Journal of Fujian Normal University, Philosophy and Social Sciences Edition*, No. 2, 1986)

At the age of 10, Chen returned to Shatoujiao, Shenzhen from Singapore with her parents and other family members. Recalling the hard life she had lived as a child, Chen suddenly choked up. Shalanxia Village, Shatoujiao, where Chen's family lived, was only one street away from Hong Kong. Before the age of 13, Chen worked in the homes of several rich families in Tai Po, Hong Kong, and suffered all kinds of cold eyes and bullying.

"Later, we came back to farm in Shatoujiao. Although I was very young, I did more work than some grown-ups. And I was very diligent. Other people rested for five minutes on a full stomach, but I never took a rest. I was voted advanced young commune member," Chen said. "I learned to plow the field at a very young age, and I often carried a burden of more than 100 catties. I did everything, but my family overspent every year."

During the collectivization period in the 20th century, at the end of a year, the production team would deduct the work points earned by the farmers in the year from the grain, goods, and loans that the production team allocated to them. When a family got more than they earned, it meant overspending. Chen's family was a well-known overspending household in Shatoujiao because there were many people in the family but few of them could work. The production team's leaders knew that it was very difficult for Chen's family, so they often gave some sweet potatoes to them.

Maybe because of the memory of hunger that formed when she was a child, Chen has always liked to eat braised pork with salted vegetables (a Hakka dish made with pickles and pork belly as the main ingredients), and she especially likes the fat part. This habit remains unchanged, although she dares not eat too much now because of poor digestion.

However, in the hard days when the family could not even afford wild vegetable porridge, Chen's mother often helped some homeless elderly people on the side of the road. "When I was five or six years old, my mother taught me to read the *Three-Character Classic* and the *Aphorisms from the Ancient Chinese*, taught me the principles of life, and told me that 'saving a life is better than building a seven-level pagoda'. It's better to bear hardships than to bully others."

"Plant a grain of millet in the spring, and harvest ten thousand seeds in the autumn." Under the guidance of her mother's words and deeds, a seed of love and help slowly took root in Chen's heart.

Paying back by doing good deeds like Lei Feng

Chen is an outstanding representative of the overseas Chinese community in Shenzhen, and a model representative of this caring city. She has won more than 100 honors of various kinds, such as the National Advanced Individual of Returned Overseas Chinese and Relatives of Overseas Chinese Nationals Residing in China, the National March 8th Red Banner Pacesetter (in 1983 and 1996), the National Contribution Award for the Elderly, the National Model in Learning from Lei Feng, the Guangdong Provincial Model in Learning from Lei Feng, the Excellent Communist Party Member of Guangdong Province, the Guangdong Provincial Model Worker, the Good Citizen of Shenzhen Municipality, and the Respected Personage in 40 Years of Shenzhen Charity...

On September 2, 2010, the results of the selection of "30 Outstanding Figures in the 30 Years of Shenzhen Special Economic Zone" were announced, and Chen was named one of the 10 "Outstanding Role Models." There was a passage in the introduction to her: "She joined the Communist Party of China in 1966. For decades, she has taken care of orphans and widows, helped the poor, helped the families of army men and martyrs, cared about the healthy growth of young people, and has been enthusiastic about public welfare. She has done a lot of good deeds and is called 'the living Lei Feng on Zhongying Street.'"

Why did Chen learn from Lei Feng and do those good deeds? This is perhaps the most asked question for her in media interviews. Her answer is two words: "paying back."

It turned out that shortly after she got married, Chen suffered from epilepsy due to a miscarriage. She was often unconscious during seizures, and even fell into river ditches and wells. It was the garrison soldiers near Shatoujiao who repeatedly pulled her back from the brink of death. "In order to thank the People's Liberation Army for saving my life, I discussed with my husband and renamed our two children as 'Yongjun' (meaning 'supporting the army') and 'Aimin' (meaning 'loving the people')." Chen revealed that in the past, on August 1, the Army Day, she would take her two children to carry firewood to visit the frontier officers and soldiers near her home. "Liantang, Shi'ao (near today's Luofang Village), Changling, and Wutong Mountain outpost. We would go wherever the troops were." Of course, after she became rich later, she continued to enthusiastically support the construction of the local garrison, either giving financial assistance to the troops, or donating money to buy books and recreational facilities.

Since the 1960s, Chen has provided free haircut for residents in Shatoujiao for decades, and has never stopped. In addition, she has volunteered to take care of 13 "five-guarantee households," sewing, washing and drying their clothes, and helping them see a doctor and get medicine. Although Chen's family was not rich in the past, when she got or cooked delicious food, she would give it to those elderly persons of no family, leaving the rest to her children and husband, so that her children were said to be like "those raised by a stepmother." Chen spent the Chinese New Year and other festivals with these elderly people, and several of them passed away holding her hand.

Chen currently lives in Zhongying Street, Shatoujiao. In the glass window of the living room on the first floor of her house, all kinds of medals, trophies, and certificates of merit she won are displayed. The walls are covered with portraits of heroic figures such as Lei Feng, Jiao Yulu, Mai Xiande, and Zhong Nanshan, as well as songs supporting the army that she copied by hand. One of the certificates is already yellowish. It reads, "To: Grandma Chen / Let the children under the same blue sky have a better tomorrow / You have sent love and warmth." According to the inscription, it was a "letter of thanks" written to her in this special way on March 12, 1995 by a student named "Zhang Suzhen" in Hebei Province.

One day in 1995, Chen couldn't sleep all night after seeing the news on TV that Zhang, a girl in Mantouying Township, Zhangbei County, Zhangjiakou, Hebei Province, had dropped out of school because of family poverty. Early the next morning, Chen rushed to the post office to send the girl a letter and 1,000 yuan. Later, Chen proposed that her family should donate to help 22 children in Zhangbei County return to school. Her charitable deeds led to the "1+1" student aid activity between Shatoujiao Township and Zhangbei County. In a short time, people from all walks of life in Shatoujiao donated more than 1.4 million yuan to build four "Shatoujiao Hope Primary Schools" and formed pairs with 519 students in Zhangbei County who were out of school or had the possibility of dropping out.

"When I accidentally make a fortune, I should donate it"

Chen told us the story about her getting rich. Many people like to hear it, but in fact, she didn't mean to get rich in the first place.

Shenzhen Development Bank (one of the predecessors of the current Ping An Bank) was the first commercial bank in China to publicly issue shares and get listed. Its predecessor can be traced back to the "Shenzhen United Credit Bank" formed in 1987 by the merger of 21 local rural credit cooperatives in Shenzhen. On May 9, 1987, even without a formal "birth certificate," the Shenzhen Municipal Government decided that the Shenzhen Branch of the People's Bank of China would approve Shenzhen Development Bank's initial public offering of 396,500 shares through free subscription, with a par value of 20 yuan per share, raising 7.93 million yuan as share capital.

However, the public had little knowledge of stocks, so it was very difficult to issue the warrants of Shenzhen Development Bank (SDB) to its depositors. After all, stocks are not like deposits, which can preserve capital. A newspaper story at that time recorded such a thing: to complete the issuance task, some units stipulated that all subscribers would pay half of the money for the shares, and the unit would subsidize another half. Those who were not Party members must subscribe for 1,000 shares each, and Party members must subscribe for 2,000 shares.

In 1987, there were not many depositors like Chen who took the initiative to buy SDB shares. A bank clerk came to mobilize her to buy the shares, and she immediately replied, "I don't gamble, and I never do bad things. But I am willing to risk my life if that can help others." The clerk told her that this was not gambling but supporting the construction of the country, because the country was not rich yet and needed everyone's support. But the clerk admitted that the capital to be invested might be gone.

In fact, Chen was not in good health at that time. She had been ill for a long time and suffered from various diseases such as gastric bleeding, gastroptosis, and duodenal ulcer. She was once told, "You can't live long enough to have the Chinese New Year's dinner." However, as soon as she heard that it was supporting the country's construction, Chen immediately transferred all his savings and the money from his brother and sister in Hong Kong to support her medical treatment to the credit cooperative, and exchanged it into 60,000 SDB shares. "I thought even if I died, this would be the last good deed I did for the people of Shenzhen Special Economic Zone."

When giving haircuts, Chen told people that she had bought the stock. Many of them said that she was "crazy." "You often need support from others. Why put yourself forward and support the construction of the country?" Three years later, Chen's health was improved, and the price of her SDB shares multiplied. Zhang Runtian, former secretary of Shatoujiao Commune, and others persuaded Chen to sell the stock. At first, she said, "I am supporting the country's construction, and I don't want money for it."

However, Chen finally cashed out the stock and got back a huge sum of 450,000 yuan. She held a family meeting that evening to donate 300,000 yuan to support needy units and poor and disabled individuals, including 50,000 yuan for the maternal and child center, 10,000 yuan for the Shatoujiao Primary School, and 3,000 yuan for the Shatoujiao Kindergarten. She stuffed the rest of the money into dozens of envelopes, ranging from 1,000 yuan and 2,000 yuan to 3,000 yuan, and remitted the money to families with difficulties, disabled people, and out-of-school children in mountainous areas she knew.

With the remaining more than 100,000 yuan, Chen built a three-story house for her younger brother and sister outside Zhongying Street, but because they were all in Hong Kong and did not come back to live, Chen rented out the house. However, she always remembers a sentence in the *Aphorisms from the Ancient Chinese*: "Money is like dung, while benevolence and righteousness are worth a thousand pieces of gold." In more than 30 years, she has donated more than 2 million yuan from renting out the house. "Our country was founded with the blood of the martyrs. Now that we are rich, there is nothing to regret when we help others," she said.

The couple scrambles to do good deeds, "covering up" large donations

Chen has been learning from Lei Feng and doing good deeds for decades. We asked her, "Have you ever been deceived by others because of your kindness?" "Yes," She replied frankly. "After knowing that I was cheated, I was a little sad at first, but I figured it out later. As a person of high status, I forgave the faults of people of low status. There are many kinds of people in society. If there were not so many bad people, the government wouldn't need to intervene or send so many people to do security work. Thinking about it this way, I accepted it and I was not very troubled."

"He wouldn't get rich by swindling me out of 100,000 or 80,000 yuan, and I wouldn't get poor after losing 100,000 or 80,000 yuan. I always believe that God knows what you did. To be a human being, one must have faith and must take the right road. We have done nothing wrong and feel no shame, so we won't be afraid if someone knocks on our door in the middle of the night."

Chen was sometimes wronged when she did good deeds. In 1969, she went to the hospital to take care of a poor cancer patient, who was a man. When she came back home, it became a big scandal. "I meant to serve the people wholeheartedly, but I almost lost my husband because of doing a good deed. At that time, I was wronged and felt deeply unfair, and I almost wanted to give up. But I thought of the 'three old articles' I had studied before (namely three short essays written by Mao Zedong, *In Memory of Norman Bethune*, *Serve the People*, and *The Foolish Old Man Removes Mountains*), as well as what Chairman Mao had said, 'It is not difficult for a person to do a few good deeds, but it is difficult to do good deeds and no bad deeds all his life.' I thought this might be the time to test me as a Communist Party member. As a result of the difficulties, we Communists must move forward and challenge difficulties without bowing our heads."

Chen's husband, named Li Guisheng, was a teacher at a school in Shatoujiao before retiring. He died of a stroke in 2013. To her surprise, when her husband was hospitalized for the stroke, a young girl came with 2,000 yuan. Then the girl said that she was now in college and asked Mr. Li not to send her money anymore.

Chen said that her husband had always been her biggest supporter of doing good deeds. Without the support of her husband and family, she could have done nothing, let alone continue to learn from Lei Feng and do good deeds for decades. "On the issue of donations, my husband and I discussed with each other when the amount was small, and 'covered up' large donations between each other. He was afraid that I wouldn't be generous enough, and I was afraid that he wouldn't be generous enough. We were afraid that it would cause conflicts." The "small amount" of donations, as she said, refers to 5,000 or 10,000 yuan, and the "large amount" is 100,000 or 80,000 yuan. "Actually, both my husband and I were generous. I was doing good deeds in secret, and so was he."

Chen has the hobby of carrying a camera with her to record everything meaningful through the lens. The digital camera she uses now was bought by her younger sister from Hong Kong. She is used to developing the photos she takes, making two copies, keeping one for herself, writing down her feelings for the other party, and sending 5 yuan as appreciation. She now spends more than 1,000 yuan a month developing photos.

Chen explained that 5 yuan represented a good harvest and a country becoming better and better. More importantly, when she was a child, her family was poor, and a soldier of the People's Liberation Army making a speech at her school gave her 5 yuan, asking her to take it home and buy rice. "I am almost 84 years old now, and it is the 5 yuan that has given me strength for my whole life, especially when I encounter difficulties."

As for writing the words of thanks, Chen always believes that, as the saying goes, a good word can make people feel warm in winter while a bad word can make them feel cold in summer. "Speaking kind words every day can drive many people to do good deeds. Sometimes even one letter can save many people." Once an unmarried girl wrote to Chen, saying that she wanted to die because she was pregnant and her boyfriend didn't want to be with her anymore. Chen immediately wrote back to persuade the girl not to commit suicide but to be strong, because nothing was a big deal. Later, the girl came round and wrote to Chen, "Auntie, you saved my life. I will live a good life and work hard in the future."

Teams of kindness grow stronger, adding to the beauty of the world

"The roses in her hand, the flavor in mine." This proverb originated from ancient India has become one of the "Top 10 Ideas in Shenzhen," and Shenzhen people are familiar with it. In fact, this sentence is a concept that Shenzhen volunteers have always adhered to.

In the Shenzhen Volunteer Association, Chen's volunteer number is "530," meaning that she is the 530th volunteer of the association. "I applied to become a volunteer in 1995 under the recommendation of Cong Fei (Shenzhen Kindness Ambassador and former head of the Shenzhen Volunteer Association Art Troupe)," Chen revealed. "After becoming a volunteer, I have felt that my life has become more enriched. I have enjoyed a wider circle and more friends." In 2005, Chen won the honorary title of "Shenzhen Five-Star Volunteer".

Now Chen is still a member of the Kindness Group of the Shenzhen Volunteer

Association. Because of cataracts, her eyes are very blurry when reading and writing, and hurt when seeing strong light, so she is used to wearing a pair of sunglasses now. In addition, she is getting older and can't walk so smoothly as before, so she goes out less. However, if her heath permits, she will keep volunteering at the Zhongying Street History Museum near her home or at the volunteer station at the entrance of Zhongying Street. As early as October 9, 2017, under the leadership of Chen, the "Lei Feng Kindness Volunteer Team on Zhongying Street of Shenzhen" was registered in the Shenzhen Volunteer Association. On April 23, 2018, the "Shenzhen Guanyu Volunteer Service Society for Learning from Lei Feng" was successfully registered in the Shenzhen Municipal Civil Affairs Bureau.

The registered address of the Lei Feng Kindness Volunteer Team on Zhongying Street is Chen's home, and the contact person is Chen's son, Li Dacheng, whom she calls "Aimin." Under the long-term guidance of his mother's precepts and deeds, he now often spends weekends doing volunteer work for the Lei Feng Kindness Volunteer Team on Zhongying Street. He is also the vice president of the Shenzhen Guanyu Volunteer Service Society for Learning from Lei Feng.

The Lei Feng Kindness Volunteer Team on Zhongying Street is mainly responsible for maintaining the entry and exit order at the customs of Zhongying Street, providing convenient services for tourists going sightseeing and shopping, and improving the urban environment. When Zhongying Street was closed due to the COVID-19 pandemic, the volunteers' main work was to patiently explain to tourists from afar. In the volunteer team, everyone calls Chen "Mother Chen." In a bid to encourage more people to join the Lei Feng Kindness Volunteer Team, "Mother Chen" continues to have photos taken with each volunteer and make exclusive work badges for them.

In the show window of the "Guanyu House" kindness station outside the entrance of Zhongying Street, there are many reflections written by members of the volunteer team. Among them, the message from a volunteer named "Xiao Liu" is particularly impressive. She wrote:

One day in 2017, through a friend's introduction, I signed up for the first time to participate in the unpaid volunteer service activity of the Lei Feng Kindness Volunteer Team on Zhongying Street.

In the blink of an eye, it has been six years. Although I have not frequently participated during these six years, I will think of my fellow volunteers once I have a little spare time! As far as participation is concerned, I cannot say that I have gone all out, but I think that at least persistence and love are needed.

When persistence and love become a habit, when people are willing to plant trees for the shade they cannot enjoy, and when extraordinary virtues become ordinary...

Think about it... How beautiful this world is.

Inspired by "Mother Chen," the Lei Feng Kindness Volunteer Team on Zhongying Street has grown rapidly. In addition to local volunteers from Shatoujiao and Yantian District, the volunteer team has also attracted some volunteers from Luohu, Futian, Nanshan and other districts. Although she is getting old now, Chen's original aspiration of "learning from Lei Feng and doing good deeds" remains unchanged. She said, "As long as my body allows, I will continue to do it."

(Photos courtesy of Chen Guanyu, except for those with credit. References: *Chinese Laborers and the Development of Malaya Before the War* and *Hearts of Overseas Chinese Turn to the Party, Pursuing Dreams for a Hundred Years.*)

杨华根

传扬中华美食与文化，
推广体育聚人心

杨华根　Wah Kun Yeung

　　杨华根，1947年出生于广东省中山县康济乡南溪村（现属珠海市香洲区凤山街道南溪社区），1958年移居香港，1972年赴荷兰发展，在阿姆斯特丹经营餐馆、旅行社等，现常居深圳和香港。现任荷比深圳总商会暨联谊会名誉会长，曾任全荷华人社团联合会主席、荷兰华人参政基金会主席、全荷华人体育总会主席、荷兰百年华人志庆基金会主席、旅荷华人联谊会理事、旅荷华人联谊会中文学校校董会主席、中国海外交流协会常务理事等职，现任全荷华人联合体育运动总会永远名誉主席、暨南大学董事会董事、暨南大学荷比卢校友会名誉会长。

　　杨华根热心公益和侨务，积极推动中荷经贸、文化、体育交流。参与组织多届全荷华人体育运动会，加强了华侨华人之间的团结合作以及世界各地侨界的联谊。主持出版《荷兰华人百年》一书，该书由荷兰首相马克·吕特撰写前言。2000年，荷兰女王授予他"奥兰治王室军官勋章"。

采访时间：2024年。

杨华根和深圳挺有缘。在荷兰，他接触了不少深圳乡亲，曾在侨团里与来自深圳的毕传友、蔡树坚等人共事。深圳的访问团去荷兰，他也曾参与座谈。

杨华根常居深圳、香港，亲眼见证了改革开放带给深圳的巨大变化。在深圳，他喜欢在住处附近散步，也喜欢坐地铁去见朋友。"有些朋友是在荷兰认识的，有些是在深圳认识的。"

深圳市民的素质给杨华根留下了深刻的印象。他坐公交、地铁时，遇到很多年轻人给他让座。这样的礼貌举动，让他觉得很舒心。

他说，在荷兰的公共交通工具上，人们也会让座给华人长者。他听老一辈说，以前，有些"老外"看不起中国，看不起华人，所以不会让座。现在，就大不一样了。从这件小事中，他也感受到了中国的强大、海外华侨华人地位的提高。

当然，这样的变化背后，也离不开各个侨团以及像杨华根这样的侨领们的付出与贡献。

2024年4月的一个午后，杨华根在深圳接受了记者的专访。旅居荷兰几十年的他，乡音未改。字正腔圆的粤语里，带着温文尔雅的气度；不疾不徐的讲述中，透着平易近人的谦逊。

闯荡荷兰，弘扬中华饮食文化

杨华根的父亲很早就背井离乡去香港谋生。抗日战争期间，日本侵略者兵临香港，杨华根的父母逃难返回家乡中山县。1947年11月，杨华根出生。1958年，他跟随家人到香港生活，在那里读完了中学。

杨华根中学毕业后就进入职场，在荷兰贸易公司（Netherlands Trading Society）香港九龙的分支机构工作，一路做到了出纳主任。荷兰贸易公司后来合并为荷兰通用银行（ABN），之后又合并为荷兰银行（ABN AMRO Bank）。

杨华根在工作中接触到一些从荷兰回来的华侨华人，觉得外面的世界很精彩，想趁着年轻出去闯一

海城大酒楼。（来源：海城大酒楼官网）
Oriental City Amsterdam. (Photo: Official website of Oriental City Amsterdam)

闯，于是，1972 年，杨华根辞去了香港的工作，远赴荷兰阿姆斯特丹发展。他的第一份工作是在香港时结识的朋友王庆棠新开业的高档粤菜餐厅——一定好酒楼，杨华根除了做会计，也在楼面跑腿。

从银行职员转行到餐饮服务业，杨华根适应得很快。"因为我本人很喜欢交朋结友，而且喜欢美食。"他解释说，"当时，我们海外华人的行业选择也比较窄，主要是开杂货店、开餐馆之类的，做其他行业比较难。我又不懂荷兰语，只能靠英语，只有这份工作比较适合。"

"一定好酒楼"后来改叫"海城大酒楼"。酒楼位于阿姆斯特丹市中心繁华地段的水坝广场附近，逐渐发展成荷兰颇具盛名的中餐厅之一。杨华根亲历了这个发展过程。他没当过厨师，但"一路做，一路学"，积累了一些心得。1979 年，王庆棠退休，把酒楼转让给了杨华根，杨华根用心经营了 40 年，直到退休。

杨华根念念不忘贵人"王老板"："得到他的提携、帮忙和协助，我才能经营海城大酒楼。"

在海外推广中华饮食文化，令杨华根很有成就感。例如，西方客人不喜欢带刺、带骨的菜肴，酒楼就会向他们解释中国菜为什么要那么做，推荐他们尝试正宗的做法，比如整条鱼清蒸或红烧。当然，订餐的客人如果对做法有特别要求，酒楼也会配合。

1996 年，香港动作电影《古惑仔 3：只手遮天》在海城大酒楼门口取景，酒楼的特色外观与电影的经典桥段一同留在了观众的时代记忆中。此后，慕名前来用餐、打卡的游客络绎不绝。

电影《古惑仔 3：只手遮天》片段。（来源：网络视频截图）
A scene of the movie *Young and Dangerous 3: Covering the Sky with One Hand*.
(Photo: Screenshot of an online video)

2013 年，海城大酒楼被荷兰皇家航空公司（KLM）选定为中餐餐品顾问合作方，为荷航从阿姆斯特丹前往中国的航班提供两年的膳食计划服务，指导食品的配置和制作。"我们提供 formula（配方），教他们荷兰的厨师怎么去做、分量多少。"杨华根回忆说。

海城大酒楼被荷航选定为中餐餐品顾问。（来源：海城大酒楼官网）
Oriental City Amsterdam is invited to be the Chinese food consultant of KLM Royal Dutch Airlines.
(Photo: Official website of Oriental City Amsterdam)

助同胞融入当地，喜看后辈百业兴

除了酒楼，杨华根还经营过其他一些实业，比如新国泰旅行社，主营机票和旅行团，为华人旅游、探亲提供便利，这家旅行社的办事处还开到过中国内地和香港。

杨华根承认，当餐厅老板是件辛苦的差事，好多事情都要亲力亲为。"我们这一辈还可以，老一辈真是好辛苦。"很多中餐厅老板的后代都不愿意接手家里的生意，也有这方面的原因。

不过，杨华根指出，很多年轻华人去从事其他行业，主要是因为他们受过良好的教育，而且现在华人的地位也提高了。时下从事餐饮业的华人比以前少了，他觉得是好事。他说，老一辈到荷兰闯荡时，语言等各方面的能力都不好，只能靠卖力工作来养家。后辈在荷兰出生、受教育，荷兰语非常好，很多人已经融入了荷兰社会，分布在各行各业，有医生，也有律师、会计师、工程师等。

由于各种有利条件，再加上思想观念的不同，年轻一辈的华人参政议政也比老一辈更容易些。杨华根曾经担任荷兰华人参政基金会的首任主席，对此深有感触。

2004 年，荷兰政府正式批准成立了"荷兰华人参议机构"，使荷兰华人群体正式成为"荷兰少数民族议会"的第八个成员，华人的参政意识大大提高。2005 年，几位侨胞牵头成立了荷兰华人参政基金会，鼓励年轻一辈参政议政。当时，基金会经常邀请议员、律师等为华侨华人子弟举办讲座。后来，在国会选举中，基金会资助了一些华人候选人印制海报等方面的费用。

回想成立这个基金会的初衷，杨华根说："我们在荷兰生活了几十年，我见到其他族裔有那么多人参政，比如摩洛哥裔、土耳其裔，为什么我们华人不可以呢？我们要争取华人的权益，是不是？我们面对的好多困难，包括老人问题、青少年问题，都是可以向政府反映的！"

杨华根说，现在很多年轻华人积极参政议政，甚至尝试地方选举、国会选举。至于成效，当然要一步步来。

杨华根为侨胞服务多年，这个基金会只是一个缩影。

1975年，他到荷兰后不久，就开始参与侨团事务。"一方面，是受到老华侨的影响；另一方面，觉得参加社团可以帮助更多人。我希望荷兰华侨华人能够团结一致，融入荷兰社会。"

他还担任过全荷华人社团联合会主席。这个组织由荷兰众多华人社团联合组成，致力于搭建荷兰政府与华人之间的桥梁，加强华人社团之间的团结和沟通。

联动多方，共庆华人移民荷兰 100 周年

2010年至2011年，荷兰各地举办一系列活动，庆祝华人移民荷兰100周年，其中一些活动是由荷兰百年华人志庆基金会组织的，杨华根就是这个基金会的主席。他谦虚地说，自己不过做了一些支持的工作。

杨华根对2011年7月9日在阿姆斯特丹举行的"百狮巡游会荷京"记忆犹新。这是当时欧洲最大规模的舞狮巡游活动，100头"狮子"在水坝广场为上万名观众献上了大型表演，一路巡游到唐人街。

"狮子"由国务院侨办、广东省侨办以及荷兰社团、商界等赠送。舞狮的500名志愿者不仅有华人，还有荷兰当地人；既有精壮小伙、活力女士，也有热情少年。他们经过半年左右的训练，聚集在一起热闹舞动，展现了华人与荷兰各族裔的友谊。

据史料记载，中国人最早抵达荷兰是在1607

2011年7月9日，100头"狮子"在阿姆斯特丹水坝广场起舞。
（来源：中新网）
A total of 100 "lions" dance in Dam Square, Amsterdam on July 9, 2011. (Photo: chinanews.com.cn)

舞狮的志愿者不仅有华人，还有荷兰当地人。
The lion dance volunteers include not only Chinese but also local Dutch people.

年，其后有零星的华人到荷兰游历或短期逗留。1911年被定为华人正式移居荷兰的年份。据杨华根介绍，那一年，有华人首次在荷兰的市政府登记注册。当时，受雇于荷兰轮船公司的华人船员明显增多，数以千计的华人在荷兰的远洋轮船上从事繁重的烧火、水手等工作。

20世纪30年代经济大萧条期间，很多华人为了生计，自制花生糖、花生饼在街头出售，他们的叫卖声"Pinda, Pinda, Lekka, Lekka（花生糖，花生糖，好吃，好吃）"还演变成了荷兰民谣，传唱至今。

2011年9月，荷兰百年华人志庆基金会组织编写的《荷兰华人百年》图书在海牙市政厅正式发行。这套中荷双语图书记录了在荷华人百年奋斗历程，展示了华人在荷兰的足迹和生活点滴。编写工作耗时一年，得到了许多侨领的大力支持。

时任荷兰首相马克·吕特在为丛书撰写的前言中写道："荷兰人常常称自己为'欧洲的中国人'，以表示我们有同中国人一样的创业及奋斗精神。"

2011年9月10日，杨华根在《荷兰华人百年》发布会上致辞。（来源：北欧绿色邮报网）
W.K. Yeung delivers a speech at the presentation of *100 Years of Chinese in the Netherlands* on September 10, 2011. (Photo: greenpost.se)

能请到这么高级别的政府官员来撰写前言，也是荷兰华人地位的体现。杨华根说，荷兰华人勤劳正直，堪称社会的榜样，而且侨界与政府保持了良好沟通。荷兰曾经洪水为患，华人也积极捐款救灾。这一切，都为华人赢得了声誉。

推动华人体育事业，凝聚侨胞力量

弘扬中华美食、促进中华文化交流、助力同胞融入社会各界，杨华根做的不止于此。早在 1985 年，杨华根就参加了第一届全荷华人体育运动会筹备组的工作。这跟他从小爱好运动有关。他认为，运动不但可以使人身心健康，还可以凝聚华侨华人的力量。

杨华根（右一）等人在第一届全荷华人体育运动会现场。
（来源：全荷华人联合体育运动总会网站）
W.K. Yeung (first from the right) and others at the venue of the first Chinese Sports Tournament. (Photo: Website of the Foundation of Chinese Sports Federation Netherlands)

1991 年，杨华根当选全荷华人联合体育运动总会副主席。1993 年，他当选主席，此后连任多次，成功组织了多届全荷华人体育运动会。他还注重国际交流，带领体育代表团遍访欧洲其他国家华人体育社团，远赴英国、美国、澳大利亚参赛。在他的倡导下，全荷华人联合体育运动总会与中国的交流也日渐频繁。

1994 年，在杨华根的主持下，第十届运动会盛况空前，不仅在荷兰社会产生了很大影响，而且在其他国家的华人社会中传为美谈，被誉为"开创性的海外华人体育运动会"。

这是一次全球华人的体育盛事，全称是"第十届全荷华人体育运动会暨世界华人友谊邀请赛"，参赛选手扩展到亚洲、美洲、大洋洲。荷兰各华人社团的代表和华人观众等共 2000 多人参加了开幕式，来自 25 个国家和地区的 1200 多名运动员参加了比赛，包括一些世界级名将，比如北京篮球代表队就是以前的中国国家队班底。

据杨华根透露，第十届运动会有大量捐款支持，许多工作人员是义务服务，有些人只领取了少许车马费。总会的日常工作中，常务理事和运动员们外出比赛、开会，都是自费旅行，但大家都乐意奉献，因为这些活动可以团结侨界力量，有助于提高华人地位。

第十届全荷华人体育运动会暨世界华人友谊邀请赛现场。
A scene of the 10th Chinese Sports Tournament of the Netherlands and the World Chinese Friendship Invitational Tournament.

2000 年，杨华根在担任第十六届运动会的主席后退居幕后。2002 年，全荷华人联合体育运动总会推举他为永远名誉主席，以感谢他对荷兰华人体育事业的卓越贡献。

传华文教育薪火，促中荷文化交流

华人重教，在荷兰也不例外。杨华根担任过旅荷华人联谊会理事，并与联谊会里热心中文教育的理事组成中文教育小组，关注旅荷华人联谊会中文学校的事务。这个中文教育小组后来发展成全荷各界人士参与的校董会，杨华根曾担任校董会的主席。这是荷兰最早的中文学校之一，1979 年创办时是一所粤语学校，2015 年开始增设普通话班，2019 年更名为华人中文学校。40 多年来，中文教育在这里薪火相传。

杨华根还是暨南大学董事会董事、暨南大学荷比卢校友会名誉会长，为中荷教育交流做了很多搭桥牵线的工作。例如，2011 年 10 月，经他联络，暨南大学访问团去了阿姆斯特丹大学、鹿特丹伊拉斯姆斯大学，洽谈达成合作意向，开始教师交流合作，还就海外中文教材编写工作、华文教育等问题与侨社及中文教育负责人展开探讨。

杨华根喜欢传统书画，他结交的中国画家们到荷兰访问时，他会跟他们交流、切磋。他还记得，曾经带着以画驴而闻名的黄胄去参观荷兰的博物馆，两人相谈甚欢。

1997 年 9 月，在阿姆斯特丹市政府和中国驻荷兰大使馆的支持下，全荷侨团在阿姆斯特丹合作举办了"九七中国周"，主要包括图片展、西安碑林文物复制品展销、中西贸易交流及洽谈。杨华根担任"九七中国周"筹备委员会主任，邀请中国的博物馆专家、画家和民间艺人等到荷兰传扬国粹，投入了很大的心力。

2000 年，荷兰女王向杨华根颁发奥兰治王室军官勋章，表彰他对中荷经济、文化、体育交流的突出贡献。

情系故园，赈灾一呼百应

荷兰侨胞奋发图强、守望相助，也心系故土，在危难时刻更是见真情。杨华根对此深有感触。比如，在 20 世纪 90 年代，他们就齐心协力捐款赈济了华东水灾。2008 年 5 月，汶川特大地震发生后，荷兰华侨华人和留学生等很快联合成立赈灾委员会，委员会的负责人就是当时的全荷华人社团联合会主席杨华根。华侨华人、留学生、中资机构及荷兰友人等积极为灾区捐款，中国驻荷兰大使馆在一个月的时间里就收到各类捐款超 71 万欧元。筹款力度之大，在荷兰侨界前所未有。"可以说是一呼百应！"杨华根回忆道，"以荷兰这么小的一个国家、这么少的华侨华人来看，我们捐得不算少。"

其中，全荷华人社团联合会捐资折合 100 万元人民币用于四川省广汉市汉州小学新建教学大楼。2010 年 3 月，"荷兰华人华侨奖教助学基金"落户该校，在随后的每一年，全荷华人社团联合会及相关社团不断强化对这所学校的支持，所捐钱物累计超过 100 万元。"鼓励那些小学生努力读书，以后多多参与社会公益工作。"杨华根在全荷华人社团联合会只当了一届主席，但一直关注着荷兰侨胞对这所学校的帮扶。

荷兰侨胞还资助了北川中学的重建。

在各项公益事业中，除了组织领导外，杨华根也解囊相助。"一点点啦！一点点啦！哈哈哈！"他一语带过，伴着爽朗的笑声。不管是服务侨胞、奉献社会还是增进国际交流，他总是尽心尽力，却又十分低调、谦让，总把成就归功于各界热心人士的群策群力。他谦虚诚恳的为人，赢得了大家的信任和尊敬。桃李不言，下自成蹊，他用行动展现了自己的赤子之心、对同胞的深切关怀、对故园的深情牵挂。

2023 年 11 月，荷兰侨胞回访广汉市汉州小学。（来源：微新广汉）
Overseas Chinese in the Netherlands return to visit Hanzhou Primary School in Guanghan City in November 2023. (Photo: Weixin Guanghan)

　　杨华根认为，海外华侨华人不应忘根，侨团工作要多邀请年轻人参与，让大家互相了解。他希望海外的年轻一辈多多了解中国，感受中国强大的综合实力以及不断提升的国际地位。

　　深圳就像一滴水，映出了今日中国的光辉。20 世纪 70 年代，杨华根见过改革开放之前的深圳是什么样子。近些年，因为有家人在这边，所以他常住深圳、香港，亲眼见证了深圳翻天覆地的变化，也体会到深圳是一座宜居之城：环境好，治安好，讲文明……他如数家珍，笑容可掬，透着由衷的欣慰与自豪。

　　（除署名外，本文图片均由受访者杨华根提供。参考资料：新华社、中国新闻网、川观新闻、《侨务工作研究》、《今日中国》、《华人》、北欧绿色邮报网、全荷华人联合体育运动总会网站、华人中文学校网站、暨南大学网站、暨南大学荷比卢校友会网站。）

Wah Kun Yeung

Spreading Chinese cuisine and culture, promoting sports to bring people together

Wah Kun Yeung, or W.K. Yeung, was born in Nanxi Village, Kangji Township, Zhongshan County, Guangdong Province in 1947. This is now part of Nanxi Community, Fengshan Subdistrict, Xiangzhou District, Zhuhai City. Yeung moved to Hong Kong in 1958 and went to the Netherlands in 1972. He previously ran a Chinese restaurant and a travel agency in Amsterdam, and now often stays in Shenzhen and Hong Kong. He is honorary president of the Shenzhen Business Association in the Netherlands and Belgium. He was chairman of the National Federation of Chinese Organizations in the Netherlands (Landelijke Federatie van Chinese Organisatie in Nederland), chairman of the Chinese Political Integration and Participation Fund (Chinese Politieke Integratie en Participatie Fonds), chairman of the Foundation of Chinese Sports Federation Netherlands (Stichting Chinese Sportfederatie Nederland), chairman of the Foundation of 100 Years of Chinese in the Netherlands (Stichting 100 Jaar Chinezen in Nederland), a director of the Fa Yin Chinese Association in the Netherlands (Fa Yin Chinese Vereniging in Nederland), chairman of the board of directors of the Chinese School Fa-Yin, and executive director of the China Overseas Exchange Association. He is one of the eternal honorary chairmen of the Foundation of Chinese Sports Federation Netherlands, a director of the board of directors of Jinan University, and honorary chairman of the Jinan University Alumni Association Benelux.

Yeung has been enthusiastic about public welfare and overseas Chinese affairs, and has actively promoted Sino-Dutch economic, trade, cultural and sports exchanges. He was one of the organizers of the Chinese Sports Tournament (Chinese Sportmanifestatie) in the Netherlands for several years, strengthening the unity and cooperation among overseas Chinese as well as the friendship of overseas Chinese communities around the world. He led the publication of the book 100 Years of Chinese in the Netherlands (100 Jaar Chinezen in Nederland), with the foreword written by Mark Rutte, the Dutch prime

---

The interview took place in 2024.

287

minister at that time. In 2000, the Dutch queen awarded him "Officer in the Order of Orange-Nassau" (Officier in de Orde van Oranje-Nassau).

Yeung has enjoyed a close relationship with Shenzhen. In the Netherlands, he met many Shenzhen migrants and worked with Chuen You But, Shu Kin Choi and others from Shenzhen in overseas Chinese groups. He also attended panel discussions when Shenzhen delegations visited the Netherlands.

Yeung has often stayed in Shenzhen and Hong Kong, and witnessed the great changes that reform and opening-up brought to Shenzhen. He likes to have a walk near his home in Shenzhen and take the metro to see friends. "Some of which I know from the Netherlands, others are new friends I have met in Shenzhen."

The well-mannered Shenzhen citizens have made a deep impression on Yeung. When he takes the bus and metro, many young people offer their seats to him. He feels very impressed by such polite actions.

While traveling on public transportation in the Netherlands, people also give up their seats to overseas Chinese elders, Yeung said. He learned from the older generation that some "foreigners" looked down on China and overseas Chinese people in the past, so they would not offer their seats. It's all different now. From this small thing, he has also seen the strength of China and the improved position of overseas Chinese.

Certainly, such changes are inseparable from the efforts and contributions of various overseas Chinese groups and overseas Chinese leaders like Yeung.

One afternoon in April 2024, we had an exclusive interview with Yeung in Shenzhen. He has lived in the Netherlands for decades, but his accent has not changed. He spoke standard Cantonese with a gentle and elegant demeanor. In his unhurried narration, there was approachable humility.

Going to the Netherlands and promoting Chinese food culture

Yeung's father left his hometown and made a living in Hong Kong at a young age. During the War of Resistance Against Japan, when the Japanese invaders approached Hong Kong, Yeung's parents fled back to their hometown, Zhongshan County. Yeung was born in November 1947. He moved to Hong Kong with his family in 1958, and finished high school there.

After graduating from high school, Yeung started his career at the branch of the Netherlands Trading Society in Kowloon, Hong Kong, working his way up to chief cashier. The Netherlands Trading Society later merged into Algemene Bank Nederland (ABN), which then merged into ABN AMRO Bank.

The job enabled Yeung to meet some overseas Chinese who had returned from the Netherlands. The outside world seemed very exciting, and he wanted to go out and explore while he was young. Therefore, Yeung quit his job in Hong Kong in 1972 and went to Amsterdam in the Netherlands. His first job there was at the "747" Chinese Restaurant, a newly opened high-end Cantonese restaurant run by Wong Hing Tong, a friend he had met in Hong Kong. Yeung worked as an accountant and a waiter.

He adapted quickly when shifting from banking to the catering industry, "because I like making friends and I like food," he explained. "Back then, overseas Chinese had a relatively narrow range of career opportunities, mainly opening grocery stores or restaurants. It was difficult for them to engage in other industries. Not knowing Dutch, I had to rely on English. So only this job was suitable."

The "747" Chinese Restaurant was later renamed Oriental City Amsterdam. The restaurant is located near Dam Square in the bustling heart of Amsterdam, and gradually developed into one of the famous Chinese restaurants in the Netherlands. Yeung experienced the whole process. He has never been a chef, but he "learned along the way" and accumulated some knowledge. Wong retired in 1979 and transferred the restaurant to Yeung, who then managed it carefully for 40 years until his retirement.

Yeung never forgets his great mentor whom he calls "Boss Wong." "Only with his guide, help and assistance, could I run Oriental City Amsterdam."

Promoting Chinese food culture overseas gave Yeung a sense of achievement. For example, when Western customers didn't like dishes with fish bones or bones, the restaurant would explain to them why Chinese food is cooked that way and recommend them to try the authentic ways of serving the dishes, such as steaming or braising the whole fish. Naturally, if the customers had special requirements for the preparation of the dish, the restaurant would readily follow.

In 1996, the movie *Young and Dangerous 3: Covering the Sky with One Hand* was filmed at the entrance of Oriental City Amsterdam. The stylish and iconic exterior of the restaurant stayed in the memory of the audiences together with the classic scene of the movie. Since then, countless tourists have come here to dine or "check in."

In 2013, Oriental City Amsterdam was invited to be the Chinese food consultant of KLM Royal Dutch Airlines, providing a two-year meal plan for KLM flights from Amsterdam to China, and guiding the arrangement and production of the food served on board. "We provided the formulas and taught their Dutch chefs how the dishes should be prepared and presented," Yeung recalled.

Helping compatriots integrate into local community, and seeing younger generations prosper in all industries

In addition to the restaurant, Yeung used to run other businesses, such as Cathay Travel, which mainly dealt with air tickets and tour groups, providing convenience for Chinese people to travel or visit relatives. The travel agency also opened offices in China's mainland and Hong Kong.

Yeung admitted that it was a hard job to be a restaurant owner, and that he had to do many things himself. "Our generation is okay, but the older generation worked really hard." That's one of the reasons why many descendants of Chinese restaurant owners are unwilling to take over their family businesses.

However, as Yeung pointed out, many young Chinese people engage in other industries mainly because they are well educated and the position of overseas Chinese people has improved. There are fewer Chinese working in the catering industry than before, which he thinks is a good thing. He said that when the older generation went to the Netherlands to make a living, they were not good at language and other aspects, and could only rely on hard work to support their families. The younger generation was born and educated in the Netherlands, and they are very good at Dutch. Many of them have integrated into Dutch society and have careers in various industries, including doctors, lawyers, accountants, engineers and so on.

Due to favorable conditions and different ideas, the younger generation of overseas Chinese has participated in politics more easily than the older one. Yeung, who served as the first chairman of the Chinese Political Integration and Participation Fund (Chinese Politieke Integratie en Participatie Fonds), feels strongly about this.

In 2004, the Dutch government officially approved the establishment of the Chinese Consultation Body (Inspraakorgaan Chinezen), making the Dutch Chinese community officially the eighth member of the National Consultation on Minorities (Landelijk Overleg Minderheden), and greatly promoting the Chinese community's awareness of participation in politics. In 2005, several overseas Chinese took the lead in establishing the Chinese Political Integration and Participation Fund to encourage the younger generation to participate in politics. The foundation often invited members of parliament, lawyers and others to give lectures to the Chinese youths. Later, in parliamentary elections, the foundation funded some Chinese candidates for poster printing and other expenses.

Recollecting the motive for establishing this foundation, Yeung said, "We had lived in the Netherlands for decades, and I had seen so many people of other ethnic groups participate in politics, such as Moroccans and Turks. Why couldn't we Chinese do the same? We should fight for the rights of Chinese, shouldn't we? Many difficulties we faced, including problems of the elderly and youngsters, should be reported to the government!"

Many young Chinese are now actively participating in politics and even becoming candidates in local elections and parliamentary elections, Yeung said. Of course progress should be achieved step by step.

Yeung has served overseas Chinese for many years, and the foundation is just a small part of his involvement in the overseas Chinese community.

In 1975, shortly after he arrived in the Netherlands, he got involved in the affairs of overseas Chinese groups. "On the one hand, I was influenced by some old overseas Chinese. On the other hand, I thought that I would be able to help more people after joining the organizations. I hoped that overseas Chinese in the Netherlands could unite and integrate into Dutch society."

He also served as chairman of the National Federation of Chinese Organizations in the Netherlands (Landelijke Federatie van Chinese Organisatie in Nederland). It is composed of many Chinese associations in the Netherlands and is committed to building a bridge between the Dutch government and the Chinese as well as strengthening the unity and communication between Chinese associations.

Working with multiple parties to celebrate 100th anniversary of Chinese immigration to the Netherlands

From 2010 to 2011, a series of events were held in various parts of the Netherlands to celebrate the 100th anniversary of Chinese immigration to the Netherlands. Some of these events were organized by the Foundation of 100 Years of Chinese in the Netherlands (Stichting 100 Jaar Chinezen in Nederland), and Yeung was its chairman. He modestly said that he only did some supporting work for those events.

Yeung still remembers the "Dance of 100 Lions in Amsterdam" held on July 9, 2011. It was the largest lion dance parade in Europe at the time. A total of 100 "lions" performed a large-scale show for tens of thousands of spectators in Dam Square and paraded all the way to Chinatown.

The "lions" were donated by the Overseas Chinese Affairs Office of the State

Council, the Overseas Chinese Affairs Office of Guangdong Province, and Dutch communities and business circles. The 500 volunteers for the lion dance included not only Chinese but also local Dutch people, not only strong young men and energetic women but also enthusiastic children. After about half a year of training, they gathered together to dance enthusiastically, showcasing the friendship between Chinese and other ethnic groups in the Netherlands.

According to historical records, the first Chinese arrived in the Netherlands in 1607. Thereafter, there was a scattering of Chinese who traveled to the Netherlands or stayed there for a short time. The year of 1911 was designated as the time when the Chinese formally immigrated to the Netherlands. It was in that year that Chinese people registered with a Dutch city government for the first time, Yeung said. At that time, the number of Chinese crew members employed by Dutch shipping companies increased significantly, and thousands of Chinese did manual work such as making fire and working as sailors on Dutch ships.

During the Great Depression of the 1930s, many Chinese in the Netherlands made peanut candies and peanut cakes and sold them on the streets for a living. Their street cries, "Pinda, Pinda, Lekka, Lekka" (peanut candy, peanut candy, delicious, delicious), evolved into a Dutch folk song, which is still sung today.

In September 2011, the book *100 Years of Chinese in the Netherlands* (*100 Jaar Chinezen in Nederland*) compiled by the Foundation of 100 Years of Chinese in the Netherlands was officially released at The Hague City Hall. This bilingual book in Chinese and Dutch recorded the striving of Chinese in the Netherlands over the last century and showed the activities and life of Chinese in the Netherlands. The compilation took a year and got strong support from many overseas Chinese leaders.

Mark Rutte, then Dutch prime minister, wrote in the foreword to the book, "The Dutch like to call themselves 'Chinese in Europe' to indicate that we have the same enterprising business spirit and work ethic as the inhabitants of China."

It was also a reflection of the position of Chinese in the Netherlands to have such a high-level government official to write the foreword. The Chinese in the Netherlands have been hardworking and upright, and can be regarded as role models for society, while the Chinese community has maintained good communication with the government, Yeung said. At a time when the Netherlands was plagued by floods, the Chinese there actively donated money for disaster relief. All of this has won a reputation for the Chinese.

Promoting sports amongst the Chinese and gathering strength of overseas Chinese

Yeung has done more besides promoting Chinese cuisine, boosting Chinese cultural exchanges, and helping compatriots integrate into all walks of life. As early as 1985, Yeung joined the preparatory group for the first Chinese Sports Tournament (Chinese Sportmanifestatie). This was related to his love of sports since childhood. He believes that sports not only make people physically and mentally healthy, but also gather the strength of overseas Chinese.

In 1991, Yeung was elected vice chairman of the Foundation of Chinese Sports Federation Netherlands (Stichting Chinese Sportfederatie Nederland). He was elected chairman in 1993 and re-elected several times after that. He successfully organized several versions of the Chinese Sports Tournament. He also placed an emphasis on international exchanges. He led sports delegations to visit Chinese sports associations in other European countries and travelled to Britain, the United States, and Australia for competitions. As a result of his advocacy, the federation has had increasingly frequent exchanges with China.

In 1994, under the chairmanship of Yeung, the 10th Chinese Sports Tournament was an unprecedented grand occasion. It not only had a great impact on Dutch society, but also became a widely told story in the Chinese communities of other countries and was praised as a "pioneering overseas Chinese sports events."

It was a sports event for Chinese people around the world. Its full name was "the 10th Chinese Sports Tournament of the Netherlands and the World Chinese Friendship Invitational Tournament," with contestants coming from Asia, America, and Oceania. More than 2,000 people, including representatives of various Chinese groups and other Chinese audiences in the Netherlands, attended the opening ceremony. More than 1,200 athletes from 25 countries and regions entered the competitions, including some world-class players, such as the Beijing basketball team, which was the former Chinese national team.

According to Yeung, the 10th Chinese Sports Tournament was supported by a large amount of donations, and many staff members served on a voluntary basis, some of whom were just reimbursed for a few travel expenses. In the daily work of the sports federation, the executive directors and athletes traveled at their own expense when they went out for competitions and meetings, but everyone was willing to contribute because these activities could unite the strength of the overseas Chinese community and help improve the status of the Chinese.

In 2000, Yeung took a back seat after serving as chairman of the 16th Chinese

Sports Tournament. In 2002, the federation elected him as eternal honorary chairman to appreciate his outstanding contribution to promoting sports amongst the Chinese in the Netherlands.

Passing on the torch of Chinese language education and promoting Sino-Dutch cultural exchanges

Chinese people attach great importance to education, with no exception in the Netherlands. Yeung served as a director of the Fa Yin Chinese Association in the Netherlands (Fa Yin Chinese Vereniging in Nederland), and formed a Chinese language education group with some directors of the association who were enthusiastic about Chinese language education. The Chinese language education group followed the affairs of the Chinese School Fa-Yin, and later developed into the school's board of directors consisting of people from all walks of life in the Netherlands, with Yeung as chairman of the board. One of the earliest Chinese schools in the Netherlands, it started as a Cantonese school in 1979. It began to add Mandarin classes in 2015 and changed its Chinese name in 2019. Chinese language has been taught here for more than 40 years.

Yeung is also a director of the board of directors of Jinan University, and honorary chairman of the Jinan University Alumni Association Benelux. He has done a lot of work in building bridges for Sino-Dutch educational exchanges. For example, he acted as an intermediary when a delegation of Jinan University visited the University Amsterdam and Erasmus University Rotterdam in October 2011. Their talks led to cooperation on teacher exchange. Discussions were also held with overseas Chinese community leaders and Chinese language education leaders on issues such as overseas Chinese language textbook compilation and Chinese language education.

Yeung likes traditional Chinese calligraphy and painting. When the Chinese painters he had known visited the Netherlands, he would communicate and exchange ideas with them. He still remembers leading Huang Zhou, who was famous for painting donkeys, to Dutch museums, and having a great conversation with him.

In September 1997, with the support of the Amsterdam City Council and the Chinese Embassy in the Netherlands, overseas Chinese groups in the Netherlands jointly held the "1997 China Week" in Amsterdam, including photo exhibitions, exhibition and sales of the replicas of cultural relics from the Stele Forest in Xi'an, and Sino-Western trade exchanges and negotiations. Yeung served as director of the preparatory committee for the "1997 China Week" and made considerable efforts, inviting Chinese museum experts, painters, and folk artists, among others, to spread the quintessence of Chinese culture in the Netherlands.

In 2000, the Dutch queen awarded Yeung "Officer in the Order of Orange-Nassau" (Officier in de Orde van Oranje-Nassau) to commend his outstanding contributions to Sino-Dutch economic, cultural and sports exchanges.

Deep love for the homeland, timely disaster relief efforts

Overseas Chinese in the Netherlands strive to be strong, help each other, and care about their homeland, showing that a friend in need is a friend indeed. Yeung has been deeply touched by this. For example, they joined together to donate money for disaster relief after the East China floods in the 1990s.

After the devastating Wenchuan earthquake in May 2008, overseas Chinese and international students in the Netherlands quickly established a joint disaster relief committee, and the head of the committee was Yeung, the chairman of the National Federation of Chinese Organizations in the Netherlands. Overseas Chinese, international students, Chinese-funded institutions and Dutch friends actively donated to the disaster area. The Chinese Embassy in the Netherlands received more than 710,000 euros in various donations within one month. The fundraising efforts were unprecedented for the overseas Chinese community in the Netherlands. "It can be said that one call had a hundred responses!" Yeung recalled, "Considering that the Netherlands is such a small country and has such a small number of overseas Chinese, our donations were not small."

Among the donations, the National Federation of Chinese Organizations in the Netherlands contributed 1 million yuan to build a new teaching building for Hanzhou Primary School in Guanghan City, Sichuan Province. The "Netherlands Overseas Chinese Fund for Teachers and Students" was established in the school in March 2010. In each subsequent year, the federation and related associations have continued to strengthen their support for the school, with donations totaling more than 1 million yuan. "We have been encouraging those primary school students to study hard and participate more in social welfare in the future." Yeung served as the federation's chairman for only one term, but he has always paid attention to the assistance provided by overseas Chinese in the Netherlands to the school.

Overseas Chinese in the Netherlands also funded the reconstruction of Beichuan Middle School.

In addition to organizing and leading public welfare activities, Yeung has also donated money to help. "A little bit! A little bit! Hahaha!" He played it down with a hearty laugh. Whether serving overseas Chinese, contributing to society or promoting international exchanges, he has always done his best, but has been very low-key and modest, always attributing his achievements to the collective wisdom and efforts of enthusiastic people from all walks of life. His modesty and sincerity have won everyone's trust and respect. Though peach and plum trees do not speak, a path is worn beneath them because of their beautiful flowers and fruits. Through his actions, Yeung has demonstrated his natural kindness, deep care for compatriots, and profound concern for the homeland.

Yeung thinks that overseas Chinese should not forget their roots, and that more young people should be invited to work for overseas Chinese groups so as to boost the understanding between overseas Chinese. He hopes that the younger generation overseas will learn more about China and feel China's strength and constantly improving international status.

Shenzhen is like a drop of water reflecting the glory of today's China. In the 1970s, Yeung saw what Shenzhen looked like before the reform and opening-up. In recent years, he has often stayed in Shenzhen and Hong Kong because he has family here. He has witnessed the huge changes in Shenzhen and realized that Shenzhen is a livable city with good surroundings, good public security and good manners, among others. He talked about the city with great familiarity and a smile, showing his sincere satisfaction and pride.

(Photos courtesy of Wah Kun Yeung, except for those with credit. References: Xinhua News Agency, chinanews.com.cn, Chuanguan News, *Research on Overseas Chinese Affairs Work*, *China Today*, *Chinese People*, greenpost.se, the website of the Foundation of Chinese Sports Federation Netherlands, the website of the Chinese School Fa-Yin, the website of Jinan University, and the website of the Jinan University Alumni Association Benelux.)

钟荣彬

为华文教育传薪火，爱国爱乡不懈奉献

钟荣彬　Raymond Chung

钟荣彬，1947 年出生，深圳大鹏王母人。1958 年到香港生活，1969 年赴荷兰谋生，1978 年到英国发展。英国华文教育基金会会长，全英华人华侨中国统一促进会副会长，英国曼城华人社团联合会名誉会长，英国共和协会名誉会长，深圳市海外交流协会海外名誉理事。1999 年获国务院侨务办公室授予"海外优秀华教工作者"称号。

钟荣彬在荷兰和英国从事餐饮业和多种经营，同时积极参与侨团和华文教育工作。1982 年在英国创办普雷斯顿中文学校，1989 年、1994 年分别创办兰开夏中文学校、黑池中文学校。2005 年牵头成立"英国华文教育基金会"，推广华文教育，搭建文化的桥梁。钟荣彬积极促进中英教育文化交流和经贸科技合作，并筹集善款和物资，参与祖国和家乡的公益慈善事业。

采访时间：2022 年。

海外华侨华人一向有重视传统、尊师重教的风气，而中华文化的薪火传承也是其中一个重要的方面。

钟荣彬自己读书不多。像他这样的家长，更是希望子女能多读书。他当年和很多华侨华人一样，苦于孩子们没地方学中文。他觉得，中文学校可以帮孩子们了解中华文化，理解中西文化的差别，尽享两种文化的优势。所以，他不但创办了中文学校，还牵头成立了英国华文教育基金会，为更多的中文学校提供支持。

他热心服务社区，促进中英友好交流。祖国和家乡有需要的时候，他发动侨胞的力量积极支援。他谦虚地说，自己喜欢到处走走看看、交朋友，所以很有兴趣做社团工作。"创业成功不忘回报故乡，报效祖国是人生最高境界。"他这样概括自己的执着追求。

辗转荷英，创业有成

钟荣彬 1947 年出生于大鹏。他幼年时，父母已经在香港谋生了。他 11 岁的时候，就和弟弟跟随奶奶去了香港，与父母团聚。

钟荣彬有 5 个弟弟、2 个妹妹，家庭条件不太好，他没有读完高中就出来工作了。据他回忆，20 世纪 60 年代，香港的生活也比较困难，很多人都去外国工作。在这股热潮中，1969 年，22 岁的他只身去了荷兰。

初到荷兰，钟荣彬听说警方要抓没有居留证的人，就干脆跑去自首，被留了一

钟荣彬的全家福。
Raymond Chung's family.

晚。警察通过翻译问钟荣彬，有没有亲戚可以雇他工作。幸好，有一位大鹏乡亲在荷兰靠近德国边境的地方开餐馆，钟荣彬就去他那里打工了，洗菜、洗碗、拖地，什么都干。每天早上 9 点起床工作到晚上 11 点，工作强度很大，他还是抓住每周休息一天的机会积极学习荷兰语。

1970 年底，钟荣彬来到荷兰首都阿姆斯特丹工作，在餐厅当服务员。业余时间，他除了继续学习荷兰语，还参加了旅荷华侨总会，和侨胞们一起致力于爱国爱乡的事业。他积极参与华人社区的各种活动，弘扬中华文化，

捐助公益事业，帮助华人融入荷兰主流社会。1973 年，钟荣彬回香港结了婚，然后又回到荷兰。凭借辛勤工作积攒的经验和资金，1975 年，他终于有了自己的餐馆，第二年又开了第二家。

1978 年，钟荣彬卖掉了荷兰的餐馆，带着妻子和 4 个子女去了英国。这主要是因为钟荣彬的家庭观念比较重。父母和弟弟妹妹在英国，弟弟妹妹们在读书，父母年纪也不小了，只有父亲在工作。钟荣彬觉得，是时候去跟他们团聚了。另一方面，去英国，也可以寻求更大的事业发展空间。早在钟荣彬去荷兰之前，就有很多乡亲去了英国。到英国后，钟荣彬在普雷斯顿落脚。开始的一段时间，他给别人打工，了解英国的生活环境。1979 年，他在普雷斯顿开办了自己的酒楼。1982 年，因为城市改造，这家酒楼被拆掉了。1983 年，他又跟弟弟合开了一家酒楼。

钟荣彬还开过中国货超市，卖过家具，做过进出口业务，当过哈尔滨啤酒的欧洲总代理商，到广东潮州开厂生产瓷器出口到英国，在广东清远跟人合作出口食用笋到英国（清远是钟荣彬妻子的家乡）。

投身华文教育，方便身边侨胞

生活安定、事业有成的钟荣彬，开始为侨胞、为家乡、为祖国投入更多的精力和心血。开办中文学校，就是他做的大事之一。

他观察发现，很多华裔子弟的思维方式和价值观在当地主流文化影响下更趋西化，父母的言传身教和家庭背景对孩子的影响有限。他觉得，侨胞们的子女如果能学好中文，再加上流利地掌握当地语言，既可以为他们未来的发展打下坚实的基础，还可以成为中国和当地社会之间沟通的桥梁。

当然，钟荣彬创办中文学校的直接原因，是当地缺乏学中文的机会。不光是他的孩子，还有附近其他华侨华人的子女，加起来有上百人，都找不到地方好好学中文。他和普雷斯顿几位志同道合的侨胞就决定自己办学校，利用周末时间带领孩子们学习中文、感受中华文化。

于是，钟荣彬在 1981 年牵头创办了普雷斯顿中文学校。这是他迈出的办学第一步，得到了当地侨胞的协助和当地政府的支持。香港地区驻英国的办事机构提供了一些中文教材。当地有些官员常去钟荣彬的餐馆吃饭，跟他比较熟，他就借机咨询办学的要求。最终，普雷斯顿中文学校借用了当地公立小学的地方。为了符合文凭方面的要求，还请来一位大学教授当名誉校长，并请这位教授的妻子担任秘书长（她有硕士学位）。

1989 年、1994 年，钟荣彬又相继创办了兰开夏中文学校、黑池中文学校。目前，他仍在管理运营兰开夏中文学校，其他两所则交给别人了。

自掏腰包办学，亲自上阵讲课

曾有段时间，钟荣彬的中文学校申请到了政府资助，所以不收学费，还提供免费午餐，这一下吸引了更多的学生，但也因此师资不足，钟荣彬就自己上阵，教孩子们学基本的汉字和《三字经》。

后来，政府资助减少乃至取消了，学校就收些学费，但仍不足以覆盖成本，钟荣彬就自掏腰包给教师和工人发工资。

为了华文教育，他出钱、出力、出时间，不仅自掏腰包，亲自上阵，还跑到学校里帮忙看着上百名学生，守护校园安全。

学校初期教的是粤语，后来教普通话，这也贴合了时代的大背景。许木在《世界教育信息》2015年第11期发表的研究文章指出，早期，英国的华裔移民主要来自广东、香港一带，英国中文学校的课程教学以粤语繁体字为主。随着中国综合国力的不断提升以及对汉语推广力度的不断加大，一定程度上促进了普通话简体字课程的发展。

钟荣彬的中文学校教学情景。
Students study at one of Raymond Chung's Chinese schools.

钟荣彬的3所中文学校的总规模一度达到300多名学生，其中还包括英国当地的孩子。"各种肤色的孩子聚集在一起学习中文，朗诵我们的经典，这是多么令人欣慰的事啊！"钟荣彬很是满足。

正是在责任感、成就感的驱使下，钟荣彬十分乐于抽出时间到学校去，跟教师、学生沟通，处理各种事务。他还教过孩子们舞麒麟。除此之外，春节时，学校还组织过舞狮活动和歌唱比赛，很热闹。深圳市侨办送过一套"狮子"给他们。看到中国文化在英国传播，钟荣彬满怀喜悦。

他的努力和贡献，也得到了祖国的认可。1999 年，中国国务院侨务办公室授予他"海外优秀华教工作者"称号。

成立基金会，促进华文教育蓬勃发展

钟荣彬没有止步于自己办学校。2005 年 6 月，他组织一群热爱华文教育的侨胞，成立了英国华文教育基金会，由他担任会长。他们希望，通过这一代的努力，推广华文教育，搭建文化的桥梁，让下一代能了解中国、了解中华文化，延续爱国爱乡的精神。

这家基金会联合了侨胞和企业家的力量，为英国的华文教育提供资金支持，并赠送教材支持教学，还举办研讨会等活动。

2006 年 11 月，基金会组织了孙中山先生诞辰 140 周年纪念活动，钟荣彬说，这类活动是为了向中文学校的校长们讲述中国历史、弘扬爱国精神。

2007 年 6 月和 2010 年 7 月，基金会在曼彻斯特举办了两届欧洲华文教育研讨会，甚至收到了英国女王的贺信。深圳市侨务代表团专程赴曼彻斯特参加了 2010 年的那次研讨会，与来自全欧的华文教育代表们共商华文教育发展大计。

钟荣彬透露，累计有 68 所中文学校接受过基金会的资助，遍布英国四大地区——北爱尔兰、苏格兰、威尔士、英格兰。

众人拾柴火焰高。钟荣彬做的这些事情，也汇入了时代的潮流。在广大旅英侨胞的共同努力下，英国华文教育得到了蓬勃发展。

2011 年有新闻报道，英国的周末中文学校有百余所，多数是由热心的侨领、社团、志愿团体等以非营利的形式筹办。

《世界教育信息》2015 年第 11 期发表的研究文章也指出，英国大多数的华文学校是在华人社团的支持下开办的，经费和场所获得了社团协会的投资和赞助，包括英国华文教育基金会、英国中文学校联合会、英国中文教育促进会等。当地留学生等团体也为华文学校及主流学校的中文教育贡献了力量。

这里提到的英国中文教育促进会是 1993 年成立的，钟荣彬也是创办人之一。会长伍善雄是 1968 年移居英国的，在纽卡斯尔发展。他曾经向媒体回忆过中文学校的筚路蓝缕：当初，老唐人街上的小补课班只有几个学生。

2014 年 5 月，时任中国驻曼彻斯特总领事出席英国华文教育基金会慈善晚会时说，海外华文教育的发展动力归根结底来自侨社。"华文教育是保持海外华侨华人

民族特性的根本保证，是维系海内外中华儿女与祖（籍）国情感联系的重要纽带，是一项'留根工程'。"

服务社区，促进中英交流

除了为英国的中文学校提供支持，钟荣彬还为中英友好交流、为当地社区做了不少事情。

英国华文教育基金会多次选派华侨华人子女到中国参加文化交流活动，促成兰开夏郡的经贸文化代表团到中国考察。钟荣彬还多次邀请中国各地政府和文化教育机构派人到英国考察，开展经贸、科技、教育等方面的交流与合作。在他促成下，兰开夏大学跟北华大学、重庆大学、青海大学等建立了友好合作关系，普雷斯顿跟青海省西宁市结为友好城市。

中国新年时，钟荣彬还邀请中国各地少年宫组织孩子到普雷斯顿进行艺术交流，参观当地主流学校，与当地青少年一起学习、建立友谊，了解英国文化。"这些孩子如果将来能到英国留学，那么，提前了解一下英国是很好的。"钟荣彬说。

他还说，自己喜欢到处走走看看、交朋友，所以很有兴趣做社团工作。他办了中文学校之后，认识的侨界朋友越来越多，他就跟普雷斯顿市长商量，又跟中国驻曼彻斯特总领事馆沟通，想成立一个社团，可以举办嘉年华（狂欢节）等节庆活动，表演舞狮、舞麒麟等。在各方支持下，1992 年，他创立了柏德斯顿及邻区华联会（后来，中文名改为"普雷斯顿及邻区华联会"）。同年，他加入了英国华人社团联合总会，后来当过副会长、执委。他曾经每年都组织华侨华人为普雷斯顿的市长基金筹款，为当地的智障儿童医院捐款。

爱国爱家乡，奉献不停歇

在服务侨胞、服务当地社会的同时，钟荣彬积极为祖国和故乡的公益慈善事业贡献力量。

1992 年，钟荣彬带着父亲，回到阔别几十年的家乡大鹏。在钟荣彬印象里，那时的故乡还比较"落后"，从深圳市区坐面包车去大鹏，摇摇晃晃 6 小时，从深圳坐车去清远，大约花了 9 小时。"那时就想着，国家什么时候可以建设得更好。"

钟荣彬不光是盼着祖国和家乡加速发展，也为此出了自己的一份力。1993 年，他为深圳大鹏华侨医院的建设捐出了 4000 英镑。那时候，英国当地人的月薪只有几十英镑。1997 年，他为清远市清城区职业中学（现为清远工贸职业技术学校）的发展建设募捐了 8000 英镑。

钟荣彬回忆，大约在 2016 年前后，他开始发现家乡大鹏有了很大的变化，他感到十分欣慰。在钟荣彬带领下，英国华文教育基金会还为中国的希望工程筹款捐建了小学，在清远市阳山县黎埠镇扶村小学、广州市海珠区芳村五凤学校设立了奖教奖学基金，奖励老师和学生。

2020 年，英国华文教育基金会在清远市阳山县黎埠镇扶村小学颁发奖教奖学金。
The UK Chinese Education Foundation presents teaching awards and scholarships at the Fucun Primary School, Libu Township, Yangshan County, Qingyuan City in 2020.

2008 年，四川汶川地震发生后，基金会捐款 1.8 万英镑。钟荣彬还记得，那时，他拿着捐款箱在街上募捐了 4 天，筹到的大多是硬币，如果自己把这 1 万多英镑硬币拿去银行处理，是要扣手续费的。"我们把收到的纸币、硬币都按面额分类打包，交给了中国驻曼彻斯特总领馆，由他们拿到中国银行处理，节省了 1000 多英镑。"

同一年，基金会又为青海玉树地震募捐了 8000 多英镑。

2020 年初，中国暴发新冠疫情，海外华侨华人通过各种渠道捐款捐物，支援这场疫情防控阻击战。钟荣彬组织筹集资金，向多家医疗保险公司预订了 3 万只 N95 口罩，但由于货源奇缺，采购计划落空，他又发动亲友与挪威、德国、法国等多方联系货源。他还通过中国的宗亲、广西玉林市侨联名誉主席、英国华文教育基金会荣誉会长钟雄组织采购了一些测温枪、KN95 口罩，捐赠给吉林、辽宁、青海、广东、广西等地一些学校，总价值27万多元，这笔资金来自多个国家的华侨华人。"基金会在荷兰、法国、中国、澳大利亚、加拿大都有名誉会长，有什么活动都很支持我。"钟荣彬说。

2021年夏天，河南郑州突遭暴雨袭击，造成洪灾。钟荣彬牵头组织普雷斯顿及邻区华联会的人士捐赠了2000多英镑。

新冠疫情之前，钟荣彬经常回中国，到处走走看看，参加各种交流活动，受邀出席过1994年和2009年国庆观礼。他去过北京、黑龙江、吉林、青海、河南、河北、广东、广西等地，曾在多个省区的海外交流协会担任理事。

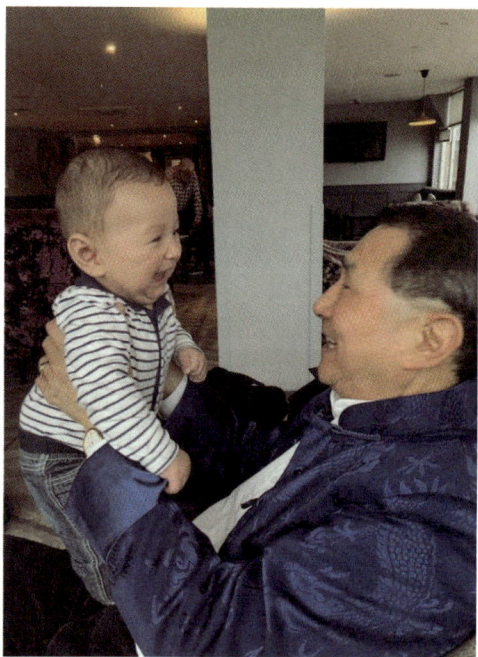

钟荣彬和小孙子。
Raymond Chung and his grandson.

作为旅英侨领，钟荣彬以自己的方式实践着对祖国、对家乡的爱。75岁的他还在操持着社团事务。2022年11月底，他又在筹划一件大事：跟兰开夏郡政府商讨中国新年庆祝活动的安排。

同时，钟荣彬也在物色爱国爱家乡的接班人。他希望，海外的华裔青少年能爱国爱乡，了解中华文化。

他说："只要地球在转，长江、黄河的水在流，我都愿意为祖国统一、中华民族伟大复兴尽心尽力，为传承中华文化和爱国爱乡传统继续努力，把这种传统一代一代传下去。"

（本文图片均由受访者钟荣彬提供。参考资料：《桑梓情深 赤子丹心——大鹏侨情口述史》、《世界教育信息》、《深圳侨报》、中新网、中国外交部网站、中国侨网、容县之声。）

Raymond Chung

Passing on the firewood for Chinese language education, dedicated to his beloved motherland and hometown

Born in 1947, Raymond Chung, or Raymond Wing Bun Chung in full, is a native of Wangmu, Dapeng, Shenzhen. He migrated to Hong Kong in 1958, to the Netherlands in 1969, and to Britain in 1978. He is president of the UK Chinese Education Foundation, vice president of the Promotion of China Re-Unification Society in UK, honorary president of the Federation of Chinese Associations of Manchester, honorary president of the Kung Ho Association, and overseas honorary director of the Shenzhen Overseas Exchange Association. In 1999, he was awarded the title of "Outstanding Overseas Chinese Language Educator" by the Overseas Chinese Affairs Office of the State Council of China.

Chung is engaged in the catering industry and various businesses in the Netherlands and Britain. At the same time, he has been actively involved in overseas Chinese groups and Chinese language education. In 1982, he founded the Preston Chinese School in Britain. In 1989 and 1994, he founded the Lancashire Chinese School and the Blackpool Chinese School respectively. In 2005, he led the establishment of the UK Chinese Education Foundation to promote Chinese language education and build a bridge of culture. Chung has actively promoted Sino-British educational and cultural exchanges and economic, trade, scientific and technological cooperation, and has raised funds and provided materials for public welfare and charity in his motherland and hometown.

Overseas Chinese have always put emphasis on tradition, respected teachers and valued education, and the inheritance of Chinese culture is an important part of their common practice.

Raymond Chung is not well-educated. Parents like him especially want their children to study more. As many overseas Chinese did back then, he suffered from the fact that his

---

The interview took place in 2022.

children had no place to learn Chinese. He believes that Chinese schools can help children understand Chinese culture, understand the differences between Chinese and Western cultures, and enjoy the advantages of both cultures. Therefore, he not only founded Chinese schools, but also led the establishment of the UK Chinese Education Foundation to provide support for more Chinese schools.

He is enthusiastic about serving the community and promoting friendly exchanges between China and Britain. When his motherland and hometown need, he mobilizes overseas Chinese to provide active support. He likes to go around and make friends, so he is very interested in doing community work, he said modestly. "After I succeeded in running my businesses, I did not forget to repay my hometown. Serving the motherland is the highest state in my life," he summed up his persistent pursuit.

A successful businessman in the Netherlands and Britain

Chung was born in Dapeng in 1947. When he was young, his parents went to Hong Kong to make a living. When he was 11 years old, he and his younger brothers went to Hong Kong with his grandmother for family reunion.

Chung has five younger brothers and two younger sisters. As the family was rather poor, he began to work without finishing high school. He recalled that life in Hong Kong was also difficult in the 1960s, and many people went to work abroad. In the heat of the boom, he went to the Netherlands alone in 1969 at the age of 22.

When he first arrived in the Netherlands, Chung heard that the police would arrest people without a residence permit, so he just surrendered himself and was detained overnight. The police asked him through an interpreter whether he had any relatives who could hire him. Fortunately, there was a Dapeng immigrant who opened a restaurant near the German border, so Chung went to work with him, doing everything from cleaning vegetables and washing dishes to mopping the floor. He got up at 9 a.m. and worked until 11 p.m. every day. With such a high workload, he still seized the opportunity to learn Dutch when taking a day off every week.

At the end of 1970, Chung went to work as a waiter in a restaurant in Amsterdam, the capital of the Netherlands. In his spare time, in addition to continuing to learn Dutch, he joined the General Chinese Association in the Netherlands (Algemene Chinese Vereniging in Nederland), working with the overseas Chinese to benefit his motherland and hometown. He actively participated in various activities in the Chinese community, promoted Chinese culture, donated to public welfare undertakings, and helped fellow

Chinese integrate into the mainstream society of the Netherlands. In 1973, he returned to Hong Kong to get married, and then went back to the Netherlands. With the experience and funds accumulated through hard work, he finally had his own restaurant in 1975 and opened another the following year.

In 1978, Chung sold his restaurants in the Netherlands and went to Britain with his wife and four children. The main reason was his traditional family concept. His parents and younger siblings were in Britain. The younger siblings were still students while his parents turned old, and his father was the only person in the family who had a job. Chung thought that it was time to reunite with them. On the other hand, he could seek more room for business development in Britain. Long before he went to the Netherlands, many Dapeng people went to Britain. After arriving in Britain, Chung settled in Preston. In the beginning, he worked for others and learned about the living environment. In 1979, he opened his own restaurant in Preston. In 1982, the restaurant was demolished because of urban reconstruction. In 1983, he co-founded a restaurant with his younger brothers.

Chung also opened a Chinese goods supermarket, sold furniture, did import and export business, worked as Harbin Beer's general agent in Europe, opened a factory in Chaozhou, Guangdong Province to produce porcelain and exported it to Britain, and cooperated with others in Qingyuan, Guangdong to export edible bamboo shoots to Britain (Qingyuan is the hometown of Chung's wife).

Engaged in Chinese language education for the convenience of overseas Chinese

With a stable life and a successful career, Chung began to devote more energy and effort to the overseas Chinese, his hometown, and the motherland. Opening Chinese schools was one of the major things he did.

He found that the way of thinking and values of many overseas Chinese children tended to be westernized under the influence of local mainstream culture, while the influence of their parents' words, deeds and family background was quite limited. He thought that if the children of overseas Chinese could learn Chinese well while being fluent in the local language, they would not only lay a solid foundation for their future development, but also serve as a bridge of communication between China and the local society.

Of course, the direct reason why Chung founded Chinese schools was the lack of opportunities to learn Chinese in the local area. Not only his children, but also the children of other overseas Chinese in the vicinity, adding up to about 100, could not find somewhere to formally learn Chinese. He and a few like-minded overseas Chinese in

Preston decided to open a school of their own, leading the children to learn Chinese and experience Chinese culture at weekends.

Therefore, Chung took the lead in founding the Preston Chinese School in 1981. This was his first step in running schools, which was assisted by local overseas Chinese and supported by the local government. Hong Kong's office in Britain gave some Chinese textbooks to the school. Some local officials often had dinner at Chung's restaurant and got familiar with him, so he took the opportunity to inquire about the requirements for running a school. Then the Preston Chinese School borrowed the venue of a local public elementary school. To meet the diploma requirements, the Chinese school invited a university professor to serve as honorary headmaster, and his wife as secretary general (she had a master's degree).

In 1989 and 1994, Chung founded the Lancashire Chinese School and the Blackpool Chinese School successively. Currently, he is still managing and running the Lancashire Chinese School, while the other two have been handed over to others.

Running schools at his own expense, sometimes giving lectures by himself

There was a time when Chung's Chinese schools successfully applied for government funding, so they did not charge tuition fees and provided free lunches. This attracted more students, but also caused a shortage of teachers. So Chung also taught classes, teaching basic Chinese characters and the *Three-character Scripture*.

Later, when the government funding was reduced and even cancelled, the schools had to charge some tuition fees, but it was not enough to cover the cost, so Chung paid salaries to the teachers and workers out of his own pocket.

He contributed money, labor, and time to Chinese language education. In addition to running the schools at his own expense and sometimes teaching classes by himself, he also helped to keep an eye on hundreds of students to ensure their safety on campus.

The schools taught Cantonese at first and Mandarin later, keeping pace with the times. Xu Mu's study published in the 11th issue of the *Journal of World Education* in 2015 pointed out that in the early days, Chinese immigrants in Britain mainly came from Guangdong and Hong Kong, and the Chinese schools in Britain mainly taught Cantonese and traditional Chinese characters. The continuous improvement of China's comprehensive national strength and the increased promotion of Chinese promoted the curriculum of Mandarin and simplified Chinese characters to a certain extent.

There were once a total of more than 300 students in Chung's three Chinese schools, including some British children. "It's so gratifying that children of all colors gather together to learn Chinese and recite our classics!" Chung was very satisfied.

Driven by a sense of responsibility and achievement, Chung has been more than happy to spare the time to go to the schools, communicating with the teachers and students, and handling various affairs. He also taught the children to play the kylin dance, or the Chinese unicorn dance. During the Spring Festival, the schools organized lion dance shows and singing competitions, which were very lively. The Overseas Chinese Affairs Office of the Shenzhen Municipal Government once gave them a set of "lion" for the dance. Chung is joyful to see the spread of Chinese culture in Britain.

His efforts and contributions have also been recognized by the motherland. In 1999, the Overseas Chinese Affairs Office of the State Council of China awarded him the title of "Outstanding Overseas Chinese Language Educator."

Establishing a foundation to promote vigorous development of Chinese language education

Chung did not stop at running schools. In June 2005, he led a group of overseas Chinese loving Chinese language education to establish the UK Chinese Education Foundation, with him as president. They hoped that through the efforts of this generation, Chinese education would be promoted and a cultural bridge would be built so that the next generation could understand China and Chinese culture, and continue the love for the motherland and their hometown.

The foundation has united the strength of overseas Chinese and entrepreneurs to provide financial support for Chinese language education in Britain. It has also donated textbooks and held seminars and other activities.

In November 2006, the foundation organized an event to commemorate the 140th anniversary of the birth of Dr. Sun Yat-sen. Such activities were to tell Chinese history to the headmasters of Chinese schools and to promote patriotism, Chung said.

In June 2007 and July 2010, the foundation held the European Chinese Education Seminar in Manchester, and the event in 2010 received a congratulatory letter from the British queen. In 2010, Shenzhen's overseas Chinese affairs delegation made a special trip to Manchester to attend the seminar, discussing the future development of Chinese language education with representatives of Chinese language educators from all over Europe.

Chung revealed that a total of 68 Chinese schools had received funding from the foundation, covering all the four major regions of the United Kingdom, namely Northern Ireland, Scotland, Wales, and England.

The more the merrier. Chung's deeds have also converged into the tide of the times. Thanks to the joint efforts of overseas Chinese in Britain, Chinese language education has developed vigorously there.

According to a news report in 2011, there were more than 100 weekend Chinese schools in Britain, most of which were non-profit ones organized by enthusiastic overseas Chinese leaders, associations, and voluntary groups, among others.

A study published in the 11th issue of the *Journal of World Education* in 2015 also pointed out that most of the Chinese schools in Britain were opened with the support of overseas Chinese associations, and the funds and venues were invested and sponsored by associations such as the UK Chinese Education Foundation, the UK Federation of Chinese Schools, and the UK Association for the Promotion of Chinese Education. Overseas students from China, as well as other groups, also contributed to the Chinese schools and the Chinese language education in mainstream schools.

The UK Association for the Promotion of Chinese Education mentioned above was established in 1993, and Chung is one of its founders. Its president, Sin Hung Ng, immigrated to Britain in 1968 and settled in Newcastle. He once recalled to the media the hardship of Chinese schools: In the early days, there were only a few students in the small after-school classes in the old Chinatown.

In May 2014, the then Chinese consul general in Manchester attended a charity gala of the UK Chinese Education Foundation and said that the driving force for the development of overseas Chinese language education came from the overseas Chinese community. "Chinese language education is the fundamental guarantee for maintaining the ethnic characteristics of overseas Chinese. It is an important link to maintain the emotional connection between Chinese people at home and abroad and their motherland or ancestral country. It is a 'project to keep the roots.'"

Serving the community and promoting Sino-British exchanges

In addition to providing support for Chinese schools in Britain, Chung has also done a lot for the friendly exchanges between China and Britain and for the local community.

The UK Chinese Education Foundation has selected and sent children of overseas Chinese to China for cultural exchange activities for many times, and has facilitated Lancashire's economic, trade and cultural delegations to visit China. Chung has repeatedly invited representatives of governments and cultural and educational institutions from all over China to visit Britain and carry out exchanges and cooperation in economy, trade, science and technology, education, and other fields. Thanks to his efforts, the University of Central Lancashire has established friendly and cooperative relations with Beihua University, Chongqing University, and Qinghai University, and Preston has become a sister city with Xining City, Qinghai Province.

During the Chinese New Year holidays, Chung has invited children's palaces from all over China to send children to Preston for art exchanges, visiting local mainstream schools, studying and making friends with local teenagers, and understanding British culture. "If these children can study in the UK in the future, it is good to know about the UK in advance," Chung said.

He likes to go around and make friends, so he is very interested in doing community work, he said. After opening Chinese schools, he met more and more friends in the overseas Chinese community. He discussed with the mayor of Preston and the Chinese consulate general in Manchester, saying that he wanted to establish an organization to hold carnivals and other festival activities such as performing the lion dance and the kylin dance. With the support of all parties, in 1992, he founded the Preston and District Chinese Community Association. He joined the Confederation of Chinese Associations UK in the same year, and later served as vice president and executive committee member. He used to organize overseas Chinese to raise funds for Preston mayor's fund every year and to donate to the local hospital for mentally handicapped children.

Loving his motherland and hometown with unremitting devotion

While serving the overseas Chinese and the local society, Chung has also actively contributed to the public welfare and charity of his motherland and hometown.

In 1992, Chung took his father back to his hometown of Dapeng, decades after their departure. Chung recalled that his hometown was relatively "backward" at that time. It took six hours for a van to bump its way from downtown Shenzhen to Dapeng, and it took about nine hours to travel from Shenzhen to Qingyuan. "At that time, I wondered when China could be built into a better country."

Chung not only looked forward to the accelerated development of his motherland and hometown, but also contributed to it. In 1993, he donated 4,000 pounds for the construction of the Shenzhen Dapeng Overseas Chinese Hospital. The monthly salary of ordinary people in Britain was only dozens of pounds back then. In 1997, he raised 8,000 pounds for the development and construction of the Qingcheng District Vocational Middle School (now the Qingyuan Industry and Trade Vocational School) in Qingyuan City.

Chung remembered that around 2016, he began to see big changes in his hometown of Dapeng, and he felt relieved. Led by Chung, the UK Chinese Education Foundation raised funds for China's Project Hope to build primary schools. It also set up teaching awards and scholarships for the teachers and students in the Fucun Primary School, Libu Township, Yangshan County, Qingyuan City, and the Wufeng School, Fangcun, Haizhu District, Guangzhou Municipality.

In 2008, after the Wenchuan earthquake in Sichuan, the foundation donated 18,000 pounds. Chung still remembered that he carried a donation box to collect donations on the street for four days, and most of the money he raised was in coins. If he took the coins, amounting to more than 10,000 pounds, to the bank for processing, a handling fee would be charged. "We sorted and packaged the banknotes and coins we received by denomination, and handed them over to the Chinese consulate general in Manchester. Then they took the money to the Bank of China for processing, saving more than 1,000 pounds."

In the same year, the foundation raised more than 8,000 pounds for the earthquake in Yushu, Qinghai.

At the beginning of 2020, when COVID-19 broke out in China, overseas Chinese donated money and materials through various channels to support the fight against the disease. Chung raised funds to order 30,000 N95 masks from several medical insurance companies. However, the procurement plan fell through due to the shortage of supplies. Then he mobilized his relatives and friends to contact sources of supplies in Norway, Germany and France, among others. He also purchased some temperature guns and KN95 masks through Zhong Xiong, who is one of his relatives, honorary president of the Yulin Federation of Returned Overseas Chinese, Guangxi, and honorary president of the UK Chinese Education Foundation, and donated them to some schools in Jilin, Liaoning, Qinghai, Guangdong, Guangxi and other places. Worth more than 270,000 yuan, the temperature guns and KN95 masks were bought using funds from overseas Chinese in many countries. "The foundation has honorary presidents in the Netherlands, France, China, Australia, and Canada, and they support me whenever we hold an activity," Chung said.

In the summer of 2021, Zhengzhou, Henan Province was suddenly hit by heavy rains, which brought floods. Chung led the Preston and District Chinese Association to donate more than 2,000 pounds.

Before the COVID-19 pandemic, Chung often returned to China to visit different places and take part in various exchange activities. He was invited to attend the National Day ceremonies in 1994 and 2009. He has been to Beijing, Heilongjiang, Jilin, Qinghai, Henan, Hebei, Guangdong, and Guangxi, among others, and served as a director of the overseas exchange associations in many provinces and autonomous regions.

As an overseas Chinese leader in Britain, Chung has practiced his love for his motherland and hometown in his own way. At the age of 75, he is still managing the affairs of his organizations. In late November 2022, he was busy planning a major event, discussing the arrangements for Chinese New Year celebrations with the Lancashire County Council.

At the same time, Chung is looking for a successor who loves his motherland and hometown. He hopes that overseas Chinese teenagers can love China and their hometown and understand Chinese culture.

He said, "As long as the earth is rotating and the water of the Yangtze River and the Yellow River is flowing, I am willing to do my best for the reunification of the motherland and the great rejuvenation of the Chinese nation, continue to work hard for the inheritance of Chinese culture and the tradition of loving the motherland and hometown, and pass on this tradition from generation to generation."

(Photos courtesy of Raymond Chung. References: *Deep Love for the Hometown and Sincere Loyalty to the Motherland: Oral History of Overseas Chinese from Dapeng*, *Journal of World Education*, *Shenzhen Overseas Chinese News*, www.chinanews.com, the website of the Ministry of Foreign Affairs of China, www.chinaqw.com, and *Voice of Rongxian County*.)

蔡树坚

走出蔡屋围，在荷兰专注推广华文教育

蔡树坚　Shu Kin Choi

　　蔡树坚，深圳罗湖蔡屋围人，1951 年 4 月出生，现为旅荷比深圳市蔡屋围同乡会会长，荷兰中文教育协会常务理事、教育咨询，荷兰华文精英教育中心高级教育顾问，全荷华人联合体育运动总会名誉主席。

　　自 1978 年定居荷兰后，在旅荷华人联谊会中文学校任校长一职长达 30 年，并积极参加各侨社的义务工作，推动中文教育和华人体育运动的发展，长期为促进中荷两国文化和运动的交流作出积极贡献。曾获国务院侨务办公室暨中国海外交流协会颁发的"海外优秀华教工作者""华文教育终身成就奖"，以及荷兰王室骑士勋章（Ridder in de Orde van Oranje-Nassau）等荣誉。

采访时间：2022 年。

少小离家老大回，乡音无改鬓毛衰。

儿童相见不相识，笑问客从何处来。

这是 1200 多年前中国唐代诗人贺知章写的《回乡偶书》组诗之一。当时，诗人刚刚辞去朝廷官职，告老返回故乡越州永兴（今浙江杭州萧山）。贺知章 37 岁左右高中进士离开家乡，回乡时已经 80 多岁，成了一个白发苍苍的老人，就是说，这个时候他离开家乡已经有近 50 年的时间了。

在旅荷比深圳市蔡屋围同乡会会长蔡树坚看来，贺知章这首诗所抒发的感喟，时空虽异，却也是他自己情怀的真实写照。

远赴荷兰生活

蔡树坚告诉记者，他父亲原来是"行船嘅"（跑船、做海员的），过去曾在荷兰渣华轮船公司的"芝大隆"号上工作。

1958 年 2 月春节期间，蔡树坚父亲工作的海外远洋轮船抵达香港，并停留几天。这个时候，他母亲申请了出境手续，带着年幼的妹妹去香港和父亲相聚，留下蔡树坚和大妹在乡下——蔡屋围。

很不巧，在香港时蔡树坚的母亲生病了，一时回不了蔡屋围，而他和大妹仍需要大人的照顾。于是，他父亲向乡里说明情况，并告知了自己家里的难处，希望能接他们兄妹一起到香港来。随后蔡树坚兄妹二人拿到了出境的通行证，跨过罗湖桥，去到香港与母亲和妹妹团聚。

至今，蔡树坚依然清楚记得，那一年他还不到 8 岁，正在蔡屋围小学读二年级。从此以后，他告别了在蔡屋围的童年故乡生活，在香港度过了寄人篱下的漫长岁月……后来蔡树坚的父母辗转到了荷兰阿姆斯特丹，在当地开了一家餐馆。不过，蔡树坚在师范大学毕业之后，仍选择留在香港，在新界的上水凤

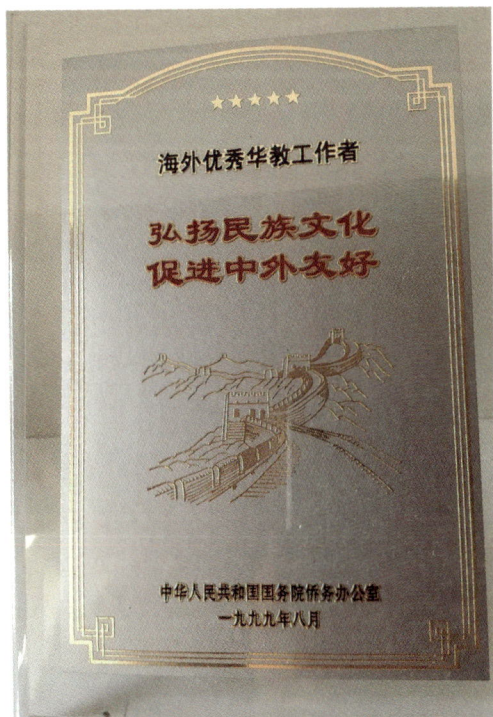

蔡树坚获得中国国务院侨务办公室颁发的"海外优秀华教工作者"称号。

Shu Kin Choi was awarded the title of "Outstanding Overseas Chinese Language Educator" by the Overseas Chinese Affairs Office of the State Council of China.

溪中学当一名教书育人的老师。到了 1978 年，由于父母年事已高，弟弟妹妹年纪小还在上学，蔡树坚不得不终止在香港的工作，与太太、女儿一起申请到荷兰和家人团聚，帮父亲打理餐馆的生意。就这样，一直坚持了十多年时间。

但是，蔡树坚的兴趣不在于此。结束了家族的餐饮生意之后，他在荷兰继续进修了会计、电脑等成人培训课程。1995 年，蔡树坚在阿姆斯特丹的新国泰旅行社找到了一份工作，并担任旅游部经理，直到 2016 年退休。

在荷兰，无论是帮忙打理家族的生意，还是后来在旅行社工作，蔡树坚也一直没有闲着。用我们现在社会上流行的说法，他其实就是一个积极向上且精力充沛的"斜杠青年"。譬如，2004 年到 2007 年期间，他就兼任着一份中文国际报章（欧航版）在荷兰办事处的总经理。不过，在众多的"兼职"当中，蔡树坚投入精力最多的还是自己的老本行——华文教育。

致力华文教育

华文教育被认为是中华文化在海外传承的"留根工程"，是海外华社繁荣发展的"希望工程"，更是惠及广大海外侨胞生存发展的"民生工程"。关于荷兰的华文教育，中国驻荷兰大使馆领事部曾称"荷兰是欧洲开展华文教育最好的国家之一"。

如此评价，可谓赞誉甚高。殊不知，这个成绩背后饱含了多少像蔡树坚这样一代又一代海外华文教育工作者的艰辛付出。

蔡树坚回忆，"荷兰的中文传授可追溯到 20 世纪 30 年代"。值得注意的是，他在这里用的是"传授"一词，而不是"教育"二字。

皆因当时在荷兰鹿特丹和阿姆斯特丹两大城市有华裔团体或家庭开设了零星的中文班或中文识字班，只是由于华裔儿童人数太少、

代表荷兰女王颁授荷兰王室骑士勋章的海尔许霍瓦德市长特尔·希格德与蔡树坚合照。

On behalf of the Dutch queen, Heerhugowaard Mayor H.M.W. ter Heegde awards Knight in the Order of Orange-Nassau (Ridder in de Orde van Oranje-Nassau) to Shu Kin Choi.

学习困难等种种因素，当时荷兰的华文教育尚未形成气候，即便是到了二十世纪五六十年代在荷兰的华人开始逐渐增多，情况依旧没有多大的改观。

现在身份是荷兰中文教育协会常务理事、教育咨询的蔡树坚认为，华文教育在荷兰有规模地发展起来，应该始于 20 世纪 70 年代以后。1973 年，荷兰鹿特丹华人教会成立中文识字班，当时学生人数已经开始逐渐增多。到了 1979 年，阿姆斯特丹相继有旅荷华人联谊会中文学校、启华书院两间中文学校创立，经过了十多年的辛勤耕耘，由幼儿班至小学、中学有十多个班别，学生人数达几百人，成为荷兰最早具有规模的中文学校，客观上也促进了荷兰华人在 20 世纪 80 年代之后的办学潮。踏入了 20 世纪 90 年代，中文识字班、中文学校如雨后春笋般地在荷兰各大城镇上出现，至今方兴未艾。

1979 年，蔡树坚就是因为带女儿到旅荷华人联谊会中文学校（2019 年该校已更名为"华人中文学校"）学习中文，师范中文系毕业的他才跟中文教育再续上前缘的。从 20 世纪 80 年代起，他就开始在旅荷华人联谊会中文学校担任高年导师兼校长职务，时间长达 30 年，不但为学校制定了一系列的规章和制度，而且也规范了学校在教材、课程、作业和考试等方面的内容。

过去在荷兰，从事华文教育，无论是理事、校长还是教师，都是无薪酬（只有少数的津贴）的志愿工作，人人都是凭着一股热情来推广华文教育的。"大家都只

庆祝中华人民共和国成立 70 周年暨 2019 第一届荷兰华校才艺汇演。

The first Talent Show of Chinese Schools in the Netherlands in 2019, which also celebrated the 70th anniversary of the People's Republic of China.

蔡树坚获得的荷兰王室骑士勋章。
The medal of Knight in the Order of Orange-Nassau
(Ridder in de Orde van Oranje-Nassau) of the
Netherlands won by Shu Kin Choi.

问耕耘不问收获，只是想让华人的子弟可以有机会去学习中文，接触自己的历史文化，不会遗忘固有的根源。"蔡树坚说道。

当然，中文学校上课的时间也都是在荷兰本地学校上正课以外的日子，通常是周六或周三下午（荷兰小学周三下午休息），又或者是在周日；上课时长则2至4个小时不等。

"随着中国国力的强盛，现今中文已成为世界语言中的一门'显学'。"如今，身处荷兰的蔡树坚同时透露了一组数据："目前全荷兰各地开办的中文学校约有40所，学生人数有5000多人，教师有300多人。大规模的中文学校，学生已超过600多人，包括不少本土荷兰人。"

在荷兰侨界，知道"蔡树坚"三个字的人或许不多，但提到"蔡校长"则几乎无人不晓。可以说，2010年之前，在阿姆斯特丹出生、成长起来的华裔年轻人，如果懂中文而且又能够把自己中文名字写得工工整整的，十有八九都是出自蔡校长的门下。

投身华人体育运动

学教育出身的蔡树坚现在还有一个头衔，那就是"全荷华人联合体育运动总会名誉主席"。全荷华人联合体育运动总会在1985年创立，蔡树坚在2005年到2010年期间，有幸成为全荷华人联合体育运动总会的主席。"其实都是一帮志同道合的华人利用个人业余的时间在周末开会、组织活动，义务为大家做一些奉献的工作。"蔡树坚谦虚地说道，全荷华人联合体育运动总会最主要的工作就是组织举办每年一次的全荷华人体育运动会。"在过去，运动会每一年一届，从不间断，只是最近几年因为疫情的缘故，所以才暂时停办了。"

关于全荷华人体育运动会，蔡树坚印象最深刻的还是在1994年举行的那一届运动会。当时全荷华人体育运动会正好进入第十个年头，组委会将运动会办成了一次全球华人体育事业的盛事，比赛也因此有了一个特别的名称——第十届全荷华人体育运动会暨世界华人友谊邀请赛。

1994 年 10 月 24 日，在荷兰阿姆斯特丹南方体育馆的室内运动场里，来自中国、美国、加拿大、泰国、新加坡、澳大利亚及欧洲等全球 25 个城市的近 1500 名华人代表出席了开幕式。运动会共设足球（室内、室外）、篮球、排球、羽毛球、乒乓球、中国象棋、保龄球和武术等 8 个项目，分青、中、老年组别，集中在阿姆斯特丹的 4 个标准运动场馆进行，盛况空前。

全荷华人体育运动会已经成为当地华人社会中一项非常重要的活动。（右一者为蔡树坚）

The Chinese Sports Tournament has become a very important event in the local Chinese community. (The first from right is Shu Kin Choi)

有一份记录第十届全荷华人体育运动会的文献资料，或许可以从侧面进一步佐证蔡树坚的说法。这篇由白金申（中国篮球名宿）和汪勇共同署名的文章《体育，把华人联结在一起——记第十届全荷华人运动会》（刊载于 1995 年第 1 期《体育博览》杂志）透露：比赛之余，他们还偶遇了率加拿大华人足球队前来参赛的著名前中国国家足球队主教练苏永舜，以及前中国香港队主教练郭家明，大家聚在一起叙旧，激动不已。白金申更是奇迹般地遇到了老朋友——1956 年便迁居海外的新中国第一代游泳名将黄鸿九。

今天，全荷华人体育运动会已经成为当地华人社会中一项非常重要的活动——"一个老少咸宜的中国人喜庆节日"：有儿童参与的游戏嘉年华，也有青少年、中年人喜欢参加的体育比赛。

除了华人之外，几乎每支参赛球队中还会有一些不同肤色、不同国籍的运动员。对此，已经身居幕后的蔡树坚解释，大部分荷兰华人从事的基本都是餐饮行业，虽然荷兰本地的体育运动非常丰富，但是以前华人能够参与的却很少。"全荷华人体育运动会除了为旅荷华侨华人提供比赛和相聚机会之外，就是希望能够促进华人和本地社群的联络，更好地帮助旅荷华侨华人融入当地社会。"

难忘蔡屋围

1987 年，中国国务院侨务办公室邀请欧美地区的中文学校代表回国访问，中国驻荷兰大使馆邀请蔡树坚和几位教师参加，他们先后在北京、西安、桂林、广州等地参观和游览。参访访问活动结束之后，蔡树坚抽空回了趟深圳，探望日夜想念的在家乡的亲人。自 1958 年离开蔡屋围，蔡树坚再一次踏上故土，已经相隔了近 30 年的光景。

蔡树坚参加 2017 "华文教育·示范学校和华教机构负责人华夏行"。
Shu Kin Choi participates in the 2017 Trip to China for Leaders of Chinese Language Education Demonstration Schools and Chinese Language Education Institutions.

后来，利用在旅行社工作的便利，蔡树坚几乎每年都会在暑假组织学生和家长一起参与的夏令营，回国参观、交流、访问。"就是希望能让在荷兰的华人子弟亲身体验一下祖国的大好河山和名胜古迹。"蔡树坚表示，荷兰的中文学校回国访问团在深圳、北京跟当地学生的面对面交流活动，是让华裔学生最为津津乐道的事。

在 1995 年之后，蔡树坚差不多每一年都会趁着带团之便回到蔡屋围（就是他口中的"乡下"）走一趟，无形中也见证了深圳从一个落后的边陲小镇发展成为一个具有全球影响力的国际化大都市的奇迹。

蔡屋围是深圳的一座古老的自然村落，始建于明朝洪武年间，至今已有 600 多年的历史。据《深圳原住民家谱》（陈宏著，深圳报业集团出版社 2011 年版）记载：解放之初的蔡屋围面积很大，从广九铁路往西到笔架山，从深圳河到八卦岭，都是蔡屋围的地盘，面积有 5000 多亩，而且有不少是在香港的境外土地。20 世纪 80 年代迄今风光无限的渔民村的土地，也是解放之初从蔡屋围靠近深圳河的一块地方剥离出来的。然而，改革开放之前，土地广袤的蔡屋围却穷得叮当响。

今天的蔡屋围已经完全蜕变成为"深圳的华尔街"。这里是中国人民银行、几大国有银行深圳总部和深圳证券交易所旧址的所在地，有早期的"亚洲第一高楼"地王大厦，还有与地王大厦相邻的 441.8 米高的京基 100 大厦，汇聚了众多全球 500 强企业。1987 年创办的深圳发展银行（现在的平安银行），是中国内地第一家面向社会公众公开发行股票并上市的商业银行（股票代码：SZ000001），就位于蔡屋围。

"如今的蔡屋围，跟我们小时候的印象完全不一样了。蔡屋围走过的路，就是深圳经济特区 40 多年建设与发展的缩影和见证。"蔡树坚感慨道。

蔡屋围是深圳著名的侨乡，蔡屋围人敢闯敢拼，为谋生计，足迹遍及世界各地，在海外的蔡屋围同乡会组织也是遍布欧美。作为旅荷比深圳市蔡屋围同乡会会长，蔡树坚表示，组织同乡会就是想让在海外的乡亲可以互相帮助，有机会聚在一起，交换信息，了解乡情，特别是将家乡发展的最新消息在第一时间跟大家一起分享。"侨居异国的蔡屋围人爱国爱乡，不但团结一致，非常支持国家的发展建设，而且群策群力，热心支持家乡的公益事业。"蔡树坚说。

（本文图片均由受访者蔡树坚提供。参考资料：《体育博览》《深圳原住民家谱》。）

Shu Kin Choi

Coming from Caiwuwei, focusing on promoting Chinese language education in the Netherlands

Shu Kin Choi, also known as Ken Choi, was born in April 1951 in Caiwuwei, Luohu, Shenzhen. He is president of the Foundation of Choi Family Association in the Netherlands and Belgium (Stichting Familie Choi in Netherlands en Belgie), executive director and education consultant of the Foundation of Chinese Education in the Netherlands (Stichting Chinees Onderwijs in Nederland), senior education consultant of the Chinese Education Center Netherlands (Chinees Onderwijscentrum Nederland), and honorary chairman of the Foundation of Chinese Sports Federation Netherlands (Stichting Chinese Sportfederatie Nederland).

After settling down in the Netherlands in 1978, he served as principal of the Chinese School Fa Yin for 30 years. He has also actively participated in the voluntary work of overseas Chinese communities, promoted the development of Chinese language education and Chinese sports, and made positive contributions to promoting cultural and sports exchanges between China and the Netherlands for a long time. He was awarded "Outstanding Overseas Chinese Language Educator" and "Lifelong Achievement Award of Chinese Language Education" by the Overseas Chinese Affairs Office of the State Council of China and the China Overseas Exchange Association, as well as Knight in the Order of Orange-Nassau (Ridder in de Orde van Oranje-Nassau) of the Netherlands.

I return to the homeland I left while young.

Thinner has grown my hair, though I speak the same tongue.

The children, whom I meet, do not know who am I.

"Where are you from, dear sir?" they ask with beaming eyes.

The interview took place in 2022.

This is one of a series of poems named "Home-Coming" written by He Zhizhang, a Chinese poet in the Tang Dynasty, more than 1,200 years ago. At that time, the poet had just resigned from his official position in the imperial court and returned to his hometown, Yongxing, Yuezhou (now Xiaoshan, Hangzhou, Zhejiang Province). He passed the highest imperial examination and left his hometown when he was almost 37 years old. When he returned, he was more than 80 years old with white hair. He had been away from his hometown for nearly 50 years.

In the opinion of Shu Kin Choi, president of the Foundation of Choi Family Association in the Netherlands and Belgium (Stichting Familie Choi in Netherlands en Belgie), the sigh expressed in this poem is a true portrayal of his own feelings despite different time and space.

Going to the Netherlands

Choi said that his father used to be "someone working on a ship" (a sailor) and used to work on a ship of Java-China-Japan Lijn N.V., a Dutch shipping company.

During the Spring Festival in February 1958, the overseas ship where Choi's father was working arrived in Hong Kong and stayed for a few days. At this time, Choi's mother applied for exit procedures, took his youngest sister to Hong Kong to meet his father, leaving Choi and a younger sister in the countryside, Caiwuwei.

Unfortunately, Choi's mother was ill in Hong Kong and couldn't return to Caiwuwei in a short time, while Choi and a younger sister still needed adults to take care of them. So, his father explained the situation to the township officials and told them about the difficulties of his family, hoping to take the two children to Hong Kong. Then the brother and sister got their exit passes and crossed the Luohu Bridge to reunite with their mother and sister in Hong Kong.

Choi still clearly remembers that he was less than 8 years old that year and was in the second grade of the Caiwuwei Primary School. From then on, he said goodbye to his childhood life in his hometown, and spent a long time of dependence in Hong Kong... Later, Choi's parents moved to Amsterdam, the Netherlands, and opened a restaurant there. However, after graduating from a normal university, Choi chose to stay in Hong Kong to work as a teacher in the Fung Kai Secondary School in Sheung Shui, New Territories. In 1978, he had to stop working in Hong Kong because his parents were old while his younger brother and sisters were still school children. He, together with his wife and daughter, applied to go to the Netherlands to reunite with his family and help his father manage the restaurant business. Then Choi ran the business for more than 10 years.

However, Choi's interest did not lie in this. After finishing his family's catering business, he went on to study accounting, computer and other adult training courses in the Netherlands. In 1995, he found a job in Cathay Travel Service B. V. in Amsterdam and served as manager of the tourism department until his retirement in 2016.

Choi has always been busy in the Netherlands, whether was helping with the family business or working in the travel agency later. In popular parlance at present, he was a positive and energetic "slash youth," with two or more concurrent careers. For example, from 2004 to 2007, he was also general manager of the Dutch office of the European airlines version of an international newspaper in Chinese. However, among his many "part-time jobs", he has devoted the most energy to his old job—Chinese language education.

Committed to Chinese language education

Chinese language education is considered the "project to keep the root" for the overseas inheritance of Chinese culture, the "Project Hope" for the prosperity and development of overseas Chinese communities, and the "livelihood project" benefiting the survival and development of overseas Chinese. Regarding Chinese language education in the Netherlands, the Consular Department of the Chinese embassy in the Netherlands once said, "the Netherlands is one of the best European countries in carrying out Chinese language education."

This is high praise indeed. In fact, such an achievement is the result of hard work of generations of overseas Chinese language educators like Choi.

"The imparting of Chinese in the Netherlands can be traced back to the 1930s," Choi recalled. It should be noted that he used the word "imparting" instead of "education."

It was all because there were just a few "Chinese classes" or "Chinese literacy classes" run by overseas Chinese groups or families in Rotterdam and Amsterdam. At that time, Chinese language education in the Netherlands did not come into fashion because of many reasons, including the small number of overseas Chinese children and the difficulties in learning Chinese. Even in the 1950s and 1960s, the number of Chinese in the Netherlands began to increase gradually, but things did not change much.

Choi, who is executive director and education consultant of the Foundation of Chinese Education in the Netherlands (Stichting Chinees Onderwijs in Nederland), believes that the large-scale development of Chinese language education in the Netherlands began in the 1970s. In 1973, Chinese literacy classes held by Chinese churches in Rotterdam saw gradually increasing students. In 1979, two Chinese schools were founded in Amsterdam, namely the Chinese School Fa Yin and the Foundation of Kai Wah Chinese School (Stichting Chinese School Kai Wah). After more than 10 years of hard work, there were more than 10 classes, for kindergarten children, primary school students and middle school students, amounting to hundreds of students. They became the first large-scale Chinese schools in the Netherlands, and, as a result, promoted the trend for Chinese in the Netherlands to run schools in the 1980s. In the 1990s, Chinese literacy classes and Chinese schools sprang up in major cities and small towns of the Netherlands. Now the trend is still on the rise.

Choi, who had graduated from the Chinese Department of a normal university, continued his old career in Chinese language education in 1979 after taking his daughter to study Chinese at the Chinese School Fa Yin. Starting in the 1980s, he served as senior grades tutor and principal of the school for 30 years, when he not only formulated a series of rules and regulations for the school, but also standardized the school's teaching materials, courses, homework and examinations.

In the past, Chinese education in the Netherlands was voluntary work without pay (with only a few allowances) for all directors, principals and teachers. Everyone promoted Chinese education with enthusiasm. "We all worked hard and asked for nothing. We just wanted to offer an opportunity for the children of overseas Chinese to learn Chinese, to touch their own history and culture, and not to forget their inherent roots," Choi said.

Of course, Chinese schools have classes on days when local Dutch schools have no regular classes, usually on Saturday or Wednesday afternoons (Dutch primary schools have no classes on Wednesday afternoons), or on Sundays. It takes two to four hours each time.

"With the prosperity of China's national strength, Chinese has now become a 'prominent learning' in the world's languages," said Choi, who is in the Netherlands now. He also revealed some data, "At present, there are about 40 Chinese schools in the Netherlands, with more than 5,000 students and more than 300 teachers. A large-scale Chinese school has more than 600 students, including many native Dutch."

In the Dutch overseas Chinese community, few people may know the name "Shu Kin Choi", but almost everyone knows "Principal Choi." We can say that before 2010, if a young Chinese born and raised in Amsterdam knew Chinese and could write his Chinese name perfectly, he would be Choi's student in nine cases out of ten.

Engaged in Chinese sports

Choi majored in education and has another title: "honorary chairman of the Foundation of Chinese Sports Federation Netherlands" (Stichting Chinese Sportfederatie Nederland). The foundation was founded in 1985, and Choi was honored to be its chairman from 2005 to 2010. "In fact, we are a group of like-minded Chinese who spend our spare time holding meetings and organizing activities on weekends, and volunteering to make a contribution," Choi said modestly. The main task of the foundation is to organize the annual Chinese Sports Tournament, he said. "In the past, the tournament was held every year without interruption. It has been suspended only in recent years because of the pandemic."

Choi was most impressed by the event held in 1994. That year marked the 10th anniversary of the event, and the organizing committee made it a grand event of global Chinese sports with a special name: the 10th Chinese Sports Tournament and the World Chinese Friendship Invitational.

On October 24, 1994, nearly 1,500 representatives of Chinese from 25 cities in different countries around the world, including China, the United States, Canada, Thailand, Singapore, Australia and some European countries, attended the opening ceremony in the indoor stadium of the Sports Halls South Amsterdam (Sporthallen Zuid Amsterdam). The tournament had eight sports, including football (indoor and outdoor), basketball, volleyball, badminton, table tennis, Chinese chess, bowling and martial arts, divided into youth, middle-aged and elderly groups. Held in four standard sports venues in Amsterdam, it was an unprecedented event.

A document recording the 10th Chinese Sports Tournament may further support Choi's statement. The article, *Sports, Linking Chinese Together—the 10th Chinese Sports Tournament* (published in the *Sports Vision* in its first issue of 1995), co-signed by Bai Jinshen (a famous Chinese basketball player) and Wang Yong, revealed that, during the event, they ran into Su Yongshun, the famous former head coach of the Chinese national football team, who led the Canadian Chinese football team to participate, and Kwok Ka Ming, former head coach of the Chinese Hong Kong team. They were excited to get together and reminisce about the past. Bai even miraculously met his old friend Huang Hongjiu, one of the first generation of famous swimmers of the People's Republic of China, who moved overseas in 1956.

Today, the Chinese Sports Tournament has become a very important event in the local Chinese society—"a festival for Chinese people of all ages," including a game carnival for children and sports competitions for teenagers and middle-aged people.

Almost each team has some athletes of different colors and nationalities besides overseas Chinese. According to Choi, who has faded into the background now, most Chinese in the Netherlands are engaged in the catering industry, and, although there are plenty of sports in the Netherlands, there were few available to the Chinese in the past. "In addition to providing opportunities for overseas Chinese in the Netherlands to compete and meet, the Chinese Sports Tournament will hopefully promote the contact between overseas Chinese and local communities, and better help overseas Chinese in the Netherlands integrate into local society."

Remembering Caiwuwei

In 1987, the Overseas Chinese Affairs Office of the State Council of China invited representatives of Chinese schools in Europe and Americas to visit China. Invited by the Chinese embassy in the Netherlands, Choi and several teachers took part in the event, and visited Beijing, Xi'an, Guilin, Guangzhou and other places. After the visit, Choi took the time to return to Shenzhen to see his relatives in his hometown, whom he had missed day and night. Once again, Choi set foot on his hometown. It had been nearly 30 years since he left Caiwuwei in 1958.

Later, with the convenience of working in the travel agency, Choi organized summer camps almost every year for students and parents to visit China and carry out exchanges. "I hoped that the children of the Chinese in the Netherlands could experience the beautiful rivers and mountains, as well as places of historic interest of the motherland." Choi also said that the face-to-face exchanges between the Dutch Chinese school delegation and local students in Shenzhen and Beijing were the most interesting for the overseas Chinese students.

After 1995, Choi returned to Caiwuwei (what he called "the countryside") almost every year when leading the tour group to China. In this way, he witnessed the miracle of Shenzhen's development from a backward border town to an international metropolis with global influence.

Caiwuwei is an ancient natural village in Shenzhen. It was built in the Hongwu period of the Ming Dynasty and has a history of more than 600 years. According to the *Family Trees of Indigenous People in Shenzhen* (written by Chen Hong, published by the Shenzhen News Group Publishing House in 2011), Caiwuwei had a large area when the People's Republic of China was established. From the Canton-Kowloon Railway to Bijia Mountain in the west, from Shenzhen River to Bagualing, Caiwuwei covered an area of more than 5,000 mu (about 3.33 square kilometers), much of which was overseas land in Hong Kong. The land of the Fishermen's Village, which has been glorious since the 1980s, was also separated from a place in Caiwuwei near Shenzhen River shortly after the People's Republic of China was founded. However, before the reform and opening-up, Caiwuwei was very poor despite its vast land.

Today, Caiwuwei has completely transformed into the "Wall Street of Shenzhen." The Shenzhen headquarters of the People's Bank of China and several major state-owned banks are located here, and the Shenzhen Stock Exchange used to be located here. There are the Diwang Mansion, the former "tallest building in Asia," and the Kingkee 100 Tower, 441.8 meters high and adjacent to the Diwang Mansion. Many of the global top 500 enterprises gather in Caiwuwei. Shenzhen Development Bank (now Ping An Bank), founded in 1987, is also located in Caiwuwei. It was the first commercial bank in China's mainland to go public (stock code: SZ000001).

"Today's Caiwuwei is completely different from our childhood impression. The road Caiwuwei has gone through is the epitome of the construction and development of Shenzhen Special Economic Zone in more than 40 years," Choi said.

Caiwuwei is a famous hometown of overseas Chinese in Shenzhen. Caiwuwei people are courageous and entrepreneurial, making a living all over the world. Overseas associations of Caiwuwei natives are also all over Europe and Americas. As president of the Foundation of Choi Family Association in the Netherlands and Belgium (Stichting Familie Choi in Netherlands en Belgie), Choi said that the association intended to enable overseas fellow villagers to help each other, get together, exchange information, and share news about their hometown, especially its latest development. "The Caiwuwei people living in foreign countries love their motherland and hometown. They not only stand united and support the development and construction of China, but also work together to enthusiastically support the public welfare undertakings of their hometown," Choi said.

(Photos courtesy of Shu Kin Choi. References: *Sports Vision* and *Family Trees of Indigenous People in Shenzhen*.)

蔡建业

乡音不改，做个具有国际视野的
"传统中国人"

蔡建业　Choi Kin Yip

　　蔡建业，1952 年出生，深圳蔡屋围人，1968 年移居比利时。安特卫普市唐人街主席、荷兰广东总会理事。曾任比利时法兰特省国际旅游协会理事、比中友好协会执行理事、中比文化协会创会会长、《华人通讯》创办人。

　　经营过餐馆、进出口和旅行社等，从多方面服务、协助华侨华人以及当地社区。20 世纪 70 年代至 90 年代，积极帮助比利时华人找工作，并提供生活便利。1999 年至 2001 年，以安特卫普市的城市更新项目为契机，推动唐人街的设立和命名。2021年，为抗击新冠疫情，组织筹款购买防护用品捐给医院、养老院等。

采访时间：2022 年。

如果用简单的几个字来概括蔡建业，那可以是"故土情结，国际视野"。

他已经在比利时生活了 50 多年，但乡音未改，能说一口纯正的粤语。在他的带领下，儿女们都会说普通话和粤语，5 岁的小外孙也能说流利的普通话了。

"我是传统的中国人。"蔡建业这样总结自己。他涉足过餐饮和文化娱乐业，还经营过通信和机票业务。"我也是做生意，但是间接帮到了我们这里的华人，这些都是小贡献。"但他也有大贡献。比如，推动比利时安特卫普市唐人街设立和命名；再比如，年轻的时候，他就帮着热心助人的父亲为侨胞提供生活上的各种帮助，包括去邮局、银行、政府跑腿，在警察局、法庭为侨胞当翻译、做担保等。

蔡建业没上过大学，但学会了用英语、荷兰语、法语和德语跟人交流，办事、做生意自然顺畅。他也不会像二十世纪六七十年代的前辈们那样，在餐馆工作十几个小时后就上楼睡觉。

"老华侨真不容易啊！我们期望的就是祖国越来越强大，国际地位和认可度越来越高！"

蔡建业欣慰地发现，这种期望正在变成现实。

少年自立，渐有所成

蔡建业很早就离开了家乡蔡屋围前往香港。1963 年，在香港生活困难的父亲接受友人聘请，前往比利时中餐馆担任厨师工作。1968 年，蔡建业 16 岁时，有了当地一位华人老板做经济承担人和监护人，他就申请以学生身份去了比利时，与父母团聚。

所谓"工字不出头"（打工者永无出头之日），两年后，父母渴望有自己的事业。为了帮父母达成意愿，蔡建业离开了学校和监护人，帮助父亲购买别人出让的一家小餐馆。餐馆位于安特卫普市贝尔赫姆区。后来，蔡建业因为要在餐馆工作，只能去私立语言学校就读。

当时，自家餐馆生意不好，蔡建业就利用周末时间，找了生意好的餐馆去当跑堂，收入很理想，自赚自花，还买了一辆二手小汽车，帮助家里餐馆运货。

1974 年，蔡建业自己开起了餐馆。从 20 世纪 70 年代到 90 年代，先后开过 6 家。1995 年，比利时影像技术巨头爱克发 – 吉华集团在无锡市设立中比合资企业，中比两国派出部长级官员在安特卫普市签约，游艇晚宴就是蔡建业的餐馆"中国楼"负责的。现在想起这事，他仍然觉得自豪。

1982 年，蔡建业考取比利时旅游执照后创办了华比旅行社。几年后，这家旅行社取得了国际旅游牌照和国际航协（IATA）代理资质，还在布鲁塞尔市中心开设了分公司。

比利时的官方语言是荷兰语、法语、德语。安特卫普市主要讲荷兰语，布鲁塞尔主要讲法语，而去航空公司开会时通常用英语，蔡建业都能应付。他还会说德语，但很少有机会用到。"语言需要 practice（实践）的。"他回忆说，在香港生活的时候，年纪还小，而且只待了 5 年，所以并没有学好英语。虽然在比利时读了 3 年语言学校，但主要还是靠实践。"为了脱离前辈寂寞无助的生活，语言沟通是我必须要达到的目标。"在学校、在工作中，他都注意与当地人用口语交流，最终功夫不负有心人。

益街坊，解乡愁

正是凭着坚定的决心、敏锐的商业头脑和不折不扣的执行力，蔡建业把事业做得风生水起，同时也便利了华侨华人的生活，帮他们一解乡愁。

粤语里有个词叫"益街坊"，字面意思是"让街坊受益"，引申为"便宜大家了"，常用来形容优惠促销。这个词里，也藏着蔡建业的生意经。

20 世纪 90 年代，比利时的华人多了起来，但生活比较单调。华人住的地方，多数是三层的小楼，一楼做生意、做餐馆，二楼一般是老板住的，三楼是伙计们住。一天工作十四五个小时，没有娱乐活动。一个星期休息一天，有时打一场麻将就过去了。

蔡建业看到眼里，计上心来：香港的电影、电视剧都很出名，如果能在比利时播放，华人就有娱乐的去处了。于是，蔡建业成立了中比文化协会，租用当地电影院的场地，播放这些片子。大部分是香港电影，以粤语为主。也有来自台湾地区的片子，是普通话对白，比如《龙门客栈》，有些片子带有英文字幕。

另外，蔡建业组织过欧洲华人新秀歌唱比赛、欧洲华裔小姐选美比赛等活动，赞助过比利时历史最悠久的华人团体"旅比华侨联合会"举办一年一度的春节晚会。他还创办过《华人通讯》，向华侨华人赠阅，内容包括比利时新闻摘要、劳工法律

2001 年 8 月，中国驻比利时大使馆、中国驻欧盟使团和比利时侨界通过《华人通讯》庆祝北京成功申办 2008 年奥运会。

In August 2001, the Chinese Embassy in Belgium, the Chinese Mission to the European Union and the Belgian overseas Chinese community celebrate Beijing's successful bid to host the 2008 Olympic Games through the *Overseas Chinese Magazine.*

须知、华人动态、侨团活动、小笑话、励志文章、艺文交流等。旅比华侨联合会在这份月刊上免费刊登过筹款广告，募集资金购置的会所一直用到现在。

早年，华人除了缺乏娱乐，打电话回老家也很困难，因为话费太贵了。蔡建业就通过中比文化协会跟当地的电话公司合作，推出长途电话卡，费用只需原先的十几二十分之一，很多华人因此受益。

更贵的乡愁，是一张机票。蔡建业还记得20世纪70年代的情景："上一代华人来比利时，你问他有没有回过乡下，结果是没有。当年华人来到这里，真的就是一辈子了，很少能回去的。因为机票太贵了。"那时，比利时来往中国的交通很不方便。香港地区和欧洲之间的航班多数是英国航空运营的。后来，国泰航空和金狮航空开始运营香港和伦敦之间的航班，这两家公司把伦敦作为它们的欧洲基地。蔡建业的旅行社趁这个机会，跟这两家航空公司接洽，争取到特价票给回乡的侨胞，便宜了近一半。这样，有些侨胞就可以两年回一次中国了。

蔡建业的旅行社还曾经捐出一些机票，在侨团的新年晚会上搞抽奖，并延伸到越南、缅甸、老挝联谊会与各侨团合办的新年晚会，也捐过机票给布鲁塞尔的餐馆同业公会。既回馈同胞，也为华侨华人广结善缘。

参与城市更新，建立唐人街

更多时候，唐人街是海外华人寄托乡愁的所在。比利时的第一条唐人街就在安特卫普市，是蔡建业推动建设起来的。

坐落在安特卫普市唐人街的石狮子以及蔡建业的华比旅行社。
Stone lions and Choi Kin Yip's Wabi Travel Agency in Antwerp Chinatown.

那个区域原本破破烂烂，有四五条街，灯光昏暗，被人嫌弃。但那儿的地段不错，靠近火车站，还有个小广场，很早就有几家中餐馆、两家小超市，蔡建业的旅行社也开在那里。除了华人，那一带也有来自越南、韩国、菲律宾甚至非洲国家的侨民。

世纪之交，那个区域也迎来了改变的机会。蔡建业说，当时，安特卫普市图书馆停车不方便，市政府想把图书馆搬到小广场那里的一座空置建筑里，同时把所在片区更新一下。他参与了更新计划，向市政府转达了华侨华人的要求：可不可以把这里变为唐人街呢？

"我想，这样也可以创造一个融洽的、和平共处的环境。全世界很多地方都有唐人街，比如美国、英国，都是偏旅游的。很多人到了一个地方，就会去唐人街走走，买点中国货，吃吃中餐。"蔡建业回忆说，"我的建议就是，不单是更新这个地方，还可以列为旅游点，增加游客，带旺我们的市区。"

政府方面的反馈是：这事可行，但你们要参与的话，就得有个组织，才师出有名啊。安特卫普市唐人街街坊会就这样应运而生，由蔡建业担任会长。街坊会注册登记好了之后，就跟政府合作推动片区的改造，重新铺了路面，改善了照明，还放置了石狮子、"龙吐珠"街灯。"都是通过这个街坊会向市政府申请的。整条街的翻新、小区的翻新，都差不多是市政府全包的。我们这个会筹集的款项仅仅买了 4 只石狮子和龙灯，从中国运到比利时的码头。其余的一切工作和费用都是当地政府负责的。"蔡建业记忆犹新。

这项城市更新计划是 1999 年开始实施的，2001 年完工。市政府同意了华侨华人的申请，正式命名为 Antwerpen China Town，意思就是"安特卫普唐人街"，也叫"安市唐人街"或者"安市华埠"。蔡建业登记注册的职务就是 Antwerpen China Town Voorzitter，即"安特卫普唐人街主席"（也可译作"安特卫普华埠主席"），也是经过宪报进行了公告的。

在 2001 年 12 月 8 日的唐人

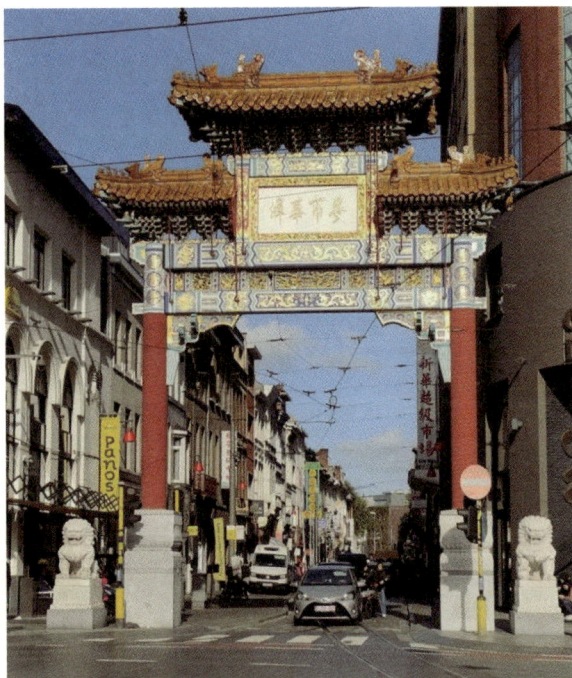

安特卫普唐人街近照。
A recent scene of Antwerp Chinatown.

街命名和揭幕仪式上，安特卫普市市长德吉尔热女士说，该市有了唐人街，表明中国文化将在比利时得到更广泛的传播，比利时和中国的友好合作将掀开新的一页。时任中国驻比利时大使关呈远说，安特卫普唐人街的诞生是旅比侨团不懈努力与当地政府大力支持和协助的结果，充分表明当地政府对华侨社团的肯定。蔡建业也在仪式上致了辞，深感荣幸。

东奔西走，无私帮助

20 世纪 70 年代至 90 年代，蔡建业在自己的学业和事业之外，持续做了一件事：为华侨华人提供各种帮助，有工作上的，也有生活上的。

据蔡建业回忆，70 年代，当地的华人还不多，大部分人还没拿到比利时的身份，找工作、出门都不方便。其中很大一部分人来自香港新界，而他们大部分又是深圳人。蔡建业的父亲蔡喜满对他们伸出了援手，帮同胞，更是帮老乡。蔡喜满当时经营着小餐馆"好彩楼"，就帮助了一些有困难的同胞，不但提供食宿，还帮助他们找工作。蔡建业课余也帮同胞们做了很多事情，包括去邮局、银行、政府机构跑腿，开车接送同胞们出入，等等。有些华侨华人因为非法逗留被警察抓到，他更是穿梭于警察局和法庭之间，承担翻译、签保之类的工作。

有一次，一位 50 多岁的老伯中了风，只能平躺。为了帮助他顺利回乡，蔡建业东奔西走筹款，凑够了买 3 张机票的钱，让老人能够躺着飞回香港。

半个多世纪，不少难忘事

抗击新冠疫情，是蔡建业近几年最难忘的经历。

2021 年春天，比利时暴发了新一波疫情，口罩等防护用品短缺，安特卫普市的一些小疗养院和社区福利社的老人院遭受疫情冲击，出现了死亡病例。3 月 27 日，心急如焚的蔡建业组织成立了安市华联辅助委员会，筹款抗疫。到 4 月 17 日筹款结束时，共募集了 2.1 万多欧元，全都用来购买防护服、口罩和洗手液等物资，送给当地的社区医院和养老院等机构。

蔡建业说，这样的关心、关爱之举，是为了维护中比一向的友好关系，也是为了消除西方某些人对中国、对华人的偏见。50 多年来，蔡建业还有不少其他的难忘事。

1971 年，中华人民共和国恢复在联合国的合法席位，消息传来，蔡建业协助比中友好协会，组织了十几位同胞相聚庆祝。人虽不多，但是他个人觉得很有意义。当时，安特卫普市的华人也就百来人。

20 世纪 80 年代，蔡建业曾代表比中友好协会到中国参观访问，拜访了北京市人民政府侨务办公室。90 年代初，蔡建业探访故乡深圳，大受震撼。"哇，完全变

疫情期间，蔡建业（右）参与派送防护用品。
Choi Kin Yip (right) distributes protective equipment during the pandemic.

了样，太漂亮了！太高兴，太惊讶了，看到很多东西都目瞪口呆。"承载了他幼年记忆的蔡屋围，就是深圳沧桑巨变的缩影。

　　蔡屋围是深圳最古老的村庄之一。改革开放后，这里崛起为深圳的金融中心，有"深圳的华尔街"之称。深圳证券交易所曾经设在这里，中国人民银行和四大国有银行在深圳的直属分支机构曾经都在这里。矗立在这里的地王大厦、京基 100 大厦都曾是深圳最高楼。这里的深圳大剧院、深圳书城、华润万象城购物中心也是深圳不同历史时期的地标。

九千公里之外，感受强国意义

　　蔡屋围西侧百米开外的地方，邓小平的画像隔街注视着蔡屋围。再往西大约 500 米，深圳市委大门外面的路边有两块标语牌，分别写着"四项基本原则是立国之本"和"改革开放是强国之路"。在直线距离 9000 多公里之外的比利时，蔡建业也能感受到"强国"的意义。"中国富强了，我们海外华侨华人的地位也高了。这个区别是很大很大很大很大的！"他连用了 4 个"很大"。

蔡建业说，早年，华人来到外国，90%多都是做餐饮业的，1%到2%的人则是经营杂货。"我自己有餐馆，但我自己没去做，都是给别人打理。我主要就是旅行社之类的，跟人打交道，还有前面说的电影、电话，跟西方人来往得多。尤其是旅行社，直接跟他们有竞争关系。我是国际旅游协会的会员，20世纪80年代的时候，我去开会，他们把中国跟非洲放在一起。你说话可以，但听不听是人家的事。握手肯定是最后握的了。到了现在，人家直接先来跟你握手。你以前讲话，人家背对着你，现在不会了。"

蔡建业如今还在旅行社担任董事长，但工作量少了很多，几乎是完全退休了。他在比利时成了家，现在已经是20多人的大家庭，一家人出去吃饭要坐两大桌。家庭成员除了华人，还有比利时人、越南人、菲律宾人，一派国际范儿。对于后辈，蔡建业的期望是：别忘本，不忘初心，脚踏实地去做人。

他还很注意在家里传承中华文化，三个儿子、两个女儿全都会说普通话和粤语。"三个儿子的粤语比较好，女儿普通话更强。五岁的小外孙去年参加了网上授课，非常棒，他已经能讲流利的普通话了。"言语间，蔡建业再次透着自豪。

既坚守文化传统，情系故土和同胞，又以国际化的姿态融入所在国，从蔡屋围走出去的蔡建业活出了自己的精彩。

（本文图片均由受访者蔡建业提供。）

Choi Kin Yip

A "traditional Chinese" with international perspectives and unchanged Cantonese accent

Choi Kin Yip, also known as Kenneth Choi K. Y. and Ken Cai, was born in 1952 in Caiwuwei, Shenzhen and moved to Belgium in 1968. He is chairman of Antwerp Chinatown and director of the Guangdong Federation Netherlands (Guangdong Federatie NL). He was the director of the Association of Flemish Travel Agencies (Vereniging Vlaamse Reisbureaus), Belgium, executive director of the Belgian-Chinese Friendship Association, founding president of the Belgian-Chinese Culture Association (Belgo-Chinese Cultuur Vereninging), and the founder of the Overseas Chinese Magazine.

He has operated restaurants, import and export, and a travel agency, among others, serving and assisting overseas Chinese and local communities in many ways. From the 1970s to the 1990s, he actively helped Chinese find jobs in Belgium and provided convenience for their life. From 1999 to 2001, taking the opportunity of an urban renewal project of Antwerp, he pushed for the establishment and naming of Chinatown. In 2021, to fight the COVID-19 pandemic, he organized fundraising to purchase personal protective equipment that was donated to hospitals, nursing homes and so on.

In a few simple words, Choi Kin Yip can be summed up as "homeland complex, international perspectives."

He has lived in Belgium for more than 50 years, but his accent has not changed. He can speak pure Cantonese, and, led by him, all his children can speak Mandarin and Cantonese, and his 5-year-old grandson can also speak Mandarin fluently.

"I am a traditional Chinese," Choi summed up. He has been engaged in the catering, culture, and entertainment industries, as well as telecommunications and air ticket sales. "I was just doing business, but indirectly helped the Chinese here. These are all small contributions." But he also made big contributions. For example, he pushed for the establishment and naming of Antwerp Chinatown, Belgium. When he was young,

---

The interview took place in 2022.

he helped his warm-hearted father provide various kinds of help for overseas Chinese, including running errands in post offices, banks and government departments, and serving as an interpreter and guarantor for overseas Chinese in police stations and courts.

Choi did not go to college, but he learned to communicate with people in English, Dutch, French and German, so, of course, he could handle affairs and do business more smoothly. He did not have to go to bed upstairs after working a dozen hours in the restaurant, as his predecessors did in the 1960s and 1970s.

"It was not easy for the old overseas Chinese! What we expect is that the motherland will become stronger and stronger, and that its international status and prestige will be higher and higher!"

Choi is pleased to find that this expectation is becoming a reality.

A self-reliant young man that gradually achieves success

Choi left his hometown Caiwuwei and went to Hong Kong very early. In 1963, his father, who was struggling to make ends meet in Hong Kong, was employed by a friend to work as a chef in a Chinese restaurant in Belgium. In 1968, when Choi was 16 years old, a Chinese boss in Belgium provided financial support and guardianship for him, so he applied to go to Belgium as a student and reunited with his parents.

Two years later, his parents were eager to have their own business, believing that "working for others will never make it to the top." In order to help his parents achieve their wishes, Choi left school and his guardian to help his father take over and run a small restaurant, which was located in Antwerpen-Berchem. Later on, because Choi needed to work in the restaurant, he could only go to a private language school.

The business of his family's restaurant was not running well. At weekends, Choi went to a busy restaurant to work as a waiter. The income was so ideal that he earned enough to cover his expenses, and he even bought a second-hand car to help his family's restaurant transport goods.

In 1974, Choi opened his own restaurant. From the 1970s to the 1990s, he opened six restaurants in total. In 1995, when the Belgian imaging technology giant Agfa-Gevaert Group established a Sino-Belgian joint venture in Wuxi, China and Belgium sent ministerial officials to sign the contract in Antwerp, and Choi's restaurant "China" provided the dinner on a Flanders yacht in Schilde Harbour Pier. Thinking of it now, he still feels proud.

In 1982, Choi founded Wabi Travel Agency after obtaining a Belgian tourism license.

Later, the travel agency obtained an international travel operator license, became an IATA accredited travel agent, and set up a branch office in the center of Brussels.

The official languages of Belgium are Dutch, French and German. People mainly speak Dutch in Antwerp and French in Brussels, while English is usually used at meetings with airlines. Choi can cope with them all. He also speaks German but has few opportunities to use it. "Language needs practice." He recalled that he was still young when he lived in Hong Kong for only five years, so he didn't learn English well. Although he studied in language schools in Belgium for three years, he mainly depended on practice. "In order to get rid of the lonely and helpless life of the older generation, language communication is the goal I must achieve." Whether in school or at work, he was active communicating with local people in oral language, and his hard work paid off in the end.

Benefiting the neighbors and relieving their homesickness

With his firm determination, sharp business acumen and serious execution ability, Choi's career has been flourishing, which has also facilitated the lives of overseas Chinese and helped them relieve their homesickness.

There is a word in Cantonese that literally means "to benefit the neighbors" and even "to benefit everyone," which is often used to describe discounts and promotions. This can also describe Choi's business logic.

In the 1990s, the number of Chinese increased in Belgium, but their life was relatively monotonous. Most of them lived in small three-story buildings, where the first floor was used for running restaurants or shops, the second floor was usually the home of the boss, and the third floor was the dormitory of the employees, who worked for 14 to 15 hours a day, without entertainment. They had one day off a week, sometimes just playing a game of mahjong.

Seeing this, Choi had an idea: as Hong Kong movies and TV series were very famous, if they could be showed in Belgium, the Chinese would have a place to go for entertainment. Therefore, he founded the Belgian-Chinese Culture Association (Belgo-Chinese Cultuur vereninging), which rented a local cinema to show these films and TV series. Most of them were Hong Kong movies, mainly in Cantonese. There were also films from Taiwan in Mandarin, such as *Dragon Inn*. Some of the films had English subtitles.

In addition, Choi organized the European Chinese New Talent Singing Championship, the Miss European Chinese beauty pageant, and other activities. He sponsored Belgium's oldest Chinese group, Verenging van Chinezen in Belgie (the Association of Chinese in

Belgium), for its annual Chinese New Year galas. He also founded the *Overseas Chinese Magazine*, which was given to overseas Chinese. It carried Belgian news summaries, labor law notices, Chinese community news, activities of overseas Chinese groups, jokes, inspirational articles, art and cultural exchanges and so on. The Association of Chinese in Belgium published a fundraising advertisement for free in this monthly magazine, and the office place purchased with the funds raised is still in use today.

In the early years, in addition to the lack of entertainment, it was also difficult for overseas Chinese in Belgium to make phone calls back to their hometown because telephone bills were too expensive. Choi cooperated with a local telecom company through the Belgian-Chinese Cultural Association to launch a long-distance phone card. The cost was only one-tenth to one-twentieth of the original price, benefiting many overseas Chinese.

The more expensive homesickness was a plane ticket. Choi still remembers the scene in the 1970s. "When you asked the older generation of Chinese in Belgium if they had ever returned to their hometown, they would say no. Back then, the Chinese came here and stayed for the rest of their life. They rarely went back to China because the air ticket was too expensive." At that time, it was very inconvenient to travel between Belgium and China. Most flights between Hong Kong and Europe were carried out by British Airways. Later, Cathay Pacific Airways and British Caledonian Airways began operating flights between Hong Kong and London, with London as their European hub. Choi's travel agency took this opportunity to approach the airlines and negotiate for almost half-price tickets for overseas Chinese to travel to their hometown. Then some overseas Chinese were able to return to China every two years.

Choi's travel agency donated some air tickets for lucky draws at the New Year's parties of overseas Chinese groups, as well as the New Year's parties jointly organized by overseas Chinese groups and Vietnamese, Burmese, and Lao friendship associations. It also donated air tickets to the restaurant industry association in Brussels. It not only gave back to overseas Chinese, but also formed good ties for them.

Founding Chinatown amid urban renewal

More often, Chinatowns are where overseas Chinese place their homesickness. Antwerp has the first Chinatown in Belgium, and Choi pushed for its establishment.

That small area, with four or five streets, used to be dark, dilapidated and disgusting. However, it enjoyed a good location. It was close to the train station, and there was a small square. Several Chinese restaurants and two small supermarkets were already there in the early days. Choi's travel agency also opened there. In addition to the Chinese, there were also expats from Vietnam, South Korea, the Philippines, and even African countries in that area.

At the turn of the century, that area also had an opportunity for change. Choi said that it was inconvenient to park near the municipal library at that time, and that the municipal government planned to relocate the library to a vacant building near the small square and renew that area at the same time. He participated in the renewal project and conveyed the request of overseas Chinese to the municipal government: can this place be turned into a Chinatown?

"I thought this could also create a harmonious environment for peaceful coexistence. There were Chinatowns in many places around the world, including the United States and the United Kingdom, all of which were tourism oriented. When arriving at a place, many people would go to its Chinatown to buy some Chinese products and eat Chinese food," Choi recalled. "My suggestion was not only updating this place, but also listing it as a tourist spot to increase tourists and bring prosperity to our urban area."

The government replied: this is feasible, but if you want to participate, please do it through an organization. The Antwerp China Town Non-profit Organization (Antwerpen China Town vzw), whose Chinese name means the "Antwerp Chinatown Neighborhood Association," was then founded, with Choi as chairman. After the organization was registered, it cooperated with the government to promote the transformation of the area. The road was re-paved, the lighting was improved, and stone lions and "dragons spitting pearls" streetlamps were placed. "We applied for all these to the municipal government through our organization. The government did almost all the renovation of the entire street and the community. Our organization raised funds to buy only four stone lions and the dragon lamps from China transported to the port in Belgium. The local government completed all other work and paid the expenses," Choi still remembers these vividly.

This urban renewal project was implemented in 1999 and completed in 2001. The municipal government approved the application of the overseas Chinese and officially named Antwerp Chinatown. Choi was registered as Antwerpen China Town Voorzitter, meaning "Antwerp Chinatown Chairman," which was also published in the gazette.

At the naming and opening ceremony of Chinatown on December 8, 2001, Antwerp Mayor Ms. Leona Maria Detiege said that the presence of Chinatown in the city indicated that Chinese culture would spread more widely in Belgium, and the friendly cooperation between Belgium and China would turn a new page. Guan Chengyuan, then Chinese ambassador to Belgium, said that the birth of Chinatown in Antwerp was the result of the unremitting efforts of the overseas Chinese groups in Belgium and the strong support and assistance of the local government, which fully demonstrated the local government's affirmation of the Chinese community. Choi also delivered a speech at the ceremony and was deeply honored.

Rushing around and giving selfless help

From the 1970s to the 1990s, in addition to his studies and career, Choi kept providing various kinds of help for overseas Chinese, both in their work and life.

He remembered that there were not many Chinese in Belgium in the 1970s, and most of them had not obtained Belgian identity yet, so it was inconvenient for them to find a job or go out. A large part of them were from New Territories of Hong Kong, and most of whom were natives of Shenzhen. His father, Choi Hei Moon, extended a helping hand to the compatriots and fellow Shenzhen immigrants. Choi Hei Moon ran a small restaurant named Restaurant Lucky at the time, and helped some Chinese with difficulties. He provided them with board and lodging, and helped them find jobs. After school, Choi Kin Yip helped the compatriots with many things, including running errands in post offices, banks and government agencies, driving the compatriots in and out, and so on. When some overseas Chinese were caught by the police due to illegal stay, he shuttled between the police station and the court, undertaking tasks such as translation and signing guarantees.

Once, an old man in his 50s had a stroke and could only lie flat. To help him return to his hometown, Choi Kin Yip ran around to raise funds and collected enough money to buy three air tickets so that the old man could fly back to Hong Kong while lying down.

Many unforgettable events in five decades

Fighting the COVID-19 pandemic is Choi's most unforgettable experience in recent years.

In the spring of 2021, a new wave of the pandemic broke out in Belgium, and there was a shortage of protective equipment such as masks. In Antwerp, deaths occurred in some small nursing homes and community welfare agencies hit by the pandemic. On March 27, the anxious Choi organized the establishment of the Antwerpen Overseas Chinese First-Aid Committee to raise funds to fight the pandemic. The fundraising ended on April 17, and more than 21,000 euros were raised in total, all of which were used to purchase supplies such as protective clothing, masks and hand sanitizer given to local community hospitals, nursing homes and other institutions.

Choi said that this action of care and love aimed to maintain the friendly relationship between China and Belgium, and to eliminate the prejudice of some people in the West against China and the Chinese. Over the past five decades, many events have been unforgettable to Choi.

In 1971, when the news came that the People's Republic of China regained its legal seat in the United Nations, Choi assisted the Belgium-China Association to gather more than a dozen compatriots for celebration. Although it was a small party, he thought it was very meaningful. At that time, the Chinese in Antwerp amounted to only 100 or so.

In the 1980s, Choi traveled to China on behalf of the Belgium-China Association, and visited the Overseas Chinese Affairs Office of the Beijing Municipal People's Government. In the early 1990s, Choi was shocked when he visited his hometown Shenzhen. "Wow, it was completely changed, and it was so beautiful! I was so happy and so surprised. I was dumbfounded when I saw a lot of things." Caiwuwei, where his childhood memories lie, is the epitome of Shenzhen's dramatic changes.

Caiwuwei is one of the oldest villages in Shenzhen. After China's reform and opening-up, it became the financial center of Shenzhen, known as "the Wall Street of Shenzhen." The Shenzhen Stock Exchange used to be here, and so did the Shenzhen headquarters of the People's Bank of China and all the four major state-owned banks. The Diwang Building standing here was once the tallest building in Shenzhen, and so was the Kingkey 100 Tower. The Shenzhen Grand Theater, the Shenzhen Book City, and the Mixc shopping mall run by China Resources are also Shenzhen's landmarks in different historical periods.

From 9,000 kilometers away, feeling the meaning of a strong country

About 100 meters away on the west side of Caiwuwei, a portrait of the late Chinese leader Deng Xiaoping, who initiated the country's reform and opening-up, looks at Caiwuwei across the street. About 500 meters further to the west, there are two placards on the side of the road outside the gate of the Shenzhen Municipal Committee of the Communist Party of China, which read "The four basic principles are the foundation of the country" and "Reform and opening-up is the road to a strong country." In Belgium, which is more than 9,000 kilometers away in a straight line, Choi can also feel the meaning of "a strong country." "China is prosperous and strong now, and the status of our overseas

Chinese is also higher. This difference is very, very, very, very big!" Choi said "very" four times in a row.

He said that in the early years, when Chinese went to foreign countries, more than 90% of them were in the catering industry, and 1% to 2% ran groceries. "I had restaurants too, but I didn't run the business myself. I had others take care of them. I focused on my travel agency, dealing with people. I also worked on film and phone services mentioned above. I have had a lot of contacts with westerners. Particularly, my travel agency is in direct competition with them. I am a member of an international tourism association, and when I went to meetings in the 1980s, they put China and Africa together. You could speak, but it was up to them whether to listen. You would be the last one they shook hands with. Now, people come to shake hands with you first. They used to turn their backs to you when you spoke, but it doesn't happen now."

Choi is still serving as chairman of his travel agency, but does much less work. He is almost completely retired. He started a family in Belgium, which is a big one of more than 20 people now. When the family goes out to eat, they need two tables. In addition to Chinese, the international family has Belgians, Vietnamese, and Filipinos. For the younger generation, Choi's expectation is: Never forget your roots and original intention. Be a down-to-earth person.

He also attaches great importance to inheriting Chinese culture at home. All his three sons and two daughters can speak Mandarin and Cantonese. "My three sons speak Cantonese well, while my daughters speak Mandarin better. My 5-year-old grandson took online classes last year, and it is very good that he can already speak Mandarin fluently," Choi once again showed pride in his words.

Choi sticks to cultural traditions and loves his hometown and compatriots while integrating into the country where he lives with an international attitude. He is a native of Caiwuwei who has lived a wonderful life.

(Photos courtesy of Choi Kin Yip.)

第五章
Chapter Five

以侨为桥
Building bridges

相知无远近，万里尚为邻。

——〔唐〕张九龄《送韦城李少府》

Distance cannot separate true friends afar; They are like neighbors although thousands of miles apart.

—*Farewell to County Captain Li of Weicheng*, by Zhang Jiuling (Tang Dynasty)

章辞修

中美洲百事通，连接深圳与巴拿马的一座"桥"

章辞修　Guillermo John Chava

　　章辞修，浙江湖州菱湖人，1927年出生于上海，中美洲暨巴拿马六国中华华侨总会联合总会会长、巴拿马中华总会永久名誉会长、苏浙同乡会创办会长、中巴文化中心副董事长，曾任巴拿马科隆自由贸易区董事会常务董事、主席等职务。已在巴拿马生活了50多年，在当地主流社会享有盛誉，并有着广泛的人际关系和影响力。

　　多年来，他为促进巴拿马华侨社会和谐、生存与发展，为加强中美洲华侨社会的联系与交往贡献良多，是中美洲地区的杰出侨领和社会活动家，曾获得巴拿马"杰出公民"荣誉称号和首枚巴拿马国家英雄"维道里安络罗年素勋章"。

采访时间：2022年。

说起巴拿马，估计很多人都会联想到举世闻名的巴拿马运河。作为中美洲和加勒比地区最重要的节点国家，虽然相隔甚远，但其实巴拿马与中国特别是广东，有着很深的历史渊源。华人抵巴最早可以追溯到清咸丰年间，距今已经有近 170 年的历史。广州市政府地方志办公室曾经向新华社提供的一份资料显示：19 世纪中叶，广东花县、香山等地的数万名华工到巴拿马修筑铁路及开凿巴拿马运河，成为中国人移居巴拿马的开端。目前，在巴拿马的华侨华人有 30 余万人，约占该国总人口的一成，而且据称"每 5 名巴拿马人中，就有一名拥有华人血统"。

95 岁的章辞修，已经在巴拿马生活工作了 50 多年，也算是一个"中美洲百事通"。章辞修是中美洲暨巴拿马六国中华华侨总会联合总会会长，在巴拿马有着广泛的人际关系和影响力，是当地一位著名的侨领。巴拿马运河有"世界桥梁"之美誉，同样，如果将章辞修比喻为"连接深圳与巴拿马的那一座桥梁"，则一点也不为过。

"深圳速度"，真是名不虚传

章辞修祖籍浙江湖州，出生在上海，但跟记者说起深圳时，他一点儿都不陌生，"我身边就起码有 40 张，从深圳来巴拿马的客人的名片"。在接受微信采访时，章辞修甚至还幽默地跟记者从普通话切换到了广东话频道："因为巴拿马到处都是广东人，你唔讲广东话，咁点同佢哋交流啊（你不说广东话，怎么跟他们交流啊）？"

章辞修告诉记者，其实他在中国还没有改革开放的时候，就已经来过当时的宝安县深圳镇。后来中国改革开放，很多国内的朋友都劝他到深圳来投资，但是，"我在巴拿马很忙，开了一家名叫'银座'的中餐馆，还要在（巴拿马）科隆自由贸易区、中巴文化中心任职，以及在巴拿马中华总会、六国中华总会做侨务服务工作"，最终，章辞修还是错过了在深圳投资的机会。

出于种种历史原因，巴拿马直到 2017 年 6 月 13 日才正式跟中国建交。不过，在此之前，两国的民间交流往来一直都在频繁进行着。作为巴拿马著名的侨领，章辞修每年都要接待两三个来自中国的侨务团体。每一次他都向来访客人请求协助，在中国给中巴文化中心下属的中山学校找一个二胡老师，可惜每一次都是无果而终。

1985 年，祖籍广东中山的著名爱国华侨陈奉天先生在巴拿马创立中巴文化中心，除建了一座极富中国特色的中巴友谊公园外，还在 1986 年建立了一间以中文、英文、西班牙文三语教学的中山学校。2007 年 10 月 26 日，巴拿马中山学校与中国广东的中山纪念中学结成了姐妹学校，目前巴拿马中山学校学生人数约有 1700 人，其中三分之二都是当地的华侨华人子弟，被公认为巴拿马历史最长、规模最大的华人学校。

巴拿马中山学校非常注重对学生进行中华文化的熏陶教育，比如学校就一直有舞狮的传统，还配备了二胡、笛子等中国传统乐器。原来学校里有一个中国台湾来的老师教学生拉二胡，但是教了大约 8 个月之后，这个二胡老师就离开了。学生很喜欢学二胡这种中国传统乐器，可是一把把二胡放在学校里却没有人来教，作为中巴文化中心副董事长的章辞修

90 多岁的章辞修热爱生活。
Guillermo John Chava enjoys life over the age of 90.

看在眼里，真是既心疼又焦急，因此，给中山学校找一个合适的二胡老师一直是他那个时候的心头大事。

有一天，在接访深圳来的祖国客人时，章辞修又说起了找二胡教师的事儿，这一次随团访问的深圳市侨办工作人员就把此事暗暗记在了心里。两个月之后，远在巴拿马的章辞修得到来自深圳的回复："我给你们找到了一个教二胡的老师！"在章辞修看来，"深圳速度"真是名不虚传。

邀来深圳音乐教师，用二胡架起民间外交工作桥梁

2013 年，在章辞修及其所在的中巴文化中心的邀请下，深圳的音乐特级教师刘宏伟受深圳市侨办委派，以"海外华文教育志愿者"的身份远赴巴拿马，在当地的中山学校承担二胡教学工作。

这是刘宏伟第一次走出国门教学。她向记者回忆了自己当时的心情："这个中南美洲国家离我们非常远，除了巴拿马运河之外，其他的我都一无所知，甚至有朋友和我说，那是个蛮荒之地，你去了之后小心

深圳音乐特级教师刘宏伟在巴拿马教当地的学生学习中国传统乐器二胡。
Liu Hongwei, a special-grade music teacher from Shenzhen, teaches the Chinese traditional instrument erhu to a local student in Panama.

刘宏伟与巴拿马当地音乐家交流。
Liu Hongwei exchanges with a local musician in Panama.

刘宏伟和巴拿马大学艺术学院院长特罗斯彻合作演奏多首中外名曲。

Liu Hongwei and Luis Troetsch, dean of the Faculty of Fine Arts of the University of Panama, jointly perform many famous Chinese and foreign songs.

不要被鳄鱼吃掉了。但是，我很好奇，就是想去看一下这是一个什么样的神秘国家，在那里怎么会有人想学二胡呢？带着这种好奇和茫然，我只身去到了巴拿马。"

踏上了遥远的陌生国度，凭借出色的二胡技艺及认真负责的教学态度，刘宏伟很快就获得了巴拿马学生及当地华侨华人的认可。从 2013 年至 2016 年，刘宏伟一共 4 次远赴巴拿马教二胡和音乐，在大洋彼岸留住了中国传统文化的根，同时也播下更多希望的种子。

"我从来没有见到一个普通人，在巴拿马会发展得这么好，她的魅力真是大。"说起刘宏伟在巴拿马传授二胡技艺的往事，章辞修非常感慨，"她非常亲和，巴拿马的侨胞尤其是那些广东人都把她当自家亲人一样，请她到家里去做客。以往中巴文化中心的教职员离开时，我们中心的董事长陈中强先生很少会请他们吃饭，但是当刘宏伟老师回国的时候，他为刘老师开了一个非常特别的大派对"。

在章辞修心中，从深圳来的刘宏伟老师真是一个奇人。"她在巴拿马除了教二胡之外，还做了很多很多民间外交工作。"在巴拿马教学期间，刘宏伟在当时的中国巴拿马贸易发展办事处官邸举办了两场音乐会，巴拿马的大法官、前审计长等政要，以及多位驻巴拿马使节和外交团代表都出席了，而为她进行钢琴伴奏的则是巴拿马大学艺术学院院长、著名钢琴家特罗斯彻。

感谢网络，让我们在今天，依然可以切身感受到当年关于其中一场音乐会的精彩场面。在中国外交部官网上，有一则题为《驻巴拿马贸易发展办事处王卫华代表举办音乐招待会》的报道这么描述：

2014年7月10日，中国巴拿马贸易发展办事处代表王卫华在官邸举办中国—巴拿马音乐招待会……40多分钟里，嘉宾们欣赏了二位音乐人（刘宏伟和特罗斯彻——编者注）的天合之作——用钢琴和二胡合作演奏的多首中外名曲，其中有《良宵》《茉莉花》《赛马》《浏阳河》《二泉映月》和《我和你》等。刘老师经过5月培养出的8名二胡优秀弟子也出场与她合作演奏了中国乐曲和歌曲。招待会以刘老师在这里学会的巴拿马名曲《爱的故事》作为结束曲。

整个演出的过程中，代表官邸大厅里时而鸦雀无声，时而掌声雷动，人们完全被中国和巴拿马的美妙音乐所吸引和陶醉。

左起：章辞修、王卫华及夫人、刘宏伟。
From the left: Guillermo John Chava, Wang Weihua, Wang's wife, and Liu Hongwei.

在巴拿马，刘宏伟还到大学去做专题讲座，介绍中国的音乐文化。到了做专辑演奏的环节，当刘宏伟再次用二胡拉起巴拿马名曲《爱的故事》（*Historia De Un Amor*，也就是中文歌曲《我的心里只有你没有他》的原曲）的时候，现场发出了阵阵掌声，不少巴拿马大学的老师都不禁热泪盈眶。

"在巴拿马，只要有交流机会我都愿意去。作为一个学习中国民族乐器的人，我觉得自己有一种天然的责任感和使命担当，就是要把中国的传统文化、中国的音乐在那里传播开来。"刘宏伟说道。

助力华为，开拓巴拿马市场

深圳是一座高科技创新之城，像华为、中兴、腾讯和大疆等高科技企业都是深圳在全球的一张又一张亮丽名片。虽然巴拿马在 2017 年才跟中国建立正式的外交关系，但是深圳的华为公司与巴拿马的渊源早在 10 余年前就已经结下了，其中少不了章辞修的牵线搭桥。

大概是 2006 年前，章辞修到多年的好友——巴拿马驻墨西哥大使阿雷曼（Ricardo Aleman）家做客游玩。中午吃饭聊天时，总领事先生过来告诉他们，有两个中国人来申请到巴拿马的签证。那个时候的巴拿马，虽然签证是大使馆签发的，但是审批权不在大使馆，首先要得到巴拿马国内的移民局批准才行。章辞修透露，过去有不少人都想移民或偷渡去巴拿马，在这种情况下，移民局的审批非常严格，要拿到签证去巴拿马进行商务活动是很难的事。

既然这两个人都已经在墨西哥，再到巴拿马应该也没什么大问题，但是为了慎重起见，巴拿马大使馆方面还是请章辞修去见一下这两个申请人，了解一下背景，毕竟都是中国人，沟通起来也比较容易。章辞修至今都还清楚记得其中一个人的名字，但是，在此之前他从来都没听说过"华为"这个公司。经过一番交谈和实地参观，他了解到华为当时已经在墨西哥开设了分公司，而且雇佣了一些墨西哥员工，在当地是一个正在蓬勃发展的大公司。于是，章辞修当场就表示，回去以后一定要好好向巴拿马方面介绍华为公司，并帮他们申请签证，到巴拿马去开拓市场。

从华为墨西哥分公司考察回来后，章辞修就去巴拿马驻墨西哥大使馆向大使汇报情况；恰好当天晚上中国驻墨西哥大使邀请巴拿马驻墨西哥大使参加晚宴，他就顺道一起出席了宴会。席间，章辞修向中国驻墨西哥大使询问了华为墨西哥分公司的情况，大使告诉他，这个华为公司是总部位于深圳的一家非常著名的高科技公司。听了中国大使的介绍之后，对于帮助华为工作人员申请巴拿马签证，并邀请他们到巴拿马开公司的事，章辞修心里就更有底了。

回到巴拿马，章辞修立即向巴当局介绍华为的实际情况。"华为这

章辞修是中美洲暨巴拿马六国中华华侨总会联合总会会长。

Guillermo is president of the Chinese Associations of Central America and Panama.

个公司如果来了，对巴拿马一定有贡献。"章辞修拍着胸脯对时任巴拿马移民局局长说，"最起码他们来了就要建办公室、雇佣职员，对巴拿马的经济一定有帮助。"就这样，华为公司在巴拿马最早的两张工作签证就顺利签了下来。

现在，巴拿马人民说起华为都会竖起大拇指

此前章辞修曾被巴拿马历史上第一位女总统米雷娅·莫斯科索（Mireya Moscoso de Gruber，任期1999—2004年）委任为巴拿马科隆自由贸易区的常务董事，再后来他又被科隆自由贸易区董事会推举为董事会主席，对巴拿马自贸区的各种运作制度可谓了如指掌。华为巴拿马公司开业之后，章辞修就热心地向他们介绍科隆自由贸易区的种种优势（如地理位置优越、交通和物流便利等），并建议他们将拉美地区的总部也移到巴拿马的自贸区里。"在这里，不但货物进出口可以免税，更重要的是，当地政府还为国际企业提供了税收等方面的良好营商环境。"章辞修补充道。

2011年10月，华为在巴拿马设立了占地3600平方米的拉美地区总部；2015年，华为继续在巴拿马加大投资力度，在科隆自由贸易区建立了供应中心。据中国驻巴拿马共和国大使馆（原为中国巴拿马贸易发展办事处）官网报道：2015年10月1日，在巴拿马科隆自由贸易区运营出现较大困难、贸易量下降的情况下，华为公司逆势而上，在这里建立了全球第六个调拨中心，不仅开展了仓储业务，还生产

2008年9月26日，章辞修（左三）与巴拿马客人一起参观华为公司。
On September 26, 2008, Guillermo John Chava (third from the left) visits Huawei with Panamanian guests.

和装配 15 类产品向 35 个国家出口，为中国与巴拿马开展产能和物流合作树立了一个成功的范例和提供了有益经验，也为中国与巴拿马经贸关系的深入发展产生了积极的影响。

"华为对巴拿马的贡献是非常非常大的，致力于协助当地运营商等的通信基础设施建设，并创造了很多就业机会。"章辞修认为，华为公司进入巴拿马市场之后，为当地做出了很多社会贡献，"最主要的是，帮助了巴拿马的年轻人到华为在深圳的总部去学习最新的技术"。

2017 年 11 月 18 日，华为创始人兼总裁任正非到访巴拿马，当时华为官方曾发布一篇新闻通稿，里面提到："华为巴拿马公司已为当地居民创造了 300 多个工作岗位，在科隆自由贸易区创造了 180 多个工作岗位。"而且华为还积极为巴拿马客户、合作伙伴和青年大学生等提供数字化培训。2015 年，华为在巴拿马成功启动了"未来种子"项目，来自巴拿马大学和巴拿马科技大学的 30 名优秀学生前往华为中国深圳总部，参加为期一周的培训，与华为的信息通信技术（ICT）专家近距离交流。2020 年，受新冠疫情影响，华为在巴拿马一直坚持的"未来种子"项目培训改为通过网络远程教育平台来完成，从面对面的直接交流变为在线的网络培训，反而给了巴拿马年轻人更多的参与机会。

今天，华为（HUAWEI）在巴拿马可以说是一个家喻户晓的品牌。巴拿马驻华大使甘林（Leonardo Kam）就曾拿出自己的手机向人免费"种草"，他说："大家都喜欢中国手机，我用的是华为手机。"2019 年 1 月 19 日，巴拿马第一家华为体验店在巴拿马购物城（Multiplaza Pacific）开业。据媒体报道，虽然体验店当时的开业时间是上午 10 时，但早上 8 时购机的队伍就已经排到了商场外面，甚至有真爱的"花粉"提前一天晚上就已经在店外排队等候了。

喝水不忘挖井人，时至今日，华为都没有忘记章辞修当初牵线搭桥的功劳，逢年过节都会给老人送上亲切的慰问。而章辞修也像十多年前一样，仍然继续看好华为这个中国科技巨头在巴拿马的发展前景。"华为在巴拿马发展得非常好，在我认识的人当中，无论是政府高层还是工程师、普通老百姓，说起华为，大家都会竖起大拇指。"章辞修自豪地说道。

（本文图片均由受访者章辞修、刘宏伟提供。参考资料：中国外交部官网、华为官网。）

Guillermo John Chava

Knowledgeable about Central America, a "bridge" connecting Shenzhen and Panama

Guillermo John Chava was born in Shanghai in 1927. His ancestral home is in Linghu, Huzhou, Zhejiang Province. He is president of the Chinese Associations of Central America and Panama, life president of the Chinese Association of Panama, founding president of the Su-Zhe Panama Charitable Association, and vice president of the Chinese-Panamanian Cultural Center. He once served as executive director and chairman of the board of directors of Colon Free Zone, Panama. He has lived in Panama for more than 50 years, enjoying a high reputation in the local mainstream society, as well as a wide range of interpersonal relationships and influence.

Over the years, he has contributed a lot to promoting the harmony, survival and development of the overseas Chinese society in Panama, and to strengthening the ties and exchanges between the overseas Chinese communities in Central America. As an outstanding overseas Chinese leader and social activist in Central America, he has won the honorary title of "Outstanding Citizen" of Panama and the first Victoria Andronicus medal of merit, named after the Panamanian national hero.

As for Panama, many people may think of the world-famous Panama Canal. As the most important node country in Central America and the Caribbean, Panama has deep historical ties with China, especially Guangdong, although it is far away. The earliest Chinese arrival in Panama can be traced back to the Xianfeng period of the Qing Dynasty, nearly 170 years ago. According to a document that the Local Chronicle Office of the Guangzhou Municipal Government provided to the Xinhua News Agency, tens of thousands of Chinese workers from Huaxian, Xiangshan and other places in Guangdong went to Panama to build railways and dig the Panama Canal in the middle of the 19th century, which was the beginning of Chinese migration to Panama. At present, there are more than 300,000 overseas Chinese in Panama, accounting for about 10% of the country's total population, and it is said

---

The interview took place in 2022.

that "one out of every five Panamanians has Chinese ancestry."

Guillermo John Chava, who is 95 years old, has lived and worked in Panama for more than 50 years. He is also very knowledgeable about Central America. He is president of the Chinese Associations of Central America and Panama. With extensive interpersonal relations and influence in Panama, he is a famous overseas Chinese leader there. The Panama Canal is hailed as "the Bridge of the World," and, similarly, it is no exaggeration to compare him to "a bridge connecting Shenzhen and Panama."

"Shenzhen Speed" deserves its reputation

Guillermo, whose ancestral home is in Huzhou, Zhejiang Province, was born in Shanghai, but he is no stranger when talking about Shenzhen. "I have at least 40 business cards of guests from Shenzhen to Panama." He even humorously switched from Mandarin to Cantonese in an interview through WeChat. "As Panama is full of Cantonese, how can you communicate with them without speaking Cantonese?"

He said that he had visited Shenzhen Township, Bao'an County before China was open to the outside world. Later, after the reform and opening-up, many friends in China urged him to invest in Shenzhen. However, he was very busy in Panama. "I opened a Chinese restaurant called Ginza, and I also worked in Colon Free Zone and the Chinese-Panamanian Cultural Center (Centro Cultural Chino Panameño), as well as the Chinese Association of Panama (Asociación China de Panamá) and the Chinese Associations of Central America and Panama to serve overseas Chinese." Finally, he missed the opportunity to invest in Shenzhen.

For various historical reasons, Panama did not establish official diplomatic relations with China until June 13, 2017. However, before that, there had been frequent non-governmental exchanges between the two countries. As a famous overseas Chinese leader in Panama, Guillermo received two or three overseas Chinese affairs groups from China every year. Each time, he would ask for help from the visitors to find an erhu teacher in China for the Sun Yat Sen Institute under the Chinese-Panamanian Cultural Center (Centro Cultural Chino Panameño—Instituto Sun Yat Sen). Unfortunately, it always ended in vain.

In 1985, Mr. Fermin Chan, a famous patriotic overseas Chinese, whose ancestral home was in Zhongshan, Guangdong Province, founded the Chinese-Panamanian Cultural Center in Panama. In addition to building a Chinese-Panamanian Friendship Park (Parque de La Amistad Chino-Panameña) in a typical Chinese style, he also established a school, the Sun Yat Sen Institute, in 1986 to teach in Chinese, English and Spanish. On October

26, 2007, the Sun Yat Sen Institute in Panama formed a sister school partnership with the Sun Yat-sen Memorial Secondary School in Guangdong, China. At present, the Sun Yat Sen Institute has about 1,700 students, two thirds of whom are children of overseas Chinese in Panama. It is recognized as the oldest and largest school for Chinese in Panama.

The Sun Yat Sen Institute in Panama attaches great importance to the edification and education of students about Chinese culture. For example, the school has the tradition of lion dancing, and is equipped with traditional Chinese instruments such as erhu and bamboo flute. There used to be a teacher from Taiwan region of China, who taught the erhu to students for about eight months and left. The students liked learning erhu, but no one could teach them. Guillermo, as vice president of the Chinese-Panamanian Cultural Center, was very distressed and anxious. Therefore, finding a suitable erhu teacher for the school was always on his mind at that time.

One day, when receiving Chinese guests from Shenzhen, Guillermo once again talked about looking for an erhu teacher. A staff member of the Overseas Chinese Affairs Office of the Shenzhen Municipal Government, who accompanied the delegation, kept this in mind. Two months later, Guillermo, who was far away in Panama, got a reply from Shenzhen, "I've found you an erhu teacher!" Guillermo realized that the so-called "Shenzhen Speed" deserved its reputation.

Inviting music teacher from Shenzhen, building a bridge for folk diplomacy with erhu

In 2013, at the invitation of Guillermo and the Chinese-Panamanian Cultural Center, Liu Hongwei, a special-grade teacher from Shenzhen, was appointed by the Overseas Chinese Affairs Office of the Shenzhen Municipal Government to teach erhu at the Sun Yat Sen Institute in Panama as a "volunteer for overseas Chinese education."

This was the first time for Liu to teach abroad. She recalled, "This Central and South American country is very far away from us. I knew nothing about it except the Panama Canal. Some friends even told me that it was a wild place, and that I should be careful not to be eaten by crocodiles after getting there. However, I was curious to see what kind of mysterious country it was. Why would anyone want to learn the erhu there? With this curiosity and confusion, I went to Panama alone."

Having set foot on this strange land far away, Liu soon won the recognition of Panamanian students and local overseas Chinese with his excellent erhu skills as well as serious and responsible teaching attitude. From 2013 to 2016, she went to Panama four times to teach erhu and music, retaining the roots of traditional Chinese culture on the other side of the ocean, while also planting more seeds of hope.

"I had never seen an ordinary person who would develop so well in Panama. She has great charm," speaking of the days when Liu taught erhu skills in Panama, Guillermo was very impressed. "She was very approachable. Overseas Chinese in Panama, especially those from Guangdong, treated her as their family member and invited her to their home. In the past, when staff members of the Chinese-Panamanian Cultural Center left, Mr. Fermin Tomas Chan, president of our center, rarely invited them to dinner. But when Ms. Liu Hongwei was about to return to China, he held a very special party for her."

In Guillermo's mind, Liu, as a teacher from Shenzhen, is really a wonder. "In addition to teaching erhu in Panama, she also did a lot of non-governmental diplomacy." During her teaching in Panama, Liu held two concerts in the official residence of the then Chinese-Panamanian Trade Development Office. Panama's magistrate, former auditor general and some other political figures, as well as several envoys and diplomatic mission representatives in Panama, attended the concerts. The pianist who accompanied her was Luis Troetsch, a famous pianist and dean of the Faculty of Fine Arts of the University of Panama.

Thanks to the Internet, we can still feel the wonderful scenes of one of the concerts. On the official website of the Ministry of Foreign Affairs of China, a story entitled *Representative Wang Weihua of the Trade Development Office in Panama hosts a music reception* described the scenes as follows:

On July 10, 2014, Representative Wang Weihua of the Chinese–Panamanian Trade Development Office held a China–Panama music reception at the official residence... In more than 40 minutes, the guests enjoyed the works jointly performed by two musicians (Liu Hongwei and Luis Troetsch—editor's note), including many famous Chinese and foreign songs played on the piano and the erhu, such as *The Nice Night*, *The Jasmine Flower*, *The Horse Race*, *Liuyang River*, *The Moon Over a Fountain* and *You and Me*. Eight outstanding erhu learners that Ms. Liu had trained for five months also appeared to play Chinese music and songs with her. The reception ended with the famous Panamanian song *Historia De Un Amor* (*A Love Story*), which Ms. Liu learned here.

During the whole performance, the hall of the trade representative's residence was sometimes silent and sometimes thunderous with applause, while the audience was completely attracted and intoxicated by the wonderful music of China and Panama.

In Panama, Liu also gave special lectures at universities to introduce Chinese music culture. When she played the famous Panamanian song *Historia De Un Amor* (*A Love Story*, which is also the original song of the Chinese song *You Are the Only One in My*

Heart) on erhu again, there were bursts of applause, and many Panamanian college teachers could not help but burst into tears.

"In Panama, I was willing to go anywhere for an opportunity for exchange. As someone learning a traditional Chinese instrument, I felt that I had a natural sense of responsibility and mission to spread traditional Chinese culture and Chinese music there," Liu said.

Helping Huawei develop Panamanian market

Shenzhen is a city of high-tech innovation. High-tech enterprises such as Huawei, ZTE, Tencent and DJI are beautiful business cards that Shenzhen shows to the world. Although Panama had no formal diplomatic relations with the People's Republic of China until 2017, the relationship between Huawei and Panama had started more than 10 years earlier with Guillermo's help.

In about 2006, Guillermo visited Ricardo Aleman, his friend of many years and Panama's ambassador to Mexico. While they were chatting during lunch, Panama's consul general came to tell them that two Chinese people were applying for visas to Panama. At that time, although the embassy issued visas, it did have the right of approval. Firstly, visas had to be approved by the National Migration Service of Panama. Guillermo revealed that many people wanted to immigrate or smuggle to Panama in the past, and that the approval by the National Migration Service was very strict. It was difficult to get a visa for business activities in Panama.

Since these two people were already in Mexico, there could be no big problems for them to go to Panama. But, as a precautionary measure, the Panamanian embassy asked Guillermo to meet the two applicants in a bid to understand their backgrounds, because it could be easier for them to communicate as Chinese. Guillermo still clearly remembers one of the two Chinese people's name. But he had never heard of Huawei before. After a talk and field visit, he learned that Huawei had set up a branch in Mexico, and, as a large and thriving company there, had hired some Mexican employees. So, he said on the spot that he would introduce Huawei to Panama and help them apply for visas to expand the market in Panama.

After visiting Huawei's Mexican branch, Guillermo went to the Panamanian embassy in Mexico to report to the ambassador. It happened that the Chinese ambassador to Mexico invited the Panamanian ambassador to Mexico to dinner that evening, and Guillermo went together. During the dinner, Guillermo asked the Chinese ambassador about Huawei's Mexican branch. The ambassador told him that Huawei was a very famous high-tech company headquartered in Shenzhen. After listening to the introduction by the Chinese ambassador, Guillermo was more confident about helping Huawei's staff apply for visas and inviting them to open a company in Panama.

Back in Panama, Guillermo immediately introduced the facts about Huawei to the Panamanian authorities. "If Huawei comes, it will definitely contribute to Panama," he patted his chest and told the then director of Panama's National Migration Service. "At least, they will build offices and hire staff when they come, which will definitely help Panama's economy." As a result, Huawei successfully got its first two work visas to Panama.

Panamanian people give the thumbs up when talking about Huawei

Guillermo was once appointed as executive director of Colon Free Zone by Mireya Moscoso de Gruber, the first female president in Panama's history, who was in office from 1999 to 2004. Later, he was elected chairman by the board of directors of Colon Free Zone. So he was familiar with various operating systems of Panama's free trade zones. After Huawei Panama opened, he enthusiastically introduced the advantages of Colon Free Zone (such as its superior location, convenient transportation and logistics, etc.), and suggested that they move their headquarters in Latin America to the free trade zone in Panama. "Here, the import and export of goods can be tax-free, and, more importantly, the local government provides a good business environment for international enterprises in terms of taxes and in other aspects," he added.

In October 2011, Huawei set up its Latin American headquarters in Panama, covering 3,600 square meters. In 2015, Huawei continued to increase its investment in Panama and established a supply center in Colon Free Zone. According to the official website of the Chinese embassy in the Republic of Panama (formerly the Chinese–Panamanian Trade Development Office), on October 1, 2015, when Colon Free Zone in Panama had trouble with its operation and saw declined trade volume, Huawei bucked the trend and established here its sixth allocation center in the world, where it not only carried out warehousing business, but also produced and assembled 15 types of products for export to 35 countries. This set a successful example and provided useful experience for Chinese–Panamanian cooperation in production capacity and logistics, and had a positive impact on the in-depth development of both countries' economic and trade relations.

"Huawei's contribution to Panama is very, very great. It is committed to assisting local operators and others in building communication infrastructure, and has created many employment opportunities." Guillermo believes that Huawei has made a lot of contributions to the local society after entering the Panamanian market. "The most important thing is that it has helped young Panamanian people learn the latest technology in Huawei's headquarters in Shenzhen."

On November 18, 2017, Ren Zhengfei, founder and president of Huawei, visited Panama. A press release by Huawei said, "Huawei Panama has created more than 300 jobs for local residents and more than 180 jobs in Colon Free Zone." Moreover, Huawei has actively provided digital training for Panamanian customers, partners and young college students. In 2015, Huawei successfully launched the "Seeds for the Future" project in Panama, with 30 excellent students from the University of Panama and the Technology University of Panama going to Huawei's headquarters in Shenzhen for a week-long training, communicating closely with Huawei's ICT experts. In 2020, because of the COVID-19 pandemic, the "Seeds for the Future" training project that Huawei had kept doing in Panama was moved to an online distance education platform. However, the change from face-to-face communication to online training gave young people in Panama more opportunities to participate.

Today, Huawei is a well-known brand in Panama. Leonardo Kam, Panama's ambassador to China, once took out his mobile phone to publicize for free. "Everyone likes Chinese mobile phones. I'm using a Huawei mobile phone," he said. On January 19, 2019, Panama's first Huawei experience store opened at a shopping mall, Multiplaza Pacific. According to media reports, although the opening time of the experience store was 10 a.m., customers were lining up outside the mall at 8 a.m., while some Huawei fans began to line up outside the store one night in advance.

As the saying goes, "When drinking water, never forget those who dug the well." To this day, Huawei has not forgotten Guillermo's contribution as a go-between in the early days, and will send warm greetings to him for New Year and other festivals. Guillermo is still optimistic about the development prospects of Huawei, a Chinese technology giant, in Panama, as he was more than a decade ago. "Huawei has developed very well in Panama. Among those I know, whether they are senior government officials, engineers or ordinary people, when it comes to Huawei, everyone will give the thumbs up," he said proudly.

(Photos courtesy of Guillermo John Chava and Liu Hongwei. References: the official website of the Ministry of Foreign Affairs of China and the official website of Huawei.)

何沈慧霞

自强不息铸就政坛传奇，
孜孜不倦搭起中澳"桥梁"

何沈慧霞　Helen Wai-Har Sham-Ho

　　何沈慧霞，祖籍深圳坪山，1943 年在香港出生，1961 年赴澳大利亚留学，1967 年大学毕业后留在澳大利亚发展，定居悉尼。新南威尔士州上议院前副议长，新南威尔士州议会亚太友好小组联合创始人，新南威尔士州议会狮子会创会会长，澳大利亚深圳社团总会荣誉顾问。

　　何沈慧霞曾从事社会工作和律师工作，1988 年当选澳大利亚立法体系里的首位华裔议员，在新南威尔士州上议院连续担任 4 届议员，时间长达 15 年。长期致力于社会和社区事务，为华人社区争取权益，促进华侨华人融入当地社会，推动中澳友好交流。曾获澳大利亚荣誉勋章（OAM）、新南威尔士州州长社会服务奖、澳中年度杰出校友奖等荣誉。

采访时间：2022 年。

何沈慧霞，人称"沈大姐"，在澳大利亚政坛和华人圈享有很高声望。听她细说奋斗史，你会发现，那些耀眼光环的背后，是一连串的优秀特质。她好学、勤奋、自信、坦率、健谈、热心，关心族群和公共利益。她自强不息，敢于接受新挑战、尝试不同的人生。没有人能随随便便成功，她也不是一直顺风顺水。她遭遇过婚变，当了十年单身母亲，含辛茹苦抚养两个孩子，但她从逆境中崛起，厚积薄发，迎来了职业生涯的高歌猛进，在政坛为华人争得一席之地。

远隔重洋，开枝散叶，最忆是故园。何沈慧霞发现，自己离开中国土地越久，就越爱中国。年近八旬的她还在努力学中文、读《易经》。她对中国的最大贡献，就是搭起了中澳交流的桥梁。她也是华侨华人和澳大利亚主流社会之间的桥梁，华侨华人群体内部的桥梁。

年少离家，赴澳求学

何沈慧霞 1943 年出生在香港。她的父亲来自深圳坪山，是客家人；她的母亲来自江门开平，那里也是广东的著名侨乡。

何沈慧霞的父亲年少时跟随叔叔去过马来西亚，在教会学校读书，学会了英语，后来移居香港，当过翻译员，然后到消防局工作，一路做到了九龙消防局的高层。他让六个孩子都去外国读书。何沈慧霞排行老五，她和两个哥哥去的是澳大利亚，大姐和小妹去了英国，二姐去了美国。"让子女去外埠读书，就厉害点嘛，浸过咸水嘛！"何沈慧霞笑着回忆。"浸过咸水"是粤语俚语，意思是曾经出国求学。以前出国基本是坐船漂洋过海，所以把留学比喻成"浸咸水"。

不过，虽然父亲收入不错，但供那么多孩子留学也不轻松。"就算是在家读书，都很辛苦了，更不要说去海外，要给钱吃住啊。所以我很感激我爸爸，我爸爸真是辛苦。"何沈慧霞说，只有大姐不用父亲给钱，因为她学的是护士，可以勤工俭学。

何沈慧霞在香港的中学读的是英文部，为日后外出闯荡打下了语言基础。她没有在香港读中学六年级（Form 6），而是在 1961 年去了澳大利亚继续读高中。不过，她不是坐船，而是坐飞机去的。第一次独自出远门的她，在飞机上哭个不停。

那时，她的大哥已经完成学业，离开澳大利亚。她跟着二哥住了半年，然后又在一个爱尔兰裔家庭寄住了两年半。读完高中，何沈慧霞进入悉尼大学，用了五年时间攻读文学和社会工作两个专业。虽然时时想家，但她没有年年回香港，因为那时没有便宜的机票和船票。她就利用假期时间去打工，比如在百货公司做售货员。她还记得，自己是在十七八岁的时候打了第一份工。

1967 年，何沈慧霞从悉尼大学毕业，取得文学学士学位和社会工作专业的文凭，并且获得了该校社会工作专业的最高奖励。这样优异的成绩，是她职业道路上很好的"敲门砖"。"我很走运，有四家医院给我选。不是我找工作，是工作找我。"

多年后，她感念母校的培养，捐资在悉尼大学设立了何沈慧霞奖学金，奖励社会工作专业的硕士生。

遭遇家变，转行法律

何沈慧霞先后在不同医院做社会工作，还从事社会福利的教学。那个年代，在澳大利亚的少数族裔女性担任专业职务并不多见，何沈慧霞凭借自己的专业能力赢得了认可。但是，一场婚变让她尝尽了生活的苦头，也改变了她的人生航向。"我有个悲剧，有段悲伤史，我很少讲出来的。"她说。

原来，她有过两段婚姻。她姓名里的"何"是第二任丈夫的姓氏。第一任丈夫是她大学同学，他们有两个女儿。在孩子年幼时，这段婚姻就结束了，她当了十年单身母亲，做三份工把女儿养大——除了做社会工作和教学，还在业余时间去一家诊所当接待员。

在当时的华人社会，女性离异是件大丑事，何沈慧霞一开始不敢告诉家人，身边也很少华人，除了两个女儿，她举目无亲，十分孤独。她忙于生计，只好请当地人当保姆照看女儿，错过了教女儿说中文的机会，这也成了她心头的一大遗憾。不过，以单身母亲的身份养大了两个女儿，还是令她感到很骄傲。

何沈慧霞这么辛苦地工作养家，是因为离婚时没有拿到赡养费。当时的法律规定，如果男方没工作，就不用给赡养费。她很不理解这点，还跟她的律师大吵了一架。她觉得，律师收费那么高，却不能解决大问题，当然不甘心。因为这件事，何沈慧霞跑到图书馆钻研法律，产生了兴趣，觉得律师这个职业很有前途。1978 年，她在工作之余报读了法律课程。

1985 年，她获得了麦考瑞大学（又译为"麦觉理大学"）的法律学士学位，然后在一家律师事务所工作。1987 年，她成为新南威尔士州最高法院的大律师，就是电影和电视剧里穿上法袍出庭的那种。

穿上法袍的何沈慧霞。
Helen Wai-Har Sham-Ho in robes.

政坛传奇，华人之光

何沈慧霞坦言，自己如果一直做律师的话，"会赚钱赚到晕"。那时，华人律师很少。"我做律师时，都要 300 澳元一个小时。现在上千澳元了。"但人生没有假设。何沈慧霞的兴趣、特长与历史机遇相交，造就了澳大利亚政坛的传奇。澳大利亚是一个移民国家，大约三分之一的人口出生在海外。但是，1901 年，澳大利亚开始实施"白澳政策"，对来自亚洲和太平洋岛屿的有色人种采取歧视、限制的态度。这也部分解释了何沈慧霞早年观察到的现象：澳大利亚的华人很少。到了 1972 年，这个政策才开始废除。何沈慧霞记得，从 20 世纪 70 年代末开始，来澳大利亚的移民逐渐增多。她一直在本职工作之余积极参与社会事务，随着华侨华人增多，她也越来越忙。回想起来，自己每天做了那么多事情，真有点不可思议。

比如，她做社会工作时，参与了华人社区的筹款等活动。她积极支持多元文化，在 20 世纪 80 年代中期成为新南威尔士州民族事务委员会的兼职委员。她在律师事务所工作时，曾有一名华人珠宝商在她办公室对面被人枪杀，她为此组织了一次集会，要求增加警力。

当时还出现了律师参政做议员的潮流，亚裔参政也有了转机。在社区里非常活跃的何沈慧霞受到带动。1988 年，她当选新南威尔士州上议院议员，成为澳大利亚立法体系里的首位华裔议员，令华人社区欢欣鼓舞。她是靠实力脱颖而出的。先是自由党内预选，从 35 名候选人中选出 10 人。很少有预选候选人第一次参选就胜出，但何沈慧霞做到了。会场里有 300 多名自由党人，只有她是华人。"别人都是出生就讲英文的，我要比他们厉害，才能被选出来。"她回忆说，"'斗'足了两天，就是'斗'说话。"

其实大家都清楚，这 10 人里，只有前 6 名真正"有戏"。何沈慧霞就是第 6 个。然后，她再接再厉，最终如愿以偿。

据何沈慧霞介绍，在澳大利亚，联邦议会和州议会都是立法机构，而为数众多的地方议会没有立法权，只是处理民生相关事务。

她说，华人特别是女性在澳大利亚从政，有很多无形的门槛，只有足够优秀者才能脱颖而出。比如，要掌握流利的英语，要善于演讲辩论，要有良好的职业背景和强大的政治后盾。她有社会工作和法律工作的经验，能说会道，在选举活动中应付

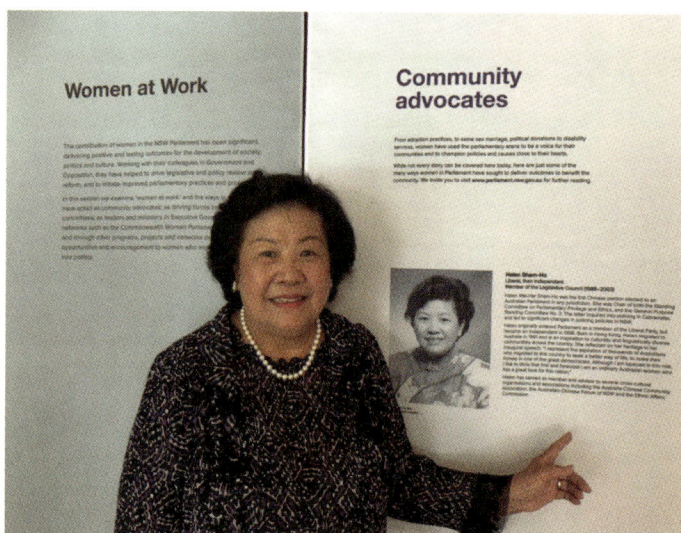

新南威尔士州议会内关于职业女性的展览收录了何沈慧霞的事迹。
An exhibition in the New South Wales Parliament on women at work includes Helen Wai-Har Sham-Ho's deeds.

自如，而且自由党和法律界都是她的后盾。

"对华人来讲，这种选战是很难的，所以很少有华人胜出。"相比之下，何沈慧霞以前做的社会工作就容易到"晕"了，要当律师也容易，"考试而已嘛"。

一生架桥，退而不休

从 1988 年到 2003 年，何沈慧霞在新南威尔士州上议院连续担任了 4 届议员，长达 15 年，十分罕见，是名副其实的政坛常青树。在这期间，她当了 8 年副议长，并在多次议会问询中担任主席。

"从头到尾，我一辈子都在做桥梁。"何沈慧霞说。她是华侨华人和澳大利亚主流社会之间的桥梁。她反映着华侨华人的诉求和呼声，还在大是大非问题上亮明立场。当选议员后不久，她做成了一件一直想做的事——为悉尼唐人街安装路灯。

早年的悉尼唐人街，晚上漆黑一片，有的地方甚至没有路灯，导致治安不好，但没有得到官方重视。何沈慧霞当了议员之后，就提出动议，让政府在那片区域装了路灯，改善了环境和治安状况，令市民和游客感到更方便、更安全了。

1998 年，她辞去了自由党的职务，成为独立议员。因为当时澳大利亚反亚裔情绪高涨，而她觉得自由党领袖对这个问题的应对不到位。她也是中澳关系的桥梁。当议员期间，她经常代表州长招待中国、新加坡等国家的代表团。她积极向新南威尔士州议员以及去中国短期学习的交换生介绍中国，两次带新南威尔士州议员访华，让他们对中国有直观的认识。"你要认识，才有感情，是不是？"何沈慧霞说，"交流越多，越容易做事，感情越深切。我做了很多这些事情。"

1999 年，新南威尔士州议会亚太友好小组创立，她是联合创始人和副主席。这个小组推动了新南威尔士州跟海外的交往，既包括中国，也包括众多太平洋小国。她是议会与社会之间的桥梁。2002 年，她创办了新南威尔士州议会狮子会，致力于社会工作和慈善事业，会员全都是议员。她还是华侨华人群体内部的桥梁。1992 年，她创办了慧贤会，这是一个华人女性团体，为她们提供联谊、交流、拓展人脉、参与慈善活动的机会。"当初，女士移民来这里，是很辛苦的，没有佣人可以请，什么事都要自己做。她们也不认识什么人，在这里可以认识一下人，互相帮助。"何沈慧霞说。

慧贤会组织女士们交流家政和美容心得，学习舞蹈，探访医院、老人院，捐助中国、柬埔寨等贫困地区的学校以及海地洪水、地震灾区，等等。

除了自己的社团，何沈慧霞也一直积极参与其他侨团的事务。

她是澳大利亚深圳社团总会的荣誉顾问，帮他们出谋划策。"我的意见很多的，因为没什么人比我更有经验了。大家都是同乡，大家互相帮助。"

广东江门的侨团也把何沈慧霞认作同乡，因为她母亲是江门开平人。何沈慧霞

2022 年 11 月 14 日，何沈慧霞在澳大利亚深圳社团总会第三届理监事会就职晚宴上发言。
Helen Wai-Har Sham-Ho speaks at the inaugural ceremony and gala dinner of the third term of the governing council of the Federation of Australian Shenzhen Community on November 14, 2022.

乐得多了个"娘家"，有活动也去捧场。2017 年，第三届世界广府人恳亲大会在江门举办，她不远万里赶去参加。江西、福建、上海……其他地方的在澳侨团邀请她开会，她也欣然赴约。"大家都是中国人，大家互相支持。""虽然我退休了，但我的地位还在。"何沈慧霞笑说。她在社会各界的人脉很广，如果侨团活动需要，她都可以帮忙邀请重量级嘉宾。"我叫的人，全都来的。因为他们对我有感情啊！"

所以，何沈慧霞继续发挥着自己独特的影响力，忙于社会事务，处于退而不休的状态。华侨华人都喜欢亲切地叫她"沈大姐"。因为对社会的卓越贡献，何沈慧霞获得了很多荣誉。她在 2006 年获得狮子会国际基金会最高荣誉——茂文钟士会员奖，2008 年获得新南威尔士州州长社会服务奖，2012 年获得澳大利亚荣誉勋章，2014 年获得西悉尼大学文学博士荣誉学位，2017 年获得澳华公会颁发的终生服务奖，2021 年获得澳中同学会颁发的澳中年度杰出校友奖。

关心女性，提携青年

何沈慧霞很关注女性权利和性别平等。她记得，20 世纪 60 年代，大学里女生很少，"大概十个里有一个"。后来她进入州议会，女议员只有五六个。侨团的会长也很少是女性。2022 年 12 月初，她参加了一个江西侨团的活动，会长是位女士，那是她见过的唯一一位女性会长。

何沈慧霞曾在公开演讲中讨论过非英语背景女性的职业发展。她举例说，在她的第一段婚姻里，她接受了"丈夫的事业优先于她的事业"这一信条，尽管她自己的事业很有前途。她当时觉得，为了丈夫事业的发展，她可以跟随他去任何地方。这在当时是理所当然的，而且来自中国文化背景的女性会毫无保留地接受。"谢天谢地，情况正在慢慢改变。"比如，她小女儿的事业就被看作至少跟丈夫的事业一样重要。"但是，许多职业已婚女性现在仍然把职业抱负放在次要位置，这是个问题。"

何沈慧霞透露，她一直在训练两个女儿独立。"家庭重要，但我觉得她们的自立也很重要。"她很欣慰的是，两个女儿都事业有成，"小女儿比我还厉害"。大女儿是建筑师；小女儿拿了律师牌照，又学了金融、读了 MBA（工商管理硕士研究生），因为读书多，所以升得快，已经在澳航（澳洲航空公司）做到了管理层。"我的女儿们不用我管了，比我更幸福。"何沈慧霞说。

何沈慧霞没有儿子，但是认了个干儿子。他叫谭凯欣，祖籍开平，从小在香港长大。从广州的暨南大学毕业后，他去悉尼大学深造，并在澳大利亚政坛崭露头角，何沈慧霞也给予了提携和帮助。

何沈慧霞和谭凯欣情同母子。

Helen Wai-Har Sham-Ho and Ian Tam are like mother and son.

猛学中文，心系故土

何沈慧霞说，她虽然很"西化"，但她深爱中国。离开中国土地越久，越爱中国。因为，她骨子里还是中国人。她为自己的中文不好感到很惭愧，所以在努力学习，已经有了很大进步。她的中文只学到了小学，后来的大部分时间生活在英语环境里，导致英语掌握得比中文好。因为中文不好，她遭到过个别人的冷遇。"我 20 年前不怎么讲中文，包括粤语，因为不流利。"何沈慧霞说，"我会讲中文就是这十年八年，因为我退休了，去中国多了。"

现在，她的粤语很流利。在采访中，她全程用粤语交谈，只有个别词汇一时想不起来，先用英语代替。

"我听得懂普通话，讲得不好。"她说，"普通交谈听得懂，演讲能听懂七八成，因为有的字眼听不懂。"

她从小就没有普通话的语言环境，现在自学达到这个程度，已经很不错了。中文水平的进步，还有个原因是她喜欢读书，很多词汇都是从书里学来的。她现在仍然在读很多书，包括深奥的《易经》，那是干儿子谭凯欣去年从香港寄给她的。

"我跟别人说，我 70 多岁才看《易经》，信不信？哈哈哈哈！"何沈慧霞笑了，"之前我都不知道什么叫《易经》，连名字都没听过。我中文只有小学毕业，哪里听过？"

何沈慧霞在祖屋的宗祠前留影。
Helen Wai-Har Sham-Ho in front of the ancestral hall at her ancestral house.

她还记得父亲的嘱咐：学无止境。"我猛学中文，因为我喜欢。喜欢的事情，就会多做点嘛。"她说。她喜欢的事情，还包括回"家"看看。她回中国有十几二十次，前几年曾经代表澳大利亚华侨华人去郑州黄帝故里拜黄帝。澳大利亚华侨华人连续多年在悉尼举办恭拜黄帝大典，她也积极参加。

"我想再去深圳的，我去过四五次。"何沈慧霞说，"四五年前，我表姑特意从香港来见我。"她指的是 2017 年 11 月那次寻根之旅。她带着家人来到位于深圳市坪山区马峦街道江岭社区远香居民小组的祖屋——香园世居，与宗亲共叙乡情。她在台湾、香港等地的一些亲戚也赶来一聚。她很是感动，同时也为家乡的欣欣向荣感到高兴。

每次回故乡，何沈慧霞还会去看看村后面的一棵树，因为她父亲小时候经常在那棵树下坐着。"我特意去看我爸爸在哪里出生、在哪里长大。"

2012 年，香园世居被坪山列为"不可移动文物"，挂牌保护。何沈慧霞对此充满感激。

寄望后辈，融汇中西

有一年，何沈慧霞有个外孙女中学毕业，祖孙三代四口人就去北京、上海、杭州等地游玩了一番。何沈慧霞说："虽然外孙女只有一半的中国血统，我也希望她认识中国，了解中国文化。"

"中国人一定要会中文。"何沈慧霞说。她支持孙辈们学中文，还资助他们去找私人老师学。"他们会说干炒牛河、炒饭、咕噜肉……"

本来，他们读的私立学校开设了第二语言的课程，但是中文班名额爆满，他们进不去，只好改学法语。何沈慧霞说，中文在澳大利亚很吃香，不同族裔都在学。她希望后辈既掌握西方礼仪，也懂得中式

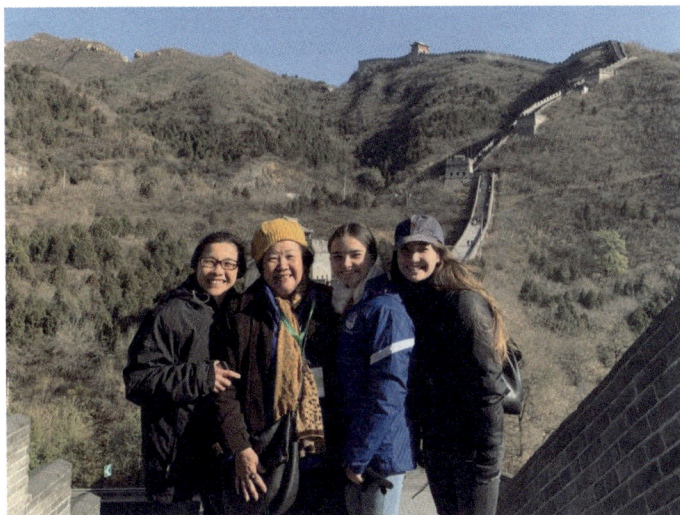

何沈慧霞（左二）带着小女儿和两个外孙女在北京游览长城。
Helen Wai-Har Sham-Ho (second from left) visits the Great Wall in Beijing with her younger daughter and two granddaughters.

礼仪，养成良好的家风，在会场等公共场合尊重他人。"最重要的是尊敬长辈。"她觉得，西方对老人家没那么尊敬，直接叫名字就是一个例子。虽然是文化差异，但她觉得不好。"我的孙子进了屋，第一句是'Hello，婆婆'，打招呼，有礼貌。""我的孙子都懂得中国礼仪，我不起筷子，他们不可以起筷子的。"何沈慧霞说，"我家不准吃饭看手机的。可以摆在那里，可以接电话。'食不言，寝不语'，我们吃饭是有聊天的，但不准看手机。不然成何体统？你看一两下不要紧，有时有些信息嘛。但不能埋头看，不吃饭。"

何沈慧霞还期待更多华人在澳大利亚政坛发光发热。近几年，大环境影响了澳大利亚华人参政的进程，但何沈慧霞觉得，华人想从政的话，练好内功是最重要

何沈慧霞的全家福。
Helen Wai-Har Sham-Ho's family portrait.

的，特别是英语水平、交流能力和对西方文化的了解。"因为我英文好，中文也讲得出，能读、能写，我就能做好沟通。"她说，"好多华人很想做，但做不了，因为对西方文化掌握不够。英文不好，词不达意。"她说，现在自己去参加"西人"的活动，一讲就是一两个小时。"他们不喜欢找其他人，因为他们英文不好。"

她建议，海外华人不管是从政，还是从事其他行业，都要认识当地的风土人情，融入当地的生活，多跟外界交往，有效地提高外语水平。"这里是英语国家，我们华侨华人在这里定居，已经把这里当作我们的第二个家乡了。"

［本文图片均由受访者何沈慧霞提供。参考资料：《深圳侨报》、《人民日报（海外版）》、新南威尔士州议会网站、新南威尔士州移民遗产中心网站、香港法学交流基金会网站、中新社、微澳洲、外交官说事儿、暨南大学国际学院网站。］

Helen Wai-Har Sham-Ho

Constantly striving to become a political legend, tirelessly building a "bridge" between China and Australia

Helen Wai-Har Sham-Ho, whose ancestral home is Pingshan, Shenzhen, was born in Hong Kong in 1943 and went to Australia to study in 1961. After graduating from university in 1967, she stayed in Australia and settled in Sydney. She was deputy-president of the New South Wales Legislative Council, co-founder of the NSW Parliament Asian Pacific Friendship Group, and charter president of the NSW Parliamentary Lions Club. She is honorary advisor to the Federation of Australian Shenzhen Community.

She was a social worker before becoming a lawyer. In 1988, she became the first elected Chinese-born parliamentarian in Australia. She served in the New South Wales Legislative Council (the Upper House of the Parliament of New South Wales) for four consecutive terms in 15 years. She has always been active in social and community affairs, fighting for the rights and interests of the Chinese community, promoting the integration of overseas Chinese into the local society, and promoting friendly exchanges between China and Australia. She has won honors such as the Medal of the Order of Australia (OAM), the New South Wales Premier's Community Service Award, and the Australia China Alumni of the Year Award.

Known as "Sister Sham," Helen Wai-Har Sham-Ho enjoys a high reputation in Australian politics and Chinese community. Listening to her detailed history of struggle, you will find a series of excellent qualities behind those dazzling auras. She is studious, hard-working, self-confident, frank, talkative and enthusiastic, and cares about the interests of her ethnic group and the public. She constantly strives to become stronger, and dares to accept new challenges and try a different life. No one can succeed casually, and her life has not always been smooth. After a divorce, she was a single mother for 10 years, enduring all the hardships to raise two children. However, she rose from adversity, accumulated her

---

The interview took place in 2022.

strength steadily, ushered in a soaring career, and won a place for the Chinese in politics.

Separated by vast oceans, her hometown is the most memorable place for her, who has a big family in Australia. She has found that the longer she left the land of China, the more she loves China. Nearly 80 years old, she is still working hard to learn Chinese and read *The Book of Changes*. Her greatest contribution to the motherland is that she has built a bridge of exchanges between China and Australia. She is also a bridge between overseas Chinese and mainstream Australian society, and a bridge within the overseas Chinese community.

Leaving home at a young age to study in Australia

Sham-Ho was born in Hong Kong in 1943. Her father is a Hakka from Pingshan, Shenzhen, while her mother is from Kaiping, Jiangmen, which is also a famous hometown of overseas Chinese in Guangdong.

When he was young, Sham-Ho's father went to Malaysia with his uncle, studied in a church school, and learned English there. Later, he moved to Hong Kong, worked as a translator, and then worked in the fire station, all the way to become a top leader of the Kowloon fire station. He sent all his six children to study abroad. Sham-Ho is the fifth child. She and two elder brothers went to Australia, her eldest sister and younger sister went to Britain, and her second-eldest sister went to the United States. "It's cool to have the children study abroad, because they will return after 'having soaked in salty water!'" Sham-Ho recalled with a smile. "To have soaked in salty water" is a Cantonese slang term, which means to have studied abroad. In the past, when going abroad, people basically traveled across the ocean by boat, so studying abroad is compared to "soaking in salty water."

However, although her father earned a good income, it was not easy for him to afford so many children's studies abroad. "Even if we studied at home, it was very hard, let alone go overseas. He needed to pay for our food and accommodation. So I have been very grateful to my father. It was really hard for him." Sham-Ho said that only her eldest sister did not need money from her father, because she studied to be a nurse and was able to work part-time.

Sham-Ho studied in the English department in a middle school in Hong Kong, which laid a language foundation for her to go out in the future. She did not study in the sixth grade of middle school (Form 6) in Hong Kong, but went to Australia to continue her high school in 1961. However, she did not go by ship, but by plane. It was the first time for her to travel alone, and she kept crying on the plane.

By then, her eldest brother had finished his studies and left Australia. She lived with her second-eldest brother for half a year, and then with an Irish family for two and a half years. After finishing high school, Sham-Ho entered The University of Sydney and spent five years studying arts and social work. Although she was homesick all the time, she did not return to Hong Kong every year because there were no cheap air tickets or ship tickets at that time. She spent her vacations working part-time, such as being a saleswoman in department stores. She still remembers that she had her first job when she was 17 or 18 years old.

In 1967, Sham-Ho graduated from The University of Sydney with a Bachelor of Arts degree and a Diploma in Social Work, winning the highest prize for the university's social work majors. Such excellent results were a good "stepping stone" for her career. "I was very lucky. I had four hospitals to choose from. I didn't look for a job, but the jobs looked for me."

Many years later, she was so grateful for her alma mater that she donated money to set up the Helen Sham Ho Encouragement Scholarship at The University of Sydney to reward postgraduate students majoring in social work.

Switching to legal profession after divorce

Sham-Ho did social work in different hospitals successively and also taught social welfare. At a time when ethnic minority women in Australia seldom held professional positions, she won recognition by virtue of her professional skills. However, a divorce forced her to taste the bitterness of life and changed the course of her life. "I had a tragedy, a sad history that I rarely talk about," she said.

She has had two marriages. The "Ho" in her name is the surname of her second husband. Her first husband was her university friend, and they had two daughters. The marriage ended when the children were young. Then she was a single mother for 10 years, raising her daughters by working three jobs. In addition to social work and teaching, she also worked as a receptionist at a clinic in her spare time.

In the Chinese society at that time, it was a shameful thing for a woman to get divorced. So she dared not tell her family at first. There were very few Chinese around her, and she had no relatives apart from two daughters. She felt very isolated. She was busy making a living, so she had to hire locals to take care of her daughters, and missed the opportunity to teach them to speak Chinese, which was a great regret for her. Still, she is proud of raising two daughters as a single mother.

Sham-Ho worked so hard to support her family because she did not get maintenance when she was divorced. The law at that time stipulated that if the man wasn't working, he would not have to give maintenance. She couldn't understand this and had a big fight with her lawyer. She thought that the lawyer's fees were so expensive but they couldn't solve big problems. She was certainly not reconciled. Because of this, Sham-Ho went to the library to study law, and got interested. She felt that the profession of lawyer would have a bright future. In 1978, she enrolled to study law in her spare time.

In 1985, she graduated with a Bachelor of Laws degree at the Macquarie University, and started working at a law firm. In 1987, she was admitted as a barrister of the Supreme Court of New South Wales. A barrister is someone wearing robes in court, as you see in movies and TV shows.

A political legend and the pride of the overseas Chinese

Sham-Ho said frankly that if she had continued to be a lawyer, she would have made so much money that she would feel perplexed. There were very few Chinese lawyers back then. "I charged 300 Australian dollars an hour when I was a lawyer. Now it's more than 1,000 Australian dollars." But life is not made up of assumptions. The intersection of Sham-Ho's interests, expertise and historical opportunities has created a legend in Australian politics. Australia is a nation of immigrants, with about a third of the population born overseas. However, in 1901, Australia began to implement the White Australia policy, adopting a discriminatory and restrictive attitude towards people of color from Asia and the Pacific Islands. This also partially explained the phenomenon that Sham-Ho observed in her early years: there were very few Chinese in Australia. It was not until 1972 that this policy began to be abolished. Sham-Ho remembers that since the late 1970s, the number of immigrants to Australia has gradually increased. She is a longstanding advocate in social affairs in her spare time. With more Chinese coming to Australia, she was getting busier. Thinking back, she can't even recall how she did so much in 24 hours.

For example, when she was doing social work, she participated in Chinese community fund raising. An active supporter of multiculturalism, she became a part-time commissioner for the Ethnic Affairs Commission of New South Wales in the mid-1980s. When she was working at a law firm, a Chinese jeweler was shot dead opposite her office, and she organized a rally demanding more police.

At that time, there was also a trend for lawyers to participate in politics as parliament members, as well as a turning point for Asians to take part in politics. Sham-Ho, who had been very active in the community, was prompted to go further. In 1988, she was elected to the Legislative Council of New South Wales and became the first elected Chinese-born member of an Australian parliament, making the Chinese community euphoric. She stood out with her capability. First, she was in the Liberal Party's pre-selection, where 10 candidates were selected from a field of 35 candidates. Very few first-time candidates can win the pre-selection, but Sham-Ho made it. There were more than 300 Liberals in the venue, and only she was Chinese. "The others spoke English from birth, and I had to do better than them to be selected," She recalled. "We fought for two whole days to see who were better at talking."

In fact, everyone knew that among these 10 people, only the top six "had a real chance." Sham-Ho was the sixth. Then, she went on to finally get her wish.

According to Sham-Ho, in Australia, both the federal parliament and the state parliaments are legislative bodies, while a large number of local councils have no legislative power and only deal with matters related to people's livelihood.

She said that there are many invisible barriers for the Chinese, especially women, to enter politics in Australia, and only those who are good enough can stand out. For example, they must speak fluent English, be good at speech and debate, and have a good professional background and strong political backing. She was a very capable speaker who had experience in social work and law, handled election campaigns with ease, and had the backing of the Liberal Party and the legal profession.

"For the Chinese, this kind of election is very difficult, so few Chinese can win." In contrast, Sham-Ho found social work "too easy," and it was also easy to become a lawyer. "It was just about taking the exams."

Building bridges in all her life, not resting after retirement

From 1988 to 2003, Sham-Ho served as a member of the New South Wales Legislative Council (the Upper House of the Parliament of New South Wales) for four consecutive terms in 15 years, which is very rare, making her a veritable "evergreen tree" in politics. During this time, she was deputy-president for 8 years and chaired a number of parliamentary enquiries.

"From beginning to end, I have been building bridges all my life," Sham-Ho said. She has been a bridge between overseas Chinese and mainstream Australian society. She has passed on the appeals and voices of overseas Chinese, and made clear her position on major issues of right and wrong. Shortly after being elected, she accomplished something she had long wanted: to install streetlights in Sydney's Chinatown.

In the early years, Sydney's Chinatown was dark at night, and there were even no streetlights somewhere in Chinatown, resulting in poor security, but the government did not take it seriously. After Sham-Ho became a parliamentarian, she proposed a motion to have the government install streetlights in that area, which improved the environment and security there, and made citizens and tourists feel more convenient and safer.

In 1998, she resigned from the Liberal Party and became an independent parliamentarian. That was because anti-Asian sentiment was running high in Australia at the time, and she felt the Liberal leader hadn't handled the issue well. She has also been a bridge between China and Australia. During her terms as a parliamentarian, she often entertained delegations from China, Singapore and other countries on behalf of the premier of New South Wales. She actively introduced China to New South Wales parliamentarians and exchange students who went to China for short-term study. She led New South Wales parliamentarians to visit China twice to give them an intuitive understanding of China. "You have to know each other before you have feelings, don't you?" Sham-Ho said. "The more you communicate, the easier it is to do things, and the deeper your feelings will be. I have done a lot of these things."

She was the co-founder and vice-president of the NSW Parliament Asian Pacific Friendship Group, which was established in 1999. This group has promoted the engagement of New South Wales with overseas, including China and many small Pacific countries. She has been a bridge between the parliament and society. In 2002, she founded the NSW Parliamentary Lions Club to be dedicated to social work and charity, with all members being MPs. She has also been a bridge within the overseas Chinese community. In 1992, she founded the Way In Network, a Chinese women's group, providing opportunities for them to socialize, communicate, expand contacts, and participate in charity activities. "In the early days, life was very hard for women who immigrated here. There were no servants to hire, and they had to do everything by themselves. They knew few people, so they could get to know people here and help each other," Sham-Ho said.

The Way In Network has organized ladies to share housekeeping and beauty experience, learn dance, visit hospitals and nursing homes, and donate to schools in poor areas, such as those in China and Cambodia, and flood and earthquake-stricken areas in Haiti.

In addition to her own organizations, Sham-Ho has also been actively involved in the affairs of other overseas Chinese groups.

She is honorary advisor to the Federation of Australian Shenzhen Community, making suggestions to them. "I have a lot of opinions to share, because no one has more experience than me. We are all from Shenzhen, and we help each other."

The groups of overseas Chinese from Jiangmen, Guangdong also recognize Sham-

Ho as a fellow immigrant, because her mother was from Kaiping, Jiangmen. Sham-Ho is happy to have one more "family of origin" and joins in their activities to show her support. In 2017, she traveled thousands of miles to attend the third Global Conference of the Cantonese held in Jiangmen. Jiangxi, Fujian, Shanghai... When other overseas Chinese groups in Australia invite her to a meeting, she also readily agrees. "We are all Chinese, and we support each other." "Although I have retired, my social status is still there," Sham-Ho said with a smile. She has a wide range of contacts in all walks of life. If the overseas Chinese groups need, she can help invite important guests to their activities. "All those I invite will come, because they have feelings for me!"

Therefore, Sham-Ho does not rest after retirement. She continues to exert her unique influence, and is busy with social affairs. Overseas Chinese like to call her "Sister Sham" affectionately. Because of her outstanding contribution to society, Sham-Ho has won many honors. She received the Melvin Jones Fellowship Award, the highest honor of the Lions Clubs International Foundation, in 2006, the New South Wales Premier's Community Service Award in 2008, and the Medal of the Order of Australia (OAM) in 2012. She was bestowed with an honorary doctorate degree of letters by the University of Western Sydney in 2014. In 2017, she was given the Lifetime Service Award by the Australian Chinese Community Association. In 2021, she received the Australia China Alumni of the Year Award from the Australia China Alumni Association.

Caring for women and supporting youth

Sham-Ho is very concerned about women's rights and gender equality. She remembers that in the 1960s, there were very few female students in colleges and universities, "probably one in ten." Later, when she entered the state parliament, there were only five or six women parliamentarians. It is rare for an overseas Chinese group to have a female president. In early December 2022, she attended an event held by a group of overseas Chinese from Jiangxi, which had a female president, the only one she has ever seen.

In a public speech, Sham-Ho discussed the career development of women from non-English-speaking background. For example, in her first marriage, she adopted the mantra that her husband's career took precedence over hers, although she had a promising career of her own. She would have followed him anywhere for his career advancement. This was then natural and accepted without question by women from Chinese culture. "Thank goodness, it is slowly changing." For example, her younger daughter's career is considered as important as, if not more important than, her husband's. "But, putting career ambitions on the back burner is still an issue for many professional married women."

Sham-Ho has been training her two daughters to be independent. "Family is important, but I think their self-reliance is also important." She is gratified that both of her daughters are successful in their careers, and "my younger daughter is better than me." The elder daughter is an architect. The younger daughter obtained a lawyer's license, studied finance and got an MBA (Master of Business Administration). She is so well-educated that she has been promoted quickly and is in the management team at Qantas Airways. "I don't need to worry about my daughters, whose lives are happier than mine," Sham-Ho said.

Sham-Ho has no son but a godson, Ian Tam. His ancestral home is Kaiping, and he grew up in Hong Kong. After graduating from Jinan University in Guangzhou, he went to The University of Sydney for further study and made his mark in Australian politics. Sham-Ho also gave him support and help.

Learning Chinese diligently, caring about her homeland

Sham-Ho said that although she is very "westernized", she loves China deeply. The longer she has left China, the more she loves China, because she is still a Chinese at heart. She used to feel ashamed of her poor Chinese, so she studied hard and has made great progress. She didn't have Chinese lessons after graduating from elementary school, and has lived in an English-speaking environment most of the time since then, which made her English better than her Chinese. She was treated coldly by some people because her Chinese was not good. "I didn't speak much Chinese 20 years ago, including Cantonese, because I was not fluent," Sham-Ho said. "I have been able to speak Chinese for the past 10 or eight years, because I retired and went to China a lot."

Now, she is fluent in Cantonese. During our interview, she spoke Cantonese all the way through. There were only a few words that she could not remember at the moment, and she used English words instead.

"I can understand Mandarin, but I can't speak it well," she said. "I can understand ordinary conversations, and 70% to 80% of speeches because I don't understand some words."

Since she was a child, she hasn't lived in a Mandarin-speaking environment. It is already very good for her to reach the current level by self-study. Another reason for the improvement of her Chinese is that she likes to read, with many words learned from books. She still reads a lot of books, including the esoteric *The Book of Changes*, which was sent from Hong Kong last year by her godson Tam.

"I told others that I began reading *The Book of Changes* when I was in my 70s.

Believe it or not? Hah, hah, hah!" Sham-Ho laughed. "I didn't know what *The Book of Changes* was, and I didn't even hear of the name of the book. My Chinese was only the level of an elementary school graduate, so how could I hear of it?"

She still remembers what her father told her: there is no end to learning. "I have studied Chinese vigorously because I like it. If you like something, you will do more," she said. She also likes to go back to "home." She has returned to China for about 20 times. A few years ago, on behalf of overseas Chinese in Australia, she went to the hometown of the Yellow Emperor in Zhengzhou to worship the Yellow Emperor. Overseas Chinese in Australia have held a ceremony of worshiping the Yellow Emperor in Sydney for several years in a row, and she has been active to take part.

"I want to go to Shenzhen again. I have been there four or five times," Sham-Ho said. "Four or five years ago, my father's cousin came from Hong Kong to see me." She was referring to a root-seeking trip in November 2017, when she took her family to her ancestral home, the Xiangyuan Ancestral Residence, a compound in Yuanxiang Residents Group, Jiangling Community, Maluan Subdistrict, Pingshan District, Shenzhen. She shared her affection for the homeland with her clan, while some of her relatives in Taiwan, Hong Kong and other places also came for the reunification. She was very moved, and at the same time happy for the prosperity of her hometown.

Every time she went back to her hometown, Sham-Ho would go to see a tree behind the village, because her father often sat under that tree when he was young. "I went there purposely to see where my dad was born and where he grew up."

In 2012, the Xiangyuan Ancestral Residence was listed as an "immovable cultural relic" by Pingshan, and a sign was hung to protect the residence. Sham-Ho is very grateful for this.

Expecting the younger generation to integrate Chinese and Western cultures

One year, when one of her granddaughters graduated from high school, Sham-Ho led a team of four from three generations to travel to Beijing, Shanghai, Hangzhou and other places. She said, "Although my granddaughter is only half Chinese, I also want her to know China and understand Chinese culture."

"Chinese people must know Chinese," Sham-Ho said. She supports her grandchildren in learning Chinese and even sponsors them to find private teachers. "They are able to say the Chinese words for dry-fried rice noodle with beef, fried rice, and sweet and sour pork..."

In fact, the private schools they attend offer second language courses, but the Chinese classes are full and they can't be enrolled, so they have to learn French instead. Chinese is very popular in Australia, and people of different ethnic groups are learning it, Sham-Ho said. She hopes that the younger generations will master both Western etiquette and Chinese etiquette, develop a good family tradition, and respect others in public places such as conference venues. "The most important thing is to respect the elders." She feels that Western people don't respect the elderly so much. For example, they call the elderly by their names. Although it is a cultural difference, she thinks that it's not good. "As soon as my grandsons come into the house, they will say, 'Hello, Grandma!' It's polite to greet people in this way." "My grandsons all understand Chinese etiquette. Before I raise my chopsticks, they can't raise theirs." Sham-Ho said, "In my family, it is not allowed to look at the mobile phone while eating. It can be placed there, and you can answer the phone. 'Eating and sleeping without talking.' We can chat while eating, but we mustn't look at the mobile phone. Otherwise, what do the rules mean for us? It doesn't matter if you take a look or two, because sometimes you get some information. But you can't always look at it and stop eating."

Sham-Ho also expects more Chinese to shine in the Australian political arena. In recent years, the general environment has affected the process of Australian Chinese participating in politics, but Sham-Ho believes that if overseas Chinese want to enter politics, it is most important for them to improve their own skills, especially English proficiency, communication skills and the understanding of Western culture. "I am good at English, I can speak Chinese, and I can read and write, so I can communicate well," she said. "Many Chinese want to do it, but they can't because they don't have enough knowledge of western culture. They are not good at English and can't express themselves." When she goes to an event of "westerners," her speech can last one or two hours. "They don't like to have others do it, because their English is not good," she said.

She suggested that overseas Chinese, whether they are engaged in politics or other industries, should understand the local customs, integrate into the local life, communicate more with the outside world, and effectively improve their foreign language proficiency. "This is an English-speaking country, where we overseas Chinese have settled. However, we have already regarded this place as our second hometown."

(Photos courtesy of Helen Wai-Har Sham-Ho. References: *Shenzhen Overseas Chinese News, People's Daily Overseas Edition*, the website of the Parliament of New South Wales, the website of the New South Wales Immigrant Heritage Centre, the website of the Hong Kong Legal Exchange Foundation, China News Agency, We Australia, Diplomats Talk, and the website of the International School of Jinan University.)

李锦贤

先辈的奋斗故事，一定要让
海外华裔年轻人知道

李锦贤（来源：《晶报》）Dato' Sri Lee Jin Xian (Photo: *Daily Sunshine*)

　　李锦贤，1948年出生，马来西亚华裔，祖籍深圳大鹏葵涌丰树山。马来西亚拿督斯里，马来西亚深圳总商会总会长，东盟—中国经贸文化促进会理事长，马来西亚惠州联合总会永久名誉会长，深圳市海外交流协会海外名誉会长，深圳市罗湖区侨联名誉会长，惠州市侨商投资企业协会副会长，惠州市归国华侨联合会荣誉主席。曾获第二届中华杰出商业领袖（企业社会责任）、深圳大鹏新区第二届"最美大鹏人"（华侨之星荣誉奖）等称号。

　　李锦贤早年经营木材业，后将企业多元化发展。从商之余，李锦贤活跃于社团、青年体育、排球运动等50余年，热心参与社区建设，推动社会发展，建树良多。

采访时间：2023年。

"深圳是我的家乡，我是深圳人。"说着李锦贤指着坐在他右边的李勇伟，又补充了一句："他也是深圳人。""我是他儿子。"李勇伟迅速但很小声地插话道。顿时，现场哄堂大笑。

这是 2023 年 5 月 23 日下午，马来西亚深圳总商会访问团在深圳宝安人才园参观考察后进行座谈交流，李锦贤作开场白时出现的欢乐一幕。

李锦贤这一次率队来深圳的访问团名字很长，叫"马来西亚深圳总商会青年海外创业拓展商机访问团"。从 5 月 21 日到 27 日，在深圳期间，访问团一行马不停蹄地与深圳各级侨务部门、深圳市企业联合会、宝安区人力资源服务中心、大鹏新区葵涌商会等多个组织或机构进行座谈交流，并实地参观考察了深圳市草根天使会及戈创学院、深圳国际会展中心、宝安人才园及宝安人才园西部中心分园、深圳国际生物谷（食品谷）坝光片区、大鹏所城、较场尾民宿小镇、金沙湾、沙鱼涌红色记忆陈列馆、葵涌侨史馆等多个地方。

李锦贤在马来西亚的身份有很多，其中最著名的就是他的"拿督斯里（Dato' Sri）"头衔，这是马来西亚州封衔中的最高封衔。不过，在深圳交流访问期间，风趣幽默的他介绍自己最常用的一个头衔就是"马来西亚深圳总商会总会长"。

2023 年 5 月 23 日，李锦贤率领的马来西亚深圳总商会青年海外创业拓展商机访问团在深圳合影。（来源：《晶报》）

The Visiting Delegation of Malaysia-Shamchun Chamber of Commerce for Youth's Overseas Entrepreneurship and Business Opportunity Exploration, led by Lee Jin Xian, has a group photo taken in Shenzhen on May 23, 2023. (Photo: *Daily Sunshine*)

24 岁就成为百万富翁

1948 年，李锦贤出生在马来西亚彭亨州关丹一个名叫"甘孟村"的华人家庭里。李锦贤的父亲李木生，是 20 世纪 20 年代初漂洋过海下南洋，然后定居在马来西亚关丹的广东客家人；其母劳观有是马来西亚出生的华人女子，祖籍广东开平，他的外公外婆都是早年从开平下南洋的四邑人。站在《晶报》记者面前的李锦贤说起话时，可以在马来语、英语、普通话、客家话、广府白话、四邑话间来回自如地切换。"在马来西亚生活的华人大多如此，拥有多种语言能力。"李锦贤说，"没有办法，在海外的华人要生活下去，就得这样。"

李锦贤小学上的是村里的甘孟培英华小，中学起初上的是彭亨州关丹中华中学，后来又去了森美

14 岁时的李锦贤。
Lee Jin Xian at the age of 14.

兰州的马口启文中学。"因为我的姑姑、表姐都住在那边。"李锦贤解释。读完初三，李锦贤的父亲就跟他说，他不能再读下去了，因为下面还有弟弟妹妹要读书。"我家有 10 个兄弟姐妹。"李锦贤说，自己那个时候其实是很不愿意的，但最后没办法还是不得不回到甘孟家中，去帮父亲干农活。在家乡待了一段时间之后，李锦贤就不想再干农务了，李父于是建议他去找表哥，学做木材生意。

回忆起自己过去的从商经历，李锦贤连说了好几次"很幸运"。"从 1966 年起，我就开始跟表哥学做木材生意，起初做的是书记员。"慢慢地，李锦贤发现，那个时候吉隆坡、怡保、新加坡的一些木材板厂商去他们那边收购木材时都是带着大量现金的。"我想这是一个商机啊。"在 1970 年，李锦贤成立了一家木材公司——建生木业贸易公司。"'建生'就是建立新生活的意思，这是我自己给自己的鼓励。"李锦贤这样阐释。

成立了自己的木业公司后，李锦贤每天起早贪黑地去森林里找可以出售的木材。当时刚好有位马来西亚的森林官员住在李锦贤家对面，或许是被他的勤奋所感染，对方将其叫上门并问他："李，你要不要申请森林的伐木许可证呀？"这种好事对初涉木材业不久的李锦贤而言，简直就是天上掉馅饼的大好事。在这名好心邻居的指导下，李锦贤以比较便宜的价格，申请到了 300 英亩的森林伐木许可证。

马来西亚森林资源丰富，是亚洲主要的木材和木材产品出口国之一，木材产品出口一直都是该国创汇的重要来源。"在马来西亚，这种森林伐木许可资格不是永久的，木材你采伐完了，森林土地就得交回政府，你再申请，政府就可能再另外批一片森林给你采伐。"李锦贤告诉《晶报》记者，他在采伐完了 300 英亩的森林后，

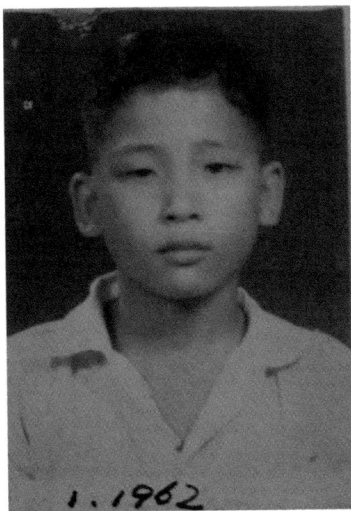

李锦贤早年从事木材生意。

Lee Jin Xian is engaged in the timber business in his early years.

很快就又申请到了300英亩的森林采伐许可资格。"就这样，我在两年内，就赚到了100万（林吉特，马来西亚货币），真的很幸运。"

那一年，李锦贤才24岁。掘到了人生的第一桶金之后，李锦贤没有乱花，而是用赚到的钱去置了一些产业。"就是买了一些土地和房产，要保值嘛！直到现在，我还有一些当年买下的房产租金收入呢。要知道，在20世纪70年代，那个时候马来西亚的房地产还是很便宜的。总之，我是一个很幸运的人。"

今天，李锦贤及其家族的企业发展更为多元化，涉猎的行业也更为广泛，涵盖了种植、旅游、建筑、物流、人力资源、电子商务以及马来西亚"第二家园"服务（马来西亚政府为了鼓励外籍人士在当地长时间居住而推出的一项计划）等。

断了近百年的血脉重新连上

据2012年出版的《深圳侨务史志》记载，深圳人移民新加坡、马来西亚始于明朝永乐年间（1405年）。早在1805年，马六甲就成立了第一个华人会馆"惠州会馆"，成员中有不少深圳籍人士，以龙岗、观澜、石岩人居多。大量移民是在18世纪后期和19世纪初期英国人莱佛士率兵占领马来亚以后，英殖民统治者为掠夺和开发马来半岛资源，采取鼓励外来移民特别是华侨移居的政策，大批中国人从闽、粤涌入，多数深圳人就是在这一时期进入马来亚的。过去深圳人去马来亚俗称"过锡山"，皆因当时移居马来亚的深圳人主要是去当锡矿工人和割胶工人。

李锦贤的父亲李木生出生于1904年，迫于生计，在16岁时就下了南洋，去寻找在那边定居的姐姐和姐夫。李木生先是借道去了香港，在茶楼找了份工作，一是筹措下南洋的路费，二是在等去新加坡的船到岸。一个月后，李木生坐船到了新加坡，然后坐火车直接到了现在马来西亚吉隆坡国际机场的所在地雪邦，在那里找到了姐姐。后来他们又去了马口，给英国人做除草等杂工，最后再辗转来到关丹甘孟村落脚。

如《深圳侨务史志》所言，"到外国谋生的深圳人，以观澜、龙岗、大鹏、葵涌、坪山、石岩、龙华等地客家人最多……能幸存下来的，大多在当地娶妻、生儿育女。由于时间久远，逐渐与家乡失去联系，但他们的后代仍保留家乡方言与生活习惯。"20世纪20年代，李木生在关丹甘孟村扎根、娶妻，一共生下了10个子女，李锦贤是李木生的二儿子。李家的孩子长大后互相帮扶，勤奋工作，家族也逐渐在马来西亚成为名门家族。

1970年的李锦贤。
Lee Jin Xian in 1970.

年轻时的李锦贤。
Lee Jin Xian in his early years.

出于种种原因，离开家乡以后，李木生始终没有回到中国认亲。"我爸爸从小就跟我们讲，他在中国的家乡就在'广东惠阳的枫树山'，还特别告诉我这个'枫'字是'枫树'的'枫'。"李锦贤说，"在爸爸近70岁的时候，我们曾劝他回中国寻亲，但他说家人都找不到，回去了也没什么意思。他经常在我们面前说一句非常经典的客家话——'沙坝打陀螺，唔得转'，意思就是在沙滩上打陀螺，真惨，转都转不动！这句话其实是有双重含义的，客家人说的'转'还有'回去'的意思，'唔得转'就是意味着他到了南洋之后，再也回不到家乡了。"

2007年12月18日，李木生在马来西亚去世，享年104岁。临终前，老人叮嘱儿子李锦贤有机会还是要回中国寻根问祖，并又一次说起了自己父母的名字、住址等信息。

为完成父亲遗愿，李锦贤多年来数次前往惠州寻亲，均没有结果，直到2013年他开始担任马来西亚惠州联合总会会长。2014年3月，当时惠州市侨联第九次侨代会举行，李锦贤作为惠州市侨联荣誉主席，在会上与时任惠州市惠阳区侨联主席陈文佳相识。在交谈中，李锦贤向陈文佳提起寻根问祖的事。但对方经过多次查询，发现惠阳区并没有"枫树山"这个地名，寻亲线索依然无果。

但惠阳区侨联并没有放弃，在多次与李锦贤沟通后，他们把寻亲范围扩大至邻近原属于惠阳地区的深圳市大鹏新区。大鹏新区侨联和葵涌办事处侨联立刻行动，查到葵丰社区有一个地方叫"丰树山"。在葵丰社区工作站工作的李文喜此时加入了协助李锦贤寻亲的队伍，并多次前往丰树山片区拜访上了年纪的老人。一次偶然的机会，李文喜与90多岁的廖维奶奶说起这件事，令人惊喜的是，廖奶奶居然知道来龙去脉——李文喜的爷爷李水生和李木生就是堂兄弟。真是"踏破铁鞋无觅处，得来全不费工夫"。

2014年，李锦贤踏上了回乡之旅，来到居住在大鹏新区葵丰社区双伍居民小组的堂哥李云茂家。兄弟相聚泪涟涟，隔断了近百年的血脉竟然又重新连上了。

创立马来西亚深圳总商会

2016年6月24日至26日，第九届世界惠州（府署）同乡恳亲大会（简称"世惠会"）在马来西亚吉隆坡举行，大会的主题是"同根同源同血脉，四海一心惠州情"。大会由马来西亚惠州联合总会主办，而作为大会主席，李锦贤为了办好世惠会，促进全球惠州同乡的联系与交流，他大胆地向惠州有关部门阐述了自己的想法，其中之一便是在"惠州"两字前加上一个"大"字，即"世界大惠州同乡恳亲大会"，可惜被否决了。经过商议，大家决定在"惠州"后面加上"府署"二字，认为这样比较合适。

"这一次的恳亲大会可以说是非常成功的。来自惠州、深圳、东莞、汕尾与河源5市的一百多名企业家也来到吉隆坡出席了大会，并进行交流。"李锦贤表示。

2023年5月23日下午，李锦贤率领的马来西亚深圳总商会访问团在宝安人才园进行交流座谈。
（来源:《晶报》）

A delegation of the Malaysia–Shamchun Chamber of Commerce, led by Lee Jin Xian, attends a panel discussion at the Bao'an Talent Park on the afternoon of May 23, 2023. (Photo: *Daily Sunshine*)

也就是在这一次的世界惠州（府署）同乡恳亲大会上，李锦贤见到了当时的深圳市侨联领导，经过交流，他就开始着手创立马来西亚深圳总商会。

2018 年 8 月 26 日晚，马来西亚深圳总商会在吉隆坡举行成立大会暨首届理事会就职典礼。在 880 名海内外嘉宾见证下，李锦贤以马来西亚深圳总商会总会长的身份率首届全体理事宣誓就职。"8 月 26 日是个特别的日子，是深圳成为经济特区的纪念日，所以我选了这个日子举行马来西亚深圳总商会成立大会。"李锦贤意味深长地说道。同样是在 2018 年这一年，李锦贤以 4 万多票（网络投票）荣获大鹏新区第二届"最美大鹏人"（华侨之星荣誉奖）的称号。要知道这可不简单，因为整个大鹏新区的常住人口也就 16 万左右。

马来西亚深圳总商会在吉隆坡顺利注册后，迅速在马来西亚吸纳了一批经济、科技、教育、文化等领域的企业家、专业人士和卓越青年成为会员。"现在我们总商会的会员数量不算多，有 100 多个，但我们重质不重量。"李锦贤表示，马来西亚深圳总商会的宗旨非常鲜明，就是要"发挥桥梁纽带作用，不遗余力推动马来西亚与深圳在经贸、文化、教育等方面的交流合作"。

2023 年 5 月 21 日到 27 日，由李锦贤率领的 11 人马来西亚深圳总商会访问团来到深圳考察交流，其间便出现本文开头的有趣一幕。这也是继 2018 年马来西亚深圳总商会商业考察团和 2019 年中马企业家经贸文化合作座谈会，推动 14 家中马企业现场签署旅游、教育、金融、建筑等多个领域合作文件后，该商会第三次到访中国。"3 年多的新冠疫情，中断我们和深圳之间太多的交往。"李锦贤遗憾地说。

希望海外华裔年轻人记住先辈的历史

2023 年 5 月 25 日，访问团在李锦贤父亲李木生 100 多年前的出生地——大鹏新区葵涌参观交流。当日上午，在位于沙鱼涌的葵涌侨史馆门口的两座铜像雕塑前，李锦贤一本正经地开起了玩笑："因为过两天我们要回马来西亚，没有钱买飞机票，我就跟讲解员说'你可以让我暂时作为讲解员吗？我只要赚一点点回家的路费'。她说可以。"现场的人见状，又哈

2023 年 5 月 25 日，李锦贤在葵涌侨史馆门口。（来源：《晶报》）

Lee Jin Xian at the entrance of the Kuichong Overseas Chinese History Museum on May 25, 2023. (Photo: *Daily Sunshine*)

在葵涌侨史馆门外，李锦贤给马来西亚同伴讲解华人过去在海外奋斗的故事。（来源：《晶报》）

Outside the Kuichong Overseas Chinese History Museum, Lee Jin Xian tells his Malaysian companions the stories of the Chinese who struggled overseas in the past. (Photo: *Daily Sunshine*)

哈大笑起来。

李锦贤扶着侨史馆门口一尊弯着腰拄着拐杖、右手抚着前额远眺的老人铜像，问到访的马来西亚同伴："你们知道这位老人在看什么吗？"

"他在看对岸有没有船回来。"有人答。

"还有吗？"等了一会儿，见没有人再回答，李锦贤便认真地讲解起来："这尊雕塑做得很传神，它实际上是想表达这样一个意思——我们的祖辈从沙鱼涌这里出海到南洋或其他地方去，他们的父母（就是这个老人）年轻时把孩子送去南洋或海外其他国家，自己就在沙鱼涌这里日日夜夜等着孩子归来，但是，很多父母由年轻盼望到老，一直都没有等到孩子回来……"说到此，或许是联想到了自己父亲在马来西亚的经历，李锦贤言语间有些哽咽。

接着李锦贤走到旁边坐着另一尊铜像的长椅上坐下。他抚摸着铜像说："这个雕像穿着西装、皮鞋，打着领带，旁边还放着一个大皮箱，就好像你们现在这样，衣锦还乡，终于回到沙鱼涌，回到家乡了。是不是很有意思？"

"这个一定要让这些年轻人知道，不然，他们回来干什么？"李锦贤告诉《晶报》记者，此次访深的主要成员是马来西亚深圳总商会"青年创业组"组员，大多是第二代、第三代马来西亚华裔，有几个还是首次跟随马来西亚深圳总商会来中国参加经贸交流活动。"要让他们都知道这些故事，这样他们以后才会多回大鹏、回深圳看看，或者投资创业。"

"我希望在我有生之年，能够参与更多的建设粤港澳大湾区的工作，这样就能够向我们的祖辈有所交代了。虽然我今年75岁了，但是我还是要继续努力。"李锦贤说。

（除署名外，本文图片均由受访者李锦贤提供。参考资料：《深圳侨务史志》《深圳侨报》《桑梓情深　赤子丹心：大鹏侨情口述史》。）

Lee Jin Xian

We must let young overseas Chinese know the struggle stories of their ancestors

Lee Jin Xian, born in 1948, is a Malaysian Chinese. His ancestral home is in Fengshushan, Kuichong, Dapeng, Shenzhen. He is bestowed the title of Dato' Sri in Malaysia. He is president of the Malaysia-Shamchun Chamber of Commerce, board chairman of the ASEAN-China Economic, Trade and Culture Promotion Association, permanent honorary president of the Federation of Fui Chiu Association Malaysia, overseas honorary president of the Shenzhen Overseas Exchange Association, honorary president of the Returned Overseas Chinese Federation of Luohu District, Shenzhen, vice president of the Huizhou Overseas Chinese Enterprises Association, honorary chairman of the Huizhou Federation of Returned Overseas Chinese. He has won honors such as the second version of China Outstanding Business Leader (Corporate Social Responsibility) and the second version of "Most Beautiful Dapeng People" (Overseas Chinese Star Honorary Award) of Dapeng New District, Shenzhen.

Lee was engaged in the timber industry in his early years, and later diversified his business. In addition to his business career, Lee has been active in social groups, youth sports, and volleyball for more than 50 years. He has enthusiastically participated in community building, promoted social development, and made many achievements.

"Shenzhen is my hometown, and I am from Shenzhen," Dato' Sri Lee Jin Xian said. Pointing to Dato' Lee David, who was sitting on his right, he added, "He is also from Shenzhen." "I am his son," David interjected quickly but quietly. Immediately, the audience roared with laughter.

This was a joyous scene on the afternoon of May 23, 2023, when Lee Jin Xian made the opening remarks as a delegation of the Malaysia–Shamchun Chamber of Commerce attended a panel discussion after visiting the Bao'an Talent Park in Shenzhen.

The delegation he led to Shenzhen this time had a very long name: "Visiting

The interview took place in 2023.

Delegation of Malaysia–Shamchun Chamber of Commerce for Youth's Overseas Entrepreneurship and Business Opportunity Exploration." During its stay in Shenzhen, from May 21 to May 27, the delegation had non-stop discussions and exchanges with overseas Chinese affairs departments at all levels in Shenzhen, the Shenzhen Enterprise Confederation, the Bao'an District Human Resources Service Center, the Dapeng New District Kuichong Chamber of Commerce and other organizations or institutions, and visited the Shenzhen Grassroots Angel Investor Club and GOBIIE (Gobi Institute of Entrepreneurship), the Shenzhen World Exhibition & Convention Center, the Bao'an Talents Park and its West Central Branch, the Baguang Area of the Shenzhen International Bio Valley (Food Valley), Dapeng Fortress, the Town of Homestay Inns in Jiaochangwei, Jinsha Bay, the Shayuchong Red Memory Exhibition Hall, the Kuichong Overseas Chinese History Museum, and many other places.

Lee Jin Xian has many identities in Malaysia, the most famous of which is Dato' Sri, the highest state title in Malaysia. However, he mostly introduced himself as "president of the Malaysia-Shamchun Chamber of Commerce" during this visit to Shenzhen. He also showed his fine sense of humor during his stay.

Becoming a millionaire at 24

In 1948, Lee Jin Xian was born in a Chinese family in a village named Gambang, in Kuantan, Pahang, Malaysia. His father, Lee Seng, was a Hakka from Guangdong, who traveled across the sea to Nanyang (Southeast Asia) in the early 1920s, and then settled in Kuantan, Malaysia. Lee Jin Xian's mother, Loo Kon Yew, was a Chinese woman born in Malaysia, and her ancestral home was in Kaiping, Guangdong. In the early years, her parents went to Nanyang from Kaiping, one of the four towns that were collectively called Siyi. Standing in front of us, Lee Jin Xian could freely switch back and forth between Malay, English, Mandarin, Hakka, Cantonese vernacular, and Siyi dialect when speaking. "Most of the Chinese living in Malaysia are like this, with multilingual skills," he said. "We have no choice. Overseas Chinese have to do this to keep life going on."

The primary school he went to was Gambang National Type School (Chinese), or Sekolah Jenis Kebangsaan (Cina) Gambang, in his village. He attended Kuantan Chong Hwa High School (Sekolah Menengah Chong Hwa Kuantan) in Pahang State, and later went to Chi Wen National High School (Sekolah Menengah Kebangsaan Chi Wen) in Negeri Sembilan State. "Because my father's sister and my cousin lived there," Lee explained. After he finished the third year of junior high school, his father told him that he could not continue studying because his younger siblings needed to go to school. "There are 10 brothers and sisters in my family." Lee said that he was actually very reluctant at that time, but in the end he had to return to his home in Gambang to help his father with farm work. After staying in his hometown for a while, Lee didn't want to do farming anymore. So his father suggested that he go to find his cousin and learn about timber business.

Recalling his past experience in business, Lee said "very lucky" several times. "In 1966, I began to learn to do timber business from my cousin. At first I worked as a clerk." Gradually, Lee found that some timber panel manufacturers from Kuala Lumpur, Ipoh and Singapore who came to buy timber carried a lot of cash with them. "I thought this was a business opportunity." In 1970, Lee established a timber trading company. "Its Chinese name meant building a new life, and this was the encouragement I gave myself," he explained.

After setting up this wood company, Lee got up early and worked late every day to find timber in the forest that could be sold. A Malaysian forest official happened to live opposite to Lee's house. Perhaps moved by Lee's diligence, he invited Lee to his home and asked, "Lee, do you want to apply for a logging permit in the forest?" For Lee, who had just been involved in the timber industry, it was a great thing like manna from heaven. Under the guidance of this kind neighbor, Lee successfully applied for a 300-acre forest logging permit at a relatively low price.

Malaysia is rich in forest resources and is one of the major exporters of timber and timber products in Asia. The export of timber products has always been an important source of foreign exchange for the country. "In Malaysia, this kind of forest logging permit is not permanent. After logging the timber, the forest land should be returned to the government. If you apply again, the government may grant another piece of forest for you to log," Lee said. After logging 300 acres of forest, he soon applied for the logging permit for another 300 acres. "In this way, I earned 1 million ringgits (the Malaysian currency) within two years. I was really lucky."

That year, Lee was only 24 years old. After finding the first pot of gold in his life, Lee didn't spend it recklessly, but used the money he earned to buy some properties. "I just bought some land and real estate to preserve the value! At present, I still have some rental income from the properties I bought back then. You know, in the 1970s, real estate in Malaysia was still very cheap. In short, I'm a very lucky person."

Today, Lee and his family's business development is more diversified. They are involved in a wider range of industries, covering planting, tourism, construction, logistics, human resources, e-commerce, and the services for Malaysia My Second Home (a program launched by the Malaysian government to encourage foreigners to live there for a long time), among others.

Roots reconnected after nearly 100 years

According to the *Historical Records of Shenzhen Overseas Chinese Affairs* published in 2012, the immigration of Shenzhen people to Singapore and Malaysia began in the Yongle period of the Ming Dynasty (1405). In 1805, the Huizhou Association, the first Chinese association, was established in Malacca. Among its members, there were many people from Shenzhen, most of whom were from Longgang, Guanlan and Shiyan. After Thomas Stamford Bingley Raffles, a British colonial official, led troops to occupy Malaya in the late 18th century and the early 19th century, the British colonial rulers adopted a policy of encouraging foreign immigrants, especially overseas Chinese, to plunder and develop the resources of the Malay Peninsula. People from Fujian and Guangdong poured in, and most of those from Shenzhen entered Malaya during this period. In the past, when people from Shenzhen went to Malaya, they were commonly known as "going to the tin mine" because they mainly went to work as tin miners and rubber tappers.

Lee Jin Xian's father, Lee Seng, was born in 1904. To make a living, he went to Nanyang at the age of 16 to find his sister and brother-in-law, who had settled there. He first went to Hong Kong and found a job in a tea house, raising the travel expenses to Nanyang while waiting for the ship to Singapore to land. A month later, he arrived in Singapore by ship, and then took a train directly to Sepang, where the Kuala Lumpur International Airport, Malaysia is now located. He found his sister there. Later, they went to Bahau to do weeding and other odd jobs for Britons, and finally settled down in Gambang Village, Kuantan.

As stated in the *Historical Records of Shenzhen Overseas Chinese Affairs*, "among the Shenzhen people who went to foreign countries to make a living, most were Hakkas in Guanlan, Longgang, Dapeng, Kuichong, Pingshan, Shiyan, Longhua and other places... Those who survived mostly got married and had children overseas. After a long time, they have gradually lost contact with their hometown, but their descendants still retain the dialect and living habits of their hometown." In the 1920s, Lee Seng took root and got married in Gambang Village, Kuantan. He had 10 children, with Lee Jin Xian as the second son. The siblings worked hard and helped each other after they grew up, and the family gradually became a well-known clan in Malaysia.

Because of various reasons, after leaving his hometown, Lee Seng never returned to China to recognize his relatives. "When we were children, my father began to tell us that his hometown in China was 'Fengshushan (Maple Mountain) in Huiyang, Guangdong,' and he emphasized to me that the Chinese character of 'feng' was for 'maple,'" Lee Jin Xian said. "When Dad was nearly 70 years old, we persuaded him to return to China to look for his relatives, but he said that his family could not be found at all, and it was meaningless to go back. He often told us a very classic Hakka saying, 'a spinning top doesn't rotate on the beach,' which means it's so miserable to play a spinning top on the beach because it won't rotate there! This sentence actually has double meanings. In the Hakka dialect, 'turn' or 'rotate' also means 'go back,' and 'not to rotate' means that after one arrives in Nanyang, he will never be able to return to his hometown."

On December 18, 2007, Lee Seng died in Malaysia at the age of 104. When he was dying, the old man told his son, Lee Jin Xian, to go back to China to find his roots and keep track of the family if possible, and once again mentioned his parents' names, address and other information.

To fulfill his father's last wish, Lee Jin Xian went to Huizhou several times over the years to find relatives, but in vain. In 2013, he began to serve as president of the Federation of Fui Chiu Association Malaysia. In March 2014, at the Ninth Overseas Chinese Conference of the Huizhou Federation of Returned Overseas Chinese, Lee, as honorary president of the federation, met Chen Wenjia, then president of the Federation of Returned Overseas Chinese of Huiyang District, Huizhou. During their conversation, Lee told Chen about searching for his roots and ancestors. But after many inquiries, Chen found no place named "Fengshushan" in Huiyang District, and the clues to find Lee's relatives were still fruitless.

However, the Federation of Returned Overseas Chinese of Huiyang District did not give up. After discussing with Lee many times, they expanded the scope of family search to Shenzhen's Dapeng New District, which used to belong to Huiyang Prefecture. The Retuned Overseas Chinese Federation of Dapeng New District and the Retuned Overseas Chinese Federation of Kuichong Office acted immediately, and found a place called "Fengshushan" in Kuifeng Community, although the Chinese character of "feng" is for "rich" instead of "maple." Li Wenxi, who worked at the Kuifeng Community Work Station, joined the team helping Lee to find his relatives, and went to the Fengshushan area to visit the elderly many times. By chance, Li talked about this matter with his grandmother, Liao Wei, who was more than 90 years old. Surprisingly, Liao knew the whole story: Li's grandfather, Li Shuisheng, and Lee Seng were cousins. It was really "a fancy finding by sheer luck after searching far and wide."

In 2014, Lee Jin Xian embarked on a trip back to his hometown and came to the home of his cousin, Li Yunmao, in Shuangwu Resident Group of Kuifeng Community, Dapeng New District. The two cousins gathered in tears, as the roots that had been cut off for nearly 100 years were reconnected.

Founding Malaysia-Shamchun Chamber of Commerce

From June 24 to June 26, 2016, the 9th Huizhou World Convention was held in Kuala Lumpur, Malaysia, with the theme of "Same root, same origin and same blood, love for Huizhou from all over the world." The convention was hosted by the Federation of Fui Chiu Association Malaysia. To run the convention well and promote the contact and exchange of Huizhou people around the world, Lee, as the chairman of the conference, boldly explained his ideas to the relevant departments in Huizhou, one of which was to add "Greater" before "Huizhou" in the Chinese name of the conventions. But, unfortunately, it was rejected. After deliberation, they decided to add "Government Office" after "Huizhou" in the Chinese name as a more appropriate change.

"This convention was very successful. More than 100 entrepreneurs from five cities, including Huizhou, Shenzhen, Dongguan, Shanwei and Heyuan, also came to Kuala Lumpur to attend the convention and exchange ideas," Lee said. During the convention, Lee also met the leader of the Shenzhen Federation of Returned Overseas Chinese. After discussions, he began to set up the Malaysia–Shamchun Chamber of Commerce (MSCC).

On the evening of August 26, 2018, the MSCC held its inaugural meeting and the inauguration ceremony of its first council in Kuala Lumpur. Witnessed by 880 guests from home and abroad, Lee, as president of the MSCC, led the inaugural directors to take the oath of office. "August 26 is a special day, the anniversary of Shenzhen becoming a special economic zone, so I chose this day to hold the inaugural meeting of the MSCC," Lee said meaningfully. Also in 2018, Lee won the second version of "Most Beautiful Dapeng People" (Overseas Chinese Star Honorary Award) of Dapeng New District with more than 40,000 online votes. It was really not easy, because the permanent population of the entire Dapeng New District is only about 160,000.

After successfully registering in Kuala Lumpur, the MSCC quickly enrolled a group of entrepreneurs, professionals and outstanding young people in economy, technology, education, culture and other fields in Malaysia as members. "At present, our chamber of commerce doesn't have too many members. There are more than 100 of them. But we focus on quality rather than quantity." The purpose of the MSCC is very clear, which is to "play the role of a bridge and a link, and spare no effort to promote the exchanges and cooperation between Malaysia and Shenzhen in economics, trade, culture, education, etc.," Lee said.

From May 21 to May 27, 2023, an 11-member delegation of the MSCC led by Lee came to Shenzhen for investigation and exchange, during which we saw the interesting scene stated at the beginning of this article. This was the third time that the MSCC had visited China, following the MSCC business investigation team in 2018 and the Sino-Malaysian Entrepreneurs' Economic, Trade and Cultural Cooperation Symposium in 2019, which promoted 14 Chinese and Malaysian enterprises to sign cooperation documents on site in multiple fields such as tourism, education, finance, and construction. "The COVID-19 pandemic for more than three years has interrupted too many exchanges between us and Shenzhen," Lee said regretfully.

Hoping young overseas Chinese to remember the history of their ancestors

On May 25, 2023, the delegation visited Kuichong, Dapeng New District, where Lee's father was born more than 100 years ago. In the morning, in front of the two bronze sculptures at the entrance of the Kuichong Overseas Chinese History Museum in Shayuchong, Lee made a serious joke, "Because we are going back to Malaysia in two days and have no money to buy plane tickets, I told the guide, 'Can you let me be the guide temporarily? I just need to earn a little money to go home.' She said yes." Hearing this, the others burst into laughter again.

Lee touched a bronze statue of an old man at the entrance of the Overseas Chinese History Museum, who bent over, leaned on a cane, and looked into the distance with his right hand in front of his forehead. Lee asked his visiting Malaysian companions, "Do you know what the old man is looking at?"

"He's checking if there's a ship coming back from the other side," someone replied.

"Any more?" After waiting for a while and seeing no more answers, Lee began to explain seriously, "This sculpture is very vivid, and it actually wants to express such a meaning: from here, Shayuchong, our ancestors started a voyage to Nanyang or other places. Their parents (such as this old man), when they were young, sent their children to Nanyang or other countries overseas. Then they waited day and night here in Shayuchong for their children to return. However, many parents became old while they were waiting, and never saw their children back home..." Speaking of this, Lee choked up. He was perhaps thinking of his father's experience in Malaysia.

Then Lee walked to the bench with another bronze statue next to him and sat down. He stroked the bronze statue and said, "This statue is wearing a suit, leather shoes, and a tie, with a big suitcase next to it, just like what you are doing now, returning to your hometown in glory, returning to Shayuchong, your hometown, at last. Isn't it very interesting?"

"This must be told to these young people. Otherwise, what do they come back for?" Lee said that the main members of this visit were members of the "Youth Entrepreneurship Group" of the MSCC, and most of them were the second or third generation of Malaysian Chinese, with several of them coming to China with the MSCC for the first time to participate in economic and trade exchange activities. "Let them all know these stories, so that they will return to Dapeng and Shenzhen more often in the future, or will invest to start a business here."

"I hope that in my lifetime, I can participate in more work in the construction of the Guangdong-Hong Kong-Macao Greater Bay Area, so that I can satisfy our ancestors to some extent. Although I am 75 years old, I still need to continue to work hard," Lee said.

(Photos courtesy of Lee Jin Xian, except for those with credit. References: *Historical Records of Shenzhen Overseas Chinese Affairs, Shenzhen Overseas Chinese News*, and *Deep Love for the Hometown and Sincere Loyalty to the Motherland: Oral History of Overseas Chinese from Dapeng*.)

陈云生

在"彩虹之国"广结善缘，为深圳企业"走出去"服务

陈云生（来源：《晶报》） Chan Wan Sang (Photo: *Daily Sunshine*)

陈云生，1949 年出生，深圳盐田大梅沙人。1969 年赴香港谋生，2000 年开始长住南非，经营外贸公司。

曾任南非客家联谊会第三、四任会长，现为荣誉会长。2017 年创立南非－中国深圳总商会，担任会长至今，积极配合深圳在南非开展各项工作，带领该商会发展成为南非影响力最大的侨团之一。2018 年，该商会主办第四届国际深圳社团大会暨南非·深圳经贸交流会，取得圆满成功。新冠疫情期间，该商会积极组织、协调抗疫物资的捐赠、接收和发放，为中国和南非抗击疫情作出了贡献。陈云生热心公益，目前还担任南非华人警民合作中心名誉主任、全非洲中国和平统一促进会顾问、广东省侨联海外委员、深圳市海外交流协会海外名誉会长等职务。

采访时间：2023 年。

2023 年 4 月，陈云生从南非约翰内斯堡回到祖国，在一个月的时间里参加了很多交流活动，见了很多老朋友。我们在深圳对他的专访，见缝插针地安排在 4 月下旬的一天。

"我不会讲话的啊！"一见面，陈云生就先打了个"预防针"。其实，这是很多侨领惯有的谦辞。对于自己在外闯荡的经历，对于自己为华侨华人和当地社会服务的心路历程，对于"彩虹之国"南非的商机，陈云生都能娓娓道来。

他是客家人。早年在深圳、香港的生活，也在他的语言里刻下了痕迹。他喜欢用粤语（俗称"白话"）交谈，当中又夹杂了客家话和普通话的发音。采访结束时，他特意选择在一面"为人民服务"的背景墙前面拍照。他说，他很喜欢这个口号。

机缘巧合，留在南非发展

陈云生 1949 年 12 月出生在深圳盐田大梅沙，家里还有个姐姐。他在深圳中学毕业后，回到盐田农村耕田。1969 年，他独自去香港谋生。

在香港，陈云生一开始是卖菜的小贩。赚到一些钱之后，他跟两位中学同学合伙开起了装修公司。后来，他又跟一位朋友合伙开了建筑公司。1980 年，改革开放的春风把陈云生吹回了久别多年的家乡深圳。陈云生跟几位在香港的同学一起筹钱，到深圳开办了一家运输公司，帮一些工厂运货。后来，他又在深圳开了贸易公司，出口中国产品。2000 年，陈云生开始长住南非，依然经营贸易，销售中国产品。之所以留在南非发展，有一个颇具戏剧性的原因：南非的气候治好了他的老毛病。

原来，他在深圳读中学的时候，经常踢足球。"踢完球，满身大汗。水龙头，叽……"他形象地模仿着往身上冲水的声音。

据陈云生回忆，那是他 14 岁的时候，差不多天天都这样，结果落下了风湿关节炎。有时，关节整夜整夜地痛，睡不着觉。为了治病，他可没少拔火罐，腿上至今还有很多疤。

他在香港的时候，就开始与南非有贸易往来了。有一次，他去南非住了 20 多天，结果发现脚和关节不怎么痛了。后来，他又去南非谈生意，住了一个多月，关节也不痛了。1998

陈云生接受专访。（来源：《晶报》）
Chan Wan Sang accepts an exclusive interview.
(Photo: *Daily Sunshine*)

年，他在南非注册了公司。2000 年 12 月，他就开始长住南非。

陈云生在南非的事业，也不是一蹴而就的。"刚到南非时，人生路不熟，要做生意，要找客户，我又不懂英文。"他说，"谈生意要翻译，有时翻译不做了，我又要去找人，好辛苦。"意想不到的是，陈云生发现，自己不懂英语、需要翻译，也带来了一定的好处：有的客户喜欢跟他做生意，觉得他是真真正正从中国来的，从他那里可以买到真真正正的中国货。

投身社会事务，助力侨胞抱团

在南非的生意做了四五年，就上了正轨，陈云生开始积极投身社会事务。

2005 年 8 月，南非客家联谊会成立，受会长李凤光邀请，陈云生担任了常务副会长。"当时不需要用很多时间去跟生意了，就有时间抽出来做客家联谊会。"陈云生说。

客家是广东的三大民系之一（另外两个是广府和潮汕）。客家人的足迹遍及海内外，国内主要分布在广东、福建、广西、江西、湖南、台湾等地，国外分散在 80 多个国家和地区。目前南非约有 3 万客家人，约占南非华侨华人的十分之一。

对于南非客家联谊会创办的主要目的，陈云生有一个通俗的概括："客家人在南非有什么事情，我们就照顾一下他们。"他举例说，客家联谊会里面有很多老华侨，经济条件不是很好，因为他们中很少有人做生意。"所以，我们就照顾他们，有什么困难就帮他们。"另外，如果有客家人来到南非后走散了，或者丢了护照、被人抢了钱，客家联谊会就去资助他们，安排他们回中国。从 2011 年开始，他担任了第三任、第四任会长，为时 6 年。接着，他组织创办了南非 – 中国深圳总商会、南非 – 中国深圳联谊会。

南非 1998 年与中国建交，中国目前是南非最大的全球贸易伙伴，南非是中国在非洲的第一大贸易伙伴。中国和南非都是金砖国家（其他 3 个国家是巴西、俄罗斯、印度），南非是 2011 年加入这个合作组织的。随着两国关系不断巩固、经贸关系和经济技术合作不断加强，旅居南非的深圳籍乡亲、曾在深圳工作生活过的海外侨胞希望有一个专门的组织帮助他们抱团发展，并且为深圳创新发展贡献力量。

2016 年，在深圳市侨办、市侨联支持下，陈云生等热心侨领开始筹备南非 – 中国深圳总商会、南非 – 中国深圳联谊会。2017 年 5 月，南非 – 中国深圳总商会、南非 – 中国深圳联谊会正式成立，陈云生被推举为会长。同年 11 月，他就率领总商会、联谊会代表团到深圳参观交流，重点考察了福田区。

重任在肩，不辱使命

创办南非 – 中国深圳总商会之后，陈云生觉得自己的担子更重了。"我们商会最重要的任务就是，将深圳的企业、产品引出去，将外国的企业引进来。"他说。

这个商会主要为深圳的企业和政府部门提供在南非的商务及政府机构沟通协调服务，也是一个互相交流的平台。接待到南非考察的深圳企业，是商会的日常。陈云生举例说，深圳市商务局、市贸促委和深圳的企业需要南非的资源时，商会就提供给他们。商会还定期与南非当地机构和企业举办线上及线下交流会，多次参与华侨华人产业交易会。

2018 年 10 月，这个商会在约翰内斯堡主办了第四届国际深圳社团大会暨南非·深圳经贸交流会，其间举行了深圳城市推介及交流座谈会、国际深圳社团圆桌会议、海外深圳社团建设微视频网络大赛等一系列活动，推动深圳、南非两地的项目签约，为全球深圳人搭建联谊及商务合作平台。深圳侨务代表团也前去参加了系列活动，与 600 多名来自五大洲 23 个国家的深圳社团的代表、企业家以及南非各界精英畅叙友情，共商合作。

2018 年 10 月 27 日，第四届国际深圳社团大会暨南非·深圳经贸交流会欢迎晚宴上的文艺表演。
（来源：非洲华媒）

An artistic performance at the welcome banquet for the 4th International Conference of Shenzhen Association & South Africa-Shenzhen Trade Conference 2018 on October 27, 2018. (Photo: African Chinese Media)

国际深圳社团大会始于 2015 年，是深圳侨务部门指导、支持海外深圳社团主办的盛会，有助于发挥深圳海外社团网络的影响力，提升深圳的形象和知名度。

南非西北大学是第四届国际深圳社团大会的参会机构之一。在大会举行之前 5 个月，这所大学的代表团就访问过深圳，对深圳的创新创业环境留下了深刻印象。

那次访问，就是陈云生促成的。当时，南非西北大学受邀组团到浙江访问，陈云生得知后，就跟组织方联系，安排代表团先到深圳进行两天访问。陈云生陪同他们走访了深圳博物馆和深圳 3 家科技型企业与研究单位。

后来，南非西北大学跟深圳方面敲定了药物检验领域的合作项目。"做了几年了！"谈起这事，陈云生言语里透着欣慰。在他带领下，短短几年，南非 – 中国深圳总商会就发展成了南非影响力最大的侨团之一。但他又谦虚地说，因为有需要，"我们不做事不行啊"。自己年纪大了，做这些好事也是回馈社会。南非 – 中国深圳总商会、南非 – 中国深圳联谊会也秉承了深圳开放包容的作风。不管是土生土长的深圳人，还是曾经在深圳生活、工作的人士，都欢迎入会。"来了就是深圳人嘛！"陈云生说。

情牵故乡，全力以赴支持两国抗疫

2023 年 4 月，陈云生拜访了深圳市贸促委，深入交流了合作设立驻外经贸联络处、展销中心和组织企业赴南非举办储能博览会、展销会等事宜，并达成共识。他说，这是他这次中国之行的主要目的之一。

这是 2020 年新冠疫情发生后，陈云生第一次回到家乡。他说，疫情前，他经常回来列席广东省和深圳市的人大或政协会议。他还应邀到北京参加过阅兵、国庆等活动。他说，自己心里是挂念着家乡的。"我是深圳人嘛！"

这次回来，他先去了宝安区，发现那里变化好大。"深圳的建设是全世界一流的，快得不得了！"他兴奋地总结道。而在疫情的严峻时刻，陈云生带领南非 – 中国深圳总商会全力以赴，为中国和南非抗击疫情作贡献，一切都历历在目。

2020 年和 2021 年，商会在组织、协调抗疫物资的捐赠、接收和发放方面做了很多工作。他们还收集疫情和社会信息，举办会员线上座谈，了解会员面临的困难，加强会员间的沟通。

疫情之初，商会协调力量，发动会员捐赠口罩，运往广东、安徽等地，支援祖国抗击疫情。其中有一批是向深圳捐赠的 3.6 万个医用口罩，从陈云生带领大家发起募捐，到物资抵达深圳，短短 4 天就完成了跨越 1 万多公里的爱心接力。原来，在南非那边，募捐、采购、联系航空快递公司等环节是同步进行的。物资运到香港机场后，卸货、清关、提货都高效完成。在南非 – 中国深圳总商会荣誉会长陈镇文的帮助下，接力运输，经皇岗口岸运抵深圳。

疫情在南非蔓延之后，商会组织力量，最大效率接收各方提供的抗疫物资，向有需要的地区、机构和社会团体发放抗疫物资和生活物资，为商会会员提供抗疫物资和疫情咨询。

2020 年到 2021 年，商会及会员个人累计捐赠口罩 20 余万个，接收口罩 10 余

南非 – 中国深圳总商会向南非国民议会捐赠 1 万个医用口罩。
The South Africa-China Shenzhen General Chamber of Commerce donates 10,000 medical masks to the National Assembly of South Africa.

万个，此外捐赠手套、防护服、生活物资等价值 50 余万南非兰特（约合 26 万元人民币）。

热心公益，惠及多方

平时，南非 – 中国深圳总商会也积极参与南非的慈善公益事业，多次向农村贫困地区积极提供慈善捐助。

2019 年 12 月，商会把年会搬到西北省马里科镇举行，并且应拉马福萨基金会号召，向当地 200 名贫困老人和 400 名小学生捐赠了价值 20 万元人民币的生活、学习用品和圣诞礼物，受到当地政府和社会各界热烈欢迎和高度评价。全场观众欢呼雀跃，用当地语言高呼"中国、中国"。当地儿童现场表演了马林巴和部族传统舞蹈，表达对中国政府和人民的感激之情。

时任中国驻南非大使林松添在捐赠仪式上说，这次活动不仅是扶危济困的慈善义举，也是中国企业积极融入和回馈当地社会的责任担当，更充分体现了中南特殊友好的兄弟情谊，彰显了中南关系源自于民、植根于民、惠及人民的根本属性。

号召举办这次捐赠的拉马福萨基金会，是南非总统拉马福萨发起的慈善组织。

2019 年 12 月 13 日，南非西北省马里科镇捐赠仪式现场。（来源：中国驻南非大使馆官网）
A donation ceremony is held in Groot Marico, North West Province, South Africa on December 13, 2019.
(Photo: Official website of the Chinese Embassy in South Africa)

南非 – 中国深圳总商会是这个基金会的会员，连续多年派出代表参加基金会的慈善晚宴。陈云生回忆说，那年，西北省省长办公室通过基金会找到商会，希望捐助一下贫困的马里科镇。陈云生灵机一动，把商会的年会也安排在那里开，让会员们一起参与公益事业。

2021 年，商会在约翰内斯堡召开年会时，也举办了慈善捐赠仪式，向一家老人院捐赠 7 万南非兰特（约合 3.5 万元人民币）和 30 包大米。

陈云生说，在南非这个第二故乡开展公益活动，既承担了社会责任，有助于华侨华人融入当地社会，也可以提升中国的形象、增进两国人民友谊。

"这些捐款，不光是对华人，对我们国家也有影响。"他说，同南非的困难群众、政府官员打交道，捐款捐物给他们，可以让他们对南非华人的印象好些，对中国印象好些。"我今年要再搞个更大型的。"他透露说。

2021 年 11 月 14 日，南非－中国深圳总商会向一家老人院捐赠 7 万南非兰特和 30 包大米。
The South Africa-China Shenzhen General Chamber of Commerce donates 70,000 South African rands and 30 bags of rice to a nursing home on November 14, 2021.

警民合作，力保侨胞平安

陈云生还曾经在南非华人警民合作中心担任要职。"做了两年干事长，做了 3 年常务副会长，现在年纪大了，是名誉主任。"

这个中心成立于 2004 年。截至 2022 年 10 月，已在南非各省、市推动建立 14 个省、市级警民中心，成为南非侨胞危难时刻首先想到的"呼救机"和"避风港"。

南非华人警民合作中心致力于维护侨胞的生命财产安全，协助南非警方侦破涉及华侨华人的案件。近年来，警民合作中心搭建了网络安全服务平台和"一键报警"系统，还组织武装保安在中国商城区域巡逻。

陈云生举例说，华侨华人如果在南非遭遇抢劫、绑架，都可以向警民合作中心求助。如果丢了护照、没钱买机票回中国，警民合作中心也会提供帮助。侨胞之间和家庭内部的纠纷，警民合作中心也会帮忙调解。总之，都是为华侨华人服务。

他说，南非是一个比较先进、开放的非洲国家，会有非洲其他国家的人偷渡到南非抢劫，有些人得手之后，就有本钱跑回自己国家当老板了。警民合作中心就是要配合警方，跟这些人作斗争。

洞悉商机，鼓励"走出去"也鼓励"回来"

虽然南非有些治安问题，但陈云生认为，南非是适合中国人去做生意的。他分析说，非洲生产落后，依赖进口，而在非洲国家里，南非的局势是比较安定的，没有内战。除了中兴、华为、大疆，深圳其他一些企业也在南非发展得不错。

他很看好太阳能的商机。南非经常停电，他家里、公司里全都靠自己用太阳能发电。现在，南非－中国深圳总商会就准备牵头筹资，帮几位会员把太阳能产品的生意做大，把深圳高科技的太阳能逆变器、电池以及东莞的太阳能板卖到南非去。那几位会员已经在南非做得不错了，但自身资金有限，所以商会打算筹一些钱让他们去做，商会也能赚些钱。

据陈云生介绍，有很多企业在南非做小型的太阳能发电设备，有些用户在家里装一台太阳能逆变器、一块太阳能板，看得了电视、煮得了饭、烧得了开水，就行了。"但我们做的不是"，而是要满足冰箱等全套家电的用电需求。

另外，广东河源也有一家工厂在跟他商量，准备在非洲开厂，生产逆变器。除了"走出去"，陈云生还希望有更多的海外华侨华人能回中国投资，留学生毕业后尽量回国工作。每逢广东省侨办、深圳市侨办邀请海外华侨华人青年来中国参加活动、了解中国，他都鼓励年轻人回来看看。

他说，南非有不少中国留学生，而南非一些大学在医药领域是很不错的，比如西北大学、开普敦大学。"在南非读书的高科技人才，做医药、当医生的，国家很需要这些人。"

　　[除署名外，本文图片均由受访者陈云生提供。参考资料：新华社、《人民日报（海外版）》、外交部官网、中国驻约翰内斯堡总领事馆官网、中国侨网、《深圳特区报》、《深圳侨报》、深圳市贸促委官网。]

Chan Wan Sang

Building good relationships in the Rainbow Nation and serving Shenzhen enterprises "going abroad"

Born in 1949, Chan Wan Sang is from Dameisha, Yantian, Shenzhen. In 1969, he went to Hong Kong to make a living. In 2000, he settled in South Africa to run foreign trade business.

He was the third and fourth president of the South African Hakka Association, and is honorary president of the association. He founded the South Africa-China Shenzhen General Chamber of Commerce in 2017 and has served as president. He has actively cooperated with Shenzhen in carrying out various tasks in South Africa and led the chamber of commerce to develop into one of the most influential overseas Chinese groups in South Africa. In 2018, the chamber of commerce hosted the 4th International Conference of Shenzhen Association & South Africa-Shenzhen Trade Conference 2018, which was a complete success. During the COVID-19 pandemic, the chamber of commerce actively organized and coordinated the donation, receipt and distribution of anti-epidemic materials, making contributions to the fight against the disease in China and South Africa. Chan has been enthusiastic about the public good. He serves as honorary director of the South Africa Chinese Community and Police Cooperation Centre, consultant to the All-Africa Association for Peaceful Reunification of China, overseas member of the Guangdong Province Federation of Returned Overseas Chinese, and overseas honorary president of the Shenzhen Overseas Exchange Association.

In April 2023, Chan Wan Sang returned to his motherland from Johannesburg, South Africa. He spent a month here participating in many exchange activities and meeting many old friends. We made use of an interval to conduct our exclusive interview with him in Shenzhen on a day in late April.

The interview took place in 2023.

"I'm not good at talking!" Chan gave a "warning" in the beginning. In fact, he was just too modest, as many overseas Chinese leaders are. Chan talked a lot about his adventure abroad, his experience of serving overseas Chinese and the local society, and the business opportunities in South Africa, known as the "Rainbow Nation."

He is a Hakka. His early life in Shenzhen and Hong Kong also left traces in his language. He likes to converse in Cantonese (commonly known as "the Canton vernacular"), with a mixture of Hakka and Mandarin pronunciations. At the end of the interview, he chose to have photos taken in front of a background wall carrying the Chinese characters of "serve the people." He likes the slogan very much.

By chance, he stayed in South Africa for development

Chan was born in Dameisha, Yantian, Shenzhen in December 1949. He had an elder sister. After graduating from Shenzhen Middle School, he returned to Yantian to raise crops. In 1969, he went to Hong Kong alone to make a living.

In Hong Kong, Chan started out as a vegetable hawker. After earning some money, he partnered with two of his middle school classmates to open a decoration company. Later, he partnered with a friend to start a construction company. In 1980, the spring breeze of the reform and opening-up brought Chan back to his hometown Shenzhen after a long absence. Chan raised money together with several classmates in Hong Kong to set up a transportation company in Shenzhen to help some factories transport goods. Later, he opened a trading company in Shenzhen to export Chinese products. In 2000, Chan began to live in South Africa, still engaged in trade and selling Chinese products. There was a rather dramatic reason why he stayed in South Africa for development: the climate there cured his chronic ailment.

When he was in middle school in Shenzhen, he often played football. "After playing football, I was sweating profusely. Then I turned on the faucet," he vividly imitated the sound of water being poured on his body.

According to Chan, he did this almost every day when he was 14 years old, and he ended up with rheumatoid arthritis. Sometimes, his joints hurt all night long, which made him sleepless. In order to cure this, he had cupping treatment frequently, leaving many scars on his legs.

When he was in Hong Kong, he started doing business with the South African side. Once, he lived in South Africa for more than 20 days, and found that his feet and joints did not hurt much. Later, he went to South Africa to discuss business and stayed there for more than a month without joint pain. In 1998, he registered a company in South Africa. In December 2000, he began to live in South Africa.

Chan's career in South Africa was not accomplished in day. "When I first arrived in South Africa, I was a stranger in an even stranger land. I wanted to do business and find clients, but I didn't know English," he said. "I needed an interpreter when I was discussing business. Sometimes the interpreter quit, and I had to find another one. It was very hard." Unexpectedly, Chan found that not knowing English and needing an interpreter also brought certain benefits: some clients liked to do business with him, thinking that he was really from China and that they could buy real Chinese goods from him.

Engaged in social affairs and helping overseas Chinese to unite

After four or five years, Chan's business in South Africa was on the right track, and he began to actively participate in social affairs.

In August 2005, the South African Hakka Association was established. At the invitation of its president, Li Fengguang, Chan served as executive vice president. "I didn't need to spend a lot of time on business, so I had time to do things for the Hakka association," Chan said.

Hakka is one of the three major ethnic groups in Guangdong (the other two are Cantonese and Chaoshan). The Hakka people have traveled all over the world. They are mainly distributed in Guangdong, Fujian, Guangxi, Jiangxi, Hunan, Taiwan and some other places in China, and they are scattered in more than 80 countries and regions abroad. At present, there are about 30,000 Hakkas in South Africa, accounting for about one-tenth of the overseas Chinese in South Africa.

Regarding the main purpose of the South African Hakka Association, Chan gave a colloquial summary: "We can take care of the Hakka people in South Africa when they are in need." For example, there are many elderly overseas Chinese in the association, whose financial conditions are not very good because few of them do business. "So, we take care of them and help them if they have any difficulty," Chan said. In addition, if some Hakka people, after coming to South Africa, got separated, lost their passport, or were robbed of their money, the Hakka association will help them and arrange for them to return to China. Beginning in 2011, Chan served as the association's third and fourth president, for six years. Then, he founded the South Africa-China Shenzhen General Chamber of Commerce and the South Africa-China Shenzhen Association.

South Africa established diplomatic relations with China in 1998. Now China is

South Africa's largest global trading partner, and South Africa is China's largest trading partner in Africa. China and South Africa are among the BRICS countries (the other three countries are Brazil, Russia, and India), a cooperation mechanism that South Africa joined in 2011. As the relationship between the two countries continued to consolidate, and their economic and trade relations as well as economic and technological cooperation continued to strengthen, Shenzhen immigrants in South Africa and the overseas Chinese in South Africa who had worked or lived in Shenzhen were in need of a special organization to help them develop together and contribute to Shenzhen's innovation and development.

In 2016, with the support of the Overseas Chinese Affairs Office of the Shenzhen Municipal Government and the Shenzhen Federation of Returned Overseas Chinese, Chan and other enthusiastic overseas Chinese leaders began to prepare for the establishment of the South Africa-China Shenzhen General Chamber of Commerce and the South Africa-China Shenzhen Association. In May 2017, the South Africa-China Shenzhen General Chamber of Commerce and the South Africa-China Shenzhen Association were formally established, and Chan was elected as president. In November of the same year, he led a delegation from the general chamber of commerce and the association to visit Shenzhen, mainly Futian District.

Shouldering heavy responsibility and fulfilling the mission

After founding the South Africa-China Shenzhen General Chamber of Commerce, Chan felt that his responsibility was even heavier. "The most important tasks of our chamber of commerce are to help Shenzhen enterprises and products go abroad and to bring foreign enterprises to Shenzhen," he said.

This chamber of commerce mainly provides business and government communication and coordination services in South Africa for enterprises and government departments in Shenzhen. It is also a platform for mutual exchanges. It is the daily routine of the chamber of commerce to receive Shenzhen enterprises that visit South Africa. For example, Chan said, when the Commerce Bureau of the Shenzhen Municipality, the China Council for the Promotion of International Trade Shenzhen Municipal Committee (CCPIT Shenzhen) and enterprises in Shenzhen need resources in South Africa, the chamber of commerce will provide them. The chamber of commerce also regularly holds online and offline exchange meetings with local institutions and enterprises in South Africa, and has participated in overseas Chinese industry fairs many times.

In October 2018, this chamber of commerce hosted the 4th International

Conference of Shenzhen Association & South Africa-Shenzhen Trade Conference 2018 in Johannesburg, including a series of activities such as the promotion and exchange symposium for Shenzhen, the international Shenzhen association roundtable conference, and the online competition of micro-videos for overseas Shenzhen association construction. The events promoted the signing of projects in Shenzhen and South Africa, and built a platform for networking and business cooperation for Shenzhen people around the world. An overseas Chinese affairs delegation of Shenzhen attended the activities, sharing friendship and discussing cooperation with more than 600 participants, including representatives of Shenzhen associations from 23 countries on five continents, entrepreneurs, and elites from all walks of life in South Africa.

Inaugurated in 2015, the International Conference of Shenzhen Association is a grand event hosted by overseas Chinese associations under the guidance and support of Shenzhen's overseas Chinese affairs departments. It helps to exert the influence of overseas Shenzhen association networks and enhance Shenzhen's image and popularity.

The North-West University of South Africa participated in the 4th International Conference of Shenzhen Association. Five months before the conference, a delegation of the university visited Shenzhen and was deeply impressed by its innovation and entrepreneurship environment. The trip was facilitated by Chan. At first, the North-West University was invited to send a delegation to visit Zhejiang Province. After learning about it, Chan contacted the organizer and arranged for the delegation to visit Shenzhen for two days before going to Zhejiang. Chan accompanied them to visit the Shenzhen Museum and three technology-based enterprises and research institutions in Shenzhen.

Later, the North-West University finalized a cooperation project with Shenzhen in drug testing. "It has been running for several years!" Chan was gratified to talk about this. Under his leadership, in just a few years, the South Africa-China Shenzhen General Chamber of Commerce has developed into one of the most influential overseas Chinese groups in South Africa. But he said modestly that they couldn't stop doing those things when the need was there. As he becomes old, he gives back to the society by doing these good deeds. The South Africa-China Shenzhen General Chamber of Commerce and the South Africa-China Shenzhen Association also uphold Shenzhen's open and inclusive style. Natives of Shenzhen and whoever used to live or work in Shenzhen are all welcome to join. "You become a Shenzhener once you come to live in Shenzhen!" Chan said.

Loving his hometown, going all out to support China and South Africa in fight against COVID-19 pandemic

In April 2023, Chan visited the China Council for the Promotion of International Trade Shenzhen Municipal Committee (CCPIT Shenzhen) for in-depth discussions on cooperation in setting up a foreign economic and trade liaison office as well as exhibition and sales centers, and organizing enterprises to hold energy storage expos and trade fairs in South Africa. A consensus was then reached on these matters. He said that it was one of the main purposes of his trip to China.

This is the first time Chan has returned to his hometown after the COVID-19 outbreak in 2020. He said that before the pandemic, he often came back to attend the annual provincial and municipal meetings of the People's Congress or the Chinese People's Political Consultative Conference in Guangdong and Shenzhen. He was also invited to Beijing for military parades, National Day celebrations and other activities. He has always been missing his hometown. "Because I'm from Shenzhen!"

This time, he visited Bao'an District first, just to find a lot of changes there. "Shenzhen's construction is top-notch in the world, and it's extremely fast!" Chan concluded excitedly. At the critical moments of COVID-19, Chan led the South Africa-China Shenzhen General Chamber of Commerce to go all out to contribute to the fight against the disease in China and South Africa. Everything is clearly remembered.

In 2020 and 2021, the chamber of commerce did a lot of work in organizing and coordinating the donation, reception and distribution of anti-epidemic materials. It also collected COVID-19 and social information, hold online forums for its members, learned about the difficulties faced by its members, and strengthened communication among the members.

At the beginning of the COVID-19 outbreak, the chamber of commerce coordinated all forces and mobilized its members to donate masks, which were sent to Guangdong, Anhui and other places in China to support the motherland in fighting the disease. Among the medical masks, 36,000 were donated to Shenzhen. From the fundraising initiated by Chan, to the arrival of the masks in Shenzhen, a relay of love spanning more than 10,000 kilometers was completed in just four days. It turned out that the South African side carried out the donations and contacted the air express company at the same time. After the masks were transported to the Hong Kong International Airport, unloading, customs clearance and delivery were all efficiently done. With the help of Chen Zhenwen, honorary president of the South Africa-China Shenzhen General Chamber of Commerce, the masks were transported to Shenzhen via Huanggang Port.

After the pandemic spread in South Africa, the chamber of commerce organized various forces to receive anti-epidemic materials provided by all parties with maximum efficiency, distributed anti-epidemic materials and living materials to regions, institutions and social groups in need, and provided anti-epidemic materials and consultation for its members.

From 2020 to 2021, the chamber of commerce and its members donated more than 200,000 masks and received more than 100,000 masks. In addition, they donated gloves, protective clothing, and daily necessities, worth more than 500,000 South African rands (about 260,000 yuan).

Enthusiastic about public good, benefiting many parties

In normal times, the South Africa-China Shenzhen General Chamber of Commerce has also actively participated in charity and public welfare undertakings in South Africa, and has actively provided charitable donations to poverty-stricken rural areas on many occasions.

In December 2019, the chamber of commerce moved its annual meeting to the town of Groot Marico in North West Province, and, at the call of the Cyril Ramaphosa Foundation, donated 200,000 yuan worth of living materials, school supplies and Christmas gifts to 200 poor elderly people and 400 primary school students there, which was warmly welcomed and highly appraised by the local government and all walks of life. The audience cheered and shouted "China, China" in the local language. Local children performed marimba and traditional tribal dances to express their gratitude to the Chinese government and people.

Lin Songtian, then Chinese ambassador to South Africa, said at the donation ceremony that this event was not only a charitable act of helping those in need, but also showed the responsibility of Chinese enterprises to actively integrate into and give back to the local society. Furthermore, he said, the event fully reflected the special friendship between China and South Africa, as well as the fundamental nature of China-South Africa relations: originating from the people, rooted in the people, and benefiting the people.

The Cyril Ramaphosa Foundation, which called for the donation, is a charitable organization initiated by South African President Matamela Cyril Ramaphosa. The South Africa-China Shenzhen General Chamber of Commerce is a member of the foundation, and has sent representatives to the foundation's charity dinner for many years. Chan recalled that in 2019, the office of the premier of North West contacted the chamber of commerce through the foundation, hoping the chamber of commerce to donate to the impoverished town of Groot Marico. Chan had a brainwave and arranged for the annual meeting of the chamber of commerce to be held there as well, enabling its members to participate in public welfare undertakings together.

In 2021, when the chamber of commerce held its annual meeting in Johannesburg, it also held a charitable donation ceremony, donating 70,000 South African rands (about 35,000 yuan) and 30 bags of rice to a nursing home.

Carrying out public welfare activities in South Africa, Chan's second hometown, not only undertakes social responsibilities, helps overseas Chinese integrate into the local society, but also enhances the image of Shenzhen and the friendship between the two peoples, he said.

"Donations and other deeds have an impact on both overseas Chinese and the country." Dealing with the needy people and government officials in South Africa and donating money and materials to them can make them have a better impression of the Chinese in South Africa and of China, Chan said. "I'm going to hold a bigger event this year," he revealed.

Cooperating with police to safeguard overseas Chinese

Chan also held an important position at the South Africa Chinese Community and Police Cooperation Centre. "I used to be secretary-general for two years, and executive vice chairman for three years. As I get old, now I am honorary director."

This center was established in 2004. By October 2022, it had prompted the establishment of 14 provincial and municipal community-police centers in various provinces and cities in South Africa, which have become a preferred way to call for help and a "safe haven" in times of crisis for overseas Chinese in South Africa.

The South Africa Chinese Community and Police Cooperation Centre is committed to safeguarding the life and property of overseas Chinese, and assisting the South African police in solving cases involving overseas Chinese. In recent years, the center has built an Internet security service platform and a system of "calling the police by one button." It also organizes armed security guards to patrol the China Malls.

For example, Chan said, if overseas Chinese are robbed or kidnapped in South Africa, they can turn to the Chinese Community and Police Cooperation Centre for help. If they lose their passports and have no money to buy a plane ticket back to China, the center will also provide assistance. The center also helps mediate disputes between overseas Chinese and within their families. In short, what the center does is to serve the overseas Chinese.

South Africa is a relatively advanced and open country in Africa, and some people from other African countries smuggle into South Africa to rob, Chan said. Some of them succeed, and they take the money back to their own countries to start a business. The Chinese Community and Police Cooperation Centre cooperates with the police to fight against these people.

Knowing business opportunities well, encouraging both "going abroad" and "coming back"

Although there are some security problems in South Africa, Chan believes that it is suitable for Chinese people to do business there. According to his analysis, Africa is backward in production and depends on imports, and, among African countries, the situation in South Africa is relatively stable, with no civil wars. In addition to ZTE, Huawei, and DJI, some other companies from Shenzhen are also developing well in South Africa.

Chan is optimistic about the business opportunities in solar energy. South Africa suffers from frequent power outages, so his home and company rely on solar power to generate electricity. Now, the South Africa-China Shenzhen General Chamber of Commerce prepares to take the lead in raising funds to help several of its members expand their business in solar products, selling Shenzhen's high-tech solar inverters and batteries and Dongguan's solar panels to South Africa. Those members have already done well in South Africa, but they have limited funds. So the chamber of commerce intends to raise some money for them, and the chamber of commerce also expects to make some money from the business.

According to Chan, there are many companies selling small-scale solar power generation equipment in South Africa. Some users just need to install a solar inverter and a solar panel at home, so that they can watch TV, cook rice, and boil water. "But we won't do that," Chan said. They aim to meet the electricity demand of a complete set of home appliances including a refrigerator.

In addition, a factory in Heyuan, Guangdong Province has also discussed with Chan to open a factory in Africa to produce inverters. In addition to "going abroad," Chan also hopes that more overseas Chinese can return to China to invest, and that international students can try their best to return to China to work after graduation. Whenever the

Overseas Chinese Affairs Office of the Guangdong Provincial Government and the Overseas Chinese Affairs Office of the Shenzhen Municipal Government invite overseas Chinese youth to come to China to participate in activities and learn about China, he encourages young people to come back to China and have a look.

There are many Chinese students in South Africa, and some universities there are very good in the field of medicine, such as the North-West University and the University of Cape Town, Chan said. "The high-tech talents who are studying in South Africa, such as those learning medicine and those to be doctors, are much needed by China."

(Photos courtesy of Chan Wan Sang, except for those with credit. References: Xinhua News Agency, *People's Daily Overseas Edition*, the official website of the Ministry of Foreign Affairs of China, the official website of the Chinese Consulate General in Johannesburg, chinaqw.com, *Shenzhen Special Zone Daily*, *Shenzhen Overseas Chinese News*, and the official website of CCPIT Shenzhen.)

吴裕光

深耕侨务工作，为 8200 多位归侨
侨眷排过忧解过难

吴裕光（来源：《晶报》）
Wu Yuguang (Photo: *Daily Sunshine*)

　　吴裕光，越南归侨，原深圳市光明新区侨联一届副主席、原深圳市光明街道侨联主席。1950 年出生于越南广宁省云屯县。1978 年底因越南排华回国，并于 1979 年 1 月被安置在深圳光明华侨畜牧场（广东省国营光明农场）。

　　数十年来，吴裕光深耕侨务工作，以为侨服务为宗旨，为光明地区归侨侨眷谋福祉，解决归侨侨眷们急难愁盼的问题，广受侨界群众肯定和好评。2005—2009 年连续 5 年获评深圳市侨联系统"先进个人"称号；2007 年被中国侨联授予"从事侨联工作 20 年以上工作者"称号；2008 年被广东省侨联授予"从事侨联工作 30 年以上工作者"称号；2009 年被国务院侨务办公室、中华全国归国华侨联合会授予"全国归侨侨眷先进个人"称号。

采访时间：2022 年。

"万丈高楼平地起，辉煌只能靠自己。"在圳美社区，吴裕光家中的墙上挂着一幅大照片，那是儿子吴强在 2012 年 3 月 23 日结婚时他们在家门口的合影，而在这张照片下面，就配着这么一句励志的话语。一直以来，吴裕光都将其作为鞭策自己和三个子女努力上进的座右铭。

圳美社区位于深圳市光明区新湖街道北片区，与东莞市的黄江镇相毗邻。这里的户籍居民中，广府原住民和归侨侨眷的比例接近 1∶1。归侨侨眷之中，大多是从越南回来的，72 岁的吴裕光就是他们中的一员。

越南记忆：上过战场，打过美国

1950 年，吴裕光出生在越南广宁省云屯县下龙乡的一个华人家庭里。云屯县位于广宁省的东部和东南部地区，60 个大大小小的岛屿星罗棋布，吴裕光在越南的老家就在其中一个岛上。云屯县距下龙市（如今的广宁省省会，市内著名的旅游景点下龙湾有"海上桂林"之美誉）约 50 公里，与越南芒街（跟中国交界）的直线距离仅 70 多公里。

吴裕光家里有兄弟姐妹一共 9 个，他排行老二。据吴裕光介绍，爷爷是中国人，在日军侵华时从广西逃难到了越南。吴裕光的父亲也是在越南出生的。吴裕光的外公是中国人，外婆是越南人，但他们在骨子里依然认为自己是中国人。

在吴裕光的记忆中，虽然那个时候是生活在越南，但是他们的根还是在中国。"很多越南人其实都是中国人的后裔，他们很多人认了祖宗，祠堂、神台上写的都是中文字。越南的很多文化习俗，像清明、端午、中秋、重阳、春节等，都跟中国差不多。"

"当时我们在越南的那个村里，基本都是华人，大家都认祖归宗，都学中文，越文学校反而开不起来，我从一年级到初中，学的都是中文。"吴裕光透露，自己的初中毕业证就是在越南那边的中文学校拿到的，"胡志明（越南无产阶级革命家，1890—1969 年）还在的时候，越南是可以随时学中文的，之后就不能再学中文了"。

1969 年，吴裕光初中毕业，随即进入了一所越文学校读高中。"那边的高中

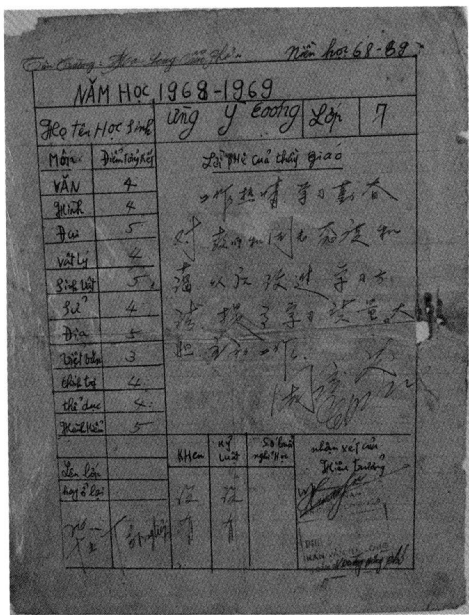

吴裕光在越南拿到的初中毕业证书。（来源：《晶报》）

Wu Yuguang's junior high school diploma obtained in Vietnam. (Photo: *Daily Sunshine*)

没有中文学校，而且当时我们在越南的乡里，读高中的人不多，也就三五个人。不过，越南的高中学校里有一门课是中文。"吴裕光顺便补充了一句："现在在越南，会中文的人可吃香了，工资很高的。"

高中毕业后，吴裕光就去参军了。他要保卫自己的家园，于是参加了越南战争。这是一场越南人民反对美国侵略、实现国家统一的民族解放战争，当然其中也少不了中国对越南人民正义事业的大力支持。用吴裕光的话来说，就是"越南打美国，他们上前线去打美国侵略者"。

1975 年 5 月，越南战争结束，越南实现了国家统一。从部队退伍回来后，吴裕光就被安排在一个合作社里当会计员。这个合作社其实是一个船运公司，男的在社里负责在海上跑运输、打鱼，女的则在家负责后勤工作。因为上过高中，也算是一个有文化的人，他成了合作社里的一名干部，手下管理着 50 多名妇女，主要负责加工面条给国家。

很可惜，这种宁静的生活很快就被打破，吴裕光及其家人的命运发生了重大的转折。

初到光明：一片荒凉，人少地多

自 1975 年越南统一以后，中越关系开始恶化，大规模的排华运动在该国蔓延开来。在 1979 年以前，当地针对华人的暴力活动司空见惯，而且在 1979 年之后仍未绝迹，甚至还相当严重。

在一篇题为《从排斥到接纳：越南华人政策的转变》的学术论文中，厦门大学历史系教授陈衍德曾一针见血地指出，这主要是"当时的越南领导集团出于对国际层面上和国家利益层面上更深的考虑，同时企图通过阻挠华人生计而达到抑制其经济发展的目的，或者通过转移对国内社会矛盾的视线而达到安抚土著民族的目的"。（参见《世界民族》2008 年第 6 期）

正是因越南政府实施全面的排华政策，20 世纪 70 年代中后期，大批华侨华人纷纷沦为难民，不得不拖家带口逃离越南，经水路和陆路回归祖国或前往第三国。1978 年底，吴裕光和家人从越南广宁省云屯县坐船到了芒街，再向北跨过北仑河，进入中国境内。他们在广西东兴逗留了一个月，次年 1 月，被安置在广东省宝安县的光明华侨畜牧场（俗称"光明农场"）。

据《深圳侨务史志》记载，光明华侨畜牧场的前身是广东省国营光明农场，始建于 1958 年，是一个国营农牧企业，也是当时深圳归侨侨眷较集中的地方。至 1977 年，农场已经接收了从印度尼西亚、马来西亚、泰国等国回来的归难侨 163 人。1978 年 7 月至 1979 年 6 月，光明华侨畜牧场又先后接收了 6 批 909 户 4349 名被越南当局驱赶的难民（大部分是华侨华人）。当时，中国政府基于人道立场，配合联合国难民署，接收了 25 万余名被越南当局驱赶出来的归难侨，安置在光明华侨畜牧场的就是其中的一部分，约占深圳归侨总数的 20%。

这些从越南回国的归难侨分别被安置在石介头、红坳下、果林、上其、凤凰、东周、木墩、北岗、红湖、圳美等自然村，共分 18 个点。另据《光明归侨 30 年》记载，当年农场按人均 6 平方米给归侨分配了砖瓦房，男未满 60 岁、女未满 50 岁的全部安排为农场职工。虽然创业初期正式职工人均工资只有 29 元，但在那个时候能当上国营农场职工还是周边乡镇农民十分羡慕的事情。

当年安置越南归侨的果林村。（来源:《光明归侨 30 年》）
Guolin Village, where returned overseas Chinese from Vietnam were housed. (Photo: *The 30 Years of Returned Overseas Chinese in Guangming*)

时至今日，吴裕光仍然清楚地记得，他们一家来到光明的时间是 1979 年 1 月 21 日，安置地点是圳美大队。"我们当时回来这里就是种稻谷，后来又种甘蔗，还有部分人去种象草，养奶牛。我们一家就住在圳美大队，当时队里有个菜场，是光明农场专门给香港供应蔬菜的，就叫圳美菜场。"吴裕光说。

只是，回忆起初到光明的场景，吴裕光连说了几个"荒凉"。"我们当时回来，光明这里还是一片荒凉的土地，有部分本地人都跑去了香港，留下这里的土地都荒废了，没有人耕种。当时的光明真是人少、地多。"吴裕光说得一点儿也没有错，原来光明在改革开放初期还有一个外号，就叫"深圳的西伯利亚"。由于条件还比较差，生产比较落后，经济不宽裕，再加上生活习惯、语言等不适应，部分归难侨人心不稳，初期还出现了个别外逃现象。

回国后不久，吴裕光夫妇与一对
女儿在深圳的合照。

Shortly after returning to China,
Wu Yuguang, his wife and their
daughters have a group photo taken
in Shenzhen.

扎根光明：生活美满，要好好珍惜

近年来，光明区开始逐渐成为深圳科研经济发展的新增长极，也正慢慢实现从一个农场到"世界一流科学城、深圳北部中心"的华丽蝶变。在吴裕光现在所居住的新湖街道圳美社区，南边是风景如画的华侨城光明小镇，北边则是中山大学深圳校区、深圳理工大学和光明科学城大科学装置集群区，一个"粤港澳大湾区国际科技创新中心"正呼之欲出。

"现在光明、深圳都发展起来了，老百姓的生活也比以前好了很多，老了可以有退休金，小孩上学也免费了。我们归侨也享受到了改革开放的红利，如今是最幸福的了。这个不是我一个人讲的，周围的老百姓也都这样讲。"吴裕光口中的"改革开放的红利"，应该是指过去 10 多年以来，省、市、区各级政府在当地实施的侨心工程、安居工程、同富裕工程、三业（学业、就业、创业）工程、华侨农场危房改造工程等重大惠民政策，不断改善着归侨侨眷的整体生活水平。

"现在家家户户住的都是洋楼，干农活儿的人也少了。"说到这里，扎根光明40 多年的吴裕光突然幸福地笑了，"我们现在的生活很美满，说明了党和政府的归侨政策在光明是真正落到了实处，这个改革红利很难得，要好好珍惜。我真的很感动，有时候说到以前经历的磨难，他们（归侨）都会忍不住流泪。"

吴裕光表示，他在越南出生的那个地方是海边，比起越南内地许多山区，经济条件已经算是不错的，但是，相较深圳而言，还是差远了。"就算是现在越南一个

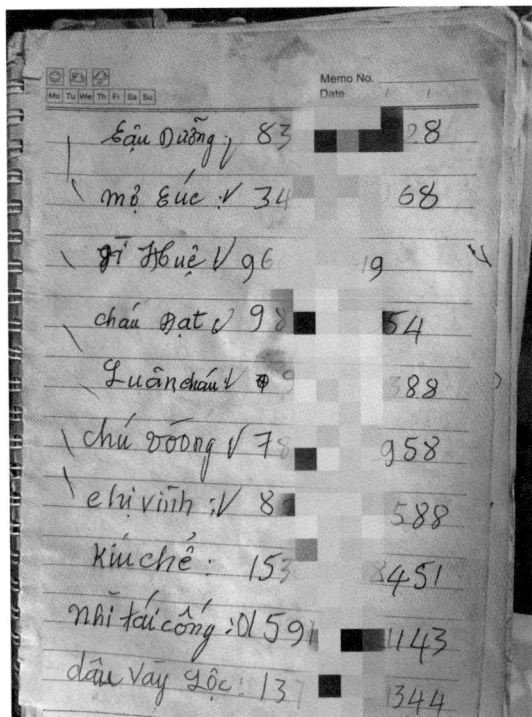

吴裕光用越文记下了越南亲友的联系电话。（来源：《晶报》）
Wu Yuguang wrote down in Vietnamese the contact numbers of his relatives and friends in Vietnam. (Photo: *Daily Sunshine*)

国家的经济全部加起来，都不如深圳一个市，对吧？"吴裕光向记者问道。

他说得一点儿都没错。网上可以查到的公开数据显示：2021 年，越南的 GDP 为 3626 亿美元，而深圳的 GDP 则达 3.07 万亿元人民币，按年度平均汇率计算，约为 4750 亿美元。

"我们现在还有不少亲戚在越南，那边的生活现在怎么样，我是了解的。"在吴裕光家中的电话旁边有个旧笔记本，上面用越文密密麻麻写满了一个个他越南亲友的联系电话。虽然已经离开出生地几十年，但是他每个星期都会与在越南的妹妹、老表、同学或战友联系一两次，以前是打长途电话，现在则是用微信沟通比较多。

令吴裕光感到高兴的是，现在深圳已经开通了直飞到他越南老家云屯县的航班，在新冠疫情之前，深圳至云屯的机票含税价还不到 700 元。"深圳飞到那边也就一个多小时，而且我们在越南的老家距离云屯国际机场就 1 公里远。"吴裕光兴奋地说。

为侨服务：做人的工作，要有感情

当初吴裕光一家被安置在光明农场圳美大队，本来是要务农的，但那个时候，在回国的越南归侨当中，读过书的人并不多，而吴裕光的中文已经是初中毕业水平，越文也有高中毕业的水平。一开始，吴裕光就被安排在队里当记工分的记分员，后来他又当了统计员、出纳员和保管员，再后来还当上了圳美菜场的副场长。

"我在越南读过中文学校，也读过越文学校，回到祖国，在深圳这边又继续读了中专（深圳市工业学校），后来还读过函授的大专、本科。我的中文是在越南学的，与在国内的人接受的中文教育还是有差距的，不提高不行，否则，肯定会对工作有影响。"吴裕光坦言，自己一辈子就喜欢读书，所以才会想着在工作之余不断去努力提高自己的文化水平。从这些话中，或许就不难理解，为何他会将"万丈高楼平地起，辉煌只能靠自己"这一句励志的话，当作时刻鞭策自己的座右铭了。

吴裕光既是归侨，也是一名侨务工作者。他常说，做好侨务工作，为侨服务，是他的职责所在，同时也是他所热爱的事业。在光明，只要见到归侨侨眷有困难，天性坦诚热情的他，都会在第一时间去提供帮助，许多归侨侨眷遇到困难也会主动请吴裕光出谋划策。

2010 年春节，吴裕光（左五）到石介头看望慰问百岁归侨老人黄五妹及其家人。（来源：《光明归侨 30 年》）

Wu Yuguang (fifth from the left) visits Huang Wumei, a centenarian returned overseas Chinese, and her family in Shijietou during the Spring Festival in 2010. (Photo: *The 30 Years of Returned Overseas Chinese in Guangming*)

2000 年，吴裕光当选光明街道侨联主席。过去，在光明街道侨务中心，吴裕光的办公室其实就是一个接待室，每当有归侨侨眷去找他诉苦、求助或者谈心，他总是笑脸相迎，并递上一杯暖暖的热茶。

吴裕光承认，其实在光明做侨办、侨联的工作压力挺大的。"因为很多地方省市的侨办、侨联都要来深圳学习交流，如果搞不好，会影响到安定团结。"

吴裕光还透露了多年以来总结出的一点工作心得："为侨服务，也是做人的工作，一定要有感情。有时候有些工作，不灵活，没有感情，一定不行。侨务工作有自己的特点，有统战性，还牵扯到海内外的关系，我们做好侨务工作也是做好统战工作的一部分，所以一定要做好做细。"

2003 年，为了给回国时因超龄没有安排工作的老归侨争取养老生活补助，吴裕光到市、区有关单位跑了一次又一次。他耐心地倾听老归侨的诉求，对他们的心声感同身受，并不厌其烦地向有关部门详细说明了归侨老人们一生的艰辛。终于，在各级政府和有关部门的高度关注下，光明地区归侨侨眷的困难情况得到根本性改善。当年 10 月，宝安区政府特批当时的光明街道 128 名回国时因超龄没有安排工作的归侨老人每人每月补助生活费 300 元。

吴裕光手捧获得的"全国归侨侨眷先进个人"荣誉证书。
（来源：《晶报》）
Wu Yuguang holds the honorary certificate of "National Advanced Individual of Returned Overseas Chinese and Relatives of Overseas Chinese Nationals Residing in China."
(Photo: *Daily Sunshine*)

2006 年 5 月，吴裕光又到当时的深圳市劳动和社会保障局依法为已退休的 872 名归侨核实退休补贴，其中为 101 名未办手续的归侨老人补办了手续，并帮助他们领到了养老补贴，从而能够在深圳安享晚年。

档案里密密麻麻的数字显示：过去几十年，吴裕光已为 8200 多位归侨侨眷排过忧、解过难。

2006 年 9 月，中国侨联成立 50 周年，给吴裕光颁发了一张"从事侨联工作 20 年以上"的证书，以表彰他不辞辛苦地为广大归侨侨眷和海外侨胞服务；2008 年 12 月，广东省侨联成立 50 周年，吴裕光又被授予"从事侨联工作 30 年以上工作者"荣誉称号；2009 年 7 月，吴裕光再被国务院侨办、中国侨联授予"全国归侨侨眷先进个人"荣誉称号。

对此，吴裕光表示："做了几十年的侨务工作，得了奖我感到非常荣幸。国家给我颁这些奖，可能是觉得我过去几十年的工作做得对，体现了党和政府对我们归侨和侨眷的关心。虽然这是对我个人工作的认可，但我也是代表归侨这个群体领的奖。"

（除署名外，本文图片均由受访者吴裕光提供。参考资料：《深圳侨务史志》《光明归侨 30 年》《世界民族》《向光而生，献礼特区：他们见证光明》《深圳侨报》。）

Wu Yuguang

Deeply involved in overseas Chinese affairs, solving problems for more than 8,200 returned overseas Chinese and relatives of overseas Chinese nationals

Wu Yuguang, or Ngo Du Quang, a returned overseas Chinese from Vietnam, is former vice chairman of the first session of the Federation of Returned Overseas Chinese of Guangming New District, Shenzhen, and former chairman of the Federation of Returned Overseas Chinese of Guangming Subdistrict, Guangming New District, Shenzhen. He was born in 1950 in Van Don County, Quang Ninh Province, Vietnam. He returned to China at the end of 1978 because of Vietnam's anti-Chinese waves, and was resettled in Shenzhen Guangming Overseas Chinese Livestock Farm (Guangdong Province State-run Guangming Farm) in January 1979.

For decades, Wu has been deeply involved in overseas Chinese affairs. With the purpose of serving overseas Chinese, he has sought the well-being of returned overseas Chinese and relatives of overseas Chinese nationals residing in the Guangming area, and solved pressing difficulties and problems that are of great concern to them. He has been widely recognized and praised by the overseas Chinese community. From 2005 to 2009, he was awarded the title of "Advanced Individual" of the Federation of Returned Overseas Chinese system in Shenzhen for five consecutive years. In 2007, he was awarded the title of "Worker in the Federation of Returned Overseas Chinese for More than 20 Years" by the All-China Federation of Returned Overseas Chinese. In 2009, he was awarded the title of "National Advanced Individual of Returned Overseas Chinese and Relatives of Overseas Chinese Nationals Residing in China" by the Overseas Chinese Affairs Office of the State Council and the All-China Federation of Returned Overseas Chinese.

The interview took place in 2022.

"Tall buildings rise from the ground, and glory should be achieved only on oneself." There is a large photo on the wall of Wu Yuguang's home in Zhenmei Community. It is a group photo taken when his son Wu Qiang got married on March 23, 2012. Under the photo, there is an inspirational sentence. For a long time, Wu Yuguang has used it as a motto to spur himself and his three children to go forward.

Zhenmei Community is in the northern area of Xinhu Subdistrict, Guangming District, Shenzhen. It is adjacent to Huangjiang Township, Dongguan City. Among the registered permanent residents here, the ratio of Cantonese locals to returned overseas Chinese and relatives of overseas Chinese nationals is close to 1:1. Most of the returned overseas Chinese and relatives of overseas Chinese nationals came back from Vietnam, and the 72-year-old Wu Yuguang is one of them.

Memories of Vietnam: fighting against the U.S. on the battlefield

In 1950, Wu was born in a Chinese family in Ha Long Township, Van Don County, Quang Ninh Province, Vietnam. Van Don County, in the east and southeast of Quang Ninh Province, is dotted with 60 big and small islands, one of which is Wu's hometown in Vietnam. Van Don County is about 50 kilometers away from Ha Long City (now the capital of Quang Ninh Province, and the famous tourist attraction Ha Long Bay in the city has the reputation of "Guilin on the sea"), and the straight-line distance from Van Don County to Mong Cai (bordering China) is just more than 70 kilometers.

There are nine brothers and sisters in Wu's family, and he is the second child. According to Wu, his grandfather is Chinese, who fled from Guangxi to Vietnam when the Japanese army invaded China. Wu's father was also born in Vietnam. Wu's maternal grandfather is Chinese, and his maternal grandmother is Vietnamese, but they still think they are Chinese in their blood.

In Wu's memory, although they lived in Vietnam at that time, their roots were still in China. "Many Vietnamese are in fact descendants of Chinese people. Many of them recognize their ancestors. Chinese characters are written on the ancestral halls and altars. Many cultural customs in Vietnam, such as the Qingming Festival, the Dragon Boat Festival, the Mid-Autumn Festival, the Double Ninth Festival, the Spring Festival and so on, are like those in China."

"Back then, in the Vietnamese village where we lived, most of the people were Chinese. We all recognized our ancestors and learned Chinese. However, they failed to run Vietnamese schools there. I learned Chinese from the first grade to junior high school."

Wu revealed that he got his junior high school diploma from a Chinese school in Vietnam. "When Ho Chi Minh (Vietnamese proletarian revolutionist, 1890–1969) was still alive, people in Vietnam could learn Chinese at any time. After that, people could no longer learn Chinese."

In 1969, Wu graduated from junior high school, and then went to a Vietnamese school for senior high school. "There was no Chinese senior high school over there. And in the town where we lived, few people were in senior high school. There were only three or five of them. However, the Chinese course was taught in senior high school in Vietnam," Wu added. "Now in Vietnam, people who can speak Chinese are very popular and enjoy very good salary."

After graduating from senior high school, Wu joined the army. To defend his homeland, he participated in the Vietnam War. This was a war of national liberation in which the Vietnamese people opposed U.S. aggression and realized national reunification. Of course, China's strong support for the just cause of the Vietnamese people was also indispensable. In Wu's words, "Vietnam fought the United States, and they went to the front to fight the American invaders."

The Vietnam War ended in May 1975, and Vietnam achieved national reunification. After returning from the army, Wu was appointed to be an accountant in a cooperative, which was in fact a shipping company, where the men were in charge of shipping and fishing at sea, while the women were in charge of logistics at home. Because he was a senior high school graduate, Wu was regarded as a well-educated person and became a cadre in the cooperative, leading more than 50 women mainly to process noodles for the country.

It was a pity that this peaceful life was soon broken, and the fate of Wu and his family took a major turning point.

Arrival at Guangming, a desolate place with few people and a lot of land

After the reunification of Vietnam in 1975, Sino-Vietnamese relations began to deteriorate, and a large-scale anti-Chinese movement spread in Vietnam. Before 1979, violence against the Chinese was commonplace. After 1979, the violence did not disappear, but was even quite serious.

In an academic paper entitled *From exclusion to acceptance: changes in Vietnam's policies toward the Chinese*, Chen Yande, a professor at the Department of History, Xiamen University, pointed out that this was mainly because "the Vietnamese leadership at the time took deeper consideration of the international situation and national interests, and, at the same time, tried to suppress the economic development of the Chinese by obstructing their livelihood, or to appease the indigenous people by diverting attention from domestic social conflicts." (See the *World Ethno-National Studies*, No. 6, 2008.)

It was precisely because the Vietnamese government implemented a comprehensive anti-Chinese policy that in the mid-to-late 1970s, many overseas Chinese became refugees and had to flee Vietnam with their families and return to the motherland or go to a third country by water or land. At the end of 1978, Wu and his family took a boat from Von Don County, Quang Ninh Province, Vietnam to Mong Cai, and then crossed the Beilun River to the north and entered China. They stayed in Dongxing, Guangxi for a month. In January of the following year, they were resettled in Guangming Overseas Chinese Livestock Farm (commonly known as "Guangming Farm") in Bao'an County, Guangdong Province.

According to the *Historical Records of Shenzhen Overseas Chinese Affairs*, the predecessor of Guangming Overseas Chinese Livestock Farm was Guangdong State-run Guangming Farm, which was founded in 1958. It was a state-run agricultural and animal husbandry enterprise, and it was also a place in Shenzhen to gather returned overseas Chinese and relatives of overseas Chinese nationals. By 1977, the farm had received 163 overseas Chinese and refugees returning from Indonesia, Malaysia, Thailand and other countries. From July 1978 to June 1979, Guangming Overseas Chinese Livestock Farm successively received, in six batches, 4,349 refugees in 909 households (mostly overseas Chinese) who were expelled by the Vietnamese authorities. Based on a humanitarian standpoint, the Chinese government cooperated with the UNHCR to receive more than 250,000 returned overseas Chinese and refugees expelled by the Vietnamese authorities. Some of them were placed in Guangming Overseas Chinese Livestock Farm, accounting for about 20% of the total number of returned overseas Chinese in Shenzhen.

These returnees from Vietnam were resettled in 18 places in some natural villages such as Shijietou, Hongaoxia, Guolin, Shangqi, Fenghuang, Dongzhou, Mudun, Beigang, Honghu and Zhenmei. According to *The 30 Years of Returned Overseas Chinese in Guangming*, the farm allocated brick houses with roof tiles to returned overseas Chinese according to a standard of six square meters per capita, and employed all the men under the age of 60 and all the women under 50. Although the average salary of formal employees was only 29 yuan in the early days of the business, being a state-run farm worker at that time was something that farmers in surrounding towns were very envious of.

To this day, Wu still clearly remembers that his family came to Guangming on January 21, 1979, and was resettled in Zhenmei Brigade. "When we came back here, we planted rice. Later we planted sugar cane, and some people planted elephant grass and raised cows. Our family lived in Zhenmei Brigade. The brigade had a vegetable farm, and Guangming Farm used it to specially supply vegetables to Hong Kong. It was called Zhenmei Vegetable Farm," Wu said.

However, recalling the scenes when he first arrived at Guangming, Wu repeatedly said "desolate." "When we came back, Guangming was still a desolate land. Some locals had fled to Hong Kong, and the land left here was abandoned, with nobody to cultivate it. At that time, there were really few people and a lot of land in Guangming." Wu was right. Guangming had the nickname of "Shenzhen's Siberia" in the early days of reform and opening-up. It was relatively poor in living conditions and backward in production, and was not financially well-to-do. Coupled with difficulties in the adaption to the living habits, language and so on, some of the returned overseas Chinese had low morale, and some even fled abroad in the early stage.

Taking root in Guangming and cherishing happy life

In recent years, Guangming District has gradually become a new growth pole for the development of Shenzhen's scientific research economy, and is gradually realizing its magnificent transformation from a farm to "a world-class science city and the center of northern Shenzhen." In Zhenmei Community, Xinhu Subdistrict, where Wu lives, the picturesque OCT Farm is to the south, and the Sun Yat-sen University Shenzhen Campus, the Shenzhen University of Advanced Technology, and the Large-scale Scientific Facilities Cluster area at the Guangming Science City are to the north. The "Guangdong-Hong Kong-Macao Greater Bay Area International Science and Technology Innovation Center" is about to emerge.

"Now Guangming and Shenzhen have developed, and the lives of ordinary people are much better than before. They can have pensions when they get old, and children can go to school for free. We, as returned overseas Chinese, have also enjoyed the dividends of reform and opening up, and it is the happiest time for us now. I am not alone in saying this, and people around me are saying the same thing." The "dividends of reform and opening-up" mentioned by Wu refers to the major policies benefiting the people, which have been implemented by the provincial, municipal and district governments over the past 10 years, such as the Overseas Chinese Heart Project, the Housing Project, the Common Prosperity

Project, the Education, Employment and Entrepreneurship Project, and the Renovation Project for the Dilapidated Buildings of the Overseas Chinese Farm. These projects have continuously improved the overall living standards of returned overseas Chinese and relatives of overseas Chinese nationals residing in Guangming.

"Now every household lives in western-style buildings, and people doing farm work are fewer than before." Speaking of this, Wu, who has been rooted in Guangming for more than 40 years, suddenly smiled happily. "Our life is very happy now, which shows that the returning overseas Chinese policies of the Party and the government have been implemented effectively in Guangming. This kind of reform dividend is precious and should be cherished. I am really touched. Sometimes they (the returned overseas Chinese) can't help crying when they talk about the hardships they experienced in the past."

The place where Wu was born in Vietnam is by the sea. Its economic conditions are relatively good, compared with many mountainous areas in the interior of Vietnam, he said. But compared with Shenzhen, it is still far behind. "Even if the economy of Vietnam is added up, it is not as good as Shenzhen, right?" Wu asked.

He is absolutely right. Public data available on the Internet shows that in 2021, Vietnam's GDP was 362.6 billion dollars, while Shenzhen's GDP reached 3.07 trillion yuan, equivalent to about 475 billion dollars based on the annual average exchange rate.

"We still have many relatives in Vietnam, so I know how life is going there." There is an old notebook next to the telephone at Wu's home, which is filled with, in Vietnamese, the contact numbers of his relatives and friends in Vietnam. Although he has been away from his birthplace for decades, he will contact his younger sister, cousins, classmates, or comrades in Vietnam once or twice a week. He used to make long-distance calls, but now he uses WeChat more often.

Wu is happy that Shenzhen has opened a direct flight to his hometown, Van Don County in Vietnam. Before the COVID-19 pandemic, the "Shenzhen-Van Don" flight cost less than 700 yuan including tax. "It takes just more than an hour to fly from Shenzhen to there, and our hometown in Vietnam is only one kilometer away from the Van Don International Airport." Wu said excitedly.

Serving overseas Chinese: dealing with people with emotions

At the beginning, Wu's family was placed in Zhenmei Brigade of Guangming Farm, and they were supposed to work on the land. But at that time, among the returned overseas Chinese from Vietnam, there were not many people who had studied in school, and Wu had graduated from junior high school in Chinese and graduated from senior high school in Vietnamese. At first, Wu was assigned to be a work point recorder in the brigade. Later he worked as a statistician, a cashier, and a custodian, before he became deputy director of the Zhenmei Vegetable Farm.

"I went to a Chinese school in Vietnam, and I also went to a Vietnamese school. After I returned to my motherland, I went on to study at a technical secondary school in Shenzhen (the Shenzhen Industrial School). Later I also took correspondence college and undergraduate courses. I learned Chinese in Vietnam, and it's not as good as the Chinese education received by people in China. If I didn't improve, it would definitely affect my work." Wu said frankly that he had loved reading all his life, so he would keep improving his educational level after work. From what he said, it may not be difficult to understand why he takes the inspirational words "Tall buildings rise from the ground, and glory should be achieved only on oneself" as a motto to spur him all the time.

Wu is both a returned overseas Chinese and an overseas Chinese affairs worker. He often says that it is his duty to do a good job in overseas Chinese affairs and to serve overseas Chinese, and it is also a career he loves. He is frank and enthusiastic by nature. In Guangming, once he sees the returned overseas Chinese and relatives of overseas Chinese nationals in difficulties, he will provide help right away. Many returned overseas Chinese and relatives of overseas Chinese nationals are also active in asking Wu for advice when encountering difficulties.

In 2000, Wu was elected chairman of the Federation of Returned Overseas Chinese of Guangming Subdistrict. His office at the Guangming Subdistrict Overseas Chinese Affairs Center acted as a reception room, where he always greeted returned overseas Chinese with a smile and a cup of warm tea whenever they came to him to complain, ask for help or have a heart-to-heart talk.

Wu admitted that there was much work pressure at the overseas Chinese affairs offices and returned overseas Chinese federations in Guangming. "Because the overseas Chinese affairs offices and returned overseas Chinese federations in many provinces and cities will come to Shenzhen to study and exchange. If the job is not well done, it will affect stability and unity."

Wu also revealed a little work experience he summed up over the years: "Serving overseas Chinese is also a job of dealing with people, so you must do it with emotions. Sometimes, when dealing with something, you can't make it if you are inflexible and unemotional. The work on overseas Chinese affairs has its own characteristics. It has the nature of the united front work, and it also involves relations at home and abroad. When we do a good job in overseas Chinese affairs, it is also part of the united front work, so we must do it well and carefully."

In 2003, Wu visited the relevant units at municipal and district levels many times to obtain pension allowances for the elderly returned overseas Chinese who had not been given a job because they were overage when they returned to China. He patiently listened to the appeals of the elderly returned overseas Chinese, empathized with their aspirations, and tirelessly explained to the relevant departments the hardships of these returned overseas Chinese in detail. Finally, when governments at all levels and relevant departments attached great importance to it, the difficult situation of the returned overseas Chinese and relatives of overseas Chinese nationals in the Guangming area was fundamentally improved. In October of that year, the Bao'an District Government specially approved a monthly allowance of 300 yuan each person for 128 elderly returned overseas Chinese in Guangming Subdistrict who had not been assigned work due to being overage when they returned to China.

In May 2006, Wu went to the then Shenzhen Municipal Labor and Social Security Bureau to verify retirement subsidies for 872 retired returned overseas Chinese according to law. There were 101 of them who had not completed the formalities, so Wu completed the procedures for them, and helped them receive pension subsidies, so that they could enjoy their sunset years in Shenzhen.

A mass of figures in the files show that in the past few decades, Wu has solved problems for more than 8,200 returned overseas Chinese and relatives of overseas Chinese nationals.

In September 2006, when the All-China Federation of Returned Overseas Chinese marked its 50th anniversary, it issued a certificate to Wu for "working in the federation of returned overseas Chinese for more than 20 years" in recognition of his tireless service for the vast number of returned overseas Chinese, relatives of overseas Chinese nationals residing in China, and Chinese nationals residing abroad. In December 2008, when the Guangdong Federation of Returned Overseas Chinese marked its 50th anniversary, Wu was awarded the honorary title of "Worker in the Federation of Returned Overseas Chinese for More than 30 Years."

In this regard, Wu said, "I have worked on overseas Chinese affairs for decades, and I am much honored to receive awards. The country gave me these awards probably because I was thought to have done the right work in the past few decades to show the Party and the government's solicitude for our returned overseas Chinese and relatives of overseas Chinese nationals residing in China. Although this is a recognition of my work, I have also received the awards on behalf of the returned overseas Chinese as a group."

(Photos courtesy of Wu Yuguang, except for those with credit. References: *Historical Records of Shenzhen Overseas Chinese Affairs*; *The 30 Years of Returned Overseas Chinese in Guangming*; *World Ethno-National Studies*; *Born to the Light, Giving Gifts to the Special Zone: They Witness Guangming's Past and Present*; and *Shenzhen Overseas Chinese News*.)

马兴锐

深圳"开荒牛"远赴苏里南，力促友好交往与合作

马兴锐在深圳前海留影。
Ma Xingrui in Qianhai, Shenzhen.

马兴锐，1958年出生于广东汕头，1982年到深圳工作，1989年赴苏里南发展。曾任苏里南华人基金会主席，现任苏里南华商联合总会会长、苏里南远洋捕捞公司总裁、苏里南国民发展供应公司董事会主席，2023年初以来兼任苏里南－中国投资协调委员会副主席、苏里南警方企业家安全监督委员会委员。

马兴锐深耕苏里南水产行业，成为领军人物之一。积极投身社会和侨界事务，在争取便利政策、培养举荐人才、改善治安等方面不遗余力地为侨胞服务。致力于加强华侨华人与苏里南其他族群的交流，促进中国与苏里南的友好交往与经贸合作。

采访时间：2023年。

位于南美洲北部的苏里南，跟深圳有着不解之缘。早期移居苏里南的华人里，很多是深圳的客家人。时至今日，苏里南仍是深圳籍华侨华人的聚集地之一。

苏里南人口有 60 多万，印度裔、克里奥尔人、印尼裔、丛林黑人的人数较多，其余是印第安人、华人、白人等。据马兴锐介绍，当地华人不算很多，加上混血的后代，约占全国总人口的 10%，但华人的经济社会地位比较高。他们大多经营超市、餐馆、小商店，近年来也有来自浙江、福建的侨胞和企业从事木材、金矿开采。

2023 年，苏里南迎来印度裔定居 150 周年、黑奴解放 160 周年、华人定居 170 周年，该国成立了国家庆典委员会，指导各种庆祝活动。庆祝华人定居苏里南 170 周年系列活动的官方开幕式和文艺晚会将在 10 月 6 日上演，由马兴锐担任总导演。

马兴锐说，深圳籍侨胞传承了客家人朴实、勤劳、谨慎、自律的优点，为华人在苏里南树立良好形象奠定了基础。"还有一点值得我们自豪：由于深圳籍侨胞传承下来的精神，苏里南华人群体的守望相助是很到位的。"

他自己也不断用行动诠释着这种精神。他参与侨团工作十几年，近几年更是把大部分精力放在社会工作上，夜以继日。在血浓于水的同胞情驱使下，他满腔热忱，为侨胞排忧解难，成为大家抱团发展的后盾。

马兴锐在深圳平安金融中心参观展览。
Ma Xingrui visits an exhibition at the Ping An Finance Center in Shenzhen.

深圳"开荒牛"远赴苏里南，创业一炮打响

马兴锐在广东汕头出生，在广州上学，学的是食品加工。1982 年，他毕业到深圳工作，成为深圳"开荒牛"。马兴锐记得，自己是 9 月份到深圳报到的，那天正好停电，人事局办公桌上的风扇没开，等他填完表出来，"的确良"衬衫已经湿透，贴在身上。当时的深圳，出门就是工地，没树、没高楼，深南路还在开挖。

马兴锐在一家小型国营企业当技术员，很快就升到了工程师，28 岁就当上了副厂长。他主持了工厂的技术改造，从设计到组织生产，都是他一肩挑。1987 年，苏里南一位经营食品厂的华侨来参观，很赏识马兴锐，邀他去苏里南提供技术援助。

经过一些波折，马兴锐在 1989 年到了苏里南，在三星食品公司当工程师。几年里，他给公司设计了一个调味品加工间，开发或改进了好几款果蔬罐头和饮料，解决了产品保存期短和滞销等问题。

由于本地市场规模小，三星食品公司的工作已不能满足马兴锐的追求，他开始尝试创业，利用业余时间研究鱼翅的精加工，几个月后拿出了产品，一炮而红。

"鱼翅大王"不停步，携手中国公司实现飞跃

过了一年半，马兴锐听从美国客商建议，给产品换上了他自己设计的塑料包装盒，借此把产品售价上调将近一半。新包装产品大受追捧，远销欧美。

苏里南老一辈华侨华人给马兴锐起了个"鱼翅大王"的绰号。但他预感到鱼翅资源量不够，就新增了鱼肚（鱼鳔）和梅香咸鱼的加工、出口业务，还往美国空运冰鲜产品，并正式离开了三星食品公司，自己创业。

1995 年，马兴锐买下一处旧厂房改造成海产加工厂，正式运营苏里南远洋捕捞公司，之后不断发展壮大，在 21 世纪之初更是实现了一次飞跃。

2005 年，首届中国－加勒比经贸合作论坛在牙买加举行，苏里南远洋捕捞公司与中国水产总公司在论坛上签署合作协议，这也是苏里南的唯一签约项目。中方随后派出 4 条船到苏里南开展合作捕捞，马兴锐的公司以市场价收购渔获，然后加工出口，年产量一下子跃升到 3000 多吨。

2013 年，银行提供全额优惠贷款，马兴锐收购了亏损多年的苏里南日本渔业公司（SUJAFI），改名为苏里南国民发展供应公司。按照收购约定，马兴锐虽收购公司，但实际仍再租给原股东们继续经营，可原股东们并未完全履行约定，在两年里只给了 5 个月的 80% 租金。于是，2015 年，马兴锐终止租约，接手了公司，亲自经营管理，当年就扭亏为盈。接着，他改造、扩建了工厂，把加工的高端水产品持续出口到日本和欧美市场。

马兴锐比较好学，是个多面手。在深圳时，他跟着深圳大学的老师们学建筑设计，然后又通过函授等方式自学。他现在住的房子，改造方案就是他自己设计的，80% 以上的图纸是他手绘的。他的两家工厂，采用的基本上都是他的设计概念，过半的图纸出自他手。

苏里南官方语言是荷兰语，民众日常使用苏里南语，英语也可以通行。马兴锐能用简单的荷兰语交流，正式场合会用英语。令人称奇的是，到苏里南的第 7 个月，他就能用苏里南语跟人交流了，有位警察与他交谈时都觉得难以置信。

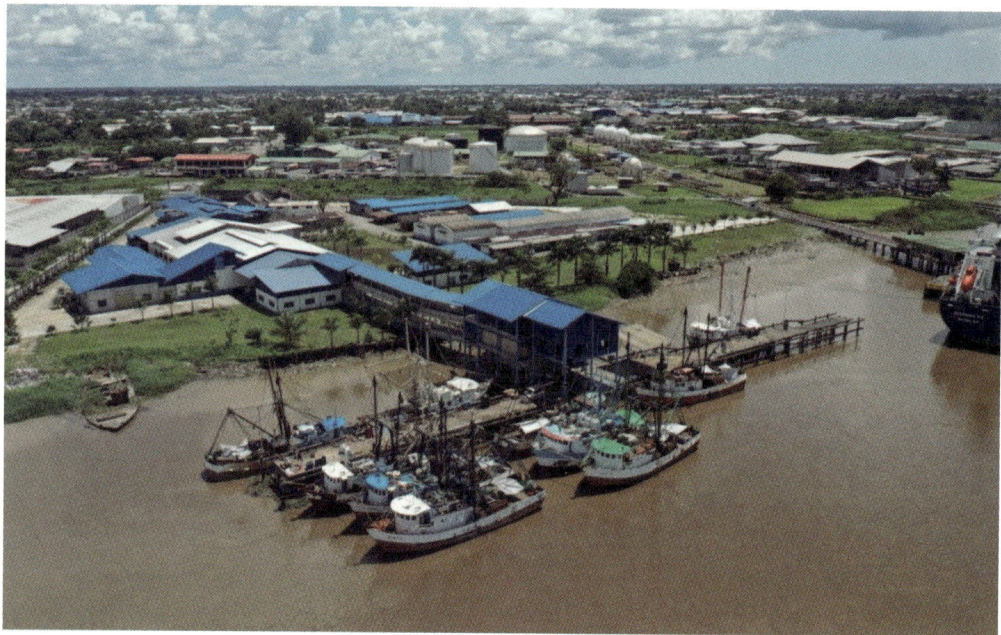

改造后的工厂。（2022 年摄） The renovated factory in 2022.

马兴锐觉得，到新的地方去发展，就得融入社会，第一道关就是掌握当地语言。他一直坚持跟妻子、儿女讲广州话，那是他到广州读书时学会的。和很多海外侨胞一样，家乡话是联系他们与故土的一条文化和情感纽带。

牵线搭桥，助力两国友好交流

马兴锐还把苏里南国民发展供应公司的设备陆续换成了"中国制造"。

2015 年改造工厂时，马兴锐考察发现，中国制造的高端专业制冷设备物美价廉。同时，出于民族情怀，他决定：能用中国货就用中国货。如今，这个工厂 90% 以上的设备、材料都是中国产的。"下一步，连建筑材料、预制件都要从中国来。"马兴锐说。

除了自己的业务往来，马兴锐还积极参与和推动苏里南与中国的交流交往。

2013 年，时任苏里南总统鲍特瑟访华，马兴锐随团访问了北京和长沙。他还曾陪同苏里南财政部长到厦门参加中国国际投资贸易洽谈会，并访问福州、呼和浩特。

2020 年初，新冠疫情暴发后，马兴锐协助筹款采购紧缺的口罩、手套，捐赠给中国。他自己也设法采购了一批，捐给深圳。后来，中国国内的疫情得到有效控制，深圳侨务部门向苏里南捐赠了一些抗疫物资，马兴锐分发给了侨胞以及军队、警察、医院等机构。

最近，马兴锐在推进一个大项目：把中国的皮卡车生产线引进苏里南，把合作生产出来的皮卡车销售到加勒比地区。他常做牵线搭桥的事情，还投入大量时间接待中国访问团。他把这些事情形容成"给大家跑跑腿"。

见证深圳侨胞移居苏里南的历史印记

从 2016 年开始，马兴锐经常应邀列席深圳市政协和深圳市人大的会议，关心深圳发展。他说，深圳跟苏里南的联系比较紧密，因为苏里南有很多深圳籍侨胞。

华人移居苏里南的历史，可以追溯到 1853 年。赴苏里南的首批 18 名中国契约劳工是在那年 7 月 2 日从印尼出发，10 月 20 日抵达苏里南的，有 4 人在漫长的航程中病逝。余下的 14 人从事甘蔗种植工作，到契约期满时，有 11 人活了下来，其中 3 人留下担任下批劳工的翻译。

1858 年至 1870 年，约有 2500 名劳工从中国前往苏里南。他们也奠定了早期苏里南华侨华人的结构基础：以客家人居多，大多来自广东的宝安县、惠阳县、东莞县。

世界各地侨团名称里的"惠东宝"或"惠东安"，指的就是旧时的这 3 个县。苏里南华商联合总会理事会的 23 位成员中，有三分之一的原籍或祖籍是"惠东宝"。而宝安县就是深圳市的前身，明朝、清朝时曾称新安县。今天深圳东部的龙岗、坪山、大鹏，曾属惠阳县管辖。所以，苏里南很多侨胞的故乡就是现在的深圳。

由于这段历史渊源，在很长一段时期里，苏里南华人社区以客家话相通。马兴锐也见证了这段历史：他 1989 年到那里的时候，华人社区依然以客家话为主，当地人甚至把客家话当作中国话。

2010 年，深圳侨务部门统计发现，当时苏里南有 5000 名祖籍深圳的华侨华人。

马兴锐介绍说，中国改革开放以来，苏里南侨胞的组成变得多样化了，但不变的是一路传承下来的朴实勤劳、守望相助等品格。

大胆改革，中秋晚会变成各族群联欢盛会

因业务关系，马兴锐早年跟侨胞打交道比较少。他的生意有了一定规模之后，在老一辈侨领提点下，他投身侨团工作，为侨胞服务。

大约在 2007 年，马兴锐加入了广义堂，随后出任理事。后来，他被派往由广义堂、中华会馆、华侨商会联合组成的三侨团基金会，作为广义堂代表组的组长。2010 年，他当选三侨团基金会主席，然后推行了大刀阔斧的改革。

那时，苏里南已经有十多个侨团。征得各方同意后，马兴锐把三侨团基金会改为华人基金会，让全部十几个侨团都派代表参与进来。另外，他把中秋体育比赛向其他族群开放，并且把中秋晚会办成了大型多族群文艺晚会。

2010 年的中秋晚会，"马导"初出茅庐，就引发了轰动。按惯例，晚会现场准备了 2000 张凳子，结果去了 5000 多人，很多人宁愿站着观看，节目结束后才不舍地离去。这场盛况空前的晚会，凝聚了马兴锐的奇思妙想。比如，请印尼裔演员表演中国舞蹈《泉水叮咚响》和《九九艳阳天》等；印度裔、非洲裔等族群也表演了节目。

2011 年，类似的中秋晚会再次成功上演。这两年中秋晚会筹集的公益捐款，是往年的两三倍。

春节活动声势浩大，凸显华侨华人地位

2021 年新冠疫情期间，苏里南大多数侨胞都盼望能接种中国产的新冠疫苗，马兴锐促成了苏里南政府批准进口中国新冠疫苗。随后，中国向苏里南援助了新冠疫苗，马兴锐发动几位企业家一起捐款，资助了国际运输费用。

2022 年 2 月 1 日，苏里南总统单多吉开创特例，同时向 7 位华人授勋，表彰他们对国家和社会的贡献。马兴锐获得了黄星军官勋章，是当天颁发的最高荣誉。

2022 年 2 月 1 日，马兴锐获颁苏里南黄星军官勋章后，与妻子合影留念。
Ma Xingrui has a photo taken with his wife after being granted Suriname's Officer in the Honorary Order of the Yellow Star on February 1, 2022.

为了更有力地维护华商权益，促进华商实现更好发展，应广大华侨华人要求，在中国驻苏里南大使馆的支持下，马兴锐牵头创办了苏里南华商联合总会并担任会长。

2022年1月30日，总会举行揭牌仪式。紧接着，2月1日，总会在苏里南总统府后花园举办了春节招待会，政界、商界、侨界代表云集。2023年1月22日，总会又在苏里南总统办公厅花园举办了春节晚会，河道上的烟花表演把晚会推向高潮，照亮了苏里南首都帕拉马里博的夜空。

2023年1月22日，苏里南华商联合总会在总统办公厅花园举办春节晚会。

The Suriname Chinese Business Alliance holds a Spring Festival Gala in the garden of the presidential office on January 22, 2023.

两场声势浩大的春节活动展现了华人的地位和影响力，让社会各界对华侨华人、对总会刮目相看。会员们反映，自此以后，去有些部门办事情，没遇到以前那么多刁难了。

截至2023年7月，总会已经有212个成员单位，包括各类企业以及侨团、基金会、行业协会等社会组织。

服务侨胞不遗余力

新冠疫情期间，总会一位副会长保持手机24小时开机，一旦接到侨胞身体严重不适且未能得到及时救治的报告，就出面和相关卫生部门协调。

有些华侨有急事须回中国，但因居留过期而无法成行，总会组织代表到总统办公室开会，并请司法警察部长到场，协调解决问题。

马兴锐前些年也协调过类似的事情。那是单多吉总统任司法警察部长的时候，马兴锐带着侨团代表和中国大使馆代表到司法警察部，希望放宽华人申请居留的条件。促成此事之后的一个周末，马兴锐到单多吉家做客，看到警卫提着两个大行李箱进来。马兴锐就问单多吉："你明天要出差呀？"对方半开玩笑地回答："这是你给我的额外工作啊！居留许可证在办公时间里签不完，就带回来审查、签名。"

2023 年 2 月 6 日，在总会等组织的推动下，苏里南司法警察部成立了企业家安全监督委员会（又称社警安保监察委员会），马兴锐等商界代表加入委员会，配合警方打击犯罪。

2 月 17 日，帕拉马里博发生暴乱，总会慰问、安抚遭洗劫的华人商户，组织他们参加总统召开的交流会。在总会推动下，司法警察部开设了华人辅警培训班。培训后，华人辅警可以配枪，震慑犯罪。3 月 11 日开课的第一期共培训 25 人，全都在 7 月 14 日顺利毕业。

着重培养新生代

马兴锐平时还帮侨胞办了很多"小事"，他觉得不值一提。"有句话叫'血浓于水'。看到同胞受难或无助时，总觉得如刺锥心。特别是一些不公平或带有一定偏见的事件，如果有条件的不出来站台，问题就会越来越严重。"马兴锐这样概括自己的心路历程。

"我的事业和工作能力可能让当地人比较认可，加上自身的双边文化背景，大家比较喜欢和我交朋友。我比较务实，又不大会讲虚假的好话，所以很多时候，他们都乐意和我交流，也比较愿意听我的建议。"他总结说。

"随着时代的变迁，中国的国际地位不断提升，我们这些海外的中华儿女应该以一种新的姿态和方式出现在地球的不同角落。"他感叹道，"如何发现、培养既有中华文化感情，又积极融入居住国的华裔新生代，是我们这一代华人人生里的最后责任和答卷。"

（本文图片均由受访者马兴锐提供。参考资料：中国外交部官网、《侨务工作研究》、《深圳侨务史志》、苏里南《中华日报》、龙岗政府在线、华人头条。）

Ma Xingrui

A "pioneering ox" of Shenzhen shines in Suriname, promoting friendly exchanges and cooperation

Ma Xingrui (or Ma Hsing Jui) was born in Shantou, Guangdong in 1958. He went to work in Shenzhen in 1982 and went to Suriname in 1989 for development. He used to be chairman of the Chinese Community Social Interests Foundation (Stichting Sociale Belangen Chinese Gemeenschap), and is chairman of the Suriname Chinese Business Alliance, managing director of Suriname Sea Catch N.V., and president of National Industrial Supplier and Development N.V. Since the beginning of 2023, he has been vice chairman of the Suriname-China Investment Coordination Committee (Suriname-China Investeringscoördinatie Comité, SCIC) and a member of the Entrepreneur Safety Monitoring Team (Monitoringsteam Veiligheid Ondernemers) of the Surinamese police.

Deeply involved in Suriname's seafood products industry, Ma has become one of the leading figures. He has actively participated in social and overseas Chinese affairs, and spared no effort to serve overseas Chinese in terms of striving for convenient policies, cultivating and recommending talents, and improving public security. He is committed to strengthening exchanges between overseas Chinese and other ethnic groups in Suriname, and promoting friendly exchanges and economic and trade cooperation between China and Suriname.

Suriname, located in the northern part of South America, has an indissoluble bond with Shenzhen. Among the early Chinese immigrants to Suriname, many were Hakkas from Shenzhen. To this day, Suriname is still one of the gathering places for overseas Chinese from Shenzhen.

Suriname has a population of more than 600,000. There are relatively more Asian-Indians, Creoles, Indonesians, and Marrons (black people of the forest), while the rest are

---

The interview took place in 2023.

Indians, Chinese, and whites, among others. According to Ma Xingrui, there are not many overseas Chinese in Suriname, accounting for about 10% of the total population of the country, including the mixed-race descendants of Chinese, but the economic and social status of the Chinese is relatively high. Most of them operate supermarkets, restaurants or small shops. In recent years, overseas Chinese and enterprises from Zhejiang and Fujian have engaged in lumbering and gold mining.

In 2023, Suriname ushers in the 150th anniversary of Indian arrival, the 160th anniversary of slave emancipation, and the 170th anniversary of Chinese settlement. Suriname has established the National Jubilee Committee to guide various celebration activities. The official opening ceremony of the activities commemorating the 170th anniversary of Chinese settlement in Suriname and an evening party will be staged on October 6, with Ma as the general director.

Ma said that the overseas Chinese from Shenzhen inherited the Hakka people's virtues of simplicity, diligence, prudence and self-discipline, which laid the foundation for the Chinese to establish a positive image in Suriname. "There is another thing that we should be proud of: because of the spirit passed down by the Chinese immigrants from Shenzhen, the Chinese community in Suriname has done well in helping each other."

He keeps interpreting this spirit with his own actions. He has participated in the work of overseas Chinese groups for more than a decade, and, in recent years, has devoted most of his time to social work, which is going on day and night. Driven by his love for compatriots, which is guided by the concept that blood is thicker than water, he is full of enthusiasm to solve problems for overseas Chinese and become the backing for them to develop together.

A "pioneering ox" of Shenzhen went to Suriname and started a business, which was an instant success

Ma was born in Shantou, Guangdong, and went to school in Guangzhou, where he studied food processing. In 1982, he graduated and went to work in Shenzhen, becoming one of Shenzhen's "pioneering oxen." He remembered that when he reported for duty in Shenzhen in September 1982, there was a power outage, and the fan on a desk in the Personnel Bureau was not turned on. When he finished filling out the form and went out, his Dacron shirt was soaked and stuck to his body. Back then, Shenzhen was full of construction sites outside. He saw no trees or tall buildings, and Shennan Road was still being excavated.

Ma worked as a technician in a small state-run enterprise, and soon became an engineer. At the age of 28, he was promoted to deputy factory director. He was in charge of a technical transformation of the factory, with all the work, from design to production organization, on his shoulders. In 1987, an overseas Chinese who ran a food factory in Suriname came to visit the factory. He appreciated Ma very much and invited him to Suriname to provide technical assistance.

After some twists and turns, Ma arrived in Suriname in 1989 to work as an engineer at Three Stars Food N.V. In a few years, he designed a condiment processing room for the company, developed or improved several beverages and canned fruits and vegetables, and solved some problems of the products, such as short shelf life and slow sales.

Because of the small size of the local market, Ma's job at Three Stars Food N.V. could no longer satisfy his pursuit. He began to try to start a business. In his spare time, he studied the fine processing of shark fins. After several months, his product came to market and became an instant hit.

"King of Shark Fins" moved on, and achieved a leap after joining hands with Chinese company

After a year and a half, Ma followed the advice of an American merchant and replaced the product's packaging with a plastic box he designed, thereby increasing the price of the product by nearly half. The product became very popular and was exported to Europe and the United States.

The older generation of overseas Chinese in Suriname nicknamed Ma the "King of Shark Fins." But he had a premonition that shark fin resources would become insufficient, so he carried out the processing and export of fish maws (dried swim bladders) and "mui heong salted fish," and also airlifted chilled fresh products to the United States. He formally left Three Stars Food N.V. to start his own business.

In 1995, Ma bought an old factory building and transformed it into a seafood processing plant, so as to officially begin the operation of Suriname Sea Catch N.V. After that, the company continued to grow and develop, and achieved a leap at the beginning of the new century.

In 2005, the first China-Caribbean Economic and Trade Cooperation Forum was held in Jamaica. Suriname Sea Catch N.V. and China National Fisheries Corporation signed a cooperation agreement, and it was Suriname's only contracted project at the forum. The Chinese side then sent four ships to Suriname for cooperative fishing. Ma's company purchased the fish at market prices and then processed them for export, with the annual output jumping to more than 3,000 tons.

In 2013, some banks provided full preferential loans for Ma to acquire Suriname Japan Fisheries NV (SUJAFI), which had been losing money for many years. The company's name was then changed to National Industrial Supplier and Development N.V. According to the acquisition agreement, although Ma acquired the company, he still leased it to the original shareholders, who continued to run it. However, the original shareholders failed to fully fulfill the agreement and paid only 80% of the rent for five months in two years. Therefore, Ma terminated the lease in 2015, took over the company, and managed it by himself, turning losses into profits in the same year. Then, he remodeled and expanded the factory, which constantly exported high-end seafood products it processed to Japan, Europe and the United States.

Ma is a studious generalist. When he was in Shenzhen, he studied architectural design with some teachers of Shenzhen University, and then taught himself by taking a correspondence course and in other ways. He designed the renovation plan of the house he lives in, with more than 80% of the drawings done by him. His two factories basically adopted his design concepts, and more than half of the drawings came from him.

The official language of Suriname is Dutch. People use Surinamese (Sranan Tongo) in daily life, while English is also widely used. Ma can communicate in simple Dutch, and uses English in formal occasions. It is amazing that he was able to speak Surinamese with others in the seventh month of his arrival, and a policeman found it unbelievable when talking with him.

Ma feels that to develop in a new place, one must integrate into the society, and the first step is to master the local language. He has always insisted on speaking Cantonese to his wife and children, which he learned when he went to study in Guangzhou. Like many overseas Chinese, their hometown dialect is a cultural and emotional link connecting them with their homeland.

Building bridges to facilitate friendly exchanges between the two countries

Ma replaced the equipment of Suriname National Industrial Supplier and Development N.V. with products made in China.

When renovating the factory in 2015, Ma found through on-the-spot investigation that the high-end professional refrigeration equipment made in China was of high quality and low price. At the same time, out of his national feelings, he decided to use Chinese products as much as he could. Today, more than 90% of the equipment and materials in this factory are made in China. "Next, even building materials and prefabricated parts will come from China," Ma said.

In addition to his own business dealings, Ma has also actively participated in and promoted exchanges between Suriname and China.

In 2013, when Desi Bouterse, then-president of Suriname, visited China, Ma came with the delegation to visit Beijing and Changsha. He also accompanied the finance minister of Suriname to Xiamen to attend the China International Fair for Investment & Trade, and to visit Fuzhou and Hohhot.

In early 2020, after COVID-19 broke out, Ma helped raise funds to purchase much needed masks and gloves, which were then donated to China. He also managed to purchase a batch of these materials to donate to Shenzhen. Later, when China effectively controlled the outbreak, the overseas Chinese affairs departments in Shenzhen donated some anti-epidemic materials to Suriname, and Ma distributed them to overseas Chinese, the army, the police, hospitals and some other institutions.

Recently, Ma has been pushing a big project: introducing China's pickup truck production lines to Suriname, and selling the pickup trucks produced in cooperation to the Caribbean region. He often builds bridges and spends a lot of time receiving Chinese delegations. He described these things as "running errands for all."

Witnessing historical imprint of Shenzhen immigrants in Suriname

Since 2016, Ma has often been invited to attend the sessions of the Shenzhen Municipal Committee of the Chinese People's Political Consultative Conference and the Shenzhen Municipal People's Congress, learning about Shenzhen's development. Shenzhen has a closer relationship with Suriname because there are many overseas Chinese from Shenzhen in Suriname, he said.

The history of Chinese immigration to Suriname can be traced back to 1853. The first 18 Chinese indentured laborers to Suriname departed from Indonesia on July 2 of that year and arrived in Suriname on October 20. Four of them died of illness during the long voyage. The remaining 14 people were engaged in sugar cane cultivation. When their contract expired, 11 people survived, and three of them stayed in Suriname to serve as translators for the next batch of Chinese workers.

From 1858 to 1870, approximately 2,500 laborers traveled from China to Suriname. They also laid the foundation for the structure of early overseas Chinese in Suriname:

the majority were Hakkas, mostly from Bao'an County, Huiyang County, and Dongguan County in Guangdong.

"Huidongbao" or "Huidong'an" in the names of overseas Chinese groups all over the world refers to these three counties in history. Among the 23 members of the council of the Suriname Chinese Business Alliance, one-third of their origin or ancestral home is Huiyang, Dongguan or Bao'an. Bao'an County is the predecessor of Shenzhen Municipality, and it was called Xin'an County in the Ming and Qing dynasties. Today's Longgang, Pingshan, and Dapeng in the eastern part of Shenzhen were once under the jurisdiction of Huiyang County. Therefore, the hometown of many overseas Chinese in Suriname is today's Shenzhen.

Due to this historical origin, for a long period of time, the Chinese community in Suriname spoke Hakka with each other. Ma also witnessed this period of history: when he arrived there in 1989, the Chinese community was still dominated by Hakka, and the locals even regarded Hakka as the Chinese language.

In 2010, statistics from Shenzhen's overseas Chinese affairs department found that there were 5,000 overseas Chinese who were originally from Shenzhen in Suriname.

According to Ma, since China's reform and opening-up, the composition of overseas Chinese in Suriname has diversified, but what remain unchanged are the characters of simplicity, diligence, and mutual assistance, which have been passed down along the way.

Bold reforms turned Mid-Autumn Festival gala into gathering of all ethnic groups

Due to his business circle, Ma didn't have much contact with overseas Chinese in early years. After his business reached a certain scale, under the guidance of the older generation of overseas Chinese leaders, he began to devote himself to the work of overseas Chinese groups and serve the overseas Chinese.

Around 2007, Ma joined the Kong Ngie Tong Sang and later served as a director. Later, he was sent to the K.C.F. Directorate (K.C.F. Directoraat), a foundation jointly formed by the Kong Ngie Tong Sang, the Chung Fa Foei Kon, and the Fa Tjauw Song Foei, as the leader of the representative team of the Kong Ngie Tong Sang. In 2010, he was elected chairman of the foundation, and then implemented drastic reforms.

There were already more than 10 overseas Chinese groups in Suriname at that time. After obtaining the consent of all parties, Ma changed the K.C.F. Directorate to the Chinese Community Social Interests Foundation (Stiching Sociale Belangen

Chinese Gemeenschap) and asked all the dozen or so overseas Chinese groups to send representatives to the new foundation. In addition, he made the Mid-Autumn Festival sports competitions open to other ethnic groups, and turned the Mid-Autumn Festival gala into a large-scale multi-ethnic cultural evening.

The Mid-Autumn Festival gala in 2010, directed by Ma for the first time, caused a sensation. As usual, 2,000 stools were prepared for the show, but more than 5,000 people came, many of whom were willing to stand there and watch, and left reluctantly after the show. This unprecedented gala condensed Ma's fantastic ideas. For example, actors of Indonesian origin were invited to perform Chinese dances such as *Tinkling Spring Water* and *Nine-Nine Sunny Days*. Indians, Africans and other ethnic groups also performed.

In 2011, a similar Mid-Autumn Festival gala was successfully staged again. The public welfare donations raised by the two Mid-Autumn Festival galas were two or three times that of previous years.

Grand Spring Festival activities highlighted status of overseas Chinese

In 2021, a time of the COVID-19 pandemic, most overseas Chinese in Suriname looked forward to being vaccinated with the Chinese vaccine. Ma prompted the Suriname government to approve the import of the Chinese vaccine. Afterwards, China donated the vaccine to Suriname, and Ma mobilized several entrepreneurs to donate together to fund the international transportation costs.

On February 1, 2022, Suriname's President Chan Santokhi created a special case by awarding honors to seven Chinese at the same time in recognition of their contributions to the country and society. Ma was granted Officer in the Honorary Order of the Yellow Star (Officier in de Ereorde van de Gele Ster), the highest honor awarded that day.

In a bid to more effectively safeguard the rights and interests of Chinese merchants and promote the better development of Chinese merchants, at the request of the overseas Chinese and with the support of the Chinese embassy in Suriname, Ma took the lead in founding the Suriname Chinese Business Alliance (SCBA) and has served as its president.

An unveiling ceremony was held for the SCBA on January 30, 2022. Soon afterwards, on February 1, the SCBA held a Spring Festival reception in the back garden of the presidential palace of Suriname, where representatives from the political, business and overseas Chinese circles gathered. On January 22, 2023, the SCBA held a Spring Festival gala in the garden of Suriname's presidential office. The fireworks show on the river pushed the party to a climax, lighting up the night sky of Paramaribo, the capital of

Suriname.

The two massive Spring Festival events demonstrated the status and influence of the Chinese in Suriname, making all walks of life hold the Chinese and the SCBA in high esteem. Members of the SCBA found that since then, when going to some departments to deal with things, they had not encountered as many difficulties as before.

As of July 2023, the SCBA had 212 member units, including various enterprises and social organizations such as overseas Chinese groups, foundations, and industry associations.

Sparing no effort in serving overseas Chinese

During the COVID-19 pandemic, a vice chairman of the SCBA kept his mobile phone on 24 hours a day. Once he received a report that an overseas Chinese was seriously unwell and could not receive timely treatment, he would come forward to coordinate with the relevant health departments.

Some overseas Chinese need to return to China for urgent matters, but are unable to make the trip because their residence permit has expired. The SCBA will send representatives to hold a meeting in the president's office and invite the minister of justice and police to be present to coordinate and resolve the problem.

Ma coordinated similar things a few years ago. When President Santokhi was the minister of justice and police, Ma led representatives of overseas Chinese groups and the Chinese embassy to the Ministry of Justice and Police, hoping to relax the conditions for Chinese to apply for residence. On a weekend after the matter was solved, Ma visited Santokhi's house and saw a guard coming in with two large suitcases. Ma asked Santokhi, "Are you going on a business trip tomorrow?" Santokhi replied half-jokingly, "This is the extra work you gave me! I was unable to sign all the residence permits during office hours, so I bring it home for review and signature."

On February 6, 2023, with the promotion of the SCBA and other organizations, the Ministry of Justice and Police of Suriname established the Entrepreneur Safety Monitoring Team (Monitoringsteam Veiligheid Ondernemers, also known as the Security Supervision Committee of Society and Police). Ma and other business representatives joined the team to cooperate with the police in fighting crime.

On February 17, riots broke out in Paramaribo. The SCBA expressed condolences and consolation to the Chinese merchants who were looted, and organized them to attend an exchange meeting held by the president. With the promotion of the SCBA, the Ministry of Justice and Police opened a training course for Chinese auxiliary police officers. After training, Chinese auxiliary police officers can be equipped with guns to deter crime. The first phase of the course, which started on March 11, trained a total of 25 people, and all of them successfully graduated on July 14.

Focusing on cultivating new generations

Ma has also helped overseas Chinese with many "little things" that he thinks not worth mentioning. "There is a saying that 'blood is thicker than water.' When seeing compatriots suffering or helpless, I have always felt like that there is a thorn in my heart. Especially in case of unfair or biased events, if someone with favorable conditions does not come out, the problem will become worse and worse," Ma summarized what he thought.

"My career and work ability may have been recognized by the local people, and, considering my bilateral cultural background, people like to make friends with me. I am quite pragmatic and I don't speak false good words, so, in many occasions, they are willing to communicate with me and listen to my suggestions," he concluded.

"As the times change and China's international status continues to rise, we overseas Chinese should appear in different corners of the earth with a new attitude and way," he sighed. "How to discover and cultivate new generations of Chinese descendants who have Chinese cultural emotions while actively integrating into the country they live is the final responsibility and answer sheet in the lives of our generation of overseas Chinese."

[Photos courtesy of Ma Xingrui. References: the official website of the Ministry of Foreign Affairs of China, *Research on Overseas Chinese Affairs*, *Historical Records of Shenzhen Overseas Chinese Affairs*, *Suriname Chinese News (Cheung Fa Daily)*, Longgang Government Online, and 52hrtt.com.]

后　记

　　深圳是一座新兴的现代化城市，但是，深圳人（或称新安人、宝安人）勇闯世界的历史最早可追溯到七百多年以前的南宋末年。

　　据《深圳侨务史志》记载，南宋灭亡后，深圳大批参加过抗元的义民及其家属为了逃避元兵的屠杀，相继逃亡海外，漂泊至南洋一带；明朝时，以南头人张政为代表的深圳人已经频繁来往于中国与南洋诸国之间，从事贸易和海上运输工作；鸦片战争失败后，观澜、龙岗、大鹏、葵涌、坪山、石岩、龙华等地大批的深圳人（客家人最多），以契约劳工的形式卖身出洋，他们或被运往东南亚、夏威夷、南美洲、加拿大，或被卖至美国的旧金山、澳大利亚的新金山（墨尔本），又或被送到欧洲、非洲；1950年前后，一批在国内受过中等教育的侨眷知识青年纷纷出国继承祖业……①

　　今天的深圳是广东省重点侨乡之一。据统计，祖籍深圳的港澳同胞、海外侨胞和归侨侨眷超过100万人。他们历来有爱国爱乡的优良传统，自辛亥革命以来，特别是改革开放以来，他们积极办教兴学、捐款捐物，倾力支持家乡建设，是深圳发展的一支不可或缺的重要力量。

　　2022年起，深圳报业集团《晶报》社联合深圳市委统战部（市侨办、市侨联）推出"记录侨故事"系列专栏，着力挖掘祖籍深圳或与深圳联系紧密的港澳同胞、海外侨胞和归侨侨眷的故事，展现广大侨胞对祖（籍）国和家乡一往情深的牵挂与眷恋。3年来，该项目团队已采访了28位老一辈的港澳同胞、海外侨胞和归侨侨眷，并将他们的"侨故事"记录成文，这是一笔非常值得保存的奋斗向上、启迪后人的宝贵记忆与精神财富。

　　在采访过程中，我们深深地感受到了身处海外的华侨华人爱家乡、爱深圳、爱祖（籍）国的强烈感情。与此同时，我们也见证了一个已经在海外形成的有影响力的"深圳华侨族群"，发现了一个又一个分布在世界不同角落的"深圳侨元素"：荷兰"海上皇宫"餐厅、旅荷比深圳市蔡屋围同乡会、纽约大鹏同乡会、纽约大鹏育英总社、澳大利亚深圳社团总会、马来西亚深圳总商会、南非-中国深圳总商会……

　　本书收录的部分"记录侨故事"系列专栏文章，全部首发于深圳市委统战部微信公众号"同心鹏城"或《晶报》等新媒体平台，这是智媒时代"讲好中国故事、

---

① 深圳市人民政府侨务办公室. 深圳侨务史志［M］. 深圳：海天出版社，2012：30-36.

后　记

深圳故事"的一个成功案例，也是新时代深圳讲好"侨故事"的一次大胆且有益的尝试。

每次在"记录侨故事"系列专栏推送之后，我们总能收到多方的热情评价，有海外侨胞甚至请采访记者帮忙将采访文章精心排版，再打印出来，以便永久珍藏。如今，在深圳市人民政府侨务办公室、深圳市归国华侨联合会、深圳市海外交流协会的大力支持下，"记录侨故事"系列专栏文章终于付梓出版，这也算是给长期关心深圳侨务工作的各方热心人士交上的一份答卷。

我们相信，本书的公开出版，对于探讨深圳侨史、侨文化，梳理深圳侨文脉，总结深圳侨精神，全力做好新时代深圳"侨"文章，都是一个很好的注解。这还有助于广大港澳同胞、海外侨胞和归侨侨眷发挥独特优势、紧跟时代步伐，做深圳改革开放创新发展的积极参与者，弘扬企业家精神、履行社会责任的践行者，讲好中国故事、深圳故事的传播者，深圳与世界各地友好交往的促进者，为深圳加快打造更具全球影响力的经济中心城市和现代化国际大都市贡献智慧和力量。

最后需要特别说明的是，"记录侨故事"系列专栏采写工作由深圳市侨办与《晶报》联合采访团队完成，深圳市侨办方面的成员有刘昕、江红、张鹏、佘堉南、张宇纯等，《晶报》团队的成员有姚宇铭、侯晓清、赖良青、赵周贤、兰小棵、白念平、曾广霖、武莹，其中兰小棵还负责了全书的英文翻译工作。这一系列侨故事的采访能够顺利完成并结集出版，得益于深圳市委统战部的精心指导，《晶报》与深圳市侨办、侨联的通力合作，各区（新区）侨务部门以及接受采访的28位港澳同胞、海外侨胞和归侨侨眷的鼎力支持。刘宏伟、黄海旋、李添奎、赖坚贞、萧燕珍、钟子威、杨依心、于仁秋、鲁星、李美花、黄文德、童锦源、汪娟而、鲜于惠子、区丽琼、李建齐、刘玉芬等人也为采写工作提供了无私的帮助，我们在此谨致谢忱。暨南大学出版社华侨华人/岭南文化编辑室主任冯琳、编辑雷晓琪和杨柳牧菁为本书的顺利出版呕心沥血，认真编校，在此一并致谢。

本书编委会

2024 年 10 月

Postscript

Shenzhen is an emerging modern city, but the history of Shenzhen people (also known as "Xin'an people" and "Bao'an people") bravely venturing into the world can be traced back to the end of the Southern Song Dynasty, which was more than 700 years ago.

According to the *Historical Records of Shenzhen Overseas Chinese Affairs*, after the fall of the Southern Song Dynasty, a large number of Shenzhen people who had participated in the anti-Yuan war fled overseas with their families to avoid being massacred Yuan soldiers and drifted to the Nanyang region (Southeast Asia). In the Ming Dynasty, some Shenzhen people, represented by Zhang Zheng from Nantou, frequently traveled between China and Nanyang countries, engaged in trade and maritime transportation. After the failure of the Opium War, a large number of Shenzhen people (mostly Hakkas) from Guanlan, Longgang, Dapeng, Kuichong, Pingshan, Shiyan, Longhua and other places sold themselves abroad as contract laborers. Some of them were shipped to Southeast Asia, Hawaii, South America, and Canada, some were sold to Old Gold Mountain (San Francisco) in the United States and New Gold Mountain (Melbourne) in Australia, and some were sent to Europe and Africa. Around 1950, a group of young intellectuals, who were relatives of overseas Chinese and had received secondary education in China, went abroad to inherit their ancestral business...

Today, Shenzhen is one of the key hometowns of overseas Chinese in Guangdong Province. Statistics show that Shenzhen is the ancestral home to more than 1 million Hong Kong and Macao compatriots, overseas Chinese, returned overseas Chinese and relatives of Chinese nationals residing overseas. They have always had a fine tradition of loving China and their hometown. Since the Revolution of 1911, especially since the reform and opening-up, they have actively run schools, donated money and materials, and devoted themselves to supporting the construction of their hometown. They are an indispensable and important force for the development of Shenzhen.

Starting from 2022, the *Daily Sunshine* of the Shenzhen News Group and the United Front Work Department of the Shenzhen Municipal Committee of the Communist Party of China (the Overseas Chinese Affairs Office of the Shenzhen Municipal People's Government and the Shenzhen Municipal Federation of Returned Overseas Chinese) launched a column named "Stories of Overseas Chinese," dedicated to discovering the stories of Hong Kong and Macao compatriots, overseas Chinese, returned overseas Chinese and relatives of Chinese nationals residing overseas whose ancestral home is

452

Shenzhen or who have close ties with Shenzhen, showing the deep concern and attachment of numerous overseas Chinese to their home country and hometown. Over the past three years, the project team has interviewed 28 persons, who are of the older generation of Hong Kong and Macao compatriots, overseas Chinese, returned overseas Chinese and relatives of Chinese nationals residing overseas, and written down their "overseas Chinese stories," which is a precious memory and spiritual wealth that is worth preserving, as it features their strive for progress and will inspire future generations.

During the interviews, we have deeply felt the strong feelings of overseas Chinese who love their hometown, Shenzhen, and their home country. At the same time, we have witnessed an influential "Shenzhen overseas Chinese community" that has been formed overseas, and found "Shenzhen overseas Chinese elements" distributed in different corners of the world, one after another: the "Sea Palace" restaurant in the Netherlands, the Foundation of Choi Family Association in the Netherlands and Belgium (Stichting Familie Choi in Netherlands en Belgie), the Tai Pun Residents Association in New York, the Yook Ying Association, New York, the Federation of Australian Shenzhen Community, the Malaysia-Shamchun Chamber of Commerce, and the South Africa-China Shenzhen General Chamber of Commerce...

This book includes some of the articles in the "Stories of Overseas Chinese" column, all of which were first published via the WeChat public account "Tongxin Pengcheng" of the United Front Work Department of the Shenzhen Municipal Committee of the Communist Party of China or new media platforms such as the *Daily Sunshine*. This is not only a successful case of telling China's stories and Shenzhen's stories well in the era of smart media, but also a bold and beneficial attempt for Shenzhen to tell "overseas Chinese stories" well in the new era.

Every time after the "Stories of Overseas Chinese" column was sent out, we would receive enthusiastic comments from multiple sources. Some overseas Chinese even asked our reporters to do them a favor by carefully typesetting the articles about them so that they could print out the articles for permanent collection. Now, with the strong support of the Overseas Chinese Affairs Office of the Shenzhen Municipal People's Government, the Shenzhen Municipal Federation of Returned Overseas Chinese, and the Shenzhen Overseas Exchange Association, the articles in the "Stories of Overseas Chinese" column is finally put into print, which can be regarded as an answer sheet presented to all the enthusiastic people who have long been concerned about Shenzhen's overseas Chinese affairs.

We believe that the publication of this book is a good annotation for exploring the history and culture of overseas Chinese from Shenzhen, sorting out the context of overseas Chinese from Shenzhen, summarizing the spirit of overseas Chinese from Shenzhen, and sparing no effort in dealing with Shenzhen's overseas Chinese affairs in the new era. It will also help overseas Chinese, returned overseas Chinese and relatives of Chinese nationals residing overseas to give full play to their unique advantages, keep up with the pace of the times, and become active participants in Shenzhen's reform, opening up, innovation and development, doers in promoting entrepreneurial spirit and fulfilling social responsibilities, conveyors in telling China's stories and Shenzhen's stories well, and promoters of friendly exchanges between Shenzhen and the world, so as to contribute their wisdom and strength to Shenzhen's accelerated creation of a more globally influential economic center city and a modern international metropolis.

Finally, it should be noted that the interviews and writing of the "Stories of Overseas Chinese" column were done by a joint team of the Overseas Chinese Affairs Office of the Shenzhen Municipal People's Government and the *Daily Sunshine*. The team members from the Overseas Chinese Affairs Office of the Shenzhen Municipal People's Government include Liu Xin, Jiang Hong, Zhang Peng, She Yunan, and Zhang Yuchun, among others, while the team members from the *Daily Sunshine* include Yao Yuming, Hou Xiaoqing, Lai Liangqing, Zhao Zhouxian, Lan Xiaoke, Bai Nianping, Zeng Guanglin and Wu Ying, as Lan Xiaoke is also responsible for the English translation of the book. The successful completion of the interviews of this series of "Stories of Overseas Chinese" and the publication of this book are due to the careful guidance of the United Front Work Department of the Shenzhen Municipal Committee of the Communist Party of China, the full cooperation of the *Daily Sunshine*, the Overseas Chinese Affairs Office of the Shenzhen Municipal People's Government and the Shenzhen Municipal Federation of Returned Overseas Chinese, and the strong support of the overseas Chinese affairs department of various districts (new districts) of Shenzhen and the 28 Hong Kong and Macao compatriots, overseas Chinese, returned overseas Chinese and relatives of Chinese nationals residing overseas who were interviewed. Liu Hongwei, Huang Haixuan, Li Tiankui, Chien Chen Yu, Catherine Y.C. Siu, Andrew Gee Wai Chung, Josje Yeung, Yu Renqiu, Lu Xing, Li Meihua, Huang Wende, Tong Jinyuan, Wang Juaner, Xianyu Huizi, Peggy Au, Li Jianqi, Liu Yufen and others also provided selfless help for our interview and writing work, to whom we would like to express our sincere gratitude. Feng Lin, director of the Overseas Chinese/Lingnan Culture Editorial Office of Jinan University Press, and editor Lei Xiaoqi and Yang Liumujing have made painstaking efforts in editing and proofreading for the successful publication of the book, to whom we would like to express our gratitude.

Editorial Committee of *Flying Far and High*
October 2024